DATE DUE

The Dark Clue

The Dark Clue

JAMES WILSON

Atlantic Monthly Press
New York

First published in Great Britain in 2001 by Faber and Faber Limited, London, England

Printed in the United States of America

FIRST AMERICAN EDITION

Library of Congress Cataloging-in-Publication Data
Wilson, James, 1949–
   The dark clue / James Wilson.—1st American ed.
      p. cm.
   ISBN 0-87113-831-X
   1. Turner, J. M. W. (Joseph Mallord William), 1775–1851——Fiction. 2. Biography as a literary form—Fiction. 3. Biographers—Fiction. 4. Painters—Fiction. 5. England—Fiction. I. Title.

PR6123.I57 D37 2001
823'.914—dc21   2001045209

Atlantic Monthly Press
841 Broadway
New York, NY 10003

01 02 03 04   10 9 8 7 6 5 4 3 2 1

For Paula
and for my mother, Tom and Kit
with love

Limmeridge, Cumberland,
21st January, 186–

This is a book begun, but not finished.
   I could not finish it.

Many times I have come close to destroying it, thinking I should
have no rest while it remained to reproach me.
   I could not bring myself to do it.

I have therefore given instructions that it should be sealed in a
box, which is to remain unopened until I, my wife, Laura, our
sister, Marian Halcombe, and all our children are dead.
   As I write these words, the man whose story I set out to tell
has already answered for his life in the highest court of all.
Before you read them, I shall have followed him there, and
made answer for my own.

Remember, as you judge us, that you shall stand there too.

   WH

Book One

I

Letter from Walter Hartright to Laura Hartright, 18th July, 185–

Brompton Grove,
Tuesday

My dearest love,

I hope you're sitting down as you read this, for I have strange news. (But don't be alarmed – *good* news, I think!) I've no time to confide it both to you and to my journal, so please keep this letter – as you'll see, I may have need of it later.

First, though, a coincidence. You are, in a way, responsible for it, for it arose from my mood yesterday, when you left. I was so melancholy at the sight of your dear faces drawing away from me that it was all I could do to stop myself jumping on to the train, and I must own that, afterwards, I cried. Feeling unequal to explaining my tears to a cabman, I decided to walk home.

As I started west along the New Road, I suddenly saw it, as I have never seen it before, as a scene from hell: the clatter of the horses; the stench of their ordure; a crossing-sweeper nearly knocked down by a brushmaker's wagon; a woman crying 'Stunning oranges!', yet so drearily you could tell she had lost all hope of selling her handful of pitifully wizened fruit, and so providing something for her child's supper; a boy turning carter-wheels, and the men on the roof of an omnibus tossing halfpennies and farthings at him, and then guffawing as he fell into the gutter. And everywhere a yellow, choking haze, so thick that, even in the middle of the morning, you could not see more than fifty paces. And all the while a stream of tilers' carts and brick merchants' drays rattling by with provisions for the armies of new houses which daily carry this new Babylon still further into the lanes and meadows of Middlesex. Even as I rejoiced that you and the children would soon be breathing purer air and seeing lovelier sights, I felt myself alone and trapped inside some great engine from which all beauty, all joy and colour and mystery, had been banished.

This feeling so oppressed me that I quickly turned off and started to zig-zag through the maze of little streets and alleys to the west of Tottenham Court Road. My principle was simple

3

enough: so long as I continued a certain distance west, and then a certain distance south, I must eventually come to Oxford Street, and avoid getting badly lost. And so it was that I crossed Portland Place (where, all those years ago, my journey to you so improbably began), entered a mean, dusty little court hung with dripping laundry that was already smudged with soot, and suddenly emerged into a street of handsome old-fashioned houses that seemed oddly familiar. But it was not the familiarity of everyday: rather the ghostly brilliance of some long-lost childish memory, or of something glimpsed once in a dream. I stood for perhaps two minutes, surveying the line of dark windows and blackened brickwork and heavy brass-handled doors. When and why had I seen them before? What was the original, of which they were suchmhbvkhvjhfv a plangent echo? Try as I might, I could not find it. All I noted was that my mind seemed somehow to associate it with feelings of powerlessness and smallness and a kind of awe.

Still musing, I set off again. After fifty yards or so I noticed a boy of eight or nine skulking in the area of one of the houses. His cap was too large for him and his jacket too small, and he wore an odd pair of boots, one black and one brown. As I turned towards him, he shrank back against the damp wall and looked up at me with the terrified stare of a cornered animal. As much to allay his fear as to satisfy my own curiosity, I called down to him:

'What street is this?'

'Queen Anne Street,' he replied.

I was none the wiser: I recognized the name, but could not recall anyone I knew ever having lived there. I took a penny from my pocket and held out my hand.

'Thank you,' I said.

He cowered like a dog, torn between hunger for a scrap of meat and dread of being kicked.

'It's all right,' I said. 'I won't hurt you.'

He hesitated a moment, before scuttling up the steps and taking the coin. Then, instead of running off as I had expected, he gazed wonderingly at me, as if even so small an act of kindness lay entirely beyond his knowledge and understanding of life. His eyes, I saw, were unhealthily large, and the pale skin was drawn into the hollows of his cheeks, as if age could not wait to put its mark upon him. And suddenly I thought of little Walter, and of the horror I should feel if I looked into *his* face and saw there such a world of want and pain and sickness. So I gave the boy sixpence more, and without a word he was gone, as if he feared that in another moment the spell would break, and the natural order of things would reassert itself, and I would change my mind and take the money back again.

And that is my coincidence. I already hear you saying: 'Walter! I see no coincidence'; but you shall, my love, I promise, if only you will be patient and read on.

I was in Brompton Grove again by three minutes to twelve. It was a sombre homecoming. The small things that spoke of our happy life here together looked already out of place, like a doll or a bonnet washed up on a beach. In the few brief hours since we'd left, the house had been occupied by an alien spirit, which now resented the return of the previous tenant. Whenever I entered a room, I seemed to feel its presence, like a silent wind, propelling me back towards the door.

Marian was still out, and only the distant murmur of the Davidsons' voices in the kitchen told me I was not entirely alone. I felt as lost and mopish as a child. I tried to draw, but could not settle to it. After ten minutes I laid aside my pencil and took up a book, only to set it down again ten minutes later. The lunch bell promised a welcome diversion, until I found myself sitting in solitary state in the dining room like an oriental despot, with Davidson hovering near as if I might need help raising the fork to my mouth. I sent him away, saying I could take care of myself and would ring if I needed anything, and then kept the poor fellow running up and down stairs with my demands for fresh water and more mustard.

When I had finished, I went into the garden, where the workmen were marking the foundations for the new studio, and solemnly reiterated all manner of things – that I must have a north light, that the entrance must be sheltered from the weather – that they knew perfectly well already from the plans. And it was here that Marian found me when she came home, and saved them from me, and me from myself.

'You cannot possibly come like that!' were her first words, delivered in such a forthright tone that the three workmen started. But she was smiling, and her black eyes shone. 'You look like a man who has walked across half London.'

'Come where?' I said.

'Why, to Lady Eastlake's,' she said, more quietly, drawing me towards the house. 'She was at the exhibition this morning, and afterwards I had lunch with her, and we talked of Laura's going away today, and my staying. And so, by a natural progression, of you.' She took my arm, and led me indoors. 'And she asked most particularly that I should bring you to meet her this afternoon.'

I was immediately struck by the notion that this might have something to do with my painting: Sir Charles is, after all, Director of the National Gallery, and I confess that for a wild moment I imagined him emerging from behind a screen in his wife's drawing room and saying: 'Ah, Hartright, I much admired *The Artist's Wife and Children at Limmeridge, in Cumberland* at the Academy this year, and would like to buy it for the nation.' I soon recognized this pitiable fantasy for what it was, however, and concluded that Marian, as good and kind as ever, was merely hoping to distract me from my separation by introducing me to one of her blue-stocking friends.

As it turned out, neither explanation was remotely as strange as the truth.

Has Marian ever described the Eastlakes' house to you? It's too late now for me to ask her (after midnight, and she must be asleep) – so, if she has, simply pass over the next paragraph.

They live in one of those fine old stone houses in Fitzroy Square (here and there on the walls you can still see patches of the original honey gold peering through the grime), with lofty windows and a front door big enough to take a horse. As we arrived, a fashionably dressed woman in a fur-trimmed jacket and a tiny pill-box hat garnished with feathers flounced down the steps (in so far as you can flounce when you are imprisoned from the waist down in a giant birdcage) and into a waiting carriage. There were angry spots on her cheeks, and she barely acknowledged us as we passed.

The front door was opened by a tall footman with grey hair and thick dark eyebrows. Marian addressed him with a natural ease which surprised me.

'Good afternoon, Stokes. Is your mistress at home?'

'She is, ma'am.' He led us through a wide hall lined with marble busts and upstairs to a large drawing room. It was furnished in the modern style, with a heavy Turkey carpet, a set of carved oak chairs, and rows of watercolours jammed together on the green walls like carriages in Piccadilly. Above the picture-rail ran a line of Japanese plates (*really* made in Japan, I fancy, and not in Stafford!), and over the fireplace was a large classical landscape which, from its treaclish colouring, I took to be one of Sir Charles's own.

As we entered, a strikingly tall woman rose from a chaise longue in the window. For a moment she was held in silhouette by the evening light, and the only distinctive feature I could make out was her head, which tilted oddly to one side, like a bird's. As she came towards us, however, I saw that she was about fifty, wearing a soft green dress edged with braid, and with her still-dark hair pulled simply back into a net. She had a wide, uneven mouth that broke into a frank smile as she held out her hand.

'Marian,' she said. 'You must have winged feet.' Her voice was soft but clear, and I thought I detected a trace of a Scotch accent. She turned to the footman. 'Thank you, Stokes. If anyone else should call, I am not at home.' She touched Marian's hand and smiled sidelong at me. 'Did you have to rope him, and drag him to a cab, to make him come?'

Marian laughed. 'Lady Eastlake, this is my brother – well, my *half*-brother-in-law – Walter Hartright.'

'*Half* in-law,' said Lady Eastlake, laughing. 'How very complicated. I'm delighted to see you, Mr. Hartright. How do you do?' As we shook hands, she glanced about her, as if suddenly dissatisfied with where she was. 'I think we'll be more comfortable in my *boudoir*' – she gave the word an ironic inflection which made Marian laugh – 'if you will forgive the clutter.'

She walked to the back of the room and threw open a pair of folding doors. Beyond them lay a light, pleasant, informal parlour, with a tall window overlooking the garden. The immediate impression was more that of an Oxford don's study than of a lady's sitting room. A range of bookcases, some crammed with books, others with what appeared simply to be stacks of papers, ran along the walls. In the corner was a bureau, the lid wedged half open by a cascade of notes and letters; on each side of the fireplace stood a large cabinet containing rocks, shells, pieces of broken pottery and half an Etruscan head; while in the centre (strangest of all) was a large mahogany table, entirely covered with more photographs than I have ever seen together in one place in my life. Despite myself, I could not stop my eyes straying across them in search of a unifying theme or a familiar image. In the first I failed, for the subjects seemed as various as life itself – portraits, a country cottage, a great mill veiled by the smoke from its own black chimney – but in the second I was successful, for there, between a haystack and a blurred carthorse, I quickly recognized a picture of Lady Eastlake herself.

She must have been watching me, for as I stooped to look at it more closely she said sharply:

'Well, Mr. Hartright, what do you think?'

'It is a fair likeness,' I said, equivocally; for I feared that, like so many people, she might resent the camera's merciless exposure of every blot and blemish, and feel it did her beauty less than justice.

'I mean', she said, 'about photography.'

'Well . . . ,' I began. I did not know how to go on, for, truth to tell, it is not something to which I have given much thought at all; but I did not wish to cause offence, either by seeming too cool, or by too warmly offering an opinion that might differ from her own. She spared me by continuing:

'Do you practise yourself?'

'No,' I replied. 'I still prefer pencil and brush.'

'And why is that, Mr. Hartright?'

This inquisition was so far from what I had expected that I was forced to consider for a moment. At length I said:

'Because it seems to me that photography can merely record facts.'

She gave me not an instant's respite. 'Whereas your pencil . . .?'

'Whereas a pencil should, I hope – in the right hands – be able to hint at the truth. Which is not perhaps the same thing.'

She fixed me with an inscrutable stare, from which I could not judge whether she thought me mad, dull, or fascinatingly original. Then she opened the bureau gingerly, to prevent the overflowing papers from spilling on to the floor, and took out a small notebook and pencil. 'Do you mind if I make a note of that?' she said, already writing. 'I am doing an article.'

'So,' said Marian, with a teasing familiarity, which again took me by surprise, 'prepare to see your words in the next issue of the *Quarterly Review*.'

Lady Eastlake laughed. 'Not unacknowledged,' she said. 'Whatever else I am, I am not a pickpocket. Besides, what makes you suppose I should want to claim Mr. Hartright's thoughts as my own?'

She put the notebook away and sat in an armchair by the fireplace, gesturing Marian to the seat next to her. She sighed, shut her eyes and sank back, in a dumbshow of tiredness. I wondered if this were some further comment on what I had said, and, despite myself, felt the heat rising to my cheeks.

'Forgive me,' said Lady Eastlake. 'I've just had to endure a duty call from Mrs. Madison. Did you see her as you came in?'

'There was a lady leaving,' said Marian.

'She can only have been here for a quarter of an hour, but it felt like three days. My stock of conversation on children's clothes is soon exhausted, I'm afraid. I did try venturing on to the weather, but even that turned out too mettlesome for her.'

Stokes entered, carrying a tea tray. He set it down on a low table by Lady Eastlake's chair. She watched warily, her head cocked, until he was out of sight again; then she went on, more quietly:

'She's one of those women who believe that a member of her own sex should have no views on anything. And certainly *never* read a book. In which, I must say, she sets a splendid example.'

Marian laughed. Lady Eastlake started to pour the tea, then put the pot down and touched Marian's arm. 'That's why I so enjoy your sister's company, Mr. Hartright. Someone to keep pace with me. She always has something fresh and interesting to say, no matter where my runaway mind has led me.'

'I know how deeply she values *your* friendship, Lady East-lake,' I said. 'I'm afraid that in our house she must often feel the want of an intellectual companion.'

9

'Oh, that's not true, Walter!' burst in Marian.

'It is not what she tells me,' said Lady Eastlake. 'You write, do you not, Mr. Hartright?'

I had just handed Marian a cup and was leaning down to take one myself. Lady Eastlake's face was barely two feet from my own, and I felt the full power of her steady gaze. Again, it was impossible to avoid the sense that I was being interrogated – although to what purpose I could not begin to imagine.

'I have written a book,' I replied. 'But it is no more than the history of a conspiracy against my wife, which my own experience qualified me to narrate. Perhaps it would be truer to call me a chronicler than a writer.'

Lady Eastlake nodded.

'Or even an editor,' I went on. 'For, wherever possible, I told the story through the words of those who were closest to the events described, and thus best able to give a true account of them. Including Marian, whose journal was an invaluable source of information.'

I glanced at Marian. I had expected her to gainsay me: *What nonsense, Walter: you are far too modest*. Instead, she was watching me intently, her dark complexion flushed with excitement. As I turned back to Lady Eastlake, I saw, out of the corner of my eye, the table laden with photographs.

'You could say', I continued, 'that I aspire to art in my painting. Whereas . . .'

'Whereas in writing,' said Lady Eastlake, 'you are a camera, perhaps?'

'Exactly,' I said. I was taken aback, both by her acuity and by her rudeness in interrupting me. I looked again at Marian: she was smiling at Lady Eastlake, as if to say: *There, I told you so*. The idea that there might be some secret understanding between them, of which I was the unwitting object, unsettled me.

'May I ask', I said (with, I own, a certain iciness), 'if this is tending towards some end?'

Lady Eastlake did not answer at once. She exchanged another furtive glance with Marian, then took a handkerchief from her sleeve and carefully smoothed it on her lap. At length she cleared her throat and said:

'Mr. Hartright, would you mind closing the doors?'

I did so. She went on:

'I would not, of course, expect you to keep anything from your wife; but I must begin by asking that you do not mention this conversation to anyone else.'

I felt I could not accept this condition without knowing more, but was hard put to find a delicate way of saying so. She must have seen what was in my mind; for she said:

'Och, you needn't worry about your honour, Mr. Hartright. I'm not going to confess to a murder, or the theft of a child. Besides, your sister's presence in this room should give you assurance enough.'

I felt the justice of this, and nodded. She continued:

'My only concern is to protect my husband. His position – which God knows he never sought – is difficult enough already, and the last thing I want to do is stir up a hornets' nest around his poor head.'

'Very well,' I said.

'Thank you.' She looked warily towards the door, and when she spoke it was in little more than a whisper. 'Do you by any chance know a man called Thornbury?'

'No,' I replied. 'Who is he?'

'A journalist,' she said. 'And, I fear, an utter scoundrel.'

'That is not surprising,' I said. 'A cynic might say that, to be the one, it is almost a requirement to be the other.'

Lady Eastlake laughed. 'I have not myself met him,' she said, 'but, so far as I have been able to learn from my friends, he is intent – for no other reason than to sell the wretched book he is writing – on slandering a poor, misunderstood body who can no longer defend himself. And the result, I'm afraid, will be a serious injury, not only to the memory of one man, but to England herself, and to English art. For his subject was – in my view, and the view of many others – the foremost genius of our age.'

And it was then, with the force of a sprung trap, that the image of Queen Anne Street re-entered my mind, and, in the same instant, I knew why it was familiar. For a moment I was a boy of eight again, and sitting in a cab next to my poor father; the winter cold turned our breath to steam, and I huddled close to him, for in his thick coat he was an island of warmth and safety. As we jolted past a tall house with dirty windows and a

11

heavy front door, he laid his gloved hand on mine and pointed out of the window. 'Look, Walter,' he said. 'That is 47 Queen Anne Street. Where the foremost genius of our age lives.'

And now, in the space of six hours, I had walked down the same street and heard the same phrase again for the first time in thirty years. Without stopping to consider, I said to Lady Eastlake: 'Do you mean Turner?'

It was her turn to be astonished. She stared at me, her mouth half open, then looked at Marian. 'Have you . . .?'

Marian was equally perplexed. 'No,' she said. 'I said nothing. Walter, how did you . . .?'

I confess I was tempted to confound them further by pretending to some mysterious knowledge, but I merely said: 'Oh, it was just a guess.' And then, to forestall more questions (for both of them still looked puzzled), I went on: 'So is Mr. Thornbury writing Turner's biography?'

'That is what he claims.'

'But if you have never met him,' I said, 'how do you know it is defamatory?'

'I have been following his progress, Mr. Hartright – with, I have to say, a sinking heart. A few of those closest to Turner have, wisely, refused to speak to him at all. Of the rest, he appears to have given most credence to a gang of malicious gossips, most of whom scarcely knew the man. And they, as is the way with these things, have in turn referred him to more of their own kind.'

I must own that my first thought was the old adage: *There's no smoke without fire*. Perhaps she saw my scepticism, for she went on:

'No man as eminent as Turner could avoid making enemies among those less successful or less gifted than himself – particularly a man with such a thoroughgoing disdain of flattery and convention. You've probably heard all manner of stories about him yourself.'

Her raised eyebrow seemed to demand an answer, but I said nothing, for – beyond a few hoary old anecdotes about his meanness, and his garbled speech, that are common currency at the Academy – in reality I was shamefully ignorant about him. She waited a moment, and then continued:

'He was, it cannot be denied, an odd, perverse, eccentric little creature, but he was not a monster, and he deserves better than to be commemorated by tittle-tattle.' She leaned confidentially towards me. 'I came to know him well in his last years. Indeed' – here her voice grew unsteady, and her eyes glittered with tears – 'I am told that as he lay dying he called my name. Which I cannot but feel as a charge upon me. To try to protect his memory.' She hastily dried her eyes, then clenched her handkerchief into a ball. 'Mr. Hartright, what I am asking . . . what I am suggesting . . . is that you might yourself consider undertaking to write a *Life of J. M. W. Turner.'*

For perhaps three seconds I was, literally, speechless with astonishment. A thousand questions crowded into my head, and then flew off again before I could find words to express them. I was conscious of Marian's gaze upon me – watchful, anxious, almost pleading – and the sense that *her* hopes and happiness were, in some way I could not yet fathom, bound up with my reply, only confused me further. Perhaps Lady Eastlake mistook my perplexity for calculation, for she said:

'I have spoken to a publisher I know, and am assured that there would be a ready market for such a book . . .'

'That is not my concern. I –'

'And I'm sure I speak for all of Turner's friends when I say we should be happy to underwrite it . . .' She broke off, suddenly noting that I was following another train of thought. 'What?' she said. 'You think there must be others better placed?'

I nodded. 'What about yourself, for instance?'

'As I explained, my connection to Sir Charles . . . Besides, there are many doors closed to a woman that a man may pass through easily and freely.'

'I cannot believe –' I began.

'What you must understand, Mr. Hartright, is that poor Turner died a recluse,' said Lady Eastlake. 'Most of those who knew him well are long dead. Of those who are still alive, Mr. Ruskin would seem to be the natural choice, but he' – here she smiled slightly – 'is too Olympian to contemplate it. My situation you already know. And as for my husband – well, it's entirely out of the question, I'm afraid.'

'Oh, I can quite see that,' I said. 'But –'

She appeared not to have heard me.

'Both Mrs. Booth, Turner's housekeeper, and his friend George Jones are good-hearted people, but . . .' She paused, and shook her head. 'Well, frankly, neither of them is equal to it. And Mr. Jones, I believe, in any case now spends most of his time dressing up as the Duke of Wellington. At best, they might both furnish you with useful memoirs.'

She paused, and again I found myself at a loss for words. It was Marian who broke the silence:

'There *is* no-one else, Walter. If you won't do it, Thornbury will carry the day unopposed.'

'And do not underestimate yourself, Mr. Hartright,' said Lady Eastlake. 'Unlike Thornbury, you are an artist, who will understand the painter in Turner . . .'

I cried – I could not stop myself – 'You cannot compare –!'

'He may have been a general, and you – forgive me – only a colonel,' replied Lady Eastlake. 'But all artists belong to the same regiment, and fight the same battles, and crave the same victory. And then', she went on, before I could protest further, 'you are also, by your own admission, a chronicler, who knows how to gather and evaluate and compile the accounts of different witnesses.'

'And a crusader, who has already proven his determination to right a great wrong,' said Marian.

Lady Eastlake nodded. 'Who could be more ideal?'

They were quiet then, leaving me to ponder what they had said. I tried, again, to impose some order on my own jangled thoughts, but they all – save one, which rang through my head with the clarity of a bell – remained in turmoil. At length Marian said:

'This is all so unexpected for poor Walter that I think we must allow him some time to consider his response.'

'Yes, of course,' said Lady Eastlake.

And so we left it. No more mention of the idea was made, and, after exchanging the usual pleasantries for a few minutes, Marian and I rose to go. Only as Stokes ushered us from the room did Lady Eastlake say:

'I may expect to hear from you soon, I hope, Mr. Hartright?'

*

We barely spoke on the way home. I was still trying to marshal my own thoughts, which were all of you and the children, and of how our lives would change if I accepted Lady Eastlake's strange proposal; but I was constantly deflected by waves of wild emotion – dread, and a kind of dizzy exhilaration, in about equal measure – which I could not trace confidently to their source, but which seemed to gush unbidden from some hidden spring in my mind.

Marian, for her part, was uncharacteristically constrained. I thought little of it at the time, beyond merely remarking the fact; but now I think she must have taken my silence to mean that I was angry; for when we were back in our own drawing room, and had shut the door, she laid a hand lightly on my arm and said:

'I do hope, Walter, that you don't think I did wrong.'

'What,' I said, 'to invite me to Lady Eastlake's?'

'Not that,' she said. 'But to invite you without telling you the reason. She insisted that you should know nothing until she had met you, and could decide for herself whether you would be suitable. But when I saw you sitting there, so bewildered, it made me feel a traitor. Or, rather, made me feel that *you* would think me a traitor.'

Poor Marian! 'I was taken aback, I must own,' I said. 'But I never suspected you of treachery, or doubted that you had my best interests at heart.'

'I'm glad.' She was silent for a moment, looking down at her bag and toying with the string. Then, as if she had decided at last to say something that had long been on her mind, she burst out: 'May we talk frankly, Walter?'

'Nothing I have ever known could prevent you talking frankly, once you were set on it,' I said. 'And I'm quite certain that it lies beyond *my* power to stop you.'

She laughed, and her voice had regained some of its old gaiety as she replied: 'I said "we", not "I".'

'Very well,' I said.

We sat together on the sofa. It was dusk, but neither of us suggested lighting the gas. Perhaps we both felt that it would be easier to open our hearts if our faces, at least, were veiled by the deepening gloom. At length she said:

'Many years ago I told you that we should always be friends, Walter, did I not?'

'Yes,' I said, taking her hand. 'And so we shall.'

'I hope so,' she said. 'At any rate, that is the spirit in which I now speak. You may think me impertinent; but please believe that I am prompted only by sisterly love for you and Laura.'

'Of course I believe it,' I said. 'I've never been surer of anything in my life.' And nor had I; but, notwithstanding, I waited with trepidation to hear what she would say next. A whole army of butterflies seemed to have taken up residence in my stomach, and my legs were so leaden that, if Davidson had rushed in at that moment shouting 'Fire! Fire!', I doubt whether they would have carried me to the door.

'Thank you,' said Marian. She breathed deeply, then went on: 'You know that, living as close together as we do, we cannot help noticing the smallest changes in each other's moods?'

'Yes,' I said.

'Well,' she said, 'recently I think I have noticed such a change in you. You have become restless, and distracted. You paint and draw less than you did. And, while you are still as loving a husband and father and brother as ever, I sometimes think it is with a greater effort than previously. As if . . . as if you have to bring yourself back from some other place in order to be with us.'

'It's difficult for me to paint here,' I said, 'until the studio is finished. And I have, as you know, been very taken up with planning it, and overseeing the work.'

'The want of a studio never stopped you painting before,' she said. 'And you may, I think, safely leave building it to the workmen. They do not require you to go out twenty times a day and tell them their job.'

I remembered where she had found me that afternoon, and was glad the darkness hid my blushes.

'No,' she went on, 'we must look for a deeper cause. And I think I know what it is.'

~~I need not burden you~~

I wish I could spare you what she said next; for it must inevitably hurt you, and make you think worse of me. But it is the truth, and you must know it – else you will cease to know *me*.

'Dear Walter,' she said, in a quieter, tenderer voice. 'You are the victim of your own sensitive nature. No-one else, knowing all the circumstances, could possibly accuse you of having benefited improperly from marrying Laura, and sharing the fortune which eventually became hers. Yet that, if I am right, is the charge with which you torment yourself. You know that your conduct has always been beyond reproach, and that you have brought her more happiness than she ever knew in her life. And yet, and yet, and yet . . . You still harbour the faint suspicion that you have somehow become a pensioner, and it is an agony to you.'

I opened my mouth to speak; but, in truth, I could not find the strength to deny it. In a moment, she had cast a light into some dark corner of my being and found a canker to which, until now, I had been unable to give a name.

'Worse still,' she continued, 'you feel a certain vacancy at the centre of your life. You have everything that, in the eyes of the world, should make a man happy: a gentle and loving wife, two beautiful children, a fine estate, and the regard of your brother artists. Yet something is lacking: a *cause* capable of stirring your soul, and carrying you beyond the concerns of family and home.'

I nodded, and I think she must have seen me; for I felt her hand tightening on mine. 'It is nothing to be ashamed of,' she said. 'It is just that, like all noble natures, you know that family and home themselves are meaningless, unless they stand in relation to some greater purpose.'

Outside, a wagon squealed and rumbled across the cobbles. I clutched at the sound gratefully, and wrapped it about me like a cloak; for my eyes were full of tears.

'For months,' said Marian, 'I have been looking for some way to relieve you. And that is why my heart leapt when Lady Eastlake told me of her anguish over Turner's life, for here at last, it seemed, was a great purpose you were perfectly fitted to fulfil.' She paused, and then went on: 'You know, I hope, that I will gladly help you, as I did once before, when fate enlisted us in the same struggle. Dear Walter, please say you will do it!'

Once, many years ago – do you remember? – I called Marian our good angel; and so she is, for like an angel she seems to know what is best and truest in us better than we know it ourselves.

17

For some moments I could not speak; and when I did, all I could say was: 'Thank you.'

And so, my love, tomorrow I shall write to Lady Eastlake, telling her that, on certain conditions, I accept. And the upshot (if she agrees) is that you will have to get to know me in yet another character. Drawing master, detective, husband, clerk of works – and now, of all things, biographer!

It is late here, and cold. I shall go to bed, and hold to myself the pillow that still bears the smell of your skin and hair.

Good night,

Walter

II

Memorandum of a letter from Walter Hartright to Lady Eastlake, 19th July, 185–

1. Thank you for your invitation; great pleasure finally to meet you.
2. After consideration, delighted to accept your proposal that I should write a *Life of J. M. W. Turner*.
3. Must, however, make one stipulation: respect your feelings towards Turner, but neither they, nor wish to thwart Thornbury, can be my guide. Shall do no more, and no less, than try to discover truth (which in biography *must*, I think, be same as facts!). Go where trail leads me, without fear or favour. Cannot promise, therefore, to paint portrait you wish.
4. Hope you will forgive bluntness, but important to be clear at outset in order to avoid misunderstanding later.

III

Letter from Lady Eastlake to Walter Hartright, 19th July, 185–

7 Fitzroy Square,
Wednesday

My dear Mr. Hartright,

Many thanks for your letter of this morning, and for so promptly putting an end to my unease.

I am very glad that you feel able to act on my suggestion, and will give you what assistance I can. And yes – of course I accept that Truth must be your only master. I would, indeed, expect no less; and, had I suspected for a moment that you would be deflected from your purpose by partisan considerations, I should not have asked you to undertake a task which so clearly requires the greatest integrity.

I hope, nonetheless, that you will not feel I am trying to influence you improperly if I recommend that – whomever else you may talk to – you should begin by approaching Mr. Ruskin, Mr. Jones and Mrs. Booth. I have given their addresses to Marian, with this letter, and I will write to Mr. Jones and Mrs. Booth myself this evening, telling them that they may expect to hear from you. Since I know that Mrs. Booth refused to speak to Mr. Thornbury, it occurs to me that – in the first instance, at least – Marian, as another woman, might have more success in winning her confidence and securing her co-operation. As to Mr. Ruskin – I fear a letter from me would not help your case, so you must take courage and disturb the great man yourself.

Yours most truly,
Eliz. Eastlake

IV

Letter from Walter Hartright to Laura Hartright,
20th July, 185–

The Reading Room, British Museum Library,
Thursday

My dearest love,

Thank you for your letter, and for Florrie's and Walter's drawings – they will soon outstrip their father if I do not look to my laurels!

Yesterday I wrote to Ruskin and to George Jones, R.A., but have received no reply from either of them. Not wishing to be idle, therefore, I have taken myself – as you can see from the address – to the new Reading Room at the British Museum Library. (It is, by the by, a prodigious building, which seems to me to belong almost to a new order of object; large and hushed and awe-inspiring enough to be a great cathedral, and yet erected not as a temple to God, but rather to our knowledge of His creation. Was such a thing ever attempted before? In Alexandria, perhaps; but what mankind then knew of the world was puny by comparison. Here, in London, for the first time, the Tree of the Knowledge of Good and Evil has been raised up in bricks and mortar; and who knows whether it will prove a blessing or a curse?)

My aim here has been to find out what I can of Turner – and, from what I have discovered so far, I think my life of him will be quick work indeed. He was born, in London, in 1775, on St. George's Day; he drew; he painted; he died. That, in essence – save for a few incidentals, such as his journeys in this country and in Europe – is more or less all we know, at the ordinary humdrum level. He never married; never fought a duel; never fomented a revolution; never declared his love for a princess – a million Englishmen must have lived such lives, and none but their families and friends thought them worthy of a second glance. All that marks Turner out is his fanatical dedication to his art, which makes for sublime paintings, but leaves only meagre pickings for a biographer. I begin to feel sorry for poor Thornbury, who has perhaps resorted to slander in a desperate attempt to make the thin gruel of his narrative more palatable.

It is for this reason that, while I understand your anxiety, I believe it to be groundless. There will, of course, be unexpected difficulties, and I must not underestimate them, but I am sure that our separation need only be prolonged by two or three weeks – and if I thought otherwise I should, I promise you, write to Lady Eastlake this instant, telling her that I had changed my mind. Turner's close acquaintance was, it seems, pitifully small, and is now much depleted by death; and seeing the few friends who are left (assuming *they* will see *me*!) should take only a matter of days. After that, I shall have to seek out diaries, letters and so on to help me – particularly for the early years, for which there are presumably no living witnesses at all; but then I should be able to return to Limmeridge with my booty, and do most of the work there. Although I may have to come back once or twice in the interim, just for a few days, I'm

sure I shall then be safe in Cumberland until we all return to
London together next season.

So please, my dearest – don't worry! And let me end with a
worry of my own: I was delighted to hear that you have been
visiting our favourite haunts on the moor, but do you think, in
your present condition, it is wise to walk so far, particularly
when you have no companion to help you, should need arise?
Please – be careful.

Your devoted husband,
Walter

V

Letter from Walter Hartright to Laura Hartright,
1st August, 185–

Brompton Grove,
Tuesday

My dearest love,

Your letter reached me this morning. Thank you! I confess I
was hoping it might arrive in company, for over the last few
days I have felt powerless to do more on the *Life* until I have
heard from Jones and Ruskin (with the result that, to Davidson's evident annoyance, I have taken to anticipating the post
by pacing about the house like a caged wolf awaiting the full
moon).

But your words galvanized me into action; and as soon as I
had finished reading them I at once resolved to go on the offensive, and try to find my own way into Turner's world. I confess
I had no very clear idea of how, or where, I should begin (I think
at the back of my mind was the notion that if all else failed I
could end up at the Athenaeum, where I might happen upon
someone who recollected him): my aim was merely to set out,
and see where the day took me. And – although it may seem
fanciful – I think my faith was rewarded.

Hyde Park was even more thronged than usual, but by avoiding
the carriage-ways, and following the narrowest paths through
clumps of bushes and over grassy rises, I was sometimes able,

21

for a moment, to imagine myself not in the centre of the greatest city on earth but in some pleasant rural Eden. My way brought me at length through a fringe of trees and out by the Serpentine, which – as if pressed flat by the heavy sky – lay as still as a newly poured bath, glowing with the surly sheen of pewter. Around the shore, as their nurses looked on, children played with hoops and sticks, or put dolls to sleep in their own perambulators, or chased after a silly dog (a bundle of white curls, with no discernible face) which had made off with a ball and chewed it half to pieces. One little boy was wailing inconsolably, and I stopped to ask him the matter.

'I've lost my duck,' he sobbed, pointing to a little wooden pintail, which had bobbed out of reach and seemed to be trying to join the real ducks in the middle of the lake.

It was here that fate first took a hand; for I went to back to the trees, broke off a small branch, and (after a good deal of getting it, and losing it, and getting it again) managed to retrieve the toy, and return it to its owner. And had it not been for this small delay, I should not still have been there five minutes later, when a voice suddenly called out:

'Hartright!'

I turned, and could not for a moment identify the fashionably dressed young man who had broken from the crowd and was advancing smiling towards me. It was only when he pointed to the stick that still hung dripping from my hand, and said, laughing, 'What? Trying to catch dinner?' that I knew him by his voice.

'Travis!' I said.

It was no wonder that I had not recognized him, for he had grown a beard, and, instead of his usual get-up, was sporting a check waistcoat and a new soft felt hat. He carried a large portfolio, which he pinioned under his arm while he removed a flawless yellow glove and shook my hand.

'Where are you going?' we both said together, and laughed.

'Sir William Butteridge,' he said. He tried to sound nonchalant, but his face shone, and in struggling to suppress his smile he distorted his next words so much that all I could make out was '. . . discuss a . . .'

'A *what*?'

'A commission.'

'Really? That's wonderful!' I said. And I was, needless to say, truly delighted for him; but I cannot deny that I felt a pang of envy, too, swiftly followed by satisfaction at the recollection of my own commission, and as swiftly again by frustration that I was sworn to secrecy, and could not, therefore, counter 'Sir William Butteridge' with 'Lady Eastlake'.

'Is it in there?' I asked, nodding towards the portfolio.

'Just a few sketches. You want to see?'

He laid the portfolio on a bench and opened it. Inside were some rough drawings of a sickly-looking young woman with flowing hair clutching a broken column for support. 'She's swooning at the sight of her lover,' Travis explained, pointing at a vague blob on the left-hand side, 'who is returning, mortally wounded, after a seven-year absence. Faith and Purity, that's what Sir William wants. I think I've got it, don't you?'

'I'm sure he'll be very pleased.' It did occur to me that, since Sir William had made his fortune dispossessing widows and orphans from the path of railways, he might stand in greater need of faith and purity than most; but I said nothing.

'There's money in mediaevalism,' said Travis, perhaps feeling he had failed to impress me as an artist, and must therefore do so as a man of the world. 'Take my advice, Hartright. Find yourself a knight and a damsel, and set to work.'

'I haven't the time, just at the moment,' I said. I hesitated, giving him an opportunity to ask me why not; but he merely busied himself with putting his sketches away, so I went on: 'Tell me, what do you remember of Turner?'

'Turner? I barely met him,' he said, closing the portfolio. 'My first Academy dinner was his last. I did see him once or twice on Varnishing Days, but it would never have occurred to me to speak to him.' He turned towards me, and a spasm of silent laughter shook his heavy chestnut curls like blossom on a tree. 'Like sauntering up to the altar, and helping yourself to communion wine.'

'Was he really so extraordinary?' I said.

'Not to look at,' he said. 'Well, yes, *extraordinary*, but not in the way you mean. Not *impressive*. He was about so tall!' – he held his hand out, below the level of his own shoulder – 'with a huge

Jew nose, and beady grey eyes, and an enormous top hat with the nap brushed the wrong way, and an old-fashioned coat with tails that almost swept the ground (and couldn't have been much dirtier if they had), and long sleeves that entirely covered his filthy hands. Like this.' He hunched forward, miming the ridiculous little figure he had described. Several passers-by stopped to stare, and a small girl erupted in uncontrollable giggles. I could not help laughing myself – Travis always looks most beatific when he is being most malicious, and seeing his pale, noble face contort into this grotesque hobgoblin was irresistibly comical – but it made me uncomfortable, as if I had joined in the mockery of some poor unfortunate whose only fault was his unusual appearance.

'I meant,' I said, 'was he really so great a genius?'

'Certainly if you equate genius with industry,' said Travis. 'He never stopped. Rain, shine, awake, asleep, in the water closet . . . He's doubtless at it now, scraping sunsets on his coffin lid.'

'Oh, come now,' I said, laughing. 'What's your true opinion?'

He did not reply at once, but stared gravely at the ground, as if seeking an answer there. Finally, he said:

'We thought so then. Or, rather, we thought he was a genius who had lost his powers, and degenerated into madness.'

'How mad?' I said.

'Just look at his late pictures,' he replied. 'Colours entirely divorced from any object. Great splotches of paint that look like nothing at all, save – splotches of paint. *Pictures of nothing*, as the critic said, *and very like.*'

'And what do you think now?' I said.

He shrugged. 'Some of the early work. The Dutch sea pieces. The engravings.'

I waited for him to go on, but he didn't: he took a watch from his pocket, looked at it, then gathered up the portfolio.

'Can you suggest anyone else,' I said, 'who might have known him better?'

'Jones?'

'I've written to him.'

He shrugged again, and shook his head. It was only after we had shaken hands, and said goodbye, and gone a few paces on our separate ways, that he turned and called:

'Try Davenant. He's in retirement now, at Hampstead. But still has his memory, and likes to open it to the public sometimes, and display the contents.'

This slight encounter had given me, in truth, little enough; but for some reason – no more, maybe, than that I had at last taken the initiative – I came away from it filled with a new spirit. Or perhaps it would be truer to say an old spirit: for, like the face in a crowd which suddenly calls to mind a long-forgotten childhood playfellow, I knew it at once for something I had known before. My heart beat faster; my legs ached with a tremulous excitement; I filled my lungs, and found in the smoky air, which only an hour ago had tasted of drudgery and sickness, an intoxicating hint of romance – I felt, in short, like a young man again, newly released from dull routine and about to embark on some great adventure. Had you seen me striding through the Regent's Park and up Avenue Road (it did not even occur to me to take a cab), you might have fancied you saw the ghost of that other Walter Hartright, who, fifteen years ago, his head full of simple purposes and grand hopes, used to walk from London to Hampstead three times a week, and think nothing of it. I seemed, indeed, to glimpse him myself sometimes, marching companionably at my side; and it was surely at his prompting that I broke my journey at a plain roadside inn, and sat with him over a plain luncheon of bread and cheese and ale – I the grave master of Limmeridge, and he the cheerful young drawing teacher, with neither the burden nor the privilege of fortune, and no prospect save the prospect of life itself.

Mr. Davenant (I learned at the post office) lived not half a mile from my mother's old cottage, in one of those quaint red-brick houses in Church Row. Its once-regular façade had started to sag and buckle with age, giving it the unsteady look of a child's drawing (Florrie, indeed, would have got the lines straighter!), as if it had tired of classical sobriety, and decided to get drunk. A big wood-clad bay window, jutting out pugnaciously from the first floor like the stern of an old man-of-war, added to the air of disorder.

The door was opened by a young manservant who still seemed pitifully uncertain of his duties. When I inquired if Mr.

Davenant was at home he said: 'I'll go and ask him'; a moment later he came back, his cheeks flaming, to ask my name; and then, after a few steps, stopped, and turned again – presumably to find out my business. He was interrupted, however, by a man's voice booming down from upstairs:

'Who is that, Lawrence?'

'Mr. Hartright, sir,' called the boy.

'Who?'

'Mr. Hartright!'

'What does he want?' shouted the man, as if he were commanding a company of troops.

'What do you want?' stammered the boy.

'To talk about Turner,' I said.

The boy relayed this to the man upstairs, who promptly roared:

'What the devil does that mean?'

'What the –?' began the boy, so thoroughly embarrassed now that you could have lit a cigar from his face. I stepped past him into the hall, to be met by a line of unsmiling family portraits and, at the foot of the stairs, a large oil-painting of what appeared to be the Battle of Waterloo. Staring down at me from the first-floor landing was a fine-looking man of seventy or so, with white whiskers, a noble nose and a heroic brow. He wore a paint-stained smock tied loosely at the neck, and was tapping the handle of a brush impatiently against the banister.

'I was told you knew Turner well,' I said.

'Oh, yes,' he said, 'and what of it?'

'I am hoping to write his biography.'

'Are you, by God?' He leant forward, peering closely at me. 'You're not that what-ye-call-him, been making such a damned nuisance of himself?'

'Do you mean Mr. Thornbury?' I said.

He grunted.

'No,' I said.

He pondered a moment, then said: 'Come up. Fifteen minutes.'

A moonlit seascape hung above the stairs, and another battle scene – showing a knot of red-coated soldiers clustered round a tattered union flag, while the shadowy enemy crept towards

them through a fog of gunsmoke – dominated the landing. I
stopped before it, and asked:

'Is that one of yours?'

He nodded abruptly. 'Can't get rid of 'em. No-one wants anything now except pretty little pictures of their families, all
scrubbed clean and dressed up like tailors' dummies. And those
damned fainting women.' He shook his head. 'Madness.'

I could not help smiling – he had skewered both Travis and
me with a single stroke – but fortunately he was too busy wiping his fingers on his smock to notice.

'It's very impressive,' I said.

He nodded again. 'There, I shan't smear you now,' he said,
and grasped my hand. 'How d'ye do?'

As if that simple formality had qualified me to be admitted to
his confidence, he turned and led me into a double room –
divided in the middle by folding doors – which ran the entire
depth of the house. At one end was the large bay, giving a distant
view of the heath and washing the walls and floor with silvery
light; at the other, a south-facing rear window, unshuttered,
but screened with a sheet, presumably to mute the effect of
the sun.

A huge unfinished canvas, held upright on a crude frame,
stood in the bay, next to a table spread with brushes and an
open paintbox. It was turned to catch the north light, and I
could consequently only half-see the subject; but I made out
enough – a woman on a horse, surrounded by armed men, and
a line of sails on the horizon – to guess that the subject was
Queen Elizabeth before the Spanish Armada. On a dais in the
centre of the room, a woman in a blue velvet cloak and a tall hat
sat for the central figure. Her 'horse' had been ingeniously constructed of three bolsters lashed together and laid between a
pair of trestles; and she held before her a wooden sword, which
– doubtless because she had been at it some time, and her arm
was tired – wavered perilously.

'Very well,' said Davenant. 'You can have a break, Mrs. Holt.'

'It would be as well, sir,' she said, taking off her hat, 'if you're
to get your dinner.'

'Never mind about my dinner,' he said. 'If I keep you here all
afternoon, it's no matter: you can send out for a pie. A cup of tea

in the kitchen, to restore you; and then back to singeing King Philip's beard.'

'Yes, sir,' she said, compliantly enough – but her eyes rolled with a comic exasperation that fell just short of outright insolence.

'Begone with you, you besom,' said Davenant, raising his hand as if to strike her. 'And tell Lawrence to bring us some wine.'

'Yes, sir,' she said, laughing.

There was a moment's silence after she had gone. Davenant glanced out of the window, then turned and fixed me with a frank gaze. With a gravity I had not heard before, he said:

'Turner was my friend, Mr. Hartright. I'll not do anything to injure him. If you want scandal, or gossip, you won't get it here.'

'I give you my word,' I said, 'I am only interested in the truth.'

'I'll tell you that, and gladly,' he said. 'But mind – I speak only of what I know.' He paused; then, pulling two chairs from the wall, muttered: 'And I could earnestly wish others would the same. Will you sit down?'

'Thank you.'

'I sometimes think you could knock on any door in London, and find someone there whose acquaintance with Turner extends, at most, to having once seen him get out of a cab – and who will cheerfully swear on that basis that he was the most crabbed, suspicious, miserable skinflint in creation.'

I laughed; and he acknowledged it with a chuckle, and a curious little bounce of the head, as if I had complimented him on some soldierly skill. He went on:

'But I knew him for thirty years, and found him as kind and sociable as any man I ever met. You certainly couldn't have asked for a tenderer friend.' He sat down, tugging at the knees of the old-fashioned breeches beneath his smock. 'I was sick as a dog, once – the doctors almost gave me up, and most of my family, too – but Turner'd come every day, to inquire after my health, and wish me better – even, I afterwards discovered, when I was too weak to receive him myself, and he got no more for his pains than two minutes' conversation with my housekeeper.' He shook his head, and his eyes sparkled with tears, which he made no effort to hide.

'But what of his supposed moroseness, and meanness?' I said.

'Why, as to that – you never saw such a fellow for merriment and hilarity, when he was easy, and among friends. Get up any little social or professional party, and he'd gladly participate, and pay his share – and sometimes, to my knowledge, he'd defray the whole expense himself, without others knowing it.'

'How then did he get such a reputation?' I asked. I was, I confess, astonished: for this genial figure bore no relation to Travis's crazed dwarf – or to the misanthropic miser I had heard of at the Academy, or to Lady Eastlake's friendless recluse.

'Oh, I won't deny there may have been reason enough, for those who judge a man by his appearance, and never trouble to look beneath the surface,' said Davenant. 'He lived most of his life with his old father, and much of the rest alone; and never learnt good domestic management – and thus could not receive his friends at his own table, as he told me on many occasions he would have liked. And he could be gruff, sometimes, too – especially if he thought you were trying improperly to find out his secrets, or interfere with his habits.'

But why (I immediately thought) should a man be at so much pains to protect his privacy, unless he has something shameful to conceal? I kept the question to myself; but, as if he could look into my mind, Davenant said:

'I don't know if you've a wife, Mr. Hartright – and, if so, how you live with her, and, if not, how you do without one – but you might well feel that it was no damned business of mine, unless you chose to tell me, and I should heartily agree with you.'

The young manservant entered, carrying a tray with a decanter and two glasses. He stood trembling while Davenant made a space for it on his painting table, and then set it down without mishap.

'Thank you, Lawrence,' said Davenant, as the boy withdrew. 'That was Turner's view,' he went on, as if there had been no interruption. 'To hate humbug, and meddling, and condemnation, was almost a religious principle with him. I never heard him speak ill of a fellow-creature, or fail to put the best construction he could on another's behaviour. If he couldn't defend you, or approve your work, he'd hold his tongue. Will you take some wine, sir?'

'Thank you.'

'He wouldn't pry into your private affairs,' he said, busying himself with the decanter, 'and asked nothing more in return than that you shouldn't pry into his. And all I can say is: I wish to God there were more like him.' He handed me a glass, full to the brim with brown sherry; then raised his own, and, looking straight before him, as if he could see Turner's face etched upon the empty air, said: 'Here's honour to your memory, you old scamp.' He drank, and turned immediately towards me. 'Your very good health, Mr. Hartright.'

'And yours,' I said. And yet I did not drink; for, in some obscure way, it seemed that to do so would be to set a kind of seal on our conversation, implying that I accepted not only his hospitality, but also his account of Turner – which, in truth, had left me more puzzled and unsatisfied than ever. I merely touched the glass to my lips, therefore, and tried feverishly to compose a question that would press him further without angering him.

Once again, he seemed to anticipate my thoughts.

'You may yet wonder', he said, sitting down again, 'how such a man could have been the butt of so much malice, and so many hateful anecdotes? And the only answer I can give you is: envy. Most people seem to conceive of artists as little less than angels, but they're not, by God! – in my experience, outside a school-room, you won't find a bigger pack of squabbling, jealous, back-stabbing cheats and bullies anywhere on earth. They all try to make themselves into geniuses; and if they can't do that, they'll say anything, and believe anything, that seems to make the geniuses more like themselves.'

He hesitated; and for a moment I considered pointing out that I was an artist myself, of sorts; but quickly thought better of it.

'And Turner *was* a genius, Mr. Hartright,' he went on. 'He was *the* genius, I'd take my oath upon it. Varnishing Days at the Academy, before the Exhibition, the rest of us'd just be putting the finishing touches to our work; but he'd send in a more or less bare canvas, and you'd see the younger members looking at it, and laughing, and saying: 'What's he going to do with that?'

And then he'd walk in, and open his little box of tricks, and get to work – never standing back, to look at what he was doing, for it was all in his head – and within a few hours he'd have conjured a picture out of nothing. If a savage had seen it, he'd have sworn it was magic. I remember, indeed, a young Scotch fellow watching it once, and going quite pale, and muttering something about sorcery.'

'But surely', I said, 'no painter could fail to admire . . .'

He gave a derisive splutter. 'Imagine, Mr. Hartright,' he said, 'you have laboured for six months on a painting, and are mightily pleased with it, and think it will get you a knighthood; and along comes Turner, and in a single day produces its nemesis, so that you are utterly eclipsed . . .'

I laughed nervously, for his words had struck a hidden weakness in me; and I suddenly found that I *could* imagine it, all too easily; and for a moment felt the chill of some bottomless desolation fall upon me like a shadow.

'If you did a bright sun or a blue sky,' he said, 'he'd as like as not try to make a brighter or a bluer. Once, I recall, he'd done a beautiful grey picture of *Helvoetsluys*, without a hint of positive colour; and next to it was Constable's *Opening of Waterloo Bridge*, which seemed to have been painted in liquid gold and silver; and Turner looked several times from one to the other, and then fetched his palette, and put a daub of red lead on his grey sea, a little bigger than a shilling, and went away without a word.' He started to laugh. 'And poor Constable groaned: "Turner's been here, and fired a gun"; for, of course, his own picture now looked weak and insipid by comparison.'

'Perhaps, then,' I said, 'it's little wonder Turner was so much disliked.'

Davenant nodded. 'But what none of them understood was, he meant no harm by it. It was but a kind of friendly rivalry, a goad to make us all strive harder, to perfect our art. If you outdid him, he'd laugh about it, and clap you on the back, and tell you to enjoy your victory. And he'd as soon help you as fight you. No man had a truer eye for what was wrong with a picture, or for how to make it right.' He got up. 'Let me show you something.'

I followed him on to the landing and halfway down the stairs, where he stopped before the moonlit seascape I had passed, not a quarter of an hour since, on my way up. I now noticed, picked out in black lettering on the frame, the title: *Dover beach: night. By John Davenant, R.A. Exhibited 1837.*

'There,' he said.

It was a dramatic enough scene, with moonlight spilling out from behind a great bank of dark cloud, and then shattering into a hundred pieces on the inky sea. Just below the horizon was a heeling merchantman, its full sails almost black in the eerie light.

'It has great power,' I said, glad to be able to praise something wholeheartedly at last.

He nodded, colouring with pleasure. 'But the power is Turner's. My first conception was quite different – no cloud at all, and the moonlight falling straight on to the ship, and making the sails glow white – and that is what I painted. But when I saw it framed, and hung at the Academy, I knew it was wrong, and so did my friends – but could any of us say where the fault lay?' He shook his head. 'Not until Turner chanced by, clutching his palette, and looked at it for half a minute, and said: "It wants depth, and contrast. You should cover over the moon – make the mass of the cloud black, and the edges silver, so you've got the brightest and the darkest next to each other – put the sails in shadow, and a dab of light on the bow." Well, I felt the truth of this, but I was naturally rather cautious, and, try as I might, I could not get the effect he meant; and after coming back once or twice to see how I was getting on, he finally lost patience with me, and seized the brushes, and did it himself – two great strokes of black, two of white' – here he mimed the words, with large sweeping gestures – 'one, two, three, four. And of course we all saw at once that he was right.'

Davenant stood back to admire the painting, chuckling and shaking his head in wonderment; but I felt faintly disturbed – not merely by the high-handedness of Turner's intervention, but also by its result: for it had instantaneously transformed a scene of bland tranquillity into one of louring menace. My thoughts, however, were at that instant disrupted by the sound of footsteps from below, and by Davenant's suddenly roaring, so loudly that I nearly leapt from my skin:

'Good God, Hartright, there's dedication for you!'

I turned, and saw Mrs. Holt coming upstairs towards us.

'She doesn't wait to be called, you note!' said Davenant. 'Can't wait to get back to harrying the dons!'

'We'll lose the light, sir, is all I was thinking,' said the cook.

'Very true, Mrs. Holt,' said Davenant. He turned to me. 'She's quite right, I fear, Mr. Hartright. You will, I hope, forgive me . . .?'

'Of course,' I said. 'It was very good of you to give me as much time as you have.'

'Nonsense,' he said. 'Delighted to help. If I have. Which I doubt . . .'

I started to speak, but he held up his hand, and went on:

'None of your damned flattery, now. Go on up, Mrs. Holt, and get on your regalia. I'll be with you in a moment.' Then he took my arm affably, and led me downstairs.

He had opened the door, and was about to shake my hand, when he stopped suddenly, and said:

'Will you wait a minute, Mr. Hartright? Something I think may assist you.'

He crossed the hall, and entered a room at the back of the house. I stood beneath his bay window, and looked about me. To the south, the smoke hung over London like a great mantle, so thick and black that just to see it was to feel the weight of it on your chest, and its woolly itch against your skin; but here a fresh breeze ruffled my hair, and there were chinks of blue between the grey-rimmed clouds that churned and tumbled above the heath. Something in their wild motion put me in mind of sporting sea creatures, and I watched, rapt, until his voice roused me from my reverie:

'Here,' he said, handing me a folded sheet of paper. 'Two more people who knew him well. But neither of them painters; so you may be sure that what they tell you will be untainted by artistic rancour. Michael Gudgeon's an antiquary, who travelled with Turner years ago on a tour of Kent and Sussex. And Amelia Bennett is old Benjamin Waley's daughter . . .'

He paused, searching my face for some sign of recognition. I shook my head.

'You're too young, I suppose,' he said, with a sigh. 'He was quite a man in his day. A great amateur, who befriended Turner when he was little more than a boy.'

I thanked him warmly, and started for Kensington in high good spirits. I had trusted to fate, and fate had amply repaid me; and some almost superstitious conviction told me that it had not done with me yet, but would repay me further still when I got home.

And I was not mistaken; for there, in the hall, was the enclosed note from Ruskin!

My love as always, to you and to the children.

Walter

VI

Letter from John Ruskin to Walter Hartright, 1st August, 185–

163 Dennmark Hill,
1st August, 185–

Dear Mr. Hartright,

Thank you for your letter of 21st July. I should have replied sooner, had I been here to receive it, but I only returned yesterday from a long absence in Italy and France.

Yes, I shall be happy to talk to you about Turner – although I am not sure how far it lies within my power (or the power of any man or woman) to light your way. I fear, however, that I shall be unable to see you this week – for, as I am sure you know, it is the inevitable consequence of travel to come back and find one's garden choked with weeds, and, if I do not set to at once, some of my tenderest plants (a book, a lecture, and a thousand shy little shoots that seem to have sprung from my words, and to want only encouragement to flourish) will surely die. Would Thursday next, at three o'clock, be convenient?

Yours very truly,

John Ruskin

VII

From the diary of Marian Halcombe, 4th August, 185–

A small cottage, with but one window on each floor, and entirely unremarkable save for a curious iron railing on the parapet, that

34

looked as if a balcony had decided to emigrate from its original home to the roof. On one side, a tavern; on the other a little shop, advertising 'ales', 'refreshments' and 'first-class ginger-beer'; next to that, a knock-kneed gateway bearing a weatherbeaten sign – all you could read was 'Ale anders Boat ard', so you had to fill in the ghosts of the missing 'x' and 'y' yourself – and leading to an untidy sprawl of spars and timbers and ropes. Facing the house, beyond the road, flowed the great river, hemmed in by a shallow embankment of rough stones, and approached by a flight of steps, which were crowded with lounging watermen smoking their pipes and waiting for custom. Further out, a desultory little army of mudlarks in ragged dress scoured the stinking mud for treasure.

'Are you sure this is the right address?' I asked the driver.

'Six Davis Place, Chelsea, miss?' he said, slowly, as if I were an idiot.

I got out. A knot of boys kicking a broken bottle stopped to stare at me, and two or three of the watermen stiffened and turned in my direction. They may simply have been bored, or hoping I would take a boat; but there seemed a kind of animal watchfulness in their unsmiling faces, as if, even at this time of day, a lone woman could have no rightful business here. I knew, though, that to show fear is to feed the monster that frightens us, so I paid the cabman and marched up the path without so much as a backward glance.

As I knocked on the door, however, I sensed a movement behind me, and, looking round, saw that the group of boys had followed me, and were pressing against the gate like a pack of wild dogs. Most of them instantly turned their heads to avoid my eyes, but one, a gangly beanpole of twelve or thirteen, held my gaze steadily.

'You want to know about Puggy?' he called.

I couldn't tell whether he was mocking me or trying to be helpful; but since I have found that, if you expect the best of people, they generally strive to live up to your expectations, I smiled and said:

'Booth. I'm looking for Mrs. Booth.'

'She won't tell you nothing about him,' said the boy.

There was no sound from within the house, so I knocked again.

The boy called: 'Ask Mr. Neave about him.'

The words were barely out of his mouth when I heard a man shouting: 'That's right, miss, I knew the Admiral!'

I turned, and saw one of the watermen (presumably Mr. Neave) crossing the road towards me. He seemed to have been drinking, for he staggered a little, and waved his arms wildly to attract my attention.

'I took them everywhere,' he said, gesturing across the river towards Battersea. 'You come with me, I'll show you where they went.'

I had no idea what they were talking about, but did not want to show it, for fear that it might encourage them to take some advantage of me, so I said nothing, and knocked for a third time. But I was beginning to lose heart. What if – as now seemed probable – Mrs. Booth were out, and I had to walk down the path again, and through the throng? My cab had long since disappeared from view, and there was not another in sight. To add to my disquiet, three or four more men, apparently attracted by the commotion, now spilled out of the tavern. One was a most impressive figure, a black-bearded giant in a red flannel shirt and pleated black French trousers, who elbowed his way to the front and bellowed, in what sounded like a Russian or Polish accent:

'I tell you about the Admiral! The bottles! The ladies!'

'You lying foreign b–!' shouted Mr. Neave. Emboldened by drink, he clenched his fists and lurched forward, scattering boys on every side, although he could barely reach his opponent's shoulder.

'Please!' I shouted. 'I have no interest in any Admiral!'

I hoped this would calm them, but it appeared to have no effect. The men jostled themselves into two groups, while the boys lined up against the fence, either because they wanted to watch or because they could not escape. I quickly formulated a plan: I would appeal to the beanpole's chivalrous instincts and offer him and his friends a penny apiece to escort me safely to the nearest cab stand.

I had already started back towards them when, at last, I heard the door opening behind me. I turned and saw a handsome, dark-haired, sturdily built woman of sixty or so, wearing a plain grey dress and a white apron. Her eyes stared past me towards the crowd at the gate. Her sallow, heavy-featured face wore an expression of infinite, exasperated sadness, such as you might see on a nurse who discovers her charges, yet again, doing something they know is wrong. To my astonishment, that look alone was enough to restore order: the two opposing factions melted away without a word, and the boys, as if suddenly released from captivity, scampered at full tilt down the street.

'Mrs. Booth?' I said.

She turned towards me. She inclined her head slightly, but did not smile.

'I am Marian Halcombe,' I said. 'I believe Lady Eastlake wrote to you . . .?'

'Yes,' she said. There was a rural lilt to her voice, but its tone was perfectly neutral, neither friendly nor unfriendly. 'Will you please come in, Miss Halcombe?'

The hall was so poky and dark that I could see almost nothing, and had to rely on the bobbing beacon of Mrs. Booth's apron string to guide me. But the little parlour she led me into was pleasant enough, with a lively fire burning in the grate, and a strange-looking tailless cat stretched on the rug before it. A canary chirruped in its cage in the window, and a stout grandfather clock ticked soothingly by the door, as if Time, too, had been caught and tamed, and put in a corner to add his voice to the domestic chorus.

'Please sit down,' said Mrs. Booth, 'while I fetch the tea.' She was immediately gone again, and a moment later I heard her clumping down into the basement. I rose, and looked about me. The room was, for the most part, quite unexceptional, and such as you might expect to find in the housekeeper's quarters of any well-run large house: neat cupboards, with white-painted panelled doors, flanked the fireplace; a cavalcade of china milkmaids, led by a Macready toby jug, marched across the mantel-shelf; and on the chimney breast above hung a watercolour of a church and some miniatures in oval frames.

It was only when I turned back towards the hall that I noticed something unusual. Two oil-paintings, stacked one behind the other and half covered by a sheet, leant against the wall between door and window. Seeing the corner of a gilt frame, and a whirl of leaden colour, I was overcome with curiosity, and immedi-

37

ately bent down and lifted the cloth. The images that greeted me were so terrible, and yet so vague, that they seemed to have been conjured from a nightmare. The first showed a wild, grey-green sea stirred into an implacable fury; in the foreground, indistinct figures clung desperately to a queer, serpentine lump of wreckage which rose from the spume like a sea-monster, and, further off, a cutter sailed to their rescue. The second, behind it, was perhaps the same scene the following day: a crowd gathered on the shore, dumbstruck at the frightful proof of nature's destructive power littered all about them; while on the horizon, lit by an ulcerous, unforgiving yellow sun, a disabled ship with two masts gone was just visible through the haze. Their impact – at least on me – was almost physical, and somewhat as I imagine the effect of mesmerism to be; I lost all thought of where I was, or what I was doing there, and was still staring when Mrs. Booth re-entered.

'Ah, yes,' she said, colouring slightly. 'Those are his. He gave them to me.'

'What, Mr. Turner!' I exclaimed. I must have sounded, I fear, more amazed than I should have done – partly because the only Turner I could remember seeing was the stately engraving in the hall at Brompton Grove of *London from Greenwich Park*, showing a tranquil classical landscape with a distant view of the smoke-covered city and its river, which seemed to bear no relation to these desolate scenes at all; and partly because it had never occurred to me that Mrs. Booth might have any of his pictures in her possession.

'Yes,' she said, setting her tray down. I expected her to go on, but she busied herself instead with the tea, pouring two cups and then perching the pot at the edge of the fire basket to keep warm. Hoping to revive the subject I said:

'That was very generous of him.'

I regretted the words even before they were out of my mouth. She coloured again, and said:

'What, you think I didn't deserve so much kindness?'

'No, of course not. I merely meant . . .' I could not, of course, say what I really meant: that few successful artists would have dealt so handsomely with a servant. To cover my confusion, I said:

'Why do you not hang them?'

'I had them upstairs, but I feared they might be stolen. My son is going to keep them safe for me.'

I confess I found myself wondering why she did not sell them, for they must surely be worth a great deal of money; and in doing so she could simultaneously remove the cause of her anxiety and ensure herself a comfortable old age. Perhaps she guessed what I was thinking, for she said:

'I could not bear to part with them.'

'They remind you of the sea?' I said.

She nodded.

'You have naval connections, perhaps?' I said. 'The boys outside mentioned –'

'The Admiral?'

'Yes.'

She nodded again, but wearily. 'That is what they called him.'

'Mr. Turner?' I said; for, though it seemed unlikely, we had talked of no-one else.

'Yes,' she said. 'They called him Admiral Booth.' She paused, and looked coolly at my astonished face; then, as if I should have divined it for myself, went on: 'They thought he was my husband.'

I felt quite lost, like a traveller who suddenly discovers he is without both map and compass. What could I ask that would not appear rude – the most obvious question, *Why?*, would certainly have fallen into this category – or, on the other hand, risk eliciting some new piece of startling information which would only bemuse me further? At length I said, cautiously:

'How long did you know Mr. Turner?'

'Twenty years,' she said. 'He first came to me when I had a boarding-house in Margate. Then, after Mr. Booth died, he wanted a retreat by the river; so he asked me to move to Chelsea, and keep house for him here.'

'He must have had great confidence in you,' I said.

She nodded, a proud woman briskly acknowledging her due. 'He used to call me the handmaiden of Art.'

'You helped him in his work, then?'

'Oh, yes, I'd set his palette every morning, and make sure everything was ready.' She said this with a certain warmth, as if she had begun to feel easier in my presence. A second or two later, the cat unexpectedly furthered my cause by getting up and jumping into my lap, where it stood lazily sinking its claws into my dress. For the first time since my arrival, Mrs. Booth smiled.

'Oh, you're very honoured,' she said. 'Jason generally only likes men. Mr. Turner, especially. He'd sit on his knee, his shoulder – even his head, sometimes.'

I laughed, and decided this would be a propitious moment to venture a little further.

'What kind of a man was Mr. Turner?'

'There were times', she said, 'when I thought he was a god.'

'A god!' I said. 'Why, did he resemble a Greek statue?'

Mrs. Booth laughed. 'Oh, I don't mean to look at!' she said. 'In his work.' She waved a hand towards the two oil-paintings. 'You or I could stand where he did, and see nothing but a rough old day, or a wintry sun. But he saw what ordinary mortal eyes can't see. He saw into the heart of things.'

I found myself thinking: *Dear Lord, I hope the heart of things doesn't look like that*. But I said:

'Yes, they are magnificent.'

That seemed to please her. She brightened, and – as if surprised by her own candour – said:

'Would you like to see the room where he died, Miss Halcombe?'

In truth, I should have preferred to stay where I was, and finish my tea, and ask her more questions; but I could not very well refuse, so I replied:

'Yes, I should. Very much.'

We went up the cramped staircase, which squeaked under our weight like a procession of complaining mice, and entered a small attic at the front of the house. The feeble sun seeped through a square, deep-set dormer, casting a watery pattern of light and shadow on the neighbouring wall. The left-hand side of the room was dominated by a simple brass bed, and a single wheelback chair stood before the window. The boards were bare, and there was no other furniture save a plain cupboard, a small table set with a bowl and ewer, and an iron ladder leading to a trapdoor in the ceiling. It looked like the kind of lodging where a struggling actor or a poor travelling salesman might seek refuge from the disappointments of the day.

'This was his room,' said Mrs. Booth. 'Every morning he would rise before dawn, and throw a blanket round him, and go up there' – here she indicated the ladder – 'on to the roof, and sketch the sunrise.'

'Ah,' I said. 'That's why the parapet's railed?'

She nodded. 'And then he'd come back to bed, and rest till breakfast time. And so he went on, right up until his last illness. He was indefatigable, Miss Halcombe. Even when I was nursing him, I had to make sure he always had pencils and paper to hand.'

'Was he still able to paint, then?' I asked.

'Not at the very end,' she said. 'But not to have the hope of it would have killed him that much sooner. So I always kept up the pretence: *Perhaps tomorrow, my dear.*'

How many housekeepers call their master 'my dear'?

'He was very lucky to have you, Mrs. Booth,' I said.

She did not answer, seemingly lost in her own thoughts. At length she said:

'I'll tell you a strange thing, Miss Halcombe. A few weeks before he died, the police dragged out of the river some poor girl, who had fallen into disgrace, and drowned herself.' She moved towards the window, and pointed down to the embankment steps, where the watermen were still idling the afternoon away. 'Just there. And Mr. Turner was very troubled by it, and kept waking me in the night, and saying he saw her face, and feared to sleep. "I must draw it," he said. "I must draw that face, or I shall have no rest." And so he drew it, and it was almost the last picture he ever made.'

'And was he still haunted by it?' I asked.

'He never spoke of it again,' she said. 'Leastways, not that I recall.'

She was quiet then, and I feared I had lost her to her own memories. I said:

'How did he come to see her, if he was in bed, and she outside?'

'It was a terrible winter,' she said. 'Nothing but fog and smoke for weeks on end. He'd say, "I wish I could see the sun again" – but he could barely more than whisper it by then, it'd break your heart to hear him. So he'd roll on to the floor, and try to crawl to the window to look for it.'

'I see,' I said. 'So he was there when the police found her?'

She nodded abstractedly, as if her mind were on something more important. 'Sometimes', she said, 'he was too weak even to go that far, and I'd find him here, by the chair, and have to help him back to bed.'

Again she was silent, and, though she faced the window, I thought I saw a tear in the corner of her eye. Finally, she sighed, and said: 'But he did see it again. One morning, it suddenly broke through; and the doctor and I got him into the wheelchair, and pushed him here to the window, so that it could shine full on his face; and an hour later, as if he was satisfied at last, he died, without a murmur, with his head against my shoulder.'

Her voice did not quaver. And yet something in the way she spoke, bringing the thoughts from the depths of her own being, and then gently replacing them there, as if they were her most cherished possessions, told me, beyond doubt, that this was a woman who had not merely served Turner, but had loved him in every sense. And I knew – however hard it might be to believe – that the man described by Lady Eastlake as the foremost genius of the day had lived and died in this mean little house, under an assumed name, as his housekeeper's husband.

If I am honest, I have to say this realization prompted in me no other feeling for Mrs. Booth than deep pity, mingled with a genuine admiration. But what, I wondered, would Walter make of it? For the old widow, I was sure, he would share my sympathy and compassion; but would he view Turner himself in the same liberal spirit? Might the discovery of his subject's eccentricities (to put it as charitably as I can) make him lose interest in writing the *Life*, even before he has begun it?

It was therefore with some trepidation that I said:

'You have been very helpful, Mrs. Booth. Would it be possible for me to call again with my brother, who, I know, would like to talk to you himself?'

And it was with relief, as well as disappointment, that I heard her reply:

'I mean no offence, Miss Halcombe, but Mr. Turner's memory is sacred to me. I do not like to talk about him; and, to speak plain, I have already said more than I meant to. So, while I shall always be pleased to see you, if you pass this way, I must ask that you do not bring your brother here; for I could tell him nothing more than I have told you today.'

VIII

Letter from Walter Hartright to Laura Hartright, 11th August, 185–

Brompton Grove,
Friday

My dearest love,

Your letter is by me as I write – I glance over, and read 'I am so proud of you, Walter'; and the words sting me like a slap, for I am sure that had you seen me today you would have been anything but proud. I am just returned from Ruskin, you see, and know not what to make of him, or of what he told me – but I fear *he* has made a fool of me, and I of myself, and the result is that I am cast down, and quite confused.

The start of my perplexity is the man himself. Strange, is it not, how a famous name may produce an image in our minds, composed of who knows what scraps and trifles and odds and ends, yet strong enough, in the absence of personal experience, to *be* that person for us? Before today, without in the least reflecting on it, I saw Ruskin as a wild shaggy creature lurking in the dark somewhere (his natural abode has always seemed a cave, or a dungeon), waiting to rush out without warning and impale some poor unsuspecting painter. Perhaps this idea arises partly from my own dread, whenever I exhibit, that he will single out something of mine for particular scorn; and partly from – do you remember it? – that verse in *Punch*:

> I paints and paints, and no complaints;
> I sells before I'm dry;
> Then savage Ruskin sticks his tusk in
> And nobody will buy.

And just think – had I had no occasion to meet him, this fancy might, through sheer force of habit, have finally established itself in my mind as the truth; and so been passed on by our grandchildren to their grandchildren as a lifelike portrait of the great man!

43

At all events, they, and I, will be spared that; for the revolution of the last twelve hours has entirely deposed all my preconceptions, and despatched them to an exile from which they will never return.

My first surprise came even before I had met him, for 163 Dennmark Hill turns out to be a tall, rambling old house which – far from shrinking into the shadows – announces its presence with the beefy self-importance of a provincial lord mayor. It has its own porter's lodge (where I was obliged to state my business to a burly man with suspicious eyes and licorice breath, who said: 'That's Mr. *John* Ruskin, is it?' and then, before I was able to reply, peered at me through the window of the cab, and answered his own question: 'Yes, it'll be Mr. John'); and a carriage sweep; and walls furred with ivy; and a front door approached by railed steps, and almost hidden in the recesses of a heavy portico. From its size, in short, and its John Bull posture – feet splayed, elbows out – it looked more like the house of one of our fox-hunting neighbours in Cumberland than the home of the world's most celebrated art critic, on the fringes of the world's greatest city.

The footman who opened the door seemed ordinary enough; but for a fleeting moment I had the odd impression that the dim square hall behind him was filled with pale, elderly faces (it was difficult to be sure, for my eyes had not yet adjusted to the gloom), which promptly scattered, as soon as they saw me, like rabbits startled by a walker.

'Is Mr. Ruskin at home?' I asked.

'Mr. *John* Ruskin?' replied the man, in a stiff parody of the lodge-keeper.

'Yes,' I said, wondering secretly how many others there might be, and whether they all had opinions on Art.

He went upstairs; and, as soon as he had gone, two of the rabbits (as I supposed) reappeared. One was an old woman in a bonnet and a black dress; the other, a stocky man with ragged white hair and thick whiskers, wearing a dark jacket and a speckled twill waistcoat. Neither looked exactly like a servant, and there was something proprietorial in their manner; yet they hovered at the margins of the hall, as if they feared to take full possession of it, smiling uneasily at me, and looking away again

44

– like prosperous innkeepers, perhaps, whose house is their own, but who must defer to others within its walls.

'Mr. Hartright,' said a soft, gracious voice; and, looking up, I saw a man descending the stairs towards me. At first glance he seemed immensely tall; but as he reached the hall, and stood level with me, I saw that in fact he was merely extremely thin, with a long, close-fitting blue coat that hugged his slender frame and emphasized all the vertical lines in his appearance. He was about my own age, or a little older, with a bright complexion, thick yellow hair and whiskers, and beetling eyebrows. There was something almost foppish – even feminine – in the way he moved, and in the evident care he had taken in arranging his watch-chain and tying his cravat; but it was entirely contradicted by his sharp nose and deep-set blue eyes, which gave him the wary, petulant look of a beast disturbed in its lair.

'How very pleasant to meet you,' he said, taking both my hands in his. His lower lip, I noticed, was slightly deformed; but his smile more than atoned for it, transforming his expression, in an instant, from bad temper to sweetness. He turned to the old people and said, with a courtly air:

'Papa, Mama, this is Mr. Hartright. He's here to talk about Turner.'

I had heard, of course, of the poor man's marital difficulties; but the idea that in his middle years, and at the height of his eminence, he should have abandoned the part of a husband only to resume that of a son was strange indeed. I thought of what Davenant had told me of Turner and his father, and Marian had learnt from Mrs. Booth; and wondered if it was a mark of genius to be incapable of normal domestic arrangements.

'How d'ye do?' said the old man; and, as he and his wife stepped forward awkwardly to shake my hand, I at last recognized their odd mixture of pride and diffidence and concern for what it was, and felt suddenly – and quite unexpectedly – like a schoolboy invited to the home of a gifted but over-sensitive friend.

'Will you indulge me, Mr. Hartright,' said Ruskin, 'and take a walk in the garden? I've been in the thick of it all morning, and can't see for the smoke, or think for the noise of the guns.'

Without waiting for a reply, he ushered me quickly out of the front door again, as if anxious to make good his escape before his parents had time to forbid it.

'In the thick of what, may I ask?' I said, as we turned on to the carriage sweep. 'A new piece of criticism?'

'I *am* struggling to finish the last volume of *Modern Painters*,' he said. 'But I'm afraid I've come to the wretched conclusion that all my critical and historical work up till now has been almost valueless.'

'Oh, come . . .!' I said.

'It *is* a sad thought,' he said. 'Especially when you've devoted your whole life to a thing, as I have. But when I look about me, and see the burden of dumb misery in the world, and calculate what an infinitesimally small fraction of it I have managed to lift with my ruminations on Turner or Veronese or the Gothic . . .' He shook his head.

'But *Modern Painters*', I said, 'has given delight – and instruction – to thousands. Millions.' I confess that I was slightly abashed, when I reflected how little of it *I* had read, and how long ago; but not sufficiently to prevent my adding: 'Myself included.'

'You are kind to try to console me, Mr. Hartright,' he said. He stopped, and turned on me a gaze of extraordinary candour. 'But – forgive me – you do not look miserable – at least, not in the way I mean. When I speak of misery, I am thinking of that great mass of suffering humanity which surrounds us, and which we see – and yet do not see – every day; and which we barely touch with all our ideals and concerns.'

He rounded the end of the house, and ducked his head to enter a dark tunnel, pungent with the scent of damp leaves, formed by a dense old laurel bush pressing against the wall.

'And that is why', he said, the words – suddenly muffled now – floating back to me in the close air, 'I have begun to turn my attention to the question of political economy.'

I was, I must admit, surprised that he should be so frank with me, and not a little flattered; yet mingled with my gratification, as I followed his stooping figure through the dimness, was a slight repugnance – although I could not, at the time, have told you the reason for it.

'You may, of course, feel I have little enough reason to complain myself,' he said with a laugh, as we emerged behind the house. He gestured languidly towards the lawn, dotted with trees and artfully laced with winding paths that stretched away below us; and at the kitchen gardens and orchards and a row of farm buildings beyond. 'Our own milk and pigs,' he said, 'and peaches from the hothouses; and a meadow for the horses. Everything a mortal could desire, in fact, save a stream – and mountains.' I glanced towards him, and saw that he was smiling, and that he had the grace to blush.

'But enough of me, Mr. Hartright,' he said, suddenly setting off again. 'I have a lecture this evening, and fear I must leave at four o'clock. So, tell me, how fares your tremendous undertaking?'

'It's scarcely begun,' I said. 'But I have spoken to a few people who knew Turner.'

'Ah, yes,' he said. 'Who?'

I told him. He made no response of any kind; so I went on:

'And my sister has been to see his housekeeper.'

'Ah, the good Mrs. Booth,' he murmured. 'Did she elucidate the mystery, or add to it?'

From his sharp sidelong look I deduced that this was a test of some kind, and that his good opinion of me depended on my making the right answer; but since I had no idea what that might be, I said lamely:

'I don't know.'

He did not reply, but nodded; and, stopping by a green gate in a wall, opened it, and led me into one of the kitchen gardens. Around the perimeter ran a pleasant grassy walk, lined with fruit trees and rambling roses, and broken here and there by an arbour with a wooden seat.

'Peace,' he said, looking round. 'And the last blessed warmth of the sun.'

We sat on one of the benches, beneath a trailing rose that was still, even now, covered with flowers. Ruskin gazed silently at two apple trees near the opposite wall, as if gathering his thoughts. At length he said:

'You do know, do you not, that you are not alone, Mr. Hartright? There is already another labourer in the vineyard?'

'You mean Mr. Thornbury?' I said.

He nodded. 'What, if you will forgive my asking, makes you think that you are better qualified than he?'

This was delicate indeed, and I hesitated before answering:

'I was approached by a friend of Turner's, who expressed some confidence in me – and none whatever, I'm sorry to say, in Mr. Thornbury.'

'And may I inquire *which* friend?'

'That, I'm afraid, I cannot tell you.'

'I see.' He tapped his fingers and nodded, as if beating time to a tune in his own head.

I had chosen my words carefully, but I was forced to acknowledge that, even to my ears, they had sounded flimsy and unconvincing; and I was not entirely surprised when he went on:

'Sometimes, Mr. Hartright, we may deceive ourselves, or allow others to deceive us, into thinking we are capable of some great task which is beyond us. I speak here as a friend, and from my own experience. I regarded Turner as my earthly master. I venerated him. I knew him personally for the last ten years of his life, and for much of that time, and for long after his death, I thought of little but him and his work. And yet in many respects I feel I did not know him at all.'

Anxious not to appear still more foolish, I said nothing. He reached out to touch a white rose which drooped above his shoulder. A drop of moisture broke free from the petal where it had taken refuge, and rolled down his finger.

'Perhaps you know, Mr. Hartright, that the first volume of *Modern Painters* was intended as a defence of Turner against his critics. It was – as I am all too keenly aware – a youthful effort, full of a young man's zeal and prejudices – but it did enjoy a certain success. Yet it gave Turner, I believe, not an ounce of pleasure. Cold and solitary though he was, the flame of my approbation did not warm him. It was a year and a half before he even mentioned the book to me; and then, indeed, he did thank me, in his way – for he invited me in, one night after dinner, and insisted that I take a glass of sherry with him, in an under-room as chilly as the tomb, and lit by a single tallow candle. Yet he always made it plain that – though I regarded him, as I still regard him, as the greatest landscape painter in the history

48

of the world – I had not grasped the meaning, or the purpose, of his work. And I fear he was right.'

A wiry, grizzled man in a white shirt entered the kitchen garden, pushing a wheelbarrow. He stopped when he saw us, and tipped his moth-eaten felt hat.

'Good afternoon, Pearce,' called Ruskin.

'Good afternoon, sir.'

'Please, don't mind Mr. Hartright and me,' said Ruskin; and the man continued on his way. Ruskin turned to me again.

'But just how *little* I saw . . .' He shook his head. '*That* I only discovered this past winter, when I undertook to catalogue and preserve his drawings and sketches – which, naturally enough, this being England, were gathering dust and mildew in a basement at the South Kensington Museum.'

An electric tremor started in my stomach, and ran tingling to my fingertips.

'What did you find?' I asked.

He sighed. 'I found such pessimism, Mr. Hartright. And such courage.' He turned suddenly, and pulled the rose down so that it was close to my face. 'He saw the flower, in all its beauty, with a truer eye than any man who ever lived. And' – here he plunged his thumb deep into the petals, prising them apart – 'he saw the canker within, just as truly, and did not flinch from it. Look at any of his pictures with discernment enough, and at its heart you will find a dark clue.'

There was something in his manner as he said this – a portentous quiver in his voice, his eyes as mournful as a bloodhound's – that made me want to laugh. I mastered the impulse, however, and said:

'Clue to what?'

He did not reply; but raised a magisterial finger, and gave me a sternly pitying look – like a schoolmaster correcting a particularly obtuse pupil who has once again failed to understand some simple point.

I tried to keep the irritation from my voice. 'Are you speaking of any works in particular?'

'There are more than nineteen thousand of them,' he said. 'You must see them yourself. I can give you a note.'

'Thank you.'

'Indeed, the best advice I can offer you, if you would hope to know Turner, is: immerse yourself in his work.'

'But what of the man himself?' I said. 'His character? His tastes? His habits?'

He did not answer at once; but, raising his hand, called out to the gardener, who was passing with his newly filled barrow:

'Pearce!'

'Yes, sir?' said the man, stopping, and squinting towards us.

'Would you go to the house, and ask Crawley to fetch my Turner self-portrait, and . . .?'

'Beg pardon, sir, but fetch your *what*?'

'My Turner self-portrait,' said Ruskin (a trifle peevishly, I thought). 'And bring it here.'

'Yes, sir.'

'What were you saying?' said Ruskin, when the man had gone; and then, before I could speak, he went on: 'Ah, yes, his character. Well, all I can do for you is what I did for Mr. Thornbury. And that is tell you what – in my view – were Turner's principal qualities.'

'That would be very helpful,' I said.

He breathed deeply; and then, looking ahead, as if the words were written on a bill on some invisible hoarding, said slowly:

'Uprightness. Generosity. Tenderness. Sensuality. Obstinacy. Irritability. Infidelity.' He turned towards me. 'And never forget: he lived and died alone and without hope, knowing that none could understand him or his power.'

And what, in heaven's name, I thought, *am I to make of that?*

'Forgive me,' said Ruskin earnestly. 'Have I been too cryptic? It's a perennial fault of mine, I'm afraid – and what makes it all the worse is that I'm equally guilty, on occasion, of its opposite' – here he suddenly laughed – 'and drive my friends mad with my discursiveness.'

Again, the same boyish ingenuousness showed in his face; and I reflected that I had never before heard a man speak so eloquently, or with such feeling, about his own failings. Yet as I looked into the limpid brilliance of his eyes, I knew suddenly why I was as much troubled as disarmed by it; for behind the patina of openness and warmth lay a kind of reptilian coldness, which put me strangely in mind of those Arctic regions where the surface thaws in summertime, but the earth beneath is permanently frozen.

'I must confess,' I said, 'I feel rather daunted.'

'I am truly sorry if that is my doing,' he said. 'I meant only to point out the deserts you must cross and the peaks you must climb on your great journey.'

'I fear', I said, smiling, and endeavouring to make light of it, 'that you think me unequal to it, and believe that I shall fall by the wayside.'

He did not (as I own I had expected) hasten to reassure me; but rather looked off into the distance again, and resumed drumming on his knee. After a few seconds he leaned towards me and lightly touched my arm: 'I think perhaps it will be best', he said, 'if you continue your inquiries, and come to see me again at a later date. It may be then that what I have to say will seem less impenetrable.'

He spoke with such ineffable condescension that I bridled, and could not entirely keep the irritation from my voice as I replied:

'And how, in the meantime, do you suggest I proceed?'

'Proceed?' he said, as if his mind were already elsewhere, and he had to force it back again. He pondered a moment, and then went on:

'Few people, you will find, had even a faint inkling of Turner's true nature. But you might write to Colonel Wyndham at Petworth, whose father knew him well –'

'You mean the Third Earl of Egremont?' I said, anxious to show that I was not entirely ignorant, and remembering – from my researches at the library – that Turner had spent some time at Petworth in the Third Earl's day. Ruskin responded with a weary blink, which perfectly conveyed that he found my interruption tiresome, and resented having to pause, even for a second, to accommodate it.

'The colonel may yet preserve some family traditions about Turner,' he went on. 'As, too, may Hawkesworth Fawkes of Farnley, the son of another patron, and himself a true lover of art, and a true friend of Turner's.'

'May I mention your name?' I asked, with some trepidation.

'Of course,' he said. 'And go to Maiden Lane; for to know

51

Turner you must see where he was born, and brought up.' He frowned, as if a new thought had struck him. 'Are you returning to London at once, Mr. Hartright? When we are finished here?'

'Yes.'

'Well, I can take you, if you wish; for I am going to Red Lion Square.'

'Thank you.'

He took his watch from his pocket, glanced at it, nodded, then hurriedly slipped it back again.

'But I must warn you that I have a great deal of preparation to do,' he said, rising, and brushing a petal from his sleeve. 'So I shall act as if you were not there; and you must promise not to be offended.'

We started together back towards the house, each occupied with his own thoughts, and had reached the lawn when we saw a manservant hurrying towards us, carrying a slim package wrapped in white muslin.

'Good heavens, Crawley!' cried Ruskin. 'Whatever is the matter?'

'Pearce said you wanted this, sir,' said the man gravely, holding out the package.

Ruskin stared at it for a moment, and then said: 'So I did, so I did. Put it in the carriage; and it can help Mr. Hartright to while away the time.'

He had not exaggerated: all the way there we sat as if in different worlds, he taking objects from a box – pieces of crystal, an apple, a ball on a chain – and consulting a notebook, or drawing (most beautifully, I have to say) a rose, on the margin of a page, as he thought; I, opposite him, at first looking out of the window, as we made our way up Vauxhall Road, and across the bridge; and then taking up the Turner picture, and unwrapping it.

To my surprise, it showed not a man, but a boy, with intense eyes looking out directly – and with something approaching insolence – from beneath dark eyebrows. The nose was long and fleshy, and there was a hint of wantonness in the full, unsmiling mouth. He was fashionably dressed in the style of sixty or seventy years ago, in a brown coat, with a white stock carefully tied at his throat, and his hair neatly parted in an inverted 'V'. On the back was a handwritten label which read: 'Turner, *æt* c. 24 years, by himself. Given by Hannah Danby.'

'Who was Hannah Danby?' I said.

'His housekeeper. At Queen Anne Street,' murmured Ruskin, without looking up.

I turned the picture over again. As I stared at it, I found myself – already unnerved by my conversation with Ruskin – thrown into turmoil; for, yet again, instead of deepening my knowledge of Turner, I seemed merely to have discovered a different version of him. This was not a portrait of Travis's buffoon, or Davenant's good fellow, or Ruskin's misunderstood martyr: it seemed to be of someone else entirely – and someone who, in the enigmatic image he had left of himself, challenged me to find him out, and declared that I should fail. For a moment, I felt something akin to panic; and only finally succeeded in bringing myself under control by reasoning that, in view of the young age at which he had drawn it, it was perhaps not surprising that it bore no resemblance to the man remembered from later life.

As we drew up in Red Lion Square, Ruskin at last looked up from his work, and closed his box, and said:

'Well, Mr. Hartright, here, I fear, we must say goodbye.'

I wrapped the picture up again, and handed it to him.

'I shall show it to my working men,' he said. 'To inspire them.'

The coachman held the door; and, as I followed Ruskin out, I said:

'Are there any other portraits of him?'

'Very few,' said Ruskin. 'He hated being painted. I believe he went several times to Mayall's photographic studio in Regent Street. You could ask there.'

And so we parted, he already nine-tenths in his lecture, and I so distracted that I barely remembered to thank him.

And all the way home my mind churned; and I found myself asking, again and again:

What is it you have undertaken to do? Where will it lead you? What if you cannot do it?

And I am still no nearer a resolution now; but it is nearly one in the morning, and, though sleep feels an impossibility, I know that if I do not go to bed I shall never think straight again.

So let me end with a kiss, and that which I *do* know:

I love you.

Walter

IX

Letter from George Jones, R.A., to Walter Hartright, 14th August, 185–

The Royal Academy, Trafalgar Square,
14th August

Dear Sir,

I write in answer to yours of July 24th. I have already communicated a brief memoir of Turner to another gentleman, whose subsequent conduct – to speak plain – has resolved me to hold my tongue in future. I fear, therefore, that I shall be unable to accommodate you with a meeting.

Yours truly,

George Jones

X

Memorandum of a letter from Walter Hartright to J. Ruskin, Esq., 14th August, 185–

1. Thank you for seeing me – very helpful.
2. Have written to Lord Egremont and Mr. Fawkes.
3. This afternoon will go to Covent Garden as you suggested (if the rain eases!)
4. If – as I feel sure it will – it would be helpful to talk further at a later date, may I accept kind offer to see me again?

XI

Letter from Walter Hartright to Laura Hartright, 15th August, 185–

Brompton Grove.
Tuesday

My dearest love,

Lord! The rain today! – it continued without let, from dawn until the middle of the afternoon. And not just a downpour, but a biblical deluge, so that you might suppose God had tired of the filth and squalor to which we have reduced His world, and sent a second Flood to wash it away. Indeed, the spectacle filled me, for an instant, with a superstitious awe; for the violence of the weather seemed of a piece with my discouraging letter from Jones (which, though it had been provoked by Thornbury, yet I could not help taking as a personal rebuff) and my pained recollections of the day before – and it was easy enough to imagine that all three had been ordained by some great force with the express purpose of thwarting me!

I soon put such unworthy thoughts behind me, however (and it was not just the fear of Marian's mockery that made me do so!), and resolved that, rather than seeing these set-backs as a deterrent, I would take them as a spur to further action. I therefore busied myself with reading and correspondence until, a little after four o'clock, the rain relented sufficiently for me to venture out of doors without being immediately soaked to the skin.

Perhaps, as it turned out, it would have been better if I had been more credulous, and stayed at home all day after all.

Maiden Lane is a narrow little street lying between Covent Garden and the Strand. I must have passed it a hundred times, on my way to and from the theatre; yet I am ashamed to own that, before today, I scarcely knew of its existence. It is, in truth, a mean, poor, dingy kind of a place – yet not entirely abject, for two or three of the houses still have vestiges of respectability which cling to them like the shreds of some finery passed on by one of their richer neighbours in Buckingham Street or Villiers Street. This afternoon, however, it looked desolate enough: for the rain seemed to have swept down all the detritus from

Covent Garden market, and knots of children squatted in the gutters, patiently making little mountains of mud and old cabbage leaves and broken fruit. They turned and looked at me as I approached; and then, as I passed, returned without a word to their game.

Turner's father, I knew, had kept a barber's shop on the corner of Hand Court; but whether Hand Court still existed, and, if so, which of the half-dozen or so gloomy little entrances (crammed here and there between the houses at odd angles, as if a giant dentist had prised the bricks apart to accommodate them) might lead to it, I had no idea. As I looked about for someone to ask, my eye fell on a girl of twelve or thirteen, standing a little apart from the rest.

'Good afternoon,' I said.

She stared at me, but said nothing. Her large eyes, I noticed, were brown, and flecked with amber. Her dark hair was matted, and there was a grey smudge on one cheek; but had you washed her, and dressed her in new clothes, and placed her in any drawing room in Harley Street or Berkeley Square, she would have been counted very striking, and made much of by the ladies.

'Can you tell me', I said, 'which is Hand Court?'

Again, she did not speak; but continued to stare, as if trying to find some meaning in my face that she had not heard in my words. At length she wiped her hand on her grubby pinafore, and jerked her cracked thumb towards a gloomy passage on the other side of the street. It was barred by an iron gate, beyond which nothing was visible save a line of discoloured wooden slats that seemed to dissolve, after a few yards, into pitch-blackness.

'Is that a barber's shop?' I asked, pointing at the corner building.

She hesitated a moment, then at last broke her silence. 'No, sir,' she said, in a flat, weary voice. 'It belongs to Parkin.'

'Parkin?'

'The grocer, sir. 'E keeps it for a warehouse.'

I walked to the window, wiped a film of soot from one of the little panes, and peered in. All I could see to start with was a heavy metal grille, but as my eyes adjusted to the meagre grey light I at length made out a row of shadowy tea chests stacked against the far wall. So much for my hope of finding the shop unchanged, and perhaps even occupied by a member of the same family.

'Does anyone live in the court?' I said, turning back to the girl.

She looked at me as if I had asked her whether the sun was warm, or water wet. 'Why, yes, sir.' She started to laugh. ''Unnerds of 'em!'

For the life of me I could not imagine where hundreds of people would fit, unless the court were a mile long; but I contented myself with asking:

'Anyone called Turner?'

'Turner? No, sir, not as I knows.'

'Any old people, who might remember how it was years ago?'

'Well, sir . . .' She frowned, and her gaze flickered towards the gate. 'There's old Jenny Watts, as I've 'eard tell is ninety . . .'

There was a sudden eagerness in her tone; and I could not help noticing that her eyes followed my hand as it reached into my pocket and drew out a shilling.

'Will you take me to her?' I said.

For answer, she glanced at the pawnbroker's across the street, then trotted to her charges playing in the gutter, and said something to the eldest girl. Then she ran back and took the money, before looking round furtively again, and muttering:

'Only I mustn't be long.'

She opened the gate easily enough, but as we passed through, a boy of perhaps fifteen suddenly emerged from the shadows and blocked our way. Without taking his eyes from us he half-turned his head and shouted a word – I could not make it out, but it sounded like 'khulim' – into the court behind him. All at once, in the darkness beyond, I saw figures hurrying about, and there was a frantic chink and scraping of metal, which led me to suppose that they had been gambling, and were gathering up the evidence.

'All's well,' said the girl. ''E's not' – and again I could not discern the word, but it might have been 'esclop', or possibly ''Islop'. The boy seemed no more inclined to let us pass; for he spread his feet, and folded his arms, and started, slowly and insolently, to whistle.

57

'Come on, Sam,' said the girl. 'We're just going to Jenny Watts'.'

The boy widened his eyes and grinned; and then, glancing behind him again, to see that his companions had finished their business, lazily stepped aside.

Perhaps it was their slang which put the idea in my head (for there seemed a distinctly Arabic ring to it), but my first thought as we entered the court was that I had been transported to some city of the East. The buildings, four or five storeys high, faced each other across a space so narrow that – as, supposedly, in Damascus or Baghdad – a woman on the top floor could shake hands with her neighbour opposite without fear of mishap. The eight or nine boys who stood about, watching me silently, only added to the impression; for, if there was nothing exotic about their clothes or their complexions, yet their blank sullen faces made it all too easy to imagine that they belonged to a different race entirely. Only when you looked up, and saw a strip of foul grey tinged with brown – made fouler and browner every second by smoke from the fires of those who could afford them – did you realize that this was not a cool refuge from the Mediterranean sun, but a part of our own city, which we have condemned to perpetual twilight.

'In 'ere, sir,' said the girl, stopping by a green door that had wrenched its hinge from the frame. She pushed it open with her shoulder, and led me into a kind of lobby which gave access to a scuffed and dirty wooden staircase. The air was cool but close, and so foetid that I had to press my handkerchief to my nose.

'Are you not well, sir?' said the girl, clearly unaccustomed to such faint-heartedness. 'It's a bit of a way; and 'ard if you ain't got your wind.'

The cause of her concern was soon apparent. Treading gingerly (for the steps were bowed and shiny with use, and I feared my boots might go through them altogether), I followed her up three flights of stairs to the top of the building, where she succumbed to a terrible fit of coughing so violent that I found myself looking for blood on the hand she held to her mouth.

It was almost a minute before she had recovered enough to knock on the door. A frail voice answered (though too faintly for me to understand what it said), and the girl pushed her face to the wood and wheezed:

'Sarah Bateman. With a gentleman to see you.'

And this time I heard, distinctly enough:

'Oh! Come in!'

The girl opened the door, and – how to describe what met my eyes? First, the light: a pearly grey haze, diffused through a grimy skylight, which almost dazzled me for a moment, after the gloom of the lower storeys; then an impression of space, which I soon saw came not from the great size of the room, but from its bareness. The floor was uncovered, and there was nothing on the walls, save – on the chimney-piece – an engraving of a sportsman and his dog. A single iron cooking pot, its bottom smeared with ash, hung above the lifeless fire. A small table, a crate which had been pressed into service as a dresser, and a crude bed in an alcove completed the domestic arrangements.

But what struck me most was the figure sitting in the small attic window. She was probably, in truth, little bigger than the girl; but her upright bearing, and her old-fashioned sea-green silk dress, gave her a kind of stateliness that made her appear too large for the Lilliput in which she found herself. Heaps of clothes were piled against the wall behind her; and she held before her a pair of black breeches, which she seemed to have just finished mending. Her face was the colour of cork, and wrinkled like a monkey's; and, as we entered, she turned and looked at me with light, curious eyes and an ingratiating smile.

I expected the girl to say something more, by way of introduction, but she merely stood aside; and, after a few seconds, I realized I must speak for myself.

'Mrs. Watts?' I began.

The woman made no response, and I wondered whether she might be deaf; but the girl said:

'Go on, she can 'ear well enough.'

'I believe', I said, 'that you remember this place as it was, many years ago?'

Again she said nothing; but cocked her head, and shifted in her chair – like Florrie preparing to hear her favourite story.

'I am interested in a family called Turner,' I continued.

She frowned; and then, after a few seconds, said: 'Toorner?'

Her voice was strong and clear; but having no teeth, she seemed to hold the word in her lips, almost squeezing the life out of it.

'They kept a barber's shop,' I said. 'On the corner of the court.'

'Oh, the *barber's*.' She nodded. 'Yes. Where Captain Wyatt went.'

'Captain Wyatt?' I asked.

'To 'ave 'is 'air dressed, o' course!' she said, as if I must as well know who Captain Wyatt was as why he would go to a barber.

'Did you know them?' I said. 'William Turner? And Mary? And their son?'

She nodded again. And then, to my surprise, she winked at me, as if she knew something remarkable about them, and was acknowledging my shrewdness in guessing it.

Even though I knew it to be foolish, the thought that I might be the first person to discover some secret about Turner's child-hood (for I could not imagine Thornbury coming here, and I fancied that she would have been less conspiratorial with me if he had) set my heart beating faster.

'Can you tell me something of them?' I said.

The woman reached down beside her chair, and brought out a little stool, which she gave to me. I sat down, and – since she said nothing more – coaxed her by going on:

'I should especially like to hear about the boy.'

'Ah!' She grimaced knowingly. ''E was a slippy one.'

'Slippy?'

'Up and down, sir. In and out.'

'Up and down the court, you mean?'

She nodded. 'Reg'lar little fish.'

The girl giggled; and, after eyeing her uncertainly for a moment, Mrs. Watts joined in – as though she thought she had made a joke, but needed confirmation to be sure.

'And what about the Strand?' I asked. 'Did he go there much, to see the river?'

'Oh, yes, sir.'

'That's well enough, for a fish,' said the girl; and they both laughed again.

I pressed ahead doggedly, anxious lest the whole interview dissolve in merriment:

'What, he liked the ships, did he?'

'Ah, yes,' said Mrs. Watts. 'The ships. They was much thicker then, before they built the new docks.'

'And did he paint them at all, or draw them, that you remember?'

'Ay, sir,' she said; yet I doubted that she did, for her tone was quite mechanical, and she immediately went on:

'My father was a purlman, and plied all the vessels 'ereabouts; but them docks pretty much ruined him, for after they was made 'e couldn't get near the boats, and when a seaman's ashore 'e don't want purl, do 'e, sir?'

'No –' I began; but before I could say more she continued:

'For nothing'll please 'im but to sit in a tavern, with 'is mates, and them women.' She laughed, and looked past me, towards the girl. 'In't Jenny right, pet?'

'Do you recall anything of the mother?' I said, hoping that a different approach might nudge her back to the subject.

'Why, yes, sir,' she said, with sudden animation, 'that I do.' She shook her head. 'She, sir – oh, my, she was a very gale –'

'A what?' I asked, thinking I had misheard her, or that this was her form of 'girl'.

'A gale, sir. You'd think the end of the world 'ad come.' She looked about her; and, her eye lighting on the little casement, seized the handle, and shook it, and then drummed her fingers on the glass. 'Like that. Captain Wyatt heard 'er once, 'owlin' up from the basement; and 'e said 'e never 'eard nothing like it, no, not in the Indies, where 'e saw a ship go down once, in a 'urricane.'

'A fish,' said Sarah, 'and 'is ma's a gale.' She giggled; and after a few seconds the woman joined in again, and soon they were whinnying and spluttering like a pair of infants, until the exertion proved too much, and sent the girl into another paroxysm of coughing. Even this Mrs. Watts seemed to take only as evidence that the child had reached some new pitch of hilarity; for she continued to watch her with streaming eyes, laughing herself, until I said:

'Can't you see the poor girl is ill?'

I sounded, perhaps, unduly harsh; for I was beginning to suspect that this had been an entirely wasted journey, and that the old woman was either too deranged or too simple to tell me anything of value. I decided, however, to make one final attempt.

'Do you recollect', I said more gently, 'any particular stories about them?'

She looked perplexed for a moment, as if she had not understood me; and then pressed her hands together and said:

'The frost fair! 'Ard to credit now, sir, what with them takin' down the bridge, but them days the river was all-over ice, 'ere to Southwark, and there was fireworks, and puppets, I even seed a 'orse-race; and after, the Captain walked me down the City Road, and stopped before a stall; and 'e said, "You're nothing but skin and bone, girl, you need a bit of meat on you." And 'e bought me a pudding.'

'How old would you have been then?' I asked.

'Ooh, let's see.' She sucked in her cheeks, and counted on her fingers. 'Sixteen, I'd say, sir, pretty near.'

And that settled the matter; for I had vivid memories of my father telling me about the last frost fair – *there was a great mall in the middle, Walter, where the ladies and gentlemen promenaded; and they called it 'City Road'* – which, I knew, had been held in the winter of 1813. If she had been sixteen at the time, she must have been born in 1797, when Turner was already a successful artist, and only two years before he had moved from Hand Court to Harley Street. There might be the remnant of some genuine anecdote or local tradition about the family in what she had told me; but, if so, it was inextricably jumbled with the recollections of her own life, like the image in a splintered looking-glass.

I rose to leave, thanked her, gave her sixpence (which she left lying on her open palm, as if I might add to it), and beckoned to the child. We had barely reached the door, however, when, from below, came the sound of hurried footsteps on the stairs, and a woman's voice calling: 'Sarah! Sarah!' The girl gasped, and stopped quite dead; then, crying, 'My ma, she'll flay me!' she ran back into the alcove, and hid herself, as best she could, behind the blanket that served as a curtain.

'Come,' I began, 'why should she be angry –?'; but before I could say more a woman rushed into the room. She was about thirty, poorly but respectably dressed, and must have been handsome once; but fatigue and disappointment, like a victorious army, had traced their advance in the lines upon her face. She looked frantically about her, and then, not immediately seeing her daughter, pointed accusingly at me.

'Where's my girl?' she said, panting heavily. Her voice was quiet, but some emotion she could barely master made t squeak and waver, and her eyes – remarkably like the child's, I now saw – were feverish with anger.

Not wishing to betray the girl, but equally unwilling to tell a lie, and a useless one at that, I said nothing. I must, though, have given her away unwittingly; for my gaze strayed towards the alcove, and the woman at once read its meaning, and pushed past me towards the bed. I managed to bar her way, but not before the child had revealed herself by whimpering, and then promptly abandoned her flimsy sanctuary to take refuge behind me.

'What 'ave you done, you little cat?' said the woman, lunging towards her, and raising her hand as if to strike her.

The girl made no reply, only pressing herself further into the narrow space between me and the wall; but Jenny Watts clapped her hands, and started to laugh again, as if this were a kind of Punch-and-Judy show, put on especially to entertain her.

'She's done no harm,' I said, laying a hand on the mother's arm to restrain her.

'I shouldn't 'ave known, save for Sam Telfer,' said the woman, ignoring me entirely, and addressing the girl. 'I'm gone ten minutes, just to get the tightner, and when I'm back 'e says 'e sees a gentleman givin' you brownies, and you takin' 'im in 'ere.'

'I only asked her to bring me to Mrs. Watts,' I said.

'Oh, so that's what you calls it now, is it?' said the woman, suddenly rounding on me.

I braced myself, for she was now swaying and trembling so violently that I thought her rage would not be contained; but having been denied the girl, must vent itself on me instead. After a second or two, however, she brought herself under control, and merely clenched her fists, and said with scalding contempt:

'"Bringin' you to Mrs. Watts!"'

I longed to cry out: *For God's sake, woman, what do you take me for? I have a daughter myself!* and yet I knew that to do so would be useless. Looking at the man before her, she saw not me but someone else entirely; for all her experience had taught her that a gentleman talks to a girl in Maiden Lane, and gives her money, with but one purpose; and nothing I could say or do would persuade her that I should have sooner died than violate her child.

'I didn't do nothin'! 'E didn't do nothin'!' screamed the girl, suddenly darting out from behind me, and lifting up her dress. ''Ere, 'ave a look if you don't believe me!'

And, without a word, the woman did so, barely pausing long enough to tug the blanket a few inches across the gap, and so afford her daughter a scrap of modesty.

At length, she grunted and stepped back. She said nothing, but looked at me; and for the first time I saw a doubt in her eyes, and she seemed somehow smaller, like a kite that has lost the wind, and begun to sag. For a moment, I felt, I had the advantage, and at once determined to make the best of it.

'I will not insult you by offering you more money,' I said, 'but Sarah has a shilling, which she earned fairly, by bringing me here; and I think you would do well to spend it on the doctor; for that is a bad cough, and should be treated.'

And before she had time to reply, or to tell the girl to give the shilling back again, I left, shutting the door behind me, and made my way back through the court, exciting no more than some whispering, and a derisive laugh, from the boys. A few moments later I was in the Strand – which, with its street-vendors, and gas-lamps, and crowds of cheerful theatre-goers, seemed like the waking world after an oppressive dream.

Forgive me, my darling, if what I have described distresses you; but – as you may imagine – it troubled me, and we have agreed that we must have no secrets from each other. I am haunted not merely by the thought of that poor child and her mother, and the knowledge that, quite unintentionally, I have brought more care into their already over-burdened lives, but also by the nagging question of why Ruskin should have suggested I go to

64

Maiden Lane at all. Surely he must have known – as I know myself, if I pause to reflect upon it – that after almost sixty years it is almost inconceivable I should find someone who remembers the Turners? Yet what, otherwise (save only malice; and I hesitate to believe he would be so cruel to a man who has done him no harm) could have prompted him to send me to a stinking slum, from which all traces of the family have been long since obliterated?

My one hope is that I shall find the answer when I see Turner's pictures – in which case, I shall know it soon enough, for Marian and I go to Marlborough House on Monday.

My love to you always,
Walter

XII

Letter from Michael Gudgeon to Walter Hartright, 15th August, 185–

Box Cottage, Storry, East Sussex,
August

Dear Mr. Hartright,

Lord, yes! – I remember Turner, though the journey I took with him must have been almost forty years ago now. If I were to draw up an inventory of my memories, I should list them under the following chief heads:

1. Being very cold.
2. Being very wet.
3. Being sick in a boat.
4. Being footsore and saddle-sore in about equal measure.
5. Being ill-housed and ill-fed.
6. Being well housed and well fed.
7. Not giving a damn about any of the above; for my companion was a Great Genius, and I a lusty, impudent, carefree young fellow.
8. Turner very silent when sober.
9. Turner very boisterous when drunk.

I fear I cannot furnish you with a long memoir, for my hand is rheumatic (my poor long-suffering wife, indeed, is taking this letter down to my dictation); and nowadays I do not go about much. My friends, however, are good enough to call upon me here; and if you think it worth the time and expense to do likewise, I should be delighted to welcome you as one of them, and to tell you all I can recall.

Yours very truly,
Michael Gudgeon

XIII

From the diary of Marian Halcombe, 16th August, 185–

Marlborough House is not, I am sure, the most magnificent palace in the world: a long, plain red-brick building in the Palladian style, it hangs back a little from Pall Mall, as if ashamed to show its dowdy façade in such distinguished company. And the crowds that throng it – now that the ground floor has become a temporary art gallery – make it feel more like a railway station hotel than a private residence. But palace it is, and the first I have ever entered; and as we walked down a long covered passage into the lofty hall (so vast that Jenny Lind has sung here, before an audience of hundreds), and paid our shilling for a guidebook, I could not but reflect on how different it was from the house in which Turner had spent his last years, and in which I had first seen one of his paintings.

Perhaps Walter was preoccupied by a similar idea; for he was unusually silent all the way there; and, when we arrived, looked about him with an almost incredulous air, as if comparing it with the scene of *his* last adventure – for surely the filthy little street where Turner had been born, though nearer in miles, must have presented an even starker contrast to this place than the cottage in which he had died?

But then we turned, and all such thoughts and calculations instantly evaporated. We had both seen individual Turners before, of course; but never – for this is the first public exhibition since his death – more than thirty of them displayed together. All at once our eyes were assailed by the most brilliant radiance I have ever seen in paintings – and far more, I have to say, than I should have conceived possible. Reds, oranges and yellows, as hot and tumultuous as burning coals, erupted from the walls, making even the brightest objects about them – a woman's gaudy green dress, a huge picture of the Battle of Blenheim above the chimney-piece – appear suddenly drab and lifeless. They seemed, indeed, more intensely real than the press of people staring at them, or the building itself – as if we were trapped in Plato's cave, and the pictures, rather than merely flat pieces of canvas hanging *inside*, were in fact holes in the rock, through which we could glimpse the unimagined world beyond.

The effect on Walter was immediate; and so dramatic that I wish I could have found some means to record it, for it would have convinced even the dourest sceptic of the power of art. He stopped dead, and drew himself up, as if someone had suddenly lifted a great weight from his back; his mouth set in a small, surprised smile, and the skin appeared to tighten across his forehead, raising his eyebrows into an expression of wonderment and pleasure. His gaze was fixed on a square picture on the opposite wall, which showed an indistinct white figure apparently emerging from the smoke and flames of a raging fire. From where we were standing it was impossible to make out more; but, rather than going closer (which, indeed, would have been difficult, so dense was the press of people), Walter remained there, seemingly uninterested in the subject, content merely to bask in the radiance of the colour, like a cat stretching itself in the sun. I waited for him a moment, and then, since he still showed no inclination to move, set off on my own to explore further.

The impressions of the next half an hour were so forceful and so contradictory that I must try to set them down here in some detail, before they disintegrate into brilliant confusion. There were more than thirty pictures in the exhibition, and what you noticed about them first was simply their enormous variety. The view I had always associated with Turner, *London from Greenwich Park*, was there – although the original had a grandeur and richness you could not have guessed from our engraving of it; and a terrifying picture of a puny cottage caught in a mountain avalanche, and crushed by a deluge of broken ice and uprooted trees and a giant rock (so ferociously painted that the pigment was as thick and ridged as mortar), recalled some of the dread and horror the pictures in Mrs. Booth's house had inspired in me. Almost everything else, however, took me by surprise. Here was a magnificent sea piece, showing distant ships heeling in a stiff breeze, which (save for the waves, which gathered menacingly in the bottom right-hand corner and threatened to spill over the frame and wet your feet) might have been by a Dutch master; there a gorgeous classical landscape saturated with honey light, or a sublime mountain darkened by angry clouds. Most striking of all were those wild swirls of paint – like those which had so captivated Walter – in which the pure colour seemed to strive for freedom, detaching itself from form like the soul leaving the body, so that you could not clearly discern a subject at all.

I think most people, confronted by such splendid profusion, would find it hard to believe that it could all have sprung from one hand. Certainly, as I embarked on my tour, that was the uppermost thought in my mind. It was only after I had examined three or four of the pictures more closely that I recognized – with that sudden dawning that comes when you at last become conscious of some insistent sound, like a dog barking in the distance – that there was, indeed, a family relationship, suggested not by obvious similarities of style, but by certain recurrent quirks and oddities. What they mean, or whether they mean anything at all, I still do not know; but they have left me with the nagging idea that they are a kind of message in code, and that I need but the right key in order to decipher it.

The first painting I looked at (for no other reason than that it was the closest) was a luminous, gold-tinged historical scene which, at a casual glance, I should have taken to be by Claude. I failed, in my eagerness, to note the exact title, but the subject was the decline of Carthage. You are standing, as it were, in the bottom left-hand corner of the picture – in the entrance, perhaps, of a great palace, for the foreground is in shadow. Immediately before you, like flotsam on the shore, lies a clutter of objects: a pile of fruit; a standard bearing a shield and a wreath of withered flowers; discarded cloaks and weapons; and a strange, bulbous brown blob with a protuberance at the top, which might be a buoy with a chain but which also – you realize after a few seconds – has a fleshly quality about it, like a giant squid, or the internal organ of a beast. Beyond that is a narrow quay, and then a dazzling strip of water, fringed in the distance by lines of hazy masts, which stretches to the horizon. Above it – almost in the centre of the canvas, but a little to the left – hangs a burning sun, filling the sky with an incandescence so bright that it stings your eyes to look at it.

On either side of the harbour, like the jaws of a vice, are clusters of classical buildings, their steps crowded with little doll-like figures. Those on the left are floridly baroque, and covered with ornate carvings, but those on the right – to which, because of the diagonal perspective, your gaze is naturally drawn – are more restrained: passing an odd little tower that looks like a dwarf lighthouse, you enter them by a narrow flight of steps (so narrow, indeed, you feel the walls will squeeze the breath from your body), and then ascend gradually until, at length, you reach a temple of Parthenon-like simplicity on the summit of a distant hill.

I could remember little about the fall of Carthage, save that she had been reduced to surrendering her arms and children to Rome, but the import of the picture seemed clear enough. It was, in effect, a moral tale, told (unlike a written narrative) from top right to bottom left: once, the Carthaginians had had the vigour and discipline to climb the straight and narrow path; but, as their wealth and power grew, they had abandoned the austere and lofty heights of greatness, neglecting their industry and defences, and descending into the flyblown city on the left, where they had dissipated their strength in idleness and luxury.

The picture was dated '1817', a mere two years after the defeat of Napoleon, and it suddenly occurred to me that Turner must have intended it as a warning to England – which, with her great trading empire, must surely be the Carthage of the modern age – against lowering her guard and sinking into complacency. Convinced (but how foolishly, I think now, looking back) that I had correctly divined his meaning, I turned to a second Claudian scene, *The Bay of Baiae, with Apollo and the Sibyl*, to see if my great perspicacity could unlock *its* secrets, too.

A simpler and more tranquil piece, this, with soft light and sweet curves in place of the other's fierce sun and harsh architectural planes. You are standing (again, a little to the left of centre) on a wide sandy path that draws you enticingly to a golden beach. A stone pier lined with boats reaches diagonally into the sea – which is no more than a long finger of blue, really, laid across the middle of the canvas, and yet enough to give you a pang of longing, and make you think you feel the warm breeze on your face, and smell its cargo of salt and the scent of wild flowers. The bay is ringed by gentle hills of a pale yellowy-green, which fades into grey on the horizon and differentiates itself into darker shrubs and bushes and leaves as it reaches the near-distance. It is only when you look closely that you see that among the rocks and foliage there are also ruined buildings: broken stone walls crumbling back into the sand, or a pair of subter-ranean archways – two great eyes separated by a brick nose, like the top of a buried skull – half hidden under a tangle of scrub. As if to heighten the air of menace, a barely visible serpent, almost the same colour as the earth, lurks in the bottom right-hand cor-ner, waiting for its prey.

The picture is dominated by a V-shaped pair of trees on the right, which start close to the bottom of the canvas and reach almost to the top, spreading a band of shadow nearly to the left-hand edge. It is here that the only creatures – apart from the snake – appear: first, immediately under the trees themselves, a tiny white rabbit (soon to be the reptile's victim?); and then, on the other side of the path, the figures of Apollo and the Sibyl. He, dressed in a wreath and a red robe, is holding his hand towards her; while she, naked from the waist up, kneels on a rock, arms outstretched, inclined slightly towards *him*. Both of them seem somehow flat, and too small, giving the odd impression that they have been cut from another picture and pasted on. And the Sibyl, in particular, has the same doll-like appearance as the figures in *The Decline of Carthage*, as if she were the work of a gifted child rather than of the genius who painted the rest of the picture. There is something strange, too, in her hands and feet, which have the blunt shape of flippers rather than the complex geome-try of human limbs. You might almost think that Turner had con-ceived her as a mermaid rather than a woman – an impression accentuated by her dress, which has a sort of scaly brightness, and clings to her legs like a skin.

Walter has several times reproached me for being too practical, and preferring dry facts to the sweeter but less substantial world

of myth and fancy; and now, for once, I felt the justice of his criticism; for if I had ever known the story of Apollo and the Sibyl, I
had quite forgotten it, and was forced to seek him out, and ask
him to explain it to me. I found him gravitating – as if drawn by
magnetic attraction – towards another of those bolts of colour
that had so struck us upon entering: a square canvas, cut in half
by a horizontal blood-red bar so vivid that you could have seen it
from half a mile away. Falling into step beside him, I said:

'What did Apollo do to the Sibyl? Or can you not tell me in
such august company?'

'Sad,' he said, 'but perfectly respectable. He granted that she
should have as many years of life as she held grains of sand.'

That at least explained what she was doing with those fin-like
hands. 'And what happened?'

'He was as good as his word; but she failed to ask for perpetual
youth, and gradually wasted away until only her voice was left.'

I felt I now understood the subject; but I was still left with the
faint consciousness – which remains with me still – of an unanswered question. It was put out of my mind at the time, however,
by the square picture, which, as we approached it, imperiously
claimed our attention with mysteries of its own. The red strip, I
now saw, was a flaming sunset, spreading, it seemed (the painting was so indistinct it was difficult to be sure) across some desolate seashore. Before it stood Napoleon, his arms folded, his eyes
cast pensively down, entirely alone save for a lone British sentry
standing behind him, and his own elongated reflection in the wet
sand. He was staring at a tiny triangular object on the ground,
which I could only identify by looking at the title: *The Exile and
the Rock Limpet, 1842.* To the right was a pile of debris that might
have been a wrecked ship, and above that the smoking ruins of a
war-torn city.

We stood looking at it in silence for a few seconds, and then
Walter sighed and said:

'"And the light shineth in darkness."'

He paused, and seemed to be waiting for me to go on; so I said:
'"And the darkness comprehended it not."?'

He nodded, but said nothing more. I am not sure what he
meant – unless, as a painter himself, he was merely admiring the
ability to create colour so radiant that it seems to burn from

within – but his words nonetheless helped to galvanize something in *my* mind; for they startled me almost as if he had uttered a profanity. After a moment's reflection I realized why: Turner had, without question, captured the beauty of the sun more gloriously than any artist I knew; but in the paintings I had seen there was always something terrible about it, too – a cruelty, a heedless power to destroy, that made it seem a fitter symbol for the bloodthirsty deity of the Aztecs than for the pure love of our Lord, expressed in that lovely passage from St. John.

I said nothing of this to Walter, for I did not wish to disturb him, at least until I had had a chance to see more, and discover if my impression was justified. I did not, however, scruple to point out another idiosyncrasy I had come to recognize; for, although the technique was entirely different from Turner's earlier works – the paint so coarse and mixed that it looked as if it had been applied by a madman in a frenzy – yet Napoleon and his guard had the familiar toylike quality, making them look more like tin soldiers than men, and I felt I could safely generalize about his figures.

'At least your people are better than his,' I said, laughing.

I thought this compliment would please Walter, but he barely even acknowledged it; and after a moment I left him again to his reverie, to continue my researches on my own. Rather than examining another picture in detail, I decided to test my theory by merely glancing at them all; and flitting rapidly from one to the next I soon persuaded myself that I was right. I cannot remember every painting now, but enough to prove the point: a gory sunset lights the last journey of an heroic old warship, *The Fighting Téméraire*, towards its destiny in a breaker's yard; terrified people flee the wrathful *Angel Standing in the Sun*, the flesh burned from their bones by his all-engulfing fire; even a sun-soaked picture of Venice, which at first sight seems like a cheerful Canaletto seen through a heat-haze, at length reveals its own tragic secret – for its subject, you realize on closer inspection, is the Bridge of Sighs, which carried condemned criminals to their death

My exploration also yielded another discovery. As I was hurrying past a dark picture – which I had already dismissed in advance as unsuitable for my purpose, since there seemed no sunlight in it at all – my eye was caught by a glint of gold, and the hint of a familiar form, in the middle of the canvas. Stopping to examine it, I saw that it was the coil of a giant serpent, emerging from a low, dark cave half hidden by brush, which immediately put me in mind of the snake and the ruins in the *Bay of Baiae*. There was more to come; for confronting the beast, in the foreground, is a man – presumably Jason, for the piece is called *Jason in Search of the Golden Fleece* – kneeling on a split and twisted fallen tree – which, when you look at it, seems to turn into a writhing monster, or two monsters, like the buoy in *The Decline of Carthage*. Less than two minutes later I happened upon *The Goddess of Discord in the Garden of the Hesperides*, where the effect is inverted: beyond a gently wooded valley, peopled with nymphs and goddesses, stand two mountainous walls of stone, leaning ominously towards each other (like the sides of a half-formed arch) across a narrow pass. In one place, the top of the rock has an odd serrated shape; which – when you examine it closely – turns out not to be rock at all, but the back of a terrifying monster guarding the entrance, with stone-coloured wings and crocodile jaws that might almost have been hollowed from the granite by wind and rain.

I had, and still have, no idea what to make of these connections, but I must confess that finding them excited me, and made me think, for a moment, that I should turn critic, and go into competition with Mr. Ruskin. At the same time, they troubled me (for they are undeniably disturbing), and put me in a quandary which I have still not resolved as I write this: should I point them out to Walter? To do so would have been to risk casting him back into gloom just at the moment when his delight in Turner's work seemed to have lifted his spirits; but to keep silent would have been to leave him in ignorance of something that might be important – and also (I must be honest!) to deny myself the chance of demonstrating my own insight.

Fate, however, spared me from having to make an immediate decision, for when I looked about for Walter I could not at first see him; and no sooner had I eventually found him again – standing in front of another lustrous canvas, in a corner I had missed – than I heard a voice behind me calling 'Marian!'

I turned, and saw Elizabeth Eastlake – her head towering above all the other women, and most of the men – making her way towards me. She was not, it seemed, alone; for as the crowd parted before her I noticed a little cavalcade in her wake: a middle-aged couple (as I supposed) and their daughter, and an old woman in a bath chair pushed by a manservant.

'Marian!' she repeated, as she drew near; and then, seeing Walter: 'Oh! And Mr. Hartright too! What a pleasant surprise!' After shaking our hands she turned towards the old woman in the bath chair, and, raising her voice, said:

'Lady Meesden, may I introduce Miss Halcombe?'

I bowed, and for a moment had the extraordinary idea that I was meeting one of Turner's doll-people; for the woman's face was chalk-white with powder, save for a dab of rouge on each cheek, and the skin seemed to have folded in about her eyes, reducing them to no more than a pair of black shining buttons. She stared at me, unsmiling, for a moment, and then bobbed her head, like a bird pecking water from a pool.

'And her brother-in-law, Mr. Hartright,' said Lady Eastlake. Walter can usually extort a smile from the stoniest misanthrope, but the old woman was as frosty with him as she had been with me; and it was, I thought, with some relief that Lady Eastlake turned away from her to present us to the other members of her party: Lady Meesden's daughter, Mrs. Kingsett; her husband (who appeared, among his other misfortunes, to be called Mauritius); and their own daughter, Florence, an awkward, coltish seventeen-year-old who blushed when you looked at her.

'Marian is a particular friend of mine, Lydia,' said Lady Eastlake.

'Indeed?' said Mrs. Kingsett. She was about fifty, with plaited greying hair coiled neatly behind her head, and wearing a loose-fitting walking dress in a fine red-and-white check that looked wonderfully free and comfortable. She was too square and craggy to be considered beautiful; but there was a certain vivacious charm to her voice when she smiled and said:

'Well, there can't be a better recommendation than that.'

'Perhaps "By Appointment to the Queen"?' said Lady Eastlake.

Mrs. Kingsett laughed; and – as if trying to make up for her mother's coldness – shook my hand in the most easy and affable manner imaginable.

'Sir Charles and I are away on our autumn visit to Italy next week,' Lady Eastlake went on. 'And I have come to remind myself what great *English* art can be.'

'What do *you* think, Miss Halcombe?' said Mrs. Kingsett, casting her eyes about her in a way that seemed to include the whole exhibition. 'Are you quite overwhelmed?'

'Quite,' I said.

'I, too.'

At this, her husband, who was standing at her elbow, gave a derisive 'tk' – which she studiedly ignored – and looked away with a long-suffering smile. Nature had not dealt kindly with him; for he had a turned-up nose like a pig, and a pulled-down mouth, with too many teeth, like a wolf; and whiskers so curled that you'd think they'd been singed by his hot and florid complexion; and in his little gesture of defiance, and his wife's pointed refusal to acknowledge it, I suddenly fancied that (as sometimes happens) I could read the whole history of their connection. Here were a plain man and a plain woman, who had married – as they thought – for mutual advantage: he for the respectability that came with her station, and her mother's title; she, poor thing, for fear that a shy and ungainly girl like herself might have no husband at all if she refused him. But over the years, both had come to realize that she was his intellectual, as well as his social, superior; and as she had grown in confidence, and blossomed into maturity, so he had dwindled into sourness and disappointment. Any true feelings they might have had for each other had been eaten away by the acid of his resentment and her contempt – leaving the marriage an empty shell, into which she had steadily expanded, by developing as independent a life as was consistent with respectability, and he had been reduced to sulking in a corner.

You could not help but feel sorry for both of them, but I must own that the balance of my sympathy lay with her – if only because her fate, or something like it, might all too easily have been my own. Perhaps Mr. Kingsett sensed this; for, though he shook my hand (he really could not do otherwise, when his wife had already done so), his grip was as slack and uninterested as a dead fish, and he immediately turned away with an inaudible mumble, and fixed his watery gaze on the fireplace. To my surprise, as I moved myself, I noticed that Lady Meesden was scowling at us, with a ferocity that suggested she had witnessed the whole episode.

Certainly, Mr. Kingsett's hostility cannot have arisen from any consciousness of social distinction, for he received Walter as one greets an old friend – or, perhaps it would be truer to say, as a drowning man greets a log, for here was a promise of rescue from the ocean of females in which the poor man found himself, and he clung to it for dear life. Within less than a minute he had manoeuvred Walter away from me and established a small gentlemen's club, with a membership of two, in the corner. A moment later I heard him opening the proceedings with: 'I think a picture should be *of* something, and you should be able to see what it is.'

Not wanting to add to Walter's embarrassment by eavesdropping on his reply, I turned back towards Mrs. Kingsett; but she – doggedly pursuing her policy of disregarding her husband altogether – was already deep in conversation with Lady Eastlake again, and I felt I could not intrude. Rather than brave the bellicose Lady Meesden or her tongue-tied granddaughter, therefore, I decided to study the picture before us.

It was another classical subject: *Ulysses Deriding Polyphemus*. Again, we are close to the bottom left-hand corner, looking diagonally across the canvas to a brilliant sunrise on the low horizon, which casts its rays into the sky, burnishing the underside of the clouds and veining them with bloodshot streaks. The foreground is dominated by Ulysses' ship, its gilded hull trimmed with stripes of black and red, moving from left to right into the centre of the canvas as it makes for the open sea. The water is soporifically calm, with tiny lapping waves that seem barely to have the energy to reach the shore, but on board everything is bustle: the decks are crowded, the oars are out, and sailors swarm up the mast and yards, frantically setting the ornately decorated sails or raising their red flags. Behind them, almost in darkness, is the dark mass of Polyphemus's island.

I knew, I think, even before I had consciously noted any of the details, that this picture was unlike the others – or, rather, that it somehow *fulfilled* the others; for, like a song, of which, up until now, you have only a few notes and half the chorus, it seemed to bring together all those peculiarities which I had glimpsed elsewhere, and miraculously fuse them into a glorious whole. Here was the beautiful but merciless sun; here the entrance to the underworld – the mouth of Polyphemus's cave, its blackness broken this time not by the gleam of a serpent, but by a single smear of reddish gold, which could be the glow of a fire within, or of the sun without; here, above all, those weird hybrid objects that seemed to be two things at once, or one thing in the process of turning into another. The prow of Ulysses' ship was a gaping fish-jaw, its shape echoed by two great arch-like rocks in the sea beyond, while about it, in the foam, played silvery figures – nymphs? spirits? – which gradually faded into transparency, until they were one with the water, and disappeared. Saluting it, on the right edge of the canvas, was the figurehead of another ship, which rose up like a clenched fist – or one of those odd flipper-limbs: fish, and flesh, and wood, all at once – before a cluster of clouds that turned out, on closer inspection, to be the horses of Apollo's chariot, drawing the sun into the sky. And the wounded giant himself, rearing in agony above his island, was so vague that he, too, might be a cloud, or the mist-covered peak of a mountain.

Each of these effects taken on its own could have been merely disturbing, but in their totality they seemed to achieve a kind of dreamlike enchantment which made me think for a moment that I had at last glimpsed (though I could not put it into words) Turner's purpose. The subject was sombre enough, and its treatment strange to the point of insanity: yet (in this picture, at least) the beauty seemed finally to outweigh the horror and the madness – and to be, indeed, all the greater for having absorbed the base elements of our experience, and transmuted them into gold. Exhilarated, I opened my notebook and wrote: 'Magician. Alchemist.'

I had barely finished when I was startled (the 't' of 'Alchemist' has a long squiggling tail to prove it) by someone speaking at my elbow:

> 'I sing the cave of Polypheme,
> Ulysses made him cry out . . .'

Astonished, I looked round. There was Lady Meesden – one

77

hand raised, to signal to the manservant that he should stop –
gliding into place at my side. Without pausing, she continued:

> 'For he ate his mutton, drank his wine,
> And then he poked his eye out.'

Her voice was rather faint, but there was something commanding about it – not the imperious tone you might imagine
from a woman in her position, but rather a kind of operatic flourish that made you think you were listening to a performance
rather than a conversation. I noticed several other people glancing at her as if they expected her to break into song; and, in truth,
I half-expected it myself, for I had no idea what she was talking
about, and it seemed as likely as anything else that she was mad,
and merely reliving some entertainment from her youth – like
Walter's old woman in Hand Court.

'Tom Dibdin,' she said, as if by way of explanation.

The name was familiar – it somehow conjured in my mind a
world of stage-coaches and sailing-ships and breezy spring
mornings, before railways and factories turned England into a
great machine, and swaddled it in smoke – but I could not for a
moment place it.

'*Melodrame Mad*. 1819.'

And then I remembered: Thomas Dibdin's *Reminiscences* had
been a great favourite of my father's when I was a child –
although, fearful that it might corrupt me, and make me run away,
and become a travelling player like its author, he forbade me to
read it. (This interdiction, of course, only increased its romance for
me, prompting me to sneak into the library whenever I could, and
stealthily devour two or three pages of an anecdote about a theatre
manager or an actress, before approaching footsteps forced me to
make my escape.) I still could not see the relevance to Turner's
work, however; and the perplexity must have shown on my face,
for, pointing a wavering finger at the picture, Lady Meesden said:

'His inspiration for that. Or so he claimed.'

'Turner, you mean?' I said.

'Of course Turner,' she snapped; but then softened it by (for a
marvel) smiling at me, and saying more gently: 'But he might not
have meant it.'

'Why should he say it, then?'

78

'Why, to shock,' she said, as if nothing could be more natural, and I must be an idiot to ask. 'It was some damned silly woman, as I recall, whispering to a clergyman. *So misty, so spiritual, so ethereal, Mr. Whatever-his-name-was. Upon my word, I don't know how Turner does it. He must be a magician.* Or some such nonsense.'

I confess I felt myself blushing, but had the grace to smile.

'And he told her he'd got the idea not from *The Odyssey*, as we'd all supposed, but from a ditty in a comic spectacle.' She shook her head, and started to laugh, almost silently. 'I bet she never dared offer another opinion in her life.'

'Were you there yourself?' I asked.

'He told me of it afterwards.'

'Oh, so you knew him personally?'

'Oh, yes, I knew Turner,' she replied, with a knowing emphasis on the 'I' and the 'Tur' that immediately made me wonder if their acquaintance had been more than mere friendship. The same thought, I fancy, must have struck the little audience that had gathered around us; for a stout woman who had been listening (and pretending not to) from the beginning, shot Lady Meesden a stern glance, and turned her back; and a man behind us took his wife by the arm and hurried her away.

'He was a great lover of the theatre,' Lady Meesden went on, entirely heedless of the stir she had created. There was something proprietorial in her tone which suggested that the theatre was *her* world, and she would therefore naturally know anyone who frequented it; and for the first time it occurred to me that – improbable as it might seem – she might, from her appearance and the way she spoke, have once been an actress.

'Did you appear there yourself?' I said – with just enough levity to be able to pretend, if necessary, that I was merely joking.

'Lord, yes,' she said, laughing; and then, to save me from the need for a further question (which I was already trying to devise): 'I'm Kitty Driver.'

'*Mrs.* Driver?'

She nodded. 'Or was, until Meesden plucked me from the green room, and set me down in the drawing room.' The phrase had a worn, over-rehearsed air, and I wondered how many times she must have resorted to it over the last fifty years, hoping that a show of wit in discussing her origins might disarm disapproval of them.

79

'I was never fortunate enough to see you –' I began.

'Of course, you're too young.'

'But Walter's mother still speaks of your Lady Wurzel.'

She shook her head, but the faintest glow of pleasure appeared beneath the white mask.

'That was the end of my career. My Mrs. Mandible, 1810, now, there was a thing. Or Lucy Lovelorn in *All in a Day*. Meesden saw it thirty-nine times.'

'Really?'

She nodded again. 'He wrote to me every night; and at the end he met me at the stage door and said: "There's no denying it, by God, you've got my heart, fair and square, Mrs. D. And if you give it back again, I'll go straight into the street and offer it to the first woman I meet there, damn me if I won't – for, if you won't have me, I don't care what happens to me."'

There was another ripple in the crowd about us, which, again, Lady Meesden seemed not to notice; for she guffawed and went on: 'What could I do but marry the dog?'

I laughed. 'And what of Turner?' I said – a trifle clumsily, for I could think of no other way to guide the conversation back to its original subject. 'Was he also an admirer?'

She did not answer directly, but rested her chin on her hand and stared at the floor for a moment, as if the idea surprised her. At length she said. 'He was a sly, secretive fellow, Miss . . . Miss . . . Miss . . .'

'Halcombe.'

'Miss Halcombe. He felt a hurt more keenly, I think, than any man I ever knew – and, as a consequence, was morbidly careful to avoid any risk of public humiliation. Few of us knew anything of his private affairs – save that he lived with his father, and had a mad housekeeper. There were *les on-dits*, of course, about a woman, but . . .' She paused, and shook her head.

'An actress?' I said, with some trepidation.

'A pretty widow, so the story went. Who gave him a bastard or two. But you can't credit everything you hear.'

A gentleman at my shoulder – of whom I was only aware because of the strong smell of cigar smoke – cleared his throat noisily, and clumped off; and I must have looked discomfited myself, for Lady Meesden said:

'Lord, woman! – what's the matter with that? It ain't natural for a man to be alone, nor yet a woman, neither.' She suddenly fixed me with her gimlet eyes, discomfiting me further. 'Sooner one warm bed than two cold.'

How foolish to feel embarrassed and confused, yet I did; and, for fear of hearing more such confidences (or rather, if I am honest, of being *seen* to hear them in that place), I started towards Walter, saying:

'My brother is writing a biography of Turner, did you know that?'

And I wish now that I hadn't; for, had I been less delicate, I might have learned more.

'Don't fetch the men,' said Lady Meesden plaintively. 'They're all such infernal prigs nowadays – like lawyers and schoolmasters.'

I paused, but it was too late. I heard Walter say, 'I, too, have a daughter called Florence' – as if all topics of conversation, beyond the coincidence of their children sharing a name, had already been exhausted – and then he caught my eye, and gave me an imploring look that would have melted an iceberg, and made it impossible for me to withdraw.

'I'm beginning to think we should have called 'em "Venice",' said Mr. Kingsett, with a snorting laugh, and a wave towards *The Bridge of Sighs*.

Walter edged in my direction, his face frankly saying what his lips could not: *Save me!*

'Lady Meesden was a friend of Turner's,' I said. 'Did you know that, Walter?'

'Oh, no,' he said, moving towards her. 'How interesting.'

But Mr. Kingsett, with a nimbleness I would not have suspected, was there before him; and a moment later, as if some signal had passed between them (though I own, if it did, I saw nothing), his wife had joined him, and was saying:

'Now, Mama, we mustn't detain Miss Halcombe and Mr. Hartright any longer. If we don't continue on our way, we shall be here all night, and most of tomorrow.'

I was, for a moment, quite furious; and then I remembered my own response to the old woman, and was forced to reflect that, had she been *my* mother, and I had heard her chattering indiscreetly to a stranger, I should probably have acted in the same way.

It was when I had shaken hands with them all, and Walter was exchanging a few polite words with Lady Eastlake on the subject of his researches, that I suddenly thought – like a sailor with time enough to snatch only one treasure from a sinking ship – of a final question for Lady Meesden. Leaning down, I said:

'Which painting here do you think is truest of Turner the man?'

And without a moment's hesitation she replied: '*Calais Pier*.'

After they had gone, Walter and I sought it out. It is another marine picture, with a marbled grey sea churning and breaking beneath a stormy sky. On the right-hand side, a ramshackle wooden pier lined with disorderly knots of figures juts out towards the horizon – where two distant ships appear in silhouette, and a crack in the clouds lays a pencil-stroke of sunlight on the water. Closer at hand, in the centre of the picture, is a chaos of boats trying to put into, or set out from, the harbour. In the nearest – which an oarsman with only one oar is frantically trying to keep from being dashed against the wooden piles – a man in the stern, far from helping, is angrily shaking a bottle of cognac at his wife on the pier above. Only the approaching English packet, its sails confidently set, appears to be under control.

The bluff, John-Bullish air – a crowd of drunken, cowardly, disorganized French people being shown up by English seamanship – is echoed by the full title: *Calais Pier, with French Poissards Preparing for Sea: An English Packet Arriving*; for, according to my dictionary, *poissard* means not (as one might suppose) 'fisherman', but 'base' or 'vulgar'.

We stood before that picture for perhaps fifteen minutes, and I must have thought of it every hour since; for although it was easy enough to imagine the author of this jaunty, humorous, patriotic satire quoting Tom Dibdin, I could find not the slightest evidence to suggest that the same artist could also have painted *Ulysses Deriding Polyphemus*.

XIV

Letter from Colonel George Wyndham to Walter Hartright, 29th August, 185–

Petworth,
29th Aug., 185–

Dear Sir,

I have received yours of 17th August, and will be glad to see you here if you are near Petworth. I fear, however, that you may find it a wasted journey, for there is very little I can tell you about Turner, or my father's dealings with him.

Yours truly,
George Wyndham

XV

Letter from Walter Hartright to Laura Hartright, 19th September, 185–

Brompton Grove,
Tuesday

My dearest love,

I fear you may have begun to grow anxious about me, so long is it since I last wrote; but the truth – which I hope you guessed – is that what with being rattled about in coaches and railway carriages, and twice nearly thrown from a fly, and having to make so early a start (on the one morning when I thought I should have leisure to write) that I was still half asleep as I left, I have scarce had thirty minutes together in which to put pen to paper. But here I am, home again at last, with nothing worse to show for my adventures than a bruise or two, and a pair of boots scuffed white by the downland chalk.

The new railway to Brighton is a marvel of speed and convenience (as you will see; for I am resolved that when we are next in town together, we shall astonish the children by taking them to the seaside, and bringing them back again, all in the same day!); but for this very reason I found that it depressed my spirits. Every mile seemed to be putting a greater distance not merely between me and London, but also between me and Turner; for *his* journey to Michael Gudgeon, all those years before, must have been an entirely different affair – a jolting, jostling, day-long lurch from one inn to the next, by dusty roads where the only sound was the clop of hooves and the squeak and rumble of wheels, and the only steam the vapour from the horses' flanks. Just at the moment when I felt I had finally glimpsed his elusive figure, in those extraordinary pictures at Marlborough House, I now seemed to be losing sight of it again, in the smoke and bustle of the modern world.

But matters soon mended after we arrived. I took a fly at the station, and within ten minutes we were driving through streets of white stuccoed boarding-houses, with square, cheerful faces, that must have been there in Turner's day; and after ten minutes more we had begun to climb into the downs – which it was hard to imagine had changed greatly since Caesar first saw them, or for a thousand years before that. On every side stretched a rolling, billowing ocean of grass; and when I looked behind, I saw, in the distance, a broadening ribbon of silver-gilt sea.

After perhaps three miles, at the entrance to a small village, we bore left down a narrow lane lined with bramble hedges. It soon dwindled into no more than a cart-track, and it was here that the first near-accident occurred; for, while the driver was momentarily distracted, the horse trotted blithely ahead on to the rough surface, where it missed its footing, and – twisting violently to right itself – dropped one of our wheels into a deep ruck with a tremendous bang that almost overturned the fly. The driver had to hurl himself across his seat to avoid being flung out. The next moment he pulled up abruptly.

'I'm sorry, sir,' he said. 'I can't go no further. Another knock like that, and I shall want a new axle.'

'Is it far?' I said.

'Not half a mile,' he said, pointing to a smoking chimney just beyond the next brow.

So I paid him, and picked up my valise, and set off on foot, picking my way carefully between the ruts. The soft wind stroked my face; and for a moment everything that connected me to the humdrum world seemed to be vanishing with the retreating fly, and I was left with nothing but the cuff and slither

of my own boots, and the cry of the larks urging me back to
some great task, or reminding me of some great grief, that I had
somehow forgotten in the noise and distraction of everyday.

As I came over the brow I saw below me what appeared to be
a small farm, with a muddy yard, bounded on two sides by
ranges of ramshackle outbuildings, and on the third by a long,
low house of whitewashed stone, protected to the rear by a line
of trees. It was so unlike the snug cottage I had expected that I
immediately supposed the driver must have brought me to the
wrong place, and by the time I reached the gate I had quite persuaded myself that I should have to retrace my steps to the village, or even go back to Brighton and start afresh.

A gaunt black-and-white dog signalled my approach by
springing up and barking furiously, jerking on the end of its
chain like a child's toy, and scattering a troupe of chickens
which were strutting across the yard. Moments later, a red-faced
woman of perhaps sixty-five, with her sleeves rolled up to the
elbows, appeared from one of the outbuildings and started rapidly towards me. She moved with the rolling, exaggerated gait
of the comic widow in a pantomime, which at first made me
think she might be drunk; but then I noticed that she was
merely working on to her feet a pair of stout wooden clogs to lift
her above the mire.

'Good morning,' I called. 'I'm looking for Mr. Gudgeon.'

The cacophony of squawks and barks must have drowned my
words; for she frowned and shook her head, and then – shooing
the last of the hens on its way, and shouting to the dog to be
quiet – cupped a hand behind her ear, and raised her eyebrows,
and opened her mouth, in a charade of "I beg your pardon?"

'Mr. Gudgeon?' I said again.

'Are you Mr. Hartright?' she asked, in a gentle Sussex brogue:
and, when I nodded, she held out her hand in a forthright manner, and said: 'I'm Alice Gudgeon.'

'How do you do?' I said.

'The man's in his study. Will you forgive me if I take you
through the back?'

She led me across the yard and into a warm kitchen filled
with steam and the tang of boiling bacon and the sweet smoky
fumes of meat roasting on a spit. From the low beamed ceiling,

and the black range cluttered with pots, and the brace of hares just visible through a half-open pantry door, you would have supposed – again – that this was the home of a prosperous yeoman. Only the table seemed out of place; for, beneath the old sheet which entirely covered its surface, you could just see four finely turned mahogany legs, which suggested that it might have once adorned a dining room, but had fallen on hard times.

We entered a cool hall, floored with polished flagstones, where Mrs. Gudgeon stopped. 'Will you leave your bag here,' she said, pointing to the foot of the stairs, 'and we'll show you to your room after?' Something in the way she spoke – slowly and loudly, and with an eye on a door opposite – made me suppose that this was as much for her husband's benefit as for mine. Having thus alerted him to my arrival, she huffed and fussed and muttered over my valise for a few seconds, before standing back with her hands on her hips and saying: 'There, no-one'll break their necks on that now.' Then, without knocking, she opened the door.

What I noticed first was the paper – single sheets, and rough heaps tied loosely together with ribbons, and old notebooks piled into rickety columns that looked as if they would collapse if you breathed on them – which seemed to cover almost every square inch of floor and furniture. The air was heavy with the smell of mildew and old leather, and the dust so thick that you could see a great funnel of it floating before the window like a muslin curtain. Here, I immediately decided, was something I had never thought to see: a room even more disorderly than Lady Eastlake's boudoir.

But this impression was immediately dispelled when I turned to Gudgeon himself. He was a slight, dapper little man, with amber eyes and a shock of white hair sweeping up from his forehead, wearing a snowy cravat (as white and plump as a swan's breast) and a well-cut brown worsted coat which made him look fastidiously neat. As he came to greet me, he picked his way carefully between the papers like a general anxious not to disturb the disposition of his troops.

'Mr. Hartright?' he said, looking at his wife. She nodded; and he extended his left hand towards me. 'How kind of you to come, sir.'

'The kindness is yours –' I began, surprised at his tone; but he stopped me with a shake of the head.

'You're an angel,' he said. 'Sent from heaven to save me.' He swept his hand about him, like a sower broadcasting seed. 'You see what I am reduced to.' He shook his head sorrowfully, and broke into a rueful smile – from which I took courage to ask:

'Why – what is all this?'

'The work of forty years,' he said. 'And it will take me forty more to organize it, if I do not make haste.'

I looked at the stack nearest to me. It was bound with a piece of twine, and beneath the knot someone (presumably Cudgeon himself, or his wife) had slipped a small card, marked with an alpha, and the number '7'. Above it, in faint pencil, was written 'Chap. 1? Chap. 3? Chap. 4?'

'You are planning to write a book?' I asked.

At this, his wife – who stood still in the doorway, watching him fondly with bright indulgent eyes – began to laugh and, after glancing sharply at her for a moment, he joined in himself, with a deep, self-mocking chuckle.

'When I was younger, Mr. Hartright,' he said, 'I was elected to the Beef-steak Club in Brighton; where, at the monthly dinner, you might be required, at the whim of the chairman, to compose an *extempore* epitaph – either for yourself, or for another member. And Jack Marwell, of the Theatre Royal, who was a humorous fellow, wrote this on me:

> Here lyeth, friend, a gentle wight
> Who did no wrong, but could not write
> Each day he'd plan – but plan in vain –
> A book – and then he'd plan again;
> Until at last his soul was took –
> Yet, though his life hath left no book,
> Pray, with his grieving friends and wife
> His name be in the Book of Life.

There were tears in his eyes when he had finished – though whether from merriment, or the recollection of his friends, or merely the melancholy that the thought of our own death must arouse in us all, I could not tell. At length, however, he chuckled again, and said: 'But I took my revenge the following month; for

87

the chairman demanded I should compose one on Marwell, and I said, "I'm still planning it"; and was excused for my wit.'

I laughed; and, looking about me, said: 'It seems to me you were slandered; for you must have the makings of at least half a dozen books here –'

'Oh, the makings!' he said. 'The makings! But how to make 'em? – that's the question! Here are graves' – pointing to one pile – 'and Roman fortifications' – indicating another – 'and a giant's thigh-bone, and druidical stones, and a thousand other curiosities; and between them they would amount to a very respectable *Guide to the Natural Wonders and Ancient Remains of the County of Sussex*, which is what I always intended them to be.' He paused a moment, perhaps because he had suddenly recalled the reason for my visit; for he went on: 'That was, indeed, part of my original object in travelling with Turner – I hoped he might furnish me with engravings.'

'And did he refuse?' I asked.

'I did not ask him outright, but I think perhaps he guessed my intention, for he told me plainly that all the pictures were destined for a publisher, who wished to make his own book. Later, I heard that failed, and I could have approached him then; but felt I was still not sufficiently advanced.' He shook his head in a sudden frenzy of frustration. 'Try as I may, I can never find a way to arrange my material; and just at the point when I seem about to manage it, damn me if something new doesn't turn up, and throw the whole thing off the road, horses and all.' He began jabbing the air, as vigorously as the conductor of an orchestra. 'If I order everything according to place, I must jumble together temples to Diana and mediaeval coins and batteries from the late war; if I do it chronologically, I make myself and my reader giddy by flying from one side of the county to the other – and back again – in a single afternoon.' He shook his head. 'It will end by making me mad.'

'Perhaps I might help?' I suggested; for I could not but feel for the poor man, and yearn to cut him free from the net in which he had enmeshed himself. 'I do have some small experience – and, indeed, am beginning to face similar problems in my *Life of Turner*.'

'Lord bless you!' said Gudgeon. 'It's uncommon good of you

to offer; but God knows I mustn't waste your life, as well as my own. Besides' – here he smiled at his wife, who coloured and smiled back, as though they had some secret understanding – 'the woman's depending on you to restore me to sanity – if only for an instant – by taking me away from the whole sorry business.' He laid a finger on my arm. 'Come, we'll go to the museum. And there, I swear, I'll talk nothing but Turner.'

From our preparations – he insisted I put on my coat again, and borrow a muffler; and he himself donned an old redingote, and seized a shepherd's crook – you'd have thought the 'museum' must be a day's journey away, and up a mountain. It turned out, however, to be no further than the corner of the yard, squeezed into an old cattle-shed between the end of the house and a tack room and stable – from which, as Gudgeon fiddled with the latch, a brown pony with a shaggy white mane watched us, tossing its head and twitching impatiently. Inside, the room (if room it may be called) was cold and damp, smelling of wet earth and old hay, and lit only by a row of small dirty windows set high in the wall, which gave it something of the feel of a gloomy church. I could see nothing clearly, but was aware of being surrounded by indistinct shapes – which nonetheless somehow conveyed a sense of bulk and presence, for they seemed to press in upon me as palpably as a crowd of people.

Gudgeon took down a lantern from the back of the door; lit it with surprising adroitness (considering that his right hand could do no more than hold the box of matches), and then slung it on to the crook.

'Would you be so good as to hold this?' he said. 'I think we shall get on better if I can point.'

I raised the staff like a bishop's crosier, spilling light on to a broken black stone slab that leant against the wall immediately before me (so immediately, indeed, that, had I taken one step more in the darkness, I should indubitably have tripped on it). There were uneven letters scratched into the surface; and bending down to read them, I saw:

> *Gaius Ter*
> *Et sua coniunx caris*
> *HSE*

'From a Roman cemetery near Lewes,' said Gudgeon. '*Gaius Tertius*, I imagine. *Et sua coniunx carissima.*' He ran his fingers gently along the top, and nodded, as if in approval; and I fancy he was thinking of *his* beloved wife – as I, most assuredly, was of mine. '*Hic Situs Est* – so he died before she did, and her name was added later.'

'I find it rather touching,' I said.

He nodded again. 'But Turner would have none of it. Said that a true painter could be married only to his art. An idea for which he gave, as I recall, no less an authority than Sir Joshua Reynolds.' He smiled, and said: 'See, I'm as good as my word! Nothing but Turner!' – and then turned abruptly, and marched off into the void.

I followed him, bearing the lantern aloft, and watching the shadows dissolve in its yellow glow. My first thought was that I had stumbled upon the cave of some demented Aladdin; for the walls were lined with rough shelves – divided into rectangular compartments, something like the berths in a ship's cabin – which appeared to overflow with the biggest hotch-potch of rubbish I have ever seen: broken pots; a horn knife-handle without a blade; the sole of an old shoe, dotted with rusty studs; half a black, fibrous wooden box (the other half, presumably having rotted clean away); a tray of flint chips that might have been crude arrowheads, but so frayed about the edges that they looked as if they had been nibbled into shape by a teething dog rather than formed by a human hand. Surely, I thought, this must be the product of some disease of the mind (had not the study, indeed, already afforded me a glimpse of it?) which renders its victim incapable of discarding anything, however small or useless, and hence of ever imposing any kind of pattern on his life?

But if this was madness there was certainly some method in it; for each section bore a neat handwritten label, stating a place and a date – 'Braysted, 1845', or (the ink here faded with age) 'Tamberlode, 1816'.

'Are these all finds that *you* made?' I asked.

He nodded curtly, and muttered something I could not hear. I could not but feel awed by his industry (if not by his discrimination!), but he seemed to think it scarcely worthy of comment, for he continued on his way without altering his pace or turning his head, and said nothing more until he had reached the end of the room, and slapped a shelf with his hand, sending up a plume of dust.

'Here's Turner for you,' he announced proudly. 'He loved this spot.'

There were, I saw, objects from four different excavations here – the earliest dated 1811, the last 1825 – yet they all appeared to come from a single place, identified by a large sign in the centre of the wall: 'Sturdy Down'.

'He never said so, for he was taciturn about such matters, but I think he liked it for its layers,' said Gudgeon.

'*Layers*?' I said, not sure if I had heard him correctly.

Gudgeon nodded. 'Stand on the top of Sturdy Down, and within two miles – if you have eyes to see – you'll find evidence of almost every stage in our island's past.' He lifted a pitted iron axe-head, and weighed it in his hand. 'Anglo-Saxon, from some princeling's grave.' Before I had had time to examine it, he set it down again, and picked up a shiny fragment of orange tile, which he dropped into my palm. 'Roman. From the hypocaust of a villa in the valley.' As quickly again, he pointed to an intricate brooch, gracefully curved like an elongated snail's shell. 'Bronze Age. Buried with some priestess or chieftain's daughter, to allow her to appear in the next world with proper dignity.' He was jabbing his finger so rapidly now that I had barely even glimpsed one treasure before he was on to the next. 'A stone from the mediaeval priory, most of which has been plundered to build that damned folly up there. A flint spear-point, which might have killed a mammoth.'

'But why was Turner so fascinated?' I asked – partly to slow him down, but partly out of genuine puzzlement – for while, in the pictures at Marlborough House, there had been abundant evidence of a taste for mythological subjects, and even more of a passion for the moods and effects of nature, I could remember none suggesting a deep interest in British history.

'He was a man of the people,' said Gudgeon. 'A man of the *labouring* people. Many times I have seen him stop to sketch a fisherman, or a shepherd – not as a curiosity, or as some fanciful figure in a classical scene, but as a fellow-man, with the sympathy born of common experience. A great part of his purpose, indeed, was to present the mass of British men and women – those who would never enter a gallery, or have the means to buy a painting – with views of their country.'

'But still –' I began.

'For he, too, you see,' said Gudgeon, interrupting me (yet with a little nod, that seemed to say that he noted my objection, and would answer it in due course) 'knew what it was to be poor, and footsore, and storm-lashed, and to work hard all the day long, and go to bed hungry.' He paused, and then went on more quietly. 'There were tears in his eyes as he stood there. Almost as if could see them, marching across the landscape – all those generations who had lived and toiled and died in that one place.' Emotion, or the raw air, had thickened Gudgeon's voice, and he had to clear his throat before continuing: 'I confess I did not truly understand it myself at the time. I was too young. It's easier for me now; for I find, as I get older, I feel closer to the people who made these things' – here he looked about him and nodded, as if he were greeting a party of old friends – 'and used them, and at length died, and left them behind for me to find.' He was silent for a few seconds; and then – perhaps in an effort to master his feelings, for he seemed close to tears himself now – turned away abruptly, and seized another object from the shelf. 'Here's something will interest you, Mr. Hartright.'

At first I could not identify it at all, but as he brought it into the light I saw that it was the lower jaw of some great animal, long and lined with jagged teeth like a crocodile's. But it was so huge that – if the rest of the body were in proportion – the brute must have been at least five or six times bigger than even the largest crocodile you have seen in the Zoological Gardens; and I confess that when I took it in my hands I let out an involuntary gasp of amazement.

'Part of an extinct dragon,' said Gudgeon, with the practised chuckle of a man who has seen the same response many times before. 'What I believe Owen now calls a *dinosaur*.'

'Owen?' I said.

'William. *Sir* William, I should say.' (You would have supposed from his emphasis that no man ever deserved a knighthood less.) 'Superintendent of the British Museum. And so, naturally, to be deferred to on every point of classification.'

He glowered round at his collection, his mouth working, like a rumbling volcano about to erupt; and I prepared myself for the long catalogue of his differences with Sir William. At length, however – perhaps again recalling his undertaking to talk of nothing but Turner – he nodded at the jawbone and said:

'At all events, Turner and I saw it being dug out of the chalk, and he stood there, quite mesmerized for a moment, his face all aglow like a schoolboy's; and then he started to sketch. Like this' – making wild thrusts with his hand – 'as if his life depended on it. Later, I believe, he clothed it in flesh, and put it in one of his pictures.'

'Yes,' I said; for, as he spoke, the monster in *The Goddess of Discord in the Garden of the Hesperides* suddenly slithered before my mind's eye, and I recognized it for this creature as surely as you may recognize a face that you have seen before only in a photograph. 'I know it.'

'And here', said Gudgeon, laughing, 'is a paintbrush, left on the down by the greatest artist of our age.' He handed me a worn wooden handle.

'You mean this was his?' I said; and, when he nodded, felt a tremor pass across my skin like a crackle of lightning, for (save, perhaps, for Mr. Ruskin's self-portrait) I had never yet held anything that Turner had held; and for a fanciful moment imagined that his power might still reside in this slender shaft of wood, and communicate itself to me, so that I might paint as he did. Then I lifted it to the lantern-light, and saw that only one bristle remained.

Gudgeon must have noticed my amazement; for he laughed again, and said: 'He was happy to keep working with only three hairs left, he told me, and content with two; but when he was reduced to one even he had to admit defeat.'

'But why?' I said, thinking with a prick of guilt how easily I will condemn a brush for the slightest fault. 'Surely he could have afforded to replace it sooner?'

Gudgeon nodded. 'Yes, he was already a rich man when I knew him. But he chose to live simply.'

'Surely,' I said, suddenly remembering some of the rumours I had heard. 'To call such behaviour "simple living", when there is no occasion for it, might seem . . .?'

'Yes,' said Gudgeon, 'I know that he was considered mean. But that is not how I should describe him. Frugal, yes. Careful – and quick to anger, undoubtedly, if he feared he was being cheated, or imposed upon. But I have seen him give five shillings to a young widow with a crying child at her breast, and tell her to buy something for it, and make sure it went to church, and learnt right from wrong.'

'Was it bravado, then?' I said, recalling Turner's delight in displaying his skill on Varnishing Days.

'In part, perhaps. He certainly took a great pride in being able to *make do*. And partly, too, that he feared losing his independence; for he told me once, when we had both drunk too much, that he detested above everything being subject to the whim of patrons.' He paused; and when he went on again, it was with a doubtful tone, as if he was giving voice to some question that had just struck him, and that he had not yet resolved. 'But there was, I think, something else, too. Something akin to a *superstition*.'

'You mean,' I said – and I don't know why, save that it seemed, of a sudden, to fit with all those recurrent images of luxury and ruin and destruction at Marlborough House – 'that he believed that if he was wasteful it might provoke some sort of a catastrophe?'

For some reason Gudgeon coloured slightly, as if I had confounded him; and then he nodded and said: 'That is very astute of you, Mr. Hartright. And not just a catastrophe for himself. But for the country. Or even for the world.' He smiled, and laid a finger impulsively on my arm. 'I think you will do very well, sir. Very well indeed.' And then, nodding towards the brush. 'Keep it, please. I should like you to have it.'

'Really?'

He nodded again.

'I shall carry it with me always,' I said, slipping it into my pocket. 'As a talisman.'

It was a small enough thing, of course, and yet I could not help feeling delighted by it; for this was the first real encouragement I had received from anyone but Lady Eastlake – Mr. Ruskin's comments, for all their ineffable condescension, having had much the same effect on my spirits as a bucket of cold water over the head. And it seemed to confirm what I had increasingly begun to feel (though still scarcely dared to hope) since seeing Turner's paintings: that I was, at last, starting to get the measure of the man. It was, in consequence, in the highest good humour that – when Gudgeon took a watch from his pocket, and looked at it, and said: 'The woman'll have dinner ready, I fancy, best not to keep her waiting; shall we go in?' – I replied, 'Gladly, sir,' and followed him back into the house.

It was a hearty, old-fashioned meal, in an old-fashioned dining room with heavy beams and a huge open fire that must have consumed a whole tree in the time it took *us* to eat a boiled fowl, a pudding, and half a leg of mutton. Since Gudgeon could not carve, I thought his wife might ask me to do it in his stead; but she took the burden on herself, and I soon saw why: when she came to her husband's portion, she discreetly cut it into little pieces, so he should not be humiliated either by his own incapacity to hold a knife, or by having to ask, like a child, to have it done for him on his own plate. Another man, perhaps, understandably reluctant to draw attention to his disability, might have chosen not to acknowledge this kindness; but Gudgeon touched the back of her hand, and thanked her with a smile of a great sweetness. I must have seen, as we sat together, twenty such instances of their mutual affection and regard. Let us hope, my love, when we are their ages, that we make such a picture!

When we had finished, Mrs. Gudgeon cleared away the dishes, and then left her husband and me alone with the wine. We talked a little of his family; and then, without my having to prompt him, he started to tell me more of his adventures with Turner: of how Turner loved storms – 'the fouler the weather, the better' – of how they took a boat once at Brighton, and a gale came up, and the sea broke over the gunwales with a sound like thunder, and all were ill, save Turner, who merely stared intently at the water, remarking its movement and colour, and muttering 'Fine! Fine!'; of how they walked twenty or thirty miles a day, in rain, shine or deluge, and put up sometimes at the meanest inns, where Turner would be content with a piece of bread and cheese, and a glass of porter, and a table to rest his head on, if there was no bed to be had. 'Those were wonderful evenings for a young man,' said Gudgeon at last, shaking his head in wonderment at the memory, 'for there was Turner, who would show you nothing of his work, and barely say a word, during the day; but when the ale had freed his tongue would sing, and make jokes (though you could hardly understand them), and boast of his success, and how he meant to be the greatest painter in the world.'

He was silent a long while after this, and I think must have fallen asleep, for he nodded, and then jerked his head up again, and stared at me for a moment, as if he did not know who I was. And then he smiled, yet still said nothing, as if our sitting there companionably were conversation enough. There was no sound save the plaintive stammering of distant sheep, and the whisper of the fire – which, like us, seemed to have grown sated and sleepy; for, though Gudgeon had thrown another log on when he had last filled our glasses, the flames had scarcely even charred it. The candles had burned low, and through the window I could see the first stars appearing in the sky; and I thought of those far-off days (yet not so far off, in truth) when young Gudgeon and not-yet-old Turner had sat together, just like this; and of how – in no more than one flickering iota of a second in a star's life – Time creeps up on us all, and overtakes us. And so at length must have fallen asleep; for the next I knew was that Mrs. Gudgeon was shaking my shoulder, and laughing, and offering to light me upstairs with a lamp.

The following day I rose late, and made a leisurely breakfast in the kitchen – at that hour, thanks to the fire, the only warm room in the house. Afterwards, I sat a while with Gudgeon in his study, and we exchanged 'Thank you's and 'It's been a great pleasure's until, at length, his wife entered, and told me that it was time to leave if I wished to be sure of the train. He came out into the yard with me – where the resourceful woman had already harnessed the trap to the brown pony, which waited, stamping its feet, as if anxious to be off. Then, sheltering in the doorway against the sharp east wind, Gudgeon unwound the cravat from his neck and stood waving it, like a scarf, in his good hand, as his wife drove me away.

In the event, she deposited me at Brighton station in ample time for the train to Chichester, by which I was to start my journey to Petworth, and I –

But no – if I embark on that now, I shall be another day in the writing. So, let Petworth be the matter of my next letter, and this one delay no longer its most important business – telling you that I am well, and that I love you.

Walter

XVI

From the journal of Walter Hartright, 19th September, 185–

Michael Gudgeon told me one thing more about Turner, which I set down here (as nearly as I can remember) exactly as he said it:

'One day, I recall, everything pleased him: a gothic ruin, a view of the sea, an effect of the light he especially loved, where the sun breaks through at a slant, and grains the cloud like a piece of slate. Late in the afternoon we stopped at an ale-house and then rolled back to the Royal Oak at Poynings, singing "I am a Friar of Orders Grey".

'Do you know the Royal Oak, Mr. Hartright? No? Well, I dare say you'd think it a simple enough house – I dare say *I* should, now – but it seemed a very palace then, after what we'd been accustomed to, for the beds were comfortable, and we had a room apiece, for a marvel.' [*A pause. A laugh.*] That night, as we sat drinking after supper, we fell into conversation with two big village girls, and Turner, I remember, told them his name was 'Jenkinson' – with a twinkle in his eye, that told me not to gainsay him – and that made me laugh; and the girls laughed too, though I am sure they didn't know why; and the upshot, by and by, was that I took the one with the brown ringlets to my room, and he took the other to his.'

[*I confess I do not know what I did to provoke this next comment; certainly I said nothing.*]

'Lord! You young people are such prudes, Mr. Hartright. Do you mean to say you've never had resort to a jolly girl?' [*Another pause, another laugh.*] 'I must say, though, Turner's didn't look so jolly the next day. Her eyes were red, and her skin was all chafed.'

XVII

Letter from Mrs. Tobias Bennett to Marian Halcombe, 21st September, 185–

Brentford,
21st September

Dear Miss Halcombe,

Thank you for your letter of 17th September. I should be delighted to see you – and your brother, if he is returned from his travels – any day next week. Thereafter we shall not be here, for the doctor orders us to the coast for my husband's health, and we may be gone some months.

Mention Turner, and my first thought always is of the Thames, and boats, and picnics. I know this time of year is famously wild and wayward, but if we should be blessed with a fine day, would you care to undertake a modest expedition with us on the river (we keep a small skiff, just big enough for four), and see some of the haunts I most fondly associate with him?

Please be so good as to let me know what day would suit best, and whether my little proposal is agreeable.

Yours very truly,
Amelia Bennett

XVIII

Letter from Walter Hartright to Laura Hartright, 22nd September, 185–

Brompton Grove,
Friday

My dearest love,

It is past three o'clock, and here I am, at last, setting about the letter I promised you yesterday. I should have started this morning; but, having woken early, I decided to take myself to the park, and try to paint the dawn. The result – as I should have foreseen – is dreadful: an overboiled egg squashed on a bed of cinders. How did the man get such colours from his palette?

So – where did I leave you? Entering the train at Brighton

railway station, I think; which proceeded to hurtle me at break-neck speed through Shoreham and Worthing, Angmering and Littlehampton, and at length – little more than an hour after I had left – delivered me, like a well-cared-for parcel, at Chichester. I was then obliged to continue my journey to Petworth by walking to the Ship Inn and taking the London coach – which, needless to say, contrived to cover only half the distance in twice the time, and lurched and bumped so much that I soon boasted a fine pair of bruises on my shoulder and forehead, and was starting to feel like a very *badly*-cared-for parcel.

Yet although I did not realize it at the time – indeed, I was inwardly cursing my ill-fortune, in terms you would have been shocked to hear! – fate was smiling on me; for among my fellow-passengers (who also included two elderly widowed sisters; and a young draughtsman with a case full of drawings, which he tried manfully to review, until a jolt sent them on to the floor; and a party of drunken students outside, who whooped and jeered with every swerve) was a pleasant-looking woman of about forty, who sat opposite me – and, as it turned out, was to play a material part in my adventure. She was well but not fashionably dressed – from her appearance, you might have supposed her to be the wife of a country doctor or attorney – and, as we bounced this way and that, smiled at me, with the conspiratorial air of a fellow-sufferer. At length (when I had received my knock on the head), she grimaced, gave a solicitous 'ooh', and said:

'Jabez Bristow.'

'I beg your pardon?' I said.

'Jabez Bristow.' I must have still looked blank, for she went on: 'You're not from these parts, then?'

'No.'

'Jabez is famous. Or infamous, rather. Can't drive unless he has a pint of brandy inside him to keep him warm. And who cares for anything after a pint of brandy?'

I smiled. I could not place her voice; it was not that of a lady, but it had a kind of confidence that spoke of prosperity, and a practised ease in conversing with people of all sorts and conditions

'How far do you go?' she said.

'Petworth.'

She nodded. Her eyes flickered towards the two widows, and then she leant towards me and said, more softly: 'Pity the poor souls who are going all the way to London. At least we shan't have to endure this much longer.'

We felt the horses slow, and then strain forward, as if their load had suddenly become heavier. Looking out of the window, I saw a little farm bounded with knobbly flint walls, and, beyond it, our road rising sharply up into the downs.

'In a year or two,' said my companion, 'we shan't have to endure it at all.'

'Why?' I said. 'Are they building a railway?'

She nodded. 'Though you'll still have to walk when you get the other end,' she said, with a smile. 'Or take a gig; for the station will be a clear two miles from the town.'

'Good Lord!' I said. 'Is it impossible to build it closer?'

She shook her head. 'The colonel won't have it near his park.'

'Colonel Wyndham?' I asked.

She nodded; and then, after a moment, said: 'Why, do you know him?' Her tone was neutral, but she studied my face intently as she spoke, as if the question was prompted by something more than mere common politeness.

'No,' I replied. 'But I am hoping to meet him.'

'Indeed?' she said non-committally, still watching me closely.

I had the strong impression that she knew something about the colonel, which might prove helpful to me, but that – like a card-player unwilling to disclose her hand until she has seen her opponent's – she would only confide it to me once she had satisfied herself as to my own purpose in visiting him, and established that it was of a purely professional nature, and that I was an entirely disinterested party, who posed no threat to her. I therefore said:

'I am writing a life of Turner.' She did not reply at once, so I added: 'The artist?'

'Oh, yes, I knew Turner,' she said. 'I knew all of them, in the Third Earl's time. Chantrey, Carew, Phillips, Haste, Constable . . .'

This was more than I had dared to hope; and, scarce able to believe my luck, I began: 'What was . . .?' At that exact moment, however – to my extreme annoyance – one of the two widows leaned towards me, scowling; and in a stern tone – as if she had caught me red-handed trying to make off with something that was rightfully hers – said:

'Are you talking about Turner?'

'Yes,' I said. I held her gaze for what seemed the minimum demanded by good manners, and then turned back decisively to the woman opposite. 'What was he like?'

'Oh,' she said – and I suppose, by now, I should have come to expect her next words – 'he was a funny little man. Ruddy face' – she paddled her fingers against her own cheek – 'and always carried a big umbrella. You'd never have thought he was an artist, to look at him. More like . . . more like a . . .'

She pondered a moment, and the hesitation was fatal; for it allowed Widow A to recharge her conversational guns, and – at the very instant my companion concluded, *like a sea captain* – to boom:

'We saw *The Fighting Téméraire*, at the Academy, in 'thirty-nine'; and then, as if I might be disinclined to believe this startling intelligence on the strength of her word alone, she turned to her sister and shouted: 'Didn't we?'

'What?' yelled Widow B.

'See *The Fighting Téméraire*!'

'What!?' repeated her poor sister, who must have been completely deaf; for even the students on the roof heard the commotion, and one of them banged on the door with a mittered hand and bellowed: 'Hoi! Less noise there below!' His fellows promptly erupted into stifled laughter, and I confess that I was suddenly possessed by a kind of desperate hilarity myself, and had to avoid catching the eye of my new friend opposite, for fear I might join them.

Widow A finally gave up on her sister, and fixed me with a gimlet eye. 'It was of particular interest to us,' she said, in the same accusing tone (which I was beginning to realize was her normal manner of address), 'for our father served with Nelson, in just such a ship as that.'

'Really?' I said. 'How fascinating.' And so, indeed, it might have been, in other circumstances; but at that instant, and in that place, it seemed nothing but a monstrous imposition, and I felt my temper rising. Once again, though, fate came to my assistance; for the young draughtsman – with a discreet wink in my direction, which said, as clearly as if he had spoken the words, *Leave this to me* – removed his hat, and held out his hand to Widow A, and said:

'Well, now, *there's* a thing – I'm in the ship-building business myself, in a small way; and it's an honour to make your acquaintance.'

In less than a minute, he had charmed both the sisters into submission – though one could not have heard what he said, and the other could barely have understood it, since the ships *he* talked of had nothing to do with the romantic old man-of-war in Turner's painting, and everything to do with the modern steam-boat tugging it to its doom. And my companion, too, was touched by his spell, if only obliquely – for, seeing our fellow-passengers engrossed in a conversation of their own, she seemed visibly to relax a little, and to be more willing to talk frankly to me.

'Yes, it was altogether different, in those days,' she said, settling back in her seat.

'Petworth House, you mean?'

She nodded. 'Liberty Hall. People would come and go as they pleased, and there'd always be a bed for them, and a meal, and a room for them to work in, if they wished.'

'Were they all artists, then?'

'Many of them. *The greatest patron in England*, the Third Earl, that's what I heard say. And with the finest collection. I wouldn't know, myself, though I liked to creep into the gallery, and look at the statues. It was quite a thing, for a fourteen-year-old girl, to see a marble man with no clothes on.'

I glanced at the widows, but they showed no sign of having heard. I wanted to ask her how she came to be there, at such an age; but since it was clear that she was not a member of the family (and to assume that she was would have been a kind of mirror-image condescension, as bad as the thing it reflected), and the only other probable explanation was that she had been a servant, I could not think of a way to frame the question without the risk of insulting her. Instead, I said:

'And was Turner there a great deal?'

'Oh, yes; his lordship gave him the use of the Old Library, as his studio; and Turner' – it suddenly struck me that she said

'Turner', rather than 'Mr. Turner', which seemed curious, when the man she was talking of was a guest in her master's house – 'Turner shut himself away there, all morning sometimes; and no-one was allowed to disturb him, save his lordship himself.' She smiled, and laughed softly. 'One time, I heard, Sir Francis –'

'Sir Francis?'

'Chantrey. The sculptor?'

'Oh, yes,' I said.

'Well, he decided to play a trick on Turner; and he imitated his lordship's footsteps in the corridor, and his special knock on the door, and did it so wonderfully well that Turner was deceived, and admitted him.'

'And what happened?' I said, impatiently. It was galling to find that even now, when I had supposed I was beginning to understand Turner, I could not guess the answer for myself. It all depended *which* Turner you believed in – the suspicious recluse, jealous of his privacy, or the hearty good fellow described by Gudgeon? The one would surely have resented such a prank; the other, equally surely, would have slapped his thigh, and made light of it.

'Oh, he took it in good part, and laughed when he saw his mistake,' said my companion. 'He and Sir Francis were old friends, so I believe, and liked to tease each other. There was much merriment about it that evening at dinner, you may be sure.'

A point, I thought, *to Gudgeon*. I smiled and said: 'That's an illuminating story. Do you suppose the colonel will remember more, and be able to tell me?'

'He might.' She hesitated, and clenched and unclenched her jaw before going on grimly: 'But he's not like his father.'

'In what way?'

'He's very shy. And has a terrible temper on him.' She paused, as if her own words had surprised her. 'Well, so did his father, come to that. But . . . but the colonel doesn't *love* like his father. That's the difference.'

'Love what, or whom?' I said.

'Everything,' she muttered, flushing slightly; and then, more confidently: 'His people.'

'Why, you make him sound like a monarch!' I said, laughing.

'And so he was!' she cried. 'Wasn't there a French king once, they called the Sun King?'

'Yes,' I said. 'Louis XIV.'

'That is how the Third Earl was,' she said. 'He was our Sun.'

We had reached the top of the hill now, and could feel the horses gaining speed, and hear the harness jingling freely again, as it eased about their shoulders. My companion glanced out of the window, but I kept my eyes on her face, in the hope that she would return to her subject. She seemed to think she had said enough, however, and after a long silence I decided I must prompt her, or risk losing her attention altogether.

'Louis was a despot,' I said.

'Hm?' She turned sharply, like a straying animal suddenly recalled by a tug on its rope.

'A tyrant,' I said. 'He ruled by fear. Hundreds died building his palace. I take it you don't mean –'

'Oh, no!' she said. She seemed genuinely shocked, and frowned, and looked this way and that, casting about for a way to explain what she meant. At length she said: 'All I meant was, the sun *shines* on you, don't it? That's what his lordship did, he shone on us all. Even the animals; for he doted on his dogs and horses and cattle, and loved to have them about him, and you could fall over a sow on your way to the kitchen garden, or even see her galloping through one of the rooms, and all her little ones behind her.' She smiled, and her eyes hazed with recollection, and she lowered her heavy eyelids to brush the moisture from them. 'And the people, too. They'd play cricket on his lawn, and walk in his park as if it were their own – Lord! you should have seen them, sometimes – the boys'd scratch their names on his walls and windows, and he'd say nothing about it.'

'Truly?' I said; for I could not conceive of any landowner *I* know willingly suffering such behaviour – and, indeed, would not tolerate it myself, at Limmeridge.

She nodded. 'And every year he'd mark his birthday with a great feast for the poor. Once, when he was past eighty, it could not be held at the usual time, because he was ill; and so he arranged a fête in the park the next May. Four thousand tickets were given, but many more came; and the old man could not bear that any should go hungry outside his gates, and went himself, and ordered the barriers taken down, so that all could enter. I've heard six thousand were fed that day – think of it! six thousand! – even our Saviour did not feed so many. I was there, and I know I shall never see such a sight again – a great half-circle of tables spread before the house, and carts full of plum puddings and loaves, piled like ammunition, and an endless army of men marching back and forth, carrying sides of mutton and beef on hurdles. And his lordship forever slipping in and out of his room, for the pleasure of looking upon it all, and reflecting what he had done.'

'Magnificent,' I began, 'but –'

'Yes, magnificent,' she said, so swept up now in the torrent of memory and feeling that she could not contain herself but must rush on. 'And he provided houses for the poor, and a doctor; and brought gas to the town, twenty years before they had it in Midhurst . . .'

'Like the sun, indeed,' I murmured.

'What?' she said, almost snappishly. Then, as if she had just caught my meaning, she laughed, and said: 'Oh, yes, I had not thought of that!'

'But a hard example', I said, returning to my theme, 'for an ordinary mortal to follow.'

'What, his son, you mean?'

I nodded; and, in truth, I did feel sorry for the colonel; for only an angel could avoid being unfavourably compared with such a splendid figure, and only a saint bear it without rancour. Before I could speak, however, the woman shook her head fiercely, and said:

'Oh, I shouldn't waste your sympathy on him.'

'Why?' I said. 'What has he done?'

'He began as he meant to go on,' she said, 'by putting me out of my place, and scores with me. For no worse offence than that we were employed by his lordship. Truly, you wouldn't think they were of the same race, let alone the same family.'

And suddenly, a question which had only been fluttering at the edge of my mind until now, like a half-seen moth, sprang into consciousness.

'Why is he only a colonel, if his father was an earl?'

'Because he is a bastard,' she said venomously.

I tried to press her further, but she evaded my every inquiry, and at length lapsed into silence. Only once, when we had stopped some time later at a lonely little tollhouse (much like the cottage in a fairy tale, with diamond-paned windows, and a tall chimney) by a country bridge, did she venture another remark; pointing to a deep scar in the valley, where a team of navvies was at work, she said:

'There! That's where Petworth station is going to be. That's how well Colonel Wyndham likes humanity!'

The guidebook mentioned three hotels in Petworth; and I had decided in advance, out of a childish fancy, that I should put up in the first of them that I saw. This proved to be the Swan Commercial Inn, a long, white, nondescript building of uncertain age – distinguished only by a great picture of its namesake fixed over the central first-floor window – which overlooked the little market square where the coach set us down. It was not, I had to own, the romantic hostelry I had envisaged – even as I looked at it, I felt I could see within, to the too-bright dining room, and the smoking room full of stale air and stale travelling salesmen; but I kept to my resolve, and having bade a grateful farewell to the draughtsman, and a fond one to my companion, I crossed the street, and went inside.

It was, if anything, drearier than I had imagined, with a dingy hall smelling of sour beer, and I approached the girl behind the desk, to ask for a room, with a sinking heart. Once again, however, luck was on my side; for she told me that all their beds were taken, and directed me to the Angel, where she was sure I should be accommodated to my satisfaction.

She was right, for the Angel turned out to be an ancient, lop-sided, timber-framed inn, with arthritic joints and drooping eaves, yet clean and well kept within, with bright scrubbed floor-tiles, and a welcoming fire in the hall. I was greeted by an old man in a stiff leather apron, who gravely took down from the rack behind him a key big enough to secure the Tower of London, and led me upstairs to a neat little room, with coals ready-laid in the fireplace, and a casement overlooking a row of quaint houses. And when he had gone, I sat on the bed, and listened to the breathy stir and thud of a herd of cattle being driven through the street below, and thanked my own good angel for bringing me here, and wondered how many travellers over the years had had the same thought, and thanked their own.

I soon had another reason to be grateful that I had ended up at the Angel; but I was not to discover that for an hour or two more, and shall come to it in its rightful place.

Nothing prepares you for Petworth House. You leave the market square by a dingy cobbled alley, lined with small shops and taverns that offer no hint of what is to come, and all at once – there it is! a mass of roofs and chimneys, of kitchens and stables and coach-houses, coiled around the northern edge of the town like a giant serpent that, having set out to crush the whole place in its embrace, has tired and fallen asleep before it could accomplish its aim.

A gate, with a small lodge beside it, stood open, from which it was apparent that in one respect, at least, Colonel Wyndham still continued the traditions of the Third Earl's day; for even now, on a cold September afternoon, a stream of people seemed to be passing through it, on their way to or from the park as freely as if they had been strolling by the Serpentine – and, while I should have been startled indeed to see any of those respectable matrons or sober-suited shopkeepers scrawling their names on the walls, they might, had they chosen, have done so with ease, since their path took them close to the side of the house for a hundred yards or more. By screwing up my eyes, and so blurring the details of their clothes, I could fancy myself back thirty years, and Turner yet in his studio – an illusion aided by the fading light, and the wistful autumn smells of fallen leaves and distant bonfires, which always seem to raise the ghost of other times so palpably that you feel its presence in a tightening of the throat and a prickling of the skin. In that hazy, magical moment, I allowed myself to hope that my companion on the coach had been exaggerating, and that I should, after all, find the son as welcoming as the father.

To enter Petworth House is to repeat, after a fashion, your experience of approaching it from the outside. The lodge-keeper directed me to a door so unassuming that I should have missed it entirely if he had not pointed it out – it stood in an odd angle of the wall, with none of the clues (steps, or columns, or a pediment) that normally suggest the entrance to a great house – and for a dizzying second or two I wondered if Petworth were so magnificent that even the tradesmen dressed as I did, and he had mistaken me for a butcher or a grocer, and sent me to the kitchens. At length, however, the most immaculate footman I have ever seen – wearing a livery of dark blue coat, yellow-and-blue striped waistcoat and moleskin breeches which would not have disgraced an ambassador – answered the bell; and, on being told that I had come to see Colonel Wyndham, nodded and ushered me inside.

I recall walking along an unremarkable passage, which would have seemed too plain for the hall of a simple country parsonage, let alone one of the grandest mansions in England. And then, without warning, we passed through another door, and all at once I found myself in a world conceived on an entirely different scale, and built on entirely different principles. We entered it beneath the first flight of a vast staircase, which rises (you see, as you emerge into the light) round three walls of a cavernous hall, until at length it reaches a great balustraded landing extending the full width of the fourth side. Above the middle section are two huge windows, each as tall as three men; but almost every other square inch of space seems cluttered with ornament: swags and festoons; medallions and urns; laughing *putti* holding shields; painted figures, in togas and laurel crowns, standing in painted niches; and marble busts, in flowing marble wigs, haughtily surveying the world from real ones. And, dominating everything, a series of enormous wall- and ceiling-paintings in the Baroque style – a gaunt Prometheus fashioning mankind from clay, Jupiter forcing Pandora to open her box, a woman (perhaps some ancestral Wyndham) drawn in state on a chariot, accompanied by earthly and celestial attendants, and a black-and-white dog. It was hard, indeed, to find a surface that someone had not somehow contrived to cover (even the underside of the stairs was panelled and painted), save only for one doorway, which – yielding to the practical necessity of allowing people to enter and escape this odd dream-state – has been cut straight through a woman's figure, leaving a great notch in the middle of her.

The effect, I have to say, is rather like being swaddled in a giant tapestry; but, for all that I found it oppressive, I should have liked to look a while longer – partly to feast my own eyes on this great dragon's hoard, and partly to try to see it through the eyes of a man brought up in Hand Court, to whom it must surely have seemed even more alien than it did to me. The footman, however – determined to prove himself a man of the world, by affecting a complete indifference to his surroundings, and clearly expecting me to do the same – marched ahead, and stood waiting for me by a door at the other end of the hall, with a bored expression that plainly said: *The master will not be kept waiting.*

When I had caught up with him, he led me quickly through two smaller rooms – which might have furnished the text for some moralist's sermon on the dangers of excess; for they were crammed with treasures, each of which individually would have repaid an hour's attention, but which seen together simply stupefied the senses, as a surfeit of fine food jades the palate – and knocked on the door of a third. After a moment, we heard a faint 'Come in!'; and, entering before me, the man announced, 'Mr. Hartright, sir,' and stood aside to admit me with the jerky grace of a mechanical toy.

After my strange introduction to the house, it was, I have to say, with some surprise (and not a little relief) that I found myself in a pleasant library, not much larger than our drawing room at Limmeridge, to which one might almost have applied the term *ordinary*. The immediate impression was of warmth – warmth from the bright coal fire in the marble fireplace, warmth from the fading sun creeping in through the windows, and giving its last lustre to the yellow-gold carpet; warmth from the ranks of leather-bound books lining the red-painted walls, and from the two hissing gas-chandeliers, hanging in the entrance to an alcove at the far end of the room, that made the polished hide and the gilt lettering sparkle. A cream-coloured cat preened itself on a large round table in the middle of the floor; and all about were thickset sofas and chairs, covered in a pretty white fabric patterned with flowers, that seemed to beg you to sit down, and take your rest.

Colonel Wyndham, however, was clearly not of the same mind. He was a broadly built man of about seventy, with sallow skin and a mane of white hair; and, from the moment he saw me walk in, he made it perfectly obvious that he would not be easy until he had seen me walk out again. He did, it is true, come forward to shake my hand; but as soon as he had done so he sprang away again – like a magnet forced close to another of the same polarity, and then suddenly released – and paced about the room, rubbing his fingers on his well-cut grey coat.

I waited for him to speak; but he remained stubbornly silent, and after a minute or so I saw that, if we were to have a conversation at all, I must initiate it.

'You may remember', I said, 'that I wrote to you. About Turner?'

He nodded.

'I was wondering if –'

'I barely remember him,' he mumbled, without looking at me (and, indeed, the whole time I was there, his eyes never met mine directly, but kept straying behind me or above me or at my feet, as if, even for him, the room had not yet revealed all its secrets, and he was constantly finding new objects of interest to distract him).

'But surely', I said, 'Turner must've been here a great deal when you were younger?'

'A soldier's away a lot, Mr. . . . Mr. . . . Mr. . . .'

'Hartright.'

'And this is a big house. People don't necessarily see each other.'

I waited for him to go on, but he turned towards the fire, pressed his hands together, and then spread them before the heat, as if the subject were closed.

'What about servants?' I said. 'Would any of them –?'

'Most of the staff came with us,' he said, shaking his head. 'From the previous house. Don't think any still here would've known him.'

Again I waited – there must, after all, be scores of servants at Petworth, and surely a moment's thought would yield the name of at least one who had been here in the Third Earl's day? – but again in vain. He continued to stare morosely at the fire; and at length I was once more forced to break the silence myself

'Would it be possible for me to see some of the paintings your father commissioned from him?'

'Afraid not,' he said, shaking his head again. 'All the pictures are being cleaned and catalogued at the moment.'

'Or the room where he worked?' I went on, nothing daunted.

'Shut up for the winter.'

'His bedroom, even?'

'The whole end of the house,' he said, flapping his hand impatiently.

This was, I suppose, a plausible answer – all those cavernous apartments, whose only purpose was to be filled with people and laughter and music, must have been a constant reproach to a solitary man like himself, reminding him only of his own puniness and isolation; and it would be natural enough to keep most of them sealed off. I could not, however, avoid the suspicion that he was lying, for he flushed slightly, and, fixing a marble bust on top of the bookcase with a trance-like gaze, set about tweaking the end of his nose between thumb and forefinger, as if it were the most absorbing occupation in the world.

But I could not, of course, challenge him; and, after waiting a few seconds, in the futile hope that his conscience might do so on my behalf, and prompt a change of heart, I saw that – as, to be fair, he had suggested – I was merely wasting my time.

'Well,' I said. 'Thank you.'

He appeared not to notice my tone – which would have turned another man to ice – but simply nodded, as if he were at last able to agree with something I had said, and gratefully seized the bell-pull. Then, as we waited, he said nothing more to me, but paced fretfully up and down the room, twining and untwining his fingers; while I, anxious to preserve my dignity, gazed out of the window at the park – which was as cunning a piece of artifice as I have seen, with a Grecian temple on a little knoll, and graceful slopes dotted with deer, and planted with copses and broad sweeps of trees. As I watched, the last few drops of crimson were seeping out of the dying sun and soaking into the horizon – making, for a moment, the sky redder, and the earth blacker, than any paint could make them; and I knew why

Turner had loved this view, and returned to it again and again.

'Where is the damned fellow?' muttered Colonel Wyndham, under his breath; and, as if in response, the door opened, and the footman reappeared. A few minutes later – less than a quarter of an hour after I had passed it on my way in – I found myself once more at the porter's lodge; and distinctly saw the lodge-keeper smirking out of the window at me, as much as to say: *I thought I should see you again, soon enough.*

It was, as you may imagine, in a thunderous mood that I retraced my steps to the Angel. It sprang, in part, from my natural disappointment at finding that my journey had been fruitless; but I was also nagged by an obscure sense of grievance, such as you might feel if you suspected that you had been cheated at cards, but had no way of proving it. A faint taint of dishonour seemed to cling to me, and I could not go down to dinner until I had washed, and put on a fresh shirt.

Once installed at a small table close to the fire, with a girl spreading a clean cloth before me, and cheerful guests all about, and the old man who had shown me to my room – now in the character of a waiter – hurrying to do my bidding, I found my spirits somewhat recovered; but I knew that this comfort was only temporary. It would keep me company as far as my bed, but forsake me in the small hours of the night, leaving me to wake all alone, and lie there in the darkness and the cold, agonizing over my humiliation.

But then, the good fortune that had aided me so often that day – call it fate, or chance, or providence, or what you will; though for myself, I cannot but see some benign power at work in it – took a hand once again. I had finished my soup, and was just making the first inroads into my steak pudding, when a woman's voice close to my shoulder suddenly said: 'Why, Mr. Hartright!' and, turning, I saw my companion on the coach, her eyes wide with surprise and pleasure, with a bearded man next to her. I was, of course, delighted to see her; but also astonished – for I could not recall telling her my name, and I certainly did not know hers. She must have seen my confusion; for she laughed, and picked up the key to my room, which I had laid next to my plate.

'There's no mystery to it,' she said. 'Giles told me a Mr. Hartright had taken room 7. Though I own I never supposed it might be you.'

'Giles?' I said.

She jerked her chin towards the porter/waiter, who was just emerging from the kitchen with a tray laden with dishes.

It took me a moment to grasp the import of what she had said; and while I did so she stood there smiling at me, like a child who has baffled you with a riddle.

'Oh,' I said, at last, 'so you're . . .?'

'Yes,' she said. 'We keep the Angel.' She gestured towards the bearded man, drawing him into our conversation. 'My dear, this is Mr. Hartright, the gentleman I was telling you about '

'How d'ye do, sir?' he said. His voice was strong and businesslike, but he flushed slightly, and briefly inclined his head.

'Mr. Hartright, my husband, Mr. Whitaker.'

I rose to shake his hand. 'Would you both sit down, and take a glass of wine with me?' I said.

'No, sir – please – do us the honour of taking one with *us*, in our own house,' said Mrs. Whitaker.

I started to protest; but she insisted, and I soon saw that I should only cause offence if I continued to refuse.

'Well, then,' I said. 'Thank you.'

'Giles!' she called. 'If you please!'

They drew chairs to my table; and, as soon as a fresh bottle of wine was before us, and the glasses poured, she leant towards me and said quietly:

'So. How was the colonel?'

'Very much as you described him,' I said. 'Only perhaps more so.'

She laughed – the delighted, mischievous laugh of one who expects to hear a piece of illicit gossip, and intends to enjoy it.

'Tell us!' she said, confidentially – as if, instead of hotel-keepers and guest, we were three friends who had chanced upon one another at their club.

And, strange as it may seem, I did; for I felt I owed Colonel Wyndham no debt of loyalty, and had nothing to lose by being frank about him, since there seemed no possibility now that he would ever help me. And it was a relief, truth to tell, to unburden myself to an attentive audience – particularly one that seemed so ready to take my part.

'Bless me!' cried Mrs. Whitaker gleefully, when I had finished. 'That's surly enough, even for him!'

Her husband chuckled, and looked into his glass – like a man embarrassed by his wife's forthrightness (for it must be perilous for a tradesman in Petworth to be heard criticizing the colonel) but powerless to stop her.

'And you must wonder', she went on, 'why you troubled to come here at all, if that was all you were going to get for your pains?'

'Yes,' I said, surprised at her perspicacity (though it shames me to admit it – for she was an intelligent woman, and why should an innkeeper know less of disappointment than we do?).

She bent towards her husband, and whispered something in his ear. He gave a startled grimace, and then, almost immediately – with such practised rapidity that you could only suppose this was not the first time he had been taken aback by one of his wife's suggestions, and subsequently forced to accede to it – nodded, and muttered something I could not hear.

'Mr. Hartright,' she said, facing me again. 'Are you game for an adventure?'

'I hope so,' I said. 'When some good may come of it.'

'Why, then,' she said, leaning closer, and dropping her voice. 'Whitaker's nephew, Paul, is a footman up at the house. And a good boy, who'd do anything to oblige us.'

'That's because he hopes to follow us here one day,' said Whitaker. 'And is conseckently more eager to please his uncle than his master.' He nodded at his wineglass, and gave a knowing little smile that seemed to say: *I may be under my wife's thumb, but don't imagine I'm a sentimental fool.*

'Oh!' said Mrs. Whitaker, mock-chidingly, tapping him playfully. She turned back to me. 'We'll get word to him that you want to see Turner's studio, and arrange for him to meet you in the cowyard.' The wine had heightened her colour and brightened her eyes, and given her voice a kind of reckless animation.

'But surely', I said, 'it would be dangerous for him. If he was found out –'

114

She shook her head. 'We'll say you're a relative, visiting from London.'

'That's right,' said her husband, with a grim little laugh. 'From the *gentry* side of the family. Come to pass a pleasant evening in the servants' hall.'

'Ssh!' said Mrs. Whitaker. She pulled back her head, and squinted at me appraisingly. like an archer taking aim. 'In one of your hats, my dear, and one of your coats, he'll look well enough.' She stared a moment longer; and then, evidently satisfied, nodded. 'Well, sir, what do you say?'

I still don't know exactly why – did I truly think I should learn something of value, or was I simply attracted by the chance to outwit the man who had humiliated me? – but I did not hesitate.

'Yes,' I said.

And so it was, an hour-and-a-half later, that I set out for my second appearance at Petworth House, wearing a curly-brimmed bowler hat, and an old muffler, and a heavy worsted coat that was too tight at the shoulders, and too baggy at the waist, and left six inches of wrist showing below the cuffs. Had you been in Petworth that night, and seen me walking towards you along one of those narrow little streets, you would not, I am certain, have known me for your husband. but thought me a different sort of man altogether, and crossed the road to avoid me.

The cowyard gate, it transpired, was on the London road, a little away from the centre of the town – which was just as well, for I had to wait there twenty minutes or more, and had I been in view of the porter's lodge, or of curious passers-by, I might have been challenged, and asked to explain what I was doing. As it was, though I managed to keep myself out of sight, I could not feel entirely easy, for I was tormented by the thought, which had not struck me before, that the Whitakers' nephew might be the footman who had admitted me that morning. It did not seem likely, for they had spoken of him as a boy; but I could no feel entirely convinced until I saw a tall young man in a blue cape hurrying out of the blackness towards me. It was, of course, quite dark now, and he kept his head lowered; but I caught a glimpse of a fresh-faced complexion, and almost-white golden hair, that told me, beyond doubt, that I had never seen him before in my life.

He glanced up and down the street, and then said, in a quiet voice:

'Good evening, sir. I'm Paul Whitaker. I'm sorry you was kept so long.'

'Not at all,' I said. 'It's good of you to help me.'

'I should have been here punctual,' he said. 'Only Mrs. Smith said to see her; and I couldn't say no, her being the house-keeper.'

'No, of course not.'

'It was only a small matter,' he said – just in case, doubtless, I should imagine he had stolen the plate, or murdered the under-butler.

He conducted me quickly across a dank, gloomy courtyard stinking of dung and wet straw, and then, through an archway, into a second, as different from the first as light from day – for it was full of the noise and smells of the kitchen, and paved with light from its windows. His policy (which I could only applaud, for I should have done the same myself) was to tread softly, and to keep as far as possible to the shadows, in order to avoid drawing unnecessary attention to himself – yet not to appear so surreptitious as to suggest, if anyone did stop him, any con-sciousness of wrongdoing.

Looking round sharply, to see if we were observed, he opened a door to the side of the kitchens, and led me into a broad, well-lit passage – which, save for the dingy yellow paintwork, and the pervasive fumes of pickles and jams and boiled cabbage, was not unlike that by which I had entered the house earlier in the day. An old man with no teeth and a moth-eaten white beard, who was just coming out as we went in, stopped dead when he saw us, and watched open-mouthed as we passed. I feared that he suspected something amiss, and would instantly report us when we had gone; but as soon as we were out of earshot, young Whitaker whispered:

'Don't mind him, he's only an old man, and won't say any-thing; and no-one will believe him if he does, for he's half mad.'

At that moment, however, he clearly sensed a greater danger; for he took my elbow, and pushed me ahead of him, just as a door to our right opened, and a surge of laughter and conversation and the heavy, drowsy scent of wine spilled into the corridor. I had time only to glimpse a stout man in a black coat, and the gracefully tapering legs of an old-fashioned mahogany sideboard, before we had turned a corner, and were descending a flight of stone steps.

'Upper servants' dining room,' muttered Whitaker. 'Best avoided if we can.'

We were now in a long, low underground tunnel, with a curved ceiling and worn flags on the floor. It was lined with pipes, and lit by gas-lamps, although there were little riches set at regular intervals in the clammy walls where, presumably, lanterns had once stood. To the right, about halfway along, was a brick arch, barred by an iron gate, which seemed to lead into the void. Whitaker jabbed his thumb towards it.

'The well,' he said; and then, as if divulging this titbit had reminded him of my ignorance, and made him feel he should explain more: 'This is the way into the main house.'

When we finally emerged, we did not continue straight ahead, but turned into a small courtyard, like one of the older and pokier quads at an Oxford college, which – from the rude construction of the surrounding walls, and the shape and alignment of the plain square windows – was clearly of an earlier date than the rest of the mansion. To my surprise, however, I felt no change in the air, such as you normally experience when you go outside; and when I looked up, instead of the stars I expected to find there, I saw a pattern of rough roof beams, and, beyond them, a blackness more profound than even the darkest sky. And in an instant I realized that this sprawling monster must have been built about an entire other house, which still stood within its walls, invisible to the outside world – like the ghostly leg-bone that, according to anatomists, lies trapped beneath the skin of a seal.

'Turner's studio's up there,' said Whitaker, nodding to a dark upper window. He opened a narrow door, and, reaching into the gloom, brought out a lantern – further evidence of his intelligence and forethought, for he must have placed it there earlier, to avoid rousing suspicion – and quickly lit it. Then, lifting it high, he led me stealthily up an old spiral stone staircase. so

117

rank with the stench of dust and mildew that it seemed to cling to the roof of my mouth like grease – and, indeed, the taste of it lingers there still, even as I write. And I was suddenly, force-fully, reminded of another place – although it was so unex-pected that it hovered for a few seconds at the edge of my mind, like a powerful but half-forgotten image from a dream, before I could put a name to it: Hand Court.

'Just a moment, sir,' whispered Whitaker, when we reached the top. He appeared far more nervous now, and peered out gin-gerly, to ensure that the coast was clear. And when he did at length stride on to the landing, beckoning me to follow, he moved so fast that my next distinct memory is of being in a large dark space, and of Whitaker closing the door and then leaning against it, half panting and half laughing softly with relief.

'Pardon me, sir, if I don't light the gas-lamps,' he said, when he had got his breath back, 'but I fear we might be seen.'

It might not have been strictly true to say that the room had been shut up for the winter, but it certainly had an unused air about it. The atmosphere was chilly and damp, and the only evi-dence of a fire was the fusty smell of long-dead coals. In the cen-tre of the end wall was a huge arched window, unshuttered and uncurtained, and against its weak grey light I could see the sil-houettes of a sofa and two or three chairs, and the outline of a convoluted statue – rising from its pedestal in the form of an enormous ragged cone, like a drunken witches' hat – which seemed to show some mythic mortal combat between man and man or man and beast. It was difficult to make out much else – for Whitaker's lantern, swinging in his hand, illuminated no more than a few square feet of carpet – but as my eyes grew more accustomed to the dimness I noticed that the walls were lined with bookshelves, and realized that this must be another library. (How many books can Colonel Wyndham own, in heaven's name?! How many of them has he read?) There was no evidence of it ever having been used as a studio – no obvious connection with painting at all, in fact, save for a few pictures hung over the fireplace.

And yet, for all that, I could not help but feel Turner's pres-ence strongly – so strongly, indeed, that for a fleeting moment I almost fancied I saw his shadowy little figure standing before an easel in the window, a brush clenched between his teeth, another in his hand, a gleam of furious pleasure in his eye. It may be that I really am starting to know him, or perhaps I was merely following the train of thought that had begun on the staircase, but I seemed, in an instant, to understand why he was easy here: it was a kind of ideal Maiden Lane, giving him, on a far grander scale, and with unimaginably greater comfort, the same relation between society and seclusion that he would have known when painting in his bedroom as a boy. The great door that so effectively protected him from the prying eyes of the world could, quite as easily, re-admit him to its company; for beyond this private island stretched a giant warren, teeming with servants and children and fellow-artists, all presided over by his kindly patron – just as, years before, Hand Court, too, must have teemed with familiar faces.

Conceive, my love, my feelings when, in the midst of these ruminations, without warning, I heard, not a dozen yards away, the stifled giggling of a girl. I defy any man, however brave – unless he be a turnip, with no imagination whatever – to deny that he, like me, would have gasped, and felt his scalp tighten with fear, and the sweat break out on his back.

'Nancy!' said Whitaker. He sounded almost as startled as I was, and his lantern shook visibly, slopping splashes of yellow light on the floor and walls. In its palsied glow I saw the girl rear up behind the sofa, patting the dust from her print skirt. She was still laughing, but it was the uncertain laughter of one who hopes to escape censure by making light of what she has done.

'I thought you wasn't here yet!' said Whitaker.

'I waited ten minutes on the stairs,' she replied, in a wronged tone. 'But when you didn't come and didn't come, I thought I'd bestest hide in here.'

He clearly felt he could not reproach her further; but could not keep his anger at being taken by surprise, and made to seem frightened, from his voice. 'Well,' he snapped. 'Have you got it?'

'Course,' she said, starting round the sofa towards us. She was walking with small, awkward steps, and as she came into the light I could see why: she was clutching something beneath her apron.

'Nancy,' said Whitaker, more gently. 'This is my cousin from London. Mr. . . . Mr. . . .'

I was, I must confess, momentarily at a loss; for if – as seemed apparent – Nancy was a fellow-conspirator, why should he not introduce me as myself? Almost in the same instant, however, I guessed the answer: he was (again with admirable prudence) trying to protect both her and us. If we were discovered, she would be less likely to betray us, and would herself appear less culpable, if she was ignorant of my true identity, but really thought that she was merely helping to entertain a visiting relative of Whitaker's.

'Jenkinson,' I said – and, had you heard me, I'm sure you would have said: *There's a man born in Covent Garden, who went on to better things.*

'How do you do, Mr. Jenkinson?' She was young – only fifteen or sixteen – with a strong, fine-featured face and an almost gypsy-brown complexion; and there was a kind of modest attentiveness in the way she took my hand that made me think she was anxious to win my good opinion, perhaps as a suitable wife for my supposed cousin.

'Let's see it, then,' said Whitaker.

Nancy crouched down, slipped an old oilskin pouch from behind her apron and laid it in the pool of lamplight on the floor. 'He gave this to my ma,' she said, drawing out a flat package covered in tissue-paper, and starting to unwrap it.

'Turner?' I said.

I don't know whether she replied or not, for at that moment I saw, beneath her fingers, the first patch of that familiar burning orange-red, and then a dark strip of foreground, and then a brilliant button of sun, furious as a raw wound, leaking its radiance into a sky ribbed with cloud.

'Here,' she said.

It was, I saw, as I took it, a little watercolour of the park, which might perhaps have served as a sketch for a larger oil. The brushwork was so rough and indistinct – sometimes an object would be suggested by no more than a line, or a single speck of paint – that it was difficult to make out anything clearly, but I was able to identify the Grecian temple; and a herd of deer (no more than a cluster of dots, really) roaming across

the hillside; and something that looked like an empty chair in
the bottom left-hand corner, on what must be the terrace in front
of the house.

'Did your mother know him well?' I said.

'She saw him often enough, I believe,' said Nancy. 'She was a
housemaid here, like me.'

'And why'd he give it to her?' I said, with a leer that made me
cringe inwardly.

'I don't know, Mr. Jenkinson,' she said. 'She never said. Why
do you suppose?' She looked me straight in the eye, and gave a
little smile, but I noticed she was blushing.

I felt I could not ask more without seeming to act out of character; so I chuckled, and gave her the picture back, and said –
with the air of a man whose limited curiosity has been satisfied
– 'That's very interesting, gel. Thank you.'

This encounter, you may think, afforded me little enough; and
yet it gave my visit to Petworth some point and purpose, which it
would have otherwise lacked, and left me feeling – whether
rightly or wrongly, I still cannot tell – that I had learnt something
of value about Turner, and gained an insight into his character.

I should, indeed, have come away quite satisfied, had it not
been for an incident on the way back, when – just as we had
emerged once more from the tunnel into the service wing, and I
was starting to breathe more easily – I saw, coming towards me,
with a tray laden with glasses and a decanter for the house the
man in all the world I most, at that moment, dreaded meeting:
the footman who had taken me to Colonel Wyndham that morning. There was no point in turning around, or pulling up my collar to hide my face, for he was already watching me, with a little
frown of puzzlement, and would have undoubtedly seen any
hesitation or evasion on my part as a confirmation of guilt My
only hope, I realized, was to make him doubt the evidence of his
own eyes; and when he slowed his pace, therefore, and made to
waylay us, I stopped, and gave him a frank smile, and said:

'Who's this, Paul?'

'Mr. Bond,' said Whitaker. 'Mr. Bond, Mr. Jenkinson. My
cousin from London.'

'It's a pleasure to meet you, Mr. Bond,' I said. I did not offer
my hand, for he could not take it; but bobbed my head respect-

fully. 'Paul's a good boy, and writes often, and never fails to say what a help you are to him, in learning his duties.'

Bond made no response, save to look deep into my eyes, and then at Whitaker, and then back again. At length he said:

'And where do you put up, Mr. Jenkinson?'

Before I could reply, Whitaker – anxious, no doubt, to show that he had not flouted the rules by inviting me to stay at the house – said:

'At the Angel, Mr. Bond.'

Bond said nothing more, and, after a moment, nodded and moved on. As he turned into the tunnel, however, he looked back at me with a cool gaze that plainly said he was not convinced; and I knew that he might tell the housekeeper what he had seen; and that she might tell Colonel Wyndham; and that the colonel might send to the Angel to make enquiries after me. I resolved, therefore, that to avoid the risk of embarrassment for my kind hosts, and of disgrace – or perhaps even dismissal – for their nephew, I must quit Petworth within the hour.

And so it was that I thanked Paul Whitaker at the cowyard gate, and gave him a sovereign for his pains, and five shillings for Nancy, and made my way back to the hotel, and ordered a fly to drive me to Horsham, where I supposed (correctly, as it turned out) that I should be able to take an early train to London. Mr. and Mrs. Whitaker implored me to stay, saying they were sure no harm would come to them or to Paul; but I would not be swayed. Then they refused payment for my room, since I should not have slept in it; but I insisted, and at length they relented, and we parted with many professions of thanks and good will on both sides.

I was so exhausted that even the cold air could not keep me fully awake on that journey through the night, and I slipped between sleep and consciousness, and half-dreamed that I was fleeing some dark confinement with Turner, who chuckled gleefully at our escape – or, rather, that I *was* Turner, and the chuckle was mine.

But now – you will be relieved to hear! – I am fully restored to myself.

Your loving husband
Walter

XIX

From the diary of Marian Halcombe, 29th September, 185–

I have been on my knees, giving thanks. I shall, I know, meet grief and pain and weariness of heart again, as surely as I have met them before; but today – let me joyfully acknowledge it – I have been truly happy. *Thank you. Lord.*

The morning, it must be said, gave little enough hint of what was to come; for I had slept poorly, and gave myself a momentary fright when I peered into the glass and saw there, instead of the lively, cheerful face I had expected, a haggard, half-familiar woman in middle life, with dark rings beneath her eyes and the first silver threads in her tangled black hair. By energetically plying the hair-brush, and smiling brightly (as you do on being introduced to a stranger), and murmuring silly little phrases of encouragement – 'You'll do very well, Marian, indeed you will' – I soon banished her; but the baleful image lingered in my memory, like an awful vision of the future.

Matters were not greatly improved when, leaving the house a little later, we suddenly found ourselves in the middle of a dense fog, as still and chilly as the tomb, which stung our eyes, and clogged our mouths and noses, and speckled our hands and faces with sharp little crystals of soot. I had – I now realized – been looking forward to our boating expedition with unreasonable, childish pleasure, and the certainty that I should be deprived of it cast me down as palpably as a physical burden, bowing my shoulders and slowing my step. I tried, however, to conceal my disappointment; and, taking Walter's arm, laughed, and said with as much bravado as I could muster:

'We shall be fortunate to find the river at this rate, let alone see anything from it.'

The journey to Brentford seemed endless, for the cabman – unable to see further than his horse's ears, and fearful, presumably, of colliding with another vehicle, or running down a child – crawled along at a snail's pace (and a cautious snail at that); and when we looked out of the window we could make out nothing to tell us where we were, or how far we had come – so that, for all we knew, we might have been travelling very slowly in a circle, and still only a hundred yards from our own front door. But then, all of a sudden, the fog thinned to reveal a line of black battlements (belonging, alas, not to the romantic old castle I at first imagined, but to a row of hideous brick villas, which seemed to think they might disguise their newness with a show of trumped-up antiquity); and then it had dwindled to a few wisps of mist; and by the time we neared Brentford, ten minutes later, you could see, through a dazzling chalky gauze, the unmistakable brilliance of a cloudless sky.

We turned into a broad, tree-lined road, and pulled up, about halfway along, in front of a modest gate crammed between a coach-house and a tall boundary wall. The house itself – which stood back a little way, behind a worn carriage sweep mottled with weeds – seemed, from the street, entirely characterless: neither large nor small, neither old nor new; quite indescribable, in fact, save as a catalogue of angles and dimensions. As soon as you walked through the door, however, you found yourself in a charming, well-proportioned hall, hung with delicately drawn portrait sketches, and freshly painted in pale, old-fashioned colours that accentuated the impression of light and space.

A stocky manservant of about thirty, with a florid complexion and a sweet smile (that peculiarity alone, surely, must make the household remarkable, for how many footmen are encouraged to *smile* at visitors?), led us to a large parlour at the rear of the building. For an instant, I had the illusion that I was entering Elizabeth Eastlake's boudoir; for this room occupied the corresponding corner of the house, and exerted, as it were, the same architectural force: you felt the shadowy bulk of hall and staircase bearing down on you, pressing you forward as insistently as a hand on the neck, and the big french window drawing you towards it, with its promise of freedom and fresh air. It took but a moment, however, to see that the presiding spirits of the two places were entirely different; for where Fitzroy Square is all oak and varnish and titanic chaos, this was brightness and elegance and classical order. The books were ranged with military discipline along their shelves, without a single mutineer on chair or table; there were no curiosities to be seen (unless you count a pair of graceful porcelain figures on the chimney-piece); and in place of the bulging bureau was a little writing desk, with fluted Grecian legs, and a drawer barely deep enough to accommodate a small family of envelopes, that looked as if it might have been used by the Empress Josephine to compose billets-doux to her husband.

A slender woman of perhaps sixty-five – who contrived somehow, to appear fashionable in a straight powder-blue dress that would have been considered *démodé* twenty years ago – rose from a scrolled chaise longue to greet us.

'Miss Halcombe! Mr. Hartright!' she said, advancing towards us with arms outstretched. 'You've brought the sun!' Her voice was soft and melodic, with none of the roughness of age – so that if you had heard it without seeing her, you would have imagined that it belonged to a woman thirty years younger. She glanced at the window, flung up her hands in a kind of priestly invocation, and then – in a single sweeping movement, as gracious as a dancer's – extended them towards us, taking Walter's hand in one and mine in the other, so that we stood like a chain of children preparing to play ring-a-ring-o'-roses.

'If we stop to be polite,' she said, 'the day will be gone. So shall we agree, this very minute, we'll take our chances, and venture out, now?'

'Yes,' said Walter and I together, without a moment's hesitation.

She coloured and nodded with evident pleasure. 'I confess I didn't entirely despair when I saw the fog,' she said, moving towards the door, 'but my poor husband was quite determined we were doomed. He'll be more than glad to hear that matters have mended.' She paused, and added, as if as an afterthought: 'You will not, I hope, object to taking the oars, Mr. Hartright? There will not be room for our man as well.'

'No, not at all.'

'Good.' She hunched her shoulders and rubbed her hands with excitement; and then – with a little 'Oh!' that was as much a cry of joy as a word – disappeared into the hall.

Sometimes, when their little one has done something especially charming, you may see parents give each other a conspiratorial smile compounded of fondness and indulgence and shared delight; and it was just such a smile that Walter and I exchanged now. Then, without a word (for why speak, when your meaning has already been so perfectly conveyed?), we gravitated to the window, and gazed out on an artful confection of paths and lawns and rose-bushes – still dotted here and there with flowers, and with the last vapours of mist clinging to them like fleece snagged on a bramble – surrounded by formal little hedges. We had been standing there, in companionable silence, for a minute or more, when Walter suddenly startled me by saying:

'He must be blind.'

'What!'

'Her husband. Look.' He gestured towards the french window; and then, realizing he might make his point more strongly, opened it. 'No. Smell.'

I did so. The air was hard and cold, and thick with the smoky residue of fog; but mingled with it, like the last echoes of a forgotten world, were the pungency of thyme, the narcotic sweetness of rosemary, and the dying breath of the roses.

'The garden is planted for scent, not sight.'

'That's a small enough foundation for a great edifice,' I said. 'Perhaps they both just prefer sweet smells to brilliant spectacle.'

Walter shook his head. 'If he could see, he would have known without being told.'

'Known what?' I said, half-laughing (and, it must be said, entirely lost).

He raised his face to the clearing sky. 'That the weather was better.'

'How do you know he didn't?'

'Because she said: "He'll be delighted to *hear* that matters have mended."'

I considered a moment. He was right, of course: Mrs. Bennett *had* said that, and it did seem curious, now I came to reflect on it, though I had paid no attention to it at the time.

'Very good,' I said. 'We shall lose you to the detective police.'

It was at that instant, I think, that I first became aware of the change in Walter – a change I should, perhaps, have noticed before, for the signs must have been there since his return from Sussex, and, once I was conscious of it, I found myself remarking it again and again. Instead of laughing, and replying in kind – as, assuredly, he would have done only a few weeks ago – he made no response at all, but continued looking out of the window, his brow slightly creased with the effort of pursuing some train of

126

thought I could not even guess at. It was not that he was cold or distant, exactly – only that our friendship, with its teasing and its affection, its rituals of mockery and self-deprecation – had been supplanted in his mind, at least for the time being, by something larger. For a few seconds, it is true (I could not help it then, and cannot deny it now), I felt wounded and bereft, like a child whose boon companion has entered the adult world, and left her behind; but, almost at once, this tincture of bitterness was swept away by a flood of joy – for had I not hoped and prayed that my dear brother would recover himself, and grow to manhood again? And was he not doing so, before my very eyes? And should we not then be truer, deeper friends yet?

'Now, I think we are quite ready,' said Mrs. Bennett's voice behind us. We turned and saw her standing in the doorway, next to a stout old man in a thick black redingote. He was almost bald, but with heavy white whiskers – as if his hair had decided to migrate, like Mrs. Booth's balcony, but in the opposite direction, from the top of his head to his cheeks – which gave the odd impression that his face was wider than it was tall.

'My dear, this is Miss Halcombe, and her brother, Mr. Hartright,' she went on. 'But time enough for proper introductions later.'

She had already started back into the hall; but her husband stayed where he was, and held out his hand, and mumbled 'How do you do?', staring at a point exactly mid-way between Walter and me with the dull milky eyes of a blind man.

Quite a spectacle we must have made, as we processed to the river: Mrs. Bennett, in a brilliant red cloak and carrying a small guitar, talking to Walter in the vanguard; then me, talking to no-one, but simply glorying in the sun that shone more brightly on us with every step; and finally the manservant, with Mr. Bennett hanging on to his elbow, and a basket of provisions and a stack of railway rugs in his arms. At length we entered a small untidy boatyard littered with planks and wood-shavings and coils of rope brittle with dried tar, where the servant vanished without a word. Mrs. Bennett was talking animatedly to Walter about cutters and skiffs and dories, her hand darting about like a frantic wren as she illustrated her argument with a mast here and a thwart there; and her husband, though he stood a little apart, as immobile as a Buddha, and could presumably see nothing, seemed to be listening with keen interest; so I ventured by myself on to a rickety wharf to admire the view.

Even this far upstream the Thames was strewn with filth, which the current had thrown against the piles of the jetty and formed into little islands – with plains made from fallen leaves and waterlogged paper, and mountains from the necks of half-submerged bottles, and, in one instance, an entire hinterland created from a drowned cat, its sodden fur as sleek as a rat's. But the far shore was another world; for there, rearing up like an exotic temple, was the new Palm House at Kew Gardens, its billowing glass roof shot through with light, and the gorgeous red leaves of an American maple flaming beside it; and beyond that, towards Richmond, the tree-fringed slopes and hollows of the Old Deer Park, rising and falling and rising again with the sweet regularity of a calm sea, or of some gentle pastoral melody. The associations with Turner were not hard to see: indeed, this whole scene was a kind of mirror image of *London from Greenwich Park*, with the foreground dominated by the mighty Thames, the father of our greatness, now reduced to little more than a stinking cesspool by the greed and venality of the modern age; while, in the distance, an Elysian landscape, restored to glorious life by the unclouded sun, seemed to show us a vision of a happier time. Less explicably, I also found myself thinking of another painting I had seen at Marlborough House. There was no sea, and no figure that might remind me of Apollo or the Sibyl; there were no ruins; and – while its character was undoubtedly classical – this vista of beech and chestnut, of copse and meadow, had none of the parched brilliance of the Mediterranean, but seemed to glow with that deep-hued, temperate lushness you see only in England. Why, then, was I so forcefully put in mind of *The Bay of Baiae*, and of the vague, troubling sense of mystery that still seemed to hang about it in my recollection? The answer must be there before me; but, try as I might, I could not find it, and was still vainly searching when the manservant returned to announce that our boat was ready.

'Thank you, Jonathan,' said Mrs. Bennett. She led the way through the yard (to my surprise, she seemed to know all the workmen personally, and greeted them by name, receiving in return a grimy thumb and forefinger raised to a frayed cap, or a muttered 'Good afternoon, ma'am') and down a flight of stone steps. At the bottom, a broad little skiff, neatly furnished with rugs and cushions, with the basket set squarely amidships and a pair of oars resting in the rowlocks, bobbed and shivered at the end of its rope. She held it steady while Jonathan handed her husband in, and settled him in the bows; then she climbed nimbly into the stern herself, helped me to the seat beside her, and smiling up at Walter said:

'Very well, Mr. Hartright, if you please.'

And so began six wonderful hours. Walter took his place amidships; and then Jonathan cast us off, and stood watching and waving from the steps (truly, he seemed more like the Bennett's son than their servant) as we glided into midstream and turned to go upriver. There was no space for a tiller, but steering expertly with a piece of ribbon attached to the rudder, and calling instructions to Walter – 'A little harder with your left, Mr. Hartright,' or 'We should not, I fear, come well out of a fight with *that*. Why don't you take a well-earned rest for a moment, and let it go?' – Mrs. Bennett brought us safely past a string of barges, and astern of a clanking collier that set us bouncing and rocking in its wake. For a moment we seemed lost in the pall of black smoke that gushed from its funnel and hung threateningly over the water, blotting out the sky and dimming the sun to no more than a pallid silver disc; but then it was gone, as miraculously as the morning's fog, and we emerged into that sunlit other world I had seen from the boatyard.

We could not, of course, entirely put the ugliness of modern life behind us: it was there in the ceaseless traffic of the river, and the broken cigar-box that slapped against the side of the boat, and the streets of mean, anonymous little houses sprawling along the north bank. But it ceased, from that moment, I think, to be the dominant reality. Lulled by the rhythmic dip and groan of the oars, delighted by the sight of a wild tangle of roots here, or the gothic ruin of some old coots' nest there, we drifted along in a kind of enchantment – saying nothing, and each of us thinking his own thoughts, of which the only outward sign was the dreamy smile on every face. I think, indeed, I must have really fallen asleep, though I have no idea for how long; for one moment I was watching Mr. Bennett put his hand over the side of the boat, with a look of beatific pleasure, as if by trailing his fingers in the water he might *feel* the colours that he could not see; and the next we had stopped with a jolt, and Walter was making us fast to an overhanging branch; and Mrs. Bennett was opening the basket, and saying:

'I hope you care for cold veal pie, Miss Halcombe?'

'Yes,' I mumbled. 'Yes, indeed.'

She took out a white cloth, and laid it, still folded (for there was not space to spread it out) in a narrow strip at our feet. 'I have chosen the bill of fare on purpose, Mr. Hartright,' she said. 'If you cannot share a picnic with Turner, you shall at least know what it would have tasted like. A pie' – here she started removing the dishes as she named them, and setting them before us – 'Beef. A chicken. A lettuce, cut this morning, if you will believe me, from our own glasshouse. Pull-bread. A cranberry tart. *Then* it would have been *strawberry* tart, but, alas, the autumn is upon us.' There was a gravity and wistfulness in her voice, as she said this, which I had not heard before, and which made me suppose she was thinking: *And not merely the autumn of the year, but the autumn of life, too.*

'I like cranberry just as well,' said Walter.

She made no response, save a shake of the head; and realizing that he would not coax her from her melancholy by making light of it, he took another approach, and tried to distract her with a simple, direct question:

'How was it that you came to know Turner?'

'Oh, his uncle was a butcher at New Brentford,' she said – and I knew instantly that Walter had judged right, for there was a renewed liveliness in her voice that told you this was a subject close to her heart, and that it was a relief to her to speak about it. 'Mr. Marshall.' She shook her head and smiled. 'I still remember him. Turner stayed with him as a child, I believe, and later continued to visit him. We lived nearby – my father was a clergyman' – here she nodded and smiled at Mr. Bennett, who, as if he mysteriously sensed it (or perhaps merely because he anticipated her next words), nodded also – 'like my husband; and a fine amateur artist. He met Turner one day when they were both sketching by the river, and saw immediately that he had genius, but that he stood in need of friends.'

'Because he was poor, you mean?' said Walter.

'Yes.' She hesitated. 'Well, I don't know about *poor*, exactly. He was, I believe, quite successful, even then. But –'

'Forgive me,' said Walter, 'but when was this?

'Oh, I don't know exactly. Some time in the middle or late 'nineties, I suppose.

Walter nodded encouragingly; and, drawing a notebook from his pocket, started to write. 'So Turner was still a young man?'

'Yes. Little more than twenty, I should say. But he had started exhibiting at the Royal Academy by then – just watercolours, you know, but still . . . And working for Dr. Monro, and . .' She smiled at some sudden recollection, and paused to grasp it before it vanished back into the abyss. 'I remember him telling me once,' she went on, 'the doctor had a great collection of pictures and employed him and Thomas Girtin to make copies of them, for two-and-sixpence or three-and-sixpence an evening, and a bowl of oysters.'

I laughed. 'I'm sorry to seem so ignorant, but who was Thomas Girtin?'

'You would have heard of him had he lived,' said Walter quickly, without taking his eyes from Mrs. Bennett. 'Another young artist, as gifted as Turner himself, supposedly. But Dr. Monro . . .?'

'Oh, he was a famous mad-doctor,' said Mrs. Bennett, with an edge of pride in her voice, as if Monro's professional eminence somehow redounded to Turner's credit. 'He helped to treat the late king.'

I could not help smiling, for there had been two 'late kings' since the one who had required the services of a mad-doctor. The strange petrifying process that had arrested her idea of fashion, and fixed it for ever about 1830, had clearly had the same effect on her notion of history.

'And he was already travelling a good deal, as well,' she went on.

'Travelling where?'

'Oh, I don't know. He couldn't go to the continent, of course, for we were still at war. But all about England and Wales – wher-

131

ever there were picturesque views to be found of lakes and mountains, or ruined abbeys, or old castles.' She laughed. 'Places where you might imagine a skeleton in a crumbling tower, or a maiden locked in a dungeon beneath the black waters of a moat. Those sorts of subjects were very popular at the time. He did not want for commissions.'

'Why then did your father think he needed friends?' said Walter. 'If he was already so successful?'

She did not answer at once, but suddenly busied herself with taking plates and glasses from the basket, as if she had only just remembered that they were there, and must attend to them at once. At length she muttered, 'I believe there were domestic difficulties'; and then, before Walter had time to reply, handed him a wine bottle and a corkscrew, and said: 'Come, Mr. Hartright, we mustn't let your sister starve. Would you be so good as to open this?'

'Of course,' said Walter. But if she had hoped thus to deter him, she must have been disappointed, for as he set to work he went on: 'What sort of domestic difficulties?'

She seemed entirely absorbed in cutting a loaf of bread, and a casual observer might have supposed that she had not heard him at all. But she was a poor actress, and could not prevent her throat working uncomfortably, or her tongue darting out to moisten her lips.

'Do you mean, perhaps, he had differences with his parents?' said Walter, gently, but with absolute determination. When she still did not reply he continued:

'You can imagine, I am sure, Mrs. Bennett, how difficult it has been to find anyone with reliable information about his early life. So anything you can tell me . . .'

'I really know very little,' she said, reddening, her eyes cast down. 'But . . . but – by all accounts – his mother had an uncontrollable temper.'

Walter's gaze suddenly lost its focus, and drifted past her. 'Like a gale,' he murmured.

'I beg your pardon?' said Mrs. Bennett. I knew Walter well enough to see that her words had recalled to his mind something he had heard or thought before, but she seemed uncertain whether or not he was joking, and half-smiled at him tentatively.

'Like a gale,' he said more loudly, returning her smile.

She nodded (though I think she was still puzzled, for her expression continued to hover between seriousness and jest) and said:

'She was, I believe, a great trial to him and his father, and died mad.'

'Really?' said Walter. 'She was committed, you mean?'

'Yes.' Her voice was barely audible. 'To Bethlem Hospital, I think. Though I – I'm not certain.' She hesitated a moment and when she went on again it was with a kind of breathless urgency that made her sound, for the first (and last) time, harassed and defensive. 'He never spoke to me about it. We all knew that he confided in my father, but it was too sacred a subject to be openly discussed.' She wrung her hands, as if she despaired of making us see. 'What you must understand, Miss Halcombe – Mr. Hartright – is that he was more like one of our family than a friend. And no family can long survive if its members do not respect each others' sensitivities and secrets.'

Walter stared at her for a moment; and then nodded and laid down his notebook and pencil.

'Shall I pour out some wine?' he said.

'If you please,' said Mrs. Bennett, with a grateful look.

At the mention of the word 'wine', I noticed, her husband held out his hand in readiness, and kept it there patiently until Walter tapped his wrist to alert him, whereupon it closed on the proffered tumbler like a sprung trap. He did not drink, however, until we were all similarly provided, and Mrs. Bennett cried:

'We should do as we always did! Raise your glasses, everybody! Here's health and happiness to us all!'

To listen to the Right Reverend Bishop of This, and Her Majesty's Secretary of State for That, telling us that *innocence* must at all cost be preserved and protected, you would think that no virtue excited greater public admiration; yet can we imagine a man of the world, or a woman of fashion – or a costermonger, or a lady's maid, come to that – freely admitting to being *innocent*, or thanking the man who so describes them? No, for to be *innocent* is not merely to be blameless – it is also, is it not, if we are entirely honest, to be childish, and foolish, and ignorant (horror of horrors!) of *how things really go on*? Yet sitting there, a tumbler of brown sherry in my hand, and seeing Mrs. Bennett's unfeigned joy at the sunshine playing on the murky water, and the caress of the cold air on her cheek; her delight at the company of friends yet living, and the memory of others now dead, I could not but reflect that *we* are the fools – for have we not, in our thoughtless desire to seem *practical* and *sensible*, taken strength for weakness, and weakness for strength? Here was an elderly woman, who had known her share of the tragedies and reverses that befall us all; and yet somehow, miraculously, they had not embittered her, or – whatever marks they had left upon her outer form – corroded the girlish loveliness of her soul. She still (you could hear it in the exuberance of that strangely young voice) took simple pleasure in the mere fact of being alive, in loving and being loved, in wondering at the beauty of God's handiwork – and surely that made her stronger, and more fitted for existence, than the most worldly-wise cynic on earth, who thinks he has seen the essential hollowness of life, and seeks only to while it away as agreeably as possible before it is taken from him?

'Health and happiness to us all!' we called back, as lustily and unselfconsciously as children, and quite impervious to the quizzical looks of the captain and his mate in a passing tug.

'Now, Miss Halcombe,' said Mrs. Bennett, taking up a plate, and searching in the basket for cutlery. 'Let me help you to something. Some beef and salad?'

'Thank you.' I had half-forgotten the purpose of our expedition already, and would have been quite content if no-one had mentioned it again all afternoon; but Walter was not to be so easily deflected, and pursued his quarry with a doggedness which – though I had seen it before, when he had been fighting for Laura's happiness and honour – still took me by surprise. Setting down his glass, and reaching once more for his notebook, he said:

'You saw him often at your house, then?'

'What, Turner?' cried Mrs. Bennett. 'Oh, yes, constantly! It seems, indeed, when I look back, that all my earliest recollections are in some way bound up with him. Truly, Mr. Hartright, you never met a merrier creature!'

The food was quite forgotten again, and she settled happily back in her seat. This, you could see, was the Turner she loved to talk about: not the madwoman's son, but the light-hearted playfellow.

'He would romp endlessly with us children,' she went on, 'making houses for us with wooden bricks, and then knocking them down, or letting us wind and unwind the long cravat about his neck as if he were a maypole.'

Walter laughed. 'And did you continue to know him in later life?'

'Oh, certainly. For a few years, indeed, we saw more of him than ever, for he built a little lodge for himself and his father at Twickenham – I can't remember when exactly, it must've been 'thirteen or 'fourteen, I suppose, there's a Miss Fletcher there now; and so we became neighbours, after a fashion, and we were forever meeting at either our house, or his, or getting up picnic parties together on the river.' She impulsively stretched a hand towards her husband, and smiled at him, though he could not see her, with her head on one side, and her eyes bright with tender recollection. 'Charles there, and his brother Tom, who became a surgeon, and me and my sisters, and our father, and Miss Phelps the singer, and Ben Fisher, who went to India, and Sam Fisher, who joined the army, and Mr. Maxwell –'

'Humph!' said her husband, loudly, startling us all; for (save when he had raised his hand to drink) he had been as impassive as a statue, and this was almost the first sound he had uttered.

'My husband did not approve of Mr. Maxwell,' said Mrs. Bennett, with a teasing laugh – which seemed, nonetheless, to contain some undercurrent of sadness, or regret.

'Why not?' I began; but she silenced me with a sharp nod towards Mr. Bennett, which plainly said: *Wait, and he will tell you himself.*

And, sure enough, after a few seconds, he said, in a ponderous, wheezing voice:

'Not so much I didn't *approve* of him, my dear. He depressed my spirits, that's all, with all his talk of rocks and bones.'

'What, he was a geologist?' said Walter.

The old man nodded. 'Every generation has its own trial. For mine it was geology.'

'Not *all* your generation, my dear,' said his wife, with a weary smile that suggested this was an old dispute, rehearsed between them many times before. Then, evidently determined to wrest the conversation back from him, she hurried on, before he had time to reply: 'It certainly wasn't a trial for Turner, Mr. Hartright. Mr. Maxwell told me he might have been a geologist himself, so great was his understanding –'

'Turner was not obliged, as I was, to sit by a dying woman,' said Mr. Bennett, suddenly, the passion of his words curiously at odds with their slothful delivery, 'and try to persuade her that she could still trust in God's love for her, and for the dead infant at her breast, despite the discovery of so much evidence that seemed to contradict His word. If He has lied to us about the age of His world, why should we believe His promise of redemption?'

There was something plaintive, even desperate, in his tone, as if the perplexity was his, and he was hoping we might ease it; but what comfort can a layman – and a stranger, at that – bring to a clergyman whose mind has become a muddy battlefield, so trampled by the ceaseless advance and retreat of faith and doubt that every argument and counter-argument must already seem wearyingly familiar? No-one spoke for a few moments; and then Walter said cautiously:

'Was Turner not, then, much occupied with religion?'

Mr. Bennett shook his head. 'He was a pagan!'

'He came to church with us, when he was staying,' remonstrated his wife, gently; but the old man only shook his head the more, and gave a disgusted 'Hah!'.

'I never discussed theology with him,' said Mrs. Bennett, pursuing her theme with some warmth now, 'but no-one could have felt the sufferings of his fellow-creatures more keenly, or tried harder to obey our Lord's injunction to love his neighbour as himself.'

This seemed to reduce her husband to speechless incredulity; for he could not make a sound, but merely continued shaking his head so vigorously that I feared he must become dizzy, and faint.

'There are, I think, some who would be surprised to hear you say that,' said Walter, mildly. 'Many people think he was cold, and mean, and –'

Mrs. Bennett reddened – she was incensed – her friend was under attack, and she must fling herself into the task of defending him, even if it meant forgetting her manners, and not allowing Walter to finish.

'They would not think so if they had known him as I did.' she said. 'He could appear rough and suspicious sometimes, I know – that was a deficiency of his early upbringing and education. But look within – and there you'd find the truest, most affectionate heart that ever beat.' She paused, searching her memory for some telling incident or characteristic to prove her point. At length she found it; and burst out:

'Another man, for instance, might have neglected us, in favour of more fashionable acquaintances, as soon as he had become wealthy, and much sought-after, might he not? History, I am sure, is full of men who have done so. But not Turner – his feelings for us were as a son for his father, and a brother for his sisters, and were not to be changed. The day my father died, Mr. Hartright' – her voice rose, and became more animated, as if this was the *coup de grâce*, and proved her case beyond all reasonable doubt – 'Turner wept like a child, and threw himself into my arms, sobbing, "Oh, Amy, I shall never have such a friend again!"'

It struck me that if Turner had been the paragon she was suggesting, he might have shown more concern for her loss, and less for his own; but Walter merely nodded, and said:

'So you never found him morose, or taciturn?'

'The kindest of us can be morose sometimes, Mr. Hartright,' she replied, glancing at Mr. Bennett. 'I've seen Turner gloomy, particularly in his last years. Once or twice I recollect coming upon him looking melancholy, and asking him the matter, and being told (here she adopted a gruff voice, with a distinct cockney twang), "I've just parted with one of my children, Amy" – by which he meant he had sold a painting. But how I remember him best – out here, in a skiff, or cooking dinner on the bank with the rest of us, or' – pointing to the shimmering park that stretched away from us, until it seemed to vanish beyond a flimsy muslin haze at a bend in the river – 'lying up there in the hay, – no! Never! He was always singing, or making jokes – though often no-one else could understand them. If he was quiet it was because he was looking at the effect of light on the water, and trying to draw it, or struggling to write a poem.'

'A poem!' said Walter, surprised.

'Oh, yes, he loved poetry.' She hesitated, and then – with a faint blush – went on: 'Once, after a picnic, I found a scrap of one of his verses on the bottom of the boat, and – I know I should have given it back, but please remember, I was very young! – I kept it.' She reached inside the collar of her dress, pulled out a little gold locket on a chain, and opened it. 'I carry it still, to this day,' she said, removing a tiny pellet of folded paper and handing it to Walter. 'Here.'

As if, in that simple act, she had broken the spell that tied her to the past, and brought herself back into the mundane present, she laid a hand on my arm and said: 'Now, I am being a miserable hostess, Miss Halcombe, and' – raising her voice, and calling indulgently – 'yes, I know, my dear, a miserable wife, too. We must all eat, without delay.' She handed me the plate she had already prepared for me, and quickly filled another. 'Mr. Hartright, would you be so good as to pass that to my husband?'

But Walter was still engrossed in reading, and seemed not to hear; and when she repeated the question he said:

'Would you mind if I transcribed this?'

'No, not at all,' said Mrs. Bennett. 'But I fear my husband will die of hunger.'

'Why don't you let me do it,' I said (for Walter, being seated in the middle of the boat, was the only means of conveying anything back and forth), 'and you can resume your proper function as a waiter?'

So he handed it to me; and I copied into his notebook the following lines:

>   pure and clear
> Past ~~meadows sweet meadows~~ tree-fring'd meadows and
>   blessèd golden glebes
> Where linger still the shades of Pope and Thomson;
> And Albion's mighty workshop, ~~wreath'd in blackest smoke~~
>   industrious yet,
> And wreath'd in blackest smoke; until at length
> He flings the fragile barks of ~~HOPE and~~ BEAUTY, HOPE
>   and JOY
> Into the raging sea, where th'ensanguined sun ~~bloodies~~
>   bloodying the clouds
> ~~Tells~~ Speaks of the storm to come

When I had done, Walter and Mr. Bennett were eating voraciously; while Mrs. Bennett, having taken one-and-a-half mouthfuls, had quite forgotten about food again, and was in the middle of a story about Turner and Miss Phelps. I had missed most of it, but it seemed to concern a debate about the refraction of light from floating objects, which Turner had tried, finally, to resolve by dropping a lettuce-leaf into the water. Standing on the bank, however, he had lost his balance, and fallen into the river himself, flapping his arms, in the vain attempt to save himself, like the wings of a bird – at which Miss Phelps (here Mrs. Bennett began to giggle at her own anecdote, something any etiquette book will tell you you should avoid doing at all costs) had cried: 'Ah, Joseph *Mallard* William Turner!'

I could not help reflecting, as I pictured the scene, and saw the simple pleasure it still brought Mrs. Bennett after so many years, on my own upbringing. Had Papa (dear man that he was) been right to protect me quite so assiduously from the unregulated company of male friends? Would I really have come to so much harm – looking at Amelia Bennett it was hard to think so – if I, too, had been allowed to mix with intellectual young men on terms of easy equality?

The meal over (most of Mrs. Bennett's disappeared over the side of the boat as she was carelessly stacking the plates, as if it had finally despaired of ever arousing her interest, and decided in a fit of pique to give itself to the ducks), she took up her guitar and announced that she would sing us some of 'the good old songs that Turner loved'. She did not, like some amateur performers, bully and embarrass us by insisting that we join in; and yet we did, of our own volition, whether we knew the words or no – for only a block of stone could have heard such unconstrained delight and remained untouched by it. It seemed, indeed, for a moment, to reach even into the depths of her husband's soul, and to bring a ray of warmth to the lump of ice that had formed there – for after half a minute or so, to my immense surprise, his wavering baritone, too, swelled the chorus.

I had never, to my knowledge, heard any of the songs before, and I can remember nothing about them now (beyond a general impression that they were all remarkably silly), save for the refrain of an absurd ditty about a nun and a gondolier:

He fiddled like the mad emperor Nero
And sang: 'O Lady, if you'll be my Hero
I'll be Leander
Tho' I stand a
Simple gondolero!'

Or something to much the same effect.

Lulled by the music, and the wine, and the sunshine and fresh
air, I at length lay down, and half-closed my eyes, and allowed
fancy to carry me back forty years. The same river, the same
songs, the same voice: not hard to imagine (the idea suddenly
filled me with a strange, intense feeling, in which joy and longing
were inextricably intertwined, that rose from the pit of my stomach, and plugged up my throat, and disturbed the motion of my
heart, like a finger laid against the pendulum of a clock) that I,
too, was of that same party of young people, lolling in the long
sweet grass, and talking of great things, when Amelia Bennett
was yet a girl, and the trees of Arcadia covered in their summer
green.

It was already twilight when we again reached the boatyard.
Walter seemed unnaturally silent as he shipped the oars, and
helped the Bennetts ashore, and I wondered whether the afternoon might have fatigued him, or made him disconsolate for
some reason; but when I glimpsed his face by a flare of light from
the open shed, I saw he was merely preoccupied with his own
thoughts, for his skin was taut and highly coloured, and his shining eyes kept wandering off in pursuit of some new idea. I was
not surprised, therefore, when he politely declined Mrs. Bennett's invitation of a glass and a light supper, and said we should
be on our way – for he intended to walk along the river, and it
would be quite dark before we got home. She, for her part,
absolutely refused his offer to carry the basket and the rugs back
to her house, saying she would not dream of taking more of our
time, when we had so little to spare, and would give sixpence to
a lad from the yard to go with them. And so we thanked and *not-
at-all*ed each other for a minute or two, until Mrs. Bennett suddenly shook Walter's hand, and (to my astonishment) kissed me
on both cheeks, and said 'Goodbye', and turned on her heel, and

hurried her husband into the night without another word or a glance over her shoulder.

I had imagined that Walter would break his silence as soon as we were alone together, but he barely spoke at all until we had gone a mile or two, and were passing a little waterside tavern, with welcoming yellow lamplight in the windows, and a wooden balcony carried out over the water on knock-kneed piles that looked as if they were about to give up the ghost, and tumble into the river, and drift off towards France. Stopping by the door, he said abruptly:

'Shall we have something to eat?'

It was not the kind of place I should normally have expected Walter to choose (or not, at least, since Laura came into her fortune), but I fancy that this evening he had had it in mind to stop here, or somewhere like it; for as we made our way through a bar parlour smelling of smoke and river-mud, where little knots of boatmen, their faces ravaged by weather and drink, turned curiously to watch our progress; and past a poky kitchen, from which the heat blasted like a furnace; and upstairs, finally, to the coffee-room, he had the satisfied look of a man whose life is unfolding perfectly to plan.

'Let's order chops,' he said, with a conspiratorial smile, as we sat at a table in the window. 'They're hard to spoil, even in a kitchen like that. And we'll have porter, don't you think, in honour of Turner?'

If I touched his skin, I thought – looking at his flushed cheeks, and feeling their warmth even across two feet of tablecloth – it would resonate like a drum, or the rind of a ripe melon: he is so *full*, so buoyed with wild excitement, that it must break out in a mad rush of words, or a flamboyant dance – or else he will strike some unsuspected rock, and explode, and all will go to waste, soaking into the barren soil.

'So what do you think? What do you think?' he said. 'Is Ruskin right?'

'About what?'

'Turner. Was he a tortured genius?'

'A genius, certainly,' I said, cautiously. 'As to *tortured* . . . Well, what do you think?'

He dismissed the question with a shake of the head.

'Come on,' he said. 'What kind of a man was he?'

'Well,' I began tentatively (for I did not wish to deter him by offering a view very different from his own, and so prove, unwittingly, to be the rock myself), 'what do we know? He was humbly born; a little eccentric, perhaps – but no more, probably, than anyone else so dedicated to his art; a man who loved England – its countryside, its coasts, its people.'

I looked questioningly at Walter, who nodded enthusiastically, giving me the courage to continue more confidently:

'He was somewhat rough-and-ready – that we must attribute to his troubled childhood – and could appear stern, or even rude, sometimes – but at bottom kind-hearted, I believe, and a loyal friend.'

Walter nodded again; but then a shadow seemed to cross his face, and he said:

'And what of his morals?'

'His morals,' I repeated slowly. His gaze was so intense that I had to look away, and was too confused for a moment to reply. Then I said:

'I wonder – I wonder, Walter, in all sincerity, whether it is possible to be a great artist, and yet live a life of monastic seclusion and purity?'

I could not tell whether he was amazed or appalled at what I had said, or merely indifferent to it, for his expression changed not one iota, and he continued to stare at me. Eventually (for I found it embarrassing to be scrutinized in that way, and doubly so when the scrutinizer was my own brother) I looked past him through the window at the Thames. The fog was silently returning, and casting a white film over the river – so you could barely see it at all, but only trace its course by the chain of reflections from gas-lamps, and oil-lamps, and the red glow of a ship's boiler, smeared on its surface like broken fruit.

At length Walter turned to see what I was looking at, and at once let out a gasp.

'Wouldn't Turner have loved that?' he said. 'The ghostliness. The *imprecision*.'

'Yes,' I said.

'Not just a great artist,' he said, facing me again, and taking my hand. 'The *greatest* artist in the history of the world!'

XX

Letter from John Farrant to Walter Hartright, 1st October, 185–

20 Trotter Street, Farringdon

Dear Sir,

I have heard you intend a life of the late Mr. J. M. W. Turner, and cannot rest easy until I have told you what I know of him; for I fear you shall never have the truth from his 'fellow artists' – I mean, Mr. Jones, Mr. Davenant &c., &c. – or from the polite ladies he kept company with at Isleworth and Brentford. They saw only the face he cared to show to the world; I saw the other.

I was an engraver by trade – and would be to this day if my sight had not failed me. You will not, I hope, think me proud when I tell you that I had a name for a good eye and a sure hand, for any who knew my work would say the same; and it was on account of that that Mr. Turner heard of me, and asked if I would make some plates for him. This was, I think, in the spring of 180–. He told me that a publisher had engaged with him for a set of coastal scenes, to be engraved and printed in a book; but they had quarrelled, and he had decided to publish them himself. I should, I suppose, have taken warning from this history, but I was young, and little acquainted with the ways of the world, and gratified that a coming artist like Turner should have chosen me to execute his design. He seemed reasonable enough, and quite businesslike, and we soon agreed terms: he would etch the outlines, and then pass the plates on to me to add aquatint, mezzotint, and any further engraving that might be necessary. For this I was to receive eight guineas a plate.

The life of an engraver is a solitary and an arduous one, even at the best of times; you spend twelve or fourteen hours a day in the closework-room, poring over a plate with a magnifying glass, trying to realize an artist's most brilliant conceptions by carefully removing small pieces of metal – and then, quite often, when you at last come to 'prove' it, you find there is some small deficiency in the plate, which obliges you to efface the effort of many days, and do it over again.

Do not think I exaggerate when I tell you that, with Mr. Turner.

143

this hard existence became a kind of hell.

Item. He did not keep his word about the outlines, but required me to do them, saying 'he was too occupied with other matters to attend to them'. He thus loaded me with a deal more work when I scarce had time enough to do what I had already undertaken with him; but when I asked for a deferment he grew angry, and said 'if I could not accommodate myself to his requirements, he believed there were other engravers in London who would be glad to do so'.

Item. He constantly found fault with my workmanship, demanding that I should re-do plates in which neither I, nor my wife, nor any other person could discern any imperfection whatever – so that I might have done five engravings for any-one else in the time it took me to complete one to his satisfaction.

Item. All this might yet have been tolerable had he treated me as an artist like himself, engaged with him in a common endeavour; but his manner towards me was always that of an irascible master towards a wilful, good-for-nothing servant. One day in November, soon after I had sent Mr. Turner the proof of a plate over which I had laboured long hours, and of which I was – I think justly – proud, and expected great things, I came into the parlour to find my wife (who was then carrying our first child) crying. On my inquiring the matter, she showed me a let-ter that had come that moment from Mr. Turner, in which he thanked me stiffly, and said (I still remember his words, tho' it is more than fifty years since I saw them) that 'he noted that I had extended the aquatint into the sea, an indulgence for which he had not asked; and he was sorry so much time had been lost, for it would not do, and I must rework it'.

My wife said she could bear no more, and begged me to go and see him, there and then, to see if I might adjust matters between us; and fearing for her health, and for that of the child (which we lost, indeed, less than a month later), I did as she asked. And so we come to the meat of my story.

Mr. Turner was living then at Harley Street, where I found him at home; but when I tried to explain to him the difficulties I was under, and told him I thought I should have ten guineas a plate, instead of eight, for all the extra work he had put me to, he grew livid, and flew into a rage, and seemed unable to speak, but only trembled, and ground his teeth, and slammed the door in my face.

I was, as you may imagine, too agitated to go straight home to my wife, and went instead to a public at the end of the street, where I had something to steady myself; but far from calming me, it only made me feel the more aggrieved, and emboldened me to think I should return to Mr. Turner's house, and confront him once more with my demands – matching his anger, if necessary, with my own.

Whether I should really have had the courage to carry this plan through I cannot now say; for as I approached his door – my legs feeling heavier, I must confess, with every step – it suddenly opened, and Mr. Turner himself emerged, dressed in his tall hat, and a long coat, and looked about him surreptitiously, as if satisfying himself that he was not observed. I was no more than fifty yards from him, and he would surely have recognized me – but for the fact that it was dusk, and a fog was starting to form, and I had the presence of mind to turn quickly into another doorway, from which I was able to watch him without his seeing me.

Mr. Turner glanced this way and that two or three times more, and then set off down the street at a quick pace. After scarcely a moment's hesitation, I began to follow him. Even at the time, I remember, I was puzzled by my own actions, and justified them to myself by reasoning that some opportunity might present itself to speak to him again, when he should not find it so easy to escape me. I now realize that this was a young man's self-delusion, and that my real motive was the hope that I might learn something which would give me greater power over him, and so assist me to redress the imbalance between us which I felt so bitterly.

Without a backward glance, Mr. Turner turned east into Weymouth Street, and, crossing Portland Road, made a dog-leg into Carburton Street, and then turned again into Norton Street Here he took me by surprise; for, about halfway along, he stopped suddenly before a certain house, and again looked about him suspiciously. I only avoided discovery by dodging quickly behind a passing brewer's cart, and crossing the street;

from where I saw him disappearing into the hall, and the front door closing behind him. My first thought was that this must be a bawdy house or an accommodation house, for why else would he wish to conceal his business there? Yet only the lower windows were lit, and I saw no-one else either entering or leaving; and after only a few minutes Mr. Turner himself came out again – too soon, I imagined, for anything in that way to have happened. He still seemed to fear detection, however; for he had taken pains to disguise himself, by putting on a heavy cloak in place of his coat, and winding a muffler about his face; and before he finally stepped into the street he once more glanced furtively about him.

He did not return to Harley Street, but instead turned back on to Carburton Street and continued east, walking with the same quick, darting gait. Wary of being taken unawares a second time, I decided to follow at a greater distance, so that if he stopped suddenly again I should be able to conceal myself; but I did not make sufficient allowance for the fog, which grew so thick, as the night came on, that I lost him altogether in Fitzroy Square. I ran to catch him up, and after half a minute or so made out a murky figure ahead of me on Grafton Street, but it seemed a little too tall for Mr. Turner, whom I concluded (or rather guessed), therefore, must have turned on to Upper John Street; and so I went that way myself. And I was right, as luck would have it, for I had not gone fifty paces – still running, and choking on the cold unwholesome air – when I came upon him suddenly.

I shall never, as long as I live, forget the picture he made standing there, the mist swirling about him, before a shabby door with the number '46' painted on it (I see it still, the '4' not quite straight, and the '6' blotched and disfigured, as if it was being consumed by mould). His hand was already on the handle; but even now he hesitated, and peered over his shoulder to make sure that no-one saw him, his little bird-like eyes turned yellow by the sulphurous haze, and burning with the most malevolent expression I have ever seen. For a moment I thought he had recognized me, for he started, as I appeared, like a frightened animal; but I immediately lowered my gaze, and hurried on, and when I glanced back he was entering the house.

There was a small public on the other side of the street, which commanded a good view of number 46, and I found myself a place by the fire, and settled there to watch. But an hour passed, and then another, and still Mr. Turner did not come out, and no-one else went in; and at length thinking I could delay going home to my wife no longer, I told the landlord I thought I had seen a friend enter a house opposite, and asked him, as casually as I could, if he knew who lived there. He could not meet my eye, but blushed (for he must have thought my 'friend' was Mr. Turner), and looked down at the mug he was wiping, and mumbled:

'There's a young widow there, sir, a Mrs. Danby. She's kept by an artist, they say, who treats her, if you'll pardon me speaking plain, as his whore – and none too kindly, by all accounts.'

This is all I know for a certainty, and I shall not lie to you, or pretend to more understanding than I have. I have heard from others, however, that in later years Mr. Turner's habits of secrecy and dishonesty became ever more vicious, until at length he deceived even his closest friends – living, unknown to them, under a false name, in a poor little cottage in Chelsea. Do not, I beg, allow yourself to be deterred by certain persons from doing your duty, and discovering what this extraordinary conduct was intended to conceal.

For my part, I can say only that J. M. W. Turner was the most tight-fisted, black-hearted devil of a man I ever met. I see him still in my dreams, and wake thanking God that he now has no other power to hurt me and my family.

Yours very truly,
John Farrant

XXI

Letter from Miss Mary Ann Fletcher to Marian Halcombe,
1st October, 185–

Sandycombe Lodge, Twickenham

Dear Miss Halcombe,

I shall be delighted to receive you and your brother here, any morning you please. I should warn you, however – lest, like the generality of visitors, you imagine it to be some great villa, that can profitably occupy you for a day – that Sandycombe Lodge is only a house in miniature, and you will be done in no more than half an hour.

I do believe, though (but you may perhaps consider me partial!) that you will find it well worth the journey: it is a charming little curiosity; and affords an interesting glimpse into Turner's mind, and into his unusual mode of life.

Yours very truly,
Mary Ann Fletcher

XXII

Letter from Walter Hartright to Laura Hartright,
2nd October, 185–

Brompton Grove,
Saturday

My dearest Laura,

Your strange letter arrived by this morning's post. You silly girl! How can you think – let alone write – such things? Do you really imagine that *I* can bear this separation any more easily than you (who at least have little Walter and Florrie to comfort you)? – or that I would willingly protract it an hour longer than was necessary?

It grieves me – as it would any man – to hear that our children ask, 'Has Papa forgotten us? Does he not love us any more?'; but what wounds me a thousand times more is that you say you are at a loss how to reply. Great God! How can you be at a loss? Does not your heart answer for you: 'Of course not, my darlings; he thinks of you, and misses you, every minute of every day; but he is engaged on some great undertaking that shall one day make you proud of him.'? Or do you think so poorly of me that you no longer believe it yourself, but really suppose that I care nothing for family and home, and that I linger in London, like some shallow, worthless man of the world, merely to indulge the whims of idleness and pleasure?

You say that my letters no longer sound like your 'old dear Walter' – that while they are addressed to you, you feel I am really directing them to someone else entirely. My dearest –

have I not explained?! I have not time enough to keep a journal *and* to write to you (if I did so, I should be always at my desk, and have to delay my return still further!), and must conse- quently depend on my letters to preserve a record of my thoughts and impressions. So, yes, others (God willing) shall one day read some of my words – but would you sooner I con- fided them all to a diary, and so excluded you, my life's com- panion, from the very marrow of my experience?

This book – let me state it plainly, when I should have hoped I had no need to – is very dear to my heart. Through it, I believe, I shall be able to say something of true value about the life of a great artist, and about the nature of art itself. If I do as you ask, however, and return to Limmeridge now, all my efforts (and the hardship we have both endured) will have been in vain; for there are more doors I must open, more cor- ners I must peer into, more questions I must ask, before I can confidently reach a judgement on this elusive man and his work. I shall not, therefore, deceive you (as I unwittingly did before) by saying: I shall be home in so many weeks. I shall be home when I have done what I must do; and that – trust me – will be as soon as I can possibly contrive it.

My love as always, and kisses to the children.
Walter

XXIII

From the notebook of Marian Halcombe, 5th October, 185–

Sandycombe Lodge, Twickenham

Neat, plain, geometrical
Whitewashed walls, low slate roof
So small, at first think it's a *real* lodge – expect to see gate, and long drive, with great man's house at end of it
Only inside see it for what it is – Lilliputian classical villa, con- ceived on different scale from modern houses surrounding it (presumably not there in Turner's time?)
Even on a dull day – first impression (like Turner's paintings): Light

Tiny hall – barrel-vault ceiling – simple decoration – entrance to an elegant dolls'-house

To left: curving staircase, lit by oval skylight, up to two bedrooms

Beyond hall, transverse corridor: dining room at one end; library at the other; in the middle, Turner's studio, with a great window overlooking garden. Light! light! light!

Miss Fletcher – answered door herself. About 40 – long, pale, anxious face, eyes rather close together. Frail, trembled, as if with cold. Sat with her while Walter went outside to sketch house and garden.

Semi-invalid – amuses herself finding out 'all I can about Turner, and his odd mode of life here'. Thinks he was 'a funny little man'. [There – 'funny' again]

Turner moved here 1813.

Why Twickenham? Air. Light. View of Sir J. Reynolds' house – also poet James Thomson's.

Solus – Solis

Blackbirdy

'Billy'

Pony & trap – sketching

'Daddy' or 'Old Daddy' – looked after house

Also gallery [strange!]

Market gardener – cart – gin

Left 1826

House sold to Mr. Ford – sold to Miss Fletcher's fath

From the diary of Marian Halcombe, 5th October, 185–

I have sat here a full hour, and written no more than '5th October' – and shall soon be obliged to change even that, for looking at the clock I see it now wants but ten minutes to be 6th October. Walter depends on me for an account of the day's events, and all I shall finally be able to give him is my notes.

And yet as soon as I start to write for myself rather than for him – see! – the words begin to come. Why? Do I all of a sudden no longer feel at ease with him? No longer trust him?

Certainly I was puzzled, and not a little embarrassed, by his manner today. He was so withdrawn, so wound about with his own thoughts, that for whole minutes together he said nothing at all, but acted as if he were quite alone, opening a cupboard door, or unfolding the shutters on the window, without question or comment. Miss Fletcher seemed not so much offended by this off-handedness as astonished by it; perhaps assuming that such behaviour would be considered quite normal in London society, she watched him open-mouthed, like a child bemused at the strangeness of the adult world but determined to learn its secrets. Only once did she try to engage him in conversation, as he stood sketching the fireplace in the dining room, and she burst out admiringly: 'Oh! I wish I could draw like that! How fortunate – to have the Muse of Art as well as of Literature!'

To which Walter did not reply at all (surely a modest 'You overstate my talents, I'm afraid', or a polite 'I'm sure you have remarkable gifts, Miss Fletcher', would have cost him little enough?); but merely looked away, with a half-smile that seemed to say: *Yes – you are right – I am infinitely your superior; and you are of so little consequence that I needn't waste breath denying it.* The poor woman was left staring and gulping like a stranded fish: until at length, unable to bear the humiliation any longer, she was forced to resort to the pitiable fiction that she had been talking to me the whole time, and muttered:

'Hm, Miss Halcombe?'

'Yes, indeed,' I said. I was debating whether to add, 'But sad that the Muse of Good Manners seems to have deserted him completely,' when Walter forestalled me.

'I think I shall go outside now, if I may,' he said suddenly. I should have liked to go with him, but decided to stay and talk to Miss Fletcher instead – partly to show my anger with him, and partly my sympathy for her.

'You must forgive my brother if he seems a little distracted,' I said as he left. 'He is very preoccupied with his book.'

'Oh! – no – I quite understand!'

'Turner is proving a difficult subject.'

'Yes, yes,' she said sorrowfully, as if living in Turner's house somehow made her responsible for his vagaries. 'But I suppose that's the privilege of genius, isn't it? To be a little odd?'

'Do you think you would have liked him?'

'What, Turner?' she said, surprised (as, indeed, I had intended she should be; for jolting her into another train of thought was the only way I could conceive of avoiding a none-too-original lecture on the artistic temperament). 'I really don't know.' She thought carefully for a moment. 'It all depends, I think. Sol*us* or Sol*is*.'

'I beg your pardon?'

'I don't know why he later changed the name to "Sandycombe Lodge", but when he first moved here he called the house "Solus" . . .'

'"Alone",' I said.

She nodded. 'But my brother thinks he meant "Solis", S-O-L-I-S. "Of the sun." Or perhaps just "Sunny". Turner'd barely been to school, you see, and didn't have Latin, so it would have been an easy enough mistake for him to make.'

My mind's eye was suddenly dazzled with the array of suns we had seen at Marlborough House. 'That seems likelier, doesn't it?'

'Perhaps,' she said. 'But you'd certainly suppose he wanted solitude, for he put bars on all the windows, and made the garden a thicket of willows.'

I looked outside. A few yards away I recognized the top of Walter's head. Beyond it, sure enough, was a thick wall of trees.

'And the boys called him "Blackbirdy",' said Miss Fletcher, 'because he wouldn't let them bird's-nest.'

That might, I thought, have simply been because he liked blackbirds; but before I could say anything she went on:

'And there were only the two of them in the house.'

Two? Was there a wife, then? A young Mrs. Booth? I could not, for a moment, think of a delicate way to phrase the question; but she must have see it in my face, for she said:

'Turner and his father.'

'His father!'

She nodded. '"Billy" and "Daddy".'

'And not even a servant?'

'Daddy *was* the servant, Miss Halcombe. I know – an eccentric arrangement, but there it is – while Billy was out in his pony and trap, sketching, Daddy was here, taking care of the house and garden. And as if being his son's cook and valet weren't enough, he was also expected to stretch his canvases, and varnish them when they were done, and go up to London to open the gallery.'

'What gallery?' I asked.

'Oh – did you not know? – Turner kept on his house in Queen Anne Street, even while he was living here; and there was a gallery there, where buyers could view his work. And Daddy of course, was a tight-fisted old man – it was something of a family trait, as I'm sure you've discovered – so to avoid paying the coach-fare he'd give a market gardener a glass of gin to take him into town on his cart.'

She started to laugh, but then stopped abruptly as Walter entered the room. All through my conversation with Miss Fletcher, one part of my mind had been silently composing a thinly veiled rebuke to him, with which I hoped, on his return, to jar him back to some semblance of politeness; but I at once saw that it would not now be necessary. His languor and aloofness seemed to have evaporated like mist before the sun, and he was once again – as he'd been on his return from Petworth, and during our visit to the Bennetts – all enthusiasm and attention. I couldn't imagine the cause of this transformation, but I quickly realized it was not simply a bad conscience: there was an unmistakable sense of direction in his manner as he sat next to Miss Fletcher on the sofa, and complimented her on her garden, and amused her with a silly anecdote about a black kitten which had leapt on him from behind a currant bush, and half-killed his boot. After a minute she started visibly to relax, and shot me a glance so brimming with gratitude – *See! He likes me, after all!* – that I shuddered with pity.

'What I was wondering', said Walter – after a tiny pause that told me that this was his true purpose – 'was where are the kitchen and the other offices?'

'Ah, yes!' said Miss Fletcher eagerly. 'A good question, Mr. Hartright. Let me show you.'

She rose, and led us back into the miniature hall.

'There,' she said, pointing to a plain, inconspicuous door beneath the stairs. 'Turner's triumph. You'd never guess it was there, would you, if you didn't know?'

'No,' said Walter.

And I must own that I hadn't noticed it before, either, and that if I had I should have assumed it was nothing more than a modest cupboard.

'Why his *triumph*?' I asked.

'Why, he designed the house,' she said, with the complacent air of a woman giving a well-tried performance, and seeing from my startled expression that it was having its usual gratifying effect. 'Oh, yes, he quite fancied himself the architect. So this' – reaching for the handle, and turning it – 'must have been in his mind.'

I confess I couldn't (and still can't) imagine what 'this' might have been – unless it was that Turner, the master of *chiaroscuro*, having contrived to make the upper floors wonderfully light, decided, by way of contrast, to leave the basement as dark as possible; for beyond the hidden door you could see nothing but the top of a mean spiral staircase, which disappeared after two or three steps into the gloomy grey haze of a dungeon. Any urge I might have had to explore further (and I felt little enough, faced by this uninviting prospect) was immediately quelled by a sickly waft of cold air, laced with the smells of stale cooking, which rose from the darkness like the breath of a dying animal; so I contented myself with turning back to Miss Fletcher and saying:

'Yes, very ingenious.'

But Walter was not to be so easily deterred; pressing past me and Miss Fletcher (who seemed on the point of closing the door again), he descended the first few steps. After a few seconds he stopped, and cried, 'This is remarkable!' and then continued on his way.

'You are wise to stay here, Miss Halcombe,' said Miss Fletcher, backing away from the doorway. 'It's rather cold down there, I'm afraid, and you might easily catch a chill.'

I have wondered, since, whether there was anything in her manner – some hint of foreboding or secret knowledge – that might have alerted me to what was about to happen; but all I can recall is a frail, hunched woman, her hands crossed and rubbing her arms, and a smile of humorous apology on her thin lips.

It cannot have been more than two minutes before we once again heard Walter's footsteps on the stairs. I shall never, I think, forget his appearance as he re-emerged a few moments later: the vigour of his movements, the vitality of his form (which seemed suddenly to have expanded, so that it risked bursting cut of his sober town clothes); above all, his face, which bore an expression I have never seen before, and don't know whether I should wish to see again – an expression compounded all at once of excitement, of satisfaction, and (as it seemed to me) of a kind of wild, desolate terror.

Perhaps this is the true root of my uneasiness: in that instant, I recognized Walter's features well enough – but not the mood, the beliefs, the thoughts they expressed. Only last week, I thought he had truly become himself again, for the first time in years (and congratulated myself, poor vain wretch that I am, on having engineered this transformation, by introducing him to Elizabeth Eastlake); now I wonder whether what then *seemed* his true self was no more than a temporary phase – not a terminus, as it were, but merely a small station, through which he has already passed on his way to somewhere else. And that somewhere else is a place I do not know, and will make him a stranger to me. Or –

Later

Heavens! Why did I stop again? A strange storm in my head – my thoughts all lashed together, so I could not unravel them.

It is now past two in the morning, and still Walter has not returned.

He told me he was going to Mayall's photographic studio in Regent Street. He cannot still be there now. Where is he?

Perhaps my anxiety has deprived me of the power to think and write about him.

This will not do.

Concentrate.

One question, naturally, preoccupied me as we got into our cab, and left Sandycombe Lodge.

What had Walter seen in the basement?

Yet I felt I could not ask him directly, for fear that in doing so I might drive him further from me. The truth was, I suddenly realized, I could no longer predict how he would behave. If I revealed that I had seen how deeply he had been affected, he

might, indeed, confide in me; but I could as soon imagine his air-
ily denying it (*You are too fanciful, Marian; I never thought I should
find you guilty of that*); or else becoming embarrassed and confused.

For a few minutes I said nothing at all, hoping that he might be
moved to fill the silence himself, and so spare me the necessity of
declaring my curiosity; but he only sat quietly staring out of the
window. At length, unable to bear it any longer, I said:

'A pretty little house, I thought. Or at least the parts of it I saw.'

An irresistible invitation, you would suppose, to describe the
parts I *hadn't* seen; but he merely nodded absently. I must either
hold my tongue, or be more direct.

'What was the basement like?' I asked.

You would think he had been struck deaf.

'What *is* it, Walter?' I said. 'Why won't you tell me?'

But again he said nothing; and after a minute or two opened
his notebook, and began studying the drawings he had made.

It was intolerable – I *must* discover what he had seen – and yet
I was at a loss to know how to prise it from him. It was clear, however, that the more desperately I pursued him now, the more
stubborn he would become; so I resolved to ponder the matter in
silence.

What might one find in a basement, to excite such a response?

Something that Turner had left there – an undiscovered picture, or pictures. But in that case, surely, Miss Fletcher would
have shown them to us, or at least mentioned their existence?

Evidence of a crime – a bloodstain (heaven help us!). Hard to
believe – but it was undeniably odd, was it not, that Miss
Fletcher seemed to be the only person in the house? Suppose
she'd fallen out with the housekeeper, and taken an axe to her in
the scullery? Or perhaps she'd had a lover, and he had spurned
her?

No, no – inconceivable – if there had been anything of the kind
there, she would not have allowed Walter to find it, and he could
not have remained silent about it.

Why was my mind running on such terrible things? Was it just
that the place made me think so powerfully of a dungeon?

A dungeon. A dungeon. A lightless room. A barred door. Dripping walls, covered in moss. A set of rusting manacles –

The cry of a hawker in the street brought me out of my reverie, and I looked out of the window and saw that we were entering Putney. The road was crowded with carriages and carts; the pavements thronged with dull, decent people thinking of nothing save whether it would rain, or where the cabbages might be best and cheapest. If they could see *my* thoughts, they would indubitably suppose I was mad.

I was somewhat chastened by this reflection (for if I have had nothing else to boast of, have I not always prided myself on my good sense?); but then it struck me that I could turn my new-found weakness to my advantage, by making light of it.

So was there a prisoner in chains there, Walter? Did you find Old Dad, still locked up after fifty years, and raving piteously about varnish?

I turned cautiously towards him, rehearsing the words in my head. He was still engrossed in his notebook, adding a line here, or a scribbled word there, whenever the motion of the cab allowed. Something in his posture, the obstinate set of his neck and shoulder, told me, beyond doubt, that he would not be amused, and I should fail again.

I was suddenly overcome with tiredness – sleep seemed to ambush me, whether I would or not, pressing me to my seat, and turning my eyelids to lead. No dreams of horrors – no dreams of anything, so far as I can recall; and I was woken again after only a few minutes – for we had gone but a mile or so, and were still a little way from home – by a sharp slapping sound. The cause, I soon discovered, was Walter's notebook, which had slipped from his lap on to the floor. I was surprised, for an instant, that he did not bend forward to retrieve it; then I saw that he, too, had fallen asleep, and I picked it up myself.

We are brought up to believe that letters and diaries are sacrosanct, and that it is the blackest dishonour to violate their secrets – but what of a notebook? Surely (I told myself) that is something else entirely – a mere collection of facts, as neutral as a column of figures, which cannot be held to belong to any person in particular. It was only as I lifted the first page that I suddenly imagined what *I* should feel if the situation were reversed, and I found Walter making free with *my* notebook without my permission.

I stopped myself, but not before I had glimpsed one of his sketches. It was not the gloomy interior I had expected, but an outside view of the garden front. There were the two little single-storey wings, with their stucco walls and trim slate roofs; there in the centre Turner's studio, where Miss Fletcher and I must have been talking even while Walter had drawn this (indeed, I could just make out two ghostly little crescents in the window, which might have been our heads).

But below it was another window, which I had not seen before: a lunette, protected by an iron grille, half hidden by a tangle of bushes. Beyond it must lie the basement.

It reminded me of something – something unexpected, though for a moment I could not say what it was. The curved top; the glass (at least in Walter's drawing) so shadowed that it looked like an empty socket – why did they seem familiar?

And then, with the force of a physical shock, it struck me: the half-buried arches in *The Bay of Baiae*.

Later still

He is back. I cannot imagine where he has been – I do not wish to imagine – but he is back. Thank God.

The sound of the door woke me. I had somehow persuaded myself that I had finished, and fallen asleep at my desk.

I have just re-read what I wrote. I had *not* finished. I had not described our homecoming.

As we descended at last from the cab, I missed my footing. Walter caught me, but not before I had twisted my ankle. The pain must have shown on my face, because, as I hobbled towards the door on Walter's arm, the driver said:

'Your missus all right, sir?'

So kindly meant. And yet those words laid bare my heart so mercilessly that even my poor self-deluded eyes could not fail to see it.

Oh God, I am so miserable.

XXIV

From the journal of Walter Hartright, 6th October, 185–

Am I mistaken? Could I be mistaken?

There is something about a photographic studio that makes you doubt the evidence of your own senses. There is the painted backdrop, telling you that you're in the library of a country house or a garden strewn with statues; there are the clamps, half hidden by a curtain, that fix the subject in a pose of apparent naturalness for long minutes together.

But surely it is childish superstition to distrust a man simply because he lives by creating illusions?

Considered rationally, is there any reason why Mayall might have lied?

I cannot think of one. He appears a plain, unaffected, business-like sort of man. Being American, he has no connections here. If he is now the most successful photographer in London ('that was, I am sure, Sir William Butteridge I saw emerging from his studio), he has become so entirely through his own efforts, and the excellence of his work. It is true that he suddenly seemed more obliging when I mentioned Lady Eastlake's name, but that, I am sure, is because she has taken such an intelligent interest in his profession.

So what exactly did he say?

'Turner came to my *atelier* several times in 'forty-seven, 'forty-eight and 'forty-nine. There was something rather mysterious about our early meetings. In one of them he told me led me to believe he was a Chancery Court Judge, and he did nothing to dispel this impression, later on.'

Led me to believe. Odd, but not inconceivable that it was simply a misunderstanding of some kind. Turner was, after all, an old man (he must have been what? – seventy-two? – when they met?) – perhaps his weak eyesight prevented him seeing the puzzlement on Mayall's face, or he mis-heard a question.

And yet . . .

'He came to see me again and again – so often, indeed, that my people used to think of him as "our Mr. Turner". And every time he had some new notion about light. One day, I remember, he sat with me three hours, talking about its curious effects on films of prepared silver. The whole subject seemed to fascinate him. He asked whether I'd ever repeated Mrs. Somerville's experiment of magnetizing a needle in the rays of the spectrum, and said he would like to see the spectral image copied.'

Not the conversation of a man with failing faculties. Nor, indeed, you would imagine, of a Master in Chancery. Surely Mayall must have been curious enough to question him further? 'If I may say so, sir, you know more about optics than any judge I ever met . . .?'

That would have been the moment for Turner to disabuse him, if it had been an honest mistake. But *he did nothing to dispel this impression, later on.*

It is true, of course, that Turner made no attempt to conceal his name – but then there was little chance it would betray him: there must be thousands of Turners in London.

What, then, of the pictures?

'At first he was very keen on trying the effects of light let in on the figure from a high position, and he sat for the studies himself. Later, I took several daguerreotype portraits of him. In one, he was reading – a favourable position for him, because his eyes were weak and bloodshot. There was a lady who accompanied him [presumably Mrs. Booth] and I recall that he gave one of these pictures to her.'

But none of the portraits was full-face; and when I asked Mayall if he still had any of them (for, apart from the early self-portrait Ruskin showed me, I have still seen no image of Turner, and can form no mental conception of him in his later years) he replied:

'Alas, no. I did set aside one curious portrait of him in profile, which of course I immediately looked up when I found out who my mysterious visitor really was. But unfortunately one of my assistants had effaced it [did Mayall hold my eyes a little too fixedly here, as people do when they lie?] without my permission.'

And how *had* he found out who his 'mysterious visitor really was'?

'Oh, I met him at the *soirée* of the Royal Society, in – I think – the spring of 1849. He greeted me very cordially, and immediately fell into his old topic of the spectrum. Then someone came up and asked if I knew Mr. Turner, and when I told him I did, my informant said, rather significantly: "Yes, but do you know that he is *the* Turner?"

'I was rather surprised, I must confess. I ventured to suggest that I might be able to help him, by carrying out some experiments for him on his ideas about the treatment of light and shade, and we parted on the understanding that he would call on me. But he never did call on me, and I never saw him again.'

Perhaps I *am* mistaken, then. If Turner's intention had really been to deceive Mayall, then surely he would not have acknowledged him at the *soirée*.

And yet and yet and yet . . .

We are still left with this:

– During his visits to the studio Turner pretended to be a judge.
– He allowed himself to be photographed, but avoided poses in which he could easily be recognized.
– Once Mayall knew his identity he never called on him again, despite having undertaken to do so.

Geniuses are not like other men.

But is not this all of a piece with Sandycombe Lodge?

You are an artist – you worship the sun – you know that no man since the beginning of time has caught its moods and effects with such fidelity and power.

You build a house so full of light that any visitor must say: *This is a temple to the sun.*

But what if Farrant is right? What if this is only the face you care to show the world, and there is another, concealed behind an almost invisible door?

As I stood in that basement, and stared out through the cavern-mouth window with its fearful iron bars, was there not but one thought that overwhelmed me: *This house was designed by a man with a secret*?

Farrant may be lying, of course. I must remember that. A letter so at odds with everything else I've learned may simply be the product of a diseased and envious mind. If that's all it is – which, let me not forget, was certainly my assumption when I first read it – then all this speculation is mere fancy, and I have evidence of nothing more sinister than eccentricity.

But if he is telling the truth . . .

There is no help for it. I must go and see him.

A mere five hours has passed since I last closed this book – but what a five hours! In that time I have changed my coat for another – changed my *name* for another – gone from the Reform Club to a low tavern, and from there to the Marston Rooms in Piccadilly (a place that even a week ago I could not have conceived of entering), where I sit now, next to a woman and a late theatre-goer at the neighbouring table who laugh drunkenly at each other's remarks as – I presume – they negotiate terms. (Small wonder that London is so full of vice, when a man seeking rest and refreshment late at night is forced to resort to an establishment such as this.)

And what to make of it all? I cannot tell – too many impressions, and speculations, and novel experiences. I must try simply to set it all down, and trust that some pattern will emerge.

The notion that Farrant was the key to resolving all my doubts had struck me with such force, and filled me with such nervous agitation, that my only thought as I set out was: *Find him!* It was only after I had gone half a mile, and the raw fog had cooled my excitement, that I realized how precipitate I was being. Suppose I *did* find him – what then? My object was to discover why he had written to me, and whether his charges against Turner were true; but a man who had lied to me on paper could as easily do so in person. Try as I might, moreover, I could think of no way to phrase the question (my best effort was: 'A story so extraordinary is hard to credit, Mr. Farrant') that would not imply I did not believe him, and so risk antagonizing him – which I was particularly anxious to avoid, since he might well be of further service to me.

But some impulse that would not be denied drove me on. I knew that if I abandoned the quest now, and returned home without the truth – or, at least, the satisfaction of knowing I had done everything in my power to get it – I should find no rest there. I had no choice but to keep going, and trust to fate and to my own wits to guide me.

This resolution seemed to clear my mind, and I immediately saw that I must consider my situation with the cool strategy of a general on the eve of battle – survey the landscape, assess the strengths and weaknesses of my forces, and order their disposition accordingly. What was at once apparent was that a direct attack would fail: if Farrant knew – or even suspected – who I was, or my motive for talking to him, I was lost. My only hope, then, was to approach him at a tangent, finding – if I could – some pretext to engage him in conversation and nudging him towards the subject of Turner. If he repeated the same story then, to a man who – so far as he knew – had no interest in the matter save natural curiosity, and no power to influence the views of others, then there must be a strong presumption that it was true. And if he *was* lying, I might detect it in his manner – for a liar often betrays himself with tell-tale gestures of unease, either revealing his dishonesty by weak smiles and fidgets, or trying to conceal it by too great a display of frankness.

My first aim must be to appear as inconspicuous as possible, so that I might enter his street, and, if necessary, station myself for some time before his house, in order to observe his habits, without drawing attention to myself. And here, at once, I encountered a difficulty: for a man dressed for business in the West End and an evening at the Reform Club cannot hope to escape notice in the back-alleys of Farringdon. I had other clothes at home, of course, but they were too formal, or too rural, or too bright – none of them suggested that sac air of straitened respectability that alone, I felt, could make me invisible.

I wrestled with this conundrum for twenty minutes or more, all the while continuing at a fast pace – for if I faltered, I knew I should be lost. I must be like the Pilgrim, confident that if my faith was great enough – but only then – every obstacle could be overcome.

And so, indeed, it turned out. As I approached Covent Garden, it suddenly struck me that Hand Court was no more than a quarter of a mile away, and that I might go by it with only the smallest deviation from my way. To see Turner's birthplace once again; to view it, this time, with the eyes of knowledge and experience rather than of ignorance – surely this might deepen my understanding of the man, and help me better to evaluate what I learned from Farrant?

Or so I argued to myself at the time; but now I wonder if I was not prompted by something else: a memory so apparently inconsequential that it could not make itself known at once, but must adopt another form entirely, until the moment when I should be able to recognize it. That moment came when I turned into Maiden Lane – and saw, of a sudden, in an illuminated shop front, three red balls on a blue ground. There! – Eureka! – the answer to my problem! The place was kept, of course, by the mother of my young guide on my last visit, and there was always the chance that she might remember me – but what if she did? She would hardly refuse to do business with me on that account; and if she questioned me directly I would simply deny I had ever been there before. Tonight I must become another man altogether; and it would be a useful test of my powers as an actor to see if I might carry off the transformation now.

As is often the case in such establishments, there were two entrances: one facing the street, and the other through a little court to the side, where those who yet retain some pride may slink in (so they hope) unobserved, and surrender their remaining treasures in the seclusion of a private booth. This second door was locked, presumably because it was thought that only the most desperate would need to avail themselves of a pawnbroker so late in the evening. Even though no-one who knew me as Walter Hartright could possibly have seen me, I confess that I hesitated a moment, and went through the pitiful charade of looking in the window, and pretending that I was contemplating buying the stuffed pheasant in a glass case, or one of the cheap rings and brooches neatly laid out like geological specimens on a card, before I finally summoned the courage to go inside.

The only gas-jet was at the front of the shop, where it could cast its light into the street, and act as a beacon to the poor souls seeking its bitter succour. The rest of the interior was lit by two oil-lamps, whose soft glow gave an unfamiliar romance to the pyramids of depressingly mundane objects – a clockwork spit, watches and snuff-boxes, cups and dishes and vases – clothing them in tantalizing shadows, and creating the illusion that somewhere among them you might stumble upon something rare and wonderful. Behind the counter were shelves lined with ticketed bundles, and another door, its presence marked only by an irregular rim of light, which must lead – I deduced from the murmur of voices beyond it – into domestic quarters.

An automatic bell announced my presence, and all at once the voices stopped, and the door at the back opened, and a figure appeared. Not the woman, but – I knew it instantly, from the slender form of the silhouette, and its rapid childish movements – the girl herself. She stopped and stared when she saw me, but whether because she recognized me (the brightness of the gaslamp was behind me, and must have made my face indistinct) or merely because she was surprised to see such a well-dressed man in the shop at such an hour, I could not say.

'Good evening,' she said after a moment, with a tentative smile.

I removed my coat. 'I should like to leave this,' I said (and was surprised to hear that, without conscious thought, I had dropped once again into the voice I had last used at Petworth). 'And take another in its place.'

She seemed puzzled, and glanced uncertainly behind her.

'Come on, girl,' I said. 'It's worth a pound, at least. You can allow me five bob for it; and must have something I could take, doesn't matter how old, older the better, for a shilling or two?'

Perhaps she wondered if I had stolen it (a thought that must occur to a pawnbroker ten times a day); for she ran her gaze over my tie and waistcoat and boots, as if to see whether they were all of a piece with the coat. At length, evidently satisfied, she said:

'What is it, then? Trouble with the 'orses?'

'That's it,' I said, simultaneously grateful that she had supplied me with a story, and angry with myself for not having had the foresight to invent my own. 'But my luck'll change tomorrow. Meantime, a man needs money to drink.'

'Yes,' she said; and then, turning her large brown eyes directly upon mine, and with a knowingness that seemed to penetrate me like a blade of ice: 'And for somethin' else, I shouldn't wonder.'

Did she, in that moment, know who I was? Had her mother convinced her, after all, that my purpose in befriending her on that earlier visit had been to debauch her? Or was this what life had taught her to assume of any man who came into the shop at night in need of money?

I looked away, affecting not to have heard her. 'So, girl, what do you say? Five bob?'

I thought she might say she needed to ask her mother; but she instantly replied, with the confidence of a seasoned haggler:

'Four.'

In truth, I should have been happy enough to take a penny, provided I could have a satisfactory replacement to go with it; but I could not tell her so, so I gruffly answered:

'Let's see what you got, then.'

She was back in a moment, with two coats. One was long and black, well cut from a fine worsted cloth, and speckled with neat darns and patches; and I was tempted to take it, for I knew it would keep me almost as warm as my own. It was so old-fashioned, however, that it could not fail to look odd on a man of my age, and in the end I chose the other – a cheap confection of brown serge and cream piping, with bound pockets and turned-back cuffs, such as a clerk with aspirations to fashion (if such a thing exists) might wear.

'That one's dearer,' said the girl. 'Three-and-six.'

I think she expected me to try to beat her down, but this was not the moment to argue, so I merely nodded and said:

'Very well.'

She handed me the ticket for my own coat, and a sixpenny piece. 'You won't get much for that,' she said, with the same knowing look, and a smile that was almost a leer. 'Couple of pots of beer, and off 'ome to your missus.'

For all I remember now of the route I took to Farringdon, or of what I saw and heard upon the way, I might as well have been sleep-walking. My every thought – beyond that required to place one foot in front of the other, and to avoid obstacles – was devoted to but one object: to try to concoct a plausible story. My want of one in the pawnbroker's shop had caused nothing worse than embarrassment – indeed, thanks to the girl, I had been spared even that – but with Farrant it would certainly prove fatal. But how to devise something that would meet every eventuality? *I am looking for a friend, who told me he lodged here.* What if he had no lodger – or, worse, *did* have one, who said he'd never seen me before in his life? *Cousin Farrant! Do you not know me? True – I was only a child when we sailed for Australia, but surely* – ? No – the stuff of melodrama; and, besides, I knew nothing of his family circumstances. In the end, I decided I must simply gather as much intelligence as possible; and then rely on fate to give me a pretext for talking to him, and my own resources to furnish me with a character appropriate to it.

Trotter Street, it turned out, barely deserves the name of 'street' at all; it is no more than a row of tall, pinched, grey houses overlooking a long straggle of workshops and builders' yards and odd pockets of waste ground. There is but a single line of gaslamps, which seem scarcely equal to the task of lighting it – at least on a night like tonight, with no moon, and with a heavy fog rolling up from the river; and even when your eyes have adjusted to the darkness, there is little enough to lift your spirits. The road is rough and treacherous, the cobbles broken here and there by black puddles; and at one end of it – just at the point where you think you should be able to turn a corner, and escape to somewhere less desolate – you find your path barred by the locked gates of a blacking works. Farrant's story might yet, of course, prove to be true; but it was easy enough to imagine how a man living here might *fancy* he had suffered a thousand wrongs, when his real grievance was against life itself, for condemning him to such a cheerless place.

Number 20 was almost indistinguishable from its neighbours, save that the painted figures on the door had faded, and you could identify it only by observing that it stood between number 19 and number 21. There was a dim glow behind the fanlight, and a brighter one in the first-floor window, but otherwise the building was dark. I looked about – as had Farrant himself, if he was to be believed, when *he* was pursuing Turner – for an inn or public, where I might make enquiries about him, and take shelter while I was watching the house; but there was none to be seen. I leaned against a buckled fence on the opposite side of the street, hoping I might see someone going in or out; but after ten minutes all that had happened was that my hands and feet had grown numb with the cold. Time, I decided, to take some other action.

There was no light in number 19; and when I approached number 21 I heard, from inside, the sound of a glass breaking, and two voices – a man's and a woman's – trying to outdo one another in

157

drunken argument. I edged away, therefore, all the while keeping my eye on Farrant's house, and knocked at number 18. After a moment, a woman of thirty or so opened the door a foot or so and peered out.

'Yes?'

'Mrs. Farrant?' I said.

Her forehead creased, and she drew in her lower lip and shook her head.

'Mr. Farrant does live here?'

'You got the wrong house,' she said.

'Oh, pardon me. Then . . .?' I pointed down the street, and raised my eyebrows.

'What you want with him?' she said. 'You a dun?'

'No,' I said; but before I could go on a child's voice behind her said:

'What is it, Ma?'

'Ssh!' she said; but the boy squeezed past her skirts, forcing the door wider open, and stood in front of her, looking up at me. He was about eight, with fair curls and curious blue eyes.

'I think he may be my uncle,' I said.

'*May* be!'

'My ma always said she had a brother who was an engraver in London,' I said. 'Only they had a difference, when they were young; and last thing she said, when she was dying, was: "Find your uncle, and make it right with him."'

If I had expected this affecting tale to melt her, I was mistaken; for she continued to skewer me with a suspicious gaze in which there was no hint of a tear. The boy, however, at that moment came to my aid.

'Who's he talking about?' he said, tugging at his mother's apron. He completed the question by forming the thumb and forefinger of each hand into a circle, and then holding them before his eyes.

'You didn't ought to make fun of him,' said the woman. 'What with all his kindness to you.'

I remember feeling a great tiredness pass through me, weighting my legs and sapping me of the will to go on. It was late – it was cold – I had come all this way, and learned nothing for my pains save that Farrant had once been kind to a child, and there seemed no prospect that I might learn anything more.

But then, the next instant – it all happened so quickly that it is still confused in my mind – the boy darted out on to the pavement, before his mother could grab him; shouted, 'Come on, I'll show you!'; ran two or three steps; and then abruptly stopped.

'There!' he said, pointing to a figure moving slowly away from us. 'There he is!' Something in the way he braced himself and tilted his head told me that he was intending to call out; but I stopped him just in time.

'Hush,' I said. 'I want it to be a surprise'; and then, before he could question me, or protest, I handed him the sixpence the girl at the pawnbroker's had given me, and left him and his mother staring after me as I set off in pursuit.

More than half a century ago, Farrant had followed Turner through the fog; now, here was I, following him. This symmetry, for some reason, exhilarated me, as the resolution of a piece of music may please the ear, or the perfect balance of a composition (think of Turner's own Ulysses Deriding Polyphemus) satisfy the eye. I was so distracted by it, indeed, that I became careless, and almost gave myself away; for – somehow foolishly conceiving him still to be the strapping young fellow he had been then, and imagining that it would be all I could do to keep up with him – I started at a tremendous pace, and came upon him far too quickly. Hearing my footsteps, he stopped and turned, and looked about him like an old bear sniffing the air; and would, I am certain, have seen me, save that – as I saw at once from his heavy spectacles, and half-closed eyes – his sight was now too weak. I stood quite still, holding my breath, until at length, hunching his shoulders, he lumbered on again, feeling his way with a stick. I had learned my lesson – as he, I recalled with a smile, had learned his in Norton Street; and waited half a minute or so before setting off once more, this time being careful to keep a prudent distance.

I did not have to continue in this manner for long. At the end of the street he turned into the main thoroughfare, and then, after fifty yards or so, into a small public house – which I must have passed on my way there, though I had no recollection of it – called the White Post. Fearing that, if I went in after him immediately, he might associate me with the footsteps he had heard, and correctly guess that I had been following him, I decided to linger outside for a few minutes. To the left of the door was a low,

uncurtained window through which I could see a crowded parlour hazy with tobacco smoke, and hear the cheerful chime of
glasses and the ebb and flow of laughter and conversation.
Although I could not stand directly before it without being
noticed, I found that if I pressed myself against the adjacent wall
and craned my neck, I still had a clear view of one half of the
room – some rustic prints; the end of a long table (the people sitting at it were largely invisible, but I could just see an assortment
of elbows, and two tankards, and a hat); and a small modern fireplace, bright with coals. In the chimney corner were two comfortable chairs – one empty, the other occupied by an old man
with a grimy red neck-tie and a round, beef-red face. Something
in the way he tapped his fingers, and then looked up questioningly, made me suppose he was waiting for Farrant; and so
indeed it proved, for a few seconds later my quarry shuffled into
view, and shook the old man's hand.

I say 'the old man's'; but as he removed his cloak, and gently
eased himself into the vacant chair, I saw that Farrant was in fact
the older of the two. Time had made sad work with him, but he
must once have been an impressive figure: even now, bent and
frail though he was, his large girth and broad shoulders made
him seem almost too big for the little room, and his big-nosed,
wide-mouthed, craggy-browed face gave him the imposing
presence of a Roman emperor – an impression accentuated by
his skin, which the cold had turned as white and luminous as
marble.

Within a few moments the two men were talking intently – Farrant leaning forward, and rotating his hand to emphasize his
words; the other nodding in agreement (though there was a certain wariness in his eyes, it seemed to me), and drumming his fingers ceaselessly against his wrist. When the barmaid brought
their mugs of beer, Red-tie looked up and smiled at her; but Farrant appeared not to notice her, and continued speaking without
pause. I waited for two or three minutes more, and then, when
Farrant at length sat back and cast about for his drink, concluded
that I might safely go in.

Two or three of the men sitting at the table glanced briefly at
me as I came through the door, but otherwise my appearance
seemed to provoke no response at all, and I knew that about the

coat, at least, I had made the right decision. The smoky warmth pressed against my face, as tangible and stifling as a blanket, and made me suddenly aware how chilled I had become. It required no great feat of acting, therefore, as I picked my way between chairs and stools, to shiver and rub my hands and mutter 'brrr' under my breath – or not, at least, until I started to come within earshot of Farrant's conversation, and heard (so I thought), amongst a torrent of words I could not make out, one that stopped me dead: 'Turner'.

My first impulse, naturally, was to stand still and listen; but to do so would be to risk alerting them to my interest; and with a great effort of will I forced myself to continue my dumbshow. They fell silent as I approached; but Red-tie looked on with a kind of distant amusement, like a man who happens by chance upon a street-entertainer, while I stationed myself before the hearth, and began stamping my feet, and blowing on my hands, and shaking the steam from my mist-sodden clothes.

'Evening,' I said, at length, seeing that if I was to get into conversation with them I must initiate it myself. They nodded, but did not reply; and after a moment – as if he thought this small show of ceremony had concluded their business with me – Farrant leant towards his companion and said, in a strangely light, womanish voice:

'Undoubtedly it would have greater weight from you.'

Whether because he felt uneasy at continuing their discussion in my presence, or merely because he was curious about me, I cannot say; but Red-tie ignored him, and continued to watch me. After a few moments he said:

'You been out all night?' He looked towards Farrant. 'You see him, Jack? He's wet as a dog.'

Farrant screwed up his eyes to look at me. The effort made him frown; but any appearance of sternness immediately vanished when he drew in his breath with a soft whistle of pity, and said:

'Oh, you poor chap. What happened to you?'

'Missus threw him out of the house,' said Red-tie, with a laugh, and I started to join in; but Farrant silenced us by lifting his big hand, and shaking his head.

'No,' he said gravely. He continued to look at me, not unkindly, as if giving me the chance to explain myself.

'I came to see my sister,' I said. 'Only she wasn't in.'

Farrant nodded. 'Where's she live?'

'Trotter Street.' That, I knew as I said it, was a mistake; but I couldn't immediately bring to mind the name of any other street in the vicinity. Cursing my own carelessness, I waited for him to ask me what my sister was called, and which her house was; but he merely nodded again, and went on:

'And where do *you* live?'

'Other side of town. Putney,' I said.

'That's a fair way,' said Farrant. He looked about him, and prodded the air with his foot until he struck a stool, and then hooked his boot under the stretcher and drew it towards me. 'Here. You don't want to stand after a walk like that.'

'Thank you,' I said, sitting down.

'Something urgent, was it?' said Farrant. 'I could give her a message, if you like. I'm just at number 20.'

For a moment, I had absolutely no idea how to reply; and then, as if someone had suddenly set off a flare, illuminating a landscape that until now had been lost in darkness, I saw with perfect clarity what I must say:

'That's very kind of you; but the fact is I'm just back from Petworth.'

Did I imagine it, or did Farrant and his companion exchange furtive glances? I went on:

'Her boy's in service at the house; and I came to tell her how he goes on there.' I paused, but neither of them spoke – though they seemed to be watching me so keenly that I felt I must comment on it, or again risk rousing their suspicion. 'Do you know Petworth, then?' I said, looking from one to the other. 'In Sussex?'

'Only by repute,' said Farrant, with a dry smile.

'Lord! you should see it! Regular catacomb of a place. Most of it empty, and the servants kept running one end of it to the other from morning to night.' I laughed. 'My nephew, he's a droll young fellow, he says it's no wonder they call them *foot*men, for that's the bit that does most of the work.'

The barmaid, a thin, dark-haired girl of eighteen or so, came to take my order. I wondered whether to offer them something, but decided it would seem too forward.

'Put a drop of something in it, Kate, to warm him up!' Red-tie called, as she was leaving. 'Else he'll take and die of a chill!'

She turned and shouted something over her shoulder, but it was lost in a sudden spasm of laughter which spread through the room, and ended with Red-tie himself.

'I'll be honest,' I said, 'I was hoping to get a position there myself; for Paul's a good boy, and I thought they might be happy enough to take another from the same stable, so to speak. But –'

Farrant raised his hand, and craned towards me. 'A position as what, Mr. . . .?'

'Jenkinson,' I said. 'Oh, you know, an upper servant. I was the under-butler in my last place' – I paused here, for effect, and lowered my voice – 'but the old man died before I could get a character from him.' I laughed – or rather Jenkinson did, for I could barely recognize the sly, cynical, man-to-man sneer that issued from my lips as my own. Red-tie chuckled too; but we were quickly shamed into silence by Farrant, who refused to ingratiate himself by joining in (surely the fellowship of facile heartlessness is the largest gentlemen's club in the world, and resisting its blandishments must have required some courage), and continued to regard me with the same unsmiling expression.

'But turns out Colonel Wyndham – that's the master now – only wants people that have come with them from their old house.' I winked at Red-tie. 'His wife's an Evangelical, you see, and very particular about the servants' morals.'

The girl brought my porter; and I winked at her, too, for good measure.

'Your health, gents.'

Farrant gravely raised his glass, but did not drink.

'I'd have done well enough there in the old days,' I said. 'If what Paul says is to be believed. Place was full of people, painters and poets and what-have-you, and Lord knows how many women – not a corner or a cubby-hole didn't have a Royal Academician in it, or one of his lordship's bastards.' I shook my head, conveying – I hoped – my deep regret at having missed such colourful goings-on.

'You're talking of the Third Earl's time?' said Farrant.

'Yes,' I said – making, I think, a fair show of surprise. 'Why? Were you acquainted with him?'

173

'I knew his name,' said Farrant. 'Everyone knew his name then, leastways in my line of business.'

'Indeed?' I was on the point of going on: *Are you an artist, then?* when I thought better of it. My 'guesses' must not appear too accurate, and I must not seem too eager to ingratiate myself. I glanced at Red-tie; and then, with a waggish little smile, and in a manner bordering on the insolent, said:

'And what business is that, Mr. . . .?'

Out of the corner of my eye, I saw Red-tie's lips twitch. Farrant still looked at me impassively, but I noticed the broken veins on his pale cheeks starting to colour.

'Farrant,' he said. 'I'm an engraver.'

'Ah,' I said, with an air of indifference. I took a deep draught of my beer, and grinned at Red-tie. 'That fortifies you, Mr. . . .'

'Hargreaves,' said Red-tie, laughing.

'Better than a warming pan.' I barely heeded the critical voice in my own head saying *That sounds foolish – warming pans don't fortify*; I was too busy trying to think of a way to direct the conversation back to Petworth, and then to artists, and then to –

'Did they say anything of Turner?' Farrant asked suddenly.

I could scarcely believe my good luck. 'Turner?' I said.

'The landscape painter,' said Farrant, looking not at me but at Hargreaves, with a meaning expression that seemed to say: *See, I know what I am about.*

'Yes, as it happens,' I said, laughing. 'Though I don't know how much of it to believe.'

Farrant leaned forward. 'Why, what did they tell you?'

'Oh,' I said, 'that he was a strange, secretive little devil, who locked himself in the library, and would admit no-one save the Earl.'

Farrant nodded. 'Is that all?'

'He had a housemaid for a . . . friend – you know the kind of friend I mean, Mr. Hargreaves? – and gave her a little picture to remember him by. That part's true at least, I think, for her daughter showed it to me – the poor girl's soft on Paul, I fancy, and thought no doubt she'd impress his uncle.'

Hargreaves guffawed lewdly.

'And I'll tell you, the funny thing – what do you think it was?'

Hargreaves shrugged, and looked away; while Farrant was so

intent on hearing the end of my story that he could not bear any distraction from it, and shook his head impatiently.

'What you or I'd have done is leave her with a sentimental miniature, wouldn't we, Mr. Hargreaves? Or a peaceful country scene? But not Turner – he had to give her a blood-red sunset, and a rising storm. "Here you are, darling. Something to remind you of me."'

Hargreaves began to laugh again, but Farrant cut him short.

'That does not surprise me,' he said. His voice was quiet but tremulous, and he clenched his fists like a man struggling to keep some great passion in check. 'Nothing of what you say surprises me – save that he gave her anything at all.'

'Why?' I said. 'Did you know him, then?'

'Well enough,' he muttered. 'Well enough.'

I said nothing, waiting for him to go on; but after a few moments he shook his head and said:

'Anyway, it is no matter.'

'No,' I said; and then – thinking it was at last safe to do so – 'I should like to hear.'

He shook his head again. 'What good's tittle-tattle? I tell you what I know, and you tell the next man, with a bit added here, and another there, to season it; and he does the same in his turn, and soon there's a hundred different stories, and no-one believes any of them. I want people to have the truth, here, in front of them, black and white. And they will, soon enough.'

His face was so grave, and his voice so urgent, that it was impossible, in that instant, to believe he had lied to me.

'What,' I said, 'are you writing a book?'

'No,' he said darkly. 'But there are others interested in Turner.'

My skin prickled, as it does at the onset of a fever. Was *others* just a rhetorical flourish, or did he mean *more than one*? If he had found out about me, of course (which was clearly the case, although I did not know how), was it not reasonable enough to suppose that he also knew something of Thornbury, and had perhaps communicated with him? But what if there was a third – or even a fourth – biographer, of whom I had never heard at all?

'Really?' I said, as casually as I could. 'Who?'

He took a leisurely sip from his glass and then set it down again, wiping the suds from his mouth. 'You will forgive me, sir,' he said with a sigh, avoiding my gaze, 'but I barely know you; and this is a delicate matter.' And I could not help noticing – dear God! how complex are our emotions, and how contradictory! – that while his shoulders were bowed under the weight of some great burden, yet his eyes shone with the consciousness of the power he enjoyed at that moment.

'The truth is,' said Hargreaves, with a wheedling smile, watching Farrant closely all the time, 'there's a value now, to stories about Turner. There's a gentleman as pays good money for them. What Mr. Farrant's saying is, you want him to tell you, you'll have to put your hand in your pocket –'

'No!' roared Farrant, so loudly that the room suddenly fell quiet, and every face turned towards us. 'I don't care anything about that. I want the facts straight, number one; and number two, no-one knows about them till they're published. That's the first rule of war: don't give your secrets to the enemy.'

'Who are the enemy?' I said.

Farrant didn't reply at once, but instead stared thoughtfully before him. At length he turned abruptly to me and said: 'Turner had powerful friends.'

'Indeed –' I began; but Farrant was already preparing to leave, pulling his coat about him and searching for his stick. 'Oh, please,' I said, touching his arm. 'Don't go. Let me buy you a drink.'

He knocked my hand away and shook his head emphatically. 'I shall wish you good night.'

My palms felt dry and empty – I longed to clasp them round his rough sleeve, and drag him back to his chair – but I knew nothing would be gained by it. If he was not angry with me yet (and it seemed to have been Hargreaves, rather than I, that had provoked him), he soon would be if I persisted in trying to detain him. All I could do, during the unconscionable time it took him to get ready, was to stare at the fire, and exchange sheepish grins with Hargreaves. At last, he fastened the final button on his coat, and without another word, began his stately progress towards the door.

'You can buy *me* a drink,' said Hargreaves, when Farrant was out of earshot. 'And I'll tell you what I know.'

'About the gentleman?'

His face took on the surly, puzzled look of a slow-witted man who suspects he is being mocked. 'What gentleman?'

'The gentleman who pays good money for stories about Turner.'

'Oh!' He clearly hadn't expected this; and he frowned as he wrestled with the troubling question of why I should want to know. Fearing that I had gone too far, and given too much away, I said hastily:

'I was thinking of my nephew. He could spin him a tale or two.'

'Ah, I see!' He smiled and nodded, and for a moment I thought he was going to tell me, for he gave me a crafty sidelong glance that seemed to say, *I get your meaning now; you're a man of the world like me*, which I interpreted as a prelude to doing business. But then he suddenly looked away and said: 'I won't deceive you – I know no more than Jack Farrant told me, and that's little enough.'

'His name?'

Hargreaves shook his head.

I cursed inwardly. Could it have been Thornbury? That was the likeliest explanation, but it failed to explain Farrant's letter to me. An author might naturally give a useful informant money; but he would scarcely pay him to send his story to a rival. Perhaps there *was* someone else . . .? Or perhaps Farrant had merely heard about me from Davenant or George Jones (for did not his letter mention both their names?) and had written to me on his own account, for his own reasons? I should gladly have given fifty pounds for the answer, though I knew better than to say so. Something of my feelings must have shown, however, for, before I had time to speak, he went on eagerly:

'But I'll tell you something else – a sight tastier – about Turner.'

I forced an indifferent smile on to my face, and said laconically: 'As good as the housemaid?'

'Oh, better!'

'Very well.'

He shook his head, and wagged a finger at me. 'Drink!'

I summoned the barmaid. The question of what he should order at my expense seemed to exercise Hargreaves terribly, and he agonized over it for some seconds before finally saying:

'A pot of porter, if you please, and a tot of brandy' – here he leered comically at me – 'just to keep it company on the way down.' And then, as if he feared I should cavil at this extravagance, and withdraw my offer, he laid his grimy fingers on my cuff, and said: 'It's worth it, Mr. Jenkinson. You'll see.'

And so, indeed, it proved; for this, as near as I can remember it, is what he told me – his face thrust forward, his eyes gazing up into mine with the anxious look of a dog that expects another biscuit if its master likes its trick, and a kick if he does not:

'I'm a waterman by trade; I was a hog-grubber once, but, what with the new bridges, there's no living to be made on that stretch of the river now; so the last fifteen year or more I mostly been plying Wapping. And that's where I saw him – oh, must've been a dozen times, at least.

'He was a rum one – you knew that the minute you laid eyes on him – not much taller'n a child, with a big hat, and a long coat. You couldn't see his face clear, for he'd wrap a scarf around it, to keep the cold out o' doors, as he'd say, and besides, it was dark more often than not; but I remember his big Jew's nose, and his eyes looking at you like a ferret, and his grey hair sticking out under his hat – for he was already an old fellow by this time.

'He liked me, he said, on account I'd been a sailor; and usually he'd ask for me special, to go to Rotherhithe. It was always the same: I'd take him across of a Saturday night, and bring him back again Monday morning. General, he wouldn't say much, just sit staring over the side of the boat, as if he was looking for something in the water; and once . . . once or twice I saw him take out a notebook, and scribble in it.

'I didn't know who he was – he never told me a name – but I wouldn't have guessed it was "Turner", for one time, as we was putting in at Rotherhithe, an old seaman who'd had a bit to drink come up to him and says: "Back again, Mr. J.? Lord, give the girls a chance!" Might have been "Jay", I suppose, but it didn't sound like that – too quick, if you know what I mean. So perhaps he went by "Jones", or "Johnson".

'But then one time, he's going ashore at Wapping, and another gentleman steps down to take the boat, and sees him, and says: "Why, Turner!"; but he just shakes his head and marches off without a word. When the other gent's settled himself, he says: "You know who that was? Turner, *the* Turner! J. M. W.? R.A.? I'd heard stories about his adventures, of course, but I never believed them before now."

'So I says, "What stories, sir?" And he says: "Why, that he'll finish painting on a Saturday night. and put a five-pound note in his pocket, and go and wallow in some low sailor's house by the river till Monday morning!"

'And the rummy thing is, after that, I never saw the old man again.'

My mouth was dry; I could hear my own heartbeat throbbing in my ears; I was filled with that strange tumbling excitement you feel when your wildest intimation suddenly becomes a certainty. Hargreaves must have seen the effect he had had, for he concluded by exhaling dramatically, and sitting back with a triumphant glint in his eye, as much as to say: *There! What did I tell you?*

'Well,' I said, still striving to sound nonchalant, even if my glowing cheeks betrayed me. 'That was tasty enough, I suppose.' I got up, squinting at the clock above the bar counter.

'Worth another pot?' he said quickly.

I hesitated, and then laughed and said:

'Oh, why not? But you'll drink it alone; for I must off home.'

It was while we were waiting for the barmaid that Hargreaves suddenly leaned over and tugged my sleeve.

'I'll tell you what,' he said, looking round to see that we were not overheard. 'The funniest thing. Fair turned my stomach. One time, we was nearly at the south bank, and Turner looking in the water as usual, when he suddenly points to something and says: "Over there! Row over there!" "What is it?" I says; for I couldn't see nothing; but he just says: "Row! Row!" And he takes out his little book, and starts to sketch something, frantic like, as if all of a sudden it's just going to vanish away.'

Hargreaves looked about him again; and when he turned back to me there was such disquiet in his eyes that I realized he was telling me this not for gain, but to unburden himself.

'I didn't see what it was until my oar struck it, Mr. Jenkinson. So help me, it was a body – a poor girl, couldn't have been more than sixteen, as'd drowned herself. And there was Turner, lost to the world, drawing her face.'

XXV

From the private notebook of Walter Hartright,
7th October, 185–

Others may read a journal.
No-one must read this.

What is a man who slips like mercury between the fingers, who is never where you think to find him, who goes abroad under an assumed name and a borrowed identity?

A man who never marries; and maintains no household; and even in those places where he hides from the world has secret chambers in which to conceal himself still more completely?

A man who consorts with whores in stinking taverns? A man who responds to seeing a corpse not with some pious exclamation of pity, but by taking out his notebook and drawing it?

He is a genius.

Last night, for the first time in my life, I was like mercury.
I have never been so free.
Leaving the White Post I might have –
What?
Gone anywhere. Done anything. Walked to the docks, and taken passage for Java. Returned to Maiden Lane and found a girl, and enjoyed her in the alley where she stood. No-one could have said: That was Walter Hartright. No-one could have blamed me. No-one could have blamed *me*.

Gravity held me by a thread. At any moment I might have snapped it, and drifted away altogether.

But I let it draw me homeward, as a child draws a kite.
Until I reached Piccadilly. And the Marston Rooms.

I did not seek her.
But I did not send her away.
I had set down my journal. I was so tired I had lost all sense of time. I was watching a drunk man lurching towards the door.
She said: 'A penny for your thoughts.'
I turned. She was perhaps twenty-five, wearing a close-fitting blue dress and crinoline. She had thick fair hair pinned loosely

over the nape of her neck. She smelt of musk.

'What are you about?' she said.

I smiled, and weighed the open journal in my hand.

'What, are you an author, then?'

I said nothing.

'Must be lonely work, being an author. I expect you feel like a bit of company, don't you, sometimes?'

I nodded.

'That's good,' she said, sitting beside me. 'I'm fond of company, too.' She leaned close. She was warm. I smelt the hot biscuit tang of powder on her cheeks.

'You going to buy me a drink, then?'

I jerked my head at the waiter.

'I like champagne,' she said. 'It makes me gay.'

The drunk man had finally stumbled into the street. Through the window, I saw a woman in a wide-brimmed hat accosting him.

'I'm Louise,' said my companion. She pouted teasingly, and gave a little nod that invited me to tell her *my* name.

I said nothing, but merely looked at her and smiled.

'Gentlemen are often shy about that,' she said. She put her head on one side and appraised me, running her tongue over her blood-red lips. 'What about *Leo*?' she said at last, in barely more than a whisper.

'Leo,' I heard myself say.

She spread her hand on the open page of my journal and caressed it, as if she might coax the meaning from it. 'So, Leo, what are you writing?' When I did not reply, she suddenly seized the book and began to read at random:

'What's this – "wallow in some low sailor's house by the river"?' She broke off, laughing. I snatched the book back.

'You bad boy,' she said. 'Is that what you get up to?'

The waiter came. His smile said: *I know what you're doing.* I wanted to hide my face in shame. I wanted to acknowledge his gaze, and bask in the warmth of his admiration.

'Champagne,' I heard myself say.

'Very good, sir.'

'And something for yourself. Make the night go a bit sweeter.'

'He's a gent, ain't he?' giggled the woman, catching the waiter's eye.

His smiled deepened. 'Thank you, sir.'

When he had gone, she took my wrist in her hot fingers and leaned closer. Her breath smelled of licorice and wine.

'I like to wallow,' she whispered.

'I bet you do.'

How can I explain it? I cannot say it was not my voice. But it was the voice of a me whose existence I had never suspected. He must have been there always, sealed away in some blackness so profound that I had never thought to try to penetrate it. But now the shutters had been thrown open, and we could see and hear each other.

'I know a nice place,' she said. Her lips brushed my cheek, and she whispered in my ear: 'What would you like to do with me?'

We were poised, Leo and Walter; balanced on a pinpoint.

It's natural enough, ain't it? A man and a woman were made to give pleasure to each other.

Think of . . .

~~*You can't pretend you don't feel*~~

You can't pretend you only want to fuck your wife.

I could see the pulse in her throat, as if some tiny creature were trapped beneath the skin.

See? Her heart's pounding, too.

If I go with her, I shall cease to be me.

Isn't that the point?

'Mm?' she murmured again. 'What would you like?' She drew my ear-lobe into her mouth, nipped it, rolled it on her tongue.

I can imagine. That is enough. I can see, and imagine.

I must freeze this moment; I must stop time; I must hold my breath; and be as adroit as an acrobat with a pole.

I laid two sovereigns on the table, and left without another word.

XXVI

Letter from Laura Hartright to Marian Halcombe, 7th October, 185–

Darling Marian,

Walter has written me such a cold, angry letter. Why is he so cross with me? Do you know? I can think of nothing I have done, save to tell him that we miss him, and long for his return. That would never have made the old Walter angry. It would have brought him back to us. I know it would.

I am so unhappy. This morning Florrie said, 'Why are you not pretty any more, Mama?' I could not tell her the answer: that I had lain awake half the night, crying about her father.

Am I – I can barely write this – am I losing him? Has he changed? I pray to God not. But I am so far away – I cannot touch him, or see his dear face, or hear his voice.

You are so much cleverer and wiser than I am. Please – is there anything you can do to make things well between us again?

Your affectionate sister,
Laura

XXVII

From the journal of Marian Halcombe, 9th October, 185–

This cannot go on.

God, is there to be nothing in life but gritting our teeth, and doing our duty?

XXVIII

Memorandum of a letter from Walter Hartright to Mr. Hawkesworth Fawkes, 10th October, 185–

1. Am engaged on *Life of Turner*.
2. Mr. Ruskin tells me you knew him well – would be able to give me invaluable information.
3. Will be passing close to Farnley on Thursday, and wondered if might call upon you?

4. Please forgive me for not giving you more warning. Will of course understand if unable to see me at such short notice.

XXIX

From the journal of Walter Hartright, 12th October, 185–

~~It is as well~~

It is as well I did not write ahead to tell her I was coming, for I shall not now be home tomorrow after all. What delayed me was a strange accident, into which I cannot but read some significance.

Just before we reached Leeds, there was a tremendous bang from the front of the train, and we jerked and rocked and squealed to a halt. My neighbour, a florid, grey-haired man of about fifty, wearing a brown suit and no overcoat, as if his own internal furnace were enough to keep him warm, lowered the window and looked out.

'Can you see what's the matter?' I said.

'Burst boiler,' he replied, turning back. 'I'm afraid, ladies and gentlemen, we're going to be here for a while. They'll need to send another engine.' And with that he leant out again, unfastened the door, and gingerly lowered himself to the ground.

I was sure this must be against company regulations, but I heard no-one remonstrating with him, and after a minute or so I took out my sketch-pad and pencil and jumped down after him – partly out of curiosity, and partly to avoid the purgatory of having to exchange grumbling platitudes with my fellow-passengers for an hour or more.

At first all I could see was a dense swirl of vapour and gritty smoke, which seemed to engulf the locomotive and half of the front carriage; but as I drew closer I could make out blurred figures hurrying about, or standing talking in little groups. Among them I saw my brown-suited companion, apparently deep in conversation with a bearded man in a round cap and white canvas trousers whom I took to be the driver. No-one seemed to have been hurt; and yet there was something undeniably awful about the scene: the flailing rods and pistons; the dreadful spouts of steam shrieking from the split boiler (it is only when they are wounded that you see the terrible power of these brutes); the ferocity of the still-raging coals, glowing red through the fog like the mouth of hell.

Awful, but strangely beautiful, too. I took out my pencil, and started to draw.

I was so engrossed in my labours that I did not notice the approach of the man in the brown suit, until he was standing at my shoulder.

'You're an artist?' he said, after a moment.

I nodded.

'You put me in mind of Turner. He loved mists, and fires, and machines. You're familiar with his work?'

'Yes,' I said. 'I admire it very much.'

'I knew him, you know,' he said. His voice sounded matter-of-fact enough, but he pushed his thumbs into his waistcoat pockets and rocked back and forth on his feet, as if his sense of self-importance, having been denied the outlet of words, must express itself in some other form. 'I'm Elijah Nisbet.'

He clearly expected me to be impressed, and I think my 'Oh!' contrived to suggest that I was, though in truth I had never heard his name before in my life.

'I have some of his later paintings,' Nisbet went on. He glanced at my drawing again, and then nodded approvingly. 'It would be a pleasure to show them to you, if you're ever near Birmingham. A professional like yourself might appreciate them better than my neighbours do.'

'Thank you. I should like that very much.'

'Let me give you my address.' He took the pad, and scribbled on the back. 'There,' he said, returning it to me. 'Now I must go and write a complaint.' He cast a speculative look towards the crippled locomotive. 'The driver's to blame. He reported it "correct" last night, but there must have been some evidence of a flaw.'

He did not explain how he came to speak with such authority, or why it was his business to complain; and I did not ask him, for fear it would reveal that I didn t really know who he was.

It was only after he had gone that I realized I hadn't told him *my* business, either. Why had I been so secretive? Was it merely that he had connected me with Turner not as a biographer, but as a fellow-artist, and I had not wished to disabuse him?

The relief engine did not finally arrive for nearly two hours, with the result that I missed the train to Arthington, and arrived in Otley too late to see Mr. Fawkes. I therefore sent a note by the carrier to say that I should call on him in the morning, and have put up for the night at the Black Bull, where I write these words.

It's easy to see why Turner loved this place. If Lord Egremont's Petworth – a Renaissance palace presided over by a Renaissance prince – appealed to the classical side of his nature, then Mr. Fawkes's Farnley must have fed his hunger for the sublime. In the streets of Petworth you are aware, above everything, of the inescapable presence of the great house; in the streets of Otley – which must be approximately the same size – you are aware only of the presence of nature. The town is bounded on one side by the River Wharfe, with majestic moors rising gradually beyond it; and on the other by an enormous hill – called 'the Chevin', according to the driver from Arthington – that seems to blot out half the western sky. The sun was setting behind it as I arrived, and I took out my notebook and did a series of quick sketches, screwing up my eyes and craning my neck to see the clutter of craggy rocks on the summit, until at length it was too dark for me to work, and I approached the inn.

The Black Bull is a solid, welcoming, unpretentious kind of place – constructed, like every other building I have seen in Otley, of rough-hewn local stone smudged with grime from the nearby mills – which stands at the corner of the main square. As I entered, the last few stalls from the day's market were being dismantled by lantern-light, and a pack of small boys was scuffling among the trampled cabbage-leaves and broken turnips on the ground. For a moment I was put in mind of my first visit to Maiden Lane – though here the children's faces glowed with health and merriment, and the cold air was misty with their breath, and rang with the sound of their laughter – and found myself wondering whether Turner had ever seen such a scene in Otley, and been moved by it to the same thought? This notion gave me a sudden start: what images, what private memories and associations – which I could never now know – might then have flitted through his consciousness; and what old pains and needs and hungers might they have stirred? And should I find any traces of this secret, inner Turner here – as I had for an instant, in Twickenham and Farringdon; or was I fated merely to discover clues to his artistic life, and hear Mr. Fawkes reiterate what I have come to see as the official line: *a strange, eccentric little fellow, but no man could have been more tender-hearted, or a truer friend.*

I was greeted in the flagged hall by a thickset, round-faced man, wearing a heavy apron, and collarless white shirt, with the sleeves rolled back to reveal a pair of massive forearms, and a sprig of grey hair showing at the unfastened throat. Through the half-open door to the right I glimpsed a trestle table lined with plainly dressed men and women, and heard the powerful thrum of twenty or thirty voices. Farmers and their wives, I thought, relaxing after market-day.

'G'd evening, sir,' said the innkeeper. 'Would you be looking for a room?'

'Yes,' I said. 'If you have one.'

'That's just about all we *do* have,' he said – not insolently, but with a kind of good-humoured relish. His eyes searched the row of hooks behind him, and at last lighted on a key.

'You want to see it first, sir?' he said.

'No, I'll take it,' I said hastily, suddenly realizing how tired I was, and how unprepared to trudge round the town looking for an alternative. 'As long as there's a bed, and a table I can sit at, and write.'

'That I think I can promise you,' he said with a smile.

Following him upstairs, I tried to guess his age. He was still hale and strong, but from the deep lines in his powerful neck, and the wisps of silvery hair about his ears, I supposed he must be about sixty. Walter Fawkes, I recalled from my researches, had died in 1825; and Turner had never again returned to Farnley, so his last visit here must have been around forty years ago. Unlikely, therefore – but not impossible. As we reached the landing, I said:

'Do you by any chance remember Turner?'

'Turner?' he said, surprised. 'What, th'ironmonger?'

'The painter.'

'Painter! Nay. What, here in Otley, was he?'

'Sometimes.'

He shook his head. 'I never knew him. But see, I only come from Ilkley fifteen year ago, like.' He opened the door to my room, and carried my bags inside. 'Here you are, sir. I'll just set the fire going for you.'

While he worked, I stood by the little casement and gazed out. The room overlooked a side-alley, but beyond it I could see the town stretching away – an irregular horizon of roofs and chimneys, oil-lamps winking in uncurtained windows, and strings of street-lights so feeble that they quickly petered out as they approached the foot of the Chevin, as if they knew they could not challenge its black looming bulk, and might as well give up altogether. Somewhere in that bewitching pattern of light and shade, I thought, there must be somebody who recalls Turner – somebody who knows something about him that will deepen my understanding of the man, and give me an advantage against Thornbury, who appears so far ahead of me in London. I had an empty evening before me; and there and then resolved to spend it trying to find this person, and learning what he – or she – could tell me.

My first thought was to join the farmers, and take my dinner with them; for among them there might well be one from the Farnley Estate, who, if he had not known Turner himself, could at least perhaps refer me to someone who had. When at last I descended again, however, and was about to enter the dining room, I found my way barred by the innkeeper.

'If you care to step into the back parlour, sir, there's a table set for you there.'

'Oh, please don't trouble yourself with that,' I said, thinking they must suppose it would be beneath my dignity to eat at the common board. 'I'm happy to sit with everyone else.'

'It's no trouble, sir,' he said – and I fancy my words had taken him aback, for he flushed, and his voice had a phlegmy edge as he went on: 'Quite the other way about; for they're nearly done in there, and my wife wants it all sided and neat like afore the lasses go home.'

And so I found myself sitting all alone at a white-clothed table before a snug coal fire, in a comfortable little room at the rear of the house. I did not, however, forget my purpose, even when it turned out – to my disappointment – that I was to be waited on by a spotty girl of fourteen or so, who would not only clearly not remember Turner herself, but whose mother had probably not even been born at the time of his last visit here.

'Tell me,' I said, when she had taken my order (standing stock-still, and frowning and biting her lower lip with concentration). 'Who is the oldest person you know in Otley?'

For some reason, this reduced her to uncontrollable giggles; and, quite unable to speak, she shook her head, and retreated to the kitchen. A couple of minutes later, however, as she reappeared with my soup and set it before me, she said:

'Mrs. says to try Druggist Thompson.'

'Why?' I said – unsure whether this was a belated answer to my question, or a reference to some other topic altogether. She froze like a frightened rabbit; so I coaxed her by saying:

'Is he very old?'

She shook her head again, and left without another word: and it was only when she brought my steak pie (a full twenty minutes later) that she said:

'Nay, but all the old folk go to him for their potions an' that. You won't have far to look. He's only out in th'market place.'

And so he was – or, rather, so his shop was; for by the time I had finished my meal, and retrieved my coat from my room, and ventured out again, 'Thompson: Druggist' was firmly closed.

There seemed nothing to be gained by returning at once to the Black Bull, so I decided to take a walk. If nothing else, I should enjoy the childish pleasure I still find in exploring new places – observing the names of shops and taverns, and looking into the houses as I pass, and imagining what it must be like to live in them; and if I was lucky, some chance encounter might yet allow me to discover something of Turner. A raw wind was starting to blow in from the north-west, carrying – above the stench of a nearby tannery – a wild moorland smell that seemed to call out the spirit of adventure; and with a sudden spasm of exhilaration I turned up my collar, and set off down the narrow path at the side of the hotel.

I found myself – as soon as my eyes had adjusted to the darkness – in a maze of mean passages, that turned and twisted and doubled back so unrelentingly that after a few minutes I should, I think, have had difficulty retracing my steps. I was not con-

189

cerned about getting lost, however; for I knew I must come out somewhere, and that that somewhere could not be very far from the Black Bull, which I would be able to approach by way of the main streets. At every lighted window I peered inside, hoping to see some elderly person sitting alone before the fire – for surely Turner, if he knew of this knot of secret alleys, must have come here again and again, drawn by the opportunities it offered for being unseen and unknown? – and someone might remember him yet, if I could but describe him well enough. Beyond one white-bearded old patriarch regaling a group of younger men in an ale-house, however, I saw nothing but rooms full of children and their mothers (including, once – through gnarled little panes of glass grey with steam – a tin bathtub before the fire, and a baby splashing in it. Why, I cannot say – but this scene stabbed me so fiercely with the recollection of my own family, and the realization of how far they have been from my thoughts lately, that I had to bite my lip to stop myself weeping.).

At length, turning a corner, I felt the wind and a spatter of rain full on my face; and a few moments later emerged in an open yard at the edge of a street I did not recognize. The Chevin rose up directly before me, no more than a mile or so away; and for a moment I had the strange impression that it had grown since I'd last seen it, for its dark mass seemed to reach as far as the eye could see. Then I saw that what appeared to be the 'top' was moving, and was in reality no more than a great black storm cloud rolling towards us at a fearful pace. I wished now that I had paid more attention to the way I had come; for it was clear that if I did not return to the hotel at once, I risked being soaked to the skin, and having to put on wet clothes in the morning.

From somewhere to my left, I heard the strains of music, and thinking there might be a hall or an assembly room nearby, where I might turn my predicament to advantage by sheltering pleasantly until the storm was past, and perhaps falling into conversation with an elderly doorkeeper, I set out briskly in that direction. After no more than two hundred yards or so, I came to a brightly lit, plain stone building which looked as if it had once been a chapel, but which now boldly announced itself to the world – by means of a large painted board above the door – as 'Otley Mechanics' Institute'. The music came from a room on the first floor; and as I drew nearer I was conscious that there was something strange about it, though for a moment I could not have said what it was. The melody was familiar – a piece by Mendelssohn, I think; the playing more than competent, for such an out-of-the-way place; and yet . . .

And then it struck me: I could identify the first two instruments easily enough – a violin and a piano – but what in heaven's name was the third? A piccolo? Too deep. A flute? Too rich and deep.

I was still wrestling with this conundrum – heedless of the rain that was now hammering the top of my head – when the door opened, and a tall, slender man peered out, and grimaced up at the sky. He held an umbrella, which he started to unfurl but as soon as he felt the wind catch it he closed it again, and set off with no other precaution than a violent shrug to lift his coat higher about his neck and shoulders. He had gone no more than five paces when he saw me. The puzzlement must have shown on my face, for his expression promptly changed from hawkish severity to a broad smile, and he said:

'You know what that is?'

I shook my head.

'Come and see.'

There was a kind of boyish eagerness in his manner that suggested he welcomed the excuse to delay his departure – either because he feared a wetting, or because he was less than enthusiastic about his next engagement; and, before I had a chance to reply, he turned abruptly and led the way back into the Institute. The ground floor was chill and gloomy, with dark-painted doors marked 'Library', 'Reading room' and 'Classroom'; but a cheerful brightness fell on the stairs, as if they rose from this world to the next. And indeed, as we ascended towards the gas-lit landing, we heard – more loudly with every step – the breath-catching tones of a tender *adagio* – which, if not quite an angelic choir, yet seemed heavenly enough in contrast to the sullen drumming of rain on roof and windows.

Directly before us, as we reached the top, was a pair of heavy panelled doors. My guide opened one, and wedged it ajar with his body so that I might see past him. A few people just inside, hearing our arrival – or else feeling the sudden blast of cold air against their necks – turned towards us, greeting me with a stare that was neither hostile nor friendly, but merely curious; and then nodding and smiling as soon as they saw my companion, who smiled and nodded back.

I found myself looking into a long room running the entire length of the building, and set out as a lecture hall, with tightly packed rows of chairs – every one, so far as I could tell, occupied – and, at the far end, four or five men sitting behind a baize-covered table on a raised dais. The musicians were clustered round the piano at one side of the stage; and one glance was enough to tell me why my guide had brought me here, and why his eyes were even now searching my face, in anticipation of some evidence of astonishment. The piano-player and the violinist were just such a young woman and a young man as you might expect to see appearing in the public hall of any small provincial town; but the third performer was something else entirely. He was no more than eighteen or nineteen, with close-set eyes, dark ringlets and a hook nose. He stood before a music stand, following a score like the others – but his only instrument was his own lips, which he was using to *whistle* his part, with a range, and a depth of feeling, that I should not – had I not seen him – believed possible.

My guide laid a finger on my arm and whispered in my ear:

'There. That's Whistling Albert.'

'*Whistling Albert*?'

'Printer Walker's boy.'

'Ah,' I said, trying to give the impression that I knew who Printer Walker was, and realized that he was an adequate explanation of the miraculous whistler. I was evidently unsuccessful, however; for my companion said:

'You haven't heard of the Printer?'

I shook my head.

'I thought maybe you'd come to see him,' he said. He backed out on to the landing, leaving just his foot in the door, and continued in a louder voice: 'We don't get many visitors in Otley, and most of them are for him. Or Dawson and Payne.'

No point in further pretence. I smiled, and shrugged helplessly.

'Why, they make "Our Own Kind",' he said; and then, seeing I was still baffled: 'The *printing* machines. That's what we're principally known for, nowadays, Mr. . . . .'

'Hartright.'

'Hartright. Yes, the Printer says in a few years Otley machines'll be known all over the world. Or rather, "celebrated in every clime and corner of the globe"; for he'll never use a simple English phrase when an ornate Latinized ore will do.' He gave a pleasant laugh, with no hint of malice in it. 'He would find it hard, I think, to rise to the challenge I once set myself, of composing a sermon entirely in words of one syllable.'

A clergyman; but of what denomination? A Methodist like as not, in a place like this. For an uncomfortable moment I imagined his sharp eyes uncovering the secrets of my soul, and making a damning catalogue of all the levity and wantonness he found there. I was relieved when at length he said:

'I'm Joshua Hart, the vicar here.' He held out his hand. 'And what *does* bring you to Otley, Mr. Hartright, if not the printing trade?'

'I'm writing a book.'

'Ah, the printing trade after all – at least, after a fashion. We should have had you here tonight.' He made a gracious little bow in the direction of the hall. 'They always like to hear literary men. Doubtless the thought of all that paper from the mill, and all that occupation for their machines.' He laughed, again without any appearance of ill-feeling. 'And what, may I ask, is your subject?'

'The life of Turner.'

His eyes brightened. 'J. M. W., R.A.?' he said; and then, before I had time to reply: 'Ah, I understand. Farnley Hall.'

'I go there tomorrow,' I said.

He nodded. Encouraged by the warmth of interest in his face – and by the sudden reflection that a vicar should be at least as well placed to advise me as a druggist – I went on: 'I was hoping tonight that I might find someone in Otley who had some reminiscence of him.'

'There, I'm afraid, I cannot help you,' he said, smiling. 'I only came here in 'thirty-sev–'

At that moment, the music ended; and a sudden explosion of clapping made all conversation impossible for the next half minute, during which time we could do nothing but stand smiling impotently at each other. As the applause finally died away, however, his eyes seemed to stray past me; and then he nodded

193

to himself, as if acknowledging some sudden insight. Leaning over and touching my arm again, he said:

'No, I *may* be able to help you.' He held up his hand, signalling me to wait, and looked towards the hall, where one of the men at the table had begun to speak in a deep, treacly voice:

'Thank you, Miss Binney; thank you, gentlemen – a charming musical interlude. We now come to the moment that certain small boys have been waiting for' – laughter from the audience – 'the lecture on electricity by Dr. Kerr and Mr. 'Druggist' Thompson. Ladies of a sensitive disposition should be warned that at some point during the demonstration an electric spark will be used to fire a concealed cannon.' (More laughter, and squeals.) 'If you want to leave now, no-one will think worse of you for that.'

'Come,' said Mr. Hart. 'Let's go before we're trampled to death by fleeing women.' As he guided me towards the staircase, he said:

'When we met just now I was on my way to see three of my parishioners. One of them, Mrs. Swinton, is a widow. No more than sixty, I should guess, or thereabouts. But she grew up at Farnley.'

'Ah.'

'She is in a sad way now, poor woman; very lonely since her husband died, and crippled by arthritis; but some company would do her good, if I can persuade her to it. Where are you putting up?'

'The Black Bull.'

There were footsteps on the stairs behind us. He glanced quickly over his shoulder, and urged me hurriedly to the door.

'If you care to wait for me there,' he said, 'I'll see what I can do, and call in on you on my way home to tell you how I've fared.'

I thanked him, and asked him

Later

Am I just seeing monsters in the dark?

God knows the soberest man might fancy he glimpsed something in the shadows after such an evening as this.

But surely

No. I must keep myself in check.

Once again – record what happened – judgement later.

*

He came for me about ten, when I had almost given him up. His face was tired and weatherbeaten, and his clothes so wet that they had abandoned all pretence of protecting him, and merely hung like dripping rags; but he seemed cheerful enough.

'I'm sorry I'm so late; my first call was a mother who's lost her boy, and these things won't be hurried. But the upshot is, Mrs. Swinton'll see you, if you're still willing. She's a strange old body, and I don't know what you'll get from her; but nothing ventured, eh?'

I followed him like a blind man, guided more by sound than by sight; for the rain was coming down so hard when we got outside that it stung my eyes; and even when I shielded my face with my hands I could see little more than an unbroken sheet of water, which all but hid the buildings on either side of us, and made it impossible to make out where we were going. Beyond the clack of his boots and the gush and gurgle of the choked gutters was another, more distant noise: an ominous rumbling, so vast and portentous that – like the Chevin – it seemed to speak of some power unimaginably greater than ourselves, which might at any moment sweep us and all our puny works from the face of the earth, leaving not a trace behind.

'What's that?' I shouted, pointing towards it.

'The weir!'

'Is it always so angry?'

He shook his head. 'There'll be floods tonight, if this don't let up.'

How long our journey took, I cannot say – for when you are as wet as it is possible to be (a state I attained in less than two minutes); and your clothes stick to you like drowning men clinging to a log; and you can discern no change in your surroundings from one moment to the next, time quickly loses all meaning. At length, however, we came to a row of small stone cottages, with roofs of tattered, dripping thatch, and odd little mismatched windows that looked as if they had been set into the walls anyhow, with no concern for symmetry or proportion. Mr. Hart paused at the second door, and knocked; and then, without waiting for an answer, lifted the latch and went inside.

A smell of smoke and fat and bacon – the feeble glimmer of two or three tallow candles – a brilliant orange fire in the grate, with the dark shape of a cooking pot cut from its heart, and a pair of old bellows hanging to one side: those were my immediate impressions. It was only after I had cast about for a few moments that I noticed *her*. She was sitting in the darkness on the far side of the hearth, wearing a black dress and a grubby old crinkled cap, with her arms protectively hugging a large bowl in her lap, as if she feared we might be robbers, and meant to take it from her. Next to her was a chair laid on its front, with planks placed across the back to form a kind of table. Her bright unsmiling eyes never left me as Mr. Hart said:

'Dolly, this is Mr. Hartright.'

'Good evening,' I said, removing my hat. She did not move or speak, but only nodded. As she did so, the light from the fire caught the contours of her face, showing a broad brow and high cheekbones and a mouth held so tightly shut that it was no more than a black crater between nose and jaw.

'Poor Mrs. Swinton – she finds it difficult to get up now,' said Mr. Hart, as if by way of explanation.

'Oh, please don't stir on my account,' I said – somewhat redundantly, for it was plain she had absolutely no intention of doing so.

'Well,' said Mr. Hart, quietly, holding his hand out to me. 'I'll leave you now.'

'Thank you,' I said.

'I hope some good may come of it.' He smiled. 'If it does, you may recompense me with a copy of your book.' He turned towards Mrs. Swinton, and raised his voice.

'Good night, Dolly.'

'G'd neet, Mr. 'Art,' she muttered – and the sound of her voice startled me, for it was almost as deep as a man's. She watched him leave, as alert as a wild animal; and then said:

''E en't put the sneck 'ome.'

'I beg your pardon?' I said.

'The sneck,' she said. She extended her hand and pivoted it at the wrist, from which I deduced she meant the latch. 'Neet like toneet, wind'll 'ave t'door off 'is 'angers if 'e's not fixed reet.'

As if to prove the point, the door flew open as I reached it, and would have knocked me off my feet if I had not jumped out of the way in time. My struggle to close it again, and to secure it firmly (no easy matter, for the wood was badly warped) must have made an entertaining spectacle; for when I turned back suddenly towards Mrs. Swinton, she was shaking with silent laughter. As soon as she saw she was observed, however, she resumed her previous dour expression; and said:

'Tha's nivver 'Artright.'

'What?' I said, too taken aback to make any other response.

'Tha reet name's not 'Artright,' she said, looking squarely into my eyes.

'What is it, then?' I said, with a sheepish smile, and an uncomfortable tightness in my throat. I held my breath, convinced, for one wild giddy instant, that she was going to say 'Jenkinson'. After studying me for a few seconds more, however, she merely shrugged and said:

"Ahsumiver, tha's sodden wi' weet. Come by t'fire, and get dry.'

I accepted gratefully, even though the stench of burnt lard and dirty clothes and unwashed flesh grew riper and more oppressive with every step. As I drew near – mastering my revulsion by breathing through my mouth, and so contriving to smell nothing at all – I saw that the makeshift table next to her was lined with rows of little freshly cooked cakes; and that suspended from the beamed ceiling was an ingenious kind of rack – much like the 'creels' I have seen in cottages in Limmeridge, save that it was attached to a pulley and a length of rope that allowed her to lower and raise it without leaving her seat – to which she had transferred a dozen or so dry. She must have seen me looking at them, for she said:

"Ayver-bread. Will tha teeaste 'un?'

In truth, the thought of it turned my stomach; but I felt I could not politely refuse, so I reached up to take one.

'Nay,' she said, 'tha oughta 'ave it 'ot, to warm tha guts; I'll make tha one fresh'; and pulling a piece of dough from the bowl in her lap, she quickly pinched and patted it into a little disc. As she laid it on the bakestone in the fireplace I tried to persuade myself that the dark smears on the surface were a trick of the dim light, rather than grime from her filthy fingers; but it was with some difficulty that I forced myself to take it from her, and bite half of it off, and say:

'Thank you, it's very good.'

'Tha don't want to stand,' she said, gesturing to an old chair –

crudely held together with thick wooden slats nailed to the legs and the back, that put me oddly in mind of a child sitting on the floor holding his knees – which was half hidden in the shadows on the other side of the hearth.

'Tha's been to th'Institute, parson says,' she said, as I pulled it out, and sat down. 'What's tha reckon to tha'?'

'I was very impressed,' I said. 'I don't know when I've heard better, even in London.'

'Oh, ay?' she said, with an odd little smile, which I could not decipher, and found slightly unsettling.

'Yes. It's a fine hall. And Whistling Albert is a phenomenon.'

She let out an almost soundless gust of derision – though whether it was directed at me, or at Whistling Albert, or at the Institute, I could not tell.

'Why,' I said. 'What do you think?'

She laughed. 'They reckon as I'm addled. And I reckon as they're a cletch o' gawbies.'

'Gawbies?'

'Don't use their yeds,' she said. 'Tha's what I mean. Think on account they don't see nowt, there b'ain't owt to see.'

Cold as I was, I suddenly felt colder. 'See what?' I said.

Perhaps she had not heard me; for she made no reply, but gazed at the fire, shaking her head sadly, and muttering 'Ay, ay' under her breath. After a few moments she picked up an ember-rake, and absently riddled the grate with it; and then, without looking at me, said:

'Hast tha bin up on t'Chevin?'

'Not yet.'

She nodded, but said no more, merely studying the flames in silence. At length I said:

'Why, what's up there?'

She laughed. 'Nowt, if tha'll credit t'Printer, and Druggist Thompson, and t'doctor man, wi' all their bangs an' flashes.'

'But *you* –' I began.

'Tha ivver 'eeard tell of t'Barguest?' she said, suddenly looking me full in the face.

'The *Barguest*?'

She nodded, and rattled the ember-rake against the cooking pot.

I was bemused for a second or two, but then all at once – miraculously, I think now – seemed to grasp her meaning.

'What?' I said. 'Is he in chains?'

She nodded. She was watching me intently now; and I knew that if my expression betrayed the slightest sign of mockery or disbelief she would clamp shut, and I should get no more from her.

'What kind of a creature is he?' I said. 'A ghost? Some poor fellow that was hanged there years ago?'

She shook her head. 'A beast,' she said, in little more than a whisper. 'I 'eeard 'im once, years sin, when the bairns was small, and we was up there bleggin'. It were a'most dark, and rawky, so's tha couldn't hardly see; and Adam, our boy, 'e were freetenin' th' lasses – tha know, "Best run, or t'Bargues'll get tha," an' sich-like – and I were tryin' to 'ush 'im, when there were this gert noise be'ind us – like a snufflin', tha'd call it, and a tiftin', and –'

'Tifting?' I said.

She pushed her tongue out, and took two or three rapid breaths, before going on: 'And 'e were roarin', and pawin'' – here she made her hands into claws, and scraped some imaginary surface – 'and jumpin' at 'is chain, so's tha could 'eear it twangin'.'

'How near?' I asked.

'Reet there,' she said, pointing towards the door. 'No more'n ten paces.'

'And did you see him?'

She shook her head. 'We was too flayed to look. We just ran, tumblin' an' bangin' all t'way down; but there were no bones brak, thank the Lord, tho' we was tha' clarty an' moithered comin' 'ome the mester a'most died o'freet to see us.'

I nodded. A dog, presumably – perhaps an escaped mastiff but if I said so I should indubitably offend her. She seemed to guess my thoughts, however, for she went on:

'Course, all tha doctors and druggists and ranters says t'were nowt – we fancied it, or t'were nobbut a dog, or a doddy, or a sheep, or some sich – but there were summat there, reet enough, an' I nivver 'eeard mortal beast make sich a noise, not afore or sin.'

'It must have been very frightening for you,' I murmured, thinking that a show of sympathy might be enough to reassure her that I took her story seriously, and so deter her from asking whether I actually believed it.

She appeared not to have heard me, however; for she was quiet for a moment, and suddenly laughed and said:

'One of them Methodies says, "Oh, Mrs. Swinton, I'm sure it was just a pow-cat." "A pow-cat!" I says to 'er; "no-one's ivver seed a pow-cat as could 'oller like tha', but there's plenty of fowks seed the Barguest – so which does tha' think is likelier *I* 'eeard?" 'Er says, all reasonable-like, "There b'ain't no sich thing as a Barguest, Mrs. Swinton." "What," I says, "and no boggards, neither, I suppose?" "Nay," she says – jus' like she's preachin' a sermon – "Truth is, there's too mich darkness in the world, Mrs. Swinton; and too mich in our een; and tha's why we 'ave street-lights and schools, so's fowks can see wha's there, and wha' b'ain't. Has tha' 'eeard tell as anyan seed a boggard sin the gas were put in?" So –'

'A boggard', I said, 'is what? A spirit of some kind?'

She nodded. 'I says to her, "Course they won't come when there's mickle light, or mickle gabble."' She sat back in her chair and scrutinized me through shrewdly narrowed eyes, trying to decide – I supposed – whether she could trust me with some still greater confidence. I held her gaze, and consciously relaxed the muscles of my face. At length, she leant towards me again.

'Oft-times, at neet,' she said, so softly I could barely hear her, 'I see the mester, a-sittin' in tha chair as tha's in now. An' I nivver leets a cannle, then, for I knows I'd only freeten him off, an' I like the company.'

I shivered – I could not help myself – my damp clothes felt suddenly as close and clammy as a shroud, and I longed to shake them off. It was all I could do not to turn, and see if the mester was standing at my shoulder, waiting to claim his place. I forced myself to breathe normally; and resolved to change the subject.

'Mr. Hart says you grew up at Farnley,' I said, my dry tongue sticking and clicking against the roof of my mouth.

She nodded.

'Do you by any chance remember Mr. Turner, the painter?'

'Ay, I remember 'im,' she said gruffly, not meeting my eyes. She took up the poker and busied herself with the fire. I waited for her to go on.

"E knew,' she muttered at last.

'Knew what?'

'Awlus about, a' sorts o'weather, he were,' she said, as if this answered my question. 'Muckier t'better. Up t'Chevin. Out on t'moors in t'rain.' She jabbed a finger towards the shut-ered window. "E were 'ere now, tha's where tha'd find 'im.'

'I imagine he was drawing, or painting–' I began.

'Ay, tha's wha' 'e said.'

'He loved stormy effects –'

She stopped me with a vigorous shake of the head.

'Why,' I said, 'what do you think he was doing?'

"E could make it come to 'im, an' do 'is biddin',' she said.

'What?' I said. I could not conceive what she was talking about. The Barguest? The *weather*?

She was silent for a few seconds; and then she said:

'Tek 'em bellowses, and give t'cowls a bit o' puff.'

I knelt before the fire. As the first shower of sparks erupted, she gave a murmur of satisfaction, as involuntary as the purr of a cat. Then she cleared her throat; and speaking in a slow, gentle voice said:

'I knew a lass once, Mary Gallimore. More like a sister to me, she were, 'an a friend; for we lived anent each other as bairns, an' was awlus lakin' together. She were nivver quite reet – a bit gaumless, tha know, cuddy-wifted, an' couldn't climm a set o' keckers wi'out she'd get ankled up at t'top, and fall down 'em again. But t'kindest body tha's ivver met. Wouldn't 'urt nee-abody or nowt, would Mary.'

She paused. I turned to look at her. She was shaking her head, and exhaling in a kind of sad noiseless whistle that was oddly affecting. She caught my eye, and continued:

'Once, I seed 'er tek th'ole mornin' tryin' to get a tom-tellalegs from out the ass-nook, for fear it'd be burned when her mother mek t'fire. Th'other bairns laughed at 'er, but she wouldn't let it bide. Tha's the way she awlus were.'

I replaced the bellows, and sat down again. Perhaps there was some impatience in my manner; for she said:

'Ay, I've no' forgot tha' Mr. Turner.'

'No, no,' I said. 'Please. What happened to her?'

'Well, owd Mr. Fawkes, 'e were a gradely man, after 'is fashion – 'e tek a interest in 'er. 'E knows she won't nivver be like rest o' us young roisters; so he says to 'er mother: "Tha send 'er to the 'all when she's thirteen, and we'll find a place for 'er there." So tha's wha' she does; an' Mary fetches up as under-'ousemaid, tekkin' out slops an' sich-like a' t'big 'ouse.'

There was an odd stirring of dread and excitement in my stomach.

'Ay,' she said. 'Yon's where she met 'im. Back-end o' th'year, it were –'

'Which year?' I said, taking out my notebook – and silently congratulating myself for having had the foresight to wrap it in oil-cloth.

'Oh, 'eleven, I should say, or 'twelve, mayhap. November, any road; for t'last time I seed 'er we was out chumpin' for Bunfire Neet, my brother an' me, down by t'river.

The last *time! Dear God! Where is this leading?*

'I'll nivver forget – we come on 'er all sudden-like, reet anent t'bank, atween a pair o' willows. We mun've freeted 'er; for she jumped an' bloddered when she 'eeard us, and a'most fell i' t'water; and when she turn' round, she were a' spew-faced – save her een, which was red fro' cryin'. "Lor', Mary," I says, "wha'ever is t'ma'er wi' tha?"; but she can' say nowt reet off, but just shaks 'er yed. So I puts my arms round 'er; an' after a minute or two she tells me.'

She paused, and fiddled with the fire again, even though it was burning brightly now, and had no need of her attentions. For a moment I felt a flush of anger: she was deliberately tormenting me by making me wait, for no good reason other than that it pleased her to do so. And then I reflected how rare this experience must be for her – to have another person hanging on her every word, and to read in his face the dramatic effect of a story that no-one else, perhaps, had ever accounted of any interest – and realized that her enjoyment was innocent and understandable enough, and that it would be churlish to begrudge it.

'There now,' she said, sitting back. 'Well, first thing she says is, "Am I a bad lass, Doll?" "No, doy," I says, "course tha b'ain't – whyivver should tha be askin' tha'?" "I's yon Mr. Turner," she

says, "as is stoppin' a' th'ouse. I goes in 'is room this mornin', an'
'e were tha" – she couldn't barely speak – "'e were tha' maungy
to me." "Why?" I says, "whativver'd 'e do?" She just sniffles an'
shaks 'er yed; but I coaxes her, like, and ends up she says: "'E
called me names – said I were a beltikite, and a buffle-yedded
greck, an' sich."'

Whatever the truth of the rest of it, I could not believe this – for
if Turner had been moved to speak at all (and he was, of course,
famously taciturn with strangers), he would surely not have
resorted to local terms such as 'beltikite' and 'buffle-head', which
must have been as unfamiliar to him as they were to me. Again,
Mrs. Swinton seemed to guess what I was thinking; for she said:

'I don' reckon tha's reet – I reckon as tha were summat else, but
she were tha' ashamed she couldn' bring 'ersel' to say it.'

'You mean you think he behaved improperly towards her?'

She shrugged. 'What does tha think? 'Im an' a thirteen-year-
old lass, in a sleepin'-room?'

It was possible – I had only to remember the girl at Petworth to
realize that. But surely it was at least equally likely that she had
merely disturbed him while he was working; and that her
description of the response this had provoked – an outburst of (to
her) quite unaccountable anger – was accurate enough, even if
she had translated the actual words Turner had used into her
own dialect?

'Ahsumivver,' Mrs. Swinton went on, 'I couldn' get nowt more
from 'er; so I kisses 'er, an' I says: "If tha's fashed about owt,
doan' keep it to thasel', else it'll go bad on tha – what tha's to do
is tell Mr. Fawkes, for 'e's a fair mester, an' a good man. Will tha
promise?" An' she does; an' at-after she's a bit bruffer, an' ivven
shows us a lahtle smile when we bahn.'

Her voice wavered suddenly, and her breathing became jerky,
as if the need for air and the urge to sob were struggling for mastery of her. She steadied herself by bunching a corner of her
apron in her hand, and continued:

'Nex' morn, I sees tha Mr. Turner, walkin' till t'Chevin in 'is
long black coat, no' lookin' to left nor reet of 'im, an' goin' tha'
quick tha'd think Jack Lob were after 'im. Soon after, it comes on
to rain; an' then it's teemin', jus' like toneet, so thick tha can't see
tha nose afooar tha; an' a' the talk's o' floods, an' t'farmers start

movin' t'beeas fro' the cloises by t'river.' Her lips trembled, and she drew them between her teeth for a moment, and clenched her fist again.

'Tha' neet, we 'eeard as 'ow Mary were missin'; an' t'men ou' in t'storm wi' lanterns, lookin' for 'er. They foun' 'er in the mornin', no' far fro' wheear we seed 'er. All ankled up in t'weeds an' willows, she were, drownded.'

'Dear God!' I said. 'What a terrible thing.'

'They carried 'er to a byre, and set 'er i' t'fodderem. And tha Mr. Turner, so I 'eeard, went there after, and drawed 'er liggin' there.'

Yet again, I thought. *Why?*

'I'm very sorry,' I said.

She said nothing, but watched me unflinchingly, as if waiting for me to draw some obvious conclusion from the evidence she had laid before me. A fearful idea suddenly struck me.

'Surely', I said, 'you don't think he was somehow *responsible* for her death? It was clearly a tragic accident – you said yourself she was clumsy, and it's all too easy to see how such a girl . . .' My voice trailed off in face of her implacable stare.

'When I were a lass,' she said slowly, 'there were an ol' woman a' Pool as could put th'evil eye on a pig, and make t'rain come.'

'Are you . . .? You're not suggesting – that Turner could – that he would . . .?'

She smiled, and I hesitated, wondering if she were laughing at me. But it was not, I decided, that kind of smile – rather the martyred, resigned grimace of a woman who sees what others are blind to, and is accustomed to being mocked for it.

'I'm sorry,' I said – knowing that in that instant I was joining the ranks of doctors and druggists and Methodists, and feeling a spasm of guilt for it – 'but I cannot believe that.'

And I couldn't. Yet as I went on to make polite small-talk for ten minutes (conscious, all the time, of her sullen coldness, and knowing that I had caused it, and that nothing I could say now would mend matters); and then at length rose and thanked her and left, and blundered back through the rain to the Black Bull, I could not get what she had told me from my thoughts.

Was it just the fact of the drowned girl, with its echoes of Hargreaves' story, and of Mrs. Booth's account of Turner's last days?

Or was it the idea of Turner as a wizard, which strangely recalled
Davenant's description of his behaviour on Varnishing Days:
If a savage had seen it, he'd have sworn it was magic.
I remember a young Scotch fellow watching it once, and muttering
something about sorcery.
I don't know.
I must go to bed.

XXX

From the journal of Walter Hartright, 13th October, ±85–

God! What a night!

I dreamed I was by a lake. It was black, and unnaturally still,
but fringed by half-submerged trees, from which I knew it had
but lately flooded. As I watched, the moon came up, and I saw
that there was something white stirring beneath the surface. At
first I thought it was a great shoal of fish; but then I noticed that
it did not move, but merely seemed to ripple in some invisible
current. And then, all at once, I knew: these were bodies – hundreds, thousands of them – broken from their graves by the
deluge.

In the same moment, I became aware that a man was standing
next to me. He was short, and wore a long black coat and a black
hat. It seems obvious, now, that he was Turner; but in my dream,
although he appeared faintly familiar, I thought he was an under-
taker. I sensed he was burdened with some great sadness. some
terrible apprehension. At length, he let out a dreadful sigh, as if he
could no longer put off the fatal moment, and began to whistle.

As though in response, a girl – so white, so dazzlingly white I
could not look at her – rose from the lake; and I knew (though
how, I cannot say, for no voice spoke) that she had been summoned to accuse her murderer.

I waited. I felt sick. I could not move.

She pointed at me.

As she did so, the Last Trump sounded.

I woke – I half-woke – in my room at the Black Bull. I could still
hear the horn: it was coming, quite distinctly, from outside. I

went to the window and peered out, but it was quite dark, and I could see nothing. I lit the lamp, and looked at my watch. It was just past five. I had slept for little more than ninety minutes.

I returned to bed and lay down; but still the horn sounded, and in my fuddled condition I could not rid myself of the idea – even as, in some part of my brain, I recognized it as ridiculous – that it was calling me. Knowing I should not sleep again, I got up after a few minutes, and dressed, and went down into the street.

I cannot account for my behaviour during the next hour, save by saying that it was as if I were simultaneously awake and asleep. My waking self knew that I was in Otley; that the storm had blown itself out overnight, leaving the cobbles wet and shiny, and tearing great rents in the clouds, through which appeared a scattering of stars; that this was the cause of the shimmering black expanse I saw before me; and that the noise I heard was made by a mortal agent, who almost certainly did not even know I existed, and was blowing his horn for some rational reason (though I could not guess what it was) that had nothing to do with me at all. And yet, at the same time, I was still in my dream; and the black expanse was the dark lake; and the horn was speaking to me alone, and drawing me, for good or ill, towards my destiny.

I could not see the pied piper; but I could hear him clearly enough, making his way through a tangle of small streets to the east. As I set off in pursuit, lights appeared in bedroom windows to either side of me, as if to confirm that I had chosen the right direction, and to show me the path ahead. After a few minutes, however, I realized that the sound of the horn was growing fainter; and when, at length, I came out in a broad thoroughfare, it had become so distant that I could no longer say with any certainty where it was coming from, or whether I must go left or right to follow it. My waking voice said: *You have lost him; go back to bed*; but to my dreaming self it seemed evident that the horn had brought me here for a purpose (for there are no accidents in the world of dreams), and I at once looked about to see if I could discover what it might be.

Before me, in the middle of the road, was a tall column like a maypole; beyond that, the louring, inescapable blackness of the Chevin. And as I looked at it – saw the knife-sharp line of its ridge; and the jumble of rocks at the top, as grim and ugly as a clot of blood – I was suddenly seized by the overwhelming conviction that I must climb it. If I could but conquer that darkness, my confusion would evaporate, and I should at last be able to see clearly.

The first mile or so – past a gasworks, and a tannery, and through an orderly little orchard, where the trees stood as still and uniform as soldiers – was easy enough; but with every pace the Chevin bulked larger and more fearful; and when at length I reached the bottom, and saw nothing but an apparently unrelieved wall of rock and scrub, I wondered if the task I had undertaken was, after all, impossible. My waking self (conscious that in a few hours I must present myself at Farnley Hall, and that I should not cut a very respectable figure if my eyes were bleary from lack of sleep, and my clothes torn and mud-stained) was all for giving up; but the hero of my dream – for whom the greatness of the obstacles to be overcome merely demonstrated the importance of the quest – would not hear of it. After a minute or two I found a narrow gap between two overgrown bushes, and saw a jagged black scar scored into the hillside above it; and concluded that this must be a path.

And so, indeed, it was, for perhaps two hundred slippery yards; but then, as the slope grew rapidly steeper, it became little more than a muddy waterfall, with last night's rain still trickling down its miry face. I hauled myself up, clutching at tufts of gorse and bramble, and feeling for rocks with my feet, until the incline eased again, and I was able to walk (arms outstretched for balance, and gingerly testing the ground with every step, in case it suddenly slid away from under me) for a hundred yards more, to the next waterfall, where I had to begin my struggle with rocks and tufts afresh.

I cannot say how long I continued in this manner, climbing and slithering, climbing and slithering; but at length the going underfoot seemed to become easier, and a cold wind started to finger my sweating face. I dimly saw, not a quarter of a mile away, the tops of three or four stunted misshapen trees jutting above the ridge; and I knew that they must be on the other side, and that I was approaching the summit. And then, without further warning, I was there, and upon the rocks.

They were larger than I had imagined, and blacker – for the dawn had just begun to lighten the sky, and they towered above me in chaotic silhouette. My first response, on seeing them this near, and realizing their size, was to wonder at the tremendous force that had placed them there; for they seemed to have been strewn along the crest as carelessly and easily as pebbles thrown by a child. But it was not this that made me pause and tremble – rather a curious, disturbed jolt of recognition. It took me but a moment to identify the cause:

What I had taken for rocks was, in fact, an enormous dragon.

I blinked, and looked again. It was unmistakable: there was its blunt head (which only a moment before I had seen as a huge crag), the mouth pulled open by the weight of the jaw, surveying the town below; behind it lay the spikes and folds and billows of the curled body.

I knew it was not a dragon; and yet I knew, in the same instant, that it was, and that I must defeat it.

I clambered to the very top, over its rough pitted skin, the bony spines of its wings, and stood there shivering. After a minute or two, the rim of the sun appeared to my right, streaking the sky with violent orange. As its first feeble rays spread along the valley, they caught the façade of a house on the other side of the river – no more than a speck of white at this distance – which I knew from its position must be Farnley Hall. A few minutes later it was gone again, lost behind a haze of vapour rising from the sodden ground. Soon the whole scene was covered in a brilliant diaphanous mist, through which blotches of brown and yellow and green appeared – pure colour, detached from any object; and I knew with absolute certainty that Turner must have stood here on such a morning as this, and taken from nature those very effects which his critics thought most unnatural.

I looked down at my feet. No scales. No wings. No talons. I was standing on rock.

I laughed with relief.

The landlord of the Black Bull made a passable job of cleaning and drying my clothes. His wife mended a tear in my sleeve.

At breakfast I asked the girl about the horn-blower.

'Oh, that's John, sir,' she said, giggling. 'Does that every mornin', when 'e knocks off t'night shift. Tell them's 'as work to go to it's time to get up.'

I was at Farnley by 11.00; but when I explained my business to the old man at the lodge he sucked his gums and shook his head. 'Tha can try, sir. But I've 'eeard as t'mester's bahn abroad today.'

It was a blow; but there was nothing to be gained by turning back now, when I had already come so far. There was always the chance that the old man was mistaken, or that, at the least, Mr. Fawkes would be able to spare me half an hour before he left and I set off down the drive at a brisk pace.

But I had not been going five minutes before I saw, coming towards me, a black carriage and pair. *Perhaps it is only a visitor,* I told myself; but even as I did so I had to admit that the evidence of my own eyes gainsaid me, for there was something in the easy movement of the horses and the relaxed attitude of the driver that made it clear they were on home ground. The carriage slowed as it drew near; and then – when I had stepped out of the way to let it pass – halted beside me. A square-jawed man of about sixty, with wavy white hair, lowered the window and looked out.

'And you're Mr. Hartright, I'll be bound,' he said.

'Mr. Fawkes?'

He nodded. 'I had your note, sir,' he said, extending his hand. 'And should have replied, had I known where you were putting up. The damnable fact is I have to go to London today.'

'I ought to have stayed a few days longer, then, and seen you there,' I said.

He laughed, and opened the door. 'If you'd care to come with me to Arthington, we can talk on the way, and afterwards Hayes can take you back to Otley, or where you will. That, I'm afraid, is the best I can offer you.'

'That's very good of you,' I said, setting my foot on the step and preparing to seat myself opposite him. As I entered, however, I saw the place was already taken by a thin, bilious-looking manservant, who shrank away from me as nervously as if I were a leper. He looked anxiously at Mr. Fawkes.

'Shall I sit with Hayes, sir?'

'If you'd be so good, Vicary.'

The man bolted through the door on the other side, and stood buttoning his coat and drawing on his gloves against the weather. Mr. Fawkes knocked on the glass, and held up his watch.

'If you please, Vicary.'

The man scuttled up on to the driver's seat.

'I fear I'm an uneasy traveller,' said Mr. Fawkes, as the carriage set off again with a lurch. 'I never much relish going from home, and always fancy a wheel will break, or one of the horses will cast a shoe, or we'll be set upon by brigands.' His face broke into a frank smile, making him appear the very image of the bluff good-hearted Englishman – until you saw that it did not reach his eyes, which remained guarded and full of shadow, as if life had indeed taught him to expect the worst. 'So I always leave early, and generally end by having to wait half an hour at the station, which vexes the servants dreadfully.' He laughed, and wagged a finger at me. 'But you, at least, should be satisfied, for it means we shall have longer together.'

And he was right; for, in the end, despite everything, I did not fare so badly. The circumstances of our meeting deprived me of the chance to see the pictures at Farnley, of course; but – by way of compensation – they seemed to have a strangely galvanic effect on Mr. Fawkes. Confined within the swaying carriage, and keenly sensible of the pressure of time, he told me more in fifty minutes than he would have done in as many hours surrounded by the distractions of a busy household. My only difficulty was that the constant motion, and the necessity of letting him speak without interruption (for the smallest pause might cost me a vital piece of information) made it hard for me to keep adequate notes.

So here, as well as I can remember them, are the most important parts of our conversation:

HF: I wish to God now I'd paid him more heed, Mr. Hartright; but you know what boys are. I cared precious little for art, I fear, and far too much for foolishness and pleasure – with the result that my early memories of him are mostly of the fun and frolic

210

and shooting we enjoyed together. [A sweeping gesture of the hand, indicating the moors]

WH: Was he a keen sportsman, then?

HF: Keen, if not entirely accurate. [*Laughs*] He once conceived – Lord knows how – to bring down a cuckoo. We taunted him mercilessly for weeks afterwards, but he took it in good part. Indeed, he was often the first to allude to it, and tell the story against himself.

I don't know what others have said to you of his temper and disposition, but in our hours of relaxation together I always found him as kindly-minded a man, and as capable of every kind of fun and enjoyment, as any that I ever knew.

[*There – I was right – the official line.*]

WH: Was he well liked by the servants?

[*HF shrugs. Plainly considers it a strange question. At length:*]

HF: They may have thought him a little eccentric.

WH: Do you remember a girl called Mary Gallimore?

HF: No. Why? Did she complain of him?

WH: She said he insulted her once in his room.

HF: *Insulted?* You mean . . .?

WH: Called her a fool.

[*HF laughs.*]

HF: He hated to be walked in on when he was working.

WH: Why?

HF: There's nothing very mysterious about it. He liked to work alone, that's all. Perhaps he feared people would think him odd, for his mode of painting was, undeniably, strange.

WH: Can you describe it?

HF: I can, as it happens, for I was once lucky enough to see it. [*Wonderful! – at last!*] One morning, at breakfast, my father challenged Turner to make him a drawing that would give some idea of the size of a man-of-war. Turner chuckled, and turned to me, and said: 'Come along Hawkey, and we will see what we can do for Papa.'

And for the next three hours I sat and watched him. At first you would have supposed he was mad; for he began by pouring wet paint on to the paper till it was saturated, and then he tore and scratched and scrabbled at it in a kind of frenzy – ripping the surface with his thumbnail, which he kept long for the purpose – and the whole thing was utter chaos. But then, as if by magic, the ship gradually took shape; and by luncheon time it was complete, every rope and spar and gunport perfect, and we carried it downstairs in triumph, and Turner said: 'Here we are! *A First-Rate Taking on Stores!*'

WH: He had no model to work from?

HF: None.

WH: Then how . . .?

HF: I've often asked myself that question; and the conclusion I've come to is that it was an unusual faculty of the brain. Just as some musicians can repeat a piece from memory after hearing it once, so he could retain an image. And then, of course, he refined his gift still further by constantly drawing and taking notes on everything he saw – so that when he stood before that piece of paper, all he had to do was move the colours about until they resembled the picture already printed on his mind.

WH: Not magic, then?

HF: [*Laughing*] It *seemed* magic, that's all I meant, to a young man. On another occasion – I must have been twelve or thirteen – I remember him calling me to the window to see a thunderstorm. It was rolling and sweeping and shafting its lightning out over the Chevin; and he was saying, 'Isn't it grand, Hawkey? Isn't it wonderful? Isn't it sublime?' and all the time making notes of its form and colour on the back of a letter. I suggested some better drawing-block, but he said: 'No, this does very well.' Presently, when it was finished, he said: 'There, Hawkey! In two years you will see this again, and call it *Hannibal Crossing the Alps.*'

And so I did. He had remembered it so exactly that he could reproduce every last detail.

[*Perhaps why we see the same motives again and again in his work? Once they were rooted in his mind he could not expunge them?*]

HF: My father, I believe it's fair to say, was Turner's closest friend while he lived; and after he died Turner couldn't mention his name without the tears coming into his eyes. It's for that reason, I think, that he never came back here in later years, even though he was often enough invited. As a result, I only saw him on my infrequent visits to London; but up to the very last time, about a year before his death, he was always the same to me – addressing me by my boy name, and showing me the greatest kindness, as if in doing so he could continue to express his attachment to my father, and his glowing recollections of his 'auld lang syne' here.

[*The official line again.*]

Yes, but that does not mean it is untrue.

Who is more likely to describe Turner accurately? A man who knew and loved him for fifty years; or one who glimpsed him once or twice in moments of weakness?

I have seen dragons where there are only rocks.

One more night at the Black Bull, to purify myself of my folly. And then, tomorrow, home.

XXXI

Letter from Walter Hartright to Marian Halcombe, 22nd October, 185–

> *Limmeridge,*
> *Sunday*

My dear Marian,

You were right – I confess it (and when were you ever not?) – this was for the best. The quest for Turner *had* temporarily disordered my mind somewhat, and to be here with my darlings is the best cure possible. I feared they would not know me – that I should not know my*self* in the gentle light and domestic calm of Limmeridge, but would mope about the house like a spectre at the feast, carrying my darkness with me. But the darkness is gone, and the spectre with it. I am truly myself again – even Florence is happy now, and as sweet and natural with me as if I had never been away!

As for Turner: I am painfully conscious of how much time I

have wasted chasing shadows – and of all that, in consequence, remains undone. (I torment myself at night sometimes, imagining what Lady Eastlake would say. *Is this all you have discovered, Mr. Hartright, in almost five months? That Turner was a strange man?*) It chastens me that I must therefore accept your offer – but accept it I do, with a grateful heart, and the certain knowledge that man never had a truer or a more generous sister. You promise to write to me regularly with your discoveries; I, for my part, swear to treat them as judiciously and dispassionately as a palaeontologist treats the bones of a dinosaur. Like his extinct titan, mine shall be resurrected on the basis of facts alone. No more unruly imagination!

    Your devoted brother,

    Walter

Book Two

XXXII

From the journal of Marian Halcombe,
October/November 185–

Monday
Nothing.

Tuesday
Letter from Walter. Sat down to answer it, but could not find the tone. At length overcome by such lassitude I could not keep my eyes open.
Tomorrow.

Wednesday
Another blank day. Tomorrow I *must* begin my work.

Thursday
This afternoon, at last, I found the courage to call. Or perhaps it was not courage, but merely foolishness; for I had finally persuaded myself, after a good deal of self-interrogation before the looking-glass, that I could carry off an interview without betraying either myself or Walter. Some part of me, I think, must have known all along that I was deceiving myself – it was Elizabeth Eastlake, after all, who drew from young Mrs. Ruskin the secrets of her unhappy marriage; and it was ludicrous to suppose that so penetrating a mind would have much difficulty in uncovering *my* misery; but without this pitiful little sop to my *amour propre* I should probably not have been able to force myself to go at all.

It was not long before I got my come-uppance.

'Marian!' she said, taking both my hands in hers. 'What a great pleasure! Tell me you are here on serious business.'

'I am, as it happens.'

She gave a gratified nod. 'Stokes, I am not at home.' She touched my arm and began leading me towards the boudoir. 'I was bracing myself for Mrs. Madison, or any one of a hundred other doughty matrons.' She waved, in passing, towards the drawing-room table. 'What do you think of my *aide-conversation*?'

217

I turned and saw a small unframed picture of a Madonna and child lying on a folded cloth. It was badly cracked and faded, but you could still see the graceful line of the Virgin's neck and the sweet simplicity of her expression.

'Filippino Lippi,' said Lady Eastlake. 'It came back from Italy with us. I shall be sorry when it goes to the Gallery, for it's been a social godsend. The dullest woman will coo at it for minutes on end, and then embark on an animated monologue about babies.'

I felt I was expected to make an amusing riposte; but my poor tired brain stubbornly refused to produce one. Lady Eastlake affected not to notice, and busied herself with clearing a pile of papers from a chair; but as soon as we were sitting down she looked at me steadily and said:

'Are you quite well, my dear?'

'Yes, thank you,' I said – aware, as I did so, that my words had a kind of leaden sluggishness that belied their meaning. 'And you?'

'Oh, yes! – I've been very blessed. Two months of mountains and buildings and pictures, and not a single dinner or at-home to irk us. But one tires eventually of all the dirt and the corruption. So it's a second blessing to come back again, and find oneself once more in a place where things are tolerably well ordered.' She smiled; but her eyes, never straying from my face, seemed to pin me to my seat, denying me the freedom to speak.

'And what of your brother?' she went on after a moment.

'He . . . he . . .' My voice was calm enough – I had rehearsed this speech again and again, to give it just the right air of nonchalance – but I could feel my traitor cheeks starting to burn, which flustered me, and caused me to lose my way. I quickly recovered myself; but it was clear from her unwavering gaze that Lady Eastlake had not missed my confusion.

'He has had to return to Cumberland for a few weeks,' I said.

She nodded, as if she knew it already, and understood the reason without my having to say it.

'I confess I did feel some anxiety about him – about both of you – while I was away. I couldn't help wondering if, after all, it was perhaps not a kindness to have asked him to undertake this book.'

'Oh no! You mustn't think that!' I said. 'He . . . he . . . he's very happy!' It was so obviously a lie (for I could not look her in the

218

eye, and my tongue rebelled, and made me stutter) that I thought she must challenge me; but she only said:

'Well, I am glad to hear it. But I fear it may have demanded more than either of you suspected. No man should be separated from his family for months at a time, if it can be helped – even the best of them finds it unsettling. And there is undoubtedly – I should probably have warned your brother of this more clearly, but I did not want to prejudice him – there is undoubtedly something disturbing about Turner. There are few people who could come close to the details of his life, and not be affected by them.'

She paused. I wanted to deny it, but it would have been as unavailing as trying to halt an advancing army by throwing sticks.

'Has that been your brother's experience?' she said.

'Perhaps. A little.'

She nodded again. 'Whom has he spoken to so far?'

I told her. She was silent for a while; and then, as it became clear that I had finished, a faint look of puzzlement crossed her face.

'No-one else?'

'Not so far as I know.'

Should I say more? Should I tell her the truth: that I could not be certain, because I had still not dared to ask Walter what he had done, or whom he had seen, on the evening of our visit to Sandycombe Lodge? I had hoped (or half-hoped and half-dreaded) that he might volunteer it; but since he had not done so, I would not force him into a position where he must either lie to me, or else tell me something he would sooner I did not know.

'And what of you, Marian?' she said. Her voice was so soft and solicitous, so removed from its usual bantering tone, that I knew at once she must somehow have looked into my very soul, and seen the desolation there. And suddenly it seemed to me that further pretence was futile – I had resisted as best I could, but the citadel had fallen, and all that remained was to surrender, and confess the secrets she had already guessed. Surely, indeed, it would be a blessed relief to do so – to share the burden of my wretchedness with another human being, and not merely with an insensible book?

I formed the words – I opened my lips – I closed them again. I could not speak without condemning Walter, as well as myself; and that I had no right to do. Or so, at least, I told myself then; but now, as I write, it seems to me that my dominant feeling at the time was *fear* – fear, I suppose, that I should become an object of pity. Dear God! how tenacious is pride, and what forms it takes to deceive us!

'It is easier for me,' I said. 'I am only his amanuensis. I merely have to gather facts for him, without reflecting on their significance. He –'

'Oh, what nonsense!' she said, laughing. 'I don't believe it for a moment!'

'No – indeed – that is why I am here,' I said (and was surprised to hear the animation suddenly returning to my own voice). 'Inevitably, most of Walter's informants remember Turner from his middle and later years. He now has the difficult task of reviewing everything they told him, and forming it into a coherent picture. I, meanwhile, am to stay in London, and learn what I can of Turner's early life and career.'

Her eyes narrowed disconcertingly. 'Personally, I should have thought *that* would have been *harder*.'

'Only in a practical sense,' I said. 'Everyone who knew Turner then is presumably dead. All I am looking for is any scraps of evidence – memoirs, letters, private papers – that may have survived, and could yield a useful insight or detail. The only art will be in knowing where to search, and getting permission to examine them. The actual business of reading them, and noting down anything of interest – that's something any competent clerk could do.'

She was not convinced. She stared at me steadily, her lips set in a kind of sceptical half-smile that seemed to say: *Very good. Now tell me the truth.* I held her gaze, however, and at length she relented.

'I am not the person to help you, then,' she said, ringing the bell. 'You should talk to my husband. He knew Turner and his circle, socially *and* professionally, for more than forty years.'

I could not help wondering why, in that case, she had not introduced us to him before; but the next moment she gave me the answer.

'I hate to trouble him, when he is so heavy-laden.' She shook her head. 'So many responsibilities – and they seem to grow more every day. He was at the palace this morning – dines with Lansdowne tonight – and tomorrow, I believe, goes to the House of Lords.' She suddenly seemed to lose her accustomed self-confidence, and turned to me with an almost pleading expression. 'He is not a young man, Marian, and I confess I fear dreadfully for his health. But what can I do?'

I was spared the necessity of replying; for at that instant the footman arrived, and Lady Eastlake, immediately recovering the habit of command, said:

'Ah, Stokes. Would you ask Sir Charles if he can spare the time to join us for a few minutes?' She was silent and thoughtful for a moment after he left; then – hoping, I fancy, that by convincing me she would convince herself – she said:

'But perhaps it will do him good, don't you think? To lay down the burdens of office for a moment?'

And certainly, from the alacrity with which Sir Charles appeared, and the affability of his manner as he greeted us, and shook my hand, you would suppose that she was right – or, at least, that *he* thought so, for he managed to convey the impression that he had but been waiting for our invitation to release him from the drudgery of duty, as a prisoner may wait for the precious few minutes in the day when he is allowed outside and can feel the sun on his face. At first I assumed that Elizabeth Eastlake – with that superior understanding that sometimes seems to exist between husband and wife – had simply judged the right moment to interrupt him; but I soon came to see that the explanation lay not in her character, but in his. He is, I think, one of the most charming men (in a quiet, melancholy, English way) that I have ever met. Not, certainly, the most handsome – his eyes are too deep-set, and his mouth too wide, for that; and yet his whole face seems to glow with such intelligence and sympathy and gentle humour as to make mere physical perfection seem shallow and commonplace next to it. It is easy to see why he has risen to such eminence, and is so much in demand, for when you are in his presence he contrives to make you feel – be you the Prince Consort, or a Royal Academician, or merely his wife's spinster *protégée* – that at that moment he would sooner be with *you* than with anyone else on earth.

'We are depending on you, my dear,' said his wife, as he seated himself opposite me, 'to help us save Turner.'

'Indeed?' he said softly, looking at me with an amused smile.

'At the moment, as you know, he is languishing in the clutches of the wretched Thornbury.'

'Poor Thornbury,' said Sir Charles, in an undertone.

His wife did not appear to hear him. 'Miss Halcombe's brother', she went on, 'has valiantly undertaken to rescue him, by writing a biography of his own.'

'Ah.' He still smiled; but – seasoned diplomat though he is – could not conceal a twitch of surprise.

Heavens! I thought. *Has she not told him even that?*

To my astonishment, Lady Eastlake suddenly blushed and started to laugh softly, like a naughty child guiltily acknowledging her misdemeanour. Sir Charles caught her eye, and gave a rueful little laugh in reply – though what the cause might have been, I could not possibly imagine.

'It must, I am sure, be difficult for him,' he murmured, turning back to me. 'I feel for any man who takes on Turner's *Life*. Even Thornbury.'

'Sir Charles is too tender-hearted,' said Lady Eastlake. 'He'd plead for the life of a rat. Thornbury is a scoundrel – and a scarcely competent one, at that. He deserves to be publicly flogged and transported.'

Sir Charles smiled and shook his head.

'A criminal colony would be just the place for an author of his sort,' said Lady Eastlake. 'With so much sensational material to hand, he'd barely have to trouble his powers of invention at all.'

'Turner is not an easy subject,' Sir Charles remonstrated good-humouredly. 'I know nothing of your brother, I'm sorry to say, Miss Halcombe, save what Elizabeth tells me' – oh, dear! poor Walter would be mortified! – 'but I'm sure he is admirably qualified. Does not he, nonetheless, occasionally find himself confounded by all the mysteries and contradictions?'

I recalled Walter's strange journey over the past few months – the moments of elation and despair, of boyish enthusiasm and silent incomprehension; and, anxious though I was that they should think well of him, and retain confidence in his abilities, I could only reply:

'Yes.'

'I sometimes think,' said Sir Charles, 'that Turner left a deliberate legacy of confusion.'

'That is, you must admit, a partial view,' said Lady Eastlake. There was a hard edge to her voice that surprised me – and perhaps it surprised her too, for she leant impulsively towards him and said more gently: 'Though, of course, entirely understandable in the circumstances.'

What circumstances? I hoped Sir Charles, realizing that I could not very well ask, might take pity on me, and explain but he merely smiled wearily and shook his head.

'He always loved riddles and enigmas, my dear,' he said. 'Think of his pictures. They're full of puns and arcane references.'

'*What You Will*,' said Lady Eastlake, dryly.

Sir Charles nodded and laughed. (It is only now, as I write this, that I see why. How slow and blind I have been!) 'Are you familiar with the painting, Miss Halcombe?'

'I don't think so.'

'It's a scene from *Twelfth Night*. Sir Toby Belch – Sir Andrew Aguecheek – Olivia and her attendants – trickery and concealment in the garden. The play had recently been illustrated by Stothard –'

'She won't know Stothard, my dear,' said Lady Eastlake.

'No, indeed. An older member of the Academy. Known for his stone deafness. And for being an enthusiastic follower of Watteau.'

He paused, and smiled at me expectantly. Clearly there must be some significance in what he had said, but try as I might I could not find it. At length Lady Eastlake came to my aid by prompting me:

'What is the alternative title of *Twelfth Night*?'

'*What You Will*.'

She nodded at me encouragingly.

'*Watteau?*' I said, utterly bemused. '*Watteau You Will?*'

They both laughed.

'The whole picture,' said Sir Charles, 'is a humorous allusion to Stothard. And, at the same time, Turner's own oblique act of homage to Stothard's master.'

I felt – as one sometimes does in dreams – as if, without warning, I had been led into a world governed by a different system of logic: a world of odd, tantalizing blind alleys and half-echoes, where a piece of string may have three ends, and none of them can ever be securely tied together. It was, undeniably, startling and disconcerting; yet exhilarating, too, for all at once it seemed to offer a possible key to understanding (if only in the most topsy-turvy way) some of the pictures and *motives* that had so baffled me since I had seen them at Marlborough House. Perhaps, indeed – it struck me – Sir Charles might even be able to explain *The Bay of Baiae*, and why it was so troubling. A month ago I should have asked him directly, without a second thought; but now I found I had not the courage to do so. Was he not, after all (I argued to myself) both Director of the National Gallery and President of the Royal Academy; and would I not be putting myself at an even greater disadvantage with him, and risking the good opinion of his wife – who had done me the honour of treating me as a friend, and as an intellectual equal – if they saw the depth of my ignorance and perplexity? There is nothing like losing your own self-respect to make you fear forfeiting the regard of others!

'Many artists do much the same, if not quite so convolutedly,' said Lady Eastlake. 'Rembrandt. Titian.'

'But it wasn't just his art,' said Sir Charles. 'You could see the same tendencies at work in his life. When he dined with us, during his last years, did he not go to extraordinary lengths to keep from us where he was living?'

'That is scarcely surprising,' said Lady Eastlake, 'when his circumstances there were so unrelievedly squalid.'

Sir Charles shook his head. 'He was always the same. Ask him at the outset of a tour where he intended to go, and like as not you'd get an evasive answer, or a downright lie.' He suddenly smiled, and laid a hand on his wife's arm. 'You won't remember this – you were still astonishing the burghers of Norwich – but in 'twenty-five or 'six he went to the continent, and while he was away there was a terrible powder explosion near Ostend. His poor father was convinced Turner must have been killed, for he'd said that was where he was going. There was even a report to that effect – in, as I recall, the *Hull Advertiser*, for some impenetrable reason. But when Turner came back, it turned out he'd gone another way altogether.'

Lady Eastlake laughed. 'You may ascribe that', she said, 'to mere perversity of character.'

A wild, barely conceivable notion, composed as much of images – the fish-jaw rocks of *Ulysses Deriding Polyphemus*, the rock-dragon of *The Goddess of Discord* – started to form in my head. I thought it would drift away before I could grasp it; but at that moment Stokes entered with the tea tray, giving me a moment to reflect. As he withdrew, and Lady Eastlake began to pour, I was startled to hear myself say:

'No – I think I see – his *life* was a kind of pun. Isn't that what you mean, Sir Charles?'

He nodded, but it was no more than a gesture of courtesy – he clearly had no idea what I was talking about. And, indeed, I had little enough myself as I went on:

'The essence of a pun, surely, is that one word, one sound, has two meanings – or more than two?'

'In that case, Turner's life was the very reverse of it,' said Lady Eastlake, laughing. 'One meaning and two words: Turner and Booth.'

'No, but . . . no, but . . .' I began, feeling my cheeks burning again, and inwardly cursing myself for having spoken.

'No, I think that's a very interesting point, Miss Halcombe,' said Sir Charles gently. 'All those contradictions contained with the same being. It *is* like a kind of pun. Would you care for some tea?'

'Thank you.'

I silently God-blessed him for his gallantry in rescuing me; but I couldn't help feeling disappointed (and not a little humiliated) that I had been so obviously in *need* of rescue. Had my observation really been so nonsensical? For all that I was embarrassed, I did not think so – and I still do not think so now, looking back.

'*Perverse*', said Sir Charles, turning to his wife, 'seems altogether too small a term for Turner. There have been times, recently, when I've found myself remembering that his mother was mad.'

Perhaps she was moved by the weariness in his face, and the sad sincerity of his voice; for instead of laughing, and saying he exaggerated (as I expected), she only looked at him in silence, her eyes wide and solemn – and lustrous, it seemed to me, with tears.

'Is it not mad, Miss Halcombe, to leave your entire fortune to charity, and your pictures to the nation – and yet to begrudge paying a few pounds to a competent lawyer to draw up your will, so that it ends up in Chancery?'

'No,' said Lady Eastlake, before I could speak. 'It is merely a poor kind of joke. Not hugely amusing, I grant you – and even less so, I know, when you're caught in the unenviable position of trying to interpret his wishes to a literal-minded judge. But a joke, nonetheless.'

Her husband made to speak, but – clearly determined to take charge of the conversation – she went on:

'I am very conscious, my dear, that we are keeping you from your work. Miss Halcombe needs to know where she may find information about Turner's early career.'

Was I imagining it, or had the talk of madness – indeed, our whole discussion about Turner's character – made her uneasy? It was, surely, exactly the kind of subject that would normally have engaged her interest, and spurred her to heights of brilliant speculation; and yet she had shied away from it as fearfully as one of those dull, unintellectual women she loves to mock.

'Well, *I* first met him', said Sir Charles, 'when I was still little more than a boy, but for many years afterwards I lived in Rome, and saw him only infrequently. We did spend a few months together in 'twenty-eight and 'nine, when he was visiting Italy – he shared my studio, and subsequently put on an exhibition of his works at the Quattro Fontane.' He laughed. 'The foreign artists, and the critics, had never seen anything like them – not just the yellowness of the pictures themselves, but how they were shown; for to save the cost of framing he nailed a length of rope round each one, and painted it ochre.'

'Turner was already past fifty by then,' said Lady Eastlake. 'Scarcely *early*.'

I thought perhaps Sir Charles had taken offence; for he did not reply at once, but stared at his long pale hands, as if he were trying to imagine how to paint them. At length, however, he looked up at his wife and said:

'What became of Haste's family?'

'*Haste?*'

'He kept a journal, I believe.'

'Not one, I'm sure, that gives a very flattering portrait of the art world.'

Sir Charles shrugged. 'Well, as to that, my dear, I think we must trust Miss Halcombe and her brother to form their own judgement. At all events, nothing else occurs to me at the moment. They're all dead – Farington, Girtin, West – all of them.' His voice trailed off, and he shook his head, as if the completeness of death's victory had ground him into despairing silence.

'And how might I find Mr. Haste's relatives?' I said quickly – for Lady Eastlake's face was set into a petulant frown, from which I could only assume she still disapproved, and might yet try to deter me.

'Well . . . well . . . Wasn't his poor son –?' muttered Sir Charles, half to himself.

'Poor!' snorted his wife.

As if to forestall an argument, Sir Charles suddenly got up. 'I shall make enquiries, and let you know.' He bowed to me, extended a languid hand to his wife, who reached out and touched the ends of his fingers; and then, murmuring how delightful it had been to meet me at last, left to return to his work.

And that is how we left matters.

After I came home I had another thought of my own. It was prompted, trivially enough, by no more than a flickering gas-jet in the hall, which sent grotesque shadows over the print of *London from Greenwich Park*, so putting me in mind of the original in Marlborough House, and then – by a natural progression – of my conversation there with Lady Meesden. She, surely, I thought, would be able to tell me more of Turner's early years; and I sat down there and then and wrote to her daughter, explaining my situation, and asking if I might call.

There. Two strings to my bow. Perhaps I shall not fare badly as a detective after all.

Friday
No post this morning.

After luncheon sat down and tried again to write to Walter. Still could not do it. I feel like a river which suddenly finds itself barred by a dam, and, no matter how hard it batters and rages, cannot break through. Perhaps I will do better when I have something definite to report.

At least, though, I have begun to feel calmer. It is a small, quiet blessing – but a blessing nonetheless – to know that I may walk easily about the house, without the dread of coming upon him unexpectedly, and feeling that awful jolt against my breast, and trying to force my thick dry tongue into making some light remark. Indeed, if I am honest, it is a relief to know that I shall come upon no-one else at all. Perhaps. (Strange that I should catch myself writing that! Are the Davidsons 'no-one'? No – they are good kind people, and as sincerely fond of me, I believe, as I am of them; yet the invisible barrier that separates their world from mine is too strong to be breached. Whatever their private thoughts, they would never say or do anything that put me at risk of revealing my true emotions, or demand anything more from me than my instructions for dinner.) Perhaps the solitary life – if that is to be my fate – may have something to commend it after all.

Tonight a letter from Sir Charles, who, as good as his word, has found where Haste's son lives (not far from Turner's birthplace in Covent Garden, it seems) and written to him to say he may expect to hear from me. Before I go to bed I shall write to him myself.

Saturday
There are many doors closed to a woman that a man may pass through freely. That, as I recall, was how Lady Eastlake explained her reluctance to undertake this work herself; and if I have discovered nothing else today, I have learnt that on that score, at least, she was right. Walter could have accomplished what I did in half the time and with a quarter of the effort. I only hope that in the event the prize turns out to be worth the trouble of getting it.

Cawley Street is a narrow little street to the east of St. Martin's Place, which – from the rigid regularity of the houses – looks as if it was intended to run in a straight line, but then had to be bent in order to fit the available space. The tall windows and delicate fanlights give the impression that it might once have been a fashionable address; but now the poverty is palpable. You can see it in the battered paintwork and rusting railings and dull windows – many of which, I noticed (either to keep the warmth in, or the prying gaze of passers-by out), were shuttered even in the early afternoon.

There was no bell at number 8, and the knocker was so arthritic I could barely lift it, with the result that, for all the noise I was able to make, I might as well have stood there clearing my throat. A young man in the street – from his peaked cap and nea brass-buttoned coat I took him for a railway guard – saw my predicament and stopped.

'May I be of assistance, miss?'

'Thank you.'

It was a struggle, even for him; but at last he managed to deliver two resounding knocks which shook the frail door. The echo from inside was so loud and vibrant that I assumed for a moment Sir Charles must have been mistaken, and the house was unoccupied; but then we heard distant footsteps descending an uncarpeted staircase.

My saviour took this as his signal to withdraw. I was on the point of offering him money, but the suave efficiency of his manner somehow conveyed the idea that he regarded helping me as no more than an extension of his official duty; and – remembering the prohibition on giving gratuities to railway staff – I thought I might offend him. Searching his face, I convinced myself that I was right, for what I saw there was not hope or disappointment but merely professional satisfaction at a job well done; but at that moment the door opened behind me, and his expression promptly changed to one of outright incredulity.

I turned, and saw a man of about fifty standing in the doorway. There was, unquestionably, something unusual and unsettling in his appearance. He was not above average height, but his body had a kind of thickset fleshiness that in other men might have suggested lethargy but which gave him an air of animal strength and menace – an impression accentuated by his moth-eaten black coat, which was far too tight and looked as if it was about to give up the long battle to contain him by bursting apart at the seams. His head was almost entirely bald, save for a close-cropped patch of silver bristles above each ear, and the veins on his throat and brow stood out so fiercely that you could see them throb. *Blood*, indeed, was the first thought that struck you when you looked at him – he seemed as full of it as a sated leech, and you could not help supposing that the smallest nick in his stretched skin might bring forth an unstoppable red torrent.

'Mr. Haste?' I said.

He did not reply, but merely scowled at me.

'I am Marian Halcombe. Did you receive my letter?'

His look went past me. 'Who's that?' His voice was loud and querulous and unexpectedly high.

I turned back. The young man was still waiting in the street – not, I am sure, for money, but only to see if I needed further help. And, indeed, I was far from confident that I didn't; but I could not very well enter the house with a railway guard in attendance, so I nodded and said:

'Thank you again.'

The young man hesitated a moment; then, raising his fingers to his cap, he said, 'Very good, miss,' and went on his way.

Haste still said nothing. He gazed at me with narrow, appraising eyes, tugging distractedly at a handkerchief clutched tightly across the knuckles of his left hand. Then, without a word, he abruptly stood aside and held the door for me.

I walked past him into a narrow hall in which there appeared to be no furniture at all. He closed the door behind me and started upstairs, the sole of one of his shoes – which had split from the upper – flapping noisily on the wooden steps.

'This house isn't fit for a lady,' he said, as we reached the landing, looking over his shoulder at me. 'It isn't fit for a gentleman, either. It isn't fit for a dog.'

He gestured roughly towards a room overlooking the street. For an instant I thought he meant me to enter; but then I realized that he had shown me merely to prove his point, for it was completely bare, and he was already on his way to the next floor.

I followed him with growing trepidation, for every step brought more evidence – the ghostly outline of a chest against the faded walls, a solitary hook abandoned on a picture rail – that the house was empty, and we were alone in it; and my unease turned into outright fear as we reached the very top and I saw before me a plain narrow door fastened with a staple and padlock. All at once – I could not stop it – I found myself thinking of the story of Bluebeard; and, while I did not imagine I should find the bodies of his previous wives inside, yet I could not help wondering why he had brought me here, or reflecting that if he meant to harm me I should be powerless to protect myself or to summon help. But I reasoned that it would be pointless to try to leave now: for if he intended anything untoward, he would certainly catch me before I made my escape; and if he did not I should miss my only certain chance of finding out more about Turner. And I took some courage, too, from *his* behaviour; for surely if there had been any grounds for my anxiety, he would have been aware of it and at pains to reassure me – and yet as he absently took a key from his pocket, and unlocked the door, and threw it open, he barely seemed conscious of my presence, let alone of my feelings.

We entered a long dingy room, as mean and functional as most attics, and yet not entirely devoid of comfort; for a frugal fire in the unadorned little grate took the edge off the cold, and a handsome old chair before it seemed to promise some respite from the prevailing atmosphere of drudgery and want. There were books, too, most with cracked spines and flaking gilt lettering – I quickly noted the plays of Shakespeare, and the *Aeneid*, and Wordsworth's *The Waggoner* among a hundred more whose titles had rubbed clean away – all squeezed into a miniature bookcase ingeniously constructed to fit against the low sloping ceiling.

'A man says you want to read my father's diary,' said Mr. Haste, staring at the dormer window.

'A man! You mean Sir Charles Eastlake?'

He did not reply, but took what appeared to be a broker chair-leg from a box by the hearth, laid it on the fire and knelt down to blow the embers into life. He had not invited me to sit down, so – uncertain what I should say or do – I waited by the door and looked about me. For all its sparseness and poverty, the room had a surprising air of neatness and purpose which saved it from seeming squalid. The mattress that served as a bed was covered with a clean white counterpane, and the stacks of papers or the floor and on the small table had clearly been arranged according to some method – although what it was I could not have said. The only discordant note came from a huge unframed painting set at an awkward angle across the end of the room (it was too big to fit the wall flat), which seemed to belong to a different order of reality, and was as intrusive and out of place in this pinched world as a giant entering a hovel. It showed King Lear on the heath, hands raised, beard matted with rain, railing at the storm as a savage fork of lightning cracked the sky.

I felt Mr. Haste's gaze upon me. 'Is that your father's?' I said.

He nodded. 'All the bailiffs left me. I secured it here and stood at the top of the stairs with the poker and told them if they tried to enter they should be sorry for it. That deterred them – they were pitiful little fellows – but I dare say they'll be back.'

So that accounts for the padlock, I thought: he must always fasten it as a precaution before answering the front door. I felt a rush of relief, and an odd sense of gratitude to the picture for providing me with such a straightforward explanation, which made me suddenly absurdly determined to like it; but when I looked at it again I could not help feeling disappointed. Perhaps it was just the oddity of seeing it here, but something about it seemed not entirely right.

'It's very striking,' I said.

If he had heard the equivocation in my voice he showed no sign of it. 'My father was a genius,' he said. 'But to be a genius in England, of course, is not enough.'

'Indeed?'

He shook his head. 'If you want to get on you must learn to grovel, and fawn, and hold your tongue. Like that man.'

'What man?' I said – realizing, in the same instant, that he must mean Sir Charles. 'Why will you not say his name?'

'Come here,' he said, moving to the window. 'Do you know what that is?'

I craned my neck to see what he was pointing at; but it was at such a sharp angle I could not manage it without standing where he did. He saw my predicament, and promptly made way for me.

'Large building. Stone,' he said.

I could just make out a square grey rim above the rooftops. 'The National Gallery?' I said.

He nodded. 'And the Royal Academy. Do you know what is behind it?'

I shook my head.

'St. Martin's workhouse. They could not say it plainer, if they carved it in stone above the door. *That is what a man of genius may expect, if he fails to ingratiate himself.* What does he want you to do?'

'I beg your pardon?'

232

He rounded on me suddenly. 'That man! Why did he send you here?'

I felt my temper rising. I wanted to tell him that his misgivings were misplaced – that Sir Charles had no other motive than kindness to me – but I feared I should only make him angrier. And I knew that if it came to a contest between his anger and mine I should assuredly lose, so I edged back into the middle of the room and said mildly:

'Did he not say in his letter?'

'A biography?'

I nodded. 'Of Turner.'

And I told him, as simply as I could, calculating that any hint of flattery or dishonesty would only inflame his suspicions more. And I think I was right; for, if he did not seem entirely convinced when I had finished, yet he did not immediately expostulate with me either, but lapsed into a pensive silence, pulling abstractedly at the handkerchief about his hand.

This, plainly, was not the moment to press him further; so I left him to his thoughts and looked about me again, discreetly searching for some clue that might help to explain his fury, and the sorry state in which he had been reduced to living. As I did so, my eye caught the papers on the table. They were of different sizes, and in different hands; and from the way they had been written and laid out it was evident that they formed the text of some magazine or journal, which in due course would be delivered to a printer. Several paragraphs bore headings – 'An Honest Man'; 'His Highness' Magpie' – in the manner of articles; and on the top sheet was written 'The Eyeglass', which I took to be the title of the publication, although I had never heard of it.

'Two shillings a day,' he said suddenly.

I could not imagine what he was talking about – unless perhaps it was the cost of the magazine, or the pittance he received for working on it. I turned towards him, with what I knew to be a foolish grin. He was clearly in the throes of some great inner turmoil, for his jaw worked, and he pulled so hard at the handkerchief that the skin about it turned white.

'Rent,' he said.

'Rent!'

'For the diary.'

The blood rose to my cheeks. Walter, I was certain, had never been expected to pay for information, and it had never occurred to me that I might be. Did Haste feel free to make such an insulting suggestion merely because I was a woman?

'I did not suppose this to be a commercial arrangement,' I said stiffly.

He started to tremble, though whether with fear or rage I could not tell. 'If a man inherits his father's house, no-one thinks ill of him for letting it.'

It was true – I could not deny it – and yet surely (I told myself indignantly) this was not quite the same? When I tried to identify the difference, however, I could not immediately do so, and ended by saying lamely:

'A diary is not a house.'

'It is all my father's estate,' said Mr. Haste. 'That and' – he gestured to the picture and the books – 'what you see here. The duns have taken the rest. Am I not to get some profit from it?'

He drew himself up, and thrust out his chest; but I was more sorry for him than afraid, for his eyes were dull and despairing, and he could not stop his hands from shaking. He looked, indeed, more than anything like a large frightened dog that hopes to win the day by a show of aggression, but is all prepared to run if its opponent stands firm. He must have seen the pity in my face, for his voice suddenly became more urgent and appealing.

'I have lost everything, Miss Halcombe. Even my family.'

'Your family!'

He nodded. 'My wife was not brought up to this, as I was. She tried, but she had no stomach for it; and at length was driven out, and took our girls to live with her sister in Surrey.'

'Oh, how dreadful!' I said, remembering the change that only a few weeks' separation from Walter had wrought on Laura and her children – and that without any of the distress of poverty, or any doubt that he would one day be returning to them.

'And there they must stay,' said Mr. Haste. 'Unless our fortunes mend.'

'And is there any prospect of that?' I asked, conscious, as I did so, that I was weakening my own bargaining position, but unable to harden my heart and affect complete indifference, as perhaps a man might have done.

'Not if . . . certain men have their way,' he said, with a grimace that was almost a smile, though a bleak and cheerless one. He waved towards the pile of papers on the table. 'But they shall not take my hope, as they took my father's.'

'What *is* that?' I said.

'A new venture.'

'A magazine?'

He nodded. 'They will try to silence me, as they have before. But even if they succeed, it will not be for long. I shall merely start another. And then another, if necessary. And another.'

Was this madness, or the heroic fortitude of a wronged man? I could not tell; and was so curious that – fearful though I was that it might only provoke a torrent of imagined grievances and fantastical allegations – felt I must try to discover more.

'What is the subject?' I said cautiously.

'Oh, my subject! My subject is always the same, Miss Halcombe. Folly and dishonesty and corruption.' He gave a sharp barking laugh, more like a cry of pain than of merriment. 'It s my destiny, it seems, to fight against them until I die.'

Mad he might be – and if, as seemed to be the case, he numbered Sir Charles Eastlake amongst his 'foolish' and 'corrupt' enemies, then mad he most undoubtedly was – and yet I could not but feel a certain admiration for his courage and determination in the face of adversity, as well as a natural sympathy for his unfortunate circumstances.

'Very well,' I said, smiling as graciously as I could. 'I agree to your terms.'

His face immediately relaxed, and took on a quite different demeanour, in which relief and triumph seemed equally mixed.

'Where is the diary?' I asked.

He pointed to six uneven volumes on the top shelf of the bookcase. I calculated that it would take me about a day to read rapidly through each, and to place a mark where I found anything of interest; and then perhaps another two or three to transcribe the passages I had selected for Walter. To be charitable (and also, I confess, to avoid the embarrassment of asking for change) I took a sovereign from my reticule and held it out to him.

'Here,' I said. 'I will take them for ten days.'

'*Take!*' he said, suddenly reverting to his bullying. 'You cannot *take* them, Miss Halcombe. You must read them here.'

It was outrageous – unreasonable – out of the question; and yet I knew I had brought it on myself by being kind to him, and so encouraging him to think he could take further advantage of me. It was time, however apprehensive and reluctant I might feel, for me to stand firm.

'No,' I said. 'Where would I work?'

'I will find you a table and chair, and put them downstairs.'

'You have scarce enough furniture for yourself,' I said. 'And what' – I started to laugh, with a confidence I did not feel – 'what if the bailiffs come?'

He shook his head, and made to protest; but before he could speak I went on:

'Besides, how shall I keep warm?'

'I'll buy coals – you must give me extra for coals,' he said; but the bluster in his voice was already being undermined by an edge of dreadful eagerness, which threatened at any moment to degenerate into outright pleading.

'Mr. Haste,' I said. 'I am not going to work in this house. I came here today in good faith, and have made what I believe is a generous offer. I'm afraid you must take it or leave it.'

'They are all I have!' he said pitifully, snatching the handkerchief from his knuckles and winding and unwinding it frenetically around his index fingers in consternation. The back of his hand, I noticed, was covered in little scabs, as if he had scraped it with a brick.

'What is it that concerns you?' I said. 'You think this is some ploy by Sir Charles to get hold of your father's diary so that he may destroy it?'

He let out an involuntary gasp, as if he had been struck, from which I deduced that I had guessed rightly.

'If that *were* Sir Charles's intention,' I went on, 'and he were prepared to act so dishonourably – which I can assure you he would not – do you really suppose he would have no better recourse than to send me?'

He could not answer, but merely stood staring at me.

'If you will trust me with them, I promise I will take good care of them; but if that is not good enough for you, then I am sorry, but I must leave empty-handed.'

He looked so desperate that I feared for a moment he would snatch the money anyway, or strike at me in a rage; but he neither moved nor spoke. Seeing the dumb misery in his eyes, I almost relented; but then I steeled myself, and – with no more than a cool 'goodbye' – turned and left the room.

Disappointment and relief – those, in about equal measure – were my dominant emotions as I began to descend the staircase, and both seemed to deepen with every step I took. But then, when I reached the last flight, I suddenly became frightened again; for above me I heard the sound of the padlock closing, and then the clatter of his footsteps following mine. What if he had decided to try to stop me? I quickened my pace, clutching my skirt in one hand and the banister in the other. I had reached the door, and was fiddling frantically with the chains and bolts, when he reached the first-floor landing and shouted:

'Wait!'

But I did not wait. I let myself into the street, slamming the door after me, and then hurried to the corner and stopped in front of a house with brightly lit windows and a cheerful sound of laughter and voices within to catch my breath.

And it was there he caught me. I had thought I was safe and did not hear him approach. I felt his hand on my arm, and almost shrieked in terror.

But when I turned I saw I had no reason to be frightened. His shoulders were sunk in defeat, and the heat and passion had left his face, making it suddenly deathly pale. He held the diaries towards me like a supplicant.

'Here,' he said.

I gave him his sovereign, and hailed a cab.

I have not opened them yet. What if, after such an adventure, they prove worthless?

Sufficient unto the day. I shall look at them tomorrow.

Sunday

Bad news. A letter from Mrs. Kingsett: her mother is very ill. I may call when she is better, but that is not likely to be for some weeks – if, that is (I cannot help thinking, in view of her age), she gets better at all. I curse myself for being such a prig at Marlborough House, and so failing to learn more then.

Prayed for Lady Meesden's recovery in church. Of course there is an element of selfishness in my prayers. I hope I may be forgiven.

Still could not bring myself to open the diaries. They are my only hope at the moment, and if they are disappointing I shall fret and be unable to sleep for worry, which will help no-one.

Tomorrow morning. I swear it.

Monday

Missing days – missing weeks – an entire missing decade – and little enough (so far, at least) about Turner. But I am not entirely despondent. Sir Charles is right: if nothing else, I am learning something of the art world fifty and sixty and seventy years ago, which can only be helpful.

And what a world it is! So different from our own! Here is the first mention of Turner's name, on 18th April, 1793:

Dined at the Old Slaughter Chop House with Perrin, then drew at the Academy from 7 till 8. Afterwards, Perrin, Hynd and Larkin came to tea, and we ended by talking half the night. Perrin was much excited by a 'young genius', William Turner, whose work he had seen yesterday. The boy is not yet eighteen – has won the Great Silver Palette for landscape drawing – is 'the bright hope of the British school', etc. etc. I said that in that case he must prepare himself for disappointment; for in a few years, when the novelty has gone off, he will find himself neglected, and another 'young genius' sought to fill his place.

'No matter!' cries Larkin (who I think was drunk, for he and Hynd had been drinking together; though it made him maudlin and reckless, not merry) – 'in a few years we shall not want hope for a British school, or for a British anything; for history has set its seal upon us, and soon we shall have come to nothing, like Venice before us.'

'Oh, what damned nonsense!' roars Hynd, like a red-faced bull.

'The world's turned upside down, and you're blind if you don't see it!' rejoins Larkin, growing heated. 'Twenty years ago, who'd have supposed that in so short a space we should have lost America, and the French king his head!'

'As to that,' says Hynd with a grim laugh. 'There's heads nearer to home might get the same treatment, and we should be none the worse for it.'

And if Perrin had not at that moment proposed a glee, and at once begun to sing, it might have come to blows.

For my own part (God forgive me!) – only grant me success, and the world may turn, or tumble, or fall about my very ears, for all I care!

This makes me think that perhaps I was right about Turner's *The Decline of Carthage* being intended as a warning to England. He painted it much later, of course; but the impressions made on a youthful mind stamp it for life; and perhaps he never lost the fear which comes from being born into a time of desperate wars and revolutions, when the very survival of your country seems in doubt.

Nothing more of note, then (save for the trials and disappointments of Haste's career), till we come to 1799:

1st *December*. An idle day. Did not work as I should.

Met Perrin tonight at Lord Meesden's. He tells me young William Turner is elected an Associate of the Royal Academy, and has removed from Covent Garden to Harley Street, having been assured by his fellow-Academicians that it is a more respectable situation.

It is painful, as I close, to reflect on our respective ages, and on our different prospects; for Perrin says that Turner, though he is but four-and-twenty, claims he has more commissions in hand than he knows how to execute, while I, nine years his senior, and with a wife and children to support, have no commissions at all, and must make up the rent for this very *un*respectable lodging by painting my landlord's cat.

God grant me strength to strive harder, that I may succeed in my great task. And keep me from the sin of Envy. Amen.

Poor Haste. As I read these words, I cannot help seeing the image of his son, and that mean little attic, and the strange overblown painting of Lear, and concluding that his petition went unanswered.

But at least he mentions Lord Meesden! That is heartening – though only, of course, if Lady Meesden lives.

Should I pray for her again? Or do we corrupt our prayers, when we want what we are asking for too much?

I must ask Mr. Palmer next Sunday.

Tomorrow I accompany Haste into the nineteenth century.

Tuesday

All morning with Haste. Sometimes I can scarcely bear to read him, so relentless is the torrent of failures and accidents and misunderstandings. And, to make it worse, as often as not they are not merely dreadful, but dreadfully *comic*, so that I find myself laughing even as I cry, and end by reproaching myself for lack of feeling.

For some reason, there is nothing at all for 1801, save a short entry for 31st December:

31st December. And what is left but once again to repent my vices, weaknesses and failings of the year past, and to pray for greater strength in the year to come?

Tonight I re-read Reynolds on Poetry and Painting. Poetry, he says, 'exerts its influence over almost all the passions', including 'one of our most prevalent dispositions, anxiety for the future'. It 'operates by raising our curiosity, engaging the mind by degrees to take an interest in the event, keeping that event suspended, and surprising at last with an unexpected catastrophe'. Painting, by contrast, 'is more confined, and has nothing that corresponds with, or perhaps is equivalent to, this power and advantage of leading the mind on till attention is totally engaged. What is done by painting must be done at one blow; curiosity has received at once all the satisfaction it can ever have . . .'

My pictures should rise to this sublime challenge – they should amaze – they should dumbfound – they should at a single unanswerable stroke attain all that a poem achieves in ten or twenty or a hundred pages.

But do they? Alas! I fear they do not. God make me worthier of the sacred cause to which you have called me.

Was not Turner, too, an admirer of Reynolds, and a lover of poetry? Might not those same thoughts have been in *his* mind?

In 1802, Turner himself reappears:

27th May. This afternoon, just when I had given up all thought of seeing him again, Sir George Beaumont called. To my astonishment, he acted as if there had been no uneasiness or estrangement between us, and our relations were as cordial as ever. On entering my painting-room he stood a long while before Lear; and my heart beat so wildly as I awaited his judgement that, had he asked me a question, I doubt if I could have answered it. At length, however, he made no comment at all, but merely asked whether I had seen the present exhibition at the Royal Academy.

Scarce able to speak – for I was starting to wonder if he might have gone mad – I said I had not; and then, pointedly, asked if he would care to give me his opinion of *that*. He plainly did not understand me; for, in the politest manner possible, he said: 'Indeed, Haste. There are some fine things there; but I don't like what I see of young Turner and his imitators. They lack *finish*.' (Was I to be denied a certain grim satisfaction at hearing this?)

And then, without a word about my work, he left, leaving me too dumbfounded to call after him.

And two years later, in 1804:

19th April. Sir George called with Perrin, who is full of Turner and all his works, having but yesterday been to the opening of Turner's private gallery. He was as excited as a child who has just seen the king. 'I is seventy feet long, Haste – and twenty wide – and stands behind his house in Harley Street, and its neighbour in Queen Anne Street' – and more in the same vein, as if a catalogue of architectural facts were the most interesting topic in the world. At length, to my relief, Sir George stopped him by saying: 'That's all very well, Perrin; but he should not shew so many pictures together. And his skies are too strong, and do not correspond with the other parts.'

'What, then,' says Perrin, aghast. 'Do you not think he has merit?'

'He has merit,' said Sir George, 'but it is of the wrong sort. There is a perversity about him – he is too rough and unnatural, and neglects the example of the immortal masters, merely for effect. The danger of it is that he may lead others into the same errors, for there's no denying his seducing skill; and that's why all men of taste and sense should oppose him.'

There were red spots on Perrin's cheeks, and I could see he wanted to take issue with him; but he held his tongue – fearful, no doubt, of losing his own commission. But I was emboldened by Sir George's words to screw my courage to the sticking-place and ask him, at last, straight out about my Lear – for here was a work built solidly on those very everlasting principles he had just so warmly praised, and – though he had not yet offered an opinion – yet surely he would not have spoken so if he had not meant to approve it?

He seemed surprised, at first, that I should even mention the matter; but then he stood and gazed at it for a minute or more. At length he said: 'It is too big, Haste.'

Too big! – I could scarce believe my ears! I should have been as politic as Perrin, and said nothing; but my indignation was roused, and the words fairly forced themselves from my lips: 'If you will recall, Sir George, it was *you* who considered my original plan too small, and asked me to paint it the size of life!' To which he made no direct response at all, but merely said: 'I should not have the space for it,' and left.

A moment later Perrin put his head back in at the door and said laughing: 'You must build a gallery to accommodate it.' And then he was gone again before I could reply.

Was ever an artist more abused? My rage and despair were so terrible I wanted to dash my own brains out, or take a knife to the picture and cut it to ribbons, but my poor Alice heard the commotion, and restrained me.

She is an angel in my distress. God bless her, and reward my exertions in spite of all!

Twenty-three months, and still he had not finished his Lear! However many years must it have taken him? Seldom can a man have laboured so long to so little effect. Or rather, not *little* – for if it is the picture I saw in the attic, no-one could complain it was too small – but rather *unsatisfying*. The style is too bombastic – the figures disproportioned – the whole somehow less than the sum of its parts. I do not agree with Sir George Beaumont about Turner, but I can fully understand his reluctance to applaud *Lear*.

But *why* do I not agree with him about Turner? Is it merely our natural inclination to venerate the past? For Beaumont, the ideal was the style of the Old Masters (who doubtless, in their turn, were reviled for flouting the accepted conventions of *their* time), and anything that diverged from it was seen as 'error'; while for me, Turner himself is already hallowed by age, and his works seem to glow with a natural beauty entirely lacking in the sickly confections of the present.

It cannot be wholly that (for otherwise, of course, I should equally admire the *Lear*); and yet it is undeniably true that I find an enchantment in Haste's world – a world of Regency bustle and elegance, in which Islington was still a village, and beaux still paraded at Vauxhall – which has not been entirely banished by the knowledge that it was vicious and depraved, and the evidence in Haste's own journal that it was as full of suffering as our own. Why are we so perverse?

Wednesday

Almost ten barren years – barren both for me and for Haste, for there is no reference to Turner, and nothing (save the birth of his son) but debt and failure for him – but at last, in 1813, I find this:

15th February. Turning into Queen Anne Street met Calcott, who had evidently just emerged from the first house. A plate by the door read: 'Benjamin Young, dentist', so I rallied him, saying: 'What! Have you broken your tooth then on Sir George's leg?'

He gave a smile that barely deserved the name and said: 'That is nearer the mark than you know. No, I am just come from Turner's.' And he pointed to a door next to the first, which I had supposed led to the dentist's mews. 'That is the entrance to his gallery.'

'I thought it was by the house in Harley Street.'

'He has moved round the corner here, and taken the next house along; and had this door made through the dentist's, so that people may reach the gallery more easily. Which is a matter of material concern for him at present; for if he is to find purchasers for his work, it is here he must find them.'

I asked him why; and he replied: 'Why, because of Sir George

Beaumont. He's so implacably furious with us – with Turner. for leading us all astray, and with me, for being led – that he's trying to stop people buying our work. Result: neither of us has sold anything at the Academy exhibition for some time now. Last year, he cut me dead at the private view, and deterred Lord Brownlow from taking one of my landscapes. And even Turner, for all his reputation, had difficulty securing a 300£ position for his *Hannibal Crossing the Alps*.'

'That', I said, 'is nothing to do with Sir George. It's to do with the Hanging Committee's being a spiteful little cabal, riven with petty jealousies and intrigues.'

Calcott did not respond – they never do, but merely sulk, for the thought that anything might be the fault of the Academy itself, and not of the patrons and connoisseurs, wounds their pride. He shrugged, and said stiffly: 'At all events, I am resolved to send nothing in this year; and Turner is minded to do the same.' And off he went, in a pet.

Perhaps I should not have spoken so; but I cannot, even now, see a great injustice and not cry out. For what is the proper object of an institution such as the Royal Academy, if not to seek out talent, wherever it is to be found, and to encourage it for the glory of art, and the renown of the country? And what does it do instead? It acts as a closed club, whose sole purpose is to promote its own members (when they are not too occupied with fighting each other) – by, for example, appointing one of their number to the position of Professor of Perspective, and then not requiring him to carry out his duties. So are men of genius excluded, and compelled to starve, while their inferiors occupy the places that should by right be theirs.

Reading that last paragraph, I was struck by how different in tone it seemed from what had gone before, as if Haste had suddenly decided to stop writing his journal and embark on a tract instead. It was little surprise to find, therefore, when I reached the entry for 11th November that year: 'Today began my satire on the Academy'; and, three months later, 'Today my satire is published. God help it to find its mark.'

He wrote under an assumed name, a rare piece of discretion for Haste, announcing his aim as 'the wholesale reform of this corrupt body'. I hope he did not suffer by it; but I know him well enough now to fear that he did.

Thursday

A letter from Mrs. Kingsett. Her mother died three days ago. A great blow for her, and – I confess it – a dreadful disappointment for me. My head is full of names that I found in Haste – Calcott,

Beaumont, Perrin – and as I read I tantalized myself with the prospect of talking to someone who could speak of them from first-hand experience. And that is quite apart, of course, from what she might have told me of Turner himself.

But I must not waste pity on myself, when there are others so much more deserving of it. Mrs. Kingsett herself sets me a fine example, for even in her grief (I am touched to find) she thinks of me, and my far smaller loss, saying that I may call next week, and look at Lady Meesden's letters and papers before they are dispersed or destroyed. I shall go, and be grateful.

All afternoon and evening with Haste. I have now reached 1827. Nothing more of Turner – nothing at all, in fact, save almost unremitting misery, made only worse by the occasional snippet of praise or promise of a commission, which raises him up just enough to ensure that the inevitable disappointment, when it comes, plunges him into yet deeper despair. He is, of course, discovered as the author of the attack on the Academy, and finds that he has contrived to alienate himself, at a stroke, from almost everybody who could help to further his career. More and more, as the years go by, and one grandiose scheme after another comes to nothing, he sees 'the great Cabal', and his own fearless honesty in denouncing it, as the cause of all his troubles.

But two small points of interest, which perhaps go some way to explaining his son's strange behaviour. On 15th May, 1814, he records:

A young artist named Eastlake called. He is still little more than a boy, but has more sense and judgement than many twice his age. He is but lately back from Paris, and as he stood before my *Caesar*, I could see what thought was passing through his mind: 'At last! – an *English* history painting worthy to hang next to those of Italy and France!'

And on 1st June, 1828:

Dear God! how corruptible are even the seemingly noblest spirits! Eastlake called to 'pay his respects' – so he said – before returning to Italy. His true purpose became apparent when I asked him to commit himself to my cause; for while conceding that the Academy 'is far from perfect', he urged me to desist from publicly attacking it, on the grounds that 'there is nothing to be gained from needlessly offending people'. 'What!' I cried. 'Is the sacred name of Art then nothing! – and the war that must be fought to protect her "needless"!?'

When he saw he would not persuade me, he soon left, without even remarking on my *Pilate*. It would not do to concede the power of my work, when you are a newly elected Associate of the Royal Academy, and hope to become a member.

Oh, dear.

Friday

It is just past eight at night, and I have this minute closed Haste's last volume. I knew I should find no more of Turner, for during his last years Haste had time and energy for nothing but the ever-growing inventory of his own sufferings – his imprisonment for debt; his desperate pleas for help; his rejections and increasingly public humiliations. I feel as if I have been sitting by a sick-bed, these last few days, helplessly watching the decline of some dear but troublesome friend, and that death has taken him at last.

He has gone, but the two last entries, in 1837, haunt me yet:

11th January. Called Arthur to me, and made him promise that, whatever may become of me, he will continue to fight for what is right, and to secure for my name that justice which, after forty years' ceaseless struggle, is its due. He was like a boy again, weeping, and begging me to remember him and his mother, and for their sakes to do nothing rash. At eleven he left, swearing to return in the morning, bringing, if he could, some hope or promise of relief.

God bless me through the troubles of this night.

12th January. I am resolved at last. My hand has been stayed by thoughts of my poor family – but now I am persuaded that when the initial pang is gone they will live easier without this great burden that has so oppressed them.

God forgive me. Amen.

I do not like to think of what happened next, but cannot put it from my mind.

Saturday

I feared I should have nightmares about poor Haste, but – as so often happens – my sleeping mind took me by surprise; for in the event the only incident from his diary that found its way into my dreams was something I had considered entirely trivial and already almost forgotten.

245

I was in a street, and saw two doors before me. One was the entrance to a dentist's; the other, though it was unmarked, I knew led to Turner's gallery. As I hesitated, wondering whether I should enter, the door opened of its own volition, and I went inside. I was not frightened – only mildly irritated that Turner had somehow contrived to admit me while remaining invisible.

The hall was dark, and completely bare. When I reached the end, I expected to find a door into the gallery before me; but instead there were only stairs down into an unlit basement. Again, I felt no fear as I descended; but I was vexed by the growing conviction that Turner was there, but would not let me see him.

At the bottom was a crude stone arch, and beyond it a kind of cave or grotto cut into the bare rock. It was suffused from above with a dim white light, which made the specks of mica in the granite glitter like a constellation in the night sky, and gave it an eerie, seductive beauty. It seemed no bigger than a cellar, but I soon realized that was deceptive; for when I reached what I took to be the end wall I found there was a small opening to the left, through which the cave continued. As I stooped to enter it, the figure of a man started from the shadows, as flittery and imprecise as a bat, and as quickly disappeared again, like a startled animal scuttling for shelter. I had barely seen him, but I somehow knew who it was: not Turner, but Walter. And my annoyance turned to outright anger: he had come here before me, and kept it a secret from me.

At length – after how many twists and turns I cannot say, and with the passage growing narrower and darker with every step – I saw a hazy yellow light before me, and a moment later found myself in an octagonal chamber. On each of the eight sides there hung a picture, but although they blazed with the familiar Turnerish golds and oranges and reds, I recognized none of them. Until, that is, I came to the seventh; for it was *The Bay of Baiae*.

At last! I thought. *I shall understand!* I stood close and studied it carefully. It was just as I remembered it. There were the sea and the sweet-smelling hills and the great tree; there the serpent and the rabbit and the skull-like ruins. And there the figures of –

I stopped suddenly; for while the figure of Apollo *was* undoubtedly there, the Sibyl was nowhere to be seen.

246

I awoke, angrier than ever, unable to shake off the disagreeable sensation that Turner and Walter were both making a fool of me, and that I was abetting them by failing to see something that was before my very eyes. It was there, like a word you know perfectly well, whose shape hovers half formed on the air, whose rhythm you can almost hear, that yet somehow eludes you. Although it was not long after four, I determined to get up, and try to discover what it was.

It was too cold to sit at the table, so I gathered my diary and notebooks and returned with them to bed. I started by thinking about the picture, looking again at my original description of it at Marlborough House, and searching for some significance to the missing figure; but, try as I might, I could not find it. I set the question on one side, therefore, and turned my attention to Queen Anne Street.

Why had I dreamt of that? Was it just chance – or was it, as I still felt strongly, even now that I was fully awake, a clue to some riddle? In real life, of course, the gallery would have been quite different – on the ground or the first floor, and lit by windows. Was there a reason for my imagining it in the basement? Or had my mind merely somehow confused it – as is the way with dreams – with Sandycombe Lodge, and Walter's experience there? Certainly that might explain my sense of anger and frustration: for my unease with Walter dates from that moment, when – for the first time – he appeared like a stranger, and refused to confide in me. (And, if I am quite honest, I must acknowledge that it was the day, too, when I first discovered feelings in myself that I could not confide to him.)

I found the notes I had taken during my interview with Miss Fletcher, and laid them side by side with Haste's account of his meeting with Calcott. On a first reading, I could see only one connection: the fact that – according to Miss Fletcher – Turner's father had travelled from Twickenham to Queen Anne Street every day to take care of the gallery.

Why should that matter? I could not imagine. I read through it again, and was on the point of giving up, when I noticed the dates.

Miss Fletcher says Turner moved to Sandycombe Lodge in 1813.

Haste says that in 1813 Turner had only recently moved to Queen Anne Street.

So: he moved to two houses at almost the same time.

And then it struck me – with a sudden rush, like stones dislodged from a river-bank – that this was not an isolated incident, but part of a broader pattern. For when Turner died, had he not been living in Chelsea, but maintaining Queen Anne Street as well, and trying to persuade the world that he lived *there*? And as a young man – if the disgruntled engraver Farrant was to be believed – did he not keep a house in Harley Street, and another in Norton Street, to which he repaired in secret?

Of course, there are families that have a house in town, where they come for the season, and another in the country; but Turner had no family (save for his father), and did not live in that way. For most of his life, moreover, *both* the houses he kept were in town – for Sandycombe Lodge was the only one that might truly be considered rural.

What, then, of women? Is it not customary for a man to install his mistress in her own establishment? Might that not be the explanation?

For Norton Street, perhaps. And possibly for Chelsea, although it is difficult to see Mrs. Booth, for all that she and Turner were not married, in the character of a 'mistress'. But not, certainly, for Twickenham; for there – Miss Fletcher was categorical on this point – there was no-one in the house but Turner and Old Dad. It is hard to avoid the impression that this tendency to live in two places at once was not merely a response to the particular circumstances of the moment, but sprang from some deeper impulse.

And what might that be? A desire to remain enigmatic – to prevent people from knowing precisely where you are?

Too fanciful? Think of Sir Charles's story about Turner's visit to Belgium. Would not his behaviour on that occasion fit perfectly with such an explanation?

I have no idea whether it is important, or even what it means, but I cannot deny a feeling of satisfaction that I have at last discovered *something*.

Sunday

At church this morning prayed for Haste, for his poor son, and for Lady Meesden. Nothing to sully the purity of my motives now.

Tuesday

Last night I was too tired even to think about writing my diary, so this entry must serve for yesterday. A day, I have to say, that I have no desire to relive, for it evokes in me nothing but feelings of weariness and frustration and unease – but relive it I must, else I shall forget the details.

The Kingsetts live in one of those large, thick-porticoed new stucco houses north of Hyde Park that look as if they have been made out of icing, and will melt entirely away at the first sign of rain. Outside, everything square-edged and dazzling white; inside, by contrast, all drapery and gloom, and glum-faced servants tip-toeing about so quietly you would think they feared a sudden noise might bring Lady Meesden back from the dead, and provoke some unpardonable breach of etiquette. When at length Mrs. Kingsett appeared, and spoke to me in a normal voice, it sounded indecently loud.

'I am glad to see you again, Miss Halcombe,' she said simply, as we shook hands. The skin about her eyes was grey and swollen, and her black dress made her appear deathly pale, but she managed a small smile, in which there was a glimmer of real warmth – and even, I thought (though I could not then imagine why) something akin to relief.

'This is very kind of you,' I said.

She shook her head quickly, as if even so slight an acknowledgement of her distress might threaten her composure, and touched my arm.

'I wasn't sure where to put you,' she said, starting to lead me back into the hall. 'But in the end I decided you'd be most comfortable in the library.'

But she was wrong. I knew it the instant we crossed the threshold: this was a foreign country. The atmosphere was both chilly (for although the fireplace was the size of a small Grecian temple, the pitiful little heap of coals in it would not have heated a bedroom) and stifling, with a dense pall of stale cigar smoke that hung in a marble haze before the half-curtained window, and made it almost impossible to breathe. In the centre of the room was a square table covered in a baize cloth, and strewn with newspapers and cigar-boxes and an open copy of *Punch*. There were, indeed, books lining the walls, but they looked so stiff and formal and unused that it was difficult to avoid the impression that they were as much strangers to the real life of this gentlemen's club world as I was, and that they had been kept merely for decoration, or to justify retaining the name 'library' for what was, in effect, now a smoking room.

Perhaps Mrs. Kingsett sensed my hesitation, for she said, almost apologetically:

'It's not ideal, I'm afraid – but you'll understand, I know, that in the present state of affairs it's difficult to arrange everything as –?'

'Of course,' I said. 'But shall I not be in your husband's way?'

'It is at his insistence,' she said, so softly that the words came out as a startling snake-like hiss. I glanced towards her: the muscles in her jaw were tight and bulging, and she clutched at her own wrist, as if trying to steady herself. And then, in an instant, she relaxed again, and said more loudly:

'I'm sure, though, that you'll do well enough here.'

She guided me towards the far end of the room, where a small table and chair had been placed next to the window. Behind them stood a lit standard lamp, and on the floor beside them were two long drawers, filled almost to overflowing with papers, which had simply been removed wholesale from a large chest. As I approached, I felt Mrs. Kingsett falling behind; and when I turned I saw that she had stopped and was staring at the floor, as if she feared even the sight of her mother's correspondence would be too painful.

'I've made no attempt to organize them, I'm afraid,' she said.

'Would you like *me* to try?' I said. 'I could at least arrange them chronologically.'

'That would be kind,' she said dully. 'Though it might be rather a waste of your time. Mauritius thinks we should just burn them.'

'Oh, no!' I cried, before I could stop myself. I should not, of course, have offered an opinion at all, for this was, in the eyes of the world, a matter for her family alone; but I was truly appalled at the idea of such wanton destruction, and no less so that such a spirited woman should feel – as the hopeless resignation in her voice suggested she did – that she must accept it merely because it was the wish of her husband. It was, after all, only three months since we had met at Marlborough House – and then it had been *she* who had seemed in control, and *he* who had been obliged to accommodate himself – however grudgingly – to her wishes. Had the death of her mother not only left Mrs. Lingsett grief-stricken, but also (in some obscure way I could not begin to understand) shifted the balance of power between them in her husband's favour?

'At all events, I hope you will find them of some use,' she said in the same flat tone, edging towards the door, as if I had again raised an unwelcome subject, and she was anxious to make her escape. 'Do ring if you need anything.' And then, with a perfunctory wave at the bell-pull by the fireplace, she was gone.

I sat down, feeling suddenly alone and dreadfully exposed like the girl in a fairy story who finds herself in the giant's castle and fears he may return at any moment. Irrational though I knew it to be – for had he not, according to his wife, proposed this arrangement himself? – I could not rid myself of the idea that he would be angry if he found me here, and angrier still if he caught me reading his mother-in-law's correspondence. It must have been a full minute before I finally mastered myself, and reached into the nearest drawer (still, I must confess, with the uneasy sense that I was trespassing), and took out a thick sheaf of papers.

The next moment, my anxiety vanished – or rather, it was temporarily dulled, as diversion may dull a toothache, by more urgent emotions – for there, in my hand, was a note from Leigh Hunt; and another from Lord Alvanley; and three or four from people I had never heard of, but supposed to be equally eminent and an order of service for the coronation of King William. Scattered among them, to be sure, was a good deal of duller matter such as you would find in anyone's effects – lawyers' letters and bills of sale, and a folded page from *The Times*, on which I could see nothing of interest at all – but it served only to show off the gems to better advantage, and make them seem all the more brilliant.

My fingertips tingling, like those of a child trying a lucky-bag at a fair, I put my hand in again, and felt, beneath the scattering of loose sheets strewn across the surface, three or four tightly bound bundles. These, presumably, were what Lady Meesden herself must have considered her greatest treasures. Trembling, I took one up at random, and set it on the table before me.

It was bound in faded red ribbon of the kind used on legal documents, and consisted of about forty letters, all in the same hand. The most recent, at the top, was dated 1823; the earliest, at the bottom, 1802. Those in between were not evenly spaced, but grouped in little clusters: 1804, 1806, 1809, 1811. It surprises me, now, that I did not pay more attention to this irregular distribution, and wonder what it might mean; but I was too occupied with trying to guess the writer's identity. Most of the letters were signed merely 'Caro'; but as I reached the last few I found two or three that bore the name 'Caroline Bibby' – and one, written in 1803, that ended: 'I cannot tell you how eagerly I look forward to next week; when I may at last sign myself, not merely your *true friend*, but your *loving sister*.' There was nothing to indicate *what*, exactly, had occurred the following week; but from that expression, and the solicitous tone of the rest of the letter, I could only assume that it must have been Lady Meesden's wedding, and that Caroline Bibby had been Lord Meesden's sister.

I took out my notebook, laid my pencil beside it, and picked up the first letter. It was my firm intention merely to cast my eye over each page in turn, and to pause only when I saw a direct reference to Turner, but after two minutes I had been waylaid into reading and relishing every word. Here, at last, was the breezy world I had hoped to find in Haste – of rides in the park and boat-trips to Greenwich; of breakfast parties and assembly-room balls; of *soirées* crowded with French *émigrés*, and ageing macaronis, and noble bankrupts, and pinks of the *ton* so tightly squeezed into their breeches that they could barely sit down, and could only hobble away discomfited when their dress was criticized, or they were worsted in repartee – and all described with the most engaging simplicity and charm. Within the space of a single day, Caro (from the beginning, I could not think of her by any other name, and soon imagined that she was *my* friend, and all this written for *my* amusement!) plays whist with a countess who loves nothing but dogs and gambling, and will not go to bed, but sleeps wherever she happens to be when she dozes off, so the servants have no idea where they will find her in the morning; calls on an old man with a rouged face and diamonds in his wig, who collects snuff-boxes, and tries to persuade her to return that night for an assignation in his *garçonnière*; and then, on her way to the theatre, is stopped by a stone-throwing mob in Westminster, who think her carriage is Lord Castlereagh's, and when they discover their mistake chalk 'Liberty' on the doors. And yet nothing seems to spoil her, or shock her, or ruffle her good humour.

I had just started to read her account of an evening at Almack's, and was so utterly engrossed in it that I had forgotten where I really was, or my purpose in being there, when I suddenly became conscious that I was no longer alone. I looked up: Mr. Kingsett was standing in the doorway. I could not clearly see his face, for my eyes had grown accustomed to the lamplight, and could not immediately adjust to the gloom beyond, but his stance – stock-still, one hand on the handle – was that of a man who had supposed he was entering an empty room, and was flabbergasted to find that it was already occupied. I told myself again that – unless his wife had been lying – he must have expected me to be there; and said, as easily I could:

'Good afternoon.'

He did not reply, but after staring at me for a few seconds more suddenly closed the door behind him, took a newspaper from the table, and settled himself in a chair by the fireplace. His posture suggested that he was reading, but it was plainly too dark for him to do so.

'You will strain your eyes, Mr. Kingsett,' I said – sounding, I hoped, good-humoured, but not over-familiar. 'Why don't you ring for someone to light the lamps?'

Again, he said nothing; so I went on:

'Would you like me to do it for you?'

Surely, I thought, he *must* answer me now – but he merely went on with his charade of reading. and showed no sign of even having heard me.

I was determined not to be intimidated, and forced myself back to work; but I felt so unnerved by Mr. Kingsett's presence, and so slighted by his behaviour towards me, that I found it almost impossible to concentrate. All at once, *this* had become the real world again, and Caro's – which before had seemed merely a romantic version of my own, like a particularly enchanting stage-set – now appeared as alien and perplexing as China or Japan. Several times, as I reached the end of a sentence, I realized I had taken in barely a word of it, and had to start again.

I had struggled through three or four letters in this way, and was beginning to wonder whether there was any point in continuing, when, as I turned a page, my eye fell upon the words 'Turner's Gallery'. I looked again, to make sure I had not made a mistake, and then – my excitement suddenly returning – copied the reference into my notebook:

All in all, my dear, I think you may count yourself fortunate to be *there* and not *here*. The only *évènement* of note that I'm sorry you missed – for I think you would have enjoyed it – was the opening of Turner's Gallery, which was splendid indeed. Never have I seen so many magnificent works by one man, in one place. The effect on walking in was rather like seeing all the members of a particularly handsome family – of whom you have previously only met two aunts and a younger son – gathered together in a single room. And there was the *grand génie* himself, the father of them all, darting about like a songless bird, presenting his favourites to the guests.

Sur ce sujet-là – I was startled to learn from Mr. Perrin, whom we met on our way out, that Turner's own mother died, not a week ago, in Bethlem Hospital. Turner is always taciturn (save, so you tell me, when he is in his cups!), and in hindsight it did strike me that perhaps he had been even quieter on that occasion than usual, but you would certainly never have supposed from his manner or his appearance that he had recently suffered such a grievous blow.

When I had finished, I turned back to note the date – 21st April, 1804 – and then set my pencil down to continue reading. As I did so I caught a movement out of the corner of my eye, and, turning slightly, saw Mr. Kingsett getting up from his chair. I fervently hoped that he was going to leave again; but instead he took a cigar from a box on the table, lit it, and then started deliberately towards me. I affected not to notice, and pretended to be getting on with my work; but when he came to a halt at my shoulder I could no longer ignore him, and glanced up.

He was standing with his back half towards me, one hand in his pocket, the other languidly holding his cigar, as if he had simply decided to stroll over and look out of the window, and was completely unaware that his vantage point was no more than six inches away from another human being. I could not think what to do: it seemed preposterous to continue acting as if he weren't there, and yet if I spoke to him, and he again refused to acknowledge me, I should feel even more embarrassed than I did now. It was only when I felt my eyes starting to smart from his cigar smoke that I decided I must say something: to have remained silent would have been tacitly to accept his violation of the normal social rules, and so put myself beyond their protection.

'Would you like me to move?' I said. 'I fear I am in your way here.'

He turned and looked at me with a kind of incredulous scowl, as if I had said something unimaginably offensive. Then, without a word, he leant his head close to mine – so close, indeed, that I was forced to crane my neck to avoid our cheeks touching – and studiedly started to read what I had written in my notebook.

I felt for a moment I must be dreaming: such astonishing conduct, in the library of a house to which I had been invited as a guest, was quite outside my experience, and seemed totally inexplicable. I wondered for a moment if he was simply exceedingly drunk, but – although he stank of tobacco – I could not detect the faintest smell of wine on his breath; and his rudeness had none of the casual bluster of a drunkard about it, but seemed rather glacially precise and calculated. And that made it all the more frightening: for drunkenness, at least, is the devil you know, and there is a certain predictability to its effects, and to the kind of chaos it may bring; but if a sober man were prepared to act so outrageously, there was no telling what else he might do

This is worse, I suddenly thought, than being at Haste's: for here I have no chance of escape, and no assets with which to bargain, and no possibility of redress if I am insulted further. And that realization made me bold: for I knew, with utter certainty, that I must assert myself now, or lose all hope of restraining him.

I took up my notebook and closed it.

He breathed in sharply, but said nothing, and did not look at me. The hand holding the cigar trembled slightly, shaking a cylinder of ash on to the pile of letters. He returned the cigar to his mouth, and then reached down unhurriedly to pick up the notebook.

I reached it before he did, and laid my hand on top of it.

Now, for the first time, he looked me in the face. I met his gaze steadily. I should, I know, have been afraid, but the instant I saw his pig-nose and weak mouth and the expression in his eyes – quite rational, but puzzled and uncertain – I knew that my will was stronger than his. After a moment, he turned away, and walked slowly from the room – trying to salvage his dignity by affecting a weary nonchalance that said: *I don't care: your notebook isn't worth the trouble of getting it.*

But I knew my victory was only temporary. I still had no idea what his motive might be, but it was inconceivable that, having created such a battle-line between us, he could now simply retreat from it. He would think twice, I imagined, before choosing to challenge me again directly, but would look for any opportunity to spite me when I could not defend myself. This meant, in all probability, that he would wait until I had left, and then remove or destroy the papers, or merely instruct the servants not to admit me again. I wondered briefly whether I might persuade Mrs. Kingsett to let me do as Haste had, and take the letters with me; but her husband would certainly forbid it, since part of his mysterious purpose had clearly been to keep them, and me, in this room, even though our presence here plainly infuriated him. And if I encouraged her to defy him, I should only end by making matters worse between them, and so adding to her misery.

For a moment, I lost sight of Turner and Walter altogether, and could think only of my struggle with Mr. Kingsett, and of how utterly intolerable (I was astonished by the savagery of my feelings on this point) defeat would be. And all at once, I knew what I must do: I must remain here for as long as necessary, and not go until I had finished.

I took out my watch: it was just past three. I looked at the two drawers, trying to estimate how long it would take me to work through them. With only the most cursory reading of the contents, I decided, perhaps two hours each. Allow a further two hours – more or less, depending on exactly what I found – to copy down any relevant references. That would take me till after nine. The Kingsetts dined, I imagined, at about seven, and would certainly expect me to leave by then; but if Mr. Kingsett could disregard convention, then so could I – and I solemnly promised myself that I would not move unless Mrs. Kingsett personally asked me to do so, or else I were physically ejected.

There was no time to reflect on this plan – I must just act on it, without delay. I skimmed the rest of Caro's letters – painfully conscious of the delights I was forced to pass over in my single-minded quest – and, finding no further mention of Turner, tied them up again, set them to one side, and picked out another bunch. This time, though, not only could I not discover the identity of the writer, but – so crabbed and cryptic was the hand – I could barely even make out one word in three. I started trying to tease out the meaning by using the characters in words I recognized as a model for deciphering the rest, but I soon realized this was a luxury I could not afford, and quickly gathered the sheets together again to re-tie them.

As I did so, something struck me: most of the dates on them were within a few days of those on Caro's letters. And almost in the same moment, I understood why: people had only written to her at length, of course, when she – or they – had been away from home. The contents of these drawers – like the negative of a photographic image, or the fossilized marks made by some vanished ancient creature – were the impressions left by *absence*.

This realization made me almost weep with frustration: for if these were only the leavings of Lady Meesden's life, how much more would I have been able to learn had I had the foresight to come here two months ago, and actually talked to her? Even as it was, thanks to Mr. Kingsett, I could not get the best from them, but must rush through at breakneck speed, picking out only the most obvious points.

For an instant, I felt close to despair; but then I rallied myself, and went on.

The next few hours are more or less undifferentiated in my recollection – an unbroken pattern of ink and paper and dust, and sore fingers, and sorer eyes – in which almost any moment might stand for them all.

With, that is, one solitary exception. I had completed my search of the first drawer, and had just taken another bundle (the last, as it turned out) from the second, when I heard Mr. and Mrs. Kingsett talking together in the hall. I could not make out what they said, but there was a kind of suppressed urgency in their voices that might, you imagined, suddenly break free of all restraint, and erupt into angry shouting. I could not but suppose that I was the subject of their conversation, and that at any second one or both of them might enter and oblige me to stop, but I willed myself to keep going.

It was not, as it happened, as hard as it might have been; for something about the new package immediately excited my interest. It was tied in a brittle black mourning ribbon – only the few notes from her husband enjoyed the same distinction – and beneath the knot someone (presumably Lady Meesden herself) had slipped a card with the name 'O'Donnell' on it. At the top was the torn and stained manuscript of a short play called *The Man of Taste* – among whose *dramatis personae*, I was intrigued to see, was a 'Mr. Over-turner'. Beneath that were perhaps fifteen long letters, written in the same strong, clear hand. The first, I saw – with a small thrill that not even my present circumstances could entirely dampen – was dated 1799, which made it the oldest document I had so far discovered. It began: 'Sweet dearest Kit', and was signed 'Your doting Richard'.

I hesitated – but only, I must confess, for an instant: for surely, if Lady Meesden had not wanted the letters to be found, she would not have kept them; and neither she nor her lover would come to much harm by my looking at them now. Before I had read more than a sentence, however, the door opened, and Mrs. Kingsett came in. As she moved into the lamplight, I saw that her eyes were red-rimmed and wet, and she was dabbing at her nose with a handkerchief.

'We are about to dine,' she said. She sounded hoarse, and could no longer even attempt a smile. 'Will you join us?'

'I'm afraid', I said, 'that I've already inconvenienced you and your husband enough.'

She did not try to gainsay me. 'But it's late. You must be tired.'

'A little. But I shall soon be done.'

'Would you not be better to come back tomorrow?'

Her voice wavered ominously. She seemed on the brink of breaking down altogether. Hoping to deflect her, I laughed, and said as lightly as I could:

'Two hours. And then, I promise, you will be rid of me for ever.'

She stared at me, as if she had exhausted all her resources, and was at a loss to know what to do next. And then her expression changed from stupefaction to fear, and – as if drawn by some unseen force – she looked towards the door. And in that gesture I suddenly thought I saw the ugly explanation of her husband's behaviour.

He was punishing her. Punishing her for creating a life in which he had no part, and protecting herself from him too effectively. Her complete indifference had reduced him (as he saw it) to no more than a cipher in his own household, robbing him even of the power to wound her. Now, at last, fate had taken his part, delivering the blow he had been incapable of inflicting himself, and leaving her, at the same time, hurt, vulnerable, and deprived of her most formidable ally. This was his chance of revenge, and he had seized it with relish. Hence his insistence that I should be in the library, and his manner towards me. By humiliating *me*, he was humiliating *her*; by demonstrating *my* powerlessness, he was exposing *hers*.

Seeing the blotches and tear-stains on her pale cheeks the frantic working of her hands, the uncontrollable tightening of her mouth, I almost relented. Had she turned back to me again, and made one last attempt to persuade me, I should have packed up at once. But she was defeated, and left without another word.

It is as well for me she did.

So hastily did I write everything down, and in such a topsy-turvy order, that I have only the haziest idea of what I have got. Today I was too exhausted to read through it all again – or, rather, too fragile, for I dread finding that after all my discoveries are worthless, and the whole ordeal of getting them consequently a waste of time. And that, when I think of what I endured – and, even more, of what I compelled poor Mrs. Kingsett to endure – would be hard to bear.

Tomorrow I shall be stronger.

XXXIII

Extract of a letter from Lord Meesden to Kitty Driver, 2nd October, 1802

Beaucoup de monde à Paris – or you might simply dispense with the 'coup' and the 'de', for the whole *beau monde* is here, or has been – Fox, Lansdowne, Morpeth, a clutch of duchesses, Ladies Conygham and Holland, and a thousand more. And all, to me, the most tremendous bore; for none possesses the only quality that can arouse my interest – being *you*.

In search of diversion from my *you*less state (no horse, I swear, ever felt the want of a driver more) I went yesterday to the Louvre. It was as tedious as being in society, and for much the same reason – whatever their merits, Titian and Rembrandt and Raphaël never painted the one face in all the world I long to see.

While there, I found your friend Turner skulking by a Poussin, and feverishly scribbling hieroglyphs into a notebook. He started when he saw me, and would, I think, have tried to make his escape if I had not gone up and asked him when he intended to return to England. I had thought perhaps to entrust him with this letter (or with the unborn twin I should then have written, beginning 'I send this by the hand of Mr. Turner'), but he seemed so displeased at being recognized that I repented of the idea. As we parted, I said:

'You know, Mr. Turner, you are the only man in Paris I envy.'

'Why?' he growled, in a suspicious sort of way.

'Because you will see Mrs. Driver before I do.'

XXXIV

Extract of a letter from Lord Meesden to Kitty Driver, 15th May, 1803

Copley tells me his tiresome compatriots are again making trouble for the King – but now, having won the colonies, they are no longer content with fighting there, but have carried the war home, to the Royal Academy. The Philadelphian President, West (I begin to fear men named after cardinal points – *North* loses us

America; *West* brings the insurrection here; what mischief may we expect from Messrs. *South* and *East*, when they appear?) has taken up arms, demanding that the Academy Council should be answerable to its own General Assembly, rather than to the Crown. I confess I can see very little purpose to its being the *Royal* Academy, if the King is to have no power within it, and his only function is to be a convenient scapegoat, on which indifferent painters may vent their fury at their own want of success; but Copley fears the democrats will carry the day.

Among the most incendiary of them, it appears, is your friend Turner, who plots against the royalists like a veritable Robesperre, and cannot contain his rage and loathing whenever he meets them. Are you certain we should invite him to the wedding? He may end by fomenting the tenants against us, and forming a committee, and turning the church into a People's Court, and declaring our bodies independent of our heads.

XXXV

Extract of a letter from Lord Meesden to Lady Meescen,
2nd February, 1809

Turner, it seems, has again excused himself from carrying out his duties as Professor of Perspective. No woman that I know would let a man off so lightly, who still showed such reluctance to enter the conjugal bed, more than a year after the ceremony; but the Academy has not even hinted at lawyers and doctors and divorce, but merely smiled demurely, and said it will be well enough for him to start *next* year.

XXXVI

Extract of a letter from Lord Meesden to Lady Meesden,
22nd January, 1810

Still the trembling bride awaits. Turner protests he has a headache, and cannot begin his lectures for a further year.

XXXVII

Extract of a letter from Lord Meesden to Lady Meesden, 1st February, 1811

Must end, & get Perkins to preen me for tonight – but before I do, a piece of droll intelligence: The marriage is consummated at last! – Turner has made his first public appearance in the character of Professor of Perspective! – & Larkin (whom I met at the B.'s) tells me it is quite the most amusing thing in London – quantities of comic business with papers, illustrative drawings &c. – sentences starting confidently in one direction, & then taking another, & so by degrees finding themselves in a dead end, by which time both the audience & Turner have long since lost any idea what they may mean, save that it plainly has nothing to do with perspective. There isn't a farce or a comedy comes close, says Larkin – the Academy could sell tickets at a guinea apiece, & would be turning people away.

XXXVIII

Extract of a letter from the Hon. Miss Lydia Bolt to Lady Meesden, 1st September, 1827

Speaking of which, dearest Mama, Mr. Turner is here, and not at all as I had supposed him to be – not brusque or withdrawn, but charming in a shy, birdish, kind of a way, and with an interesting observation to make on almost any subject, from *Childe Harold* to the reflection of light from wet feathers. He found me in the garden, trying to sketch the sea and Portsmouth beyond. I was, I own, embarrassed that *he* of all people should see it, but he was very kind, and took great pains to help me, without a single word of discouragement or criticism.

He, by the by, painted one of our *conversazziones*. Imagine a scene by Watteau, blurred by the rain before it is dry, and you have it.

XXXIX

Extract of a letter from Cynthia [Lady?] Abbott to Lady Meesden, 13th April, 1813

I wish you had been with us last night – we dined at the Nuthampsteads' – the dinner indifferent enough, but great hilarity – young Mr. Smiley, *qui veut devenir artiste*, as he says, entertained us hugely with his imitation of Turner giving a lecture at the Academy. His napkin became Turner's notes, which he proceeded to 'lose'. and discover at last under my chair – one of the footmen was transformed into Turner's assistant (to whom, apparently, he invariably delivers his oration, rather than to the audience) – and his words, when they were audible. had Turner's jumbled sense and execrable pronunciation to perfection. I cannot remember everything he said, but an orange, I recall, was a 'spearide form' – the (semi-circular) arch on the window a 'semi-ellipsis' – and the 'young gen'lmen' of the Academy were 'hex'orted to raise the hart of landscape to the poetical 'eights of 'istory painting, for the glory of Britain hand 'er Hempire'. There was a deal more in the same vein. but I missed much of it, alas, *de trop rire*.

XL

Extract from Act II, scene ii of *The Man of Taste*, a privately performed farce by Richard O'Donnell [1810?]

[Tom Wilde sees Lucy Luckwell at the theatre, and falls in love with her. He follows her to the country house of her guardian, the connoisseur LORD DABBLE, where he gains admission by presenting himself as an artist, and offering to paint Lucy's portrait. Instead of being left alone with her as he had hoped, however, he is constantly interrupted by a stream of painters and connoisseurs offering advice.]

Enter SPEED.

SPEED: No, no, no, no. no.

TOM: Why, what's amiss now?

SPEED: It's too small.

LUCY: Oh, no, Mr. Speed, surely not!

SPEED: And can you not dress her as Boadicea, or Britannia? Portraits aren't worth a fig, unless you *dignify* 'em, as Sir Ocular said. *History*, now, that's the thing. Wait. I'll fetch a crown, and a ladder.

Goes off.

TOM: Dear Miss Luckwell!

LUCY: Dear Mr. Wilde!

TOM: Dear Lucy!

Takes her hand.

LUCY: Oh! oh! oh!

TOM: I have, I fear, a confession to make.

LUCY: Oh, pray, don't be fearful! I shall be happy, dear, dear Mr. Wilde, to receive *any* confidence you may care to repose in me.

TOM: Why, then, I am not really –

Enter OVER-TURNER *and* COLD-CUT. *They stand stock-still, staring at the picture.*

TOM: Well?

COLD-CUT: *(looking at Over-Turner)* Um um um um um.

OVER-TURNER: It wants yeller.

COLD-CUT: Indeed, yellow would improve it mightily.

OVER-TURNER: An' a burnin' sun.

COLD-CUT: A sun! Of course!

OVER-TURNER: An' a sea-monster.

COLD-CUT: The very thing I was about to propose.

OVER-TURNER: Where's your colours?

Tom hands him his palette.

OVER-TURNER: Cold-cut, you make out the bill. Now then.

He starts mixing paints furiously with his brush. Enter SIR GILES BOOMER *and* MR. MEASURE.

SIR GILES: No! No! No! No! No!

TOM: What's the matter now?

SIR GILES: Ho! Stop! Seduction!

TOM: (*aside*) What, am I discovered?

SIR GILES: Mr. Wilde, you must not allow yourself to be led into unnatural error!

TOM: Error it may be, Sir Giles, but nothing connected with Miss Luckwell could be considered unnatural.

SIR GILES: Let me see. Where's my Claude-glass, Measure?

Measure hands him a Claude-glass. Sir Giles examines the picture through it, slowly walking backwards.

OVER-TURNER: Claude? 'E does misappre'end, as Sir Ocular 'ad it, taste may usurp genius, all is bespoke, nothing allowed, when that which 'eretofore is 'eld up as perfection.

SIR GILES: Your picture is fine, Mr. Wilde, very fine – I would only say it could be browner, especially in the skin and teeth, for Nature, you know, is *exceedingly* brown, as the Old Masters taught us, though a common eye may miss it. But all in all I should say – only avoid the excesses of Over-Turnerism and you will be the great hope of the British School!

TOM: But as I was just trying to explain to Miss Luckwell –

SPEED: (*off*) I thought *I* was the great hope of the British School!

Enter SPEED, carrying a ladder, with which he inadvertently hits Sir Giles, knocking him to the ground.

SIR GILES: That was last year.

XLI

Extract of a letter from Richard O'Donnell to Kitty Driver,
4th September, 1799

William Turner is also here. Do you know him? He certainly knows *you* – has seen you in everything, and is evidently a great admirer of yours, but won't come out and say so directly. I hope I have no cause for jealousy – it would be displeasing indeed for a man to know he had been usurped by a dwarf. The last I knew of him, he was painting scenes at the Pantheon in '92, but now it seems he is quite the coming artist, and has been engaged by Mr. Beckford to make watercolour drawings of the estate.

And why, you are doubtless wondering, am *I* at Fonthill? Because Mr. Beckford stands in pressing need of monks; and unding himself unable to procure the real thing (to which his avowed atheism, and his enthusiasm for catamites, have proved an obstacle), has turned to a popish Irish theatre manager to coin some counterfeits. Every morning, I assemble the 'lads', as Mr. Beckford calls them, in a vast unfinished hall, and drill them in chanting and singing and processing until I can no longer keep my temper with them – which happens often enough, for they are the least apt pupils you ever saw, having been selected more with an eye to their fawn-like looks than to their thespian ability.

And what does he want with monks? you say (nay, you whisper it, you trollop; I hear you as I write) – why, he wants them to fill his house, which when it is finished is to be the greatest gothick palace in the world – 350 feet long, and with a tower taller than the spire of Salisbury Cathedral. He plans *une grande ouverture* next year – though what he will do for guests I cannot conceive, for he is so notorious for keeping butterflies that no respectable member of society will set foot here – and work continues day and night to get it ready. Last evening, after dinner, I looked from my window, and thought I had never seen a more ridiculous scene: the labourers scuttling back and forth by flickering torchlight; Beckford, dressed as an abbot, prowling among them, with poor Wyatt, the architect, hovering in attendance like a nervous novice; and Turner behind, shrinking into the shadows as if they were his natural home, then darting out again like a little elf, drawing so quickly that his hand was but a blur. I should have laughed out loud, had I not recalled that this monument to folly is being erected on the poor scarred backs of those wretched Negroes in the Indies, from whom all Beckford's fortune comes.

XLII

Extract of a letter from Richard O'Donnell to Lady Meesden, 4th September, 1829

Jollet is a good man – cannot do much for me, but makes me as comfortable as he can, tho' he knows he won't be paid for it in this world.

You know your time is near when patterns start to complete themselves before your eyes. Today I had a fancy to see the sea again, and Mme. Sylvestre's son pushed me in my chair to the harbour. Some English passengers arriving – one seemed familiar – a little red-faced fellow in a long coat and scarf, pressing forward with some other purpose in his gait than mere pleasure. I thought for a wild moment he must be a dun, sent here to persecute me before it was too late. And then I knew him.

'Turner,' I said.

He did not recognize me, or pretended not to, but hurried on his way.

It must be thirty years to the day since I last wrote to you of Turner.

It is a hard thing to die. When you hear I am gone, wait a little while, and I shall come to you again.

XLIII

From the journal of Marian Halcombe, November 185–

Wednesday

Have just finished reviewing my discoveries, and find myself less disheartened than I'd feared. A distinct feeling that I've made progress. But *what*, exactly?

To begin with – confirmation of what I already knew:

- Turner's mother *did* die mad, as both Amelia Bennett and Sir Charles told me. And I have a date for it: April 1804.
- Turner *was* vilified by Sir George Beaumont and other connoisseurs – Haste's diaries and O'Donnell's play (Turner/Over-turner, Boomer/Beaumont) bear each other out on this point.
- He was – or at least was perceived as being – tight-fisted. ('Cold-cut, you make out the bill.' And Sir Charles's account of his 'begrudging a few pounds' to have his will properly drawn.)
- He did move about a great deal, and disliked people recognizing him, or knowing where he was, when he did so – a peculiarity attested to not only by Sir Charles, but also now by Meesden and O'Donnell.

Such corroborations are encouraging – they point to a modest foundation of fact on which I can build.

And what else?

I feel (to my own great surprise) that in a small, haphazard way I am starting to *know* him. Where before all was obscure, I now see unexpected glimmers of light.

Take, for instance, his elusiveness. Since it is mentioned in the earliest letters we have, the roots of it must presumably lie in his very early life – about which I still know almost nothing (beyond the fact that he was a scene-painter), and have little prospect of learning more. And yet might not part of the reason also be the knowledge that (as the letters to Lady Meesden make clear) he was regarded as a laughing-stock, and knew that whenever he appeared in public *as himself* he might be derided for his dress, or his tradesman's manner, or his inability to express his thoughts?

As time went on, moreover, he must have become increasingly aware that these eccentricities were adversely affecting not merely his social relations, but also his professional prospects. Why, for example, was Charles Eastlake (who, though a dear man, is not a quarter the artist) knighted, and elected President of the Royal Academy, while Turner received no formal recognition at all? It can only be because gentlemanliness, rather than talent, is the key to preferment.

All of which, surely, would be enough to breed habits of secrecy and concealment in *any* man – particularly one so painfully sensitive and shy?

His supposed meanness, too, seems more understandable when you know something of the world in which he worked. To be an artist in the first years of the century – as evidenced by the example of poor Haste, which Turner must have had constantly in his mind – was a perilous undertaking, in which your name and your fortune might at any moment be destroyed at the whim of a powerful connoisseur. Only by making yourself independent could you hope to defy a man such as Sir George Beaumont, and so continue following the dictates of your own genius – and the cost of that independence must be to practise the utmost economy, and allow no indulgence either to yourself or others.

It is undeniably satisfying to be able to ascribe comprehensible motives to behaviour that had previously seemed unaccountable, or even mad. But I must not be too pleased with myself – there is still much I do not even begin to understand.

And what of the *pictures*?

Thursday

An exhilarating day – but its fruits so tantalizing and insubstantial I scarce dare write them down, for fear they turn out chimeras, and evaporate before my eyes.

I had intended copying out what I have gathered so far and sending it to Walter (for after my recent adventures I can no longer content myself with being merely a scribe, but have begun to seek Turner on my account; and to part with my notebooks now would be the equivalent of a detective throwing away his evidence); but I was diverted from my plans by two letters. The first was from Haste's son, reminding me that I have now had his father's diaries for more than ten days, and demanding to know – with a kind of frozen rage that cut me like an icicle – when he might have the honour to expect them back again. In truth, I had not exactly forgotten our agreement; but had somehow persuaded myself, in the excitement over Lady Meesden's papers, that I need not adhere to its exact terms, and that a delay of a day or two would not be fatal. It pained me to realize what I should have known all along – that by this thoughtlessness I had only justified his suspicions, and left him feeling more embittered and besieged than ever; and I resolved that after luncheon I should call on him in person, and try to make amends.

The second letter was from Mrs. Kingsett:

> My dear Miss Halcombe,
> I found this today on my mother's writing table, and thought it might be of interest to you.
> Yours very truly,
> Lydia Kingsett

My first response was not so much curiosity as relief – for although there was no mention of what happened on Monday, yet the mere fact that she had written at all suggested that her husband had not yet entirely succeeded in breaking her spirit, and that she was not (as I had feared) aggrieved at me for being so stubborn, and so unwittingly adding to her difficulties. Her note, indeed, seemed a kind of salve to Mr. Haste's anger, from which I was still smarting; and I re-read it two or three times before finally unfolding the sheet she had enclosed, to see what it was:

> 1 Oliver Buildings, Hammersmith,
> 15th September, 185–

Dearest Kitty,

Pie and pheasant both arrived in excellent health – and we did not neglect to pledge *yours*, you may be sure, as we despatched them! How good you are to me! I do not believe you have once forgotten my birthday in more than sixty years. It seems little short of a miracle that you still remember your Romeo after so long.

I often think fondly of our days together in Drury Lane and Dublin. I won't say they were the happiest of my life, for – thank God – most of my days have been happy; but I'll swear I never knew a handsomer woman than you were then, or a truer friend.

May God bless you always,

James Padmore

I was, for a moment, frankly puzzled as to why Mrs. Kingsett had sent this to me (I must have been particularly slow-witted this morning, though I like to think I have made up for it since!); and it was only when I reached the words 'Drury Lane' on the second reading that it struck me. A great wave seemed suddenly to break over me, tumbling me this way and that, leaving me feeling excited and giddy and sick all at once. Here, at last, was what I had given up all hope of finding: someone who had known the world of Turner's youth. But in the two short months since his letter had been written, sickness and death had already cheated me of its recipient. Might not the writer now also be dead, or at least too ill to speak to me?

Without delay, I scribbled a short note to Mr. Padmore, saying I intend to call on him tomorrow; and an even shorter one to Mrs. Kingsett, to thank her for her help. Then I asked Davidson to take them to the post, and myself set out for Cawley Street with Haste's diaries.

It is strange now to look back, and reflect on my thoughts in the cab. They revolved entirely around Mr. Haste: whether or not he would be at home; whether – if he was – I could expect a civil interview, or must prepare myself for abuse and recrimination; and whether, in the latter case, I should respond by abjectly apologizing (which might mollify him, but might equally only enrage him further; for the sorrier I seemed, the more reason I should be giving him for supposing he had been deeply wronged), or alternatively by adopting an air of mild surprise that he should make so great a fuss about so small a matter.

In the event – how pitiful our belief that we can foresee the future, and our attempts to prepare for it! – Mr. Haste's behaviour proved of almost no consequence to me whatever, and the most important outcome of my visit had nothing to do with him at all.

He was, indeed, at home, and (perhaps in anticipation of my return) had even made the small concession of greasing the knocker, so that I was able to rouse him without having to press-gang a passer-by into helping me. I heard him clattering down the stairs, and then charging through the hall so furiously that I feared he must be in a very paroxysm of rage, and unable to defer even for a moment the opportunity of venting it. If he was, however, it was plain that I was not its object; for he started, as if he were surprised to see me, and then immediately glanced up and down the street, clearly looking for someone else. And not, I fancy, the bailiffs this time – for his expression was not surly and defiant, as it had been before, but rather eager and impatient.

'I am sorry I could not come sooner,' I said. 'It took me longer than I'd expected to finish. There was so much of interest and your father wrote so well.'

If I had hoped this explanation would please him, I was disappointed; for he merely nodded and grunted, mechanically reaching out his hands for the books even as his eyes continued to search the street. His fingers, I saw, were stained with ink, and there were two or three little blots on his shirt.

'I hope you will accept another ten shillings, by way of compensation,' I said.

He nodded again, and extended his palm, still gazing past me.

It was as I rummaged in my reticule that something at the corner of my vision caught my attention. It was nothing more than a triangle of split and splintered floorboard, dully illuminated by the afternoon light; but it suddenly rekindled a powerful and unexpected memory. This was the bare hallway of my dream; and for a brief vivid moment I again saw it not as the way to Haste's attic but as the entrance to a mica-spangled subterranean grotto where, I knew, I should find the secret of Turner's paintings.

'What is below here?' I asked, handing him a half-sovereign.

'Hm?'

'A basement? A cellar?'

He nodded distractedly.

I gazed down into the cramped area. The windows were grey and opaque with dirt, and one of the panes was broken, and had been roughly reinforced with a board. A tangle of almost leafless ivy spread up the walls, insinuating itself so aggressively into every gap and fissure that the bricks were starting to buckle and crack, and you could already half-see them as the ruin that they were destined to become in fifty or a hundred or two hundred years.

I was conscious of rapid footsteps behind me, and then a breathless voice calling 'I'm sorry. Sorry. Sorry. Sorry.' I turned and saw a plump man, as bald as Haste himself, hurrying towards us, clutching a carpet-bag filled to overflowing with papers. Haste admitted him, and then closed the door without another word to me, or a glance in my direction.

But I did not feel affronted – I was too elated for that. For I suddenly thought I had understood what it was that had been nagging me about *The Bay of Baiae*.

I had instructed the cabman to wait, thinking I might need to make to a quick escape; and now I told him to take me as fast as possible to Marlborough House. It was a nightmare journey – I could not remember what time the exhibition closed, and feared I should arrive too late to see the picture today; yet every time we seemed to break free of the traffic and pick up speed, we shook to a standstill again after only a few moments, and remained there for what felt like an ever-longer eternity. As we approached Trafalgar Square, the tangle of omnibuses and carriages and horses became so knotted and impenetrable that I decided it would be quicker to walk; and, having paid my fare, I got out and set off into the *mêlée*.

I was in luck. Fighting the great tide of humanity one moment, being swept along by a counter-current the next, I found myself in less than ten minutes at the end of Pall Mall. The gallery was still open, the painting where I remembered it. And when – after a good deal of gentle shouldering and 'excuse me'ing – I had breached the wall of people before it and could see it plain, I knew in an instant that I had been right.

It was so obvious, indeed, that I marvelled that I had not grasped it before. *The Bay of Baiae* is not one picture, but two. On my first visit here, I had been struck by how out of place the figures of Apollo and the Sibyl had seemed – as if they had been transposed from another scene altogether; and seeing them again now, I realized that that is exactly what had happened. For Turner portrays *them* at the start of their story, when the Sibyl, still young and beautiful, has been granted her wish, and is sifting the grains of sand in her hand, and counting the years of life she is to have; but the landscape, with its half-hidden serpent, and broken columns, and skull-like arches, shows the inevitable end: the destruction and decay to which she must eventually come.

A letter from Walter when I got home. Why has he not heard from me? I cannot write to him now.

Friday

No matter it is late. I am like a general, who, flushed with success, feels he must press on to final victory before his fortune changes.

First: Mr. Padmore. Thank God! – he is still alive, and well, and in possession of his wits – or, at least, he was until three hours ago. And more than that – has told me more than I could have possibly hoped.

From the name, I had imagined Oliver Buildings to be a dingy, stinking tenement; but in fact it turns out to be a group of single-storey alms-houses, built in red brick in the gothic style, and arranged around three sides of a grassy square, with a wrought-iron gate and a railed fence on the fourth.

My heart was beating so hard as I knocked at number 1 that I could feel it in my throat, and feared I should have difficulty in speaking normally; but there was something so soothing and reassuring about the answering 'Come in!' that I at once began to relax. It was, I know, irrational: there was no guarantee that the speaker was Mr. Padmore, for if he had died, another resident might have been given his place; and yet from those two words I felt certain that it *was* him, and that we were destined to be friends.

I entered, and found myself in a neat room, running the whole depth of the little house, that seemed to serve as parlour, kitchen and library all at once. The fire was a kind of open range, with a small oven to one side of it, and a deep grate so crammed with glowing coals that the atmosphere was as oppressive as a hot-house. To the left of it was a bookcase, and to the right a dresser lined with stout red-and-gilt china that glowed prettily in the light from the back window. A slender-legged table covered in a clean white cloth stood in the centre of the room. It was spread with cups and a sugar-bowl and a pile of papers – among which I recognized my letter. Around it was an odd assortment of oak and walnut chairs. In one of them – a heavy, old-fashioned piece with brawny arms and splayed feet, that looked as if it had been designed to accommodate the greedy squire from a Fielding novel – sat a very old man so thin that he occupied barely half the seat. He had clearly been expecting me, for he immediately said:

'Miss Halcombe?'

He tried to get up, but having pulled himself to a half-sitting position he could go no further. He looked so uncomfortable, with his head poked forward and his hands clutching the scrolled ends of the chair arms, that I immediately begged him to sit down again; and he at once subsided with a grateful smile.

'The spirit is willing,' he said. 'But the joints now – they're the sticking-point.' He held out his hand. 'How'd you do?'

'How do you do?' His fingers were as light and fleshless as a bird's claw, as if nature, resolved to waste nothing on a body so close to the grave, had reduced everything to its barest function.

'I am very glad to see you,' he said. He pulled a clean red hand-kerchief from his pocket and held it towards me. 'Would you be so good as to place this in the window by the door?'

'Of course,' I said, trying to sound as if this were the most nat-ural thing in the world, and exactly what I should have expected. But he must have seen my perplexity; for as I took it he said:

274

'It is our *billet* for tea.'

I hung it on the casement latch, where it drooped unimpressively like a limp flag; but the effect seemed to satisfy him, for he nodded and said:

'Thank you. Will you sit down?'

I took a chair next to him, and at once nearly cried out; for now that I saw him steadily I realized that he was not merely old – he was unimaginably, impossibly ancient. I should have noticed it before, save for the trouble which – presumably in my honour – he had taken with his appearance. His well-cut, brass-buttoned blue coat suggested a much younger man, until you saw how his body had shrunk away from it, leaving great empty folds about his chest and shoulders. His sparse hair, as fine and lustrous as spun silver, had been skilfully trained across the top of his head to disguise the freckled scalp beneath. Most striking of all were the discreet dabs of rouge on his cheeks, which I confess I found quite shocking – until I saw the sweetness in his eyes, and realized that what had prompted him to adorn himself in this way was not vanity, but a gracious desire to look as agreeable as possible within his limited means. (A cynic might argue that the two motives are the same; but the object of vanity, surely, is to inspire admiration? – while his, plainly, was merely to give pleasure to a guest.)

I was prepared for a long preamble of pleasantries and idle reminiscences, such as is generally necessary with old people who live alone; but, as if to confirm my good opinion of him, he at once said:

'My memory's well enough, ma'am, at least for the old days; but I tire easy now, I fear – very easy. So don't stand on ceremony – just ask what you will.' He laughed. 'Else by the time we get to the meat, you'll find I'm asleep.'

'Very well, then. I was wondering if you could tell me about Covent Garden? When you were a young man?'

'Covent Garden – oh, well, now! Just imagine – a boy no more than eighteen – seen nothing of the world but Hampshire and Margate – suddenly whisked to London, and taken to the greatest theatre in the land, and given the *entrée* of the house. All the great names of the day. Charles Bannister. Mrs. Gibbs.' He shook his head, still marvelling at his good fortune. 'I was giddy. Miss

275

Halcombe. The smell of it! Even now – mix me a bit of sawdust and a bit of paint, and the fumes of a lamp or two – not gas, mind, it must be the old oil, warm and smoky – and I can't quell a flutter down here.' He pointed to his stomach, and chuckled.

I hadn't, of course, meant the theatre, but rather the area in which it stood; but I felt I could not say so now without seeming rude.

'Did you live nearby?' I asked.

'I was with my brother at first, in Holborn. But then I had rooms of my own, in Maiden Lane.'

'Indeed?' I said, trying to keep the excitement from my voice. 'And who did you have for neighbours?'

'Well, now.' His eyes narrowed with the effort of recollection. 'Downstairs we had a German musician, what was his name? – Herr, Herr . . . I forget – and a man who made flutes, and Potter the bone-doctor, and – Schussel, that was it, Herr Schussel, lived with an Irish woman, she wasn't his wife, Mrs. Malone . . .'

'And what of the rest of the street?' I said.

'Oh, we were a pretty mixed company, taken all in all. Actors and actresses; a plasterer; a poet; an architect; two or three tavern-keepers; a coach-maker; shopkeepers; fair . . . fair' – he hesitated, and the rouge on his cheeks was reinforced by a tinge of natural colour – 'fair Cyprians, if you take my meaning?'

'Women of . . . ?'

He nodded. 'There was a deal of those.'

'And do you recall any of the shops?'

He took a deep breath, and then let out an unsteady sigh.

'Miss Halcombe,' he said, lightening his words with an indulgent smile. 'I feel I am being made to play "Twenty Questions", and cannot guess the thought in your mind. I pray you, for your own sake – be plain with me.'

And I was. For the first few seconds I hesitated and stumbled; but I soon heard myself talking about Turner and Walter and my own research with an ease and directness that startled me – for I had not spoken so freely to *anyone* since the day of our visit to Sandycombe Lodge, and could not conceive why I suddenly felt able to be candid with *him*. And I still cannot account for it now, save that I was drawn on by the interest and sympathy in his face – and perhaps by the knowledge that a crippled old man in a Hammersmith alms-house would be unlikely to betray me.

I had just finished when a short, thickset woman suddenly entered without knocking. She wore a grey dress and a crimped bonnet, and carried a white apron, which she started to tie about her waist even as she leant against the door to close it.

'Betty,' said Mr. Padmore fondly. He looked at me, and pointed to the handkerchief in the window. 'Whenever we hoist the signal, Betty takes pity on us. Betty' – turning back to her – 'this is Miss Halcombe. Miss Halcombe, Mrs. Chambers.'

'How do you do?' she said briskly, extending her hand. She was about seventy, with a heart-shaped face that might once have been very striking, but now looked weatherbeaten and neglected – as if, once her beauty had started to fade, she no longer thought it worth the trouble of tending. There was no trace either of insolence or deference in her manner, from which I deduced that she was not a servant; and yet if she had been a member of Mr. Padmore's family, surely that is how he would have introduced her?

'I live over there,' she said, as if by way of explanation, pointing out of the window.

'Ah.'

She must have seen my puzzlement; for she went on:

'With the women.' She took a kettle from the hearth, and filled it from an enamelled water-jug. 'You learn to care for one another in a company.'

'A company?' I said.

She nodded, and set the kettle to boil on the fire.

'Do you mean, then, that everyone here is an actor or an actress?' I said, half-laughing with surprise, and with an odd kind of delight at the idea.

'*Was*,' she said. 'We are all *decayed*.' She began to laugh, and after a moment Mr. Padmore joined in.

'Or so the Theatrical Benevolent Society tell us,' she said, reaching down a tea caddy from the mantelpiece.

Mr. Padmore seemed so absorbed in watching her preparations that I feared I had lost him; but, just as I was about to try to nudge him back to our conversation, he said:

'No, I have not forgotten.' He closed his eyes, and collected his thoughts in silence for a few moments. Then he looked at me again and said:

'You are in luck; for I remember the barber's shop quite distinctly.'

I gave a little yelp of triumph – I could not help it – which surprised even myself, and startled Mrs. Chambers so much that she almost dropped the teapot; but Mr. Padmore merely smiled and nodded.

'Yes, indeed,' he went on. 'Several of the older men went to Turner, or engaged Turner to come to them; and I thought I could do worse than go there myself. So I took my wigs to him, until I noticed the young whips were no longer wearing them; and then I grew my hair, and took *that* to him instead.' He shook his head. 'I wish I had the power of painting myself, Miss Halcombe, so I could show it to you. There was a long low window on the street, full of grinning dummies in bob and cauliflower wigs; but you couldn't go in that way – you entered by a side-door in the court – the name's gone, I fear . . .'

'Hand Court?'

'Yes, that was it.' He shut his eyes again, and began tracing an invisible plan with his hand. 'A narrow hall – stairs up and down – the shop in a dark little room to the left. Rows of blue bottles against the wall – a table here, with towels, and razors, and a bowl – a spiral machine there, for frizzing, I suppose – and all about powder-puffs, and crimping-irons, and braiding-pins, and leather rolls for making curls, and heaven knows what. And the *smell*. Scorched hair. Soap. Pomade.' His nostrils twitched, trying to recapture some long-lost fragrance. 'And *powder*. Yes.' He opened his eyes suddenly. 'Do you know the smell of wig-powder, Miss Halcombe?'

I shook my head.

'Not unpleasant. Sneezy. And there always seemed to be the most tremendous noise, at least when I was there. As much inside as out. Water boiling. Tongs clacking.' He laughed. '*Tongues* clacking. Oh, yes, a deal of tongues.'

'Was Mr. Turner very garrulous, then?'

He inclined his head, and scratched the lobe of his ear, as if it might stimulate thought or memory. After a moment he said:

'Do you know, I can't recall? But *someone* must have been; for there was always talk. Or so it seems, at any rate, when I think back to it now.' He smiled wonderingly, like a traveller who has paused in his journey to look behind him, and is amazed to see how far he has come. 'We did not want for subjects – the colonists in America, the *sans-culottes* in France. Or for men of consequence to discuss 'em.' He leaned a little towards me, as if confiding a secret. 'I once saw a portly-looking gentleman coming out, with the whitest wig I ever set eyes on; and Mr. Barrington, who was with me, said he was the Prince of Wales' private chaplain.'

'Really?' I said; for it is hard to imagine so exalted a person today going to a dingy establishment in Maiden Lane (or at least one where he does not fear to be recognized) and being obliged to rub shoulders there with impoverished actors and tradesmen.

Mr. Padmore nodded solemnly. 'And Dr. Monro, who was the King's –'

'Mad-doctor!' I cried, remembering Mrs. Bennett.

He nodded and beamed – not, I think, with admiration at my knowledge, but rather with satisfaction at the discovery that his world had not yet entirely vanished, and that a man who had been famous in his time was still remembered in mine.

'Did you know', I said, 'that he was one of Turner's first patrons?'

He shook his head. 'But I'm not surprised to hear it; for he was known as a collector, as I recall, and as something of an artist himself. And he must have seen the boy's drawings at the shop, for old Mr. Turner used to pin them up in the window and around the door, and sell them for two or three shillings apiece. He was also, did you know –?'

But at that moment Mrs. Chambers set the tea before us, and he stopped talking, and watched appreciatively as she poured.

'There, now,' she said, when she was done. 'It was a pleasure to meet you, Miss Halcombe.' She collected the handkerchief from the window and handed it to me. 'Perhaps you'd be good enough to show this again when you leave, and I shall know to come and tidy up.'

'Bless you, Betty,' murmured Mr. Padmore, as she left. 'She is so . . . she is so . . .' And then, quite suddenly, his eyelids fluttered and drooped, and his head dropped forward.

'You were saying . . .' I began loudly; but he did not stir.

The thought that sleep might succeed where death had not, and deprive me at the last of some vital piece of information, reduced me to a kind of panic, and without pausing to consider I leapt up and tapped him on the shoulder. It was enough, thank

God. He twitched, and opened his eyes, and looked up at me. For an instant he did not seem to know who I was; but then he said:

'Ah, Miss Halcombe, Miss Halcombe, forgive me. Were we progressing?'

'Indeed,' I said, feeling the tears start in my eyes.

He laughed apologetically. 'I grow foolish, I fear. I entirely forget where . . .'

'Dr. Monro.'

'Oh, yes, yes. He was a great connoisseur –'

'Yes,' I said, impatience getting the better of me. 'But you were about to tell me something else about him.'

'Was I?' He frowned thoughtfully. 'Ah! He tended the King during his –?'

'I know that!' I tried to soften the effect by laughing, but he seemed somewhat taken aback, and sank into perplexed silence.

I vowed I should not interrupt him again. And I was rewarded, for after a few seconds he said:

'The Hospital?'

'What Hospital?'

'I must have mentioned that. Or perhaps I assumed you knew? The *Bethlem* Hospital.'

'What of it?'

'Why, Dr. Monro worked there. He was director, or physician, or some such.'

I knew his words had some great significance – I knew they closed a circle I had thought destined to remain incomplete – but I was too busy writing them down to see their full implications. At length, Mr. Padmore himself saved me the trouble; for after gazing out of the window for half a minute or so, he said falteringly, as if he had only just grasped it himself:

'And do you know, that was a strange coincidence; for Mrs. Turner herself went mad, I believe, and ended up under his care.'

My mouth was dry with excitement, and I forced myself to take a sip of tea before asking:

'Do you remember her at all?'

'Barely. I think perhaps she was kept out of sight; for by all accounts she had an ungovernable temper, and might have troubled the customers. I do recall . . . I do recall . . .' He paused and grimaced, visibly struggling to retrieve the fragments of something that had happened almost seventy years ago. At length he nodded, as if he were finally satisfied that he had got them in order, and said:

'The family, I think, lived mostly in the cellar or basement. And I do recall one day hearing the most blood-curdling screams and howls coming from downstairs. Mr. Turner was setting my curls, or something like – he was a spry, cheerful little fellow, always bouncing about on his toes, like a sparrow; and at first he just laughed and tried to make light of it. But then the boy came rushing up, white as death, and ran into the street; and Turner made some excuse, and went down to soothe her.'

'When was this?'

He shrugged, as much with his eyebrows as with his shoulders. ''Eighty-nine. 'Ninety. 'Ninety-one. I don't think I ever saw or heard anything of her again. But a year or two later Turner did tell me his son had taken a painting-room at the other end of the court, and I remember thinking it must have been to get away from the mother.' He paused, and sighed. 'Oh! but Bethlen Hospital, Miss Halcombe. That wasn't kind. It is more humane now, I believe, but then it was a hell – as I can testify, for I went there once, to see a poor friend of mine, who after hanged himself. In the winter he was shut up like a stalled beast, with a straw mattress to lie on; in the summer he was purged and bled and doused in cold water.' He shook his head, as if that were the only protest he could make. Tears filled his eyes, and his voice broke as he went on: 'Our Saviour cast out demons, but not by bleeding or half-drowning the wretches they tormented.'

'I'm sorry,' I said. 'I did not mean to distress you.'

He shook his head again, and started to weep silently.

'Let us talk of something else,' I said. 'The theatre. Lacy Meesden.'

He nodded; but then, as suddenly as before, his eyes closed, and his chin sank to his chest; and all at once the agitation left his face, and he became so still that – save for his breathing – you might have supposed that he had finally crossed the almost imperceptible boundary separating him from death.

I did not try to rouse him again. I set the handkerchief in the window, and left.

*

281

I wrestled with myself all the way back to Kensington. Should I, or shouldn't I? It was late – I was tired – I had done enough for one day. And yet my curiosity would not be quieted. In the end, just before we turned into Brompton Grove, I stopped the cab, and told the driver to take me to Maiden Lane.

I repented of my decision the moment we entered the street. It had started to rain, and the wheels bumped over mounds of rotting leaves which had washed down from the market, filling the air – I could smell it even through the closed windows – with the stench of putrefaction. Crowds of blank-faced children stared in as we passed. Two middle-aged drunkards, their eyes as dull and slithery as oysters, leered and pointed from the steps of the Cider Cellar tavern. Realizing how vulnerable I should be if I got out, I hastily reduced the scale of my ambitions, and told myself that perhaps it would be enough if I saw the shop from the cab.

But since I knew from Walter that it was no longer a barber's, my only hope of picking it out was to discover which of the dark little alleys leading off the street was Hand Court – and this, try as I might, I could not do: for some were unmarked, and the names of the others so worn and covered in soot that I could not read them from so far away. When we reached the end, therefore, I told the driver to turn round, and to stop outside a pawnbroker's shop I had noticed as we passed, which I thought I might safely enter (for while my apparent motives might be discreditable, they would at least be easily understood, and not open me to unwanted attentions), and where I could expect a civil answer.

No sooner had I closed the door behind me than a girl of thirteen or fourteen appeared from the back of the shop. She had large brown eyes, and a pale pretty face that was already hardening into calculation and suspicion. She looked at me unsmilingly, saying nothing.

'I wonder', I said, 'if you could tell me where Hand Court is?'

She jerked her thumb towards a narrow arch on the other side of the street.

'Thank you,' I said.

'You want to see old Jenny?' she said, as I reached the door again. 'I'll take you for a tanner.'

'No, thank you,' I said (for the thought of leaving this twilight world and plunging into the evil-smelling darkness of the court filled me with horror). 'But here's sixpence for your trouble.'

She took the money without a word, and scowled at me as I left, as if she feared I had somehow got the better of her, and duped her into parting with something at less than its true value.

I asked the driver to wait a minute or two more, and crossed the street, pulling my cloak about me to protect myself as best I could from the fine penetrating rain. The entrance to the court was a plain classical arch with a heavy keystone; and through the iron gate barring it I could see huddles of people talking in the dull lamplight glow from doors and windows. I had no trouble identifying which had been the barber's shop – for had not Mr. Padmore said it was to the left of the hall, which meant it must have been the building on the left-hand side of the gateway? – but the 'long low' window of his description had long since disappeared, and been replaced by a tall modern double sash extending the full width of the house.

But what caught my attention was what lay below it. For there, at right-angles to a grating set into the pavement, was an elliptical basement window, covered with a prison-like iron grille.

The echoes were unmistakable.

Sandycombe Lodge.

The Bay of Baiae.

Thursday
Six days – almost a week – since I last opened this journal. Six days in a darkened room, with Mrs. Davidson almost always at my bedside. Six days of chattering teeth, and a thirst that would not be satisfied, and delirious dreams – of which I can remember almost nothing, save that for some reason I felt horrified by the thinness of my own sheet, which I experienced not only as a chill against the skin, but also as a sick numbness in my mouth, and as a kind of warped moral quality, as if it were the work of the devil.

I should not have gone to Maiden Lane. That is what Dr. Hampson says. To get wet in such an insanitary place, when I was already tired from days of reading and writing and staying up half the night, was little short of madness. The fever could

283

well have proved fatal. I must think myself lucky, and treat it as a salutary warning.

I try to do as he says, and thank God with a grateful heart. Too often, though, I think of it as a week lost, and of how easily I might have avoided losing it, rather than as a life gained.

But at least today I was finally able to send a note to Walter. I excused myself from recounting all my adventures, on the grounds that I am still too weak to write at length. Which is, indeed, true enough; but I cannot deny that I am also aware of a certain reluctance in myself to tell him everything, though I am at a loss to explain it. Am I just being petty-minded and mean-spirited, or will I be more forthcoming once I am confident about my own conclusions?

Tuesday

On Sunday I worked for two hours – yesterday four – today six. Dr. Hampson would not approve, but I must note down my thoughts while they are still in my mind.

There will always be mysteries about Turner. And yet I feel I have come closer to the truth than I could have possibly hoped only a month ago.

What follows is no more than conjecture; but does it not make sense of what we know?

His first memories of the world were of a dark basement, and of a wild, uncontrollable woman who terrified him. She could not give him the love and comfort that any child must crave from his mother – and yet he was powerless before her, and could not escape.

Any wonder, then, that he seems to have had a lifelong horror of intimacy? Or that in later life he painted women not as living individuals, with all the wondrous beauty and variety that he found in landscape, but rather as pale, inert objects – corpses, or dolls, or the dummies he remembered seeing in his father's window, which had no power to hurt him?

Any wonder, too, that basements and cellars and caverns were always especially sinister for him (think how all those stories of dragons and monsters in caves must have struck his childish mind!), and associated in his work with menace and ruin? Perhaps that is why, when he came to design his own house, he effectively hid the basement out of sight, so excluding its troubling presence from the light-filled rooms where he lived and worked (Is this what Walter saw when we went to Sandycombe Lodge? Did it make him suppose that Turner was trying to conceal some shameful secret, rather than the painful memory of his own childhood?)

To the same cause, I think, we may ascribe the beginnings of Turner's taste for mystery and elusiveness. To be at home, as a boy – or in any place where his whereabouts were definitely known by his mother – was to risk, at any moment, having his fragile world invaded and destroyed by a hurricane. Hence his early decision to move to the other end of Hand Court, and then – when he could – to Harley Street. Hence his insistence on privacy, and his anger at being disturbed. Hence his travels, perhaps, and his reputation for reclusiveness, and his flitting back and forth between two or three places, often without letting even those closest to him know exactly where he was.

What now of the pictures? Does what I have learned help me to say anything more about them?

I think it does. For might not the genesis of all those storms and shipwrecks and avalanches lie in his mother's madness? (Is it even possible to see, perhaps, in those bleeding suns and dripping sea-monsters, a tortured reflection of her eventual fate?)

The tempests he could not subdue at home he sought to portray – and so to master – in his paintings. This may seem fanciful; and yet is it not a very natural human impulse?

At the same time, paint gave him mastery of another world: a glorious, sun-filled Eden where, for a while, he could take refuge. But 'in the midst of life, we are in death'. Is that not the meaning of The Bay of Baiae, and all those other ruin-infested landscapes? Flee and work and hide as you may, sooner or later the outbursts of a disordered mind and a violent nature, or merely the ineluctable progress of Time and decay, will find you out and destroy you.

We know he had friends – men and women who were able to take him as they found him, and offer him some of the domestic comfort and security he could not find in his own home. These people aroused in him what were perhaps his strongest human emotions – feelings of gratitude and affection so intense that in many cases (Amelia Bennett's father; Walter Fawkes; Lord Egremont) they seem to have been undiminished even by death itself.

But what of his family?

His *art* provided his family – a substitute for the human family which (aside from his father) he never had as a child, and never acquired as an adult. Did not Amelia Bennett say he spoke of his pictures as his 'children', and mourned them when they were gone? Did not Caro Bibby use the same image, in her description of his gallery? Might it not have been the intensity of his parental feelings that drove him to treat the unfortunate engraver, Farrant, with such uncharacteristic harshness? – for any mother may become a tyrant when she feels her young are threatened. Even gentle Laura, I am certain, would kill, if she had to, to protect Florrie and little Walter.

The idea holds, I think, when we turn to the Royal Academy. Surely his concern for its affairs and traditions, and the deep (if eccentric) seriousness with which he took his obligations as a teacher there, suggest that he felt bound to it by ties far stronger than mere self-interest – as if it were his fellow-practitioners, rather than his parents and uncles and cousins, who constituted the body which most profoundly defined him, and which commanded his most abiding loyalty?

We know that – whether or not he liked them, and whether or not he admired their work – he refused to criticize other artists, and so inflict on them the pain he had suffered himself. Such heroic restraint – which must have been immensely hard to maintain in the gossipy, back-biting, hothouse atmosphere of the Academy – is surely consistent with the idea that he viewed them more as relations (the tiresome aunt we loathe, but must nonetheless tolerate for the sake of family unity) than as professional rivals?

To whom do we leave our possessions? To our families.

Did not Sir Charles say that Turner's will left his 'children' to the nation, and his fortune to provide for his 'brother' artists in distress?

Such despair. Such loneliness. Such bitterness. Such devotion. Such meanness. Such generosity.

Such hope that he might at length be understood.

To take such a man, at the end of his days, and by patience and kindness and devotion to overcome his suspicion, and penetrate the dark thickets that have grown up about his heart, and free the love imprisoned there – that is no mean achievement.

Poor Turner.

His poor mother.

Good Mrs. Booth.

Wednesday

An idle morning. Tired from yesterday.

This afternoon Elizabeth Eastlake called, to ask after my health. My mind was still full of Turner; and so eager was I to put my conclusions to the test that I thoughtlessly started to tell her about them over tea. By the time I realized how foolish I was being, it was too late to stop; and I blundered on, desperately hoping I could still somehow avoid the trap that I had created for myself.

But no sooner had I finished than she drew me into it. Giving no indication of whether or not she agreed with what I had said, she asked:

'These are your views, or your brother's?'

'Both of ours,' I said, having already decided that this was the lesser of two evils. 'But predominantly his, naturally.'

In reality, of course, Walter has not even heard them yet and – as I am only too uncomfortably aware – may well disown them when he has. But the only alternative would have been to claim them entirely as my own, and so risk suggesting that the book's central conception – if he *does* accept them – is more mine than his, which would be a devastating blow to his pride.

I am not sure, even so, that she believed me; for she searched my face intently, and there was a caustic edge in her voice as she said:

'Well, he *has* certainly made great progress since we last spoke. Remarkable to think that it came merely from sitting in Cumberland, and reflecting. Something in the air, perhaps.' She smiled. 'At all events, please give him my congratulations, and tell him this is exactly what I had hoped for. Perhaps you and he would care to come to dinner with us next week, and discuss his ideas further?'

It cannot be helped – we must go, and he must make a good impression; or Lady Eastlake will lose confidence in him, and the whole undertaking will be jeopardized at precisely the moment we begin to make headway.

As soon as she had gone, I settled down and wrote to him, saying he must come back.

A small but disquieting epilogue. Davidson had taken the letter to the post, and I was heeding Dr. Hampson's advice by taking a rest after my exertions, when I heard the doorbell ring. It seemed late for someone to be calling, but I got up and readied myself to receive a visitor. After a minute or two Mrs. Davidson came in, and began making up the fire.

'Who was that at the door just now?' I said.

'A woman, miss.'

I waited for her to go on, but she merely busied herself making a good deal of unnecessary racket with the poker. At length I said:

'What kind of woman?'

She hesitated, and swallowed noisily. 'Not what you'd call respectable, miss. And nervous.'

'What did she want?'

'She wanted to see Mr. Hartright,' she said, so quietly I could scarcely hear her.

'Why?'

'She would not say, miss.' She turned, and her eyes briefly met mine, as if she hoped I would see the disapproval in them, and so spare her the necessity of putting it into words. 'Except to Mr. Hartright.'

'Is she still there?' I said, moving towards the door. 'Let me see her.'

'I sent her away, miss. I did not think you should be disturbed.'

But I am disturbed. I cannot help it. Six months ago I should have assumed she *was* simply some poor wretch Walter had helped, and thought no more about it. But now . . .

But it is no use dwelling on it. We must get this book finished, and out of the way – and pray that we can do so without causing lasting damage to our own lives.

Book Three

XLIV

Memorandum of a letter from Walter Hartright to
Mr. Elijah Nisbet, 1st December, 185–

1. May remember we met when locomotive broke down near
Leeds.
2. Very kindly suggested might call to see your Turners.
3. Shall be passing through Birmingham *en route* to London next
week. May I accept invitation then?

XLV

Letter from Walter Hartright to Marian Halcombe,
1st December, 185–

Limmeridge,
Friday

My dear Marian,

You are a marvel! To have made such astonishing progress, in
less than two months!

Unfortunately, I shall not be able to return in time for the
proposed dinner on Monday. I realize this may place you in a
difficult situation, and I am sorry for it; but since I had not heard
from you for so long (please do not take this as a criticism – I
can quite see that it would have been impossible to write, when
you have been so occupied), I naturally had no idea of what, if
anything, you had discovered, and no inkling that you might
have made plans involving me. I have, in consequence, been
pursuing my own independent research, which I fear obliges
me to stop in Birmingham on my way back to town. Would it be
possible, do you think, to postpone our engagement with the
Eastlakes for a few days?

With love from your devoted brother,
Walter

XLVI

Letter from Walter Hartright to Laura Hartright, 4th December, 185–

Heaven knows where,
Monday

My dearest love,

See! I am being as good as my word! – though with some difficulty, I must confess – the train lurches from side to side like a
ship at sea – can only put pen to paper in half-second when it is
equidistant between the two. But now or never – for when we
arrive at Willenhall (shortly) must go directly to the inn, and
thence to Mr. Nisbet's. So please forgive brief note. More tomorrow, I promise.

Meanwhile – don't be anxious about me. I am well. I have forgotten nothing. I love you.

Walter

XLVII

From the journal of Walter Hartright, 4th December, 185–

The rest can wait for my letter, but this, I know, would upset her.

When he came in from seeing the poor fellow, Nisbet was
clearly shocked – his face pale beneath the smudges of soot, his
left hand grasping his right wrist, as if for support. He looked out
of the window at the vision of hell beyond; and then steadied
himself, and shrugged, and turned back towards me.

'The price of Progress,' he said. 'Everything has its price.' He
nodded, as if this catechism had restored his faith. 'Turner knew
that. Now, will you take a glass of wine, Mr. Hartright?'

XLVIII

Letter from Walter Hartright to Laura Hartright,
5th December, 185–

A little past Rugby,
Tuesday

My dearest love,

The North-Western Railway, thank God, is kinder to correspondents than the Birmingham and Derby. My writing-box stays on my knee (most of the time) of its own volition; the pen makes only occasional unauthorized forays across the paper; and my elbow even has the luxury of unimpeded movement, thanks to the seat next to mine being empty. All in all, in fact, aside from the cold, I'm almost as comfortable as I should be in my study at home. So here, at last, is a proper letter.

I had always supposed that the name 'Black Country' was a kind of poetical exaggeration, but it turns out to be as bald and literal a description as 'Canal Street' or 'Station Road'. The ground is black with coal and cinders – the air with smoke – the very trees and blades of grass are black with soot, with just a flash of green here and there to remind you of their former state, like an old bright handkerchief glimpsed unexpectedly amidst the drabness of a workhouse. Mr. Nisbet, it transpires, is an iron-master; and while his house – a nightmare confection of gothic spires and Tudor windows, standing not half a mile from his works – is barely ten years old, it is already so caked with dust that you can only tell by the close-mesh pattern of the mortar that it is built of brick rather than stone.

The door was opened by a middle-aged woman, who led me into a large octagonal hall. The walls were bare, save only for a few sombre portraits, and a picture of Nisbet and his family or the monumental chimney-breast. In the centre of the room was a huge table that might have been intended for King Arthur and his knights, but otherwise it was sparingly furnished, with a few seats set against the sides, and three wing-chairs arranged in a semi-circle in front of the fire blazing in the great stone hearth. A smoky light filtered down from a ring of small windows in the tower above, giving the place a kind of airy solemnity, like the interior of a church.

'I'll tell the master you're here,' said the woman.

But she had not gone three paces before Nisbet himself entered, talking animatedly to another man who – from his heavy boots, and coal-stained brown suit – I took to be his agent. Nisbet was red-faced, and repeatedly shook a sheaf of papers in his hand for emphasis; while his companion listened gravely, head bowed, occasionally nodding, and all the time casting his eyes about the room, like an animal searching for some means of escape. In due course, they fell on me, and settled there; whereupon Nisbet paused, and glanced towards me to see what he was looking at.

'Ah, Mr. Hartright,' he said. 'I shall be with you directly.' He turned back to the man in the brown suit. 'Tell him to think of his wife, Harkness,' he said. 'Tell him to ask her opinion. He must understand – they must all understand – I will not have it.'

Harkness flushed, and stared at his feet. I thought for a moment he was going to protest; but at length he nodded abruptly, and started towards the front door at such a pace that the woman had to scuttle behind him to keep up.

'Now then,' said Nisbet, giving my hand a perfunctory shake. 'How are you?' He did not meet my gaze, but merely looked about the hall, as if making an inventory of its contents. After a few seconds he sat down before the fire, indicating with a casual wave that I should do the same. 'We'll do well enough in here for the time being, I think,' he said. 'My father-in-law's dozing in the library, and I don't want to disturb him.'

His tone was pleasant enough, but there was no hint of apology, and he did not even pretend to consult my wishes, but simply assumed I should fall in with his. I was conscious, too, that he was looking at me in an odd way, staring at my legs and hands and at the back of my chair, with as little embarrassment as a farmer examining a horse he has been offered for sale. At length he sat back, with a faint air of puzzlement, and said:

'So, did you work it up?'

'I beg your pardon?'

'The locomotive?'

'The loco–?' I began. And then I recalled the circumstances of our last meeting, and realized that he must be talking about my drawing of the broken railway engine.

'No,' I said, without pausing to think. 'I've been engaged in other things.'

'Yes?' he said impatiently. His eyes started to search the area round my chair again.

And all at once I knew: he was looking for a portfolio. He had assumed I was a professional artist, and I had not corrected him; and now he supposed that I had come here to try to sell him something. Hence his off-hand manner towards me – a manner which I had last experienced, it suddenly struck me, as a young man, when applying for the post of a drawing-master, and which implied that while I was something more than a trades-man, I was certainly less than a guest.

How to explain the truth, without embarrassment to us both? Matter-of-factly, making nothing of it? Humorously, with an easy laugh at such a foolish misunderstanding? I was still trying to decide when he went on:

'Anything in the same vein? Engines? Machines?'

'No,' I said. 'Not at the moment.'

'Have you then nothing to show me?'

I shook my head. 'I simply came to see your Turners, since you were kind enough to invite me.'

I had not meant to sound reproachful, but perhaps I did; for he at once said:

'Oh, of course! of course!' He nodded and smiled. 'Forgive me if I mistook your purpose, but men in your line of business seldom lose an opportunity to advertise their wares, I find.'

Perhaps, even now, I should have told him what my *real* purpose was, but having just disavowed one ulterior motive I felt I could not very easily admit to another; so I merely laughed, and said:

'Even Turner?'

'I knew him only as an old man,' he replied. 'When he had no need to play the salesman. But even then he liked his money.' He frowned, and thrust out his lower lip, as if making some nice judgement, or recollecting some disagreeable memory. 'If truth be told, he was something of a miser.'

'Indeed?' I said – as innocently, I like to think, as if the idea were entirely new to me.

He nodded. 'He'd never part with a penny unless he had to,

or spend sixpence to save a shilling. The –' He stopped himself, reluctantly, I thought. 'But there. You don't want to hear about the man. You want to see the pictures.'

'No, please,' I said. 'He is something of a hero of mine.'

He went on immediately, like a machine that needs only the smallest nudge to set it in motion again.

'Well, the gallery in Queen Anne Street was a sight to behold. I have workmen keep their houses in better repair.' He shook his head incredulously. 'I was passing once when it came on to rain, and I thought I'd take shelter inside; but when I got upstairs it was so wet I had to keep my umbrella up. Water coming through the broken skylights – water in puddles on the floor – water streaming down the pictures. The wall-covering – some kind of red fabric – was coming off in handfuls. There was a painting of some great classical scene – Carthage, I think it was – and when I got close I saw the sky was all cracked like breaking ice, and in some places it was peeling away altogether. Another canvas was being used as a kind of door, covering a hole in the window, through which the cats would come and go.'

'Cats!'

'Oh, yes, they were everywhere. The place stank of them. They belonged to the housekeeper – a hag of a woman, to give you nightmares.'

'What, Mrs. Booth, you mean?'

'No, Danby, her name was. Hannah Danby.' He mimed wrapping a bandage about his head. 'Her face was so disfigured she had to keep it covered.'

It was all I could do not to laugh at such a relentless catalogue of gothic detail; but he seemed deadly serious as he went on:

'The cats, I suppose, were the only creatures who could tolerate her company. And she rewarded them by letting them walk and sleep where they pleased, and sharpen their claws on the picture-frames, and harry visitors. While I was standing there one of them jumped without warning on my neck, making me drop my umbrella in surprise – and suddenly four or five more appeared, attracted by the noise, and began pressing themselves about my legs.'

He must at last have noticed my efforts to keep a straight face, for he smiled in response, and said: 'And if it wasn't the cats it'd be Turner himself, creeping out of his studio and taking you unawares.'

He chuckled, which I took as a licence finally to laugh myself; and we both guffawed, egging each other on, until we had half-forgotten the original cause of our merriment. After thirty seconds or so, however, he stopped abruptly and said:

'But I shouldn't make fun of him. I wouldn't have lived as he did – but then I couldn't have painted as he did, either. And for all his oddities, he was a pleasure to do business with. Always absolutely straight – you'd agree a price, or a date, and he'd stick to it without fail.' He paused, and pondered a moment, and then acknowledged some new thought by raising his finger. 'I'll tell you something else. He was the only painter I ever met who could talk intelligently about *my* world. The uses of different kinds of coal for smelting. The design of a new pump-engine. He was always fascinated by those kinds of subjects. He had an unshakeable belief in the industrial progress of our nation. As you'll see in –'

He suddenly stopped, and cocked his head. For a moment I could not imagine what had disturbed him. And then I heard it myself: a hubbub of cries and shouts and clanking metal, some way off but impossible to ignore, like the clamour of an approaching army.

Nisbet drew in his breath sharply, and jumped to his feet. 'Excuse me,' he said, barely audibly; and started to leave at a run. But after a few steps he made a visible effort to master himself, and slowed to a walk.

'Come on,' he said, turning to me with a grim smile. 'Dad must be awake now anyway.'

He led me out of the hall and into a square room at the back of the house. It was plainly meant as a library; but it felt more like a small museum or gallery, for half the shelves were taken up not with books but with architectural and mechanical models, and there were pictures covering every scrap of wall. An elderly man in high boots and a plum-coloured riding coat sat before the fire, with the wide-eyed look of someone who has been startled awake.

'What is it?' he asked Nisbet.

Nisbet shook his head brusquely, and strode to the window. The curtains had already been drawn, but he threw them open again, and looked out.

Do you recall the picture of Pandemonium in my father's copy of *Paradise Lost*? If not, find it in my study; for it will give you some idea of the scene that now confronted us. My immediate thought was that the earth itself must be on fire; for, beyond a line of bare trees at the end of the garden, I could at first see nothing but flames, and plumes of black smoke, and some heavier, yellowish vapour that curled this way and that across the ground, as if it were too lethargic to rise into the air. As my eyes grew more accustomed to the dusk, however, I could make out huge black mounds, as big as hills; and the silhouettes of tall chimneys, and engines with great wheels for winding up the coal, and clusters of sheds and cottages and stables – all strewn about as if they had been placed there with as little thought for order or beauty as pins stuck in a pin-cushion.

At the centre were three or four raging furnaces, surrounded by a tangle of tramways lined with laden trucks – which were probably carrying nothing more fearful than blocks of limestone, but might, from their appearance, have been conveying the souls of the damned to hell (an impression accentuated by the rhythmic thump of the engines, which sounded as solemn and ominous as a death march). As we watched, men seemed to be running towards them from every direction – yelling, dropping tools and buckets and gesticulating as they went – and gathering in an ever-bigger knot about something, or someone, on the ground.

I heard Nisbet mutter, under his breath, 'Damn!'

'Is it another accident?' said the old man. He was still in his chair, twisting his head towards us, as if he was too frightened to see the truth for himself.

'Looks like it,' said Nisbet, flatly.

'Oh, Eli!' said the old man, shaking his head. He looked very pale. A strand of thin white hair fell into his eyes, but he did not try to remove it.

Nisbet looked down at his hands, flexing the fingers abstractedly; and then turned to me with a brittle smile and said, with a creditable attempt at normality:

'You'll see, Mr. Hartright, that I've not done a great deal for authors and booksellers.' He waved towards the half-empty shelves, and then to the paintings crowded between them. 'But your fraternity has no reason to complain of me.'

Looking around, I saw that there were perhaps thirty pictures altogether – oils and watercolours, prints and drawings, in almost every conceivable size and shape and manner. The only principle linking them seemed to be their subject matter: every one of them showed a machine, or an industrial process.

'You see my taste,' said Nisbet, trying to sound humorous. 'It's the taste of a man with an interest in two railways and a shipping company.'

'Eli,' said the old man, before I had time to reply. 'Should you not go out there?'

'I'm not going to faffle about like a woman,' said Nisbet quietly. He narrowed his eyes, and looked out of the window again. 'There's a bridge-stocker there. There's a manager. There's Harkness. They know where to find me if I'm wanted.' He returned to me, and, touching my elbow, moved me towards a picture over the fireplace. 'There you are. There's a Turner for you.'

It was a large marine scene: a turbulent grey sea, churned up by the wind, with an embattled steamer struggling against the storm. Everything was extraordinarily imprecise, even by Turner's standards – the waves no more than a few thick, ridged swirls laid on a brilliant white ground – the ship a fuzzy black blur, of which the most clearly defined feature was the torrent of smoke streaming from its funnel. And yet the effect was somehow so vivid that you could feel the lurch of the deck under your feet, and the sting of the spray on your face, and smell the hot sour reek of coal-smoke, and hear the wheels thrashing and the engine throbbing in your ears.

'What do you think?' asked Nisbet.

'It's very fine.'

'Is that an honest opinion?'

'Yes,' I said, somewhat taken aback by his bluntness.

'Then you must fight the whole neighbourhood. Including my father-in-law.' He turned to the old man. 'This is Mr. Hartright, Dad. Mr. Hartright, Sam Bligh.'

'How d'ye do?' said the old man. His hand trembled as it took mine.

'Mr. Hartright's an artist, Dad,' said Nisbet. He pointed towards the Turner. 'Tell him what you think of that.'

Mr. Bligh attempted a smile. 'It's all froth and splutter,' he said, like a child encouraged to repeat some amusing remark before visitors.

'And you'd as soon . . .?' prompted Nisbet.

'I'd as soon sit in the laundry, and watch the bubbles on the copper.'

'There,' said Nisbet, laughing. 'That is what I must contend with. And his daughter's no better. She thinks –'

But I never discovered what Mrs. Nisbet thought; for at that moment the man in the brown suit entered without knocking. He was out of breath; his hair was wet and tousled, his red face blotched with dirt; and there were scorch-marks on his sleeves.

'What is it?' snapped Nisbet.

Harkness glanced covertly at me. 'I think you should come, sir,' he said softly.

'What *is* it?' roared Nisbet. He was white and shaking, and spat out the words so furiously that he had to wipe the spittle from his mouth with the back of his hand.

I struggled to hold my tongue; for poor Harkness had clearly been through some terrible ordeal, and Nisbet's behaviour seemed akin to the Roman tyrant's monstrous practice of killing the bearer of bad news. But Harkness himself appeared quite unmoved by it – as if, having bolted the doors and put up the shutters to protect himself against some great catastrophe, he was not now going to be intimidated by a mere show of temper.

'Well, sir,' he said, drawing himself up and looking his employer calmly in the eye, 'I told him what you said. And *he* said, he was a free man, and if you wouldn't have him there's others as would. And he stormed off.'

'Is that all?' said Nisbet, his eyes lightening, like a condemned man who had suddenly glimpsed the possibility of reprieve.

Harkness shook his head. 'There was a barrow by the filling-hole, barring his way. He couldn't see it clearly, what with the dark, and him drunk. I suppose he must have thought it was full, for he seized it with all his might, to throw it clear. But it was empty, and gave way too easily, and the force of his own movement sent him into the furnace.'

'Oh!' whimpered the old man, turning away, and pressing his fingers anguishedly against his brow. Nisbet's gaze did not waver; but his face paled and seemed to tighten, as if some unwelcome presence had insinuated itself beneath the skin.

'Two of the other men pulled him out again, almost at once,' said Harkness. 'But he's bad. Very bad.'

'Has the doctor been called?' asked Nisbet.

'Of course,' said Harkness. 'But . . .' He dropped his eyes, finally admitting defeat.

'And what of his wife?'

Harkness shook his head.

'Give her five pounds, and tell her I shall see her tomorrow,' said Nisbet, shooing him towards the door. He started to follow, then stopped and turned to his father-in-law. 'Dad, look after Mr. Hartright, will you?'

But, try as he might, poor Mr. Bligh had not the heart to play the host; and after enquiring where I had come from, and where I was going, and making two or three feeble observations about the pictures, he gave up altogether, and gravitated towards the window, where he stood with his hands clasped behind him like an elderly Bonaparte surveying the field of Waterloo. Secretly relieved (for I did not feel much like making conversation myself), I lingered at the other end of the room, and tried to divert myself by looking at the remaining Turners. They were, undeniably, magnificent – the interior of a foundry, a dazzling contrast of dark and light; and a fiery railway train appearing through a curtain of smoke and rain – but even their drama seemed somehow flat and lifeless compared with the tragedy unfolding outside, and after a few minutes I found myself standing next to Mr. Bligh and looking out.

The commotion by the furnace seemed to have died down – the swarming throng had stabilized, and ordered itself into a long line, as dark and immobile as a wall. As we watched, it slowly parted, and four minuscule doll-figures emerged carrying what looked like an untidy heap of blankets on a gate. They moved at a regular, deliberate plod, without urgency, towards a horse and cart standing at the edge of the crowd. Clearly, the victim was either out of danger – or, as I feared, beyond help.

I looked away, but a pitying moan from my companion made me turn back immediately. It took me a moment to make out what he had seen: a woman, running and stumbling across the rough ground, who hurled herself down before the makeshift litter, forcing the men to stop. She hugged herself – then threw her arms in the air – then rose again, and did a strange distraught dance, stamping her feet, and flinging her head from side to side. We, of course, saw this only as a kind of dumbshow, for she was too far away for us to hear the accompanying wails and sobs – which (contrary to what you might suppose) actually made matters worse; for it heightened our feelings of powerlessness and detachment, while underscoring the awful solitariness of human suffering.

But enough – I do not want to distress you, or myself. Suffice it to say that I felt I must avert my eyes, and yet knew that I must not. For a moment I was paralysed by this *impasse*; and then I suddenly saw that by *drawing* the dreadful scene before me I might somehow make it tolerable. I could not be of material aid to my fellow creatures; but it seemed to me that by bearing witness to their agony I might – in some tiny, mysterious way – share it with them, and give it meaning.

My notebook was too small to be serviceable; so I turned to Mr. Bligh and said:

'Do you think I might have some paper?'

I think he, too, was glad to be doing something; for he at once went to the writing table in the corner, and brought me five or six sheets – and then, seeing the speed at which I worked, went back for more, and stood attentively at my side, like the assistant who turns the pages for a musician, in case I should run out again.

I do not know how long I stood there, or how many drawings I made, but I was still labouring when Nisbet at length returned. He seemed shaken, but after a minute or two recovered somewhat, and, recalling his duties as a host, offered me a glass of wine – which I was only too happy to accept. As he handed it to me, his eye fell on my drawings, and he picked them up, and silently scrutinized them for a minute or more. At length he returned them to me, saying:

'Send me a sketch of the finished painting when you've done it. The locomotive, too. I might be interested in buying.'

Heavens! We are almost there My love to you always, and to the children.

Walter

XLIX

Letter from Laura Hartright to Walter Hartright, 7th December, 185–

Limmeridge,
Thursday

My darling boy,

Your letter quite frightened me. Such a horrible accident! That unfortunate man, and his poor wife! I scarce dare think about it.

Please, my darling, be careful.

Your loving wife,

Laura

L

From the journal of Walter Hartright, 10th December, 185–

Prepared the canvas today. Reviewed my drawings. Worked up two or three preliminary watercolour sketches.

But I cannot settle to it.

There is something disturbing about being back in London. Sometimes – most of the time – I still feel myself. But occasionally I seem to glimpse the world through the eyes of someone else entirely – someone I supposed I had cast off for ever, but who appears to have been waiting for me here, and to have gained strength from my return.

Perhaps I am just suffering from wounded pride. For I feel I have been ordered here like a performing animal, to go through my tricks before Lady Eastlake, and parrot Marian's views as my own.

I must force myself back to the picture. If I can but make *that* work, I shall truly know more of Turner than they ever could.

LI

From the journal of Marian Halcombe,
13th December, 185–

Thank God. My prayers have been answered.

How easily do we lose our sense of proportion. Twelve hours ago, had I been able to foresee the circumstances in which I write this, I should have been utterly distraught. But my heart, instead, is full of gratitude – for what I have lost, I can see, is as nothing compared with what I *thought* I had lost, and has been miraculously restored to me.

Now. I must be as good as my word, and set to work.

From this side of the abyss, it is hard to recognize the woman arriving in Fitzroy Square last night as myself. I observe her coldly (as a stranger would) being helped by Walter from the cab, and glancing expectantly towards the front door, and then devoting a full minute or more to smoothing her dress, settling her bonnet, and hoisting her skirts above the mire, as if a wrinkle or a stray hair or a muddy hem were the worst disaster that could befall her. There is something contemptible about such a petty display; and yet it moves me to pity, too – for I know what she in her blithe ignorance cannot even suspect: that her vanity is about to get its come-uppance.

I had supposed, from Elizabeth Eastlake's invitation, that we should be dining with them alone; and I was therefore surprised to find, on entering the drawing room, that there were two other people already there. At first glance you might have supposed them to be an elderly couple; for both were grey-haired, and they shared a kind of plain, no-nonsense demeanour that marked them out as members of the high-minded, rather than the fashionable, portion of the Eastlakes' acquaintance. Something in the way they stood, however – she talking animatedly, he stooping formally towards her, with the intent expression of someone who has difficulty hearing, but does not want to admit it – suggested that they were people who did not know each other well; and as they separated and turned towards us, preparing to be introduced, I saw that in fact she was a full twenty years older than he was. Her lively spirits, plainly, had enabled her to preserve the manner and appearance of a much younger woman; while he (by some strange law of complementarity), though still only in his fifties, seemed to be hurrying into old age as fast as his stiff limbs could carry him.

'Mrs. Somerville,' said Sir Charles. 'I don't believe you know Miss Halcombe?'

But of course I knew her name (it is impossible to spend ten minutes in the company of a blue-stocking like Elizabeth Eastlake without hearing it mentioned at least once), and was keenly conscious, as we shook hands, that it was a great honour to meet her. And yet I could not but feel a spasm of disappointment, too, that the Eastlakes had not considered us worthy of an evening by ourselves, but had merely seen us as one more social duty that must somehow be accommodated with all the others.

'Mrs. Somerville, Mr. Hartright,' murmured Sir Charles. 'Miss Halcombe, Mr. Cussons.'

The next moment, disappointment gave way to outright dismay; for, turning towards Mr. Cussons, I glimpsed out of the corner of my eye another couple arriving. I could not, for an instant, believe my first impression of them; but a second glance confirmed it:

Mr. and Mrs. Kingsett.

I don't know if Mr. Cussons noticed my shocked expression, for it was impossible to deduce anything from *his* face whatsoever. He was a tall, distinguished-looking man, with a high domed forehead fringed with feathery hair, and the alert unsmiling eyes of a bird of prey.

'How do you do?' I said.

'How do you do?'

I was painfully aware of the approaching Kingsetts, and frantically wondering how I should conduct myself towards them; but realizing I could not break free from Mr. Cussons just yet without seeming rude, I lingered beside him, waiting for him to go on. He, however, seemed to feel under no compulsion to say anything more, and merely continued to stare – intently enough, but entirely without interest, so that you felt he wasn't really looking at you at all, but merely keeping watch in case a mouse or a rabbit suddenly broke cover, and scuttled across the carpet. After fifteen seconds I felt I had earned my release – for surely a man must exercise his claim to a woman's attention by speaking within a reasonable time, or else forfeit it altogether? – and, muttering an excuse, bowed to the inevitable, and turned to Lydia Kingsett.

I knew at once that matters had not improved since our last meeting. She looked more worn than ever, and her hands were deathly cold as she clasped mine – although she was, I think, genuinely glad to see me, and even managed a little smile as she said, with pathetic eagerness:

'Miss Halcombe, Miss Halcombe, I'm so . . .'

But then she caught her husband's eye, and stopped abruptly.

'You're what?' I said, laughing, and trying to encourage her with a tone of easy familiarity. 'Come on, tell me.'

She mumbled, shook her head, stared at the floor. I touched her wrist, and bent close to her, as you would to a troubled child.

'Hmm?'

But still she said nothing. In the awkward lull that followed, I felt her husband's gaze upon me, as palpable as heat from a fire, challenging me to turn and discover what had silenced her. I tried to resist, but after a few seconds curiosity got the better of me.

It was disagreeable enough just to see him again, like suddenly smelling some foul half-forgotten odour; but what made it worse was the leering way he was looking at me, which was so frankly insulting that I thought one of the other gentlemen must see it, and come to my defence. Mr. Cussons, however, was still surveying the world from his perch, and Walter and Sir Charles were engaged in conversations of their own; so I had no alternative but to try to deter Kingsett myself, by scowling imperiously at him.

For answer – to my amazement – he protruded his tongue an inch or two from his lips, and ran a finger unhurriedly along it, in a gesture of unmistakable depravity – all the while eyeing me with a shameless smirk. If anyone else observed it (and I pray they did not), they could not but have seen it as evidence of some past intimacy between us; and, although I knew myself to be guiltless, I could not help blushing furiously.

I was, for a moment, transfixed; and then, as I saw him starting to advance towards me, preparing to extend the hand he had just licked, I turned tail and fled. Elizabeth Eastlake was, mercifully, talking to Walter, and I felt no compunction in intruding on them and drawing her to one side.

'Please,' I said. 'Do not ask Mr. Kingsett to take me down to dinner.'

'Why?' she said, surprised, with a surreptitious glance in his direction.

'I'll tell you later,' I whispered urgently – for already he had changed course, and was bearing down on us again.

She nodded, and – woman of the world that she is – promptly turned to intercept Kingsett, allowing me to make my escape. I don't know what she said to him, but when, a few minutes later, she whispered something to Sir Charles, and then slipped quietly from the room (presumably to change the place-names on the dinner table) he made no attempt to approach me again.

I stood in a corner, silently congratulating myself. This was not what I had imagined it would be – it might turn out to be a dull and worthless evening – but at least I had averted the worst harm it could do me.

Or so I thought.

I was spared Mr. Kingsett; but in all other respects the dinner turned out every bit as gruesome as I had feared. The price I paid for my deliverance was to be seated next to Mr. Cussons, who for most of the meal showed as little inclination to talk as he had done before it. I did try to breach the silence with a trivial comment or two, but they were as futile as pebbles flung against a castle wall; for he seemed to regard human communication as an unnecessary distraction, and merely grunted and glowered at me when I spoke, as though I had interrupted an important business meeting between him and his soup.

Sir Charles sat to my right, and was pleasant enough; but he was largely taken up with rescuing Mrs. Somerville from Mr. Kingsett, who – under the revised arrangement – was now between her and Lady Eastlake. Kingsett was almost as silent as Mr. Cussons – though not, in his case, out of aloofness, but rather from a kind of sulky petulance. The conversation, when it caught fire at all, was about photography, and prisms, and optical effects; and knowing himself unqualified to contribute to it, it was, quite literally above his head; for Elizabeth Eastlake is at least three inches taller than he is), he did his best to extinguish it altogether. Whenever either of his neighbours said anything, he would sigh, and shift in his chair, and clatter his knife and fork; or gaze absently into space; or appear to listen, with a foolish, put-upon little smile that said: *It's all nonsense, and I won't be taken in by it.* But his principal occupation, which he resumed whenever there was a lull, was terrorizing his wife – staring at her with such undisguised loathing and contempt that the poor woman was almost paralysed with misery and fear, and could only respond to Walter's repeated attempts to draw her out with a few stammered words. I cannot deny being relieved that it was she, and not I, who was the object of this relentless persecution; and yet it left me feeling desperately angry and frustrated, too – as if I were being forced to witness some dreadful unequal battle, while being quite powerless to help the victims.

I was also, I own, haunted by another, less worthy thought: how was I going to explain this disaster to Walter? From his easy, cheerful manner you would never have guessed that he felt there was anything wrong, or that he was less than delighted with the company in which he found himself; but once or twice I caught him looking at me curiously down the length of the table, as if to say: *Why did you summon me back to London for* this? To which I could not think of a reply – save to confess candidly that I had over-estimated both Lady Eastlake's enthusiasm for my ideas, and her regard for me personally. Six months ago I might have made such an admission easily enough – indeed, I should have hastened to do so, knowing that he would reassure me, and soothe my bruised *amour propre* – but now the chasm between us seemed to make it impossible.

On only one occasion did the conversation veer in the direction I had hoped. Mrs. Somerville was reminiscing about Italy with Sir Charles when – suddenly observing that no-one had said a word to me for five minutes – she decided to take pity on me.

'Do you know Italy, Miss Halcombe?'

'Not well, I'm afraid.'

'You should, you should. I am obliged to live there, for my husband's health. But I cannot say it is a great sacrifice.'

She laughed, and Sir Charles smiled and nodded in agreement. 'The buildings,' she went on. 'The landscape.' She shook her head, as if such sublime beauty were altogether beyond her powers of description. 'And the quality of the light. Truly remarkable.'

'That, doubtless,' I said, seizing my chance, 'is why Turner was so drawn to it?'

'Oh, indeed, indeed. I discussed it with him often.'

She paused, busying herself with something on her plate; and, before she could go on, Sir Charles said mildly:

'And you, I think, are fond of Italy too, Mr. Cussons?'

Mr. Cussons glared – his eyebrows shot up – his head jerked to one side.

'I beg your pardon?'

'You are fond of Italy?'

Mr. Cussons sat back – looked about him – settled himself on his perch. He had seen his rabbit. He pounced.

'Not fond!' he boomed, in the over-loud voice of the deaf. 'Filthy dirty. Corrupt. Squalid's not the word for it.'

And then he embarked on a seemingly interminable anecdote about how he had been obliged to go to Naples on business (nothing less would have induced him to set foot in the place); how he had acquired there a Botticelli *Virgin and Child*, of whose true value the shifty peasant who sold it to him had not had the faintest conception; and how he intended to leave it to the National Gallery, together with the rest of his collection – the whole to be known as 'The Cussons Bequest'.

This, at least, answered one question that had been perplexing me all evening: why the Eastlakes had invited such a morose and unsociable individual to dinner? But by the time he had finished, Turner had entirely disappeared from view.

Most hostesses, at the end of such a meal, would have either apologized *sotto voce* to the other ladies while they were withdrawing, or else tried brightly to pretend that nothing was amiss. Elizabeth Eastlake did neither; which surprised me (for I felt the ordeal we had passed through demanded some acknowledgement), until I saw that it arose not from thoughtlessness but from delicacy – for both courses, in this instance, would have only further compounded Mrs. Kingsett's anguish: the first by criticizing her husband in front of other people, and the second by requiring her to affect normality and make polite small talk when she was clearly too upset to do so. Instead, Lady Eastlake calmly helped her friend upstairs (even then, Mrs. Kingsett was so close to collapse that she had to clutch the banister rail like an old woman), and settled her in a quiet corner in the boudoir before returning to Mrs. Somerville and myself in the drawing room.

'My poor Marian,' she said. 'This is not at all what you imagined, I'm afraid.'

'Oh, no,' I said, wondering at my own mendacity. 'It's been very pleasant.'

'Don't lie,' she mouthed, tapping me in mock reproach (at which I heard Mrs. Somerville laughing softly at my side). 'Did you bring your notes?'

'Well . . .'

Her eye fell on my reticule; and she must have seen the bulge of my notebook, for she nodded.

'Only because you asked me to . . .' I began.

She pulled a rueful face. 'I know I did.'

'But it doesn't matter. It can . . .'

'I'm so sorry, my dear.' She touched my elbow impulsively, then turned to Mrs. Somerville. 'I'm afraid I shall have to leave you to your own devices.' She glanced discreetly towards Mrs. Kingsett. 'You do understand . . .'

'Of course.'

She nodded gratefully, then started back towards the boudoir, with the quiet purposefulness of a doctor approaching his patient.

'I dare say we shall manage, Miss Halcombe, don't you?' said Mrs. Somerville. She sat on the sofa, and patted the place beside her. 'Come. Please. I fear nowadays I don't hear very well.'

I sat next to her. She smiled conspiratorially.

'Just think what the gentlemen are having to endure,' she said – with a stress on *gentlemen* that clearly implied: *At least we don't have to suffer that.*

I laughed, and sat next to her. Here at last, I thought, was an opportunity to retrieve something from the evening. I was about to raise the subject of Turner again when she spared me the trouble:

'And what, may I ask, do your notes concern?'

I briefly explained.

'The Eastlakes are always so busy,' she said, in the gentle tone of someone trying to excuse a friend's behaviour. 'They try heroically to attend to everything, they really do, but . . .' she shook her head . . . 'but I should be delighted to hear your ideas, if you'd care to tell me.'

And with some trepidation, I took out my notebook.

I began with my (or rather, since I felt I must maintain the fiction that these views were Walter's as well as my own, with 'our') earliest findings; and at first her response was very gratifying. When I spoke of Turner's relations with the Regency art world, and why they might have made him careful about money she nodded approvingly, and murmured, 'Yes, yes, how true.' My delineation of his character – his sensitivity to criticism; his shyness about his odd appearance and uncouth speech – seemed to please her even more; and she clapped her hands with delight when I concluded:

'Small wonder, then, that he shrank from the eyes of the world and was willing that people should think him a miser and a fool if only they would leave him alone.'

'Excellent, Miss Halcombe!' she cried out. 'May I ask – was that your phrase, or your brother's?'

'I beg your pardon?'

'"Shrank from the eyes of the world"?'

'Mine, I think,' I said. 'Though I fear it's an unremarkable enough image.'

'Not at all,' she said. 'Very apt. The watchful eye. The cold eye. The censorious eye.'

Perhaps I looked perplexed; for she smiled, and touched the corner of her own eye, as if to clarify the point. 'That's what he feared. But it's also what fascinated him.'

I only half-saw her meaning; but the ghostly outline of one of Turner's doll-figures suddenly entered my mind, like a bookmark placed in a page that may repay further attention.

'And he was very knowledgeable about it. I have seldom known anyone – besides other scientists – with such a keen interest in optics, and in the theory of light and colour. Or with such a sound grasp of the principles. You'd see him at Rogers', deep –'

'Roger?' I said; and then, before she had time to reply, realized

I had misheard her. 'Oh, you mean *Rogers'*?'

She nodded.

'The banker,' I said, recalling that I had heard Lady Eastlake talk of him more than once.

'I think he would have preferred to be remembered as a poet,' she said, with a wistful smile. 'At all events, we all regularly met at his house. My husband and myself; Herschel, Faraday, Babbage, Tom Moore, Campbell. And Turner could speak to any one of us on our own subjects, and with great authority.'

'Indeed?' I said, astonished; for this seemed entirely at odds with the impression I had gained from Lady Meesden's papers.

She nodded. 'Most of the great men I have known – and Turner was, indisputably, a great man – have possessed the same quality. Which leads me to wonder whether genius is not so much a highly developed aptitude for one thing, but rather a kind of general intellectual capacity, that may be more or less equally applied to any field. Certainly Turner might have been a successful scientist or engineer, had he chosen. Anyway –'

'But what, then, of the people who said he was inarticulate?'

She shrugged. 'He could be hard to understand when he spoke publicly. But not when he was relaxed, and among friends.' She paused, struck by a sudden recollection. 'The only complaints you ever heard then were from dullards, who could not soar to the same heights. I remember once we were at a *conversazione*, and I had been snared by a gentleman who talked of nothing but the funds, and the price of corn. And Turner came up to me, and plucked from his pocket a yellow handkerchief. "Now, Mrs. Somerville," he said' – and here, to my surprise, she dropped into a gruff cockney voice that I took to be a fair imitation of Turner's – '"what d'you say this is?"

'"Why, a handkerchief, of course."

'He put it back in his pocket. "And where is it?"

'"In your coat."

'"And what colour is it?"

'"Yellow."

'"You're sure?"

'Naturally, I was laughing by this point – I had some idea what was in his mind – but I said: "Of course."

'He wagged a finger at me and shook his head. "A conscious-

314

ness of the fallacy of our judgement is one of the most important consequences of the study of nature, which teaches us that no object is seen by us in its true place. And that colours are solely the effects of the action of matter upon light, and that light itself is not a real being."

'Well, needless to say, Miss Halcombe, my dull companion had been shifting from one foot to the other during this performance and rolling his eyes; and now he could contain himself no longer

'"If you don't mind my saying so," he said, "that's absolute gibberish."

'"Really?" said Turner. "Then perhaps you should read Mrs. Somerville's book."'

She laughed, with a complicit glint in her eye, as if I were in on the joke with her and Turner – rather than (as I had shamefully to admit to myself) in the same predicament as the gentleman who talked of funds and the price of corn.

'I'm sorry . . .' I stumbled. 'I –'

'It was a quotation, almost word for word, from *On the Connexion of the Physical Sciences*.'

'I'm afraid I didn't quite understand . . .' I said. 'Could you perhaps explain . . .?'

'I was talking about the constraints of the scientific method,' she replied. 'Which Turner, I think, found disturbing. Despite making light of it.'

'Because . . .? Because . . .?' I said, hoping to tempt her into saying something more before *I* had to.

'Because *thought* – the exercise of reason – will only take us so far,' she said at length. 'And then we reach the limit of its competence. For my part, I am content to leave it to faith – the grace and cohesion of what we *do* know, through mathematics, are enough to convince me of . . . of . . .' she hesitated, carefully formulating the right words . . . 'of the unity and omniscience of the Deity. But Turner, I suspect, didn't have that consolation.'

'He was not a believer?'

'We did not discuss it,' she said shortly. 'But I think he saw the chaos and destruction in Nature before he saw the beauty – or rather I think he saw them together, as expressions of the same awful power. And our incapacity to grasp it, to understand it, was humiliating confirmation of our fundamental impotence.'

'That's very interesting,' I said. And I immediately started to explain my conjectures about Turner's childhood – his mother's madness; his terror of storms, both natural and human – which seemed to accord precisely with what she had just told me. To my surprise and disappointment, however, she regarded me with an expression of growing distaste; and, when I had finished, said:

'Forgive me if I am being old-fashioned, Miss Halcombe, but I think a biographer should confine himself to ascertainable facts, and to the recollections of those who knew his subject.' Her tone was measured, but two little angry spots on her cheeks betrayed her. 'This, it appears to me, is neither; but merely unfounded speculation.'

I was about to try to defend myself; but before I could do so the gentlemen entered.

I am unclear exactly what happened next, and in what order; for this (or so it seems, looking back) is the moment when the waking world suddenly gave way to nightmare, and from now on everything has the jumbled logic of a dream. I recall Mr. Kingsett, very drunk, stumbling on a rug by the fire; I remember Lady Eastlake reappearing from the boudoir, and saying, 'I hope, gentlemen, you're going to entertain us; for we've been a bit sombre'; I remember Mrs. Kingsett standing like a spectre in the doorway behind her.

And then we are all sitting, and one of the gentlemen is saying something about a new American medium called Mrs. Mast, who has been doing a brisk trade among fashionable ladies in London – 'for she doesn't use rapping or table-turning like the others, but talks in the voices of the dead themselves'. Lady Eastlake laughs – 'People are so *gullible*' – but Sir Charles mentions a Mrs. Somebody-or-other who swears she heard her dead son speaking to her. 'What's the harm', he says, 'if it gives her comfort?'

Lady Eastlake snorts.

Mr. Kingsett looks at his wife, and says:

'We could employ Mrs. Mast permanently, my dear, could we not? To communicate with your mother. Might improve your spirits, to hear her complaining about me.'

Then confusion: sharp intakes of breath; Mrs. Kingsett crying; Mr. Kingsett saying she is unwell, and must go home; Walter and me both, simultaneously, offering to go with them (for the thought of their being incarcerated alone in a cab together is unbearable); Mr. Kingsett saying it is quite unnecessary; Lady Eastlake thanking us, and insisting on our behalf.

The street outside: helping Mrs. Kingsett into the Eastlakes' carriage. And then her husband – as if he had not insulted me enough already – suddenly putting his arm about my waist, and saying (why?), *'Please*, Miss Halcombe, we shall do perfectly well by ourselves.'

And then, as I have recovered myself, and put one foot on the step, it happens: a figure appears from nowhere – I am conscious only of a warm, dark bulk too close to me, and the stench of gin and dirty clothes – and there is a tremendous tug on my wrist, and my reticule is gone.

Running footsteps. Two sets of running footsteps. Walter crying 'Stop, thief!', and disappearing after him round the corner of the square.

I wept. I shook. I could not help myself. Elizabeth Eastlake was very kind, and sat up with me, and said I might stay the night; but when Walter had still not returned after an hour, I thanked her and returned to Brompton Grove, thinking I might find him there.

I didn't.

I could not sleep. I sat at my writing table, waiting – as I had on the night of our visit to Sandycombe Lodge – for the sound of his key in the door.

It never came.

I tried not to imagine what might have happened to him, but I could not keep his image from my mind – injured, or murdered, or broken in some dreadful accident; nor the awful reflection that in some way this was my doing.

If only I had been more alert. Taken more care. Never introduced him to Elizabeth Eastlake.

I knew I should distract myself by writing my diary, but I could not do it.

I prayed: *Return him to me, and I will be good. Make normal life possible again, and I will embrace it – joyfully; and never again complain of drudgery, or duty, or the ache of disappointment.*

*

317

A little before dawn I must have drifted off to sleep. I was woken by a sound from the garden. I looked out and saw a light in the window of his studio.

It did not even occur to me it might be an intruder. I ran downstairs, and outside, and flung open the door.

Walter stood before a huge canvas smeared with black and red. He was unshaven, his cheek bruised, his hair tousled, his eyes bloodshot and unnaturally bright. For a moment he seemed not to know me. Then he said quietly:

'You should be asleep.'

'How could I sleep! I didn't know where you were!'

I cried, and took him in my arms. He set down his palette, and stroked my hair like a child's.

'I have your reticule,' he said. 'There. On the table.'

'Never mind that! What happened to you?'

'I got lost, that's all,' he said gently. 'I'll tell you about it later. Now. Please. Go and rest.'

I could not speak what I felt. I left and returned to my room.

LII

From the private notebook of Walter Hartright,
13th December, 185–

I have crossed the bar. Today. 13th December. A little after 1.00 a.m.

We think we are our own masters, but something drives us or draws us to our destiny.

I thought I was pursuing a common thief. I followed him out of the square, down Carburton Street, across Portland Place. What was in my mind? Nothing – save that I was doing what I must do.

And that luck, or God, was on my side. For every time I seemed to have lost the fellow, I saw him again.

We ran the length of Queen Anne Street, and then my quarry (pilot?) vanished into a small dimly lit court at the end. I went after him, but could not immediately see him, and – since there was no way out but the narrow alley by which we had gone in – assumed he must have entered one of the tenements, where I had no chance of finding him. But then I heard an urgent clacking sound, and, looking towards it, was just able to make out his figure in the shadows. He was desperately rattling at a latch, as if he were intending to escape inside but found the door locked. He glanced over his shoulder as I sprang towards him, and turned to face me.

I should have seen the warning in his eyes. They were not frightened, as they should have been, but satisfied – almost triumphant.

But I had not time to heed it. I pushed him roughly against the wall, seized the reticule, and – fearing he might try to snatch it back – thrust it into my pocket.

Then I heard the door opening, and steps, and hoarse, rapid breathing. I tried to turn, but was jostled off balance. Before I could recover myself, someone was tying my hands behind me. And then someone else slipped a hood over my head, and whispered:

'Come along, sir.'

There was a man on either side of me, and a third behind. They edged me back towards the street, rearranging themselves into single file in order to pass through the alley. When we emerged they stopped for a second or two. I heard the stamp and snuffle of a stationary horse, and murmured voices, and a door opening; and then I felt myself being lifted and bundled into a cab.

Only one man, I felt fairly certain, got in with me; but in my present helpless state I could not hope to tackle even one, so as we moved off I forced myself to stay calm, and await a more favourable opportunity to get away. It was not easy, not only because I was naturally confused and disoriented, but also because my pinioned arms prevented me from sitting back in my seat, so making me prey to every lurch and bump in the road. But I determined not to protest – or indeed to speak at all, unless my captor spoke first; for to do so would have been to throw away the only weapon I had.

I think he must have seen things in the same light; for several times I heard him drawing in his breath, or clicking his tongue, as if he were on the point of saying something – but in the event he always appeared to think better of it, and kept his peace. From which I deduced, first, that he was hoping by remaining silent to break my nerve; and, second, that his own nerve was far from steady – both of which only stiffened my resolve.

I thus had ample time to reflect on who he might be, and why he had gone to such lengths to abduct me. The most obvious motive was robbery – but surely he and his friends might easily enough have accomplished that in the little court? I could think of no-one who might have a reason to murder me – and, in any case, for that, too, the cab was a quite unnecessary contrivance. I could only conclude that he had taken me for someone else, and that in due course – if I had not managed to get away first – his mistake would be discovered.

We had been going, I should guess, about ten minutes, when a particularly savage jolt flung me to the floor, knocking my face (for of course I could not put up my hands to protect it), and wrenching my shoulder. At this, my companion's firmness finally deserted him, and he cried out:

'Oh! Are you 'urt, sir?'

Hurt and dazed as I was, I was conscious of a certain exhilaration at having won the battle of wills between us. I did not reply, which made him still more anxious.

''Ere,' he said, helping me back to my seat. His hands were trembling, and his breath was rancid with gin. He laid two fingers against my throat. I felt something hard and sharp protruding between them.

'This 'ere's a spike,' he said. 'You understand?'

I nodded. Perhaps the hood prevented him seeing, for he gave me a small jab and repeated:

'You understand?'

'Yes.'

'Very well, then. Now, I'm going to undo your 'ands, and tie 'em again in front of you, so's you can sit straight. But you tries any dodges, and I swear as you'll get this' – another prick – 'in 'ere. Understand?'

'Yes.'

But for all the bravado of his words, he spoke them with a tremulousness that suggested he was far from confident, and which tempted me, for a moment, to take advantage of my freed hands to try to overpower him. Then I reflected that he could see, and I could not; and that even a drunk and irresolute man might have plucked

320

up the courage to stab me before I had been able to tear off the hood. I therefore decided to bide my time, and meekly let him go about his business – which he conducted with surprising deftness, loosening the rope in a moment, and fixing it again in a moment more, with such assurance that I could only suppose he was, or had been, a sailor. When he had finished, he sat back, and said

'I'm sorry, sir, but there was no other way to make you see 'er.'

His voice was quite different now: sad, and almost gentle.

'See who?'

'My wife, sir. As 'as something to say to you. She called at your 'ouse, but was turned away.'

'My house!' I exclaimed, suddenly seeing a chance to demonstrate that I was not the man he thought. 'And where is that?'

'Brompton Grove, sir. That's what she told me.'

I was dumbfounded. I had no recollection of sending anybody away. And I could not think of any woman who might have sought me out in this manner. The prostitute I had met at the Marston Rooms? True – I had left her abruptly – but not before paying her, so she had no cause for complaint – unless she had been as consumed with lust as I had been, an idea which I immediately saw was absurd. And how, anyway, could she have known where to find me?

Then I remembered the pawnbroker in Maiden Lane. I might unwittingly have left some evidence of my address in the pocket of my coat. But why might she want to see me? And why had she waited so long?

Finally, at a loss for any plausible explanation, and with a growing feeling of alarm, I said:

'Why does your wife want to see me?'

'She'll tell you that 'erself, sir.'

To have pressed him further would have been to betray my fear, so I held my tongue. I did not speak to him again.

I had long since lost any sense of direction; and without my eyes to help me, had to rely on hearing alone for clues as to where we were going. Once or twice I made out the steady beat and splash of steam-boats, from which I knew we were close to the river; but none of the other sounds I could pick out – the rumble of passing vehicles, a drunken bellow, a barking dog – was specific enough to tell me anything useful, save that we were still in the city. I was, however, conscious of a gradual change in the *quality* of what I heard; for everything – even the thrum of our own wheels, and the clatter of the horse's hooves – seemed by degrees to become softer, as if we were being slowly wrapped in a blanket, and so cut off from everything around us. At the same time, the air grew stiller and colder, numbing my bound hands, and making me long for the gloves and the little flask of brandy in my pocket (though I would not demean myself by asking for them) – from all of which I guessed it must be snowing.

And I was right; for when we at length arrived – after heaven knows how long – I could smell it through the fabric of the hood, and feel it underfoot when my captor helped me down. I heard him mutter something to the driver, and then he took my arm and began to guide me across some rough cobbles, taking care to prevent me slipping. Behind us I heard the cab driving away, at which my heart sank – for with it went any hope that this might only be a short interview, and that they intended I should be taken home immediately afterwards.

We appeared to be approaching a public house, for from just ahead of us came the unmistakable sound of singing and raucous laughter; but we stopped before we reached it, and I heard the secretive patter of fingers knocking on a window, and then, after a few seconds, a door opening. A woman's voice, so quiet that I could barely make out the words, said:

'This the man?'

There was no reply that I could hear, but a moment later I was led into an uncarpeted hall, and thence into what seemed to be a parlour, for I could feel the welcome warmth of a fire. I heard the rustle of the woman's dress as she came towards me, and then felt her fingers quickly squeeze mine – like a strange token of the handshake she would have given me if my wrists had not been bound, and this were merely a normal social occasion.

'I'm the lady of the house,' she said. She spoke softly, with the trace of an Irish accent; and I knew at once that I had never met her before in my life. 'Mary'll do for a name, if you want one. Please sit down.'

The man helped me into a comfortable chair close to the fire. I heard her settle herself opposite me.

'I'm sorry I can't take that off,' she said. 'But I cannot run the risk.'

I wanted to ask: *Of what?* – but I felt that to enter into conversation would be to suggest that I accepted this situation, and so somehow make it appear legitimate.

'But I'll not be making excuses,' she continued. 'You're wanting something, and I'm going to help you to it.' She paused a moment, for effect: 'The truth about Turner, am I right?'

I still said nothing. She sighed, like a mother cajoling a sulky child – which instantly made me feel a little like one. Finally she repeated:

'Am I *right*?'

'What of it?' I said, as carelessly as I could.

'I knew him,' she said. 'He used to come here.'

'And what is "here"?'

'A lodging-house,' she replied simply. 'Most of the boarders is sailors' women.'

'And he presented himself as "Turner"?' I said, instantly suspicious – for anyone who had really known him would have realized that such recklessness was quite out of character.

'No. I'd no idea who he was, till the fellow who keeps the Ship and Bladebone saw him one day by chance, and said "You'll never guess who that is."'

'And how did *he* know?'

'Turner was his landlord.'

'What! You mean he *owned* the place?' I cried; although – as I privately had to admit to myself – the very improbability of the idea gave it an odd sort of credibility, for it was the kind of detail no-one would think to invent.

'That's what Mr. Hodgson told me,' she said defensively.

At that moment – as if the mention of a public house had put the notion in his head – the man suddenly mumbled:

'I think I'll just slip next door for a drop of somethin' short.'

He had the shifty, off-hand manner of someone who fears he may be stopped, and thus hopes to escape attention; but the woman was having none of it. As he started to edge away, she said, lethally quiet:

'What, are you still afeared?'

'Don't a man deserve a drink?' wheedled my captor.

323

'You take another one, you won't be able to stand,' she replied.
'I brought 'im 'ere, didn't I?'

'Afterwards,' she said, relenting slightly.

'Oh, come on!' he said. "E ain't going to cut it now!'

'In a minute. After he's gone upstairs.'

My skin prickled with contradictory emotions: dread, and outrage, and excitement.

'He had his own ways, Turner,' she said. 'His own tastes.'

'What kind of tastes?' I said.

'You'll be seeing one of his women shortly,' she said. 'She'll show you.'

Show, not *tell*. My mouth was dry. I said: 'May I have some water?'

'Upstairs,' she said. 'In just a moment. But first I wants to tell you something about her. About poor Lucy. She's not got a great head on her, and what she has's been all but fuddled away, for she's a terrible one for the crater. That's why we keep her in, and I lay out her money for her, when her sailor-friend sends it; for she'd drink it all else, and then try to make away with herself after. But you can trust her. She won't lie to you. You understand?'

'Yes.'

'Come along, then.'

She went ahead of me, and the man came behind, pushing me out into the hall and up the stairs. When we reached the landing we paused for a moment, and I heard the woman unlocking a door and opening it.

'Now, Lu,' she said gently. 'You know what is expected of you?'

There was no answer, as far as I could tell; but the woman must have been satisfied, for I was promptly thrust forward again. All at once, the light outside the hood seemed brighter. I was conscious of the smell of cheap scent and cheap coals – and then, suddenly, of a shrill squeal, half surprised and half amused, which made me fear for my safety – for there was something uncontrolled, even mad, about it.

'We'll come for you in a little while,' whispered the woman, close to my ear. And then I heard the door closing behind me, and the key being turned again from the outside.

The squealing continued for a few moments, but all the time

subsiding into giggles, like a pot going off the boil, until at length it had become no more than a kind of breathless, bubbling trill. Then I heard – or rather felt – her approaching; smelt the violet cachou on her breath, and the *eau de Cologne* on her skin, and beneath them both, like a half-buried secret, a rank hint of animal heat. She said nothing; but as she touched my icy fingers she winced, and put them to her lips, and rubbed them to restore the circulation, before finally turning her attention to untying them. As she fiddled clumsily with the knots, I could not but reflect that we had never met – never seen each other's faces – never even heard each other speak; and yet that I was closer to her than I have been to any woman save Laura in my adult life.

She at last managed to free my hands, and then quickly plucked the hood from my head. I blinked; for even the light of the gas-lamp was enough to dazzle me after so long in darkness. She seemed to emerge, in consequence, through a kind of fuzzy mist: first a squat, rather full figure in a low-cut blue dress; then a wide, pale face, puffy from drink or tiredness; deep-set blue eyes and a bright red mouth; the thick brown ringlets untidily pinned up behind her head. She had one hand on the bed – which was not the mean object I should have expected, but a four-poster hung with a dirty chintz curtain. She caught me looking at it, and smiled with a quite uncoquettish frankness, and then shook her head and laughed, as if my presence there still bemused her.

'You got anything to drink?' she said. Her speech was low and slurred.

I had, of course; but was unsure whether I should own to it. I seemed churlish to deny her; and yet had not the woman downstairs said she was a drunkard, and must be prevented from tippling? She must correctly have interpreted this hesitation as meaning 'yes'; for she immediately said, 'You 'ave, ain't you?' and began rifling through my pockets with the frantic single-mindedness of a dog digging up a bone. When she plucked out Marian's reticule she held it up for an instant like an exhibit in a court case, laughing 'You're a sly one, ain't you?'; and then flung it to one side and resumed her search. Within a matter of seconds she had found the flask, unscrewed the cap and sucked it dry, running her tongue around the little nozzle to catch any stray drops that might have escaped her.

'Nothing more?' she said, before she had had time to catch her breath again.

'That's enough,' I said, conscious even as I did so of a jarring note of priggishness in my voice.

She looked at me curiously, focusing her eyes with some difficulty.

'What's your name?'

'Did they not tell you?'

She seemed surprised that I should ask, and shook her head emphatically – until it seemed to make her dizzy, and she stopped abruptly.

'Jenkinson,' I said.

She drew in her breath sharply; and then her confused expression slowly cleared.

'Ah, I gets it,' she said. 'You likes the same.'

She picked up the hood and the ropes from where she had dropped them on the floor, and dangled them before me. I could not begin to guess her meaning, and merely stared stupidly back at her.

''Ere you are, then,' she said impatiently. 'Take 'em.'

I did so, and stood holding them helplessly. She turned towards the wall opposite me, where a round looking-glass in a rosewood frame hung above a small chair. Then slowly, without a word, she started to unhook her dress.

I could not move. I thought I should faint. And yet some part of me – the Walter Hartright that the world saw, and that until two months ago I had always supposed myself to be – would still not accept that this was desire, but clung doggedly to the notion that I was there for some perfectly respectable purpose – much as a shipwrecked sailor clings to some pitiful fragment of his smashed boat, in the hope that it will keep him from being swept away. I did not avert my eyes as she let the dress drop to the floor and stepped out of it – I could not; but I tried to persuade myself (God! what madness!) that I was looking simply in order to try to establish her age. From her broad plump hips and thighs, and the slight slackness of the skin on her arms, I guessed between thirty and thirty-five. Though I could barely speak, I said:

'How old were you when Turner came here?'

She did not turn, but her eyes found my reflection in the glass. "Oo?'

'The other Mr. Jenkinson.'

'Oh, must've be twelve or thirteen when 'e first 'ad me. 'E come reg'lar after that.'

'For how long?'

She shrugged. 'Five, six years?'

'And how old are you now?'

She giggled; and then unpinned her hair, and shook it free, so that it tumbled down her back. "Ere, you want to talk, or what?'

I tried to say something.

I could not.

She unlaced her corset and pulled it away, as a sculptor may remove a mould; and then drew her chemise over her head, and laid both on the chair. All she was wearing now was a pair of grubby stockings. She pulled at one of the garters.

'On or off?' When I did not reply she brusquely repeated the gesture. 'Hm?'

'What did . . .? What did *he* . . .?'

'Oh, it were all one to 'im. Weren't my legs as fussed 'im. On or off?'

'Off.'

She bent down and took them off as matter-of-factly as if I had asked her to remove a tea tray.

'There,' she said, flinging them on the chair. As she did so I saw the bounce of her heavy breast, and glimpsed the thicket of darker hair beneath her belly. She appeared entirely unselfconscious, as if she felt no shame in her nakedness, and no pride either.

But to me . . .

To me it was a miracle.

I had never seen a woman undress before.

She threw herself on the bed and lay there, turning her head from side to side, gently rolling her hips so that her legs fell open.

'Come on,' she said.

And then I knew the depth of my own folly. The folly of thinking I might see another life – imagine another life – but not cross the threshold into living it.

The folly of denying my own fate.

327

For I had not chosen this. I had resisted, indeed, as I have been resisting for months. But fate had overruled me, and delivered me here.

No-one I knew had seen me.

This woman did not know my name.

I was free.

She watched me approach, but then, as I drew near, laid an arm across her face. I sat beside her, uncertain what to do.

'Put it on, then,' she said.

She removed her arm, but kept her eyes closed.

'Put it on,' she repeated.

I slipped the hood over her head. She stretched out her arms in a parody of crucifixion, blindly adjusting them until each wrist was lying against one of the bed-posts.

The meaning was plain enough. I tied one hand with the rope. She did not murmur. For the other I used one of her stockings.

I stared at her. She could not stare back. She had no eyes.

There was so much of her. Such an ocean of skin – as still now as cream, and as smooth, save where it was creased and printed with the stamp of her corset.

Not my wife. Not a woman I knew. Just woman.

I took off my clothes slowly, looking at her the whole time. Why hurry? I did not need to entice her, or persuade her, or ask her permission. She could not escape me. She was entirely within my power.

When I entered her she sighed, and yielded up a cry that seemed extorted from her against her will.

And when I had done she shuddered, and whispered:

'You're more of a man than 'e was. You want to do it again? Or you going to untie me?'

I did not sleep when she did. I have never been more awake. I got up and listened at the door. I heard nothing, except a distant noise of snoring. My captor must have drunk too much at the public, and passed out in a stupor.

I went to the window. The cloud had cleared, and there was a moon. I could see a steep roof, with what appeared to be an out-house or shed below it, from which – I thought – I could easily enough reach the ground. The snow lay thick everywhere. It would, I thought, break my fall, and muffle the sound of it.

328

I had no fear. I knew I must trust my fate.

I quietly dressed, put a sovereign on the pillow, and cracked open the casement. It was too small for me to get through fully clothed, so I had to remove my coat and drop it out before me. For a moment it snagged on a broken gutter, but then its own weight freed it and it fell on to the lower roof. And it was as well it did – for when I landed on it, I felt a sharp grazing pain, and found that beneath the snow the whole surface was covered with pieces of broken glass, which had doubtless been put there to stop boys climbing on it. The coat was badly torn, but the reticule and my flask were undamaged, and I sustained no more than a few scratches.

Trust your fate, and no harm will come to you.

I dropped down, and found myself in a little alley behind a row of houses. At the end I could see a line of rickety buildings thrown into silhouette by the moonlight. I made my way towards them, and emerged into a mean street of wharves and taverns and warehouses. I had no idea where I was, or which way I should take; but it seemed slightly lighter and more open towards the left, so I struck out in that direction. And once again fate rewarded me; for after a few minutes I came out in a main road, and almost immediately spied a cab.

The driver hesitated a moment when he saw the state of my clothes, but the sight of my purse soon convinced him.

'What street is that?' I asked him, pointing to the way I had just come.

'New Gravel Lane, sir.'

So I have been in Wapping, where Turner went. I have known the freedom he knew. I have partaken of his power.

LIII

Letter from Laura Hartright to Walter Hartright, 14th December, 185–

Limmeridge,
Thursday

My darling Walter,

You bad boy! Did you not promise you would write every day? Or has dining with Sir Charles Eastlake quite turned your head, and made you forget your poor family altogether!

We are well, save that we miss you so much. Would it were Christmas already – for that will bring us the best present of all.

Your loving wife,
Laura

LIV

From the diary of Marian Halcombe, 14th December, 185–

An odd postscript to yesterday, which I was too tired and upset to note down before I went to bed:

I spent most of the day writing my journal, and resting. About six, having not heard Walter enter the house, I returned to his studio, to ask whether he would be coming in to dinner. I think I took him by surprise; for he was engrossed in writing himself, but stopped as soon as he heard me, and stood before the table, as if he were hiding something from my gaze. He was wilder-eyed and more dishevelled than ever, having plainly neither slept nor changed his clothes since the morning.

'Are you unwell?' I said.

He shook his head. As he did so, the light caught his cheek, and I saw that the bruise there had grown into an ugly swelling.

'Oh, you are! You're injured!' I cried, moving towards him impulsively.

He shook his head again, and put out his hands to keep me from him. Perhaps he was merely being delicate, for he smelt vile, and might have been trying to spare me the stale fishy sweetness that clung to him like a fog, and still lingers in my nose as I write these words; but from the way he flinched, and the

330

coldness in his eyes, it was difficult to avoid the impression that his motive was to protect not me, but himself.

Of course I was hurt. But worse – far worse: I suddenly caught myself calculating the distance between here and the house, and wondering whether Davidson would hear me if I cried out, and come to my aid. I have grown used, these last few months, to feeling I could not completely trust Walter, or guess what was in his mind. But never before have I doubted my own safety with him.

What did I fear he might be capable of doing?

I cannot bring myself to write – to think it, even.

My judgement must have been disordered by anxiety. And lack of sleep. And a night of terrible imaginings.

As I backed away he reached behind him and then moved quickly in front of the painting I had seen that morning. His aim, presumably, was to prevent me from seeing it; but he succeeded only in drawing my attention to it, for it was far too big for him to conceal. It was quite unlike anything I have known Walter attempt before, with none of his customary care and sweetness and faithful attention to detail. The paint seemed to have been flung against the canvas, where it hung in great pools and drips as thick as icicles – as if the artist's job were merely to get it out of the pot, and he had no obligation to do anything with it once it was there. I can only assume he was trying for a Turnerish effect, for there was a jagged red smear in the middle, surrounded by black – but it entirely lacked Turner's lucidity and brilliance. The red wasn't red enough; the black wasn't black enough; they bled into each other around the edges, and suggested no natural object or effect I have ever seen in my life.

But something about it reminded me of another picture. Not the style – not the subject-matter – but the grandiose scale. The *not-quite-rightness* of it.

What was it?

And then I remembered. Poor Haste's huge picture of Lear.

Perhaps Walter saw my reaction; for he snapped: 'It's not finished!' and then, without giving me a chance to reply:

'What do you want?' From the tone of his voice you might have supposed I was a naughty child, who had been told that in no circumstances was Papa to be disturbed.

'I forgot my reticule,' I said hastily – which was true enough.

though I had only that moment thought of it.

He nodded towards the table where it still lay. I picked it up, and knew at once that it was too light.

'Where's my notebook?'

He shrugged. '*I* don't know.'

I pulled it open, and looked inside. Nothing else was missing. I took out my purse. Two sovereigns and some change. Just as I remembered.

'Could it have fallen out?'

He shook his head.

'Are you sure?'

'The thief had the string round his wrist.' He rotated his own wrist impatiently for emphasis. I noticed that it was red and chafed, but knew better now than to ask why. 'And after that it was in my pocket.'

'What about when you took it back from him?'

He shook his head again. 'You must have left it at the East-lakes'.'

'I didn't.'

'You *must* have!' He seemed taken aback by his own vehemence, and made an effort to calm himself before going on, more reasonably:

'It would have been easy enough to forget, wouldn't it? In the circumstances.'

'Perhaps,' I said, moving towards the door; for I could see there was no point in discussing it further. 'I'll write to Elizabeth Eastlake about it.'

And I will. But I still find it difficult to believe that I would have left my notebook there, even in all the confusion – for usually, whether I am thinking consciously of it or not, I am as aware of its whereabouts as I am of my own hand.

Walter did not come in to dinner.

LV

From the private notebook of Walter Hartright,
14th December, 185–

To live as Turner did you need a basement.

I did not think to provide myself with one when I designed the studio. As a result, Marian surprised me today when I was writing, and saw the *Ironworks Accident* before it was ready.

There is not a great deal I can do about the painting, save to deter further visits. But for this notebook there is a simple remedy. I shall go out tomorrow and get a box.

LVI

Letter from Lady Eastlake to Marian Halcombe,
15th December, 185–

7 Fitzroy Square,
Friday

My dear Marian,

Thank you for your note. I am so glad that your brother was able to retrieve your reticule, which has a little restored my faith in Fortune's taste, if not in her morals – for had she deprived you of *that*, after heaping on us all the other disasters of the evening, I should have considered her guilty of vulgar excess and avoided her society altogether. Did the wretch who tried to steal it escape, or was Mr. Hartright able to deliver him to the police?

No sign, I fear, of your notebook. I have made a fleeting search of the drawing room myself, and made enquiries of the servants, without success; but we shall keep looking, and if the fugitive is found will put it securely under lock and key, and return it to you under armed guard.

We must – we will – meet soon, and make good what we so signally failed to do on Tuesday; though it will not now, I am afraid, be until some time after Christmas.

In haste,

Yours very truly,

Eliz. Eastlake

LVII

From the private notebook of Walter Hartright,
15th December, 185–

I am like an engine. Pulled and pushed by so many conflicting pressures I fear the rivets will break, and I shall fly apart.

But if I can hold myself together this will be a great book. Not just the life of an artist, but – for the first time – his soul.

People will ask me how I know.

I shall say nothing.

They will see the answer in my painting. *Chiaroscuro*.

LVIII

Letter from Laura Hartright to Walter Hartright,
16th December, 185–

> *Limmeridge,*
> *Saturday*

My darling Walter,

Still nothing from you. Is something the matter?

I thought things were well between us again, but now I fear they are not.

Please write soon.

Your loving wife,

Laura

LIX

From the private notebook of Walter Hartright,
17th December, 185–

Sunday

A dreadful night. Dreamed of Laura. She was crying. She said: *If that's what you wanted, you had but to ask.*

Another letter from her this morning. Did not open it. Have not opened the last one.

Tried to reassure myself with Nisbet's words: 'Everything has its price. Turner knew that.'

But what if the price is unbearable?

The worst of it is not being able to talk to anyone. This after-noon, in desperation, I called on Travis. He is a man of the world, I think. But his wife said he had gone to the Athenaeum. I was not dressed for the Athenaeum.

Spent the evening working on the *Accident*. It still would not come; and at length I could not bear to look at it any more, and retreated to my room. But I will not be defeated.

If I have learned anything, it is that victory or defeat is all a question of will. Tomorrow I shall return to it, and *force* it to express what is in my mind.

LX

Letter from Laura Hartright to Walter Hartright
18th December, 185–

Limmeridge
Monday

My darling Walter,

Why do you not answer me? I can scarce see the paper for weeping.

Remember my condition.

Please.

Your loving wife,

Laura

LXI

From the private notebook of Walter Hartright,
18th–20th December, 185–

Monday

It is a monster, but I must face it.

Travis appeared about three o'clock. I was doing well enough until then.

'Kate told me you called yesterday,' he said. One raised eye-brow asked: *Why?*

I did not feel I could tell him at once. 'Yes.'

He did not press me, but whistled under his breath, and looked about him at the studio, nodding approvingly. Then his eye fell on the *Accident*. He did not say anything, but gave a knowing smirk that galled me.

'It isn't finished,' I said hotly. I am growing tired of having to explain it.

'No,' he drawled. He did not add: *I can see that*, but he might just as well have done. 'So you are still pursuing Turner?'

'Yes,' I said, wiping my hands, and edging him away from the canvas. 'I am writing his biography.'

'Are you, indeed?' He pursed his lips, and rolled the notion round in his mouth, as a man will savour a wine before pronouncing on its quality. 'What a good idea,' he said at last – in a manner that perfectly conveyed: *Or better, at least, than trying to paint as he did.*

His condescension was insufferable; but I managed to contain my rage, and even to give a fair impression of genial hospitality as I gestured him to a chair, and took one myself.

'And what have you found out?' he said.

'A good deal. Did you, for instance, know that he used to patronize a brothel in Wapping? Where he tied the girls up, and made them hide their faces?'

His response astonished me. I had expected surprise – disbelief – a cry of *Gracious, man! How do you know that?* and then the glorious relief of telling him. Instead, he merely chuckled, and said:

'Oh, yes! – I've heard those stories!'

'You have?'

He nodded and smiled superciliously, like a schoolboy amused at the naïveté of one of his fellows.

'And you do not believe them?'

He shrugged. 'I really don't know. And I don't greatly care.' He took a cigar-case from his pocket and opened it. 'It's not my taste at all. The wilder and freer the better, so far as I'm concerned.' He laughed. 'Smoke?'

'Thank you.'

'It's possible, I suppose. We're all rather strange, aren't we? And Turner was stranger than most.' He lit our cigars, and then meditatively tapped the match until it went out. 'But it's equally possible there are people who want *us* to believe it.'

I almost choked.

'Too strong for you?' he said.

'*Who* would want us to believe it?'

'Oh, I could give you a hundred names. Many of them titled. Most of them powerful.' He shrugged again, as if the point were too obvious to need further elucidation. 'And what else?'

'Wait!' I held up my hand to silence him, while I struggled to order my thoughts. Which was no easy task: for suddenly a whole clamour of doubts and misgivings, which up until now I had successfully kept at bay, breached my defences, and broke in upon my conscious mind.

Had my captors really gone to all that risk and trouble merely in order that I should know the truth? Even the cost of the cab, surely, would have been prohibitive for them?

Was it not far more probable that someone else had paid them to do it?

And then I remembered Farrant. And the man I had met with him, Hargreaves. *There's a value now, to stories about Turner. There's a gentleman as pays good money for them.*

I said:

'Why?'

'Why what?'

'Would they want . . .?'

'Oh, because of the will, of course.'

'Turner's will, you mean?'

'Well, certainly I don't think *mine* would have roused their interest,' he murmured. 'And' – here he looked about her, and smiled languorously – 'forgive me, but I rather doubt whether yours would, either.'

I gritted my teeth. 'And what of it?'

'You don't know?' he said, as if it were the first thing a biographer should have discovered.

'Well, naturally . . .' I began, trying frantically to recall what Marian had told me of her conversation at the Eastlakes 'Naturally, I realize he made things difficult. By being too mean to pay a competent lawyer to draw it up.'

'And who is your source for that?' simpered Travis. 'Sir Charles Eastlake?'

I could have hit him. 'In part,' I said. 'Why? Is he not to be trusted?'

He shrugged. 'He certainly has an interest in promoting that view.' He hesitated; and then, as if he had finally decided he had played with me enough, stuck his cigar between his teeth, and leant forward purposefully.

'Look,' he said, picking up the cigar case. 'Here is Turner's fortune. Houses, money, and so on. Mm?'

I nodded. He took the matchbox in his other hand.

'And here are his pictures. Some unfinished. Some unsold. But also many of his most famous works, which he's painstakingly bought back over the years, often at excessive prices.' He opened the box, and spilled matches on the table. 'See. There are hundreds of them. Thousands, if you include the drawings. Now' – tapping the cigar case – 'this, apart from a few small legacies, he leaves to charity. To build alms-houses for decayed or unsuccessful artists. While these' – sweeping the matches to one side – 'he leaves to the nation. On condition that, within ten years of his death, a "Turner Gallery" is built to house them. Do you follow me?'

'It's an undeniable challenge, for a man of my limited powers. But I think I can keep up.'

I had landed a small blow. He smiled and nodded – and even, if I am not mistaken, blushed slightly.

'But the family – a gaggle of cousins and what-not, whom Turner hadn't seen for years – contest it. First they claim he was mad. When that fails, they take it to Chancery, saying the wording of the will is too unclear to be understood. After three years there's a compromise. The charitable scheme is overturned on a technicality. So the family get this.' He lifted the cigar case. 'And the nation gets these.' He drummed his fingers on the matches, scattering them across the table. 'Only it doesn't want to go to the trouble of fulfilling his condition.'

'Why ever not?'

'Why do you suppose? Money. Only conceive the unspeakable suffering of one of Her Majesty's ministers obliged to stand up in Parliament and propose spending £25,000 on art! But Eastlake's determined to hold on to them nonetheless.'

'I don't see how he can.'

'By resorting to the most bare-faced sophistry. His argument – he actually had the audacity to say this, can you believe it, to an ex-Lord Chancellor! – is that, since the will was overturned, the

National Gallery can keep the collection without having to do anything at all.'

'But surely – it was only because of the will that he got them in the first place!'

'Exactly. As the ex-Lord Chancellor did not hesitate to point out. So Eastlake's in a ticklish situation.'

I nodded. 'But I don't see how blackening Turner's name would help him.'

'Don't you, indeed?' He absently swept the sticks together again. 'Well, now. Just imagine – for a moment – that it's not Turner we're talking about, but the Duke of Wellington. He has made a munificent bequest to the nation, but the government refuses to honour its terms. What would be the result?'

'A public outcry.'

'Yes. Questions in the House. A resignation or two. Articles in *The Times. Disgrace. Stain on the national honour. An Englishman's word* . . .

'Yes,' I said; for it was undeniable. 'Go on.'

'Of course, Turner was only a painter, which any patriotic Englishman knows is a far lesser thing than a soldier. But still – he was, by common consent, our *greatest* painter. So what's poor Eastlake to do? How does he walk the tightrope?'

He gave me a moment to answer; but my mind was in such tumult I could not order my thoughts.

'What view of Turner best serves his purpose?' he prompted. And then I saw it.

'The flawed genius!'

He nodded. 'If not a genius, then why go to the trouble of keeping his collection? But if not flawed, then how can we justify disregarding his will? Sir Charles, after all, as everybody knows, is a gentleman, and would never do anything dishonourable So the fault must lie in *Turner.*'

'The problem, you mean,' I burst out, 'is not *our* meanness, but *his!*'

'Precisely. And not just meanness, either. The man was depraved' – here he dropped for a moment into a melodramatic whisper – 'or even mad. So it's quite legitimate for us to flout his wishes. Indeed, seen aright, it is surely our duty to do so, in the interests of public morality?'

He sounded so cruelly like Sir Charles – had captured so perfectly the gentle melancholy, the tone of pious, more-in-sorrow-than-in-anger pain at the folly of the world – that I could not help laughing. But even as I did so I felt myself starting to fall – as if a wall that I had assumed to be quite solid had suddenly given way before my weight.

'*Ergo*,' said Travis, 'Sir Charles, and his trustees, and the government all have a material interest in what you say in your book. If you present Turner –'

'Yes, yes,' I said.

He sat back with a self-satisfied smile, and a little flourish of the hand: *Voilà*.

I could barely speak. It was impossible to think while he was still there. I sat mute while he told me about Sir William Butteridge's rapture at his swooning damsel; and Lady Emery's commission for a fresco; and the favourable reviews of his work, by which, of course, he sets no store at all – could I imagine anything sillier than being called 'the English Botticelli'? Eventually, having exhausted the catalogue of his triumphs, and drawn nothing from me in return but the occasional nod or 'well done, I'm delighted for you', he gave up, and left.

Since when

Since when I have been a battlefield.

At first it seemed irrefutable. I had allowed myself to be comprehensively duped. Even my own picture testified against me. It seemed to glower down on me, reproaching my foolishness and pride. In my self-loathing, I could not take my eyes from it.

But then, as I hesitated on the brink of complete despair, doubts began to set in. They started with Farrant. I had not naïvely accepted his word: I had tested him, quite ingeniously, and found him honest. I was certain I had not been deceived about that.

And then the prostitute's story: it was unsubstantiated – but quite credible, surely, nonetheless? Did it not square with Hargreaves' claim that Turner had *wallowed in sailors' houses*? Had not Gudgeon said that Turner sometimes used the name 'Jenkinson'? And did not the use of the hood seem fitting for a man so anxious not to be seen, and so incapable of painting others?

And what if someone else *had* encouraged, or even paid, the informants? That did not necessarily make what they had told me untrue.

For two hours or more I debated – struggled – fought with myself. First one side, then the other, gained the upper hand; until at length my mind seemed to have been trampled into mud, and I could make out nothing distinctly in it at all.

But I must know.

Tuesday
This is a monster.

So I wrote yesterday.

But then I had only glimpsed the head. I had not penetrated the darkness, and made out the dreadful bulk of the body.

But which monster is it?

This morning I tried to work on the *Accident*, but could not concentrate. No sooner had I composed a figure, or attempted yet another new technique to make the furnace glow, than some word or phrase of Travis's erupted in my head, and I would suddenly find myself again wrestling with the conundrum he had set me. I knew it was hopeless – that I could not resolve it without further information – and yet I could not leave it alone. Finally I saw that I was simply wasting my time, and, bowing to the inevitable, gave up the pretence of painting altogether, and turned my full attention to Turner.

But what could I do? There was no point in returning to the woman in Wapping (assuming, that is, that I could even find her), or to Farrant. They would not say who, if anyone, had paid them. In any case, if it were someone of Sir Charles's stature, they almost wouldn't know themselves, since it was inconceivable that he would have failed to protect himself by using intermediaries.

What I needed, above all, was an accomplice: someone I could confide in – who would tell me if my doubts and suspicions appeared reasonable – who would help me to form and execute a plan of campaign. The obvious choice, of course, was Marian; and for one lunatic moment it did occur to me that I might tell her everything, and throw myself on her mercy. But a half-second's reflection told me that it was impossible, and that – however painful it may be – I must accept that our easy relations are gone for ever, and I must act without her – for the events of the last few days have created a barrier between us that can never be penetrated.

Travis again? No – he would only take it as another occasion to demonstrate his superiority. And besides, I could not trust him to resist the temptation of gossiping to his friends at the Athenaeum about it.

Ruskin? For a minute or so I did seriously think of it. But it would be humiliating to have to confirm his low opinion of me by admitting that I needed his help. And would a man so maddeningly vague and discursive be willing, or able, to give me a straight answer?

In the end I concluded there was but one course of action I could take. After luncheon I must go and see Lady Eastlake.

Despite the cold, and the treacherous patches of packed, filthy snow underfoot, I decided to walk. The conventions of polite society, which had always seemed entirely natural to me, now appeared cumbersome and artificial, as if in the space of less than a week I had become a foreigner. I needed time to think myself into them again, and to rehearse what I was going to say. Even in the best of circumstances – and these were very far from the best – it would have been a difficult interview, requiring great tact and perception and mental agility. Somehow I must contrive to hint at the possible existence of a conspiracy, without either revealing my grounds for suspecting it, or naming its probable instigator. I made a little store of phrases: *Delicate matter – you will appreciate – questions of confidence – felt I must apprise you.* Undoubtedly, she would respond no more directly; but from her manner and appearance as she did so (angry or dismissive? blushing or turning pale?) I should be able to gauge whether or not she thought it likely there *was* a plot – and whether, if so, she believed her husband might be involved in it.

In the event, these preparations were in vain. Lady Eastlake was not at home. I was already halfway down the steps again, when a sudden thought struck me:

'Stokes,' I said, turning back. 'Did my sister by any chance leave her notebook here last week? It's small – about so big – red morocco cover?'

He pondered for a second. 'I don't know, sir, but I think I may have seen it. If you would just wait a moment?'

He was back in half a minute.

'Is this the one, sir?'

In his hand was Marian's notebook.

'Oh, thank you, Stokes! Miss Halcombe *will* be relieved. Where was it?'

For a second he forgot his footmanly duty. Smiling, he said:

'Where most things are in Lady Eastlake's boudoir. Beneath a pile of papers.'

Beneath a pile of papers.

All the way back to Brompton Grove I wondered what it meant.

Perhaps there was an innocent enough explanation. Lady Eastlake had found it in the drawing room – taken it to the boudoir for safe-keeping – put something on top, and forgotten it. It was, after all, a small thing, and she was a busy woman.

But then, when Marian had written, surely she would have remembered?

Very well. It was a *servant* who had found it and taken it to the boudoir, on the reasonable assumption that it was Lady Eastlake's. It at once became part of the undifferentiated clutter on the table, and in due course was covered up. Lady Eastlake did not even know it was there.

It was possible.

But at least equally possible, surely, that she *did* know it was there. In which case, why had she not returned it to Marian? Had even, perhaps, gone to the trouble of hiding it – if not very successfully?

I could not immediately think of an answer, so when I got home I wedged the studio door shut with a chair, and then sat down and opened the notebook.

At first I was as baffled as ever. It seemed to contain nothing but Marian's jottings about Turner – what people had told her, or facts she had gleaned from diaries and letters. But then, towards

343

the end, I found a long summary of her conclusions. It was so full of false starts and crossings-out that in places it was barely legible, but I could make out enough to recognize the bare bones of the character sketch of Turner that she had sent to me in Cumberland. Eight words, in particular, caught my attention:

Poor Turner.
His poor mother.
Good Mrs. Booth.

Poor Turner. *Good* Mrs. Booth. If Travis was right, these were not judgements that would please Sir Charles. Too much sympathy. Too much understanding.

And then, suddenly, a whole torrent of thoughts, each more monstrous than the last, squealed and tumbled into my mind like rats loosed from a cage.

What if Lady Eastlake is not ignorant of the plot, but party to it?

What if *she* is the instigator? What if, knowing how principled her husband is, she resolved to do what his scruples would not permit him to do himself? She is, after all, famously devoted to him, is she not – and jealously protective of his interests?

When she hears Marian's views, then (which she naturally supposes to be mine as well), she is thoroughly alarmed by them. So that when fate presents her with the notebook, she decides to keep it, in order to see the evidence on which they are based, and so be able the more effectively to counter them.

Or perhaps, if she was that determined, she hadn't left it to fate. Until now, I had assumed that Marian's reticule had been snatched merely as a decoy, to lure me to a place where I could be safely captured. But perhaps it had served a double purpose. Marian has always insisted that she would not have left the notebook behind; and certainly there were several occasions when the thief was lost to my view, and he would have had the opportunity to pass it to an accomplice.

At this point, the clamour of the rats abated for a moment; for I had seen an objection. Neither Lady Eastlake nor any of her intimates could possibly have known my abductor or his wife, or any of *their* intimates; and while it was easy enough to imagine Sir Charles using his power and connections to discover them, and buy their compliance, it was hard to see how she could have done so without running the risk of exposure. Whom could she rely on to act on her behalf, who . . .?

And then another rat appeared:

What if it were Mr. Kingsett?

Perhaps that is why he and his wife were there; and why Lady Eastlake tolerated his appalling behaviour.

Perhaps that is why he touched Marian, and said *Please, Miss Halcombe*, the moment before the thief appeared – so that he should know which reticule to take.

I am giddy. I had hoped for resolution. All I have got is more perplexity.

Davidson has just brought me another letter from Laura. I have put it with all the others. I cannot face it.

These distractions are my enemies. They keep me from my work. I must drive them from my mind, and take up my brush.

Wednesday

Perhaps the monster is what I see when I look in the glass.

Two hours last night I tried to paint, but to no avail.

I went to bed, but could not sleep. I felt myself hemmed in on every side. Disarmed. The will and energy draining from me.

I thought: *You must act, to regain your power.*

So I got dressed again, and went out. I assumed I was entirely alone and unnoticed, but from what came later I wonder now if I was observed.

There was no wind, but the cold took my breath away. It paid no heed to coat and skin and flesh, but straightway touched my bones, as if they were already in the grave, and it were merely claiming its own.

But death at least is certain. Better to walk with death inside you than nothing.

My first thoughts were of the Marston Rooms. I should find my musky whore, and get what I had paid for.

But as I neared the lights and crowds of the Haymarket I began to falter. It wasn't so much the fear of being seen that deterred me

345

– I didn't think anyone would know me in my present state, and no longer cared greatly if they did – but a horror of the dreadful charade of artifice and politeness. She wouldn't say: *Fuck me for five bob* – not in Piccadilly. In Piccadilly there would still have to be preambles: sly glances, giggles, arch comments, drinks and waiters, an exchange of names, a pretence of personal interest. The very thought of it filled me with weariness, and something close to disgust.

Without pausing to consider, I turned south again, and then east into Trafalgar Square. The great blank façade of the National Gallery and the Royal Academy looked as grim as a mausoleum, and as unlikely to yield up its secrets. I raised my hat in passing to Sir Charles, and crossed into Duncannon Street. Ten minutes later I was entering Maiden Lane.

It was impossible to be sure, for the two or three half-hearted gas-lamps did no more than fray the edges of the darkness, but so far as I could tell it was completely deserted. Slowly, slowly, I picked my way over the piles of frozen detritus, looking left and right for any sign of life: a movement, a crack of light in a shuttered window.

Nothing. The gate to Hand Court was shut. The pawnbroker's locked and unlighted.

More slowly, then. More slowly. Give fate time to meet you.

There was a sudden noise behind me. My heart was battering in my ears so loudly I could not tell what it was. I looked back, but there was nothing to be seen. A cat or a rat, probably, I decided, scuttling for safety.

I continued on my way. And then – unmistakably – heard footsteps hurrying after me; and, as I turned, a young, half-whispered voice:

'You lookin' for somethin'?'

I can't be certain it was the same girl, but I think it was. She was dressed as a woman now, and her lips were reddened; but I caught the glitter of her large brown eyes, and her cheeks were still as white and unblemished as a china doll's.

'What you after, darlin'?'

She did not seem to recognize me, but that is no surprise: the light was poor, and the intervening weeks have changed me as much as they have her. I said nothing, but held out five shillings.

She had to move and squint to see it; but when she did so, and realized how much it was, she gave a little laugh of pleasure.

'All right.' She took the money and slipped it into a pocket. Then she moved close and put her arms round me – impetuously, inexpertly, like a child thanking her uncle for a present.

'What's your name?'

She must have felt me stiffen and pull away; for she said: 'What's the matter?'

I shook my head. She looked into my eyes, with a little frown of concentration, trying to see what I wanted.

'That's all right,' she said. 'You don't 'ave to say nothin'. She glanced about her, to see we were not watched, and then lifted her skirt and placed my hand against her quim, wincing despite herself at the cold touch of my fingers. Then, without speaking, she turned and led me back down the street, and through the side-entrance by the pawnbroker's into a little court, and thence into an unlit room on the ground floor.

I could see nothing; and, even if I had, I should not remember it. I remember only the Babel of voices in my head:

How can you do this?

Is she not a whore, like the other?

She is a child, and you sought her out.

There is a price for everything.

Why should she pay it?

She is as eager as I am. Having come so far, I will only distress her more if I withdraw now. And what difference will one man more or less make to her?

What difference to you?

I must be free. Is it not natural – merely one piece of flesh enfolding another? Besides, is it not what Turner did?

Is it?

I feared this ceaseless attrition would sap me, and make me incapable at the last; and so indeed it might have done, had she made any response, or reminded me, by even the faintest gesture, that we were two people, and not merely the impersonal, mechanical conjunction of complementary organs.

But she was quick to learn, and had already understood what she must do. She stood with her back to me, and bent forward, and braced herself against the wall, with barely a movement or a murmur or a sigh. And when I was done, she guided me to the door without a word, and gently pushed me outside, locking the door behind me.

The voices were silent on my way home. I was conscious of nothing, not even the cold. Death itself had forsaken me.

Until I turned into Brompton Grove. For a moment I sensed only an animal apprehension that something was different and unexpected. Then I saw it: standing in front of the house was a black carriage. The windows were curtained, as if for a funeral. A squat coachman in a tall hat sat with his back towards me, so swaddled in blankets that he looked as improvised and immobile as a snowman. The horses themselves were invisible in the gloom, but I could see the haze of their breath on the still air.

I instantly thought of Laura – of the children – of Marian. Somehow, by my faithlessness, I had killed one of them, or made them ill. The horror of the idea stopped me dead, and I had to fight the urge to run away. But then I steadied myself. That was the voice of weakness and superstition. Dr. Hampson would have come by cab. And if someone had died, there would have been a telegram, not a carriage at the door in the middle of the night.

I started walking again, trying to convince myself that for some reason the man had simply decided to rest his horses in Brompton Grove, and that it was nothing to do with me. And had almost succeeded when, as I drew alongside, the carriage door opened abruptly in front of me, barring my path.

'Mr. Hartright?'

It was a high, frail, man's voice that I didn't recognize. I peered into the interior, but could see nothing.

'Mr. Hartright, get in, please. I have something to tell you.'

'Can you not tell me out here?'

There was a small, dry sound that might equally have been a cough or a laugh.

'I should die of the cold.' He paused, as if his supply of breath were exhausted, and must be replenished before he could continue. 'You'll come to no harm, I promise. What could I do, even if I were minded? A brute like you would snuff me out as easily as a candle.'

I hesitated, but only for a moment. If he meant to abduct me why did he not simply take me by force, as my previous attackers had done? And even if that were his intention, might I not still learn something of value? A few hours' loss of liberty would be a small price to pay, if it helped to end my uncertainty.

'Very well,' I said, pulling myself up.

In the glimmer of light from the street I half-saw a bundle of rugs and wraps and muffs huddled in the corner. I should not have known it was a man, save for the eyes, which appeared for a moment in the narrow gap between fur hat and upturned collar, and immediately flickered away again. They were more shadow than substance, so sunken that they seemed to be trying to retreat inside his skull; and somehow managed to convey, in the brief instant I glimpsed them, an impression of infinite weariness.

'Sit down, please, and close the door.'

I did so. It was now completely dark.

'Thank you.' He had to pause again. I heard the pitiful whistle and splutter of his chest as he struggled for breath. 'I wish to speak to you, Mr. Hartright,' he went on at last, 'on the matter of genius. You are writing, I believe, a life of Turner?'

I did not reply, but waited for him to reveal more of his hand before I showed my own.

'Please, Mr. Hartright,' he wheezed. 'You must assist me. I am a sick man. Every word is a battle. I cannot afford to throw them away.'

'Yes,' I said.

'Very well. I was privileged to see something of him. Something, I think, you will learn from no-one else.'

'Why?' I said. 'Who are you?'

'You may call me Simpson. That will do for now.'

'It is not your real name?'

'Why should a name I choose for myself be less real than the one given me by my parents?'

True, I thought. *Is Jenkinson not as real as Hartright?*

'*That* I had to abandon a long time ago,' he continued, 'when an indiscretion obliged me to leave England. Since then I have been living in Venice, and whenever I have returned it has always been under a *nom de voyage.*' He sucked in breath, slowly, so as

349

not to provoke a fit of coughing. When he spoke again, it was in a whisper.

'Can you still hear me, Mr. Hartright?'

'Just.'

'It's better for me to talk like this, if that is agreeable to you. Less taxing. Shan't have to stop so often.'

'Very well.'

'Well, then,' he whispered. 'You will appreciate that a man in my situation must always be careful. Make it his business to learn everything he can of his travelling companions, while giving away nothing about himself. There may be spies. Agents. Hm?'

'Yes.'

'Well, once I was crossing the Alps by Mount Cenis, and there was a small fellow in the carriage with me who at once roused my suspicions. Never said anything, unless someone spoke to him first, and then only brusquely. Never answered questions directly. Spent most of his time looking out of the window, and making sketches, as if he were preparing for a military campaign.'

He had to pause again. I was puzzled. Why was he going to the trouble of telling me this? Did he suppose I had not already heard countless stories of Turner's solitariness and eccentricity?

'Well, it took me a day or two,' he went on, 'but I found him out, little by little. The initials "J. M. W. T." on his valise. A letter interleaved with his sketchbook. A few fragments of conversation, in which he unwittingly let slip that he knew Lord Egremont, and most of the Royal Academy.'

'We travelled together several times after that. I never said anything, of course, and he never recognized me – it would have mortified him to know that I had uncovered his secret, when he had failed to penetrate mine.'

'Scarcely a secret,' I said. 'At least in his case.'

His voice was so attenuated that the reply came out as no more than a kind of ghostly sigh:

'Oh, yes! A great secret, Mr. Hartright. The secret of genius.'

My skin prickled, despite the cold.

'I saw him often in Venice. Sometimes when he thought himself completely unobserved. And I can testify that he was a remarkable man. Peep out of your window at dawn, and there he'd be, drawing away. Take a gondola for your evening cigar, and damn me if you wouldn't see him there still, scribbling till the last crack of the sun had gone. And then – then he needs must be away, to make sure that it rose again the next day.'

'Rose again?'

He could not reply at once. I had to clench my fists to prevent myself trying to shake the words from him. Slowly, painstakingly, he drew the air into his lungs.

'You know what sun-worshippers are. Their god must be satisfied with blood, else he will grow angry, and return no more.'

'Blood!'

'I'm talking about girls, Mr. Hartright. It was common knowledge in less conventional circles. I saw them taking one out of the canal myself. There were rope marks on her wrists and ankles, a sack over her face. She'd been held under till she drowned.'

For a moment I could not speak. I could not move. Then I heard myself whispering:

'Why are you telling me this?'

There was no answer. I waited. After perhaps fifteen seconds I felt something brush gropingly against my knee. I put my hand down and found his fingers. They were as cold as stone. The instant I touched them, they started to flutter towards my wrist.

I pulled away, and opened the door, and dropped to the ground.

I did not dream it. There is horse-shit on the ground where the carriage stood.

Can it be true?
Can it possibly be true?

Who is Simpson?
Could Kingsett have sent him?

Could it have *been* Kingsett?

LXII

Letter from Laura Hartright to Walter Hartright, 20th December, 185–

Wednesday

I dreamed last night you met a clever woman, who talked to you of all the things I cannot, and took you from me.

Dreams are often true, are they not?

Laura

LXIII

From the private notebook of Walter Hartright, 21st–22nd December, 185–

Thursday

Record. I must record.

Stamp order on the chaos.

Today I went to see a medium.

As I waited in her drawing room, I could scarce believe I found myself there. I looked down from the window at the press of people milling along Brook Street and thought how easily, even now, I might run outside again and lose myself among them.

But then the maid reappeared. 'Mrs. Mast will see you now, sir.'

She led me into a small parlour at the rear of the house. The curtains were already drawn, and the gas-lamps lit. The fire had burned low, and there was a marked chill in the air.

Two women sat at a round table in the middle of the room. One was thin and elderly, long-faced and big-nosed, so grey and angular she might have been made out of iron. The other plump and matronly, perhaps thirty years younger, with pink cheeks and bright eyes.

'Mr. Hartright, ma'am,' said the maid.

'How d'ye do, Mr. Hartright?' said the younger woman, thrusting her hand out as forthrightly as a man. 'I'm Euphemia Mast.'

'How do you do?'

'This is my mother.'

'How do you do?'

'She will assist me,' said Mrs. Mast. 'Please sit down.' Her voice was brisk and businesslike, with a hard nasal American twang she made no attempt to soften. As I drew up my chair she asked:

'Have you attended a consultation before, Mr. Hartright?'

'Not of this kind.'

'And why, may I ask, did you come to *me*?'

'I wish' – was I really saying it? – 'to speak – to make contact with a dead man.'

I bit my tongue. I had resolved to disclose nothing about my purpose; for if – as I still more than half-believed – she were no more than a skilful conjuror who had grown rich by preying on the gullible, she might well be able to construct a convincing 'spirit' simply from what I unwittingly let slip about him. But then I relaxed a little: for, surely, to know only his sex would be a small enough advantage for even the most accomplished fraud?

'We do not call them "dead",' she said, as matter-of-factly as if she were an engineer correcting me for saying 'piston' rather than 'valve', 'but "passed over". Is he someone you have lost?'

'In a manner of speaking.'

'Well, I shall do what I can, Mr. Hartright, but I hope you understand that I can guarantee nothing. I am no more than the channel. Some spirits find it impossible to communicate from the other side. Some do not wish to.' She was suddenly grave and earnest. 'It's most important that you realize that, before we begin.'

I nodded.

'You are a sensitive man, Mr. Hartright' – from the way she said it, you would have thought it was as evident and incontrovertible as the colour of my eyes – 'and sensitive people are sometimes alarmed by what happens when I enter the trance state. So let me explain. My physical body will still be here, but someone else will be controlling it. Most probably it will be one of my guides from the Other Side – Running Deer, or Mops. Just talk to her as you would to a friend. You may find it strange at first, but to her it will seem perfectly normal, I promise you. And as for me: whatever you see or hear, I shall not even be aware of it – so don't imagine that something is amiss, and I need help. Just allow things to take their course, and at the right moment I shall return.'

She waited for me to respond. I hesitated; and then – realizing that there was no point in being here at all if I did not at least pretend to assent to the reality of the spiritual world – nodded again.

'Very well. Have you brought anything with you that belonged to him, or is connected with him in any way? That sometimes helps.'

I knew this to be a usual request; and had anticipated it by slipping the old paintbrush Gudgeon had given me into my pocket before setting out. But now I hesitated. It was a clue – a large clue. Should I risk giving so much away?

She must have noticed my uncertainty; for she said: 'Please give it to me.'

I handed it to her, vowing to reveal nothing more.

'Thank you.'

She held it in both hands, gently running her fingers over the shaft. After a few moments, as if to concentrate better, she shut her eyes. The older woman, I noticed, was watching her closely, occasionally casting a warning glance in my direction that said: *Say nothing.* After a minute or more Mrs. Mast began to slump and nod, like a traveller falling asleep on a train. As if this were a signal, her mother got up, and, moving so quietly I could scarcely hear her, turned off the lamps and sat down again next to her daughter. The only light now came from the dying embers in the grate, and from where I was sitting the two women were no more than a blotchy silhouette.

Almost at once Mrs. Mast started to babble. To begin with it was just a torrent of groans and nonsense words, as if she were talking in her sleep; but then she began to twitch quite violently, and I heard snippets of two female voices which – though they indisputably came from her mouth – were nothing like hers at all.

You –
My –
The Turk –
I help –
Not her –

And then Mrs. Mast's head dropped suddenly against her mother's shoulder. And one of the voices said, quite clearly:

'There. *'Er's* gone. *'Er* didn't even know what tha wants. *I* knows.'

It sounded like a girl, eleven or twelve perhaps. Not American. From the north somewhere, I thought – Yorkshire or Lancashire, maybe – though some of the words had a kind of guttural thickness that seemed slightly foreign. The effect was so strange that I shivered despite myself.

'Go on, then,' whispered the old woman. 'Ask her something.'

Why could I not speak? What was I afraid of?

'Go *on,'* hissed the old woman.

'Who are you?' I said.

'Mops,' replied the voice.

'And why are you talking to me?'

'I goes. For 'er.'

'Who is *she?'*

'Tha knows. Mrs. Wosser. Wossername. Mast. I goes and finds 'em for 'er. She thinks it's *'er,* or one o' t'others, but it's awlus me.'

'Find the *spirits,* you mean?'

'Ay, tha's it.' Her tone was surprised, as if she'd supposed it was too obvious to need pointing out.

Tha. 'Er. Awlus. Where had I heard those words recently?

'Why are you there?'

'Wha', this side?'

'Yes.'

'Ay ay I drownded.'

Drownded.

That was it. The mad old woman in Otley, talking about her childhood friend.

I was drenched and cold with sweat. I said:

'What happened to you? Did someone –?'

'Drownded.' She sounded impatient, as if the subject were distasteful to her. 'I drownded.'

'Is Mops your real name?' I could not remember what the friend was called, but thought I should know it if I heard it.

'Mops. Mobs. Meg.'

Meg. And now it came to me: the friend had been *Mary*. Close – so close it was hard to believe it was mere coincidence – but not the same.

'Meg?' I said, in case I had mistaken her.

'I'm a good lass, I am,' she said, as if she hadn't understood. 'I can 'elp tha. I know what tha wants.'

It was maddening, but there was no point pursuing it. I gritted my teeth. 'What do I want?'

'Tha wants 'e.'

This sounded like a ploy to draw me out further, so – remembering my resolution – I said nothing, but waited for her to continue.

'I sees . . . canvas,' she said uncertainly, at length. 'I sees paint . . .'

And so would anyone, I thought, *who had first seen a brush.*

'I sees a name . . . the beginnin' of a name . . . I think i's a "T".'

I started; but then told myself it was not such a wonder – 'T' is a common enough letter, and there is a reasonable chance that at least one part of an English name will start with it.

'I' that right?'

'Maybe,' I said.

'Or is i' . . . is i' . . . "J"? Ay, I think tha's i'! "J". An' then "O". No, "E".'

I started again; and this time could not stop myself blurting out: 'Jenkinson!'

'Ay,' she said (though what 'she' was, exactly, I still could not say), '"Jen" summat, all right. Oh, but 'old 'ard.'

'What is it?'

'Sssh!' A pause; then, puzzled: 'I' tha' tha, or 'e?'

'What?'

'That "Jen"? Tha name, or 'is?'

I could not answer. After a moment she said:

'I'm a' felted.'

And then I seemed again to be half-hearing a distant conversation between her and somebody else. But this time the other voice was a man's, gruff and short.

Eerily, I have to confess, as I imagine Turner's.

I forced myself not to reflect on where I was, or what I was doing; but merely to hear and remember what they were saying, like a scientist or a reporter, without judging it. But try as I might, I could still only pick out fragments:

Slippin'

Taste
Why won't –?
Appre'end
'O'?
Windsor
Usurp
Aloud (allowed?)
A moment's hesitation. Then the girl's voice:
'There's no call for tha'.'

I could hear her clearly enough now, but the indignant tone suggested she was still talking to somebody else.

'Ask him,' I said. 'Ask him –'

'Wha'?' she snapped irritably.

'Ask him his occupation.'

A pause. Then:

'P . . . p . . . pain . . .'

Painter. But again, of course, the brush had effectively told me that.

'In what medium?'

'Mrs. Mrs. Wosser –'

I shook with frustration. 'What kind of paint?'

'Oi . . . oi . . .'

'Is that all?'

Silence.

'Ask him to name one of his pictures.'

'See . . . see . . .'

'See what?'

'No! *See!*'

'Oh, *sea!* Waves, you mean? Water?'

'Ay . . . ay . . . war. Wa'er. Wa'ercolour.'

I saw I must take another approach, or risk losing my mind altogether. I said:

'Lu.'

She seemed to wait for me to continue. When I didn't, she said:

'Wha tha mean?'

'Did he know a woman called Lu?'

'Mm.' There was a kind of frowning puzzlement in her voice, as if she were struggling to make sense of something – an impression strangely belied by the placid vacancy of Mrs.

357

Mast's face. 'By t'river?'

'Yes.'

There was a murmur I couldn't make out, and then a giggle.

'What is it?' I said.

''E says *Wa'erloo.*'

She laughed again. It took me a second to see why. Then an odd spasm – half fear, half exaltation – passed through me: for surely there was something unmistakably Turnerish about this reply? It could just be coincidence, of course; or it could be that Mrs. Mast was an exceptionally gifted fraud, who had guessed whom I was trying to contact, and had sufficient knowledge of him to make his 'spirit' speak in Napoleonic puns, and refer repeatedly to water – but at that instant, for the first time, I believed I really might be communicating with him.

The thought of it – the hope of it – made me reckless.

'Is it true – is it true,' I said – for a moment forgetting entirely about Mrs. Mast and her mother – 'that he bound her, and placed a hood over her head?'

Silence.

'What does he say?'

''E don' say nowt.'

I wanted to beg. I wanted to plead for my sanity. Only by a great effort of will did I stop myself.

'What of Sandycombe Lodge, then?' I said. 'Why did he design the basement so?'

Silence. I took a deep breath.

'Very well,' I said. 'One question. One question only. What does he know of a man who calls himself Simpson?'

There was no response. I waited, resolving to say nothing more. As I did so, an image drifted into my mind, so suddenly and powerfully that it was as if someone had placed it there directly.

A Turner picture. *Ulysses Deriding Polyphemus.*

But I was not merely watching the scene, I was a part of it. Everything moved before me – the jeering figures on the ship, the horses bearing the sun into the sky, the giant clutching his eyeless face in agony.

I whispered: 'Are you there?'

Still nothing. Just an unbroken silence, that seemed to grow deeper and more final by the second.

Remembering Mrs. Mast's injunction at the beginning, I did not move or interfere. But as the minutes passed I could not help wondering if this were entirely normal. And when at length the old woman – who up until now had remained calm and still – suddenly shifted in her chair, and looked (or so it appeared in the darkness) into her daughter's face, I concluded that something must be wrong.

And then, without warning, it happened. From less than a foot in front of me, the man's voice spoke again. No more than a whisper, this time, and only three words – but they were absolutely clear:

'Leave me be!'

I somehow found the strength to sit there quietly as Mrs. Mast returned to consciousness, grunting and muttering as before, and her mother relit the lamps, and the familiar shapes and colours of this world once again formed before my eyes. I contrived to answer politely when she asked if the séance had been helpful, and to offer to pay, and to find two guineas when she told me she did not charge, but would accept a contribution from those she had assisted, in order that she might be able to further her work and bring consolation to those who mourned.

But once outside I began to weep – to sob and quake and wail uncontrollably, so that people looked strangely at me, and stepped off the pavement to avoid me.

I have no pride left. Tomorrow I shall go to see Ruskin.

Friday
Record.
Just record.

I take a cab to Dennmark Hill. 'Young Mr. Ruskin is not at home. You will find him working at the National Gallery.'

Another cab, to Trafalgar Square. A half-deaf functionary, who at first affects not to understand me. Then he sees murder in my eyes, and conducts me to the basement.

It is dark and humid and close. The walls are lined with boxes, piled two or three high. In the feeble glow of the two gas-lights I can see that behind them the plaster is stained with mould and moisture.

Ruskin sits at a table, working by the light of a single oil-lamp. Before him are stacks of notebooks, hundreds of them – mildewed, tattered, frayed into holes, eaten away by damp and mice. He is painstakingly unbinding one of them, and does not pay us any attention as we enter.

'Mr. Hartright,' grumbles the functionary.

Ruskin raises his head. The blue eyes are as brilliant as ever, but he is pale with tiredness. He stares into my face for a moment – fails to recognize it – looks at the functionary for an explanation.

But the functionary is already leaving. Closing the door.

'The biography of Turner,' I say. 'I came to see you about it, a few months ago.'

'Ah, yes, yes, of course.' He half-rises, leans across the table, touches my hand. 'How are you?'

I say nothing, and he does not press me. He slumps back in his seat, his eyes already returning to his work.

'You said I might talk to you again, when I had gone further.'

He nods without looking at me. He lifts a page from the open notebook, carefully blows the dust from it, and lays it on a sheet of clean writing-paper. I can see nothing of it but a disc of radiant orange dissolving in darkness, but it is enough to jolt me. To shame me.

'Why are you not at home, preparing for Christmas, like the rest of the world?' he says, taking out another page and peering at it.

I have not the energy to ask him the same question. 'I am desperate.'

He sighs. 'I cannot say I am entirely surprised.'

'No. You warned me.'

'Did I?'

There are two other chairs. I clutch the back of one of them, hoping he will invite me to sit down.

'*Sometimes,*' I say, '*we may deceive ourselves into thinking we are capable of some great task which is beyond us.*'

'Is that what I said? Dear me.' He waves a hand at the laden table, and tugs his misshapen mouth into a smile. 'If hypocrisy were a capital offence, my prospects would be poor indeed.'

'It *was* beyond me. I need your help.'

At last he looks at me. 'That is a sad state for any man to find himself in,' he says slowly. 'And if it is the case I am truly sorry for it.'

'What is the truth about him?'

'Ah, the truth!' He shakes his head morosely. 'How do you find the truth about a man who eschewed the literal, and spoke in riddles? It will end by making you mad.'

'I fear it already has.'

He stares deep into my eyes, and then nods. 'The truth about Turner', he says, 'is never direct. Always oblique. There are hints of it in the pictures, of course, but you can never fully comprehend it. It cannot be reduced to its component parts, or to any simple proposition. There will always be something beyond, that defies our attempts to imprison it in words.'

I feel I am about to faint. I drop on to the chair. He appears not to notice.

'Perhaps the same might be said of all of us. I certainly hope it may be said of me. But most of us may be represented by a kind of tapestry, in which the principal elements – honesty, dishonesty, intelligence, stupidity – are clearly visible. In Turner, by contrast, the cloth is twisted and folded and wound in on itself. When you glimpse a thread you never know whether it is a part of the subject, or a chance trick of the weaver's art, or a false trail deliberately woven into the fabric to puzzle or mislead.' He pauses. Examines his own fingers. Fastidiously blows the chalk dust from them. 'You are familiar, of course, with the fallacies of hope?'

An odd expression, but the meaning is plain enough. 'If I wasn't before, the last five months have made me so.'

He cannot resist a smile. 'I was not referring to your own experiences, Mr. Hartright, but to Turner's poetic *magnum opus*.'

'*The Fallacies of Hope*?'

He nods. 'You have not heard of it?'

'No.'

He raises one shaggy eyebrow. I have fallen still further in his estimation, if such a thing is possible. He shuts his eyes, in the effort of remembering, and declaims:

'Craft, treachery, and fraud – Salassian force,
Hung on the fainting rear! – then Plunder seiz'd
The victor and the captive, – Saguntum's spoils
Alike, became their prey . . .

'That was the start of it. The caption to *Hannibal Crossing the Alps* in 1812. He'd used verses as captions to his pictures before, of course, but they were always taken from other poets, though often garbled or misquoted. The attribution here was: *MS. Fallacies of Hope*. Thereafter, it appeared on his paintings again and again, each time with a different verse. So what does everyone naturally assume?'

It is too remote from my thoughts for me to grasp it immediately.

He prompts me: 'What is the implication?'

'That . . . that . . . he has – or has written – a poem. An unpublished poem. And is extracting pertinent passages from it, to serve as captions.'

'Exactly. And he must have known that was the impression he was giving. But it wasn't true.'

'It didn't exist?'

'Not in its entirety. He merely composed lines, or adapted them from other writers, when he needed them. It's a false trail, you see?' He lifts his finger, and traces its progress on an imaginary tapestry. 'A flash of colour here – a flash there – you think they belong to the same continuous strand, but they don't. It's an illusion.'

I can barely muster the strength to ask:

'Can we then trust nothing?'

He shrugs, and looks at me curiously, as if he were seeing me for the first time. At length he says:

'What is troubling you, Mr. Hartright?'

And I tell him. I tell him about Farrant and Hargreaves – about our dinner at Fitzroy Square, and my abduction afterwards – about Lucy, and the hood and the ropes. I tell him about Travis, and Marian's notebook, and my growing suspicion of the Eastlakes (at which he cannot suppress a wintry smile). And about my meeting with Simpson, and my uncertainty as to whether or not it was a dream, and the séance with Mrs. Mast. I tell him I don't know what to believe.

But I do not tell him I fucked two whores, thinking it would make me a genius.

He does not even seem surprised. He nods, and then stares at me in silence.

And I am conscious only of the relief of having said so much and not being vilified or rejected or laughed at for it. And of the intolerable burden of what I have *not* said, which sits in my belly like a small hot coal.

O, God, to be rid of that too! To have said it all – to have revealed those things in myself so dark and terrible that ever I had not suspected their existence, and to find myself still accepted – that would be a kind of redemption. The only kind I can now conceive.

But it is impossible. Even as I write these words I know

O God

Write. Write. Record.

At length he gets up. He surveys the wall of boxes, finds the one he is looking for, and carefully removes it. Then he brings it to the table and – reaching in his pocket for a key – unlocks it.

'He was, unquestionably, a man of deep, strange errors and failures,' he says. 'And I find myself more and more helpless to explain them. Save that they all arose from his faithlessness, or despair. For this is the century of despair; and it has corroded the greatest minds as perniciously as it has the lowest.'

He opens the box, takes out another notebook, and turns to the last few pages. Sketch after sketch of men and women in bed together. Nothing is complete – a pair of buttocks here, a raised leg there, a hand clutching a bare shoulder – and the faces cannot be seen at all; but it is plain enough to what they refer. Pictures not of people – not even of entire bodies – but merely of an act.

'Yes,' I say. 'It's ugly. But is there any evidence that he – that he could have been capable of . . . of . . .?'

'I am an art critic, Mr. Hartright, not a detective. I can only tell you – as I told you before – that there is a dark clue running through Turner's art, and it is the darkness of death. There is another running through his life, and it is the darkness of England.' He pauses, and shakes his head sorrowfully. 'What he might have done for us had he received help and love, I can hardly trust myself to imagine. But we disdained him. For seventy-six grinding years we tortured his spirit, as we torture the spirits of all our brightest children. And we are torturing it still, now that he is dead.'

'Because of the will, you mean?'

'Ah, yes, the will. We *say* it is the will, because a will concerns money and the law, and those are things we can comprehend. They are *all* we can comprehend. But Turner stirred something deeper in this blind, tormented country – something of which, with our bluff good sense, we are barely aware in ourselves. Turner foresaw our end, which few of us can face. Worse still, he dared to love the light – something without a price on it, which could not be defined and contained in the dreary little counting-house of our minds. And we punished him for it. Whatever he was guilty of, it is we who drove him to it.'

I struggle for breath. I have to whisper it:

'But what do you believe?'

'One thing one moment, another thing the next, like most men. Only *I* accept it, with as much grace as I can. To contradict yourself is no more than to acknowledge the complexity of life.' He gets up again. 'Let me show you something.'

He picks up the lamp, leads me out into the stairwell and into a room on the other side. It is absolutely dark, save for the soft glow of burning oil. Leaning against the wall is a stack of unframed canvases, five or six deep.

'These are his last works,' says Ruskin in a hushed voice, as if we have entered a church. 'The last works of our greatest genius. See how we value them.' He runs a finger down one and then turns it towards me. It is glistening with water. 'See what they tell us about ourselves.'

He hands me the lamp, and slowly pulls the canvases away, one at a time, to let me view them.

~~I have never seen~~

Write

Nothing. Swirls of nothing. Smear

Whirlpools. Pulling you into nothing.

Whirl

Nothing

Whirl

LXIV

From the diary of Marian Halcombe,
23rd–26th December, 185–

Saturday
I shall not kill myself.
  But I know now why people do.
  Nothing rational keeps me from it.

Today we were meant to be travelling to Cumberland, to join
Laura and the family for Christmas.
  Instead

Some time in the night I was woken by the sound of my door
opening. There was a little light left from the fire. The figure of a
man crossed before it and then stopped and looked at me. No
more than a dim silhouette, but I knew him at once – though to
see him there, and at such a time, was as strange as looking in the
glass and finding another face where my own should have been.
  'Walter?' I said.
  He did not answer. I thought perhaps I was dreaming, and
reached for the box of matches to light the lamp. Immediately he
lunged towards me and put his hand over mine.
  'No.'
  'Why?' I said. 'Walter, what are you doing?'
  He said nothing, but sat on the bed, with his face turned away
from me. After a few moments his shoulders hunched and his
neck arched and he started to sob.
  'What's the matter?'
  He dropped forward, his head in his hands, crying almost silently.
  'What is it?'
  He tried to speak, but could not catch his breath. I stroked his
back.
  'Tell me!'
  After perhaps half a minute he said:
  'Futile.'
  'What is?'
  'Life.'

'Your life? My life?'

'Ev–' he began; and then had to gulp for air, and broke off abruptly.

'There! You've given yourself hiccups,' I said, in the smiling voice I have heard Walter himself use, to cajole his children from tears. But instead of soothing him, I succeeded only in provoking a renewed outburst of sobs.

'It's not futile,' I said, hastily changing tack, 'it's not!' – though since I had no idea what 'it' was, I felt as foolish as a doctor trying to treat a wound he could not see.

Walter did not respond at first; but then suddenly turned, and laid his face on my breast.

As a child must on his mother. A man must on his wife.

And like a mother and a wife I comforted him. Without reflecting. I held his head against my cheek. I fondled his hair. I whispered: 'Ssh. There. There.'

He grew quieter. I thought perhaps he had fallen asleep; but then I was conscious that his arms had tightened about me, and he was starting to caress me, as I have never been caressed.

Dear God, what did I think? That he was incapable of harming me? That it was normal for a brother to touch his sister so?

The truth is I did not think anything. I merely obeyed some impulse in me that must have lain slumbering all my life, and now awoke, and told me what to do. I caressed him too, as I have never caressed anyone. There was no beginning to it, and no clear notion in my head of any end. We seemed suspended – as if someone had abstracted us from the world, and set us down in a strange place where we could act without consequences.

Until Walter began pulling at my covers.

'No,' I whispered.

But he did not stop.

'No!' I said more loudly, trying to push him away.

But he was too strong for me. In a moment the blankets were gone, and he was tearing at my nightgown.

'Walt–!' I began; but he drew the nightgown over my eyes and mouth, forcing the word back between my lips, and held it there.

'Do you not love me?' he whispered.

I heard his boots clatter to the floor; and then he was struggling to remove his own clothes. But with only one hand he was slow

366

and clumsy, and at length, in his frenzy, he forgot himself for a moment, and uncovered my face.

All these years I have called him my brother.

He is not my brother. He is –

He was staring at me. Staring at what no man has ever seen. But not like a man. His mouth was wet. He was panting. I thought of a cat about to eat.

I could have cried out again, but what then? The only help at hand was Davidson. How could *he* intervene between Walter and me?

I tried to appeal: 'Walter. Please.'

He dragged my hair across my face, pressing it down so tightly I could barely breathe.

I did not try to speak again. I feared he would hurt me.

I had not known before what the gospels mean by *possession*. I had thought it perhaps no more than a primitive word for *madness*.

But Walter was possessed. A demon had subdued his true nature, and taken control of his faculties and his will. A demon that was not content to destroy innocence and trust and hope, but must enter every cranny, and turn what it found there to evil.

Not only in Walter, but in myself.

For was not this the hellish parody of something that – despite myself – I had thought of? Had I not sometimes dreamed about it, even; and for a moment after I'd woken fancied I felt him beside me?

I had pitied myself for it, and cursed my own folly – but not *hated* myself, for by bearing it alone I was, in my own small way, heeding our Saviour's injunction to take up my cross and follow him. As He had died to save the world, so by my own inward death I might keep those I loved from harm.

But even this consolation was taken from me. For mixed with the horror and the pain – I cannot deny it – there was throb of pleasure too. A mockery – an inversion, like a Black Mass – of the joy I had imagined.

So it was not enough that Walter should betray me, his wife, his children, himself.

I must betray them all, too.

He gave a cry. It was not even his voice, but the desolate yell of a beast. And then he lay there, so rigid that I thought the demon had fled, leaving him insensible or dead.

I was weeping too much to speak or shout for help, but at length I found the strength to move, and try to push him from me.

At once, without a word, he got up, and left the room.

My sense of time is awry. My sense of everything.

A moment ago Mrs. D. knocked.

'Pardon me, miss, but we were just wondering . . .?'

Wondering what?

I looked at my clock and saw that it was past eleven.

'I'm sorry, I'm not well,' I said.

'Oh, dear. Can I get you anything, miss?'

'No. Thank you.'

'Shall I call Dr. Hampson?'

'I think I'll just rest.'

'Very good.' Footsteps receding, then returning. 'Did Mr. Hartright say he was going out early, miss?'

'Not that I know of.'

'Only he didn't come down to breakfast this morning. And Davidson says he isn't in his bedroom, or in the studio.'

I have washed. And washed and washed. But I cannot look at myself in the glass.

Cannot even pray.

Later

It is after four-thirty. Mrs. D. again. Was I sure she could not bring me anything? Yes. Was there anything else? Yes – could they please telegraph my sister, to tell her we have been delayed? Very good.

A pause. Then: Mr. Hartright has still not returned. Did I think he would be requiring dinner? I could not say.

I hope not.

Let him go hungry. Let him know he can never enter this house again. Let him understand that what he did has put him for ever beyond the protection of society, the comfort of home, the love of family, the respect of friends.

Let him suffer.

Just midnight. He is still not back.

I feel as if I have just passed two sleepless nights without an intervening day. And now am beginning yet another.

Each has its own mood. The first: horror. The second: rage. The third:

What?

I am standing at the edge of a great ocean, that stretches as far as the eye I can see. If I lived for a thousand years, I should not be able to pass to the other side.

Sadness.

Is he out there somewhere, cold and wretched and at his wits' end? Aghast at what he has done, and utterly at a loss to know what he should do now?

Is he dead, even?

Six hours ago I should have been happy enough to think so. Six hours ago I should have been glad to kill him myself, had I had the means to do so.

To know that he had been punished. That I should never have the anguish of seeing him or talking to him again. That *my* power, in the end, had turned out to be greater than his.

But now I cannot help remembering him, not as he was last night, but as the Walter I knew before. Or rather, the many Walters – for over the past ten years he has been to me teacher, friend confidant, colleague and brother. And in every one of those characters I would have trusted him – more completely than any man I have ever met – with my honour and my life.

What drove him then to act as he did?

Am I in some part to blame?

Sunday
I can scarce hold the pen.

I have never known such fury or such shame.

He did not return during the night. At nine o'clock this morning I forced myself down to his studio, thinking he might have let

369

himself in by the garden gate and gone there rather than to the house.

But he hadn't. The air was cold and stale. The great murky picture was still on its easel, and looked no more finished than before. When I touched it the paint was not quite dry, but a skin had started to form on the surface.

It was as I turned away from it that my foot struck something heavy beneath the painting table. I could not tell what it was, for it was hidden behind the old sheet Walter uses as a cover. I bent down and lifted the cloth.

There, jammed against the leg, was a small locked deed-box.

I drew it out. It was shiny and unblemished, and so light that at first I thought it was empty. Perhaps Walter had only just bought it, and not had a chance to use it yet. Or removed the contents, and taken them with him.

But as I set it down again, I heard something slither along the bottom, and knock against the end.

Not loose papers. Too solid for that.

A diary?

I scoured the room for a key. I opened drawers, peered into the chipped jug he uses as a brush-holder, looked under rags. Nothing.

I carried the box into the house and ordered Davidson to break it open. At first he was reluctant; but when I said, 'Mr. Hartright's life may depend on it,' he immediately went and fetched a poker, and set to with something like enthusiasm – for he is now desperately anxious about Walter, though he is at pains not to show it, and was clearly relieved to feel he might at last do something to help him. When he was done, I took it to my room, and locked the door behind me.

Inside was nothing but a plain notebook. I opened it at random. The first lines I saw were:

Others may read a journal. No-one must read this.

I felt a small bitter shudder of revenge.

I told myself I should try to be dispassionate, like a doctor examining a patient, with but one end in view: to diagnose the disease that had changed him so dreadfully.

But I could not do it. I would master myself for a few pages, and then come upon something that suddenly swept away my puny defences, and made me weep and tremble. When I reached his account of what happened after my reticule was stolen, I was sick in the wash-bowl.

I still cannot bring myself to set down the details of what I read.

But I think I can now at least partially understand why he acted as he did.

~~And I know I must accept some responsibil~~

When I had finished I went down again to the studio. I found the scalpel he uses to sharpen pencils, and stood before that vile picture, and slashed it until it was no more than a tangle of stained threads.

Then I steeled myself, and wrote to Laura:

Walter is not well.

Must remain in London for the time being.

Return as soon as it is safe to do so.

My poor sister.

Later

After an early luncheon (no more than a plate of soup and some bread; but enough to fortify me, and to persuade Mrs. Davidson that I was strong enough to go out) I returned to my room, and put on a mourning dress. My greatest horror was of people brushing against me, for my skin felt so sensitive that I feared even the slightest contact would make me sick. Wearing black, I thought, would protect me. since people shrink instinctively from grief; and if without warning I suddenly started to weep — as I have done often over the last two days – the veil would both account for, and partially conceal, my tears. I waited on the landing until I heard the Davidsons going into the kitchen (for to explain my appearance to them in the present circumstances would have been quite beyond my power) and then crept downstairs and out into the street.

I had no definite plan: only the certainty that to take action of some kind – however fruitless it might turn out to be – would be preferable to staying passively in my room, with nothing but Walter's notebook and my own tortured reflections to occupy me. I had thought of walking through the park, and hoping some inspiration would strike me; but as soon as I stepped outside I realized that it was too cold, and too slippery underfoot. I went only as far as the end of the road, therefore (where I knew I should not be visible from the house), and looked about me for a cab.

But there was not a cab to be seen. Or, rather, there were hundreds to be *seen*, but none to be *had*; for they were all taken. I watched them pass in an almost unbroken stream: men going about their business; mothers returning from the shops with presents for their children; servants sent out at the last minute to get a bottle of sherry or some more glasses or another side of beef for tomorrow.

All that purpose. All those places to go. What should mine be?

I pondered the question for perhaps a quarter of an hour as I stood there, stamping my feet and rubbing my hands together inside my muff. I had almost given up all hope of finding either a destination or a vehicle to get me there when a hansom drew up on the other side of the street and a woman laden with parcels got out. And all at once I seemed to have the answer.

I struggled across the road and called to the cabman: 'Are you free?'

He nodded. 'Where to, miss?'

'Fitzroy Square. And then to wherever I tell you.'

He looked at me curiously for a moment, and then nodded again.

'Long as you got the money,' he said, with the off-handed assurance of a man who knew he could find another customer more easily than I could find another cab. 'Get in.'

I had, of course, no intention of calling on Elizabeth Eastlake. Wherever else Walter was, he would not be with her. And in my present state she would succeed in prising my secrets from me in ten minutes, whereas I had no prospect of learning *her* secrets at all.

But 7 Fitzroy Square was where this quest began, and I felt a sudden urge to see it again – to see again *all* the places to which the search for Turner had taken us. Partly, I think (though I was barely conscious of it) because of a primitive belief in coincidence, which made me suppose I was more likely to find him again where I had seen him before – as a child will seek his dead mother in the rooms and haunts he associates with her in life. But partly also because, after being trapped for so long in the confusion of my own inner world, I felt that seeing the *outer* world again – the solid, incontrovertible world of stones and bricks, of streets and crowds – would help to clarify my mind, and perhaps offer me a clue to Walter's own thinking, and to his probable whereabouts now. And I think – I hope – I was right.

The last few days have made me a stranger to myself. Before, when setting out to revisit some familiar place, I have generally known what response it was likely to evoke in my breast – elation or gloom, relief or regret. Now, though the register of my emotions is pitifully shrunk, I can no longer predict with any certainty which part of it will be touched. I had supposed that seeing 7 Fitzroy Square again would make me anxious, or depressed, or even weaken my resolve, and tempt me to confide in Elizabeth Eastlake after all; but I had not imagined it would make me angry.

Everything – the imperious windows; the well-swept steps; the wide front door – looked exactly the same, as if it were altogether too grand and self-satisfied even to notice the cataclysm that had struck me in the two weeks since I had seen it last. And I was scandalized by it. I wanted to break the glass – splinter the wood – mar the perfect paintwork.

But I did not get out. After glowering at it for a few moments, with something like hatred in my heart, I told the driver to take me to Queen Anne Street. Turner's house was still there, though (unlike the Eastlakes') it seemed to have borne its share of the world's suffering. It looked careworn and dilapidated, and the windows were covered with a fine dust, which gave them the dull opacity of a blind man's eyes. I wondered whether the gallery still stood behind it – the gallery where Calcott and Beaumont and Caro Bibby had once marvelled and debated. I could not help picturing them there; and thinking how those passionate lives, which but forty years ago had burned so hotly, and felt the causes they espoused so fiercely, were already cold and forgotten – as if a man is of no greater moment than a match, that gives a second's brilliance, and is spent. Somehow, *their* stories, and Turner's story, and our story, worked themselves together into a kind of melancholy thread, and I began to follow it, like Theseus – though with no thought or hope of slaying the monster when I reached the end.

I followed it across the sluggish tide of traffic in Oxford Street; and down New Bond Street, where the brightly lit shops were decked with sprigs of holly and ivy, and seemed to taunt me with their promise of innocence and merriment. I followed it into Piccadilly, where I saw the Marston Rooms, and thought for a moment of the woman Walter had met there, and of how even now she must be dressing, and putting on her musk in preparation for her night's work; and then down St. James's and into Pall Mall, and so past Marlborough House, where we had first glimpsed the unimaginable beauty of Turner's work, and its dreadful power.

I followed it into Trafalgar Square, where it wound into the National Gallery and the Royal Academy, and became more complex yet – twisting into itself the machinations of Sir Charles, and the furious martyrdom of Ruskin, and the despair of Haste; and so by a natural progression to Haste's house in Cawley Street, where I stopped the cab. The lower windows were all boarded up, and it struck me with a jolt (the force of my own feelings again took me by surprise; for the thought of it made me cry) that Haste's son must have finally lost his long battle against the bailiffs. But then I glanced up, and saw a defiant glimmer from the attic casement, and felt suddenly quite unreasonably cheered.

I descended from the cab, and gazed up at the tiny flickering light (no gas here; not even a lamp; only a candle) as a storm-lashed sailor must gaze at a distant beacon. Here was a man who had been robbed of almost everything that most people consider essential to human existence, and yet who still had the spirit to fight on. For a moment I wanted to rush inside and join him. Since our last encounter, life had reduced me almost to his level – or beneath it, even, since no-one, at least, had deprived him of his honour; and now, I suddenly thought, we might make common cause. Leading a life of monastic simplicity – labouring together in some great enterprise – might not *that* become my cross, and restore to me my self-regard?

The cabman must have heard my sobs, and observed my efforts to stem my tears.

'Something the matter, miss?' he said.

I shook my head, and turned to climb back into the hansom.

'Take me to Twickenham,' I managed to say.

He stared at me. I took out my purse and shook it like a rattle.

'That weren't what I were thinking, miss,' he said finally; and resumed his place.

And so we followed the thread again: edging our way along the north side of the park – only a stone's throw from the house where Mr. Kingsett had insulted me, and was doubtless still torturing his wife – and into Hammersmith, where Turner had once lived, and where the roads were now clogged with people trudging home to their one holiday of the year, and knots of excited children stood before the brilliantly lit fruiterers, gawping at their displays of oranges and apples and bowls of gold and silver fish, spilling out on to the pavement. And thence through Chiswick to Brentford, and past Amelia Bennett's house (it was quite dark, which startled me, until I remembered that her husband's health required them to spend the winters by the sea); and at length to Twickenham.

I told the driver to stop before Sandycombe Lodge. I looked at the dolls'-house door, and the dolls'-house windows – one of them bright with gaslight; and the plain white dolls'-house walls, and the dark bushes pressing upon them from every side. And I thought of what I could not see: the basement where Walter's madness had begun; its barred window, which had recalled to me *The Bay of Baiae*, and led me (I still believe) to the recesses of Turner's mind; and my stumbling discovery of my own love

The pain of it took everything from me: speech, tears movement. And yet as I sat there paralysed, I realized there was worse still to be faced, if I were to follow the trail all the way to the Minotaur. Like a child that can put its finger anywhere but the place that truly hurts, I had gone round the problem without touching its heart.

And in that moment I thought I knew where I should find Walter.

We came back along the river and through Chelsea – past Mrs. Booth's cottage (dear God! had I really supposed that Walter was too delicate to be told of Turner's life there?) and so home. As I paid him, the cabman nodded towards my mourning dress and said:

'I couldn't help noticing, miss. I'm sorry. I lost my own girl a few month back.'

On a sudden impulse, I said:

'Are you working tomorrow?'

He shook his head.

'Got to 'ave dinner, miss, with the missus and the young 'uns. I promised 'em that.'

'Of course,' I said. 'But after that?'

'Well,' he said uncertainly. 'I suppose I could come out for a bit.'

'Would you call for me here? As early as you are able?'

'Very good, miss.' He turned, and then looked back. 'A Merry Christmas to you.'

I managed to slip in without the Davidsons seeing me; but they must have heard me, for a few minutes later there was a knock on my door.

'Do you require anything, miss?'

'No, thank you, Mrs. Davidson.'

A pause. Then:

'Is there any news of Mr. Hartright, miss?'

Her voice was tight, choked with the anxieties she dared not put into words.

'Not yet,' I said. 'But I hope I may have some tomorrow.'

Please God I may.

Monday

I have a photograph of him, taken a year ago. From the openness of the expression, you'd suppose it was a different man. But the features are still recognizable.

I wrapped it in a shawl, to take with me. Then, while I waited, I looked through yesterday's *Times*. Two bodies found in the river. I raced through the descriptions: a pregnant woman, and an old man dressed as a seaman. A relief, of course. And yet I

376

could not help feeling something akin to disappointment, too. Death is at least final. It spares you the need to trouble yourself further.

At last, at four, there was a knock at the door. I went outside. It was already dark, and a heavy fog was hanging in the street. The driver peered at me in the lamplight, and grinned.

"Ow do, miss,' he said, in a mock-pompous voice, touching his cap. 'Compliments of the season.'

I could not laugh. I could not even smile. 'Was it a good dinner?' I said.

He nodded and patted his stomach. 'Very satisfactory, thank you.' He gave a burlesque bow, and gestured towards the cab. 'Where to now, miss?'

I could smell the beer on his breath.

'Maiden Lane.'

The pawnbroker's shop was closed, but a tired-looking woman was just going in by the side-door. I called to her, and showed her the picture.

'Have you seen this man?'

She narrowed her eyes. After a moment she nodded.

'Yesterday. Early. I think it was the same feller. I remembers 'im, on account of 'im bein' so, well, queer.'

'Why, what did he do?'

'I don't mean 'is manner. 'E were a gentleman, there's no denyin' that. But that's what's so funny about it. 'E says: " wants a new suit o' clothes, cheap as you got." An' 'e takes a worn velveteen tog, and an old shirt, and a pair of kerseymere kicksies.'

'Perhaps he had no money?'

'I don't think that's it. You should 'a' seen the stuff 'e was wearin' when 'e come in. *Very* serious. Must 'a' cost – she shook her head – 'I don't know what.'

'Did he leave it here?' I said.

She nodded.

'A shilling if you'll show it to me.'

She unlocked the door.

There was no question. Walter's hat. Walter's suit. Walter's shirt, with one of the buttons missing where he had torn it off in his frenzy.

377

I paid her, and turned back to the cabman.

'New Gravel Lane, Wapping,' I said.

It was a relentless journey, taking us by slow degrees from the power and splendour of the Strand to a world of such abject squalor and despair that even Maiden Lane seemed prosperous and hopeful beside it.

And with every yard I became more convinced that it was the journey Walter had taken.

For what he had done to me was an act of despair.

As we made our way down Fleet Street and Cannon Street and Eastcheap, and past the Tower, and into the teeming rat-cage beyond, I could hear his voice in my head:

That is where I thought I had met my fate.

Nothing will do but to go back there, and meet my fate again, and abandon myself to it.

I should find him there, I knew that now.

But whether living or dead, I could not guess.

After perhaps forty minutes we suddenly stopped. I looked out of the window, but could see nothing but fog and the blur of distant lights.

'Where are we?' I said.

'Ratcliffe 'Ighway. The New Gravel's just over there.' He cleared his hoarse throat. 'What is it you want there, miss?'

'I'm looking for my brother.'

He whistled softly. ''E must've done something bad.'

'Yes,' I said, getting out. 'Find somewhere you can rest the horse, and have some refreshment yourself.' I gave him a sovereign, thinking that if some accident befell me I might not have another chance to pay him. 'And meet me here again in an hour.'

'You can't go there alone, miss!' he protested.

But he took the money anyway. And when he called after me, it was not to urge me to think again, or to offer his assistance, but merely to say:

'Thank you, miss!'

What had I imagined?

Murky, ill-lit streets, half deserted. For today, of all days, surely, anyone who had a family and a home must have returned to them, leaving none but the wretched dregs among whom I thought to discover Walter.

But the desolation I found was of another sort. The people of New Gravel Lane were wretched indeed – but rather than shrinking into the shadows to suffer their misery in isolation, they seemed to have gathered in a great throng to proclaim it in public. I could hear their hubbub even before I could clearly see them: shouts and cries; snatches of song; the squeal of a tormented cat; a bullish roar that erupted suddenly out of the mist and then subsided in uneasy laughter. The beer-houses and taverns were open, and a constant stream of drunken men and women spilled out of them and staggered bellicosely into the jeering crowd, as loudly and heedlessly as if this were just another raucous Saturday night. Save that some of the shops were closed, in fact, and that the merrymaking had a kind of heightened, feverish, desperate edge to it, there was nothing to suggest that it was Christmas Day at all.

Perhaps this is how they keep Christmas in Hell.

I had feared that I should be conspicuous; but no-one paid me the slightest heed as I entered the press. My first difficulty, indeed, I soon saw, would be to attract anyone's attention for long enough to ask a question; for everyone seemed entirely occupied with bawling and singing and swaggering his own way to ruin. A dizzying procession of faces – sunken and bloated, pale and drink-reddened, scabbed and scarred – propelled themselves towards me out of the fog, and were gone again in an instant. Even had I succeeded in stopping one of them for a moment, the swell of people would have parted us before I had had time to explain my purpose.

At length, I saw a dim forest of masts and spars looming through the mist, and realized I must be nearing the river. The crowd here was slightly less dense, and I saw a knot of capless and bonnetless women talking together at the mouth of the Thames tunnel, like crows waiting for carrion. One of them turned and looked idly towards me as I approached. I raised a hand to detain her.

'I am looking for a man,' I said.

'Ain't we all of us, darlin'?' she said.

The others laughed, and I felt myself blushing behind my veil.

'Here is a picture of him,' I said, unwrapping the photograph.

The woman took it, tilted it to catch the light from the street-lamp, and let out a long whistling sigh.

'I'd be lookin' for 'im, if I 'ad one like that,' she said. She smiled ruefully – and seemed in that moment to age twenty years, for I suddenly saw that she had no teeth.

'Let's cool 'im, Lizzie,' said one of her companions, moving to her side. She stared at the photograph for a moment, and then glanced oddly at me.

'You sure you lost 'im 'ere?'

'Yes.'

'Well, I ain't seed 'im. I'd 'a' remembered if I 'ad.'

The others gathered round, and the picture was slowly passed from hand to hand. Most of the women merely shook their heads; but one – a squat, dark-haired sloven in a torn dress – held on to it for so long, and looked at it so intently, that Lizzie at last burst out:

'What is it, Lu? 'E the one promised to marry yer?'

Lu! Was not that the name . . .?

'*Which* one?' cried one of the others: and they all laughed.

But Lu continued staring at the photograph, and I at her. She *might* have been the woman in the hood, I thought; but the light was so poor, and my mind had suppressed the details of Walter's description so successfully, that I could not be even reasonably sure. I craned forward, trying to make out her features.

'Watch out, Lu, she'll 'ave yer ears off!' Lizzie called out, half jokingly. For a moment I was puzzled; and then – with a shock that made me giddy – I understood: she supposed that I saw Lu as a rival, and was about to fling myself on her in a jealous rage. I tried to dismiss the idea as entirely ludicrous, and found to my horror that I could not do so – for the last few months have broken down the impenetrable wall that I had always supposed separated me from such women. Of course, my relations with Walter were of a different order; and yet had we not both known him in the same bestial, illicit way? And did that not intimately connect us, and give us – at the basest level – a similar claim upon him?

'Give it back, please,' I said coldly, holding out my hand with as much authority as I could muster.

But she glared at me instead, and folded the picture to her breast.

'Come on, Lu,' said Lizzie. 'Give it 'er. She ain't get nothing else.'

Lu still made no response; but at that moment fate intervened for there was a sudden cry of 'Stop! Thief!' and a second later a boy burst in among us, darting between boots and skirts as he looked frantically over his shoulder. I glimpsed a mat of dirty hair – a pinched face, entirely white save for a great purple sore on one cheek – and then a pair of worn soles as he disappeared into the tunnel.

Lizzie took advantage of the commotion to snatch the picture and thrust it into my hands.

'There you are, darlin',' she muttered hurriedly. 'Off you go, smartish. And good luck to you.'

I did not hesitate, but set off immediately back the way I had come. Behind me, I heard Lu swearing and protesting; but before she could give chase a Jew in a black coat sped past in pursuit of the boy, scattering the women again like startled chickens, and allowing me to make my escape.

I have only vague and disconnected recollections of my adventures during the next half an hour. A black sailor in a fur cap who shook his head sorrowfully as he looked at the picture, and said: 'I have no money' – as if he had supposed I was trying to sell it to him, and would have liked to buy it if he could. Three tars who refused to looked at it at all, and jostled me aside, with oaths and yelps of derision. A little girl, who said she was sure her aunt knew the gentleman; and then led me to a bare room above a shoe-shop, where the air was thick with some sickly sweetness, and a lascar dozed on the floor, and a woman rocked back and forth on her heels, so stupefied that she could not focus her eyes on the photograph, or answer my questions.

At length I was forced to admit that I was wasting my time, and found my way back to Ratcliffe Highway. Whether I had been gone more or less than an hour I could not say; but the cab was waiting. The driver was squinting anxiously into the fog, and seemed relieved when he saw me.

'Well?' he said.

'No.'

'But you ain't 'urt or nothin'?'

I shook my head.

'Where now, then? 'Ome again, 'ome again?'

'No. The nearest police station.'

Of course, I had thought of it before – indeed, it had been almost my *first* thought – but I had been deterred by fear. What if I should walk in, and see a bill proclaiming the discovery of a body that could only be Walter's? What if some gruff sergeant took one look at the photograph and said: 'Oh, yes, miss! We brought *him* in not an hour since. But he don't look like that no more. Twenty-four hours in the river changes a man wonderful.' To learn it there, in the bright lights of a public place, and under the indifferent gaze of a tired official!

But now I saw I had no choice. I *must* know, one way or the other.

I *must* know. As I write those words, I am struck by the irony – for did not Walter use them too, when speaking of *his* predicament? But at the time I was too exhausted and upset even to remark it.

We drove back along the north side of the dock, and then turned south and east again. The streets seemed emptier here, and I could see little beyond the fog until we drew up before the brilliant lamp of the police station. I got out, and opened the wicket gate.

The entrance was lined with the descriptions of people lost and corpses found, but I decided not to torture myself by reading them. Instead, I went straight into the office – a plain, white-walled room that seemed almost impossibly bright and warm after the freezing gloom outside.

Before the desk stood a constable, and two figures I recognized immediately: the boy with the sore on his face, who was cowering and trembling with fear, and his black-coated pursuer. Behind it sat the Night Inspector: a lean, balding man with ginger whiskers, who was writing in a ledger. He looked up as I approached, and said wearily:

'Yes, miss?'

'I am looking for my brother.'

He nodded. From somewhere to my right I heard a soft cough and the creak of a chair. I turned slightly, and out of the corner of my eye saw another man, whom I had not observed before. He

was thickset, with a high domed forehead and a fringe of spik-
dark hair about each ear. From his neat, sober dress and the open
notebook on his knee, you might have supposed him to be a successful lawyer. But he did not seem to be connected with the boy
or his accuser; and, indeed, it was difficult to believe that either of
them would have been able to command the services of such a
man. He watched with a kind of detached curiosity as I set down
the picture on the counter – although it was too far away and too
high up for him to see it from where he was sitting.

The Night Inspector drew the photograph towards him without a word, and stared at it for so long that I felt certain he must
recognize it, and was thinking how best to tell me the dreadful
news. But at length he shook his head, and slid it back to me.

I had begun to wrap it again when the young thief suddenly
blurted out:

'I knows 'im!' He tried to lunge towards me, but the constable
grabbed his shoulder and gave him a cuff that made him squawk
with pain.

'What?' I said.

'I knows 'im,' snivelled the boy, between sobs. 'I seed 'im!'

'Where!?'

'I can show yer!'

The constable caught hold of his ear and shook it. The boy
squirmed and howled:

'Leave off! Leave off!'

'Please . . .' I laid a hand on the man's arm.

He shook his head, with the worn look of a man tired of having
to explain the wicked ways of the world to innocents like me. It's
just a dodge, miss.'

'It ain't, it ain't!' shrieked the boy. 'I seed 'im! 'E's stalled where
I dossed last night! 'E scared me!'

'And where is that?' said a deep, soothing voice. The legal-
looking gentleman had got up without my noticing it, and was
now standing at my elbow.

'Tench Street crib,' said the boy.

The gentleman nodded, and turned to me. 'My name is Mayhew, madam. And I shall be happy to show you the way.' And
with a small bow, first to the Night Inspector, and then to the boy,
he ushered me towards the door.

383

We barely spoke in the cab. My companion – though I sensed he was curious about me, and would have liked to hear my story – was too delicate to question me; and I was too dazed, and too troubled by my own thoughts and feelings, to say anything at all. I dreaded discovering that the boy was wrong; and yet doubted whether I had the strength and energy to do what must be done if he was right – for if Walter *was* there, how should I act towards him? Could I marshal enough civility even to get him away from the place, and take him to where he could be safely delivered into other hands?

After about ten minutes we turned into a dark winding street and stopped at the entrance to a narrow court.

I remember walking through it, and out into an open yard cluttered with barrows and costermongers' carts. I remember entering a huge, smoky kitchen, with soot-blackened beams, and a rude iron gas-jet in the ceiling, and haggard men lolling about on the benches and tables that ran around the walls. I remember one of them crying out: "'Ere's Mr. May'ew, gents!' and a handful of the others breaking into a desultory cheer; and my companion smiling, as if this was no more than his due, and whispering in my ear:

'I provided their Christmas dinner.'

I remember him speaking to the man who had greeted him. I remember the man nodding, and picking up a lamp, and giving it to me; and Mr. Mayhew murmuring, 'Go on!' and urging me on with a wave of his hand, as if he knew this were a quest I must undertake alone.

I remember a barn-like room lined – no, packed – *crammed* – with sleeping-stalls. I remember thinking: *This is what the inside of a slave-ship must have looked like*. I remember peering into the first three or four, and wondering if even a slave-ship could have afforded such images of want.

And then I remember nothing but Walter.

He was lying on his back on a leather cover. In the two days since I had seen him last he seemed to have shrunk, and beneath his unshaven beard his face was as white as parchment. His eyes were open, but he gave no sign of recognizing me. For a moment I feared he was dead; and then I saw him blink.

'Walter?' I said.

He made no response. I moved towards him. As I did so I felt a hand close on my wrist, and heard a voice say:

'Leave it!'

I turned back. A small man with copper-coloured hair and a face marred by giant freckles was leaning out of the neighbouring booth.

'Leave it,' he said again. His nose was running, and he wiped it with the back of his hand. ''E may want it later.'

I looked back at Walter, and noticed a tin plate lying next to him on the bed. All I could see on it were an uneaten potato and a slab of grey that might have been beef.

'Do you mean the food?' I said.

He nodded.

'I won't touch it,' I said. 'I've come to take him home.'

The man nodded again. ''E'll die else.'

'How long has he been in this place?' I said.

'Since yesterday,' said the man. 'But 'e won't eat nothing.

'And how did he come here?'

'I brung 'im. I sees 'im on the bridge, just starin' down at the river. And – I'll be honest with yer – 'e's looking so lost I thinks: *There's an easy one. Why don't you do 'is pocket?* So I'm tryin' to flare' 'is purse, but I can't find it, and while I'm pokin' and pattin' 'e notices me. But stead of shoutin' at me, or tryin' to stop me, e just looks at me. There's a namesclop the other side, 'e could 'ave 'ad me just like that, but 'e don't do nothin'.

'So I thinks: *'E must be pretty bad.* And I says to 'im: "You ain't thinkin' o' doin' it, are you? Not – *doin' away* with yourself?"

'But still 'e don't say nothin'. So I says: "You didn't ought to do it, mate. You come with me, and I'll give you twopence for a ticket, and things'll look brighter in the mornin', you see if they don't." And 'e come along as meek as a lamb, as though 'e didn't care whether 'e lived or died.'

He paused, and wiped his nose again; and then with an almost tender glance at Walter, said:

'And I don't think you do much, do you, mate?'

'Thank you,' I said.

I took Walter's hand, and pulled him up. He was quite unresisting, and did nothing either to assist us or impede us as the pickpocket and I helped him to his feet, and led him towards the kitchen.

I do not recall seeing Mr. Mayhew again on our way out. I do not recall seeing anyone, in fact, until we emerged from the court, and found the driver standing by his cab, stamping his feet and smacking his gloved hands against the cold. He made no comment when he saw us, but touched his cap, and said 'Good evening, sir', as we helped Walter inside – as if it was the most natural thing in the world for my brother to sleep in a Wapping lodging-house, and he had known all along that this was where we should find him.

On the way home, I at last found the words to say:

'You are ill, Walter. I am going to arrange for you to go somewhere where you will get better. After that, we will return to Limmeridge, and resume our lives. You may talk to me of what happened between us if you will, but neither you nor I will ever mention it to Laura or to any other living soul, and it will never happen again.'

He merely slumped in his seat, and gazed listlessly out of the window. Only when we were almost home did he turn towards me, and – shrinking into his corner, as if to prove he did not mean to touch me – whispered:

'I'm sorry. I'm sorry. You were right. Vacancy.'

'What do you mean? What have I ever said of *vacancy*?'

'My emptiness.'

Fearing he might be delirious, I affected not to hear, and said nothing.

Postscript

From the journal of Marian Halcombe, 15th July 186–

A year to the day since Walter came back to us. The doctors warned us that progress would be slow, and so it has been – agonizingly slow. But week by week he *is* growing stronger – and so, I think, am I. He walks with greater purpose. The children no longer shrink from him in fear. Indeed, he has even begun to play w th them again – though with a kind of solemn watchfulness, as if he has forgotten how it is done, and must learn all over again by observing them. And when, a few days since, we entered the nursery, and young Amy suddenly chortled at him, and pointed and – for the first time – cried 'Papa!', he almost smiled.

As for Laura: she must wonder constantly at the dreadful change in him, and yet I have never heard her complain of it or ask me its cause. Perhaps she is afraid to do so; or perhaps it is simply her nature to accept things as they are. I fear she is often still hurt and baffled; and yet several times over the last month or so I have also seen her flush with delight, as he forces himself to answer her gaze, or to accept the touch of her hand, or to compliment her with fumbling courtesy on her dress or her hair.

Life here will never be normal again – if 'normality' is how we lived before. There will always be a pain between us. But with every day that passes it feels more like a shared pain, such as soldiers may feel who have endured a battle together. And like the bass notes of a piece of music, it seems to deepen as well as darken our experience. We think and talk less of the past and of the future, and more of the present. Yesterday I found Walter on the terrace, sniffing the smell of rain on earth; and when he saw I smelt it too, and rejoiced in it, we both found – strange the invisible threads that run between us, and the messages they convey! – that our eyes were full of tears.

This morning I heard from Lydia Kingsett. Her husband, it appears, is in prison, awaiting trial (she did not say for what, but how many women would have said even that?) and – for all the shame and embarrassment she must feel – she seems much happier for it. She enclosed with her letter a copy of the *Quarterly Review*, saying there was an article in it by Elizabeth Eastlake – 'which, if you have not seen it already, I think you might find of

389

interest'. I confess I could not bring myself to read it at once, and left it unopened where it lay.

And would, doubtless, have thought no more about it – but that this afternoon, as I was on my way to the garden, I heard a strange sound from the library. *So* strange that I had to stop, and think for a moment what it was.

It was Walter. Laughing.

I opened the door. He was sitting at the table, looking at the *Quarterly*. When he saw me, he got up, and handed it to me.

At first I could not see what had caught his attention. And then I found it: a review of *The Life and Correspondence of J. M. W. Turner*, by Walter Thornbury.

I tried to read it; but it was nothing but a blur of words.

Until Walter pointed me to the last paragraph:

It is even possible that, by requesting some competent friend to draw up a modest memoir of him, and furnishing the necessary information, Turner might have saved himself from the worst of his posthumous misfortunes – that of falling victim to such a biographer as Mr. Thornbury. Perhaps the appearance of this wretched book may be the means of calling forth some writer qualified, by knowledge of the man and of his art, to investigate the truth and to tell it as it ought to be told.

Hans Christian Andersen: A BIOGRAPHY

Hans Christian Andersen

A BIOGRAPHY

by Fredrik Böök

TRANSLATED FROM THE SWEDISH BY

GEORGE C. SCHOOLFIELD

University of Oklahoma Press

Norman

Library of Congress Catalog Card Number: 62-10765

Coypright 1962 by the University of Oklahoma Press,
Publishing Division of the University.
Composed and printed at Norman, Oklahoma, U.S.A.,
by the University of Oklahoma Press.
First edition.

❧❧❧❧❧❧❧❧❧❧❧❧❧❧❧❧❧❧❧❧❧❧❧❧❧❧❧❧❧❧❧❧

*I wish to dedicate this translation of Fredrik Böök's
biography of Hans Christian Andersen to
the memory of my father,
Raymond Roy Schoolfield*—G.C.S.

Translator's Preface

THE PRESENT BIOGRAPHY of Hans Christian Andersen is the first work of Fredrik Böök, the dean of Sweden's literary critics, to appear in English. The translation is based upon the second—revised and augmented—edition of 1955; the first edition appeared in 1938. The final chapter of the second edition, *"Det danska hos H. C. Andersen"* ("H. C. Andersen's Danishness"), has been omitted in the translation; it discusses problems not altogether comprehensible, or important, to a non-Scandinavian audience.

The photographs reproduced herein were obtained from H. C. Andersens Hus in Odense, Denmark. They were all copyrighted by that institution, and have been used with their permission. The illustrations of Andersen's fairy tales which are printed along with the text of this book are all through the courtesy of The Bettmann Archive.

The translator would like to express thanks to Professor Böök himself and to Fil. Lic. Rolf Arvidsson of the University Library at Lund, Sweden, for their interest in the undertaking.

GEORGE C. SCHOOLFIELD

Cincinnati, Ohio
February 7, 1962

Contents

ix

Illustrations

Drawings

Hans Christian Andersen: A BIOGRAPHY

CHAPTER I

The Proletarian Family from Odense

T̲HE FAIRY TALES which have made Hans Christian
Andersen famous are not merely the products of their author's
imagination; they are part of his personal experience, something
he has lived through. They have their roots in his life story; as a
matter of fact, his life story represents, in essence, the fairy tales'
primary form. In looking back over his past in the 1850's, Andersen himself saw the matter in this light. "Rich and serenely
happy, my life is a beautiful fairy tale"—thus his account of himself began, and he gave the great work the title *Mit Livs Eventyr
("The Fairy Tale of My Life")*. The mood, the poetic thought,
even the very distribution of light and shade in Andersen's fairy-
tale world stem from this source. "The story of my life is intended
to teach the world the lesson it teaches me: that there is a loving
God Who arranges everything for the best." This was the opinion

3

of the fifty-year-old author. But much earlier, at the age of twenty-seven, he had written another autobiography, which has become known only in our time, under the title *Levnedsbog ("Book of My Life")*; and in the introduction to it he emphasizes the same standpoint: "It seems to me that life itself is a wonderful, poetic tale. I feel that an invisible and loving hand directs the whole of it; that it was not blind chance which helped me on my way, but that an invisible and fatherly heart has beat for me!" The religious optimism, the romantic sorcery which put their stamp of supernal enchantment upon the realm of the fairy tales thus appear to be reflections of the poet's own fate.

The delineation of this exciting and unusual fate is a tempting task. Information for the undertaking can be acquired, first and foremost, from Andersen's two autobiographies and from his letters and papers—few people have been more prone than he to confess both to their contemporaries and to posterity. But no matter how candid he may have been, there are points on which he remained reticent. In many cases he did not wish—or was not able —to present reality in its full extent or its correct light. Scholarly research in Denmark has made many valuable contributions to Hans Christian Andersen's biography; personal and literary history, topography, psychiatry, folklore, and the history of religion have vied with one onother in acuteness. Aided by all these investigations, it is possible to compose a picture of Andersen's life, based in the main upon his own accounts, but judicious in its use of factual information and in the illumination and evaluation of these facts. The fairy tale must be tested to determine its content of reality.

Hans Christian Andersen was born in Odense, Denmark, on April 2, 1805; his parents were a twenty-three-year-old master shoemaker, variously called Hans Andersen and Hans Hansen, and the shoemaker's wife, Anne Marie Andersdatter, who was between thirty and forty years old. The wedding, for the rest, had taken place only two months before the boy's birth, and it seems that the young couple was able to set up a common household only some six months later. For obvious reasons, both of these circumstances are passed over in *The Fairy Tale of My Life,* and perhaps Andersen was not even aware of them.

By birth Hans Christian belonged to the masses, to the truly poor; employing a modern term, one should say: to the "unpropertied proletariat." His father, to be sure, was called "master shoemaker," but he was merely a "free master," holding a kind of second-rate mastership—the possessor of the title did not belong to the guild; he was allowed to exercise his trade independently, but could not have anyone in his employ. The most extreme poverty prevailed in his home, a fact which Hans Christian has not concealed:

A single little room, its floor space almost completely taken up by the shoemaker's workbench, the bed, and the turn-up bench on which I slept, comprised my childhood home; but the walls were covered with pictures, on the chest of drawers there stood beautiful cups, glasses, and knickknacks, and above the workbench, by the window, there was a shelf with books and songs. In the tiny kitchen a row of pewter plates hung above the food-cupboard; the little chamber seemed both large and splendid to me; and the very door, on which a landscape had been painted, meant as much for me as a whole picture gallery would now. From the kitchen a ladder led up to the loft, and there, in the eaves trough between our house and the neighbor's, one found a box of earth with leeks and parsley—my mother's entire garden; in my fairy tale, *The Snow Queen,* it is blooming still.

5

Here one sees how Hans Christian endeavors to cast an aura of poetry and contentment over his home's unprepossessing reality —and he succeeds brilliantly. Even today the luster he created surrounds the little half-timbered house on Munkemøllestræde, to which the tourists make their pilgrimages; on the poet's seventieth birthday a commemorative tablet was put up by the municipality of Odense—the bishop himself led the delegation—and on it one may read the words: "The dearest childhood memories of the poet Hans Christian Andersen are linked to this house." A woodcut of the home was also issued during Andersen's lifetime, and the poet composed a lyric text, "My Childhood Home," describing it:

> Where the cloister had fallen to ruin,
> Near Odense's Monk-Mill there stood
> (As you see in the picture) a cottage,
> Small, half of plaster, half wood.
>
> How festive the mood was within it
> When the Whitsuntide bells were rung;
> The little white curtains of summer
> In the sun round the windows were hung.
>
> The orpine was tied to the rafters,
> The tile stove was scrubbed to a shine,
> And sweet-smelling boughs of the birch tree
> Were there with the woodruff entwined.
>
> A chamber, a little kitchen—
> And yet all so great and so good;
> And I played better games there at Christmas
> Than later in castles I should.
>
> What a feast! The rice pudding, the gnaw-bag,
> The goose on the board—we know best,

The Proletarian Family from Odense

When we think of the home of our childhood,
How richly our earth has been blest.

Accustomed to the homage rendered him at the Danish castles
where he usually celebrated Christmas, the poet, old and famous,
has employed the simplest means in this poem—the sound of bells
from the near-by church, sunshine, white curtains, flowers and
leaves and stove-blacking—to conjure up a radiantly festive image.
And the poem contains a discreet tribute to his mother as well: in
the midst of all her poverty, she saw to it that the home was spick
and span; one likes to think that Hans Christian Andersen's aesthetic bent, his meticulosity which extended even to purely material affairs, was a legacy from his mother, as he had known her
in her best days—for she ended in alcoholic misery, and her son,
still a struggling author, could do but little to help her. But he
guarded her memory to the best of his powers, and the five stanzas
on his childhood home, with their implicit glorification of her
abilities as wife and mother, represent, as it were, a part of his stewardship. If she was really able to put a roast goose on the table every
Christmas Eve, in accordance with Danish custom, then one must
admire her skill as a housekeeper. It is possible, to be sure, that the
son's and the poet's imagination idealized the situation a little.
His mention of the "gnaw-bag" is worth noticing—*Gnav,* "gnaw,"
was a game played with pawns, something like our parcheesi; it
was associated with Christmas and cookies, and the winnings were
usually composed of good things to eat. He wishes to suggest that
in his little, poverty-stricken home there was also a place for the
superfluous, for games, freedom, art, the whims of the imagination; there were books, songs, a painted landscape, knickknacks,
shining plates, flowers. It cannot have been so depressing, so oppressive and wretched, after all—an appeal of this sort lies con-

7

cealed in Hans Christian's depiction. One must grant that he is right—his childhood home was evidently neither barren nor gloomy, since he, growing up in it, turned out as he did.

But there were some special circumstances which made the idyll of Andersen's childhood possible. One of them was the boy's propitious situation: he was an only child, both his father and his mother were gentle and tenderhearted, and did their best to spoil their child. If he had had brothers and sisters, and if the atmosphere in the home had been sterner, then his life would have been marked by want and deprivation in quite a different way. And furthermore one must take into account the sunny and unassuming mood of people in those days. Bitterness and discontent were not a part of the spirit of the age.

> My mother told me that I was much more fortunate than she had ever been—I led the life of a child of the nobility! When she was small her parents had driven her out on the streets to beg, and since she had not been able to bring herself to do it, she had sat all day weeping under a bridge by the Odense River. In my childish mind I saw the scene so clearly that I wept.

There is a cruel proverb which goes: "Everyone is someone's master"; but one can also say, at the sight of the weeping Hans Christian: "No one is so poor, so forlorn, that he cannot find someone else to feel sorry for."

Thus it is an idyllic, an almost poetic, and above all an honest poverty which Andersen depicts in the very first chapter of *The Fairy Tale of My Life*. Concerning his father he writes that he was a "remarkably gifted man, a truly poetic nature," his mother is described as being "some years older, ignorant of the world and of life, but full of warmth," and the newlyweds were "enormously

8

devoted to one another." The young master shoemaker spent his free hours making toys for his son; during the evenings he read aloud to him from, among other things, *The Arabian Nights* and Holberg—he is supposed to have been a particularly zealous admirer of the great Danish playwright, knowing long passages from Holberg's works by heart. According to his son's account, he was dissatisfied with his craft, and tears once came into his eyes when a customer, a pupil at the Latin school, showed him his learned tomes—"That's the path I should have taken, too," he burst out, kissed his son, and then remained silent for a long time. The anecdote's intention is clear: talents which the father had had no chance to develop flourished in the son. Hans Christian gave a similar presentation of the matter in a poem on Odense, written in February, 1875, some months before his death:

> *In wooden shoes I walked these ways,*
> *And went to pauper's classes,*
> *But all the world before me lay,*
> *Seen through a baron's glasses!*
> *I was no child of poverty,*
> *And neither was my father,*
> *For he read fairy tales to me,*
> *And I became their author.*

It was not material but spiritual poverty whose existence Hans Christian wished to deny. He tells about strolling through the forest in the summer, together with his father; in May when the beeches had their first leaves, his mother came along, wearing the flowered cotton dress otherwise reserved for taking Communion. The little boy had toys: pictures which were transformed if one pulled a thread, a mill that really turned, jumping-jacks—all these things were his father's work. He did not like to play with other

9

children; instead he stayed at home and sewed dolls' clothes. One of his richest sources of enjoyment was the gooseberry bush which grew in the court behind their house; with the aid of a broomstick, the boy stretched his mother's apron out from the wall like a tent, and, sitting under it in rain and sunshine, he peered into the branches of the gooseberry, followed the foliage's development from small green buds to sere and yellow leaves—and was happy.

The happiness of Hans Christian's childhood really consisted, it is plain, in the delight he took in his powers of imagination. He recounts that he often went about with his eyes closed. The reality which lay closest to hand was, after all, by no means so bright or festive. If one keeps to the hard facts, then it could be depicted in quite another light—gloomy, hideous, frightening.

In a letter to his friend Henriette Wulff, written on February 16, 1833, Andersen calls himself *Sumpplanten* ("the swampplant") —the word betrays a more bitter and disenchanted view of the milieu in which he had grown up than that which was presented in *The Fairy Tale of My Life*.

When she married the "free master," many years younger than herself, Hans Christian's mother already had an illegitimate child, a daughter, Karen Marie, born six years earlier, in 1799. Karen Marie's father was a journeyman potter with the poetic name Rosenvind or Rosenvinge; in 1798, 1799, and 1800 he was named by various women as the father of their children, and was regularly sentenced to contribute to the children's support—yet he was so poor that there was scarcely anything to be had from him. Anne Marie Andersdatter seems to have taken work as a wet nurse; what she did with her daughter is uncertain. In February, 1807— when both she and the journeyman potter were married to their respective spouses—she registered a complaint with the mayor of

Odense concerning Rosenvinge's failure to pay the six rix-dollars
to which she annually was entitled. He had taken refuge as a
grenadier in a regiment stationed at Kiel, leaving both his wife
and his other obligations in the lurch.

When, in 1816, Anne Marie Andersdatter was widowed by the
death of the master shoemaker Hans Andersen, the court observed
that the insignificant estate was not sufficient to pay the family's
debts. No more than two years passed before she got married once
again to another master shoemaker, he too a "free master," and
only thirty-one years old. This Niels Jørgensen Gundersen, who
became Hans Christian's stepfather, is given sympathetic mention
in *The Fairy Tale of My Life,* and seems to have been an obliging
and innocuous person. Hans Christian left Odense in 1819; by 1822
his stepfather had died. The entire estate of the household was
estimated at being little more than four rix-dollars; clothes and
tools had already been sold to defray the expenses of the funeral,
and there had been other debts as well. The inventory sheet offers
a heart-rending picture of utter poverty: "one bedstead, knocked
down," some bedclothes, a small table, two old chairs, an old
kitchen cupboard, an old bureau of fir, chipped chinaware and
glassware, an old pair of trousers, and an old vest. The widow was
allowed to keep all these items, probably because none of the
creditors wanted them. In the same year, supported by royal charity,
her Hans Christian was able to begin his studies at Slagelse's Latin
School.

One can guess that things had gone downhill for poor Anne
Marie Andersdatter—in comparison, at any event, with the days
when she was proud of the white curtains in Hans Christian's
childhood home. And gradually they grew still worse. She landed
in a charitable institution—the Gray Brothers' Hospital of Odense,
the so-called "Doctor's Stalls"—and toward the end she became

addicted to alcohol. She died in 1833, in delirium tremens, according to reports. In her best days she had been thrifty and industrious; she could neither read nor write, and was extremely superstitious. Considering her hard life and her many misfortunes, one can easily understand why she sought consolation in the bottle—Hans Christian gave the matter an exculpatory turn in his fairy tale *She Was Good for Nothing*—and a competent medical authority (Hjalmar Helweg) therefore hesitates to state that her alcoholism derived from degeneration. Nevertheless, Andersen did not receive an especially good heritage from his mother's side.

Of her earlier history her son tells us nothing, save that she had had a hard life and as a child had been sent out to beg. Perhaps he did not know much more than that. But now research has succeeded in tracking down his maternal grandmother; her name was Anna Sørensdatter. She gave birth to Hans Christian's mother out of wedlock, and seems herself to have been an illegitimate child. On three different occasions she bore illegitimate children, by different men; and as soon as she had finished nursing the last of them, she was sentenced to a week's confinement on bread and water in the Odense town hall, in order to atone for her sins. That was in 1783; directly thereafter she married the tailor Jens Pedersen, who had just been released from the Odense house of correction.

After Jens Pedersen's death she got married a second time, to one Jørgen Rasmussen, glovemaker, mason, dragoon, and night watchman, as circumstances demanded. Hans Christian's half-sister, Karen Marie, was intermittently taken care of by the maternal grandmother, who died at the Bogense poorhouse in 1825. If Hans Christian knew something about this grandmother's existence, if he even—as has been surmised—visited her, then he at all events took pains to conceal it.

He was more communicative about his father and his father's family. His account in *The Fairy Tale of My Life* of the young master shoemaker's enthusiasm for Napoleon and of his enlisting during the war of 1813 in hopes that he might become an officer sounds very romantic. But authoritative inquiry has proved that Hans Andersen did not actually enlist, but rather let himself be purchased as a substitute, and that shining coins probably played a greater role for him than hero-worship did. He never took part in the fighting of 1813–14, but he did lose his health during marches and hardships in Holstein, came home a broken man, and died in 1816 at the age of thirty-four. He was obviously a little strange, a little unusual; he was happy neither in his task nor in his station, and had always cherished ambitious dreams which came to nothing. Evidence exists that Hans Christian's sober and realistic mother regarded her dreaming husband with troubled and critical eyes. When he became a soldier, she is supposed to have remarked: "He's not right in his head, he's getting like his father."

This father, Hans Christian's paternal grandfather, was, as a matter of fact, patently insane, and in *The Fairy Tale of My Life* the poet makes no attempt whatsoever to conceal the fact. Of Anders Hansen he writes:

> I was terribly afraid of my weak-minded grandfather. He had only spoken to me once, and on that occasion had used the word of address *De,* to which I was not accustomed. He carved strange images in wood, men with the heads of animals, animals with wings, and strange birds; these he packed into a basket and went out into the country with them, where all the peasants' wives gave him treats, yes, even provided him with grits and ham to take home, since he presented them and their children with his ingenious toys. One day,

when he was coming home to Odense, I heard the street urchins crying out after him. Terrified, I hid behind a flight of steps while the noisy crowd passed by. I knew that I was of his flesh and blood.

In other accounts one sees Anders Hansen, nicknamed "the Woodman," coming home from the forest with a wreath of blossoms on his head and swathed in beech leaves and flowers; singing at the top of his lungs, he wandered through the streets of the city. On another occasion he wore a large three-cornered hat of paper, and the urchins followed him cheering.

A certain poetic bent and a kind of artistic imagination seem thus to have characterized the deranged Anders Hansen, and the poet was plainly conscious of having taken after his grandfather to a certain extent. In several fairy tales, and above all in *Holger Danske,* allusions are made to the untutored sculptor's ability to create images; in his old age Hans Christian is supposed to have remarked, upon seeing himself in the mirror, that he resembled his paternal grandfather. In *The Fairy Tale of My Life* he presents the fate of his paternal grandparents as a moving and tragic one: they had been well-to-do peasants, but misfortune had come upon them like an avalanche: "The stock died, the farm burned, and at last the man lost his mind"; his wife moved to Odense with him, and their son, Hans Christian's father, was apprenticed to a shoemaker instead of being allowed to attend the Latin School in accordance with his talents. This account, however, will not hold water, as Hans Brix has proved; but in all probability Hans Christian wrote it in good faith: the imaginative coloring ought rather to be attributed to his grandmother. Neither the fire nor the cattle plague seems to have had any counterpart in reality, and Anders Hansen seems from the beginning to have been a shoemaker like his son; it is scarcely likely that he at any time was a

14

landowning peasant. This of course does not preclude his having possessed a certain prosperity, before mental illness kept him from carrying out his trade. He became a widower in 1822, and the next year the poor old man, for all his intractability and his attempts to escape, was admitted to the Gray Brothers' Hospital in Odense, where he died in 1827. He had cached away, it turned out, some hundred rix-dollars in national bank notes, which had become valueless since they had not been cashed in at the proper time. Psychiatric investigators seem unable to arrive at a final decision concerning the nature of his derangement; but it is clear that the grandson received a dangerous heritage from his paternal grandfather, and that his father bordered on the psychopathic. And it must be added that his maternal grandmother also exhibited features which at the least can be called unhealthy.

In *The Fairy Tale of My Life* the paternal grandmother, Anne Cathrine Nommensdatter, the daughter of the Odense town drummer, is presented in a very sympathetic light, a "quiet and extremely sweet old woman, with gentle blue eyes and a refined figure." She bestowed a tender love upon her grandson, and was deeply distressed when he had to endure need or adversity, or suffered humiliation. The old woman had, to be sure, seen better days. It emerges, however, from the stories that Andersen told Nicolaj Bøgh that his grandmother was also vain and ambitious. She was probably the source of the legend about the farm, the fire, and the cattle plague. Sighing, she was wont to tell Hans Christian stories about her maternal grandmother: the latter was supposed to have been a noble lady in a large German city, which Anne Cathrine identified as Cassel, and there she married a "strolling player"— she had left her home and her parents, and her descendants now had to pay for this false step of hers. "Had she stayed with her fine family, then things would be altogether different for poor Hans

15

Christian," she lamented. The tale has been proved to be pure invention; her maternal grandmother, named Karen Nielsdatter, had married the Assens postrider. Her narration betrays, of course, both a lively imagination and a certain confusion in her mental processes; and similar facets of her personality must also have been at work when she pieced together a perfectly splendid vest of gaudy scraps for her grandson, or when she was mortified at his mother's having him wear wooden shoes or sending him to fetch the milk. Obviously, she wished to make herself seem finer than she was, and she did not show any great care in her choice of means. One guesses that Andersen's often discussed vanity, his social aspirations, and also his power of invention are connected with the heritage he got from his paternal grandmother; but she was hardly of a well-balanced and healthy nature.

Take it all in all: it was a dangerous heritage, and the surroundings amidst which the child of the Odense proletariat was growing

Illustration from *The Ugly Duckling*.

up could well have inspired gloomy predictions. On his father's side madness lurked, and his mother came from a stratum of society where whoring, bread and water in the town hall's cellar, and sojourns in the Odense house of correction were among the occurrences of everyday life. Hans Christian had no opportunity to forget that he had his origins in this world. He had a maternal aunt—one of his grandmother's illegitimate children—whose name was Christiane; she is not mentioned in *The Fairy Tale of My Life,* but in the *Book of My Life,* from 1832, he tells that during his earliest childhood she came to Odense from Copenhagen, where she was residing; she was "very showy" and gave him a silver coin, but Hans Christian's mother spoke of her riches and her ostentation in such sharp terms that the half-sisters parted as enemies. Later on, when the adolescent Hans Christian struck out on his own in Copenhagen, he looked up his aunt. She lived in a well-kept house and gave herself out as the widow of a rich sea captain; in her rooms—according to the information the aunt herself furnished—an elegant lady sat waiting for her beloved. But the aunt did not have a good word for her sister in Odense, partly because of the old quarrel, partly because her sister had now saddled her with her child—"and, to top it all off, a boy—it might at least have been a girl." She obviously had more use for girls. Hans Christian did not stay in her house and never saw her again; and he claims to have forgotten her name. Research into his personal history (by H. G. Olrik) has, however, tracked her down just the same; her name was Christiane Sørensen, and she was never married. When she died in 1830, she left behind her, despite that well-kept house she maintained, nothing save two illegitimate daughters, whose fathers are just as unknown as their subsequent fates. These wretched girls, swallowed up by the darkness, were the cousins of Hans Christian Andersen.

Another reminder of what he had escaped was incorporated in his half-sister, Karen Marie, six years older than Hans Christian. In *The Fairy Tale of My Life* not a word betrays her existence, and for a long time she was so well concealed that one could say she had disappeared. When in 1882, Edvard Collin, Andersen's closest friend, published a diary entry in which reference was made to her, he, as editor, did not know, or pretended not to know, who she was—he interpreted the passage as if it concerned a daughter of Hans Christian's stepfather. But Karen Marie was Hans Christian's real half-sister. She was, to be sure, not present in his childhood home, but he must certainly have known about her, he must have met her. When as an adolescent he moved to Copenhagen to make his fortune, Karen Marie insisted upon following him, evidently in order to make her way in the world with her half-brother's help; but for a long time her old mother refused to give her Hans Christian's address, no doubt because she realized that this encumbrance would only mean new cares, new difficulties for her boy. As a matter of fact, the young adventurer's vessel was so fragile that it could not have borne an extra cargo. One could suspect that the twenty-three-year-old Karen Marie would have compromised her half-brother beyond repair: in a letter to his mother he expressed his misgivings concerning her virtue. Karen Marie came to Copenhagen just the same, but Hans Christian seems to have avoided a meeting by the skin of his teeth; at the very moment of her arrival he left for Slagelse, where he was to begin preparing for the matriculation examination. Evidently Karen Marie wanted to track down a faithless lover in Copenhagen —we do not know if she succeeded, and her later fortunes are likewise unknown. Back home in Odense, in 1833, the mother wrote to her son that she was ignorant of Karen's whereabouts.

What sort of feelings Hans Christian entertained toward his

sister becomes apparent from an entry which he made with deepest secrecy in his almanac for November, 1825. At the time he was boarding with the family of his school rector in Slagelse; when he heard that the rector was expecting a new servant girl from Copenhagen, by the name of Marie, the poor youth was seized by the panic fear that this unknown Marie would turn out to be his half-sister. He could not catch a free breath until, upon her arrival, he determined how unfounded his suspicions had been. But all his life long he obviously thought of his half-sister with fear and dread —he thought of all she represented for him, of poverty and vice and dishonor and the Odense house of correction, of the whole swamp on whose edge he had grown up. Hans Brix has shown how this motif appears again and again in his fairy tales and his other works; the complex received its most complete artistic expression in the novel *O.T.*, where the hero is tormented by the fear that a coarse and vicious girl will prove to be his sister, and where he, bearing the two mystic initials tattooed upon his body, fears that they attest to his previous connections with the Odense house of correction.[1] The symbolism is transparent.

Strangely enough, the wretched Karen Marie did at last crop up in his life in 1842, six years after he had published *O.T.* Emerging into the light of day, the ghost turned out to be not quite so terrifying as expected. On the eighth of February he noted in his diary that, upon returning to his lodgings, he had found "a letter from the daughter of my mother"—he avoids the word "sister." Then he added: "I experienced what I depicted in *O.T.*; sick with fever; a dreadful night." In his despair he sought advice from Jonas Collin. However Karen and, especially, her so-called husband behaved very reasonably and decently, and, poor as they were, were content to receive modest gifts of money. It is significant that Andersen

[1] In Danish, *"Odense Tugthus."*—G. C. S.

could not force himself to enter into a more friendly relationship with them; they disappeared from the pages of the diary, and nothing indicates that he even learned of his sister's death, which took place in 1846. No facts can be adduced to support the rumors that in her day she was a prostitute in Copenhagen; when she died, she was living with a laborer in a poor part of the city, and she is said to have been a laundress—the same hard task which Hans Christian has his and Karen Marie's mother perform in the fairy tale *She Was Good for Nothing.* Dying of consumption, Karen Marie was buried in the potter's field; she left nothing behind—not even children, as far as one knows. The man who had shared the life of the deceased did not even appear when inventory of her goods was taken, and her landlord, the only person present able to provide information, gave an incorrect Christian name for the dead woman.

H. G. Olrik has made the pertinent observation that while Andersen had many feminine friends whom he loved to call "sister," he called his true sister "my mother's daughter." Otherwise so gentle and affectionate, he shunned her like the plague. His reaction will give some idea of the horror he felt at the aspects of his childhood milieu Karen Marie incorporated—in his imagination, at any event—aspects he zealously and skillfully disguised in *The Fairy Tale of My Life,* inspired by shame, by discretion, by devotion, and perhaps also a little by vanity.

That Hans Christian Andersen's life took such a different form from the existences led by his sister and his other relatives, that it led him from the swamps to the heights, of both the social and the intellectual world—here lies the miracle, the fairy tale, the original fairy tale, the source of all the others and especially of that immortal one which teaches that it does no harm to have been born in a duck yard, provided one is hatched from the egg of a swan.

In retrospect the matter is clear enough; but how perilous and ambiguous young Andersen's birthright must have seemed to the people of Odense who chanced to take notice of the boy—who would have dared to cast a favorable horoscope for him? One can imagine him in a variety of situations: It is evening, the lamp is lit in the shoemaker-family's single room, which doubles as a workshop, the mother and father are conversing, the son has been put into his parents' big bed for the time being—there is still not enough space free to fix his bench for the night. Lying in the twilight behind the cotton curtains, he listens dreamily to his parents' voices. "Yet I was as alone in my thoughts and dreams as I should have been if the real world did not exist at all. 'He's lying there so nice and still,' my mother said. 'He's safely out of the way, no harm can befall him.'" Actually, her remarks do not sound very hopeful—it seems as though he were outside the world of normal human beings. His father died, his mother took work as a laundress, Hans Christian was left almost entirely to himself—he sat alone at home with the little theater his father had made him, sewed clothes for his dolls, and read plays. Now he was tall, gangling, and clumsy, with a shock of bright yellow hair; he ran around the streets bareheaded, wooden shoes on his feet. Most of the neighbors shook their heads at his strange manner. While attending elementary school he told a girl in his class that he owned a castle, that he was the changeling child of a distinguished family, and that angels came down to earth to talk to him. The girl, who dreamed of becoming a milkmaid, looked at Hans Christian with an odd glance; then, quite dryly, she remarked to one of the other boys: "He's crazy, just like his grandfather." An icy shudder ran through Hans Christian. Later on, going to paupers' schools, he once again told his companions strange stories in which he played a major role. He also visited the homes of well-to-do citizens, where he acted and recited; people listened to him and were amused. But one day he was chased through the streets by a gang of boys, who called out mockingly: "There goes the comedy writer!" At home he hid in a corner, wept, and prayed to God.

It could seem, after all, that he took most after his paternal grandfather, who was also accustomed to have street urchins at his heels.

CHAPTER II

Childhood Life

"I WAS A CURIOUSLY DREAMY CHILD," Andersen says in *The Fairy Tale of My Life*. "As I walked about, I kept my eyes closed as often as not, so that people finally believed I had poor vision, despite the fact that this one of my senses was and is especially keen."

One must agree: Hans Christian was not blind. No matter how preoccupied and inattentive he seemed as he wandered through Odense's streets, he drank up the whole drama surrounding him, and it was a colorful and entertaining play indeed. Denmark's cities have always been more picturesque and more conservative than Sweden's, to a large extent simply because middle-class culture bloomed more richly than in Sweden, and created handsome and characteristic forms better able to withstand leveling influences. However, Odense at the beginning of the nineteenth century must have offered a spectacle unusually old-fashioned even for Denmark, preserving many features which seem almost medieval to us. Andersen has very often called attention to this phenomenon. In *Only a Fiddler* he speaks of the old houses with their courtyards and their thick walls and their oriel windows, their scutcheons, their carved timber-butts, and the sculptured figures of the apostles on their façades; in the town's streets were still to be seen figures in knee breeches and with shiny metal buttons on their coats, with queues and little three-cornered hats, bearing in their hands long canes adorned with single balls of amber. *L'ancien régime* had lingered in the provincial town. "In those days people there were a hundred years behind the times, I think," a sentence in *The Fairy Tale of My Life* runs. "In Odense a number of customs still prevailed which had long since disappeared in the capital." What a lot of things Hans Christian had the chance to see! Twice he beheld one of the guilds "move its sign"—this meant that its members exchanged one guildhall for another. All the practitioners of the trade marched through the streets in solemn procession, banners flying and drums beating, lemons and silken ribbons on their swords—one is reminded of a scene painted by Rembrandt or some other Dutch master. A harlequin with bells and a fool's bauble sprang ahead of the parade, his face blackened with soot and his nose tinted a brilliant red. The merry-andrew, whom everybody roared at, was called Hans Drud, and Hans Christian's mother insisted that she was distantly related to him—but her little boy, already sensitive and ambitious, obstinately refused to claim any kinship with the fool. After the sign of the guild had been hung before the new hall, a journeyman in his shirt sleeves stepped forward to recite a speech in verse before the assembled throng; Hans Christian paid particular attention to the phrase "Vulcan was the first of blacksmiths"—he thought it sounded fascinating, and asked a boy from the Latin school about the names of other gods.

On Shrove Monday, the butchers drove a fattened ox, adorned with Shrovetide scourges and wreaths of flowers, through the streets of the town; a little boy in a white shirt and with angels' wings rode on the back of the steer. The sailors and fishermen also came into the city during Lent, marched around with flags and music, and ended their celebration by arranging a duel on a gang-plank laid between two boats: the two boldest lads among the sailors wrestled until one of them fell into the ice-cold water. One of these wrestlers was so upset by his defeat, Hans Christian heard tell, that he disappeared forever from his fishing village; and from that day on it was decreed that both should fall into the water at the close. The new year was solemnly drummed in by the town musicians, dressed in striped trousers and yellow bandoleers; there-after they marched out into the country on the same praiseworthy errand, and came back to town with pork and sausages hanging round their drums. Every Easter morning the Nunnebacke was thronged with simple people who had gone there to see the sun dance for joy at Christ's resurrection; unfortunately there was usually a cloud in the way, but no one doubted that the sun was dancing behind the cloud. Once a year the citizen's rifle club drew up on the heath outside of town; the way thither led under trium-phal arches, all the schools and workshops had a free day, the boys ran around cheering with green branches in their hands and on the march home in the evening the target was borne along in triumph, while the whole town followed the bacchantic train. "To be sure, I never took part, but stood instead on a high staircase and watched the whole happy scene," Andersen commented in the *Book of My Life*. Hans Christian himself was no doubt too shy to join the wild boys who swung their leafy branches as they sang.

"All these scenes compose my earliest and most vivid memories," he wrote in the *Book of My Life*. "My old grandmother, who loved me more than tongue could tell, always took me along to watch; she carried me in her arms or led me by the hand to all the amusements which could be had without money." The old woman and the little boy evidently had the same taste, the same love for pomp and circumstance. These old customs and popular festivals, the twenty-seven-year-old poet remarks, "have surely had a deep influence on my whole nature, and have given my childhood a strangely poetic atmosphere—it seems as though I had lived in a much more distant time." And once again he repeats: "Thus the local ways nourished my imagination, and my childhood has a romantic quality which a person born in Copenhagen is not familiar with. It was from these memories of childhood with their kaleidoscopical richness that he took the colorful and ingeniously graphic motifs from which he created his fairy-tale world. Behind the everyday life of petty tradesmen one is forever catching sight of the realm of fancy and myths and rites, the realm of magical scenes and medieval symbols.

It was a remarkable town indeed, and one could experience remarkable things in Odense. One building was regarded by Hans Christian with terror and dread: the Odense house of correction, full of robbers and thieves and ghastly stories. He heard songs from behind its walls, the voices of men and women—the prisoners, singing at their spinning wheels. He stood quite still and listened, not daring to go too near. But one day he and his parents were invited to a party by the gatekeeper of the Odense jail. The great iron-sheathed door was opened and closed, the bunch of keys rattled, the way led up a steep flight of stairs; two prisoners waited on table, but Hans Christian could not bring himself to try even the tastiest morsels. His mother explained that he was sick, and he was put to bed for a nap; but fear and excitement would not let go of him—he thought he heard rousing songs and the hum of spinning wheels. It was terrible, but, at the same time, not disagreeable.

He went to the lunatic asylum with his grandmother—the old woman took care of a garden there. The quiet patients, allowed to move about freely on the grounds, often came up to chat with the grandmother, and Hans Christian listened, both curious and terrified, to their speech and their songs; now and then he strolled with them along the green pathways, and once, when the guards were present, he ventured into the building where the violent cases were confined. Going through the long corridor between the cells, he peeked into the door-chinks: on a straw pallet he saw a naked woman with her hair hanging down over her shoulders. She was singing in a clear voice, but when she caught sight of the boy, she plunged at the door with a shriek, and stretched her arms out toward him through the open food-hole. Screaming, Hans Christian pressed himself against the floor, her fingertips touched his clothes, and he was half dead with fright by the time the guard arrived.

One is struck by the irresistible attraction which everything strange and mystical exerted upon the little boy. He crept into the spinning room in which Odense's poor old women were afforded a retreat: they told him tales, and he lectured them about the insides of the human body, a subject concerning which he had picked up some confused information. His knowledge was just of the right sort for the poor biddies; as he sketched the heart, the lungs, and the entrails with chalk on the spinning room's wooden door, the wretched old souls were amazed at his eloquence, and declared that such a wise child would not have long to live. He was flattered at the news, and the association thus offered pleasure and profit to both sides. He accompanied his mother to the country for the hop harvest, and was allowed to take part in the hop-picking; sitting around a big vat in the barn, the peasants recounted stories, or fairy tales, or simply their own unusual experiences. During the harvest he went out into the fields with his mother to collect ears of grain —an age-old privilege of the poor, but one not respected everywhere. Once a certain farm-steward, one with a bad reputation for sternness, came rushing toward them with his terrible dog whip raised to strike; the mother and her unhappy companions took to their heels, but Hans Christian, losing his wooden shoes, could not run fast enough across the stubble in his bare feet. As the whip was lifted above his head, the little boy looked the steward in the face and said: "How can you dare strike me when God is watching?" The steward lowered the whip, Hans Christian got a pat on his cheek, had to tell his name, and was given some coins to boot. "My Hans Christian is a remarkable child," his mother is supposed to have said. It must have been music to the little boy's ears.

In 1808—Hans Christian was scarcely three years old at the time —Napoleon's Spanish auxiliaries under Bernadotte's command came to Fyn to prepare landing operations against Sweden. Odense's streets were filled with the swarthy Spaniards, who set up camp on the sidewalks and on sheaves of straw in the Gray Brothers' Church, which had been half destroyed by fire. This was one of Hans Christian's oldest memories; single features, staying alive in his imagination, found their way into his narratives and his plays. He saw a Spaniard who had murdered a Frenchman being led away to the gallows hill for execution: the scene reappears in the moving little poem "The Soldier," which Chamisso translated into German and which gained popularity more or less in the manner of a folk song.

Thus the world which revealed itself to Hans Christian was infinitely rich and infinitely picturesque; but it would not have possessed such dizzying depth or such tremendous excitement, if he had not been born in poverty and want, at the very bottom of society—otherwise he would not have seen slums and alleyways, lunatic asylums and houses of correction and spinning rooms; he would not have known how it feels to run barefoot across the stubble or to go to bed hungry or to lack the proper clothes to cover one's nakedness. Existence never becomes truly romantic or wondrous for the person who enjoys it in comfort from the middle of the social ladder; how remarkable the view is, though, from the swamp, amidst the sick, the unemployed, the starving, the prisoners, the lunatics, the homeless, the common soldiers, the vagrants—in those nether regions where Hans Christian lived! But his glance also found its way to the respectable society resident behind the shining windowpanes; in Odense the poor lived wall to wall with the prosperous and affluent. Hans Christian had a remarkable ability for insinuating himself into all sorts of milieus, not just into spinning rooms and poorhouses; he was received by many distinguished families, among them Colonel Høegh-Guldberg's. Once the good-natured colonel brought his protégé to Odense Castle where, amidst pomp and splendor, dwelt Prince Christian, the provincial governor, later to become King Christian VIII. And the Prince carried on a friendly conversation with the lanky boy from the poor shoemaker's home. It was just like a fairy tale. Odense was indeed a rich and wonderful town.

If the background of Andersen's childhood was Romantic, his young spirit also lived in an immediate world of strange and extravagant concepts. His mother was ignorant and superstitious; Hans Christian was confronted on every side by the odd beliefs of the Danish peasantry. During hop-picking he heard tales about ghosts and portents and the devil with his cloven hoof; coming

29

home from the spinning room, where he listened to the old wives' tales, he trembled so badly that he dared not stick his nose outside the door after nightfall. When the great comet of 1811 appeared, Hans Christian, his mother, and the neighbor women, standing on the slope before the church, gazed in fascination at the fiery ball and its tail—dreadful events stood in the offing, the comet would destroy the earth, even as the Sibyl had foretold. Wise old crones, prophetesses, and miracle workers played a great role in the lives of the poor, above all when disease and want were at hand. In the *Book of My Life* he recounts that every Midsummer Eve he went to the spring with a pail, filled it, and then carried the water to his home, half a league away; some supernatural power must have been ascribed to it, for he adds: "I was very superstitious, and my mother no less so." When his father was heard to express doubts concerning the devil's existence, this lack of faith gave rise to real despair and terror in both his wife and the neighbor women, and Hans Christian shared their fear. One morning his father found three scratches on his arm when he awoke; he had no doubt caught himself on a nail as he slept, but the mother and her friends declared unanimously that the devil had paid a nocturnal visit in order to prove his existence. So the story is told in *The Fairy Tale of My Life;* perhaps the actual course of events was somewhat different. When the father, after his return from the Holstein campaign, lay sick, Hans Christian was sent by his mother to get help from a crone who lived half a league outside Odense. She engaged in various kinds of hocus-pocus with the boy, measured his arms with woolen thread, put on his breast a branch of the wood used for the cross of Christ, and sent him away with these instructions: "Walk along the river! If your father is to die this time, you'll meet his ghost on the way." Hans Christian undertook the return journey in mortal terror, but when he got home, his

30

heart pounding, he could assure his mother that he had not met a ghost. A few evenings later his father died just the same; during the night, while the corpse lay in the room, the sound of a cricket was heard. "He is dead," the mother told the cricket. "You don't need to sing for him, the ice maiden has taken him!" Andersen adds: "I understood what she meant." A person unfamiliar with these primitive and magical modes of thought has much more difficulty in understanding her statement, but Andersen's explanation is this: "I remember that when our windows had been frozen over the winter before, my father had shown us that the frost on the pane was shaped like a maiden stretching out her arms. 'She wants me, I think,' he said in jest; now, as he lay dead in his bed, the happening came back to my mother, and my thoughts too were occupied with what she said." Here the connection between superstition and the poetry of the fairy tales lies quite exposed.

True superstition, generally speaking, can become poetry of the first rank, and a vulgar belief in magic can become a charming idyll. St.-John's-wort—orpine, *sedum telephium*—made a pretty decoration, hung from the roof beams, but there was also a magic meaning connected with this custom. The boy's mind was ready to receive the fantastic, the unexpected, the marvelous. He dwelt in Monks' Mill Street, near the mill beside the Odense River. That in itself was enough to excite his imagination:

> Three large wheels turned beneath the falling water; then, when the sluices were closed, they suddenly stood still. The water vanished from the river, which became a dry bed, with fish thrashing about in the puddles—I could catch them with my bare hands—and the sleek water rats came out from under the great mill wheels to drink. All at once the sluice gates were drawn up, the water plunged out

foaming and roaring, the rats were no more to be seen, the course of the river was filled, and I, who had been standing in the middle of it, ran splashing through the water toward the bank.

It is one of those realistic back-yard scenes, so typical for H. C. Andersen, which depict the reality poor children experience—something quite different from traditional nature poetry. But Romantic perspectives loom up behind this unconventional realism. Above the river lies St. Knut's Church; as Hans Christian went past it, he closed his eyes, and then he saw the murdered king, a crown of gold on his bloody head and dressed in a coat of ermine and velvet, walking under the arch toward the altar. His youthful fear of the dark became the poetry of his manhood. In the river there was the bottomless "Bell-Hole," which concealed a bell which had flown thither from the church—now and then one could hear its sound from the depths. Many an evening Hans Christian tried in earnest to hear it ringing, and at last its sound became a poetic symbol for him. He was accustomed to stand on a big stone beside the river, singing at the top of his lungs. An old woman who rinsed her laundry in the river had told him that the empire of China lay right under the Odense River; and he thought it to be not at all unlikely that, one moonlit evening as he stood singing there, a Chinese prince would dig his way up through the earth to the stone, hear his song, and take him back to his kingdom. There he would become rich and distinguished, but he would also be allowed to visit Odense, and to build a castle in the town—a castle, no doubt, something like Prince Christian's, with which he was acquainted. All through the long evenings he sat absorbed in making sketches and plans for the castle he would build with the help of the Chinese prince. He lived in the supernatural.

Thus popular beliefs and peasant superstitions nourished Hans Christian's budding intellectual life, but there was also a rationalistic element in his world, and it stemmed from his father. The "free shoemaker" Hans Andersen—the title is supposed to have been painted on his sign—small of stature, blond, and with a round face, was obviously a thinking man, intellectually far more gifted than the tall, thin mother in her peasant clothes, whom Hans Christian took after in his appearance. It seems as though the "free shoemaker" espoused an attitude of mind not unlike that of the liberal artisans of the 1830's and 1840's, and in this case he would be ahead of his time; one could suspect that the son, on whose information one must depend entirely, idealized and modernized his father's figure a little. According to *The Fairy Tale of My Life,* he sat reading in the Bible one day; suddenly he slammed the book shut with the outcry: "Christ was a human being just like us, but an unusual human being!" Another quotation from him goes: "There is no devil save the one we have in our own hearts." In the *Book of My Life* it is stated that he denied the divine origin of the Bible and the existence of hell, while declaring quite openly: "I am a free thinker." According to what Andersen later confided to Nicolaj Bøgh, his mother became so filled with despair at one such blasphemous outburst that, pulling her son behind her, she ran out to the woodshed, threw her apron over his head—evidently to protect him against evil spirits—and said: "It was the devil who was in our cottage talking that way, Hans Christian, it wasn't your father, and you must forget what he said, for he didn't mean it." Then they had a good cry together, and recited the Lord's Prayer —a scene of touching innocence, which Andersen was to employ in one of his tales (*What Old Johanna Told*), but which he did not wish to reveal in his autobiography. There are faint indications that the "free shoemaker" also stood in opposition to the social conditions of the day; at any event, he took a bold and bitter tone toward the lady of one of Fyn's estates who criticized his workmanship. And there is a hint of budding anticlericalism in the anecdote which Nicolaj Bøgh preserved, but which, like the episode with the Bible mentioned above, was not allowed to appear in the autobiography. The mother had got a job washing for a family of wellborn Odense officials whose son had just returned from Copenhagen after taking his degree as Master of Theology. Marie came running home with the report that the son had tried to seduce her and had offered her money for her services. "What did you do then, Marie?" asked her husband, who stood there with clenched fists and threatening face. "I ran away as fast as I could, Our Lord Jesus Christ knows that I did," she answered, "I ran straight home to you." After a while she added: "But it was a lot of money, after all." Her husband lifted his clenched fist toward the sky and cried out: "And a person like that will be a minister—a minister!"

Seen against this background, the story about the "free shoemaker's" enthusiasm for Napoleon and his desire to serve under the Emperor's banners gets a deeper meaning: it can be interpreted as a sympathy with the Jacobinic principles of freedom. It is plain that the shoemaker stood above his surroundings; his wife did not understand why he eagerly followed Napoleon's exploits in the newspapers, just as she did not understand why he laughed out loud when he read Holberg's comedies. When she and her neighborhood friends told stories about comets and portents, he remarked: "The two worst comets I know are the lottery and liquor." He meant to say: in reality it is from them that misfortune and death arise.

A spark of the intellect's clear flame glimmered in the little shoemaker who could not feel at home in his dark and narrow world, who longed for something nobler and better, who grieved at not having had a chance to study, and who at the end made a desperate attempt to break out of his confinement—an attempt that killed him. The ice maiden on the windowpane was coming to fetch him, he feebly jested as he lay on his deathbed. She was in fact superstition, his mortal enemy. And according to what Andersen told Nicolaj Bøgh, the three scratches appeared not on his living body but on his corpse—the widow pointed to them and said: "Look there, Hans Christian, because he said what he did about Christ, the Evil One seized him and wanted to take him away." In *The Fairy Tale of My Life,* the writer has given a much milder version, which veils his father's tragic defeat. His final hours were darkened by fear of ghosts and by exorcisms, by belief in the devil and by blind credulity. On the way home from the witch-woman's house, the son had trembled with terror at the thought of meeting his father's ghost, and in the little room, as he watched over the corpse, his mother's voice was heard in the silent night, talking with the cricket about the ice maiden.

Everything indicates that as a child Hans Christian stood entirely on his mother's side—pious and superstitious. But the seed which his father had planted in his mind would not die. The man and the poet, who succeeded in combining a fanciful and magical primitivism with a lucid and liberal rationalism to form a kind of romantic philosophy, saw the seed bloom within himself; he became neither an orthodox believer nor a reactionary, but a free thinker, placing his faith in reason quite as H. C. Ørsted and Fredrika Bremer did. The two legacies, from the mother and the father, had become one in the son.

The father had not been a happy man. He had been ill at ease in his calling and in his class. From morning to night he sat bent over his work in the light of the water-filled globe, yet he remained as poor and as helpless as ever. He had nothing to do with his equals, and no one in his surroundings understood him. He was profoundly lonely; reading and dreaming, he never accommodated himself to the world, and was finally wrecked by it. The feeling Hans Christian entertained toward his father was, according to what he told Nicolaj Bøgh, an infinite sympathy. Even the boy knew that being a mere "free shoemaker" was something a little shabby, and he thought he realized that his father was created for something better. From this root there grew the instinctive conviction that he was intended to accomplish the things his father had been unable to do.

This instinct—fiercely strong and frantically compelling, but for a long time irresolute and blind, groping in every direction in the dark—provided the content of Hans Christian Andersen's childhood. Circumstances had already rendered this childhood poverty-stricken and insecure; it was surrounded by dangers and threatened by shadows from the family's past; but the boy's own tyrannical instinct made it grotesquely distorted, morbid, and monomaniacal as well.

CHAPTER III

The Departure

In a material sense, Andersen does not seem to have suffered any real want during his Odense childhood. Of course, one must take into consideration the fact that the autobiography presents a rather beautified and idealized picture of the circumstances in which he lived. Meager rations were evidently not an everyday occurrence in the "free shoemaker's" crowded home, but one cannot help detecting the thin little boy's hunger, involuntarily revealed, in a variety of connections. Hans Christian liked to accompany his paternal grandmother to the asylum, the story goes, because he got better food there than at home, and he admits that he valued the hospital's food still more highly than he did the poetic games he played with the flowers in the hospital's garden. He speaks in the same way of his childish pleasure at life on a manorial estate near Bogense, where he went on a visit with

37

his mother: his enthusiasm was directed at, among other things, the wonderful food. One can surmise that, at home, he did not go to bed with a full stomach every evening. This condition is divulged in an ingenious way by the outcry which burst from his lips when he first visited the Odense theater. A German *Singspiel* was being performed. Astonished at the number of spectators, Hans Christian is supposed to have remarked in a loud voice: "If we had as many firkins of butter as there are people here, then I'd really get enough to eat." Andersen included the little scene in his autobiography for amusement's sake, but the startling association of ideas betrays a good deal about his childhood.

The Fairy Tale of My Life also implies that the boy in no wise lacked good clothes; yet elsewhere one learns that he ran about on the streets bareheaded and in wooden shoes. On solemn occasions everything possible was done to see that he made an elegant impression. "An old woman altered my father's cast-off clothing for me; three or four big pieces of silk, belonging to my mother, were pinned crosswise on my breast and were intended to represent a vest, and a strip of black cloth was put around my neck and tied into a huge bow." It was his paternal grandmother, more than anyone else, who wanted to make a fine gentleman out of him; the result was obviously a little curious.

His education turned out to be very spotty. He first attended a school run by an old woman, who taught the children, little girls for the most part, to spell and read correctly, a job performed now and then with the aid of the switch; but Hans Christian's mother had insisted that her boy be exempt from beatings, and when, one day, the teacher gave him a smack just the same, he immediately rose, picked up his primer, and went home to his mother. He was spoiled; one could even say he was a sissy. Next he was enrolled in a boys' school directed by a man named Carstens; as the smallest pupil there, he became the teacher's pet. During the recesses, while the other boys played rough-and-tumble, Carstens—taking Hans Christian by the hand so that he would not be knocked down—gave him cakes and toys. Hans Christian's self-esteem was awakened early; he grew accustomed to being the object of attention.

On the other hand, he had scarcely any playmates; he went his own way, alone in his surroundings just as his father had been; he grew delicate and sensitive, and in essence he was timid, afraid of the brutal reality and the hardhanded people surrounding him; he felt content only when being fondled or made over. He sat at home, playing with his pictures, his puppets, and his little theater, and his greatest pleasure consisted in sewing clothes for his puppets out of gaudy pieces of material. He was, all in all, a stranger to his milieu and to reality itself. He was drawn irresistibly to the world of fancy, to the realm of sweet illusion. After his first visit at the Odense theater he was as if enchanted. Only on one occasion during the whole winter did he have a chance to attend a performance, but he consoled himself for the loss by making friends with the handbill man; Hans Christian helped him distribute his papers, and as a reward received a handbill for each performance. At home he curled up in a corner with his treasure, and, aided by the title and the cast of characters, put together a whole play out of his imagination. Soon he also began to give plays in his puppet theater. In the neighborhood there lived a pastor's widow named Bunkeflod; her husband had been a well-known poet whose spinning songs were still sung. In her home, to which, somehow or other, Hans Christian had obtained entry, he heard the word "poet" for the first time. "My brother, the poet," Bunkeflod's aged sister would say, her eyes shining, and the boy realized that a poet must be something fine and splendid. However, nothing indicates that he dreamed of becoming a poet himself. Instead, the marvelous world

39

of the theater had captured his fancy; at the Bunkeflod house he had the chance to read Shakespeare in an execrable translation, and for his puppet theater he wrote a play which he called *Abor and Elvira*. The play was based on the tale of Pyramus and Thisbe, but was even bloodier than the original. Hans Christian was so proud of *Abor and Elvira* that he read the work aloud for anyone who cared to listen, and perhaps for others, too; a neighbor woman remarked that *Perch and Cod*[1] would be a more appropriate title, and her heartless criticism made Hans Christian extremely depressed. He soon recovered, however, and wrote a new play, meant to be still finer than the first, for a king and a princess would appear in it. He was, to be sure, unfamiliar with the way kings talked, and so he asked his mother and the women of the neighborhood about it; they were of the opinion that kings no doubt expressed themselves in foreign languages. (The old women of Odense were not completely on the wrong track: German had for a long time been the principal language of the Danish court.) Hans Christian got hold of an old dictionary, in which German, French, and English words appeared together with their Danish equivalents, and with its aid he wrote the dialogue of the king and the princess in a tongue quite suitable to Babel.

However indulgent the mother may have been toward her Hans Christian, she must nonetheless have had her worries about the fatherless boy's future; when all was said and done, he would have to find some reasonable occupation, he could not sit at home all day playing with puppets, while his mother was out doing the laundry of Odense's good citizens. The neighbor's boy, for example, had got a job in a cloth factory, and came home every week with a little money. Hans Christian was also taken to the cloth factory by his paternal grandmother, but she was deeply grieved: she had

[1] In Danish, *"Aborre og Torsk."*—G. C. S.

40

not imagined that she would live to see her grandson sharing the
fate of such wretched creatures. With her high-born grandmother
from Cassel, she was, of course, not free from pride; and Hans
Christian's mother herself is supposed to have declared: "It's not
for the sake of the pay, but just so that I'll know where he is." The
excuse seems strange, coming from the mouth of a laundress. But
the frail boy did not earn any pay in the cloth factory after all, nor
did he do any real work. Hans Christian had a beautiful high soprano voice, and his songs pleased the rough journeymen so much
that they made the other boys do Hans Christian's work while he
gave a concert. After the songs were over, Hans Christian called
attention to the fact that he could act, too, and began to present
scenes, which he knew by heart, from Holberg and Shakespeare—
presumably a rather simple repertoire. His acting was received with
laughter and applause, and Hans Christian spent a few happy days
in the factory, until the coarse jests and practical jokes of the journeymen put the little fellow, blushing and in tears, to flight. When
the mother heard of the journeymen's indecent tricks, she promised
immediately that he henceforth should be spared the cloth factory.
According to the *Book of My Life,* an attempt was made directly
thereafter to employ Hans Christian at a factory where chewing
tobacco and snuff were produced; the apprentices and journeymen
there were said to be extremely well mannered. Here the boy was
better treated, but his work continued to consist mostly of singing
and acting; when he could not quite remember the numbers on
his program, he made up both words and music himself. "He ought
to be an actor," his entranced listeners declared, and Hans Christian pricked up his ears. However the mother soon discovered that
the air in the tobacco mill was bad for her son's lungs, and she was
afraid it would mean the death of him; so it happened that he
stayed at home again, more or less without employment. He was

tall for his eleven years, with blond, almost white hair; his eyes were unusually small, his feet unusually big, and the wooden shoes he wore on weekdays—and his Sunday shoes too—were measured with a thought for his future growth. Hans Christian was neither handsome nor graceful, and, as far as his appearance was concerned, he scarcely seemed to be made for the theater. He visited the Bunkeflods and other friendly old ladies of the middle class; they lent him books, had him read or recite for them, and taught him how to sew clothes for his puppets. When he had seen the tightrope-walker Casorti do his act and give his pantomimes in Odense, he went home, did a Harlequin's dance for his mother, and told her he wanted to devote himself to this career. Her answer was a warning: the person who wants to be a tightrope-walker has to live on a diet of oil in order to get supple joints! However Hans Christian was not frightened by the information, and his mother threatened to beat him if he did not abandon his notions. She was determined to make a tailor of him at all costs, and she begged him to pay a visit to a master tailor named Stegmann, Odense's finest, who lived on Korsgade and had big panes of glass in his windows and journeymen sitting on his tables: imagine how wonderful it would be if he could become a journeyman tailor like them! This was hardly a prospect to appeal to Hans Christian; the only consoling thing about it was the thought that in such case he could get his hands on many a remnant for his theatrical wardrobe.

As the years passed by, one could perhaps, and with a certain justice, characterize the strange and gangling son of the shoemaker's widow as work-shy; for, according to prevalent opinions, poor boys of his age were to be kept hard at work. In their simplicity, his mother and his paternal grandmother knew no better than to bolster him in his evil ways. While his contemporaries were already gainfully employed in workshops and factories, he attended the paupers' school, which was located in the poorhouse, but there was little he could learn there—Scripture, orthography, a dash of arithmetic. Hans Christian never learned to spell correctly, and he cared only enough about his lessons to study them on the way from home to school. But this was a source of pride to his mother. "Look at the neighbor's boy," she boasted. "He studies from morning to night, so that everything goes round and round in his head, but my Hans Christian never opens his schoolbooks, and he gets along just the same." She was right enough: the boy had a quick comprehension and a good memory, but he lacked industry and aptitude for methodical work; he did not entertain any intellectual ambitions, and although he read a great deal— plays, novels, and poems—it seems never to have occurred to him that he ought to study for a career.

On the other hand, he by no means lacked ambition and self-esteem; one could even call him vain. He wished above all else to be admired, and he uncompromisingly employed his singing voice and his mimic and dramatic talents to this end. He made a practice of standing on a big stone down by the Odense River and singing; he began with songs from his theatrical repertoire, and went from them to products of his own inspiration, with melodies and words which no one could really understand. Surely it was the whole content of his child's soul, with all its fear, unrest, and longing, which found expression in the lyric and musical improvisations; but the innocent little singer knew very well that, in the river-side garden behind the board fence, people listened with astonishment and fascination to his unusual concert. Privy Councillor Falbe, whose wife had been a well-known actress, lived there; on beautiful summer evenings the Falbes often had visitors in their garden, and they had the curious pleasure of listening to the clear boyish

43

soprano rising from the river's edge. Hans Christian never sang better and more eagerly than when he knew he had a large and interested audience. He was not shy.

When he was fourteen, he had to be confirmed; it was customary for children from the town's first families and pupils from the Latin School to be instructed by the archdeacon, while the poor children reported to the curate. But Hans Christian went, quite simply, to the archdeacon, who could not refuse his application; in this way the shoemaker's son got to stand in church among the scions of the town's most distinguished families, a group in whose midst he seemed a strange bird indeed. For his first Communion he got dressed up in a brown coat which, having belonged to his father, had been altered to fit him, and on his feet he had the first boots he had ever worn in his life. He was so delighted at his finery that he stuffed his trousers into his boot tops, so that the boots could be seen all the better. As he went up to the altar rail, the boots squeaked, and he rejoiced at the thought that the whole congregation could hear how new they were; yet at the same time he suffered dreadful pangs of conscience, since he felt that the noise was disturbing the devotional spirit. The archdeacon, of course, tacitly disapproved of the poor boy's bumptiousness, and let Hans Christian sense his displeasure. In *The Fairy Tale of My Life* no secret is made of that fact that vanity was one of the boy's driving forces, but Andersen indicates that there were also other reasons for his behavior. He writes:

I was afraid of the poor boys who had made fun of me, I constantly felt an inner urge to associate with the pupils of the Latin School, whom I at that time regarded as being much better than the others. When they played inside the yard of the church, I stood watching them from outside the fence, and I wished that I could have been

44

one of their fortunate number, not for the sake of their games but because they had so many books and could become so many things in life.

Hans Christian's case is like his father's: he feels lonely, isolated, his natural milieu, in which he ought to feel at home, repels him, frightens him; he longs for something higher and better. There is a frantic note in the eagerness with which Hans Christian, in order to save himself from the swamp, clutches at objects far up on its banks. The gesture reveals his true frame of mind: the terror which makes him so bold and reckless that he defies the archdeacon's displeasure.

However strangely Hans Christian behaved, pitiable one moment and ridiculous the next, he nonetheless had a remarkable skill at attracting attention, and not a few Odense families took an interest in him, receiving him into their circle of friends, listening to his songs, and watching his performances; many of them would have liked to help him a little, too—but how should one go about it? One fine day Colonel Høegh-Guldberg took the boy along with him to see Prince Christian at Odense Castle. "If the Prince asks you what you want, then you must say that your fondest wish is to attend the Latin School," the kindly colonel instructed his protégé. Hans Christian did his best, acting out scenes from Holberg and improvising songs; but when the Prince asked him about his plans for the future, he could contain himself no longer. His benefactor wanted him to attend the Latin School, he said, but, as for himself, he wanted to go on the stage! Thus he transgressed against his instructions, as the *Book of My Life* makes clear, although he concealed the fact in *The Fairy Tale of My Life*. The Prince, a clever and sensible man, waxed enthusiastic neither at Colonel Høegh-Guldberg's proposal nor the boy's own. It was very nice to be able to sing and to recite a poet's words, the Prince said, but having these talents did not make one a genius; and as for the pursuit of knowledge, that was a long and costly road. "As a poor boy" (these were the Prince's words, according to the *Book of My Life*), Hans Christian ought rather to consider some comfortable trade—what about becoming a turner?

Oddly enough, Hans Christian did not cherish the least desire to become a turner, and the audience seems to have come to a rather chilly end. As leaves were being taken, the Prince repeated that the boy had only to speak up if he thought better of his decision—then the Prince would hit upon some appropriate solution to the problem. But Hans Christian went his way, anything but satisfied with the interview, and never returned. This clumsy and outspoken Simple Simon, in contrast to the eponymous hero of Andersen's fairy tale to come, had *not* won princess, crown, and throne with his bluntness.

As a matter of fact, the Prince had been completely right. It was not easy to help this strange boy who, like his mad grandfather, loved to be the center of laughter and attention; who, like his poor, misguided father, longed to escape from everyday life and its traditional occupations; who, like his ambitious grandmother, imagined he was the scion of aristocracy, born for some unusual fate. He did not want to become a shoemaker, a tailor, a turner, a clerk; and so his worried mother asked: "What will become of you?" "I shall be famous," was the answer. He had read and heard tell of great men who were born in poverty, and the idea struck him like a bolt of lightning: such was his case. He explained the matter to his mother: "First you have a terribly hard time of it, and then you become famous." The only way to begin the process was to set out for Copenhagen—the sooner the better. With the tenacious energy and the remarkable purposefulness so characteristic of him, the boy, in the midst of penury, had begun to collect funds for the journey; breaking open his savings bank, he discovered that it contained thirteen rix-dollars.

It was not easy for an ignorant laundress to form an opinion about the bold notion of sending a fourteen-year-old boy to Copenhagen for the express purpose of becoming famous. While the father was still alive, an old woman at the poorhouse, an unhappy soul who now and then got leftovers from the shoemaker's scanty table and who enjoyed the reputation of being able both to work magic spells and to tell the future, had said of Hans Christian that: "He will become a wild bird, flying high, admired by all the world —someday Odense will be decked with lights for him." His mother had wept for joy at the prediction, and now that he had to win permission for the journey, Hans Christian reminded her of the episode, and then adduced still another argument to clinch the matter: "Father always said that I should never be forced to do anything against my will; he wanted me to choose my own calling." The mother had to give way before this attack; she agreed to the undertaking, weeping all the while. The hazards were many and great.

No one in his right mind could imagine that the old woman's prophecy would come true.

Thus it happened that in the fall of 1819, Hans Christian Andersen prepared to journey to Copenhagen. Those who heard the plan discussed asked the fourteen-year-old what acquaintances he had in the great city, and to whom he planned to turn; when Hans Christian answered that he did not know anyone at all, he was advised at least to get a letter of recommendation from some influential person. Hans Christian had nothing against the suggestion; but the most distinguished of his protectors, Colonel Høegh-Guldberg, unfortunately was out of town. Hans Christian conceived the idea of applying to an old printer instead—a certain Iversen, one of the town's most respected citizens. Hans Christian did not know the printer, to be sure, but it was Iversen's wont to entertain most of the famous Copenhagen actors who came to Odense for guest performances; and it had always been Hans Christian's notion that he would win fame and fortune on the boards. One peaceful Sunday afternoon the boy climbed the stairs to the apartment of the old printer, who must have gaped with astonishment when he opened the door. Given a friendly reception nonetheless, the boy presented his plan. Quite naturally, Iversen advised against such a foolhardy undertaking in no uncertain terms; like Prince Christian, he suggested that his visitor learn a trade instead. "That would really be a great shame!" answered Hans Christian. The bold reply stamped itself on the startled printer's memory, and was repeated by members of his family for a long time to come.

But, significantly, he complied with the boy's wishes, whatever he may have thought of the fourteen-year-old's mental condition in general and self-esteem in particular. To whom should the letter of recommendation be addressed? The boy suggested Madam Schall, the Copenhagen ballet's most famous danseuse; her reputation had reached Odense, although she had never honored the town with her presence. Consequently, Iversen was not acquainted with her; but he wrote her the required letter notwithstanding, and, armed with it, a jubilant Hans Christian went home. His mother packed his clothes into a bundle—not a very bulky one—and arranged with the postilion for her son's journey to the capital. Against the payment of three rix-dollars Hans Christian was to be allowed to ride the post coach over Nyborg and the Great Belt all the way to Copenhagen; the fare was actually more than the sum paid, but Hans Christian was to be taken along as a sort of stowaway—he could not get aboard until the coach had passed Odense's town limits, and he had to climb down before it entered the streets of Copenhagen.

So Hans Christian left his home one sunny autumn day, in high spirits and confident that he was going to meet his fortune. At the town gates he came upon his aged grandmother, who, tears in her blue eyes, embraced him without saying a word; she did not have much time left, and they would never see one another again. The coach left Odense's confines, the postilion sounded his horn, Hans Christian clambered into his place, and went rolling out into the world; he was on his way to Copenhagen—where he did not know a soul—with ten rix-dollars in his pocket.

In his mind's eye he beheld a message written with letters of fire: he would become famous. This alone was sure; he had only the very vaguest notions about what sort of fame it was to be. Somehow he intended to give expression and form to the feelings and moods and ideas which filled that childish, yearning, ambitious soul of his; he would seek liberation—in dance and song, or in notes and words—for all the forces seething in him; he would be the object of men's attention, he would be loved, praised, admired. But his fear of being extinguished in the darkness, of drowning in the swamp, of perishing in misery, was as wild and fierce as his thirst for growth and fortune and honor. Thus yearning and fear were his traveling companions. When, having crossed the Great Belt, he set foot on Zealand's soil, he went behind a shed on the beach, fell to his knees, and begged God for aid and protection. The prayer made him feel better. He trusted his luck.

CHAPTER IV

Adrift in Copenhagen

O<small>N ONE OF THE</small> first days of September, 1819, early in the morning, the fourteen-year-old boy from Odense climbed down from the post coach on Frederiksberg Hill: he had not, of course, paid for a regular ticket, and so was forbidden to cross the city limits by chaise. Before him lay many-towered Copenhagen, and the boy burst into tears at the sight: in this vast city, so very different from Odense with its seven thousand inhabitants, his fate would be decided. His little bundle of clothes in his hand, Hans Christian walked through Frederiksberg Park, through the long avenue and the suburb, and entered the city proper by the West Gate. On Vestergade there lay a hostelry, the Guardsman's Inn, where he got a room by surrendering his pass as security. Then, not wasting a moment of his precious time, he went out into the city. The streets were crowded with people, and down on Østergade he

came upon such a throng that he could scarcely slip through, thin
as he was; but all the noise and confusion did not surprise the boy
from Odense: he had always imagined Copenhagen to be just as
lively as he now found it. As a matter of fact, the city *was* in an up-
roar; the so-called "Jew Feud," with its mobs and its plundering,
had just broken out.[1]

He asked the old flower-women for directions to the theater—
the magnet which drew him on. Having reached his goal, he went
all around the building, looking at it from every side; someday he
would be at home here, with God's help he would become a superb
actor—but, in the meantime, how was he to gain admittance? He
had hardly finished his thought before one of the ticket sharks
loitering on a near-by corner made straight for him and asked him
if he wanted a seat. His prayer had been heard immediately—this
was not a bad beginning at all, and Hans Christian thanked his
unknown benefactor in the warmest terms. Which place would
suit him best?—there were several to choose from. The guileless
Hans Christian answered that the location depended entirely on
the donor's kindness; and strangely enough, the friendly gentleman now lost his temper, called Hans Christian a gawky scoundrel
who was trying to be funny, and frightened the boy so badly that
he took to his heels.

By the next day he had rallied his courage once again. Decked
out in his brown confirmation suit, his trousers tucked inside his
boots and his hat so big that it fell down over his eyes, he marched
down to Bredgade, there to deliver his letter of recommendation
at the residence of Madam Schall, the *première danseuse*. This was
his great chance: Iversen the printer, who knew very little about
Hans Christian Andersen, had written to Madam Schall, who did

---

[1] In 1819, Copenhagen was the scene of a number of anti-semitic demonstrations.
—G. C. S.

51

not know the printer at all. Before pulling the bell cord, Hans Christian fell to his knees and prayed God that he might succeed in getting help. Just then a cheerful servant girl, her market basket on her arm, came down the steps; she favored the boy with a friendly smile and, as she went past, handed him a six-shilling piece. The poor wretch pulled a long face, even longer than usual: so that was the way he looked in his confirmation finery—like a beggar! His protests died away unheard. "Go ahead and keep it," the girl cried over her shoulder, and vanished. After having been forced to wait a good while on the steps, he was at last given entrance by the famous danseuse, who was somewhat astonished—partly at the letter from the unknown Iversen, partly at the young man's appearance. He expressed a burning desire to go on the stage, and, in order to prove his calling, he immediately offered to act out the main role of *Cinderella* in Madam Schall's presence. The Royal Theater had given the play in Odense; Hans Christian, although he had seen it twice, had never read the text or practiced the music, but he was convinced that he knew the role by heart, and he blithely improvised wherever something was missing in the words or the notes. Arriving at the scene where Cinderella dances, he asked for permission to put his boots in a corner; then he took his graceful steps in his stocking feet, beat on his big hat as if it were a tambourine, and in his boyish soporano sang:

> *What indeed can be wealth's meaning?*
> *What is splendor? What is fame?*

This dramatic and musical scene made a strong impression on Madam Schall, as one might expect. She hurried him outside and, taking leave of him, promised him that he could come by for a meal now and then—an offer he never made use of. Weeping, he went away. Later on in life Madam Schall mentioned this first meeting to Andersen and confessed that she thought a madman had come to see her.

But Hans Christian would not give up. He made his way to Professor Rahbek, the literary patriarch of Bakkehus; he got no consolation from him, but was referred instead to the director of the theater, Chamberlain Holstein. This distinguished gentleman, after likewise having got a good look at the applicant, declared that the boy was too thin; such a figure would be laughable on the stage. "Oh, I'd get fat soon enough if I were appointed with a salary of a hundred rix-dollars!" was Hans Christian's optimistic reply; then

Illustration from *The Emperor's New Clothes.*

the chamberlain remarked that the theater only engaged young men of education. The boy asked if he could have a place in the ballet? No, the first appointments there would be made in the coming May. "Dear God in Heaven," thought Hans Christian, "it's only September now, and I have just a couple of rix-dollars left; they dwindle every day that passes."

In the post coach he had had the company of a Madam Hermansen, who was returning to Copenhagen after a visit in Odense; when he approached her later on, she had helped him a little in both word and deed. Now, learning how things were going with him, she admonished him to leave for Odense by the first boat sailing in that direction. Her suggestion was undeniably a reasonable one; but Hans Christian said to himself, "I'd rather die," and decided to stay on. In order to escape, as it were, from painful reality, he bought a ticket to the theater, although the purchase came near to wrecking his finances. The operetta *Paul and Virginia* was being performed; having arrived at the entrance at three in the afternoon, he succeeded in capturing a seat in the second row of the gallery. The play made such a deep impression on him that he burst out in a fit of weeping: just as Paul must perforce leave his Virginia, so he was compelled to say farewell to the theater and to his lovely dream. The middle-aged women sitting around him consoled him with apples, sandwiches, and cakes, and he lightened his heart still further by telling the story of his tragic fate, a tale by which he harvested still more free victuals. When, on the stage, Paul at last found happiness with his Virginia, Hans Christian smiled once again through his tears.

On the following day, however, reality once again reared its austere head. Hans Christian had only one rix-dollar left, and his second visits to Chamberlain Holstein and Madam Schall proved to be in vain. Something had to be done; he would have to come creeping back to one of those trades he detested, just as his father had been forced to return from the adventures of a soldier's life to the shoemaker's workshop. But at least he would not be the object of Odense's ridicule; he preferred instead to find an apprenticeship in Copenhagen. Madam Hermansen helped him by buying a newspaper, and in its pages they found the announcement of one Madsen, a master carpenter on Borgergade, who needed an apprentice. The master turned out to be a pleasant man who promised Hans Christian food and clothing if he would bind himself for nine years' service. When the master saw how destitute the boy was, he let him begin work immediately; his baptismal certificate and his other papers could be forwarded from Odense later on. At six o'clock the next morning Hans Christian Andersen appeared at the carpentry shop. The journeymen and the apprentices used indecent language, the jokes they played on the new boy were crude, and the first day's experiences were so crushing that Hans Christian, going to the master carpenter in tears, asked to be freed from his bargain. The request was granted.

Once again he walked the streets of Copenhagen, helpless and perplexed. True to his wont, he fell down on his knees and begged God for protection. "After all," he thought, "I have never done an evil deed." He got the idea of displaying his voice a second time for someone connected with the theater; everyone in Odense had praised its timbre. In the newspapers he had read of Siboni, an Italian *Kapellmeister* who had been appointed director of "The Royal Singing Academy"; Hans Christian decided to visit him. If the attempt failed, there was nothing left to do but board a vessel bound for Fyn that very evening. By four in the afternoon Hans Christian had made his way to Vingårdsstræde, where Siboni lived. As chance would have it, a banquet was being held there; and this piece of apparent bad luck led to a happy ending. The maid who opened the door was told not only the reason for Hans Christian's visit but the whole story of his life, and the impression it made upon her can be measured by the fact that she went straight in to the guests and described the visitor for them. "The guests came plunging out to see me as if I were a curiosity," Andersen commented in the *Book of My Life*. Admitted to the dining room, the boy was given the chance to sing and recite; in the company were Jens Baggesen, the famous poet, and Weyse, the great composer. Hans Christian was appearing before Denmark's most distinguished public. There was laughter and applause, directed, to be sure, for the most part at the silliness, the absurdity, of the boy's performance; but when he read some sad poems, his true feelings broke through. The tears he shed were authentic, and it became apparent to this audience of artists that the boy was not simply a figure of fun. Baggesen is supposed to have predicted that he would become a person of note, and Siboni promised to try to train his voice. The maid who had let him in accompanied him to the door too, patted him on the cheek, and, learning that he had only seven shillings to his name, advised him to visit Professor Weyse the next morning; of all those present, Weyse, in her opinion, had betrayed the deepest interest. At Weyse's house Hans Christian learned that the collection, which had been taken up forthwith among the guests the afternoon before, amounted to no less than seventy rix-dollars; it was Weyse, himself a poor boy once upon a time, who had struck while the iron was hot. For the time being, Hans Christian would receive an allowance of ten rix-dollars a month; Siboni would give him singing lessons and had promised to provide him with food as well.

Hans Christian went almost insane with joy. He was rich! A job at the theater was practically his! The *Book of My Life* says: "I can still remember how I, standing alone on the stairs after having left Weyse's, kissed my own hand in my childlike joy and then lifted it up to heaven, thus to show God the gratitude of my bursting heart." His religious concepts did not lack concreteness. He wrote his mother a jubilant letter. He thought his days of trial were past.

His jubilation was, of course, premature—after six months Siboni was forced to abandon his efforts; he had to tell his pupil that his voice was growing worse instead of better, that his appearance was unprepossessing, that he lacked education, that he could not expect to be employed by the theater, and that he under no circumstances could remain in the Siboni ménage. Hans Christian was left once again without friends, without aid; for the next three years he was adrift in the streets of Copenhagen. The beginning of this period has been depicted in both *The Fairy Tale of My Life* and the *Book of My Life,* but these two sources differ from each other a great deal in their details. It is only natural that the poet's memories could not be completely clear, and that they must have undergone certain changes between 1832, when the *Book of My Life* was written, and 1855, when *The Fairy Tale of My Life* came into being; further, one must also take into account the fact that Andersen neither could nor would tell the whole truth about his life in Copenhagen. He has removed or muted its repellent and its humiliating aspects, and the entire period has been given a certain poetic harmony; by 1855 this process of transformation had progressed further than it had in 1832.

His existence in the capital city was, in every respect, appalling. He had his quarters on Holmensgade, which at that time was called Ulkegade, a street populated to a great extent by prostitutes. The house where he lived, with a certain Madam Thorgesen, was irreproachable from the standpoint of morals, to be sure, but it lay in the disreputable part of the street, the so-called narrow end, and the neighborhood was questionable. Hans Christian thus came into contact at an early age with the most sordid side of life; how much he, in his innocence, understood of what was happening around him is another question. In the *Book of My Life* he tells of a visit he paid to his mother's half-sister, a woman who evidently maintained a bawdyhouse—he never went back again, for to his horror he had discovered the nature of the place. This episode is omitted from *The Fairy Tale of My Life,* which, in contrast to the *Book of My Life,* was intended for publication. To Nicolaj Bøgh he told the story of a Madam Olsen, whose acquaintance he had made on the trip from Odense to Copenhagen—she is no doubt identical with the Madam Hermansen mentioned in the *Book of My Life.* This woman gave the youth the job of delivering an epistle which seems to have been half a begging letter and half an attempt at blackmail; Hans Christian was thus drawn into a fraudulent act without being aware of it. He has employed the memory of this experience, which he did not admit in the autobiographies, in his novel, *The Two Baronesses.* In Major General Holten's memoirs it is stated that a certain Krøyer, precentor at Odense Castle, told the following story about Andersen's arrival in Copenhagen: On Lille Kongensgade he was approached by a woman who strolled back and forth on the sidewalk and who took pleasure in the half-grown youth's remarkable naïveté; Andersen lived in her quarters for the first three days of his stay in the Danish capital. No proofs at all exist for the story, but it may not be completely without foundation, for Andersen's own statements about his lodgings during his early days in Copenhagen are somewhat ambiguous, and his report from 1832 does not altogether agree with that from 1855. One could even conjecture that the anecdote about the ticket shark is a disguised narration of this event, since the *Book of My*

Life represents, after all, a confession for the chaste ears of Louise Collin. In each case the innocent country boy misunderstands the friendly advances, interpreting them as a sign of sympathy, although they are in fact part of a cynical design against his purse.

However the case may be, in the *Book of My Life,* Andersen says of his surroundings that he indeed quite literally played and dreamed on the edge of an abyss. At Madam Thorgesen's he was accustomed to open the door for an elderly gentleman who came to visit "his daughter"; later in life he once met the same gentleman, decked out with medals and keeping his countenance quite as well as Andersen did, in one of Copenhagen's distinguished homes. The episode, which seems a little artificial and which in essence does not reveal any bottomless pits of vice, is told rather differently in the two autobiographies; but it indicates at any event that the son of the proletariat, resident in the Ulkegade, caught a glimpse of realities which not every young poet has the chance to see. Madam Thorgesen distinguished herself by her freedom from various sorts of prejudice. On one occasion, when Hans Christian had received a fresh sum of money collected for him among his goodhearted benefactors, his landlady offered to give him room and board, so that he could have a trusty shield against the evil of the world and its inhabitants; in return for this service of love she would accept twenty rix-dollars a month, to be paid in advance. The room he lived in was actually an empty pantry, without windows—the only light came through the two air holes in the door to the kitchen—and thus one could not call her terms especially favorable; Hans Christian begged and implored her to let him off with a lower sum, all the more since he could not dispose of more than sixteen rix-dollars a month under the best of conditions. But the good woman was adamant: either she got her twenty rix-dollars or he had to leave! Having unburdened herself of this statement, she went out to do some errands; Hans Christian was to give her a reply upon her return—provided that he did not want to move directly. After she had departed, the poor boy sat alone in her room—he had permission to do so—with tears running down his cheeks. On the wall there hung a portrait of Madam Thorgesen's late husband; and in his despair Hans Christian turned to the picture: he begged the dead man to move his widow's heart to kindness toward a destitute child—wetting his fingers in his tears, he rubbed them against the picture's eyes, in order that the late Thorgesen might truly sense his grief. The scene is as grotesque as it is moving; as Edvard Lehmann has correctly observed, it is an expression of the animal magnetism which forms the basis of the religion of the Australian bushmen and of the superstition of peasant societies, and it also has points of contact with Catholicism's teachings about the intercession of saints—and the scene reveals the same brilliant and poetic plasticity as that one did in which Hans Christian lifted his hand, bearing the mark of his own kiss, toward Heaven as a thank-offering to God. In his hour of uttermost despair the adolescent boy called up his last spiritual reserve: his imagination, which someday would ennoble his superstitious beliefs, transforming them into the poetry of the fairy tales.

Nor did the sympathy cure fail. Coming home to find the exhausted boy asleep, Madam Thorgesen allowed herself to be coaxed out of her original stand—perhaps pity moved her; perhaps she had thought better of the matter—and she promised to be content with whatever coins the boy could scrape together. Filled with gratitude and joy at having got something which resembled a home, he sank down before her and kissed her hand; "But as for myself, I had not a single shilling for shoes, clothes, or similar necessities," the passage in *The Fairy Tale of My Life* concludes.

As a matter of fact, Hans Christian was a kind of beggar during these Copenhagen years—he existed by appealing to the charity of his betters; he was forever making written or oral application for support. However planless and confused his life may have been, he had a remarkable talent for arousing the interest of the people around him, for insinuating himself everywhere. For a number of months Siboni allowed him to stay at his house, where he frequented the kitchen and ran errands during the time he was not listening to the rehearsals of the opera's personnel or trying to sing a scale himself. Colonel Høegh-Guldberg, his benefactor in Odense, had a brother, the poet Frederik Høegh-Guldberg, resident in Copenhagen; the brother, likewise taking an interest in Hans Christian, gave him the proceeds of a piece of occasional writing he had done, and endeavored to teach him Danish grammar and orthography. In addition, Høegh-Guldberg arranged for the boy to get instruction from Lindgreen, the actor; but after a few trials Lindgreen dismissed his pupil with the following declaration: "You don't lack feeling, but you aren't made to be an actor—Heaven knows what you are made to be! Talk to Guldberg about having a chance to learn Latin—that's always a step along the road to the matriculation examination!" The idea did not appeal to Hans Christian, for the theater was his only passion; but Høegh-Guldberg, kindly as he was, made arrangements just the same for the boy to get free instruction in Latin from a theology student. Unfortunately, he did not live up to the trust placed in him; he studied the grammar in a slovenly way and occasionally did not even come to his lessons. In his opinion, his appearances as an extra or as a member of the theater chorus were far more pressing: and by now he could also creep into the empty places in the parterre. He was drawn to the theater as the moth to the flame. The theater's leading male dancer, Dahlén, who had also interested himself in the boy's case, allowed him to attend his ballet school—he stood at the exercise rail all morning long, stretching his skinny legs and performing the *battement* with an industry and a zeal the likes of which his Latin teacher had never seen. However, Dahlén could never give him any encouragement—the boy had his figure against him. On one single occasion he got to play a roll in the ballet *Armida,* and his name was included in the program; in the evening, his candle still lit, he lay awake in his bed, staring blissfully at the handbill on which his name was printed. Beside it another name, Hanne Petcher, was to be read; she was a little girl who had not succeeded in explaining that her name was Hanna Pätges. One day, under the name Johanna Luise Heiberg, she would become famous.

When Høegh-Guldberg learned of Hans Christian's indifference, he grew so exasperated that he cancelled the Latin lessons. The benefactor had grown tired of his incorrigible protégé, who at sixteen played with puppets in his toy theater and sewed the puppets' clothes himself—roving around in the shops of Østergade and Købmagergade, he had begged colorful samples, patches, and silken ribbons from their owners. He did some reading, to be sure, but only plays, novels, and the like, things which gave fuel to his gluttonous imagination; despite his intelligence, he gave no indication of a real interest in his studies. His appearance must have been extremely strange. One of his acquaintances from this period, Jules Jürgensen, has described his attire: he went around in a hat he got from *Kapellmeister* Siboni, tight trousers and a vest he had received from various sources, and finally a coat with a fox-skin collar, Jürgensen's own contribution. The young man was very proud of the collar, the adjustment of which he made his constant occupation. His movements were extremely awkward, but there was a good reason for this, as *The Fairy Tale of My Life* makes apparent: "I did not dare to stand up straight, for then it became evident that the vest was too short, nor was my posture helped by the fact that the heels of my boots were crooked. Tall and thin as I was, I had learned that people could easily make fun of me."

The figure of amusement did not lead an amusing life. He knew hardship, he suffered from the cold: he lost his voice, he declared, because he had to go about each winter and spring with leaky shoes and wet feet, and he lacked warm clothes as well. He half starved for long periods of time; still living in a doubtful section of town, his residence now was with a Madam Henckel, the wife of a sailing master, in a room without windows, but, according to the *Book of My Life,* "with unlimited rights to sit in the living room amidst the family's many children." His landlady assumed that he went out to eat dinner; but often, chilled and penniless, he wandered through the King's Park until he could return to the house and the meager supper he got there. In all likelihood, these deprivations —this self-neglect—worsened his health, preparing the ground for the hyperesthesia which would pursue him for the rest of his life. But despite these torments and humiliations, despite the insecurity in which he lived, the foolish young man would not—by returning to Odense or devoting himself to a respectable trade—make the best of a bad situation. He clung to his mania and, saying his prayers of an evening, he would make direct application to God with the hopeful and somehow ingratiating hint: "It will get better soon, of course."

Moreover, in his childish piety he by no means scorned the possibility of using magical devices to get the Almighty on the right track. As a child he had been told that, whatever one did on New Year's Day, one would do all year long. Thus, on New Year's Day, 1822, he resolved to appear on the boards of the Royal Theater, cost what it may; since no performance was scheduled, he slipped in by a back way early in the morning. "Not a living soul was in the building; trembling as if I were committing a sin, I advanced to the footlights, folded my hands, said the Lord's Prayer, and crept out just as quietly as I had crept in, convinced in my heart that I should surely have a chance to appear during the year to come." The tale is recounted in the *Book of My Life.*

This time his pious trick did not succeed. Springtime came, and in May, Hans Christian Andersen received a communication from the theater's administration that his services as an extra were no longer required. His employment had not been dignified with a salary, to be sure, but all his hopes for the future were connected with it, just the same. Now, after three years of tribulations, he was left quite empty-handed.

He was in despair. But his thoughts turned neither to Odense nor to a trade.

CHAPTER V

The Deliverance

S INGER, DANCER, ACTOR, DECLAIMER—Hans Christian Andersen, making his way from Odense to Copenhagen, had intended to become one of these. It is difficult to determine just how much talent he had along these lines. In his memoirs Major General Holten records that Colonel Høegh-Guldberg once sent the boy up to Odense Castle to give a sample of his thespian talents. Hans Christian, who persisted in waving his hands during the recitation, looked very much like a cartoon character, and Holten, then serving as the prince's secretary, was moved to sum up his opinions in the proverb, "Shoemaker, stick by your last." and the judgment, "You will never learn to be an actor." In fact, Andersen would have had trouble in finding witnesses to gainsay Holten's crushing criticism. His occasional appearances as an extra at the Royal Theater never led to a clear-cut success, and he was finally given his walking papers. The poet Baggesen and the actor Lind-green, who agreed that the strange boy had some kind of talent, were equally in agreement that he was not a born actor. His lanky figure—indeed, his whole appearance—kept him from finding his fortune as a ballet dancer, and he had recently lost his voice, no matter whether the loss had been caused by the youth's eternally wet feet or stemmed from other sources. But, despite these adverse experiences, Hans Christian long persisted in regarding a stage career as his life's calling; he gave theatrical performances for all the circles, all the families, into whose favor he had succeeded in worming his way, and out at Bakkehus, the Rahbeks' estate, he had been given the pet name (or perhaps it was a nickname) *"der kleine Deklamator."* People laughed at him, and in his innocence he took their ridicule as applause; as a matter of fact, he would be a victim of misapprehension—that he did not always realize when he was being made fun of—for a long time to come. Evident-ly, he had such a strong need of attention that he preferred derision to obscurity. Yet it was not always so easy to draw a line between the foolish and the genuinely pathetic. In *The Fairy Tale of My Life* he remarks:

> I was a curiosity; people were amused at me, and I—well, I took every smile as a sign of approval. A friend I made in later life has told me that he first saw me at about this time, in the salon of a prom-inent and well-to-do merchant; there, in order for me to make a fool of myself, I was asked to recite one of my own poems, and my friend tells me that I read with such emotion, with such unaffected and sincere expression, that scorn was transformed to sympathy.

No doubt he won his friends and protectors in this way.

His zeal—and his boldness—knew no bounds. In Copenhagen he

succeeded in tracking down Frøken Tønder-Lund, a young lady who, when they were fellow students in the confirmation class at Odense, had shown a certain friendliness to the poor boy. Frøken Tønder-Lund, presently residing at the home of an admiral on Gammelholm, wept a little upon catching sight of her wretched visitor; she gave him her pin money, and saw to it that some of her distinguished acquaintances became interested in his case. Thus he came to the attention of Fru Colbjørnsen, the aforesaid admiral's sister-in-law and widow of the great statesman; she gave him various articles of clothing and introduced him to the Rahbeks at Bakkehus. Her daughter, Fru van der Maase, was lady-in-waiting to Crown Princess Caroline, and, thanks to Fru van der Maase, he was summoned to Frederiksberg Castle, from which, after having sung and recited for the Crown Princess, he departed with a paper cone full of candy, grapes, and peaches, as well as ten rix-dollars in cash. He had succeeded in pressing all these treasures from the rose which Frøken Tønder-Lund had once handed him in the goodness of her heart. It was dangerous to give Hans Christian Andersen an inch, lest he take a mile.

He was accustomed to spend his time in the home of Madam Jürgensen, a distinguished old lady in whose childhood home Holberg had been a guest; he made more or less fleeting acquaintanceships with the librarian, Professor Rasmus Nyerup, who allowed him to borrow books, with the poets Ingemann and Oehlenschläger, who listened to him with an air of friendly distraction, and with Peter Wulff, director of the naval academy and admiral-to-be, who translated Shakespeare and demonstrated his freedom from prejudice by opening his doors to all and sundry. Hans Christian had entered his home under his own power, and the same was true in the case of H. C. Ørsted, the great natural scientist: it is difficult to say how the youth was able to arouse the interest of the brilliant physicist, but from him he received encouragement, consolation, a chance to borrow books, and even a little money.

However, all these indications of sympathy were nothing to depend upon; they did not keep Hans Christian from going hungry now and then. For the majority of his friends and acquaintances he must, in the long run, have been a torment and a trial. He composed petitions, addressed to "noble-hearted friends of humanity," in which he begged for "monthly or quarterly support." Hans Christian Andersen's failure, under these humiliating and desperate circumstances, to develop into a little adventurer, a mendacious cheat who misused human sympathies, must be regarded as proof of the good stuff of which he was made. He kept to the truth. When on one occasion Høegh-Guldberg thought he had been tricked—Hans Christian had neglected his Latin lessons—the youth fell into such despair that he walked for half the night by the Peblingesø in the moonlight, thinking thoughts of suicide; his conscience told him: "You won't amount to anything! You have become an evil person! God is angry at you, and you must die." Thus he was neither corrupt nor immoral, but he may have received physical harm, and his psychic health, too, was not of the best. He lived like a sick child amidst his hopes and his fantasies, in wild, exalted dreams of a great good fortune which should fall to his lot in some way or another; but he had no notion of how he should attain this good fortune, and no one seemed to be able to show him the way. Indeed, he had come no farther than when he stood beside Odense River, singing and waiting for the Chinese prince, who, digging his way up from beneath the earth, would give him a castle.

Only after the dreams of a dramatic and musical future had turned out to be false does Hans Christian seem to have begun

Born in 1805 in circumstances of extreme poverty, by the end of his life Hans Christian Andersen was able to say, "Rich and serenely happy, my life is a beautiful fairy tale."

From a painting by C. A. Jensen, 1836

"A single room . . . comprised my childhood home; but . . . the little chamber seemed both large and splendid to me." Later in his life, Andersen succeeded in casting an aura of poetry and contentment over his childhood home in Odense, Denmark.

From a lithograph, 1868

to think that he was perhaps born to be a poet, that he would attain fame in this capacity—for he could have doubts about his coming celebrity only in brief moments of dejection. He had, of course, always been a little of the poet, that is to say, in so far as he was an improviser: if he did not remember the text, he made up his replies himself, and, in order that he might have roles to act and scenes to perform, he wrote his own plays. It also took a long time for his poetic ambitions, liberated from his theatrical ones, to achieve an independent existence. Out at Bakkehus the kind Kamma Rahbek was merciful enough to listen to him—he had written a comedy which he wanted to read out loud. But during the very first scenes she burst out: "Why, you have copied the whole play from Oehlenschläger and Ingemann!" Hans Christian gave her the disarming answer: "Yes, but they are so beautiful, too!" The episode shows how ignorant the boy was of the abstract concept of authorship; for him everything was theater, materials, scenes, effects, something altogether concrete. Gradually, however, he realized that there existed some invisible and lofty realm behind and perhaps above the world of actors: the realm of the poet. It is characteristic of his nature that ambition put him on the right track. Even in Odense he had noticed that Bunkeflod's sister had spoken of her brother, the poet, with reverent voice and shining eyes; it happened one day that Fru Rahbek sent him to Fru Colbjørnsen with a bouquet of roses, and that she jestingly said: "Fru Colbjørnsen will be delighted to receive them from a poet's hand." The youth pricked up his ears at these words, and—something that was easy for him—he began to weep. "I know that from this moment on my thoughts were awakened to authorship and to poetry; previously poetry had only been a game for me, a kind of change from the puppet theater—now it stood higher, now it was the goal." He makes the confession in *The Fairy Tale of My Life*.

He did not acquire a deeper insight into the nature of authorship all at once, and originality was still not his strong point. A German tale, *The Chapel in the Forest,* was transformed by him into a tragedy in unrhymed verse, and he was chagrined when Høegh-Guldberg forbade him to submit it to the theater. In all secrecy he composed a new play, "a patriotic tragedy" with the title *The Robbers at Vissenberg,* built on a popular legend and cut after the pattern of Schiller's *Die Räuber.* It had taken Hans Christian two weeks to complete it, but there was scarcely a correctly spelled word in the whole manuscript. Initiated into the secret, the good-natured Frøken Tønder-Lund prepared a copy in which the spelling mistakes were corrected, after which it was sent to the theater management; six weeks later the play came back, rejected. The accompanying opinion was to the effect that the management did not wish to receive plays which betrayed such a complete absence of even the most elementary education. The words were crushing. It was poor consolation when, some time later, the first scene was anonymously printed in a literary magazine. This was Andersen's debut. It was not especially promising.

But the author had as much industry and enterprise as had the actor. Taking as his source a tale about ancient Scandinavia by a certain Suhm, he wrote a tragedy called *The Elves' Sun,* and, armed with this manuscript, he rushed to Peter Wulff, the naval officer and Shakespeare translator mentioned earlier. Subsequently, Admiral Wulff was accustomed to tell of his first meeting with Andersen in more or less the following way: As soon as the youth was inside the door, he cried: "You've translated Shakespeare, and I'm enthralled by him too, but I have also written a tragedy, if you'll only listen"—and so the reading began. Trying to get a chance to collect his wits, the tough old sea dog invited the aspiring poet to have breakfast with him, but his visitor declined; he did not have time, he said—and continued to read at a gallop. When he had finished, he asked: "Can't I turn out to be somebody?—I want so badly to be famous." Hereupon the author of *The Elves' Sun* stuffed his manuscript into his pocket and was about to depart when the kindly Wulff asked him to come for another visit. Young Andersen replied that he would be glad to—he'd come back as soon as he had written a new tragedy. Assuming, quite naturally, that the composition would take a rather long time, Wulff expressed his regrets. "Oh, no," the poet rejoined. "I'm sure I'll have it ready two weeks from now."

It is not hard to understand why Shakespeare and his Danish translator had become the focal points of Andersen's interest; Shakespeare was also a poor boy who first became an actor, then won world-wide fame as a poet—a striking parallel to the career Hans Christian had in mind for himself. But there was another model closer at hand: Oehlenschläger, he too a child of the people —although from an infinitely more prosperous layer of society than Andersen—who had also enjoyed close connections with the Royal Theater. Oehlenschläger's reputation was already considerable; Hans Christian made the personal acquaintance both of him and of the other great poet, Ingemann. Listening to Hans Christian's first verses and tragedies, old Madam Jürgensen had been so overwhelmed that she proclaimed in deep earnestness: "You're a poet, perhaps one like Oehlenschläger! In ten years— I'll be dead and gone then, but think of me."

Oehlenschläger no doubt exerted a decisive influence upon Hans Christian Andersen. He set the example which lifted the youth's interests from the material to the spiritual plane in art; Oehlenschläger, Ingemann, and Denmark's other great poets, the dead writers of Classicism as well as the living Romantics, led the impressionable boy from Odense out of the theater's realm and into that of poetry. During these Copenhagen years, filled with want and humiliation, H. C. Andersen acquired his literary education. He discovered the novels of Sir Walter Scott, novels which so entranced him that he saw the whole world in a new and profusely colored light; he directly set about writing a novel, called *The Ghost at Palnatoke's Grave,* in the manner of Scott. However, the master who spoke most intimately to him was his great compatriot Oehlenschläger. Even at this time he must have read *Aladdin,* and the wonderful fairy-tale play must have charmed, disturbed, moved, and edified him. For did he not find his own story here? Was not Aladdin a poor fatherless boy, the object of an unhappy and ignorant mother's blind and steadfast love? Did not Morgiane wish to put her lanky son to work in a tailor's shop, while the boy himself, dreaming of great good fortune, thrived only in the colorful world of whim and fantasy? And, at the end did not Aladdin turn out to be right—had he not been chosen by fate for great things, to be admired of men and, after hard trials and cruel deprivation, to bear the crown itself?

Throughout his whole life Hans Christian Andersen felt himself to be an Aladdin. When people shrugged their shoulders at him, when they scorned him and laughed at him, he must have thought of the scenes in which Aladdin, robbed of strength and reason, surrounded by the rabble, by a howling pack of street boys, gropes for his vanished lamp—Hans Christian's unhappy grandfather had been jeered at in quite the same way on the streets of Odense, and the boy himself had shuddered with terror lest the same fate befall him. But the hero of the fairy-tale play conquers all adversities. And in Andersen's own moments of greatest triumph, receiving the homage of monarchs and their men, he was wont to repeat to himself Oehlenschläger's solemn concluding words, the words with which Aladdin, now the sultan, gazes down from his palace windows onto the streets of Ispahan: "A poor boy, I too walked along those streets."

Hans Christian, the half-starved boy, must have seen his kinship to *Aladdin's* author in this light; later in life, they felt a mutual congeniality—they were both naïve geniuses. One wonders if Hans Christian, seeing the colorful backdrops of *Aladdin* pass before him, could guess that his own life-work would have such a close affinity to Oehlenschläger's wonderful masterpiece—that the same rare mixture of burgeoning fantasy, Oriental splendor, Danish realism, graceful wit, exuberant humor, and soulful lyricism would come alive once again in his fairy tales, and make its victorious way throughout the world. The fact that the earliest of the fairy tales, *The Tinder Box,* is nothing other than Andersen's own formulation of the Aladdin motif would seem to be a kind of symbolic confirmation of the inner resemblance between the two poets' works.

But if Hans Christian Andersen was now firmly convinced that he would become a great and famous poet like Adam Oehlenschläger, and that the wonderful lamp which would put the world at his feet consisted in poetic fantasy, a certain question was still bound to arise: how could he acquire the knowledge and training necessary for the new vocation? As long as he had dreamed of a performer's life alone, he had imagined he could escape tiresome and demanding studies, and Høegh-Guldberg had helped to prove how little interested in Latin grammar his protégé was. Seventeen years old, Andersen was hopelessly ill-taught, ignorant even of the elements of spelling; that he was able nonetheless to put together plays and stories from the crumbs he managed to pick up shows how clever he was and how quick to comprehend. However, it was high time that he had a chance to make up for all the lost years, and high time to leave his helter-skelter life as a mendicant bohemian for more orderly circumstances. Among his friends and protectors were evidently those who realized that Hans Christian was doomed if he did not find someone willing to take charge of him, seriously and completely. But who would wish to shoulder the responsibility for an unknown and ridiculous youth, full of great notions about himself but with extremely uncertain prospects for the future? In order to overcome all the misgivings which quite naturally might arise, both unique psychological sensitivity and moral genius were required. It was not very likely that a person thus combining perception with goodness should appear at the right moment to save Hans Christian Andersen.

But it happened just the same, and the event must be characterized as the best piece of luck Hans Christian Andersen ever had.

The savior was Jonas Collin; he was one of Danish absolutism's mightiest and most prominent officials, a director of the department of the treasury, weighed down by public charges and undertakings involving great responsibility. Among other things he was a member of the management of the Royal Theater, and in this capacity he had signed a negative reply to the anonymous author of the play *The Robbers at Vissenberg*. Perhaps it was he who adduced a friendly hint to the otherwise crushing critique, indicating that the young man, should he contemplate a continuation of his poetic career, stood in need of guidance; and in this connection a tacit appeal was made to the unknown author's presumptive "friends and protectors."

Shortly thereafter Hans Christian submitted his new tragedy, *The Elves' Sun*. Having read it, the poet Rahbek found it unplayable, to be sure, but expressed the opinion that the author revealed unmistakable talents which could deserve support. On September 13, 1822, the author of *The Elves' Sun* presented himself to the management of the theater; the minutes of the proceedings run as follows: "It was announced to him that the management intended to recommend him for royal support, so that he might pursue a course of studies, and he received the news with gratitude." Collin was one of the four distinguished gentlemen present, and it was he, supported by Rahbek and another member of the directorate, G. H. Olsen, who became the spokesman of the seventeen-year-old's cause: he would personally talk with the King about the matter. In consideration of the great confidence which Collin enjoyed, a refusal did not need to be feared.

Simultaneously Hans Christian Andersen was summoned to the home of Jonas Collin. It was his first real visit to the house which he in his maturity should regard as his true home. (In April, 1821, he had vainly attempted to arouse Collin's interest by paying him a call and giving him a poem.) On the outside the Collin establishment was unprepossessing, a half-timbered house with wooden galleries, located at the corner of Bredgade and Store Strandstræde, and in former times facing on the open piece of rough ground which was jestingly called "the Halland Ridge"[1]—the present Kongens Nytorv. In *The Fairy Tale of My Life* the meeting is described in the following way:

> I went there and Collin talked with me, but I saw only the official in him; he did not say much, and his speech was earnest and almost stern; I left without any expectations of sympathy from this man; and yet Collin was the man who had my interest most sincerely at heart, and quietly worked on my behalf. . . . He touched upon the play I had submitted only fleetingly, although many others had

[1] The boundary between the Swedish provinces of Halland (which made its definitive passage from Danish to Swedish hands only in 1658) and Småland is marked by a range of hills called "Hallandsåsen" ("the Halland Ridge").—G. C. S.

praised it to the skies, and so I regarded him as an enemy rather than a protector.

Actions, not words and phrases, were Jonas Collin's strong point. Not hesitating a moment, he arranged every detail. Frederick VI set aside an annual payment of 350 rix-dollars for three years; the ministry of education granted free instruction at Slagelse's Latin School, where a new and energetic rector had just been appointed; Collin had informed the rector, named Meisling, of the decisions taken and had arranged for board and room—Hans Christian had merely to betake himself to Slagelse by the first diligence. "I was almost dumb with amazement; I had never thought that my life would take this course." There was not only joy in his speechlessness; a little anxiety lurked in it too. Before his departure he paid another visit to Jonas Collin, who now revealed a little more of his feelings; with gentle cordiality he urged the youth to write to him, telling of his needs and depicting his circumstances. One wonders if the gawky, overgrown schoolboy fully realized what a privilege it was to correspond with one of Denmark's leading citizens.

Danish absolutism had its practical advantages. Hans Christian rolled away to the learned institution at Slagelse in October, 1822; it was only on December 2 that the official communication from the theater management reached the directors of the fund called "*Ad usus publicos.*" Since Jonas Collin was not only one of the dispatchers but also one of the recipients of the communication—he was the secretary of the foundation, which arranged all financial support for scholarship and the arts—one can be sure that the good cause did not meet with opposition. Yet the King's formal decision and the hard cash were not available until December 31; before this time everything was done on Jonas Collin's personal authority and at his private expense. In the communication mentioned above there is contained an account of Hans Christian Andersen's unsuccessful theatrical career, and in it the opinions which formed Jonas Collin's decision are indicated with the following words:

> Since the aforesaid Andersen, who is completely devoid of any personal fortune and exists only through the aid of private charity, would fall into some misfortune and be lost to respectable society, if he were allowed to continue to idle away his time in this manner, and since, on the other hand, there exists the well-founded hope that he, given scholarly training, could become a useful citizen, he was summoned to the directorate, where, having been shown the literary aberrations in which he had become involved, he was promised that he should be recommended for His Majesty's most gracious support, with the purpose of enabling him to pursue his studies, if he would exclusively apply his energy and time to the acquisition of the knowledge necessary for him.

Thus Hans Christian Andersen had not become the object of indiscriminate benevolence. Jonas Collin did not have a high opinion of his previous literary activity, and required that he cease his writing during the immediate future. Embarrassingly enough, Hans Christian had just at this very time made arrangements for the publication of an entire book, with the title, *Youthful Experiments: Part I.* It contained a prologue, a tale by his own hand, *The Ghost at Palnatoke's Grave,* and an original tragedy, *The Elves' Sun;* in order to soften the printer's heart, he had tried to collect subscribers among his acquaintances. However he had had but little success in this attempt, and no one knows whether or not the printer put the completed edition on the market; at any event, no bother was taken with it, and when it was distributed five years later with a new title page, not a single copy was sold, so that it was finally used as waste paper. This fate was devoutly to be wished, for on the title page one William Christian Walter was named as the author. The Danish Christian presented himself with William Shakespeare on his one side and Walter Scott on the other. Had Jonas Collin caught sight of the product, he would surely have shaken his head and thought some worried thoughts about his protégé, a goodhearted youth, but one not lacking ambitions.

But how in the world did Jonas Collin arrive at his calm, unshakable conviction that Hans Christian Andersen was worth all the sacrifices of time, energy, and money which were lavished upon him? Collin himself, although overburdened with work, gave generously, year after year, without ever betraying a trace of doubt. The stern, sensible, intelligent statesman (one could even call him dry), unselfish, unassuming, objective, the foe of every piece of sentimentality and every unbalanced nature—where did he get his warm sympathy for the eccentric young poet, who had so many weak sides and who was, in every essentiality, his direct opposite? There is absolutely no indication that he sensed the great genius in the strange figure before him; on the contrary, Jonas Collin was never exceedingly interested in the genius Hans Christian Andersen, and when Andersen's world fame arrived, it left Collin quite indifferent.

No, there must have been something else, something belonging to the mysteries of personal life. Perhaps it was the feeling that a human soul, a unique force, was on the point of being distorted and corrupted, of being destroyed in disorder and misery. Jonas Collin, the great economist, detested confusion, ruin, aimlessness. In the communication of the theater's directorate there becomes apparent a moral indignation at the false paths Andersen had begun to follow, and annoyance at his slovenly, irresponsible way of life ("idling away his time"). In Jonas Collin, that rational and practical man, lay an element of moral enthusiasm bordering on

Fichte's mystique of the will. In his youth he had translated Fichte's lectures on *The Vocation of the Scholar,* in the epilogue of which one finds the words: "It is womanish to stand complaining about the decay of men without seeking to lessen it. It is ungracious to mock and punish men without telling them how they might be better. Act! Act! For that is why we exist."

Jonas Collin was just such a fanatic of action, and that is why he seized the task of saving Hans Christian Andersen. He did not help the youth for the sake of the latter's present perfection.

CHAPTER VI

The School and Rector Meisling

ON OCTOBER 26, 1822, a Saturday, the seventeen-year-old Hans Christian Andersen traveled from Copenhagen to Slagelse in southwestern Zealand, and two days later he wrote in his first certificate-book that he had been enrolled in the second class of Slagelse's Latin School.

Edvard Collin has called this event the real turning point of Andersen's destinies. In our own days, one of the poet's most distinguished biographers, H. G. Olrik, has formulated the matter thus: here the seventeen-year-old youth leapt from the realm of the proletariat into the upper layers of society.

Both statements are true. Previously, to be sure, the boy, at once bold and clinging, had succeeded in obtaining many acquaintances among Copenhagen's cultured and distinguished families; he had, to be sure, been admitted to their homes, and had been given meals, shiny coins of silver, secondhand clothes, good advice, and friendly interest. But, as Olrik has so pertinently remarked, the moment Hans Christian left their threshholds, he became once again a proletarian, the next best thing to homeless, possessing as his only sanctuary a coop in the city's worst section: dressed in shabby clothes and worn-out shoes, he ate his dry bread on a bench in the Royal Park—often he had no other dinner.

This precarious existence at the edge of the abyss was now at an end. He was a duly installed pupil at Slagelse's Latin School, and the King's personal favor shone like a sun above his head. Jonas Collin, one of the most powerful men in the kingdom, had taken personal charge of his welfare, giving directions to the rector of the school and arranging proper lodgings for him at the home of a respectable widow in the little city. Her name was Madam Henneberg. At her house Hans Christian occupied a chamber facing on the garden, and around the windowpanes of bottle glass the wild vine's tendrils grew. He need no longer go cold or hungry; he was given clothes and books. He could look toward the future with quite as much composure as the scion of a normal middle-class family. He was assured the royal stipend of 350 rix-dollars for the next three years; but in 1826, Councillor Collin had it extended for another two years, and in 1828, for still another year. Altogether, the Danish government spent 2,100 rix-dollars on Hans Christian Andersen's scholarly training—not a small sum, if one considers the monetary values of those days, and one which was undeniably well applied.

It is only natural that Hans Christian, presented with this change in his fortunes, must have felt an indescribable happiness, an overpowering sense of gratitude partly directed to his benefactor, Councillor Collin, and partly—and above all—to the Heavenly Father whom he had assailed with his burning and childlike prayers.

Finally, too, he must have been filled with triumph and pride. At Christmas, 1822, he was allowed to accompany the rector and his family to Copenhagen, and for the first time in his life he was invited to take a meal at the Collins' house—this also bears witness to his advancement on the social scale. Strikingly enough, the reception he got from the members of the family in general can scarcely be termed a very friendly one; it was the paterfamilias himself who held his protecting hand above the youth's head. In the *Book of My Life* one reads the following description:

> Everyone in the family was somewhat cool toward me, but Collin was kindness itself: he gave me encouragement and comfort, calmed my worries about my studies, expressed satisfaction at my grades—for I had my certificate-book with me; he asked me to inform him of my progress every month, and he said that I should never fail to tell him frankly how things were going. I placed my heartfelt trust in him, but at the same time he seemed to me to be an entity bearing my life and my fate in his hand; I felt a strange fear and veneration in his presence.

Some months later, at Easter, 1823, Hans Christian Andersen paid a visit to the city of his birth. Writing to Iversen the printer, who had of course been friendly toward him before, he asked quite openly to be allowed to stay at Iversen's house, for his mother did not have a bed to put at his disposal, and it would cost entirely too much to stay at an inn. The letter also says that Hans Christian had not wished to appear in Odense until he could come dressed in sufficiently good clothes, and "now, thank God, I am in a position to do so." The way he gives his address also reveals a certain self-esteem: "*Studiosus Actium* [sic] Andersen, Pupel [sic] in the Latin School at Slagelse—Lodger at Fru Henneberg's." Iversen the printer may have smiled a little at the mistakes in spelling; but he

82

gave his guest a friendly reception, making him feel, according to the *Book of My Life,* like a child of the family. "I could now show myself with honor," this source says. Hans Christian got up one morning at three o'clock, put on his best clothes, picked up his little linen pack, walked from Slagelse to Korsør, and, having sailed across the Great Belt, continued his way toward Odense like a wandering scholar. When he caught sight of the tower of Saint Knut's, he fell to his knees, wept with joy, and sent up a prayer to God. The return to the town of his fathers after a three-year absence was like a dream; on the very first street he met his mother, who, beside herself with joy, took him around to all her acquaintances so that she might bask in the sun of his greatness. He paid visits to such distinguished families as that of Colonel Høegh-Guldberg; but the unimportant people and the servants who comprised his mother's circle of acquaintances were not neglected either: here they called him, not without embarrassment, Herr Christian. "In the narrow back streets I saw people opening their windows to gaze after me, for they all knew that things had gone remarkably well with me, yes, that I was studying now at the expense of the King." Perhaps some of his previous benefactors in Odense asked themselves how it could have happened that no one ever thought seriously of having the shoemaker's boy study at Odense's school. As far as Hans Christian's laundress-mother was concerned, she had recently become a widow for the second time, and his paternal grandmother had also passed away. An attempt to have his lunatic grandfather admitted to the Gray Brothers' Hospital had succeeded. Whenever he had a coin to spare, Hans Christian did not fail to help his poor mother; he does not seem to have been ashamed to be seen together with her, although her degeneration became more evident from day to day; and he made efforts to have her accepted at some more attractive institution than the poorhouse.

He was a good son; in Odense he also visited the pauper's grave in which his father lay—it was already level with the ground.

If grandeur and glory surrounded him during his stay in Odense, he could also empty the cup of success upon coming to the capital for a few days. Councillor Collin's decisive intervention had made it possible for Hans Christian's many high-ranking patrons to give open expression to their friendly feelings: since the strange boy was already taken care of, they no longer ran the risk of being saddled with him. At Christmas, 1825, Fru Wulff invited him to spend the holidays at her home. Her husband, the Shakespeare-translator, was now a commodore of the fleet and director of the naval academy; in the latter capacity he had taken quarters in one of Amalienborg's two royal palaces. Thus it happened that the twenty-year-old schoolboy from Slagelse had a pair of rooms at the castle placed at his disposal; one was his bedroom, the other his study, and in this second chamber his Christmas present awaited him—a handsomely bound edition of Shakespeare in three volumes. Arriving in the evening, he was received as though he were the Wulffs' own child, although, as it happened, the commodore and his wife had to pay a call on the Oehlenschlägers; after being richly fed, the boy was led to his room by a servant. Left alone, he went forward to the windows, and gazing down at the magnificent square and its equestrian statue, he was overcome by a host of feelings. In his diary he wrote:

Oh, how much God has done for me! My situation is Aladdin's, as he looks down through the castle's windows at the end of the play: "A poor boy, I too walked along those streets!" I too walked along down there five or six years ago, I did not know a soul in the city, and now, dwelling here in the castle with a dear and respected family, I can sit and enjoy my Shakespeare edition. Oh, God is good, a drop

84

In May, 1822, three years after Hans Christian Andersen had gone to Copenhagen to—he hoped—become a famous actor, he received a notice that his services were no longer required at this, the Royal Theater.

From a drawing by C. F. Christensen, ca.1825–30

Simon Meisling was the new rector of Slagelse's Latin School when young Andersen began his studies there. Andersen later said of him, "I had almost broken down under [the Rector's] treatment which became ever crueler . . . . In the school the Rector took pleasure in mocking me, making fun of my person, and discussing my lack of talent."

of the honey of gladness makes me forget all the gall I have tasted, oh, God will not desert me, He has made me so happy.

Six years later, when Hans Christian copied this page from his diary into the *Book of My Life,* he added, in naïve blasphemy: "I could kiss Thee!"

In such a moment as this, Andersen had quite boldly drawn an advance payment upon his life's great victory.

This happy frenzy quickly vanished, however, and then Andersen's situation seemed by no means so rosy. Just twelve days after his Aladdin-like triumph, on January 1, 1826, he confided to his diary—he was back in Slagelse now—the following message: "God, shall the whole year become even as this day was? Fear and dejection torment me, I wrote some bitter letters to the Collins and the Wulffs. Oh God, let this be my last New Year's Day." And the suicidal mood still prevails on January 2: "Things are the way they were yesterday."

It is peculiar (and indicative of the purely biological importance of the emotions) that such moods of dejection and despair are scarcely to be found in the period of Andersen's life when he was wretched and unfortunate in actual fact. In those days he had kept up his courage, in those days he had been sanguine—for otherwise he would have been lost without hope of salvation. Yet he has hardly received a little aid, a little relief, before he uses the moment of respite for the doleful laments which often fill his letters to Councillor Collin and his other benefactors. Now—contrary to what had earlier been the case—it is worth while to fall into despair, for an announcement of that despair can lead to an improvement of the situation. It is, of course, a kind of ruse; but it is not Andersen's personal cunning which is at work here; instead, it is the great and profound ruse of nature itself, of the will to survive, a ruse to which each human being is subject.

The situation in which he found himself during and after the autumn of 1822, subsequent to his salvation, was actually not an easy one. Seventeen years old, he was compelled to take his place behind a school desk, surrounded by small boys who were his superiors in factual knowledge. He could scarcely read or write, he could not spell at all, he had never seen a geometry book, and, standing before a map, he was unable to point out Copenhagen. Suddenly he had to begin with everything at once—Latin, Greek, history, geography. To be sure, he had suffered want in Copenhagen, but his bohemian existence had been free and unrestricted, he had only concerned himself with things that interested him, with his fantasy's illusory games; and now he was suddenly compelled to submit himself to the stern discipline of a school—the work-shy youth had to work from dawn till dusk. Was he intelligent? He was, without doubt, but he did not possess methodical intelligence of the sort customary among poor schoolboys who began their education somewhat belatedly. Hans Christian had no gift for exact learning, for grammatical formalities, despite his keen memory; there was something fleeting, something hasty, in his whole intellectual make-up, something which could not be made to harmonize with scientific and pedagogical pursuits.

Councillor Jonas Collin had sent him to Slagelse because the school there had just got a new rector, a man regarded as being especially skillful and energetic. His name was Simon Meisling, he was thirty-five years old, a classical philologist by profession and something of a poet, besides; one might guess that he was the right person to handle an author in process of becoming. True to his wont, Hans Christian read the rector his tragedy *The Elves' Sun* and *The Ghost at Palnatoke's Grave* upon their first meeting; "I was proud to show what sort of fellow I was." However, it is unlikely that he thereby made any great impression on Rector Meisling. The latter was in complete agreement with Councilor Collin and all Andersen's other patrons: they each thought that the boy should devote himself entirely to his studies, restraining himself from every poetic extravagance. Concerning this point Hans Christian had had to make formal promises, promises which were very difficult for him to keep completely. A *poème d'occasion* could scarcely be avoided now and then—among other things he wrote a cantata for Meisling's installation as rector—but when Hans Christian sent a song to Jonas Collin in the summer of 1823, he received the inexorable answer: "I am convinced, for the rest, that this effort, although not unsuccessful, will not encourage you to make still further experiments, something which would be ill-fitted to your present occupations." The youth ought to study, and to do nothing but study, in order to make up for all he had missed.

He did not lack industry or zeal, nor can the results he attained be called bad ones; the Rector expressed a rather favorable opinion of his work, and Councillor Collin declared that he was satisfied with the marks which Hans Christian conscientiously reported to him. Nevertheless, Andersen's school days were anything but serene, and the relationship between him and Simon Meisling finally took a drastic turn for the worse.

One of the chief causes for this sudden deterioration was, of course, Andersen's truly abnormal sensitivity, the extraordinary lability of his emotional life: on Christmas Eve he was Aladdin triumphant, by New Year's he was ready to commit suicide, although his external circumstances were unchanged, on the whole. A schoolmate of his, Jens Hviid, once said in a letter: "I know you well: first you dream that you 're in the world of the fairies, swimming about in a great sea of bliss, and then you dream that you're the worst nincompoop on God's green earth; but *medio tutissimus ibis*—that is to say, if you walk a middle path, you'll come closest to the truth." His words were correct. The difficulties and adversities which the overgrown schoolboy was bound to meet, the criticism and the censure which rained down upon him as he sat behind his desk, crushed him and brought him to despair; he vented his pain in his diary and in his letters to his many benefactors and patrons. He had as hard a time with his teachers and tutors as he later did with his reviewers, and he was firmly convinced that praise, sunshine, and warmth were the only elements in which he could thrive In a diary from the autumn of 1825 one can follow the shifts in his emotional course. On September 19 he notes that he has made a dismal showing in Latin: "You'll never reach the fourth class, you'll be thrown out of school—it's your destiny to become an artisan or a corpse—God, God, art Thou really present?" Several hours later things are a little better, for he has made some progress in Latin grammar; but before the setting of the sun he curses his fate anew, expressing the wish that he might be allowed to remain a member of the broad masses who earn their keep by the sweat of their brow—indeed, he even longs for death: "Life without hope is a hell—seeing my comrades rise while I sink—tearing myself from the world of cultured people—oh God, no, it's too hard a fate." The extent to which he is ruled by ambition is noteworthy. The next day, September 20, he bursts out: "What I could become—and what am I becoming? My strong imagination will bring me to the madhouse, my violent emotions will make a suicide of me—united, these two things could transform me into a great poet instead. Oh God, are these really Thy ways on earth?" He quarrels with God as though with an opponent; but then he repents: "Pardon me, God, I am ungrateful toward Thee, Who hast shown me such infinite favor, forgive me as Thou hast forgiven me before, oh God, and help me in the future." In order to put an end to all discord, he even suggests to the Lord that they make a contract: "God, by my eternal bliss I promise Thee that in my heart I shall never again doubt Thy paternal hand, provided that on this occasion I am promoted to the fourth class and am allowed to go to Helsingør." The offer was accepted to the extent that Hans Christian really was transferred; but his critical attitude toward the Almighty was nevertheless not conquered for all time to come. On December 8 he is still lamenting about the misfortune which makes him melancholy, dispirited, and dull, while good luck gives him hope and the will to work; the Lord is presented with the following instructions: "God, forgive me for passing judgment on Thy ways, but I believe that I can be purified by a little more kindness; thankful and humble, I shall of course feel Thy favor."

It is quite possible that a skillful teacher could have gotten along splendidly with Hans Christian Andersen, but Rector Simon Meisling was unfortunately very little suited to the task. He was a learned humanist, and even today there are those who have a high opinion of his translations of Greek and Latin literature but his attitude as an aristocrat of the intellect was flavored with a good measure of conceit and with brutal arrogance. He gave his bad humor and his polemic inclinations free reins in the presence of his disciples, and no one suffered more from his satire, his severity, and his lack of warmth than Hans Christian. It is touching to see what earnest exertions Andersen makes to like Rector Meisling; in his diary for November 29, 1825, he writes: "I'm beginning to like him, he cannot treat me otherwise than he does; Oh God, how happy I am." But in the long run it was impossible even for a person of Andersen's sanguine nature to transform the petty tyrant into a paternal friend.

The fact of the matter was that Meisling lacked sympathy for his fellow creatures in general, and in particular he felt an instinctive antipathy to the young man. At times Meisling succeeded in concealing this aversion, and he had good reasons for doing so: above all, it was an advantage for him to have a connection, through his pupil, with Councillor Collin, who distributed the bounties of the *Ad usus publicos* fund, and furthermore the Rector and his wife could harvest economic profits from getting Hans Christian as a lodger in their home. Therefore it took only a couple of years before they suggested the move, and poor Hans Christian, forced to make the best of it, had to leave Madam Henneberg, in whose house, where he had been very happy, conditions were much more favorable than they could ever be at the Rector's. In theory, of course, there were advantages to living at the Rector's house, where one could get help with one's schoolwork; besides, there was the chance to accompany Meisling to Helsingør, at which city he accepted a rectorship in the summer of 1826. In reality, however, the disadvantages were much greater. The Meisling ménage was not a pleasant place; it was distinguished, first of all, by an enormous dirtiness. A grotesque figure in his appearance, the Rector went about in filthy clothes and never washed his hands; only his fingertips customarily maintained the shine of cleanliness: they were whitened as he squeezed lemons for the strong punch which was often brewed in the home. Vulgar and pleasure-loving, Fru Meisling made regular attempts to seduce Hans Christian, but his virtue withstood the test. The family's economic difficulties, the eternal arguments with the servants, the flock of small children, whom the good-natured lodger frequently tended, caused the sojourn in the Meisling home to be turbulent and difficult. But its worst feature was unquestionably the lack of friendliness from Meisling's side.

Of course, one may not ignore the fact that Andersen could be very irritating. A skillful philologist like Meisling must have found his pupil's deficiency in formal exactness a trial; Latin and Greek, Meisling's own subjects, were the hardest for the boy. According to the *Book of My Life,* Meisling cried: "You're a stupid yokel who'll never amount to anything!" and upon being called "Shakespeare with vampire eyes," Hans Christian burst into tears. Meisling's bitterness was directed in particular at Andersen's poetic nature and poetic pretensions, which he absolutely refused to recognize. He forbade his pupil to write, forbade him to circulate amongst Slagelse's leading families for the purpose of reciting verse—as a matter of fact, he even forbade him to answer when those persons who had friendly inclinations toward him addressed him on Slagelse's streets; the Rector evidently had the notion that Hans Christian's personal ambitiousness, and his literary and social vanities, should be suppressed with an iron hand. The youth was to work dutifully and methodically, instead of running from family to family in an attempt to attract the attention of prosperous patrons. A good deal of Meisling's pedagogical and moral pathos may have been authentic enough, but unfortunately it also contained an admixture of envy and bad humor: the Rector himself, whose career was declining, had all sorts of difficulties, and it irritated him to see young Andersen taken care of by the Collins, the Wulffs, and the Oehlenschlägers in Copenhagen, and by the poet Ingemann in near-by Sorø. By humiliating and browbeating and frightening the timid youth, he could alleviate his own miseries.

There was no trick to turning Hans Christian's life into a hell: Meisling, for example, would take Andersen up to his room and there would demonstrate to him that he could never become a university student, and that he possessed not the slightest spark of poetic talent—had the spark but existed, Meisling, who was himself a poet, would have gladly ignored his pupil's weaknesses. After such scenes Andersen, falling into utter despair, would write immeasurably doleful letters to Councillor Collin and his friends. It would not have been surprising if they had lost patience with their difficult protégé. However Jonas Collin, his head filled with tasks of state, and so rigorously occupied that his endurance seems incomprehensible, found time just the same to answer the schoolboy in Slagelse, calming and consoling him, and even taking care of his purely practical needs, such as the acquisition of shoes, clothes, and textbooks. With inalterable wisdom and kindness he wrote, for example, on July 10, 1842: "In some dark moment or another, let the thought console you that you enjoy the esteem of various good people"—this was precisely the human warmth which Andersen, starved for affection, needed. On August 19, 1826, Collin wrote:

> Be calm and reasonable, Andersen, take things in the world as they are, and not the way you imagine they ought to be! One meets discomforts on every path of life, but that is no reason for abandoning the path. The scholar's career requires special endurance. The written opinion concerning you which the rector gave me was very favorable, and so you must neither lose your head nor your courage if he speaks to you in an earnest or perhaps even a harsh tone: at present he is your direct superior, and you must accommodate yourself to his wishes. Farewell! Your Collin, who is well-disposed toward you.

The term "well-disposed" was not an empty epistolary formula. Collin's good will was put to severe tests, and not only from Andersen's side. As soon as Hans Christian's case came under discussion, Meisling revealed such arrogance and irritability that the Councillor was forced to cloak himself in the high official's chilly dignity. Here as elsewhere Collin tried for the longest time to make peace, but after the move to Helsingør the situation finally became untenable. On October 24, 1826, Andersen had reported that Meisling had showered him with insults, and now he was so broken in spirit that he confessed: "Oh dear benefactor, I'll never amount to anything, I am stupid, confused, and superficial in my work." He wishes to give up his studies altogether, but since it seems too late for him to become an artisan, he will take any work whatsoever, perhaps at a commercial office in Norway or the West Indies. In other words: he is ready to abandon his dream of greatness. On October 31 he wrote to a schoolfellow in Slagelse:

> Oh Emil, never read the poets, for the dream world you find in their works does not exist anywhere. Would that my father had burned every book I had at my disposal, forcing me to make shoes instead; for then I should never have gone mad, nor should I have found myself in the plight of disappointing my benefactors.

If Hans Christian Andersen declares that he is willing to return to the shoemaker's bench from which even his father had sought to escape—then his despair must be great indeed. In *The Fairy Tale of My Life* he depicts this period in the following way:

> The life I led during these days still comes back to me in bad dreams. Once again I sit in a fever on the school bench, I cannot answer, I dare not, and angry eyes stare at me, laughter and gibes echo around me. These were hard and bitter times: I dwelt in the Rector's house at Helsingør for fifteen months, and I had almost broken down under treatment which became ever crueler, all too cruel to be borne. Each morning I prayed God that He should let this cup pass from me, or that I should be spared the day to come! In the school the Rector took pleasure in mocking me, making fun of my person, and discussing my lack of talent. And when school was over, I found myself in his house.

No one visited Hans Christian, for the Rector was feared and shunned—or, as a matter of fact, boycotted.

This situation lasted until the spring of 1827; as long as he could, Jonas Collin hesitated to allow Hans Christian to abandon Meisling and his school. The youth's deliverance was effected by a friendly and understanding teacher, Christian Werliin, an assistant master who was only a year older than his pupil. Traveling to Copenhagen, Werliin succeeded in doing what Hans Christian could not: in the course of a conversation he changed Councillor Collin's mind. He gave, no doubt, some factual information about Meisling and his school. It was decided that Hans Christian should move to Copenhagen, where he would receive private tutoring toward the matriculation examination under the direction of Werliin's friend, L. C. Müller.

Beaming with happiness, Andersen returned to Helsingør; he was just as overjoyed at being released from the Latin School as he had been upon his admission to it. His farewells to Meisling were taken, according to the *Book of My Life,* in the following way. Going into Meisling's library one morning, he said: "I'd like to say good-by, and to thank you for all the good things you've done for me." "Go to hell," the rector answered. According to what Andersen later told the younger Jonas Collin, Meisling's parting shot was the following epigram or, if one will, improvised poem: "You think that you have fantasy, but it is naught but foolery. You would yourself a genius call: you'll end inside a madhouse wall."

The poem corresponds perfectly to the conception of Andersen which Rector Simon Meisling, the highly cultured humanist and learned classical scholar, had professed in word and deed during all the years the youth had been at the school. For a long time, the verdict which Denmark's prevailing intellectual culture and orthodox taste rendered in the Andersen case had very much

94

the same sound as Meisling's; and it should not be forgotten that much seemed to argue for the correctness of Meisling's views.

The extent to which Andersen's depiction of his school years and of Rector Meisling is objectively accurate has been much disputed. Even Edvard Collin made a lively defense of Meisling, and ever since then a certain influence has been exerted by the understandable tendency to be a little generous toward the weaker of the two combatants—for there is no doubt that Meisling in the long run has come out second best. However, a Danish literary historian, Kjeld Galster, has taken the trouble to make an exhaustive investigation of Meisling's case on the basis of original documents. His research has resulted in the conclusion that Andersen in *The Fairy Tale of My Life*—the only autobiographical account he intended for publication—has given a truthful, tactful, even friendly picture of his former rector; he could have employed much harsher colors. The depictions of Meisling in the letters and the unprinted *Book of My Life* do not appear to be exaggerated. Meisling's faults of character, his arrogance and his severity, coupled with unscrupulousness in money matters, gradually made him unbearable in all quarters and then led to his downfall. As he wrote *The Fairy Tale of My Life,* Andersen was fully aware that a logical interpretation of the facts would put him in the right against Meisling, and in his concluding verdict he could therefore express himself in a manner both gentlemanly and just: "The Rector, a learned and gifted man who has afforded our literature some splendid reproductions of the classical poets of antiquity, was nevertheless, *as time has shown* [italics added], not at all suited to bring up young people." Not a word can be changed in this judgment; and the italicized clause betrays that Andersen indeed knew all about the sad story of Meisling's later years, a story which, after-

95

ward forgotten, made its appearance again only in 1933 with Kjeld Galster's book.

No, Andersen had no cause at all to reproach himself concerning his treatment of his erstwhile rector, even though Meisling's grotesque figure did play a certain role, under various disguises, in his literary work. It happened that they later met for one final time. On January 5, 1838, Andersen wrote to the poet Ingemann, whose home in Sorø had been an oasis of help for the boy during his school years:

> I had a pleasant experience at Christmas; Meisling came up to me on the street and said that he felt compelled to tell me that he had not been kind to me in school, but that he had been mistaken about me, that he was sorry, and that (as he expressed himself) I stood far above him; begging me to forget his severity, he said concerning himself: "Yours is the honor and mine is the shame!" Oh, how it touched me!

Andersen was not implacable. At the time of the above incident, Meisling was in the process of being removed from the school in Helsingør, which he had mismanaged. He spent his declining years in Copenhagen, neglected and half-destitute; he died in 1856, the year after the publication of *The Fairy Tale of My Life,* and was soon forgotten.

The last person to retain a memory of the broken old schoolmaster was surely Andersen himself—Meisling had his given place in the poet's imagination and his dreams. On June 4, 1870, the sixty-five-year-old man noted in his diary:

> Slept badly last night. Once again I dreamt of subservience: I ran from Meisling, was frightened of old Collin, since dissatisfaction

with me prevailed in the new school. To think that I can still have such dreams! How oppressed I was in the days of my youth!

Just having come back from Bregentved Castle in the summer of 1874, where Count and Countess Moltke had done everything within their power for their honored guest, he made the following entry in his diary for July 30: "An unpleasant dream about Meisling, in which I appeared timid and confused." The humiliations of youth continue to exist in the author turning seventy. Yet Hans Christian Andersen would not be Hans Christian Andersen if this lifelong disharmony had not finally been resolved in reconciliation and pious serenity. During his last year on earth, on the night of December 8–9, 1874—at a time when he, suffering from bronchitis, was given morphine to make him sleep—he had the following dream (subsequently noted down in his diary), to which Danish students of his life have called attention:

> The morphine must have had a very strong effect, I had splendid dreams, and one of them was particularly pleasant; I was quick-witted and spunky in my examination, and Meisling came in, and I declared that he was not to listen while I was being examined, for in that case I should feel so self-conscious that I'd give stupid answers—which I then proceeded to do. A little later I took a walk with Meisling, he made his usual jokes, I felt quick-witted and full of life, we soon began to talk about art and beauty, and at last we became good friends, he seemed to appreciate me and I him. When I awakened, I was heartily pleased by this conciliatory dream.

CHAPTER VII

The Poet in the Classroom

Iₙ APRIL, 1827, Hans Christian left the school at Helsingør and escaped the power of Rector Meisling. In Copenhagen he breathed a sigh of relief, rented a little attic room on Vingårdsstræde, got free board from various distinguished families (on Mondays he ate dinner with Commodore Wulff, on Tuesdays with Councillor Collin, and so on throughout the rest of the week), studied under the personal direction of the amiable, understanding, and deeply religious Ludvig Christian Müller, had nonetheless a good deal of time left over for writing, and found himself in a frame of mind which he depicted in the *Book of My Life* with these words:

> In my heart and soul I now resembled a bird in flight; all my cares and notions were forgotten, and it seemed as if my inherent facetious-

ness, suppressed until now, burst forth in almost too wild a way. Everything appeared funny or foolish to me; my exaggeratedly strong emotions, which in their purest expression of pain had been mocked and ridiculed by Meisling, now seemed to be unreasonable in my eyes, too! Life was so wonderful, after all.

In October, 1828, Hans Christian thus underwent his entrance examinations at the university, and, receiving reasonably good marks, was passed. He had taken the regents' examination in arts, he had become a university student at the age of twenty-three, and, if he so desired, he could carry out advanced studies. The next month, November, was the last in which he received his royal scholarship. It had fulfilled its purpose, transforming the stray proletarian boy into a cultured man.

He had not been an outstanding pupil. In his arts examination he did not even get a high grade in Danish composition, for his style was blemished by various mistakes in spelling. He was weak in grammar and in languages generally, not only the classical but also the modern ones. He learned to read German fluently and could also understand it when it was spoken, but he never learned to write it correctly; he acquired some French and English during his travels, but was never able to speak them halfway satisfactorily. The groundwork he had laid in school was too flimsy. The scorn which Rector Meisling entertained toward him has a certain counterpart, for example, in Edvard Collin, who got an insight into his weaknesses while helping him practice Latin composition before the arts examination. In his classic work on Andersen he gives the following summary:

> He was industrious, he read a great deal—but how did he read? He learned many things, but he never learned the correct method of learning. He acquired information in many fields but thoroughness

in none; his splendid memory won good marks for him in every field that can be learned by heart; but grammar is uncompromising, it has to be understood. Herein is contained, as far as I can see, the only explanation needed for the fact that Andersen did not and could not fulfill the requirements made by the higher education of that day.

One hundred years later we can repeat Edvard Collin's decree, but with the addition of the word "fortunately." The school could not transform Hans Christian into a classical philologist or a speculative philosopher or a Hegelian logician, into someone like Madvig or Kierkegaard or Heiberg. If the school had succeeded, then Andersen would never have been able to write the fairy tales. One must therefore be distinctly thankful that young Andersen did not profit by the finest educational training of his day; as compensation, he absorbed the literary and aesthetic culture which permeated the air of Copenhagen and Denmark during the post-Romantic age.

One can even detect a certain kind of strength in his individual weaknesses. He learned to spell correctly neither during his school days nor later in life—something which caused him to suffer a good deal of ignominy in the Collin ménage. But his failure to master orthography had an intimate connection with his fine ear for language, his strong feeling for the spoken word: this was the main thing for him, he did not need rules or analyses to help him find the appropriate expression. In a historical novel, of which he wrote several chapters during his school days at Slagelse, the following passage occurs: " 'That's horrible!' Thora burst out and dry that tear [*sic*] from her dark blue eyes as she left the hall." The phrase "dry that tear" is quite puzzling; Tage Høeg, the editor of the text, has solved the problem by taking it to read "dried a tear."[1] The

[1] In Danish, *"tørre den Taare"* ("dry that tear") and *"tørrede en Taare"* ("dried a tear").—G. C. S.

100

difference in pronunciation of these two phrases is insignificant: Andersen evidently heard the sentence with his subconscious ear. This quality subsequently enabled him to write the fairy tales —not in the conventional, formalized language of books, but in a living spoken language, following the dictation, as it were, of the invisible genius of his mother tongue which dwelt in his ear. Linguistic reflections had not destroyed his spontaneous and brilliant instinct.

Reading ahead but a single page in the same fragment of a novel, one comes upon the following description of the execution of Meta, the presumptive witch: " The hangman, a big, strong, fleshy man with an African face, a flat nose and large, thick, protruding lips; his little green vampire eyes showed up strangely beneath his bushy red eyebrows; he untied Meta from the cart, and the pastor stepped up and made a speech to her." The punctuation is noteworthy, and the syntax is not wholly above reproach—the subject "he" is repeated after the graphic interjected sentence about the hangman's colorful countenance—but to what a remarkable extent the sentence is spoken Danish, living and burgeoning, completely untainted by the artificial syntax of Latin! It was through the aid of this stylistic sense that Andersen created a new and revolutionary Danish literary language in his fairy tales. If he had acquired the elements of the language bent over his school desk, from manuals of style and grammars, instead of snatching up bits of conversation from the stage or mingling—as supplicant, beggar, and adventurer —with all classes of society, hanging upon the lips of men so that he might catch and make use of their every word, then he would never have learned to express himself with the bold, direct, and concrete veracity which gives the fairy tales their eternal freshness. Even his ridiculous failing, his everlasting declamation and recitation, is nothing other than his flight from the written page, from its dry letters and stiff phrases, to the fresh and living source of language: speech.

In his absurdity, in his foolishness, Hans Christian knew better than those who protected and trained and corrected him. Not even Jonas Collin, good and wise as he was, could give him pertinent advice about his education as an artist. It is touching to read a letter which Jonas Collin wrote to his protégé during the latter's first extended trip abroad. From Rome, Andersen had informed him that he was studying history, poring over a popular history of the world by the Frenchman Millot. Jonas Collin answered him on December 21, 1833: reading Millot, he wrote, is not the same as studying history.

> Read Livy and Tacitus, and read them in Latin. Study Hume, Ferguson, Schlözer, Heeren, Spittler, Johannes Müller, and other authors of this sort; thus you will obtain solid historical knowledge. Learn everything thoroughly, my dear Andersen; this is also true of languages. . . . If you wish to have any profit from your journey, you must not use your time only—or principally—for sightseeing, but rather for industrious work in your room; and this industry shall not consist of writing but of reading, and of reading after a plan. Read Latin too, the prose writers and the poets, understand every word and at the same time the meaning of the whole.

Erudition, classical philology, skill in Latin—these were useful, honorable, and solid attainments, in Collin's eyes as in Meisling's. How could they have guessed that providence intended Hans Christian Andersen to become not a man with a classical training, but instead a classic himself, something for which quite different qualities were necessary. He was not to understand the fine points of Latin prose, lest his own prose from Fyn become false and wooden.

No one could give him good advice, and in some strange way he succeeded, for all his mildness, in making himself immune to every influence from the outside. He was destined to become world-famous, a great poet—this was a thought he clung to even in the classroom, even as he writhed like a worm beneath Meisling's scorn. Everyone tried to cure him of this fixed idea. Even his poor mother laid down the law to him upon his matriculation at Slagelse; it is difficult, of course, to determine how much of the letter's message one must attribute to the unknown secretary who put it on paper, for the old woman herself could not write. It is too early to brag about being a credit to literature, a letter of December 12, 1822, says: "Dear Christian, get to know people, and don't be too proud about your own little person, for it is still very unimportant indeed, as you realize." A couple of months later, on March 7, 1823, the distinguished widow of Privy Councillor Colbjørnsen, the great statesman, wrote a letter to the schoolboy in Slagelse; the letter contained ten rix-dollars, a personal gift from the Crown Princess. Fru Colbjørnsen mentions in passing that the Princess had read "the little song" and found it nice; but at the letter's conclusion one finds the following sentences:

> I wish, my dear Andersen, to make one request of you: do not let the thought of becoming what you call something great, yes, something very great, become all too deeply rooted in your soul, for in such case it could perhaps do you a great deal of harm. Try instead to learn something thoroughly, so that you perhaps in time can acquire a minor office, the duties of which you can discharge efficiently. This is my advice, given in all friendliness. You know that I always make a practice of speaking my mind.

Andersen's mother and the lady from society's highest layer, the peasant woman and the widow of the statesman who had liberated Denmark's peasantry, were thus in touching agreement with one another: "Little Hans Christian, give up your big ideas." Some months later, on November 15, 1823, Andersen's motherly friend, Henriette Wulff, wrote to the schoolboy whom she had received in her apartments at Amalienborg Castle. Her letter, a long one, is filled with warmth and good will, but with admonitions, too: "You think, my dear Andersen, that you are intended to become something great, a great poet. No, you are not, and you least of all have the right to think so." She gives her young friend a thorough going over: his poetry is monotonous, his ideas are repetitive, her husband, the naval officer who translates Shakespeare, has read Andersen's poem in hexameters, but says the would-be poet has not written hexameters at all. The only genre for which Andersen has talent is that of the comical tale in prose, Fru Wulff writes with surprising perspicacity: "Whatever you do, my dear Andersen, don't flatter yourself by believing you'll become an Oehlenschläger, a Walter Scott, a Shakespeare, a Goethe, or a Schiller, and never again ask which one of them should be your model, for you won't become the equal of any of them!" The brisk lady then closes her letter by telling Hans Christian to gain some weight.

She continues in the same fashion during the ensuing years; she battles to save the youth's soul from megalomania, to instill him with courage when he is in despair, and to keep him on life's healthy middle path. "You're a good person with good, natural, normal qualities; although you began your education belatedly, you can still become a useful citizen of the state," she writes to Andersen on September 4, 1824. "You won't become a cabinet minister or the leading poet of the land, and you won't become a tailor or a shoemaker either; but aren't there a hundred other jobs besides these?" She exhorts him not to read his poetic works before too many people (June 4, 1826). With growing zeal, almost with maternal fear, she addresses herself to correcting his ridiculous aspects and his faults of character. On January 4, 1827, she gives him the following charge: that he must strive to win respect, not merely sympathy.

> Your poetry is like your prose—monotonous and filled with complaints; be a man with strength in both body and soul! Do not think exclusively about yourself, for that but weakens both parts, and above all, my dear Andersen, do not talk so much about yourself, do not make so many appearances as a singer and declaimer, use moderation in all your expressions; allow me to say that you read German poorly, but your Danish is still worse; you read and declaim so affectedly, in the fond belief that you are demonstrating animation and feeling, that I am compelled to tell the truth, however cruel it may be: everyone laughs at you without your noticing it.

The letter sounds as though Fru Wulff were trying to arouse a sleepwalker, a madman, to a consciousness of the world about him: "For God's sake, my dear Andersen, wake up, and cease your dreams of immortality, for they only make you seem absurd; do not dream of a poet's crown or of taking your place among the world's great men." She stigmatizes his boundless egoism: "Don't always think of just yourself, yourself, yourself" (March 8, 1827).

Colonel Høegh-Guldberg, his old friend from his Odense days who once had taken the fatherless boy by the hand and led him to the castle to see the Prince, now wrote him admonishingly: "Fight against the terrible adversary of your vanity, the most boundless vanity I have ever seen in a human being" (December 22, 1827). Not even Hans Christian Andersen himself could remain unconscious of the peculiarity of his nature. On November 20, 1825, he read a biography of Lord Byron, which inspired him to note in his diary:

Oh, he even resembled me in his talkativeness, my spirit is ambitious just as his was, it knows happiness only when it is admired by everyone, the least check can make me disheartened. Fame is the spur which drives my poet's soul, yet I myself recognize the weak and mistaken aspects of this attitude.

Nothing can help him, neither the criticism of others nor the self-criticism he himself employed in moments of candor. Friends and benefactors may shake their heads, Meisling may rant and rage, mocking laughter may resound, Fru Wulff may take the sleepwalker by his shoulders and shake him; he continues on his dangerous path. "Take heart—'*Aut Cæsar aut nihil*' shall be my motto. God's Will be done." He addressed these words on May 16, 1826, to the poet Ingemann, the person who in Andersen's opinion had the least hostile attitude toward his dreams of greatness.

Ingemann sent him a friendly and sympathetic answer, wished him luck for his stay in Helsingør, whither he was now about to move, and then added:

I deem your bold *"Aut Cæsar aut nihil"* a rather pagan tenet—in the realm of truth the last can be first and the least the greatest. On the whole, it matters little what reputation one has—*"Esse non videri"* is a good motto—God may decide how little or how much one is; one does not exist in vain if one really lives up to what one can be and should be."

Thus spake the pious bard of Sorø, but Hans Christian Andersen was deaf in the ear he addressed.

He had promised his friends and benefactors that he would make no literary efforts as long as he sat in the classroom. The pause during these years did him good, without any doubt. But it is only natural that he could not remain absolutely true to his intention; during this time a number of lyric poems and a few fragmentary attempts at historical novels were produced despite Hans Christian Andersen's resolve.

Danish and German Romanticism nourished his intellectual life: the Romantic strain harmonized nicely, of course, with his child-like piety, with the realm of primitive faith in which he had grown up, and with his own innermost reliance on deliverance by miracle. One of his first longer poems, written in 1825, is called *The Soul;* according to Andersen, it aroused approval and encouragement on the part of the great Oehlenschläger himself. The poem incontest-ably shows that the nineteen-year-old had availed himself of the thoughts and style of his age, and with a great deal of talent: it gives expression to spiritualism and to a hope for immortality, and the religious mood is essentially a sublimation or disguise of the hapless youth's strong desire for happiness, of his overwhelming vitality. If this vitality is denied satisfaction in the actual world, then it will ascend on the wings of the imagination into the realms of heaven, into eternity.

An identical psychological process forms the core of *The Dying Child*, the first of Andersen's poems to become famous. Written in 1826, it expresses the sick despair Hans Christian felt as he saw himself being destroyed in the school and in Meisling's home; in his distress, he dreams that he once again lies in his mother's arms:

> *Mother, I am tired, I want to slumber,*
> *Let me fall asleep beside your heart.*

But the dying child sees the colorful dreams of the imagination shining, the angelic forms of its pious faith hover before its eyes: the Sandman has opened the magical umbrella of fairyland over the deathbed of the human child. For all its weepy supersensibility, the poem is a moving one and a perfect example of its genre, simple, pure, cast like a relief of Thorwaldsen, in the most classically objective form. The twenty-year-old schoolboy who could dress his feelings of loneliness and abandonment in such a form gave sure signs of being a great artist.

It is also significant that the poem immediately found its way into the broadest circles. In Helsingør, the young author showed the poem to a Baltic German consular official named Schley, the very Schley who translated Tegnér's *Fritjof's Saga.* Having rendered Andersen's lyric into German, Schley got it published, anonymously, in a Libau newspaper. And Andersen, who had not dared to show the poem to his patrons in Copenhagen—after all, he was forbidden to write poetry—now had to reveal his authorship, cost what it might; and in September, 1827, both the Danish original and the German translation were printed in *The Copenhagen Post.* Since then the poem has traveled the length and breadth of the world: wherever Hans Christian went on his journeys abroad, he found *The Dying Child* in countless translations. In Denmark, many generations have learned it by heart, and it has been sold as a handbill at fairs. A popularity of this sort means something; it is not the result of pure chance.

While the sojourn in Slagelse was, on the whole, depressing for Hans Christian, the move to Helsingør had worked as a stimulant, a fact which Kjeld Galster has correctly emphasized. The very first sight of Helsingør's setting made him enraptured, and there is evidence of his reaction scattered throughout the *Book of My Life* and the letters. As soon as he arrived, he depicted the city by the Sound in a letter to Jonas Collin (May 27, 1826):

What activity! What a lot of excitement on the docks! Here some fat Dutchmen are speaking their hollow sounding tongue, and there I hear the musical sounds of Italian, and further along coal is being unloaded from an English brig, so that I think I smell London. The Sound is covered with vessels, they hover along the coasts like sea gulls. Yesterday I visited Marienlyst with Meisling, oh, it's one of the most splendid things I've ever seen. It all seemed like Switzerland to me, and I felt so inexpressibly happy; oh, upon seeing that wonderful landscape one must become a poet or a painter. Oh, my benefactor, thanks for each happy moment! Life is wonderful, after all!

In a letter to Ingemann written a little more than a week later (June 8), he depicts the enchanting view across the Øresund from the highest terrace behind the town. He fancies that the towers of Landskrona belong to Naples, Kronborg Castle lies at his feet, on the other side of the straits the cliffs of Kullen rise through the blue haze, English men-of-war pass by, their bands playing, and fire a salute to the fortress, a steamboat belches coal smoke, Italians sing, and from a fishing smack he hears the laughter of Swedish girls. "Happy the man who could fly away with the ships and see all the beautiful places in the world. I like to imagine that this will be one of our first steps in bliss after death—that the liberated soul, soaring away, can see each beauty spot on earth." The *Weltfreudigkeit* of the poet and travel-writer and teller of tales has tasted first blood in the lively port of Helsingør—but it is characteristic of Romanticism's incurable urge toward the afterlife, and of poverty's humble resignation, that Hans Christian thinks he must be dead before he can get a good look at the beauties and riches of the world. One is reminded of two lines in *The Dying Child*:

> *Shall I have wings the while I still am living,*
> *Or, mother, shall I get them when I die?*

Andersen got wings while he lived—he soared about the world in a manner allowed to only very few of his Danish compatriots.

However, it was in Helsingør that these sunny, outgoing, inquisitive moods, this bursting joy at the colorful pageant of existence, for the first time erupted in Hans Christian— and it is strange to think that the breaking of the spiritual ice occurred simultaneously with the crisis in the relations with Rector Meisling, at a time when life in Meisling's school had become unbearable. To his many friends and acquaintances Andersen wrote letters which depicted his impressions of his journey and of the landscape around Helsingør in cheerful colors; these were not merely individual communications but also literary products of a sort—and old Professor Rasmus Nyerup proved that he saw the matter in this light by having an excerpt from his young friend's letter printed in one of Copenhagen's newspapers, *Copenhagen Scenes*. Andersen's situation was somewhat embarrassing, and among the reasons for his embarrassment was the fact that he had sent Nyerup just about the same description as he had to many other correspondents —and now they all had a chance to read in print what they had earlier read in private letters.

The schoolboy, sternly tried as he was, not only betrayed a gift of observation and an interest in the external world's many variegated and amusing dramas; he also showed roguishness and wit and humor. His long battle for existence had been so hard, and his exertion of will so convulsive, that he had had the time to look neither to the right nor the left, and a smile had never passed over his thin face; it had been his task to watch carefully for each opportunity, to look deeply and with doglike devotion into the eyes of his powerful superiors, while at the same time keeping a close watch on their fingers. Now, however, he began to feel other moods too— freedom, pleasure, and lightness of heart—moods that alternated with despair, anxiety, dejection, and ambitious zeal, just as in the case of other healthy and normal youths. One July day during the summer vacation of 1826 he got up at three in the morning in order to go to Copenhagen on foot, and upon his arrival there he was hospitably received by the Commodore Wulffs. Lying in bed the next morning, he composed a poem about the previous day's wonderful hike through the Danish summer landscape. (Our information comes from a letter of August 4 to Ingemann.) The poem, called *The Evening,* bears the bold motto *"Anch'io son pittore,"* no mere boasting on Andersen's part; for the landscape is rendered with an exuberant brush:

> *Violets send their scent from tender grass,*
> *And farther on the pastor's white geese pass.*

The lines do not present the conventional Romantic picture of nature, which would admit wild swans alone, while excluding the pastor's white geese—Andersen was familiar with both factions. The following tableau possesses a strikingly direct truth:

> *How picturesque there stands the fisher's hut,*
> *Where, bulging, half the windowpanes seem dimmer,*
> *And where, between the half old rags have shut,*
> *The other half glows in the late sun's glimmer!*
> *And round the hut there grows the hawthorne's wall*
> *With socks and stockings as its lace and ruffles;*
> *And clear and blue, the sky embraces all,*
> *Home from the beach the fisherwoman shuffles.*

Andersen uses the same style to depict an old peasant on his way home, stopping under a beech tree to count the money he carries in a little mitten—and yearning all the while to get home to the porridge bowl in the cottage amidst the hazel bushes. Nothing more is said about the peasant, a lyric and decorative figure, but the reader cannot keep himself from thinking that it could easily be the peasant from *Little Claus and Big Claus,* the one who did not like the sexton; *The Evening*'s peasant has a promisingly humorous air about him. And in the last stanza the poet presents still another figure:

> *Behold, on yonder scarpment there does rise*
> *(Like our late Werther pale) a gawky creature:*
> *He has a nose that's grown to cannon-size,*
> *And tiny eyes, like green peas, grace his features.*

It is a self-portrait, and it reveals that humor, personal ironization, and even badinage are beginning to break through the poetic mood, through sentimental Romanticism.

In 1827, *The Evening* received the honor of being printed by that stern critic, Johan Ludvig Heiberg, in his journal, *The Flying Post,* and the honor was not undeserved. If a perspicacious judge had put this picturesque and witty poem beside the boundlessly emotional yet plastic verses of *The Dying Child,* he would have been justified in saying that the eccentric youth who had written both pieces did not lack talent—that he in fact possessed future possibilities, however uncertain they might be.

CHAPTER VIII

The Student

THE HANS CHRISTIAN ANDERSEN who came to Copenhagen from Helsingør in the spring of 1827 and became a student at the university in the fall of 1828 was both outwardly and inwardly an altogether different person from the seedy theatrical extra and the shivering schoolboy. Edvard Collin, who only now got to know him well—from this time on he was, according to the younger Collin's great source-book, *H. C. Andersen and the Collin Home,* "an almost daily guest in my father's house"—offers important testimony of the change:

I had, of course, often seen Andersen during his first stay in Copenhagen, but whatever image I had of him from those days is now rather thoroughly erased from my mind; I have only a dim memory of an overgrown boy with a long, oldish face, pale eyes, and pale

113

hair, dressed in a pair of yellow nankeen trousers which reached only halfway down his shins. But at the time of his return to the city I quite naturally had a good notion of his earlier appearance, and with astonishment I was forced to notice the change for the better which had taken place with respect to his physical development.

In other words, he no longer attracted attention by his ridiculous appearance; his dress and his behavior were not all too different from those of his fellow students. One can guess that his health, which must have suffered harm during his early adolescence and especially during his hand-to-mouth existence as a member of the Copenhagen plebs, had been substantially improved by the regular life he led during his school days. To be sure, he never became healthy in the word's strict sense, he was perpetually at the mercy of a feeling of nervous impotence, he must keep exerting all his strength in order to fill his place in the world and carry out his tasks; but despite this disposition, which the physicians (*cf.* Hjalmar Helweg) call asthenia, he by no means lacked energy or enterprise. In the new and milder climate he bloomed both in body and in soul; *The Fairy Tale of My Life* says: "A complete change had taken place within me; the crushed flower, transplanted, had begun to bear fresh shoots."

He had even become capable of asserting his personal opinions in opposition to those of his friends and benefactors. Ludvig Christian Müller, the theologian who gave him private tutoring in preparation for the matriculation examination, won his pupil's heart through his kindness and gentleness; but Müller was a religious zealot, a follower of Grundtvig; and as he unfolded his stern and orthodox theories, breaking a lance for, among other things, the doctrine of eternal punishment in hell, he was unable to persuade his disciple: the result was violent disputes. Hans Christian was a liberal rationalist like his poor father before him, and not even the authority of the Bible could get him to recognize a vengeful and punitive God. In the *Book of My Life* he speaks of the champagne of freedom which bubbled in his veins, while in *The Fairy Tale of My Life* he writes: "From a cowed creature of the classroom, I became a free and independent individual, stepping forward with these expressions of my belief: I spoke like a child of nature."

This collegiate boldness also took the form of persiflage and wit. In Andersen's childhood and earlier youth, poetically sentimental moods had had the upper hand—his very situation had, after all, been one that inspired pathos—but now humor begins to stir within him. This characteristic becomes especially apparent in his relations with Henriette Wulff, Commodore Wulff's daughter, and thus the child of parents who were among his most faithful friends. Henriette, called "Jette" for short, was about the same age as young Andersen; although unfortunate in her external appearance—she was hunchbacked—she was intellectually gifted, sprightly and humorous, and a real friendship arose between her and Andersen. In the *Book of My Life* he counts her as being among the exciting and invigorating factors in his existence: "To this must be added Jette Wulff's humorous way of looking at life, her innocent persiflage—these things rubbed off on me, from them I got a happy frame of mind, a merry nature, and an inclination to have fun." A letter to her from August 14, 1828, shows that both correspondents were pretending that she resided in Constantinople, near the Hippodrome—the very first occasion on which Andersen tries to acclimate himself to the Turkish milieu, of which he would later give such a splendid depiction in *The Flying Trunk*. Many emotional and even despairing accents find their way into the high-spirited letter, of course—Andersen was on the verge of taking the matriculation examination, and he said that he would be ruined if he failed—but the whole epistle dances along the edge of self-irony, and the signature runs: "Written by young Werther from the caves of misfortune and the mansions of misery." A bad novel by a certain Spiess had treated of the caves of misfortune and the mansions of misery: the element of literary parody is apparent. Jette Wulff was extremely interested in belles-lettres.

There were not many students in Copenhagen who had as rich a treasure of impressions from reality to look back on as H. C. Andersen did. He had been a part of the existence of peasantry and proletariat, of the artisan and the middle class, both in a small town and in the capital; he had moved in theatrical circles and in neighborhoods where vice was a profession; and he had been and done these things perhaps even more thoroughly than Spiess, the German novelist. During his school years in Slagelse and Helsingør he had received a deep insight into conditions of the Meisling ménage and of other homes as well; little by little he had become a frequent guest of patrician families, too, and had been received in several of Copenhagen's most respected and also most distinguished houses. In *The Fairy Tale of My Life* he writes of his free-board days as a student: "The practice involved variety, and I received a knowledge of family life in various circles which was also useful for me." Hans Christian Andersen was no longer estranged from reality, no longer naïvely innocent: he kept his eyes open. At the Collin home he obtained entrance to a highly cultured circle, in which old and young competed in ironic wit, repartee, and a soundly realistic interpretation of men and affairs. These circumstances developed his ability to observe and widen his horizon to the greatest degree imaginable. In his associations with the Collins and Jette Wulff, with his fellow students and his friends, he absorbed —as it were, almost unconsciously—the whole *esprit* of the Danish patriciate, clear-sighted and resourceful, free of illusions and fond

116

Jonas Collin, about whom Andersen said, "He gave me encouragement and comfort . . . I placed my heartfelt trust in him," became the youthful poet's benefactor in 1822 and remained so until
his own death in 1861.

From a painting by J. V. Gertner, 1840

Edvard Collin, son of Jonas, and his wife Henriette. Edvard and
Hans Christian Andersen were lifelong friends; when both were
elderly, Andersen wrote to Edvard, "I have many friends . . . but
you, dear friend, are the oldest . . . . You are infinitely dear to
me, and I shall pray Our Lord to let you survive me, for I cannot
do without you."

From a painting by W. Marstrand, 1842

of reality. As a background he retained the strong and profound feeling for life he had acquired in his childhood, with its infusion of magic idealism and its Romantic yearning for a happiness and bliss beyond all human understanding.

He was to become a poet; in a poem such as *The Dying Child* his sentimentally Romantic vein had found expression, and his realistically ironic vein had done the same in *The Evening*. But there was still another element in his nature, his power of invention, his delight in the imagination, the bold and light *élan* of his fancy—the qualities that revealed themselves as the boy sat by the river in Odense, waiting for the Chinese prince, or as quite ordinary theatrical handbills unfolded themselves in a dazzling display of colors, like a peacock's tail, before his childish eyes. The Collins did not have much understanding for such phantasmagorias—they were quite satisfied with solid reality—but hunchbacked Jette Wulff, herself also something of a stepchild of life, gladly joined Andersen in his games in these enchanted gardens of the imagination.

While preparing for the matriculation examination, Hans Christian Andersen had lived in an attic above Vingårdsstræde; his teacher, Müller, had moved out to Christianshavn. Twice a day Andersen had to walk over to Amager. On the way there he only thought of his lessons and of Latin compositions, but going home, relieved that the task was over, "I let my imagination amuse me," as it says in the *Book of My Life,* while in *The Fairy Tale of My Life* one finds the passage: "All sorts of colorful poetic images went through my head." He jotted down a description of some of the amusements his imagination afforded him, but he kept the majority of them in his head for the time being, since he had promised, of course, not to write anything before his examination. As soon as this critical point had been passed, however, in October, 1828, he sat down at his desk and began to write at a furious speed; and in January, 1829, his first work of any importance, *A Journey on Foot from Holmens Canal to the Eastern Point of Amager,* came off the press.

The book is a capriccio, a playful arabesque, a lyric causerie in prose about everything under the sun. The style bears many traces of Andersen's studies, although it is not the Latin quotations which give the composition its character, but rather the connections with German Romanticism, with the world of legends and of miracles which had recently come to life in literary form. Every page reveals how familiar Hans Christian had become with these authors, with E. T. A. Hoffmann and Tieck and Chamisso. When he set out on his wanderings, the first chapter says, he stuffed Hoffmann's *Die Elixiere des Teufels* into his pocket, thinking in this way to have a little imagination in reserve in case his own went on strike. He also borrowed ideas and characters whenever he needed them: he gets the seven-league boots from the Wandering Jew in return for the pawn of his shadow, and the transaction occurs just about as it did when Chamisso let Peter Schlemihl sell *his* shadow.

The whole thing is amusing, piquant, cheerful, now and then rather childish, but just as frequently of an undeniable wittiness. One may speak of a collegiate pleasure in practical jokes, but that quality which is most inimitably Andersen's lies in the deep inner satisfaction which the author experiences at letting his imagination create and invent freely, at pleasing and enchanting his viewers and listeners with surprising spectacles. In his childhood he had received themes from the realms of faith and superstition, from religion and from folk tales; now, in his youth, he had made the acquaintance of literary Romanticism, with authors who gave their narrative ability free rein. The artist will be complete—and ready to write the fairy tales—on the day when he succeeds in uniting all these elements, elements impregnated by his realistic observations and his humorous concept of mankind. If *The Dying Child* marks the first step along the way and *The Evening* the second, then *A Journey on Foot* is without doubt the third.

The zany little booklet of the newly fledged student aroused attention and became a success. In the *Book of My Life,* Andersen records that he offered Reitzel's publishing house the manuscript for a hundred rix-dollars, but Reitzel only wished to pay seventy. The great critic J. L. Heiberg, whom Andersen had succeeded in approaching, hereupon advised the young author to become his own publisher, and his advice was followed. As matters turned out, the first edition of five hundred copies was quickly sold; his hands raised in supplication, Reitzel offered to pay a hundred rix-dollars for a second edition. Such success meant a good deal for the attic poet, who led a life of touching thrift, received free board from various respectable families, and secretly put aside shilling after shilling in order to be able to afford a longer journey than that to Amager. Hans Christian had thus already learned that he was able to win the public's favor. His *Journey on Foot* had won him a kind of fame: it is almost comical to note that even as late as 1841 it was being printed in Danish in Sweden, a distinction seldom conferred upon Danish books. But cultured opinion in Denmark was also favorably impressed. J. L. Heiberg put the hallmark of his authority on the book's success by writing a friendly review of it in *The Literary Monthly,* a review which recognized the beginner's talent and felicitous imagination. Andersen hastened to have Heiberg's judgment reprinted in the new editions of *A Journey on Foot.* He was anxious to cash in his triumphs; he was twenty-four years old, and had wasted a great deal of time.

"The success of my first piece of literary work made me bolder," the *Book of My Life* says. "Now I saw everything from the comical side, I wanted to parody all my cares and worries." From this mood was born the musical comedy, *Love in St. Nicolai Church Tower,* which, in rhymed verse, was written down in eight days, and which was performed at the Royal Theater on April 25, 1829. The trifling piece received quite a friendly reception, especially from Andersen's fellow students, who composed a dependable claque. The author took up his post in the wings, in seventh heaven at seeing his play being performed at the theater in front of whose locked gates he had once stood penniless and lonely, and where he had sought refuge as an extra. But the clapping and the shouts of approval made him run away in terror; he dashed to the Collins' house and there, weeping convulsively, collapsed on a chair. Fru Collin, the only member of the family at home, tried to console him by pointing out that Oehlenschläger and many another great poet had seen their works whistled off the stage. "Yes, but I wasn't whistled off stage," sobbed Hans Christian. "They clapped and cried 'bravo.' " At least that is the way the story is told in *The Fairy Tale of My Life.*

In the last analysis, however, his success was not a tremendous one—the theater, the first enticing goal of the young man's dreams of greatness, would never, in fact, provide him with any really great triumphs. But he did not lose heart; he continued to read and he continued to write. In the summer of 1829 he took a trip through Denmark which led him to Møn and to Odense, where he paid a visit to his aged mother. It was the first of his many journeys. He had a romantic wanderlust in his blood; the journey on foot to Amager and the trips into the realms of the imagination did not satisfy him; but for the time being he had to content himself with modest summer excursions within Denmark's boundaries. During the same summer of 1829, however, he was invited to stay at Nør-ager, the Zealand estate of Chamberlain Bang—his entrance into

the world of country squires and manorial estates, a world in which
he would eventually become a regular guest. In the fall of 1829 he
took his so-called second examination, *"philologicum et philoso-
phicum,"* with good results; but by this time he had decided not to
continue his studies. Even Councillor Collin had reconciled himself to the thought that his protégé would not pursue one of the
accepted callings. "Walk then in God's name the path for which
you evidently have been created; it's no doubt for the best," he is
supposed to have remarked, according to the *Book of My Life.*
At New Year's, 1830, a collection of poetry by H. C. Andersen
appeared, and with the beginning of summer he set out on a literary tour of Jutland and Fyn. He planned to write a historical novel
in the manner of Walter Scott, and to this end he had even done
some research in the libraries of Copenhagen; now he wished to
see with his own eyes the regions of Jutland where the action was
to take place. The possessor of savings to the amount of four hundred rix-dollars, which he had earned with his literary works, he
could go about his task thoroughly and methodically. Nor did he
travel in the manner of a tramp or an unknown student, but rather
as a promising young author; moreover, Councillor Collin, inspired by paternal benevolence, had given him a letter of recommendation, something which must have had a good effect upon the
officials in the cities round about the land. Andersen awaited his
departure eagerly; he longed to see the heaths of Jutland, populated by wandering gypsies and other romantic figures; he looked
forward with anticipation to the sea journey, the dunes, the gales,
and the breakers, impressive backdrops for the novel he planned
to write. At the end of May he went on board the steamer *Dania;*
the Kattegat gave him enough—and more than enough—of the
sea's poetry before he disembarked at Aarhus.

On this first longer journey of his it happened, however, that he experienced something different from what he had expected.

He was hospitably received in Jutland: an Aarhus newspaper had mentioned his visit, and he had been welcomed both in towns and on country estates. In August, on the way back to Copenhagen, he interrupted his journey on the island of Fyn; there he lingered for a few days in the little town of Faaborg as a guest of Christian Voigt, a friend from his university days and son of a well-to-do merchant. The friend's family gave the guest a hearty reception. The daughter of the house, Riborg Voigt, a twenty-four-year-old beauty with flashing brown eyes, had read *A Journey on Foot* and the poems, and had formed a high opinion of them. Hans Christian took a lively interest in her, and she cannot be said to have remained indifferent toward her brother's friend, the poet who was but a year older than herself. As the two young people walked in the garden on the third and final day of the Faaborg sojourn, Andersen half jestingly told her that the heroine of his novel would bear her name; blushing, she asked him for a poem. Upon his departure the same day she gave him a bouquet; sadly having taken his place in the coach, he saw her gentle face nodding good-by to him from a window of the house. In Copenhagen he became the sedulous companion of Christian Voigt, and toward the close of the fall learned that Voigt's sister was coming to the capital on a visit. They met, and Andersen realized that he loved Riborg Voigt, He handed her the following four lines, written on a scrap of paper:

> *You have become my thinking's single thought,*
> *My heart's first love: it had no love before.*
> *I love you as no love on earth is wrought,*
> *I love you now and love you evermore.*

At their next meeting she was friendly, but a little embarrassed. As a matter of fact, she was no longer free, but rather half-engaged to a young man in Faaborg, the son of the town apothecary. Hans Christian was hard beset by uncertainty and suspense. On October 30, 1830, when her departure from Copenhagen was imminent, he sent her an indignant letter, a sketch of which has been preserved in the *Book of My Life*. He knew nothing of her engagement, he says; otherwise he should have surpressed his feelings in good time; now, having learned of the engagement from her brother, he puts a delicate question to her: "Do you really love this other man?" If this is the case, then he will pray God that He make fortune smile upon them. But if she is not sure about her love for his rival, then he implores her: "Do not make me unhappy! With your help I can become anything! I'll work, I'll do everything you and your parents desire of me." Yet despite these fiery assurances the letter closes on an almost resigned note: "May the two of you be happy! And forget a creature who can never, never forget you. If my letter has not offended you, then allow me to see you just once more, and I shall read my fate in every expression of your face. Farewell! Farewell—perhaps forever!"

As poor Riborg Voigt read this letter she burst into tears; still, it did not give her the strength to break with the person she regarded as her fiancé. She was of the opinion that duty required her to remain faithful to the friend of her youth. Hans Christian and Riborg Voigt pressed one another's hands as they said good-by; and she gave him a note with the lines: "Farewell, Farewell! I hope that Christian will soon be able to tell me that you once again are as happy and calm as you were before. With sincere friendship, Riborg."

This is the text of Riborg Voigt's parting words as they are included in the *Book of My Life* from 1832. However, it is quite possible that she sent a longer and more direct message to Andersen, possibly by the indirect means of a letter to her brother, for when Andersen died at the age of seventy, a leather bag was found attached to a string around his neck, and the bag contained a letter from his first love. In accordance with his last wishes, the letter was burned unread.

It is not likely that he had borne this relic on his breast his whole life through; one should rather imagine that the old man, standing face to face with death, was seized by the memory of an episode in his youth, a memory which had never withered, and that he felt an urge to confirm the truth of the feelings he had once confessed in the words: "You have become my thinking's single thought." Actually, he had been in love many times since the days when he was a twenty-five-year-old student, and he had even had a reunion with Riborg Voigt, happily married to her Faaborg friend, without being upset by the experience. Yet nothing had stirred his innermost being as deeply as his first love.

Thus if one knows that his feelings were strong and deep, one cannot help being surprised at Andersen's failure to win the object of these feelings. Andersen considered himself to have been turned down by Riborg Voigt, but the letters which he wrote to Ingemann and to another friend in 1831 reveal quite plainly that she told Andersen she loved him—it was only a sense of duty which made her persist in her earlier alliance. Hans Christian needed merely to act with greater determination, with something of the passionate zeal he showed in other matters, and Riborg Voigt would have fallen into his arms; the observer cannot escape this impression. Even that fateful letter, the draft of which has been quoted here from the pages of the *Book of My Life,* was not composed in a way to strengthen the heart of a hesitant and timid girl; Hans Christian accommodates himself in advance, as it were, to the melancholy role of the unrequited lover. He invites Riborg Voigt to partake of his resignation—considerable time will elapse before he begins his complaints that she did not love him sufficiently, that she no doubt found him too ugly and too poor.

What lies at the core of this perhaps unconscious duplicity? What inhibits Andersen, what keeps him from taking the final decisive step? One suspects that a hint of an answer to these questions may be found in the letter, in the passage which goes: "With your help I can become anything! I'll work, I'll do everything you and your parents desire of me!" The words sound a little thin. If Andersen had become engaged to the daughter of the wealthy merchant, he would certainly have had to undertake a respectable career, to pass examinations, to choose a calling. As husband and father, it would have been impossible for him to concentrate all his forces on the achievement of the great, the all-devouring dream: the dream of becoming a great poet, of winning world-wide fame. Throughout the whole of his youth he had put all his hopes on this single card—should he trade it now for another?

It is not unlikely that Hans Christian was clear-sighted enough —or, if one will, cynical enough—to see through himself. Yet the passionate and irresistible instinct which drove him along his way had just as sure an effect. This instinct commanded him to seek poetry and honor—not power, not wealth, not a happy home. Therefore something within him felt relief when Riborg Voigt— tears in her lovely brown eyes, touching in her virtuous self-denial —took her exit from his life, setting him free that he might pursue his destiny.

His whole life long he would be abandoned by love in quite the same way he had been abandoned by this girl, whom he himself had secretly played false in his heart of hearts. His flame burned before another divinity; and it did not burn in vain. But, bent beneath his laurels, the gray-haired poet still bore Riborg Voigt's single love letter next to his heart, as if in his final hours he repented the sacrifice the twenty-five-year-old student had made for his life's calling.

CHAPTER IX

Loneliness and Family Life

FROM the early 1830's onward, Hans Christian Andersen is no longer an unknown young man, a poor student, but
rather a talented and ambitious author who neglects no means
which will help him carve out a career, and who knows how to
attract attention to himself. His productivity was considerable. At
New Year's, 1830, he had published a volume called *Poems,* and a
year later, in January, 1831, a new collection of poetry appeared
with the title *Fantasies and Sketches.* During May and June, 1831,
he made his first trip abroad, to Germany, and by September the
bookstores were selling *Silhouettes of a Trip to the Harz, Saxon
Switzerland, etc., in the Summer of 1831*—and not only the title
was reminiscent of Heine's *Harzreise.* A month later, on October
5, the musical comedy *The Ship* was performed at the Royal
Theater, and in December a new collection of poetry, *Vignettes for*

Danish Poets, was published. In May, 1832, the opera *The Bride of Lammermoor* had its *première*—it had been submitted by Andersen in February, 1831—and by June, 1832, he had completed the libretto of a new opera, *The Festival at Kenilworth,* which was refused, however, and reached the boards only in 1836, in a revised form. In September, 1832, a new work was submitted to the theater, the patriotic Singspiel, *The Second of April,* but it was also turned down. On the other hand, the opera *The Fox* was produced in October of the same year, and in December a cycle of poems, *The Twelve Months of the Year,* came out. In March, 1833, Andersen submitted two musical comedies to the theater, *The Spaniards in Odense* and *Twenty-five Years Later,* both of which, like so many of their brothers and sisters, fell victim to the grim criticisms of Christian Molbech, who functioned as reader of all pieces presented to the Royal Theater. Directly thereafter, in April, Andersen, now supported by a public stipend, undertook his first journey to the south; he went by way of Paris and Switzerland to Italy, spending the winter in Rome, the spring in Florence, the summer in Austria and Germany, and returning to Denmark only in August, 1834. But he did not remain silent during this journey, either: in August, 1833, his *Collected Poems* appeared, and in December, 1833, came his poetic drama, *Agnete and the Merman,* begun in Paris and completed in Switzerland. A pause was signaled only by 1834, with its many journeys, and that pause was a brief one; in April, 1835, the novel *The Improvisator* appeared, the fruit of the impressions received during the Italian journey, and a work which the reading public greeted with interest and warmth—Andersen's first pronounced success since *A Journey on Foot* of 1829. And in the same year, 1835, the first two thin numbers of *Fairy Tales Told for Children* saw the light of day.

This enumeration will suffice to show the almost feverish zeal with which Hans Christian devoted himself to his poet's calling. It seemed as though he were attempting to storm Parnassus from every side, and if he was repulsed at one bastion, then he immediately made his attack from another and surprising direction. People who were critically inclined made fun of him, and even his friends shook their heads. Andersen indeed was considered to be hasty and superficial, and it is quite true that his whole turn of mind was characterized by a certain nervous restlessness. Yet there was a second cause for his working at top speed: he lived from his pen, and such matters as economic irresponsibility and the incurrence of debts were repugnant to him. And then, in his heart of hearts, a spur was at work whose point he never ceased to feel: his ambition, his thirst for immortality.

He was a poet, and, seen with the eyes of a respectable citizen, he now belonged to the higher classes of society, to the circles of the cultured. There was no longer anything in his circumstances to arouse pity; even if he had to count his money carefully, he by no means led a life of want. And at this time, too, his last direct connection with the proletarian depths was broken: his mother died.

She had been a patient at the charitable institution in Odense, the "Doctor's Stalls," from 1825 on, and she had caused her son worries of many sorts—worries he had tried to bear alone. Concerning this subject, Edvard Collin writes in his classic work that: "He was very restrained when he discussed her, but I know that she and her circumstances were a heavy burden for him. From her side he heard constant reproaches that he did too little for her."

In July, 1832, he visited her for the last time. He was a guest at Colonel Høegh-Guldberg's house, he was festively received at the manorial estates in the vicinity of Odense—it was not easy for him to maintain contact with the drunken old asylum-patient at the same time. Nor does he say a word about his mother in his letters to his friends. But he does complain about his health, writing to Edvard Collin that: "I haven't felt really well here in Odense, it's a strange exhaustion, a tenseness in my nerves, I get tired at the least bit of exertion, and am in a bad humor. Everyone does all he can to amuse me, the most distinguished families show me the greatest attentiveness imaginable, but it doesn't help." The thought of his mother and her misery hangs over him like a black cloud, and keeps him from enjoying his pleasant surroundings.

He cared for her as best he could, sending her money and clothes. A letter written by Pastor Ascanius at Vejlby in the autumn of 1832 shows that he had planned to arrange lodgings in the country for her, but that her drunkenness had caused hesitation on the part of her intended hosts. Evidently, she often transformed the gifts she received into liquor, and she seems to have been quite imaginative in her techniques. On one occasion she begs for money so that she can buy shoes and a shift to wear to communion, and in another letter she complains about the food, which is too thin, and the linen for the shift, which is too coarse—she prefers to receive money intended for her support directly, instead of through a middleman, and she asseverates that she will leave the bottle alone, while simultaneously protesting against the slanders circulated about her.

One can only guess what pain all this caused Hans Christian. Yet he tried, all the same, to preserve appearances, and he tried to make her happy. She was proud of his successes. In the *Book of My Life* he tells how the governor general of Fyn, Christian Frederick—the very Prince who had advised the fatherless boy to choose the turner's trade, and who in the course of time would become King Christian VIII—visited the Odense asylum in the summer of 1832: while he was there he asked to be allowed to see Andersen's old mother. When she was presented to him, he said: "Your son does you much honor!" a remark which, according to the *Book of My Life,* "delighted her to the depths of her soul, especially since the people around her were listening."

The next year, on October 7, 1833, there died, according to the church register of the Gray Brothers' Hospital, "Marie Jørgensen, member of the Doctor's Stalls, widow of Shoemaker Andersen, mother of the Poet H. C. Andersen." On November 14, more than a month later, H. C. Andersen wrote a letter from Rome to Madam Iversen in Odense, in which he says, amidst all the descriptions of roses and oranges, the Sabine Mountains and the waterfalls at Tivoli: "Please be so kind as to send the little note herewith enclosed to my old mother, seeing that I am forever taking the liberty of recommending her a little to your care." It was only on December 17 that Andersen wrote to Henriette Wulff:

> Yesterday evening I received a letter from Father Collin in which he told me of my old mother's death; her plight was hard, and I could do almost nothing for her; I have often been saddened by this, back home in Denmark, but I could never talk about it! Now Our Lord has taken her into His care, and I offer filial thanks for His deed; but her death has moved me deeply, just the same. Now I am really quite alone for the first time—no loving creature is required by nature to love me.

The following day Edvard Collin wrote from Copenhagen:

> I cannot console you, dear friend; the knowledge that you have been a good son, a son who did not forget his poor old mother upon entering into a new sphere, should offer you a great deal of consolation. If there is something among her effects—these have presumably become the hospital's property—which could have sentimental value for you, something from your childhood which could be of interest to you, then I shall be happy to acquire it for you.

Andersen does not seem to have sent an answer to Collin's offer, perhaps because he did not wish to be reminded of his childhood at this time or because he was convinced that his destitute mother could not have left anything of material value behind.

The day before he had noted in his diary the message he sent to his hunch-backed *correspondante;* his first reaction upon hearing of his mother's death was to offer thanks to God, but then another thought came to him: "However, I cannot accustom myself to the idea of being absolutely alone, without a single person who *must* love me on account of ties of blood."

This profound sense of loneliness and abandonment forms the background of the numerous friendships which Hans Christian took so many pains to establish, not least with members of the upper classes. He wanted to leave the swamp, he wanted to be admired as a poet, he wanted to acquire mighty patrons; but he also wanted to feel human warmth. Since the days of his youth he had possessed a series of maternal protectresses, Madam Iversen, Fru Wulff, Fru Signe Læssøe, Fru Colbjørnsen, who by turns scolded him and spoiled him, who gave him some of the things he could not get from his unhappy mother. He also had sisterly friends his whole life through, and he loved to call himself their "brother"; the only person who had the actual right to name him thus, his half-sister, he shunned like the plague and buried in oblivion. He was a frequent visitor in many Danish homes, and stood on an intimate footing with some of Denmark's best and most distinguished men: the poet Ingemann at Sorø, the brilliant physicist H. C. Ørsted, General Høegh-Guldberg, Admiral Wulff—the list one can compose of the families which opened their doors to the young poet is, in its length alone, a very imposing one; and the longer he lived, the more overwhelming this list became: kings

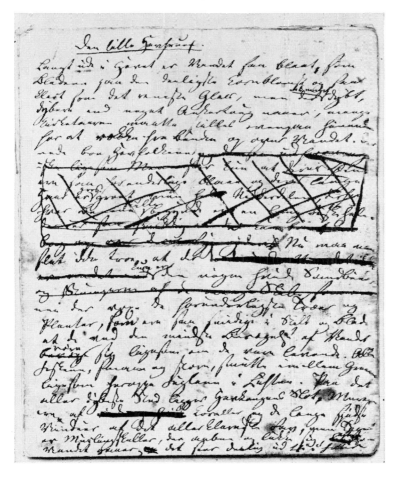

In Andersen's own handwriting, this is the first page of his manuscript of *The Little Mermaid*. Published in April, 1873, it was one of his early fairy tales.

During all of Andersen's journeys he made small pen sketches, in which he preserved the memory of landscapes and views that had charmed him. He made his drawings nowhere with more energy than in Italy; this one is of Tasso's house in Sorrento, done in 1834.

and queens, both of earthly realms and the empires of the spirit, became his hosts. Nevertheless, all these strong and sometimes intimate friendships serve merely to emphasize the fact that Andersen felt himself to be lonely and homeless, a wayfarer; in Copenhagen, between his many and extended journeys, he lived in furnished apartments, and, later on, in hotels; he would have to be hard pressed before he would acquire his own ménage and his own furniture. He was accustomed, of course, to compare himself to the stork, the long-legged bird of passage.

The comparison is all the more suitable because the stork is simultaneously a kind of symbol for the poetry of the home, a subject for which Andersen possessed a truly infinite sensitivity. Like the stork, he also had a favorite house, a house on whose roof he had built the nest to which he faithfully returned after his long journeys to distant lands and his short excursions around the neighborhood. This house was the Collins' home, around which his activities revolved for decades, which he loved and revered, which he called his "home of homes," and which granted him many of the purest joys, and some of the worst disappointments, of his life.

Jonas Collin was his savior and his paternal friend, the person to whom, of all on earth, he owed the most gratitude; it was thanks to Collin alone that the doors of the house were opened for Hans Christian—a great and an unusual distinction. Edvard Collin, the son, followed successfully in his father's footsteps as an official; witty, levelheaded, and solid, in the beginning he had shown very little active sympathy for Andersen, whose shortcomings—the two young men were about the same age—aroused his sense of the ridiculous. However, the head of the house wished his children to treat the guest in a friendly fashion, and his wishes were carried out. The author's lovable, good-natured, and naïvely appealing sides soon won him the affection of the entire family, and in this cheerful and intelligent circle Andersen's own inventive wit was especially treasured. The influence of the Collins on the development of his humorous genius cannot be overestimated. One of the most *spirituel* of his fairy tales, *The Ugly Duckling,* is full of the Collin wit and also treats mainly of the Collin family. The Collins not infrequently poked fun at the poet—in this tale he repaid them in kind.

The next to last of the five Collin children, Louise, was still quite young when Hans Christian began his regular visits to the home. Born in 1813, she was thus eight years younger than the poet; she was both beautiful and gifted, although not of as original a mind as Ingeborg, the eldest of the brood. It is not surprising that young Andersen, who had worshipped Riborg Voigt not so long before, immediately fell in love with Louise Collin. The choice of such an object for his affections was in itself presumptuous; and this fact alone was sufficient reason to keep Andersen from declaring his passion; besides, he simply did not have it in him to seek a woman's favor with decisive forcefulness. In the present case, to be sure, his hesitant innermost self had no reason to fear an all too swift and unambiguous success: it was rather unlikely that Louise Collin could bring herself to view Andersen with infatuated eyes. On September 8, 1832, he writes to her:

> You and all the other members of your family make me feel every day that I belong to you—oh, you can't imagine how much sunshine this casts into my life. It's so hard to be a stranger and alone in this world. Sitting alone in my room of an evening, I am so profoundly and terrifyingly aware of this. Just think how you would feel if you had neither parents nor brothers nor sisters . . . . Thanks for all the friendliness and all the sisterly feelings you have shown me recently, Heaven knows that I am filled with gratitude, I think of you more

than you imagine—or can imagine, but of course one doesn't dare say something of this sort to a young lady.

He begs her to put her brother Edvard into a pleasant and affectionate frame of mind: "I'm really very sensitive in this respect, a dark glance can upset me for a long time." In order to win Louise, or at least to awaken her interest and sympathy, he gave her, in the autumn of 1832, the manuscript of his first extended autobiography, the often cited *Book of My Life*. However the expected effect failed to appear; in a letter of October 27 he complains:

> Now you have read the story of my childhood, trustingly I have shown you everything, yet you are more distant toward me than ever before. I thought of you as I wrote it, oh, you still haven't said a friendly word to me about it. This has saddened me very much; many a night, while you are sleeping peacefully, I am so filled with worries, so unhappy. That's just being high-strung, people say; I know it, of course! Why haven't you spoken to me at all since I showed you the entire story of my youth?—why haven't you said the slightest word? Is there something in my nature which makes me so repulsive, so unworthy of—your friendship? You and Edvard are the two members of your whole dear family whom I trust most— may I dare say this? There isn't anything wrong with it, is there?

If—and to what extent—Andersen ever became more explicit than he was in this letter, whether in writing or by word of mouth, cannot be determined at this distance; Louise had quite sensibly informed him that she would show his letters to her sister Ingeborg, and had thereby put a limit to his confidences. At New Year's, 1833, she became engaged to a judge advocate named J. W. Lind, and with the aid of Jonas Collin, Hans Christian received a traveling fellowship—he would forget Louise in Paris and Italy. During the following years he signed his letters to her with "H. C. Andersen, in brotherly devotion"; in an especially excited moment, when she had showed him more understanding and sympathy than the other members of the family, he wrote—on November 18, 1839—"My kindhearted sister" at the beginning of a letter to her, concluding with "Your brother." Things were arranged so that Andersen would begin a journey to southern Europe and the Orient in the very month, November, 1840, when Louise's marriage to Lind was celebrated. On her wedding day, November 25, Andersen was in Munich, and there he wrote the following two stanzas, which he sent to the bride:

> At home, sadly glad in your bridal gown,
> You sit arrayed.
> A foreigner, I see a foreign town's
> Delights displayed.
> At the altar his hand in yours is laid,
> Now for the couple glass rings against stem,
> And the happy throng
> Sings a wedding song,
> But I—I pray for them!

> And those left at home: shall I see them again
> When my journey's run?
> Mild and good, you were my sister then—
> God's Will be done!
> Tomorrow my way through the Alps is begun,
> I'll see roses and think of the bridal pair,
> Of the friendly words said,
> Of each dream the North bred,
> And then—repeat my prayer.

136

He addressed her with the familiar *"du"* only in verse. Henceforth, in everyday life, he called Fru Louise Lind by the formal *"De";* he was invited to dinner at her house, and amused her children by telling them stories and cutting out pictures for them. He was never granted the privilege of becoming as intimate a member of the family as Judge Advocate Lind.

The relationship to Edvard Collin runs almost exactly parallel to that with Edvard's sister—Hans Christian likewise felt such a strong attraction to him that one is justified in terming it love. The poet was evidently captivated by all the solidly respectable qualities which he himself lacked: the sure sense of discernment, the confident tranquility, the objective trustworthiness. The plebeian upstart's fondest wish was to become the intimate friend of his contemporary, the son of a patrician family. Edvard Collin seems to have overcome his original antipathy quite quickly—provided that he felt such antipathy at all—and he gradually became a sincere friend of Andersen; his friendship, however, must necessarily have taken the form of attempts to train and harden and guide the inexperienced and hypersensitive poet. For example, Edvard Collin went to a great deal of trouble to combat Andersen's vanity: he wished to inculcate him with self-control and pride in its stead. When Andersen, anxious to get a chance to recite, allowed himself to be made the laughing stock of social gatherings, Edvard could threaten to depart forthwith. He wished to see an Andersen less irritable and less concerned with himself, but, in return, less humble and submissive. In all practical matters Edvard Collin was not merely an invaluable adviser but a helper, a guardian, providence itself; he demonstrated his very real friendship for Andersen not primarily in words but in deeds, in patience, and in self-sacrificing labor. In this respect he was like his great father. That, later on, Edvard failed to attain the same degree of moral perfection as his father, the incomparable Jonas Collin, is another matter; unable to curb his critical urge, he behaved in a sharp and irritated manner whenever Andersen made too open a show of his weak and silly characteristics. A certain disdain is easily detectible in Edvard Collin.

On June 19, 1830, Edvard Collin signed a letter to Hans Christian with "your devoted friend," and the recipient was elated: "This was the first time, although you had often shown yourself to be my friend in reality—this little detail is infinitely dear to me." Andersen's words are touching. Then, during his German trip of 1831, the poet took a bold and—as it turned out—fateful step. From Hamburg, on May 19, he assailed Edvard Collin with protestations of friendship and pleas for the same, and continued:

> And I have another favor to ask—perhaps you'll smile—but if you want to make me really happy some day, to give me real proof of your esteem, when I deserve it—then—you mustn't get angry—say *"du"* to me! I'll never ask you for this favor to your face, it must happen now, while I'm away. . . . Now I'll discover from the first letter you send me if you have wished to please me. Are you angry? You can't guess how my heart throbs as I write this, even though you aren't here.

These words are still more touching.

Edvard Collin replied from Copenhagen on May 28; his answer was a very friendly refusal. He gave various subtle reasons for not wanting to call Hans Christian by the familiar mode of address; he even went so far as to compare his aversion to the pronoun with the inexplicable dislike which some ladies felt for bleached writing paper. He concludes by saying that he would give in if his friend should sincerely feel hurt by his refusal; and he makes express assurances that he has in no wise become angry at Andersen. One must admit that the proposition's unhappy author bore his rejection with Christian humility. On June 11, in Berlin, he wrote his thanks for the dear, dear letter:

> Yes, I am as devoted to you as I'd be to a brother, and I thank you for every line; no, I haven't misunderstood you, and you have revealed your heart to me so plainly that I can't even feel depressed. Oh, if I only had your character, your whole being—I am amply aware of how inferior I am to you in so many respects! But remain forever what you are to me today, my *true* and perhaps my most honest friend—I have real need of that.

Here the correspondence reaches its pathetic climax.

It is of course impossible to determine what caused Edvard Collin to behave in so callous a manner, a manner which one at times is even tempted to call brutal; perhaps he could not have explained his actions himself. He felt a distinct necessity to keep Andersen at a distance—so much is sure. In his old age he said that the use of the familiar pronoun, unless begun during a boyhood friendship, was something to which he generally had an instinctive aversion; but in the same breath he confessed that the determining factor had been Hans Christian's personality in relation to his own. "I was young and loved life and wanted a comrade—something which he, plagued as he often was with melancholy fantasies, was incapable of being. *He* dreamed of finding in me the sort of friend one discovers in novels; but I was no good at all for that."

Edvard Collin was restored to perfect calmness by Andersen's humble and loving submission in the letter of June 11, 1831. He believed that the painful matter was settled once and for all. His astonishment was unfeigned when, after his friend's death, he found among his effects a letter, dated Stockholm, October 3, 1865, but never mailed, which Andersen had written just after having had dinner with his dear friend, Bernhard von Beskow—Andersen and Beskow used *"du"* to one another. In this letter, addressed to Edvard Collin's wife, he returns to the unhappy episode of his youth, an episode which had occurred thirty-four years before. "He did not want to call me *'du,'* but at the same time he drank a toast of brotherhood with a highly respectable paper dealer named Wanscher—I have never forgotten it."

Then the letter continues: "He is just as dear to me today as he was when I saw in him a son of the mighty Collin, and I was Andersen, a poor fellow everyone dared to kick at and spit on." Asking himself why he writes of these matters now, he receives the answer: it flames up within him now and then. But the letter was not mailed. When Edvard Collin read the letter after his friend's demise, he wondered if Andersen had not suffered from some "disease," and he meant thereby some mental illness.

Here Edvard Collin, balanced soul that he was, revealed too little imagination. For others it is not so very difficult to realize that Andersen received a wound in 1831 which never really healed, which broke open again and again; one can detect it in countless passages in his correspondence and his literary work, and in the fairy tale *The Shadow,* as well as elsewhere, he has given vent to his feelings. Despite everything he was rejected, humiliated, an outcast. In bitter hours he asked himself what it had profited him that he was treated like a son of the family by the Collins, that he was allowed to share their festivals and their everyday life—he could never become their true equal. Louise and Edvard Collin, each in a special way, had given him proof of that.

In the midst of the world of men, surrounded by the many friends to whom he eagerly—or almost frightenedly—attached himself, he still had what he in that unposted letted of 1865 called "the whole feeling of my loneliness," quite like a man sick with fever, who at uniform intervals feels a secret chill. He was happy when he could forget this sensation in the mild warmth of home and hearth-side. Say what one will, the Collins' ménage was still his surest sanctuary. The person who, more than any other, could make him feel secure was his erstwhile savior from the abyss, old Jonas Collin. Wise and affectionate, Jonas reconciled Andersen and Edvard Collin when they were on the point of an open break; no one could have been more tactful or sensitive than this man of authority, accustomed to command. One May night in 1845, when his wife fell suddenly ill and it became plain that her hours were numbered, he sent a servant to Andersen with the message: "My wife is very ill, all the children are gathered here."

Hans Christian came, and was allowed to stand in the circle around the deathbed, with the children and the grandchildren. How thankful and how moved he must have been! A healing balm was poured upon the wounds he had received at the hands of Louise and Edvard: homeless, he had been given rights of domicile.

CHAPTER X

The Traveler Afar

∫✻

GRADUALLY H. C. ANDERSEN became one of the most widely traveled men in Denmark; without exaggeration one can say that he led a roving life. His first journey abroad, which led him to the Harz and Saxon Switzerland (on the Elbe), took place in 1831. Aided by the Collins, he got a traveling fellowship in 1833 —six hundred rix-dollars a year for two years and, in April, 1834, an additional two hundred rix-dollars; thanks to these funds he could travel all the way to Italy, staying abroad for a year and a half. During the years immediately following he contented himself with summertime excursions to the Danish provinces, but in 1837 he visited Sweden, and in 1840 he traveled to Skåne, Sweden's south-ernmost province, and Germany; in 1841 he once again received a traveling fellowship, this time to the amount of six hundred rix-dollars—quite separate from the annual poet's stipend which, be-

142

ginning in 1838 with four hundred rix-dollars, was increased in 1845 to six hundred and in 1860 to a thousand rix-dollars—and he used it for his great Oriental trip to Greece, Turkey, and Vienna, described in 1842 in *A Poet's Bazaar*. By 1843 he was in Germany and France again, and hereafter it is easier simply to count up the years in which he contented himself with odysseys to Danish estates and country towns. He often made several foreign journeys in the course of a year; in 1847 he visited Holland and England, in 1849, back in Sweden, he got all the way to Dalecarlia, in 1857 he was in England once again. He went to Spain and Portugal and North Africa, he became the experienced tourist, at home in hotels and in *le grand monde*, for all his ability at the art of saving money.

Andersen's mania for travel is somehow typical of his time; by the beginning of the nineteenth century communications had become so good and so sure that European travel could be a pleasure, not just a series of adventures and hardships. Hans Christian used both steamships and railroads, the latter with rapture; no one could persuade him that the era of the stagecoach had contained more poetry, for he was thoroughly familiar with that instrument of torture. He enjoyed railroad travel to the full, and his impatient dreams toyed constantly with the idea of flying machines. At the beginning of the nineteenth century there had also existed a psychological attitude which encouraged the blossoming of tourism; Romanticism, with its enthusiasm for the acquisition of culture, its love for art and the customs of the various peoples, its passion for nature, and its interest in local color and historical atmosphere, had given a new and more profound content to travel. And Andersen is Denmark's most prominent Romantic tourist, corresponding to Nicander, Böttiger, and Snoilsky in Sweden. In this field he could successfully compete with the great Danish authors of his age—as far as bookish knowledge, intellectual keenness, and class-cal studies were concerned, he was at a distinct disadvantage when compared with such giants as J. L. Heiberg, Molbech, Paludan-Müller, and Kierkegaard, but he could vie with them, yes, he could surpass them in practical knowledge of the concrete world. He had sharp eyes, lightning-fast comprehension, and an active imagination; with the instinctive wisdom which characterized him, he chose this path from the very beginning. He did not acquire a large library, in the first place because he lacked a fixed abode. Thinking of many of Andersen's contemporary poet-colleagues, one involuntarily imagines them, pipe in hand, against a background of bookshelves in the peace of their study. In Odense's H. C. Andersen Museum, on the contrary, one's attention is most strongly attracted to the poet's worn traveling bag and his big cotton umbrella.

Andersen's religious feelings took the form of an aesthetic rapture at the splendor and beauty of all of God's creation, of which he wanted to see as much as possible. He himself often emphasized that his journeys provided him with his real life, his education, his opportunities to collect experiences and materials. In a letter of August 27, 1836, to Jonas Collin he wrote: "My training school is life and the world, I have the ability to apprehend and to represent, but I must have my workshop too, and that is comprised of my rovings throughout the world." On another occasion he said that life becomes rich only during travel—"one does not need to feed himself with his own blood like the pelican." Karl Larsen, who called attention to this last remark, correctly observes that travel thus served Andersen as a counterbalance to his sickly fascination with his own self, its sufferings, and its problems. Traveling expanded and renewed his sphere of interest, it gave him a new freshness. As an example one can take a figure who appears in his first travel book, the *Silhouettes* of 1831. In the coach from Hamburg

144

he finds among his companions an elderly, pock-marked lady, principal of a school in Lüneburg, and without actually knowing much about her, he paints her portrait, depicts her everyday life, and lets us feel what this single great journey, now coming to an end, means in her lonely existence. In all its brevity and restraint the sketch is a masterpiece of psychological imagination and sympathy; yet the owner of such subtle sensitivity, of such tender interest for his fellow creatures, is the same H. C. Andersen whom even his most intimate friends accused of being hopelessly egocentric. Why should he not have breathed more deeply on his journeys, when, opening his eyes to the world around him, he could forget the sick child that dwelt within him? As another instance, a Swedish reader could look up the little chapter about Sala in the travel book *In Sweden* (1851). The forlornness and the tomblike quiet of an old Swedish country town are reproduced in an absolutely brilliant fashion, and the whole vignette is concentrated in the person of a lonely boy, clerk in a hardware store, who, standing behind the counter, gazes after the departing traveler for a long time. And the traveler who could experience such things on his journeys must have been profoundly happy. These apparent trifles have surely played a very much greater role in Andersen's inner life than all the marvelously beautiful scenes he saw and all the famous people he met—the classical works of art and the landscapes of historical import, the meetings with Ludwig Tieck and Franz Liszt, Heinrich Heine and Victor Hugo, Rahel Varnhagen and Charles Dickens.

Of course, one must not underestimate these more normal experiences of a tourist, which in any event made Andersen's cultural life and store of facts, his knowledge of men and his experience of the world, more profound. As for himself, he regarded his Italian sojourn of 1833–34 as having been of radical importance for his whole intellectual life. He came to Rome on the day when Raphael—whose vault in the Pantheon had been opened—was being buried for the second time, and in the solemn procession he saw his great countryman Thorvaldsen striding slowly past with a candle in his hand. In Rome, Hans Christian began his friendship with the great sculptor, who listened patiently to the reading of *Agnete and the Merman*. He also became acquainted with many other members of Rome's artist colony, and he industriously studied the classical masterworks. In Copenhagen he had become familiar with literature, music, and the theater, partaking of an aesthetic culture which, fostered in peaceful Denmark's politically inactive capital, can scarcely be said to have had its superior anywhere in Europe. In Rome he completed his education with the study of painting, architecture, and sculpture. Nature had provided him with a fine artist's eye. During all his journeys he made small pen sketches, in which he preserved the memory of landscapes and views that had charmed him, pictures of cities and monuments, scenes and figures from the life of the people—there were no cameras in those days, and it was not easy to acquire pictures done by a professional hand. For all their simplicity, these sketches reveal lively interest and natural talent. He made his drawings nowhere with more energy than in Italy, where everything, the landscape, the people, the buildings, put him into a state of ecstasy—where he imagined that he walked through an earthly paradise. All his letters are filled with rejoicing; Italy is a land of beauty and fantasy. These changing impressions from various climes, the whole of this visual attitude and formal schooling, which Andersen acquired during his journeys, have doubtless been of great importance for the burgeoning imaginary world of the fairy tales. He had material and motifs to spare, he had colors and lines, natural lights and illuminations—there is a wealth of cosmopolitan ma-

146

terial, and of cosmic perspectives, in his fairy tales. They are composed by a globe-trotter. Nowhere does this become clearer than in the little fantasy which shows rich Americans "doing Europe" in a week by flying machine. He called the fairy tale *Thousands of Years from Now,* for, even though endowed with the penetration of genius, he could not foresee that his vision would be realized a mere hundred years later.

And yet, however much material there is in the fairy tales which Andersen collected during his journeys, the center of gravity never lies in that which is foreign, but rather is deeply embedded in the inimitably Danish quality of the stories. Indeed, Andersen is the most national of all his country's poets, despite the fact that he alone belongs to world literature. No one has had a more infallible sense for what is intimately peculiar to the nature, life, and atmosphere of Denmark; even though it cannot be defined, one obtains a purely physical sensation of it from almost every line Andersen ever wrote. But it is precisely this unique acuteness to Danish individuality which Andersen's constant journeys fostered and refined: if he had not become so thoroughly familiar with foreign lands, how could he have experienced that which was Danish with such intuitive keenness? He himself has given the classic formula for the influence of his life as a traveler upon his spiritual life in a little episode woven into *The Fairy Tale of My Life.* In the summer of 1841 he came home from the Orient, where he had been quarantined at Orsova, on the boundary between Turkey and the Austrian Empire. The passage goes:

> I was especially moved when outside of Slagelse, the town of my school days, I was surprised by a meeting with the past. While I was a pupil at the school there, I saw the dignified Pastor Bastholm and his wife take the same walk every evening, from the back gate in

their garden along the path through the fields of grain and then home again along the highway. Now, many years later, I returned from Greece and Turkey, and, riding along the Slagelse Road, I saw the old couple taking their customary promenade through the fields. I was strangely moved. They had continued to walk along that little path year in and year out, and I had flown far and wide; the great contrast between us left a strange impression on my mind.

Thus the stork returns from the sources of the Nile to his low-lying meadow, to his crooked wheel-perch on the farm of a peasant of Fyn, and rejoices at being home again, and is, because of this feeling, the most Danish of birds, although he is gone more than half the year.

In 1823 the good Pastor Bastholm had written a letter to the Slagelse schoolboy in which, lamenting the publication of the immature experiments of youth, he admonished him to look to his studies; yet recognizing Andersen's poetic talent, he gave him the following literary advice—one of the wisest and truest sermons an older man has ever preached to a young author:

> Observe nature, human life, and your own being with an attentive eye, in order to acquire original material for your depictions; choose small themes from among the things which surround you, observe everything you see from all possible standpoints before you take up your pen—become a poet, as if no poet had ever existed before you and as if you had no poet from whom to learn—and at all times preserve that nobility, that purity and loftiness of soul, without which a mortal can never win the poet's wreath.

One cannot accurately say that Andersen had always followed the idyllic pastor's very reasonable pieces of advice—and they indicate the mature result rather than the meandering way which led to it. During his first years of freedom Andersen scarcely made any great advance on the effervescent *Journey on Foot.* His musical comedies and opera librettos were aimed at achieving popular successes in the theater—he blithely took his themes from the works of other poets, now from Walter Scott, now from Gozzi. His lyric poems were rich in imagination and emotion, but they hardly possessed any deeper originality. The poem cycle *The Twelve Months of the Year,* which appeared at New Year's, 1833, pictures Danish nature in all the seasons, it lives and breathes, and is filled with figures and dramatic scenes and bold landscapes, but it does not give the impression of a harmonious whole—it is desultory, restless, fleeting. With his characteristic intrepidity the poet Andersen dedi-

Illustration from *Thumbelina.*

cated the book to the King. "A poor man's child I was, and no one knew me," the prefatory poem begins; it concludes by detecting paternal affection in the monarch's eye. The story of the audience during which the book was presented to Frederick VI is recounted in *The Fairy Tale of My Life,* and is distinguished by a subtle humor. Coming rapidly toward the poet, the King asked what kind of a book it was. "A cycle of poems," Andersen answered, but the old King did not understand: "A cycle? A cycle? What do you mean by that?" Dismayed, the poet attempted an explanation: "It's some verses about Denmark," and to this the King smilingly replied, "Well, that's no doubt very nice, thank you, thank you," intending thereby to put an end to the audience. However, Andersen succeeded in protracting their interview, spoke of his studies, and finally managed to say that he wanted a traveling fellowship. "Well then, submit an application," came the reply. " 'Yes, Your Majesty,' I burst out in all my naïveté, 'I have it right here, and that's just what I think is so dreadful—that I have to submit it together with my book; but people have told me I should do it that way, such is the custom; but I think it's so ugly, it goes against my grain—!' Tears came into my eyes."

Hans Christian knew how to employ his naturalness, his naïveté, his childlike excitability with just such skill; quite in accordance with Scripture, he combined the wisdom of the serpent with the harmlessness of the dove. And he got the traveling fellowship.

The fellowship was certainly not wasted. *Agnete and the Merman,* the Romantic verse-drama he wrote during the journey, was not a success, to be sure. It was based upon the old folk song, and had many poetic sections; the fantasies about life at the bottom of the sea would later on be used to great effect by Andersen in many of his fairy tales, above all in *The Little Mermaid*. But the symbolism of the drama was confused, and the delineation of character was vague; in all essentials, one must agree with Edvard Collin who, although he faithfully copied the manuscript and saw to its printing, gave open expression to his disappointment, thereby arousing embitterment and despair on the part of his friend. Nor was J. L. Heiberg's scathing criticism of the piece unjust. There was a purely personal element in *Agnete and the Merman*: the wandering musician Hemming, Agnete's unsuccessful suitor, plainly utters the sorrow which Andersen felt at having been rejected both by Riborg Voigt and Louise Collin. He complains bitterly at not being handsome enough and rich enough to win a woman's heart, at being all too soft and weak and accommodating; and the painful experience with Edvard Collin is reflected in the following lines:

"Thou" of soul is "You" of speech:
That's the dream of friendship!

If *Agnete and the Merman* had thus created the impression in Denmark that the poet Andersen's newly risen star was already on the wane, the situation was reversed when *The Improvisator* appeared in April, 1835. In Rome, H. C. Andersen had heard that J. L. Heiberg had called him an "improvisator," a term chosen, of course, to characterize the superficial and hastily thought-out aspects of his literary production. The expression made Andersen catch fire, and in the novel he depicted himself in the disguise of an Italian *improvvisatore*—poets of this sort were of course still common in Italy. Behind the shield of the Italian milieu Andersen could employ all his personal experiences, he could depict his childhood and his poor mother and his wealthy benefactors: the home of a Danish patrician was changed into the Palazzo Borghese, Rector Meisling into Professor Maretti, and the great tyrant Habbas

Dahdah had a striking resemblance to Andersen's implacable critic, Christian Molbech. *The Improvisator* expresses the poet's deepest feelings, his intense need of being appreciated and praised, his firm conviction that criticism is ruinous for an artist. The book reveals all the suffering and humiliation which Hans Christian underwent as a protégé of the distinguished and the powerful, but it also bears witness to his gratitude and devotion toward those who had been kind to him. For his contemporaries, however, it was hardly the novel's psychological content which stood in the foreground; the novel's forte was rather the colorful, picturesque, and vital portrayal of the Italian landscape and Italian life. All the impressions which the tourist Andersen had perceived with his unique virtuosity were now fused into a novel of the artist's life, and were thereby given a doubled force. Preparing, as it were, a film in diverse colors, the Danish storyteller had mobilized all the rewarding and popular motives which Swedish poets, from Atterbom and Nicander to Böttiger and Snoilsky, had treated in lyric form. In contrast to outpourings in verse, a story can be translated, and *The Improvisator* appeared both in German and English; it took Europe by storm. The outstanding English critic John Lockhart, Walter Scott's son-in-law, compared the novel with Madam de Staël's famous *Corinne,* but gave precedence to Andersen's work; and another critic ranked it with *Childe Harold*. As a matter of fact it was immediately read and appreciated even in Denmark, and ultimately was even praised there. *The Improvisator* was provided with the following dedication: "To Councillor Collin and his noble wife, in whom I found parents, and to his children, in whom I found brothers and sisters—I bring the best I possess to the home of homes!" One can imagine what satisfaction Andersen must have gained from thus honoring the house of Collin, and from offering public proof that the Collins had not wasted their kindness upon an unworthy recipient.

With infinite pleasure, into which there crept a little tinge of irony, Andersen noted a change from coolness to warmth in the air. To Henriette Hanck, a friend from his Odense days, he wrote on January 19, 1836:

> Never before has a winter passed along as calmly and as happily as this one. *The Improvisator* has won me the esteem of Denmark's best and noblest minds, and even the masses have learned more respect. I do not need to worry, thank Heaven, about keeping myself fed, I can even go as far as to say that I've been able to get some pleasure out of life. The newspapers give me free subscriptions, Reitzel [Andersen's publisher] sends me books and etchings; I sit in colorful slippers and lounging robe with my legs on the sofa, the tile stove hums, the teapot is singing on the table, and the incense smells good. I think of the poor boy in Odense who walked about in wooden shoes, and my heart grows soft, and I bless God in His goodness.

In this passage Andersen represents himself as a solid Philistine, indulging in an epicurean enjoyment of his pleasant existence. One knows the situation from the oldest of his fairy tales, *The Tinderbox,* which treats of fortune's darling. In the beginning the soldier was happy and rich, went to the theater, and had many friends; but when his money was at an end, he had to move up to the attic, and his friends were unable to climb the many flights of stairs. Discovering the magical power of the tinderbox, the soldier became rich again; he moved back to his handsome rooms, bought fine clothes, and straightaway was recognized by all his friends, "and they liked him very much." *The Tinderbox* is in the first volume of the fairy tales, which came out in May, 1835, a month after *The Improvisator;* Hans Brix, the perspicacious interpreter and commentator, says that *The Tinderbox* was written under the influence of *The Improvisator's* success. Andersen's tinderbox was his creative fantasy.

However, one should be careful not to give unhesitating credence to the Philistine contentment Andersen portrays in the letter to Henriette Hanck. He has his tongue in his cheek, and although he likes his elegant lounging robe and his handsome clothes, although he carefully curls his hair and enjoys being noticed on Østergade, he nonetheless regards all these respectable causes for happiness with a secret contempt. It was not part of his nature to feel satisfied, to indulge in a careless enjoyment of the goods he had acquired. His ambition, which once upon a time drove him from Odense to Copenhagen, is by no means satiated. On May 13, 1836, he wrote Henriette Hanck: "I wish to be Denmark's most distinguished novelist." And six months later, on January 4, 1837, he confessed to Madam Iversen, the widow of the Odense printer —once again, significantly enough, it is an inhabitant of Odense who enjoys his confidence—that he is a long way from his goal:

> People *have* to list me among the *good* poets of the age; but I want still more! May God give me the strength for the task: I wish to be called one of Denmark's greatest poets, the equal of Holberg and Oehlenschläger! But I still have a good piece to go, I know that very well, although I don't like to talk about it. Our Lord must lift me up; it won't help if I try to climb myself.

He still believes in miracles, as when he waited for the Chinese prince to come.

If the wise old friends at the Collins' house, if the great critic J.

L. Heiberg, if Ingemann and Hauch and other poetic colleagues had heard Andersen's confession to Madam Iversen, they would have said that he suffered from megalomania. The equal of Helberg and Oehlenschläger, indeed! As a matter of fact, a little contentedness and a little self-criticism were called for; Andersen could be happy at having come as far as he had. But he was like the soldier with the tinderbox: money and friends and visits to the theater did not suffice for him; in the darkness of the night he longed for the princess and the crown, and that is why he had to pass the prison cells and the gallows hill, and laughter and criticism and disgrace—until the sparkling tinderbox awakened his mighty allies, who would bring him succor and victory.

CHAPTER XI

The Cup of Humiliation

H. C. ANDERSEN WAS NOT SLOW in following up *The Improvisator's* success of 1835. In 1836 a new novel, *O.T.*, appeared —the title consists of the initials of the hero, Otto Thostrup, but also contains a mysterious reference to *Odense Tugthus,* the Odense house of correction; and this work was followed in 1837 by *Only a Fiddler.*

Regarded from the standpoint of its material, *O.T.* offers an effective contrast to *The Improvisator*: it depicts Denmark, the homeland, instead of the splendors of the south. It offers pictures from the student milieu and from the everyday life of the middle class, both in Copenhagen and in the provinces; it also presents scenes from country estates and tells of adventure on the highways. Its motifs are taken from the author's local travels, not from his extended journeys abroad. In it, one already comes upon H. C. Andersen's ironic view of the society surrounding him; the protagonist unburdens himself of a number of reflections comparing life in the capital with the more Philistine existence to be led in the small town of Lemvig; and the result turns out to be six of one and half a dozen of the other. With an ambiguous smile, Andersen adds that these thoughts of Otto Thostrup's betray his great youth and his superficial acquaintance with Copenhagen—if he had stayed there for more than just a year, he would have entertained altogether different opinions. Andersen himself knew the whole story; he would give felicitous and convincing proof of that when he wrote the fairy tales.

The personal main theme of *O.T.* is terror of squalor and degradation: elements amidst which Hans Christian grew up and from which he barely succeeded in rescuing himself; but the poet does not dare to get too close to the realities of the matter for fear of betraying the book's autobiographical core. He makes do with the symbolism of the initials *O.T.*, and at the end he frees Otto Thostrup from the suspicion of being a brother to the sinister, malformed, and thievish Sidsel; instead it is the poetic ideal, Eva, who is his sister. In the last lines of the novel Otto Thostrup declares that he cannot feel perfectly happy until he knows that German Heinrich, the blackmailer villain who witnessed his unhappy childhood, is dead; at that moment he does not know that both German Heinrich and ugly Sidsel are already drowned—drowned so that the hero's sky can shine with the true blue of happiness. The Lord has fulfilled his wishes even before they are spoken! In this clever trick Andersen's naïve egoism is revealed.

O.T. was without question an exciting and entertaining novel, and the Danish local coloring was highly esteemed abroad; among other things, H. C. Andersen had depicted the Odense of his childhood, and the old town looked very picturesque indeed. The whole story has something of the same tourist's Romanticism as *The Improvisator;* the representative of life's sober prose is a coarse and uninteresting *Kammerjunker,* blindly devoted to his agricultural pursuits, and one cannot suppress the thought that, in reality, altogether different variants of the type existed: Stjernsvärd, Maclean, and all the agricultural pioneers whom the Danish nobility produced. In this novel, a realistic one from the technical point of view, Andersen showed that he was more beholden to Romantic stereotypes, and less receptive to reality, than he would be in the fairy tales, for all their wealth of fantasy. In essence, this judgment applies to all his novels.

Only a Fiddler combines *O.T.'s* depiction of the Danish milieu with the autobiographical inspiration of *The Improvisator;* but, in order to keep the novel's hero, the musical genius Christian, from becoming identical with the author, Hans Christian, the musician has been given a fate in direct contradiction of the true facts about his creator—Christian does not become a great artist; poor and misunderstood, he ends as a failure. No small measure of self-pity found its vent in *Only a Fiddler.* Hans Christian Andersen was never afraid to draw materials from his own breast. In Christian's person is reflected the innocence with which the author once moved through Copenhagen's streets of ill repute, and the demonic spell which the theater once cast upon the boy from Odense, and the sense of being a pariah with which he gazed in at the wealthy *bourgeoisie's* sheltered realms: hanging in the rigging of a ship at dock, the wretched cabin boy stares through the windows of a brilliantly lighted apartment in a near-by house. The spiritual portrait contains the rudiments of candor. Christian makes a fool of himself in order to win attention and gifts, he is superstitious, his courage is not beyond discussion, although his ambition is. "I want to become famous, otherwise I don't care about living," Christian cries on one occasion, and he dreams that someday everyone will bow before his genius, as the sheaves bowed before Joseph in the Biblical dream. The novel's real pathos cannot be mistaken; it is bluntly proclaimed: "Do not let true talent perish in material misery."

The thought is father to the deed, and two months after the publication of *Only a Fiddler,* on January 10, 1838, Andersen applied to the King for a regular poet's salary, so that he could cease "writing in less felicitous moments in order to get money." In May he received his four hundred rix-dollars, "not a bounteous income, but one sufficing for the bare necessities," and the annual salary gradually came to be more than doubled. He had escaped sharing the hard fate of Christian, the musical genius.

It is significant that this somewhat lacrimose novel was received in Denmark only with "chilly indulgence," according to Edvard Collin, while in Germany it became the object of wild enthusiasm, and was, for the rest, esteemed almost as highly in England and Sweden. From these facts Hans Christian concluded that his fellow countrymen were more unfavorably disposed toward him than foreigners were; but perhaps one should also reckon with the possibility that taste was surer and aesthetic judgment more carefully developed in the land of Heiberg and Kierkegaard.

Andersen, however, by no means contented himself simply with the production of his novels, which made an ever wider wake, even in Danish waters. Indefatigably he submitted play after play to the Royal Theater, in the directorate of which his fatherly friend Jonas Collin had assumed more and more of a leading position, but where as a reader Andersen had his implacable foe, Christian Molbech. He wrote Singspiels, musical comedies, opera librettos, comedies, *divertissements*, original works and adaptations, one after the other; many were refused, many were produced, some were successes. The jest in dramatic form, *The Invisible Man on Language Island,* came out in 1829 and was given twenty-three times, but it, of course, was a harmless trifle. The Romantic drama, *The Mulatto,* made considerably greater claims to seriousness; Molbech, to be sure, had called it vacuous and trivial, but it had its *première* in February, 1840, nonetheless, and was given twenty-one times. This noteworthy success was brought about in part by Fru Heiberg, who played one of the leading roles with her customary unfailing talent, although she thought the play to be an essentially hollow and weak work. She and her husband were not so far wrong in making this judgment; but confronted by his detractors, Andersen could rejoice in the fact that he had the general public on his side. He had called *The Mulatto* "an original Romantic drama," and his critics rather pettily pointed out that he had taken the plot from a French novelette. The author could have contented himself with a reference to Oehlenschläger's *Aladdin,* which was not a product of the virgin imagination either; but a spirit of defiance enticed him into writing a drama, the action of which was entirely of his own devising. This turned out to be *The Moorish Maiden,* a Spanish tragedy in the grand style following on the heels of the Creole play. *The Mulatto* had contained a personal element: H. C. Andersen's own sense of being an outcast, a pariah, gave heat and flames to the enamored mulatto's outbursts. *The Moorish Maiden,* on the contrary, was a structure erected by reason alone, and reason was not Andersen's strong point. Molbech was deprecatory in this case, too, but Jonas Collin maintained that the Moorish girl would probably be received with the same applause as the mulatto—that the play would be a box-office triumph. The tragedy was produced in December, 1840, but, to Andersen's great despair—and even rage—Fru Heiberg had steadfastly refused to play the Moorish maiden: the play was a fiasco and had to be removed from the stage after three performances.

On the whole, the theater caused Andersen many vexations and disappointments throughout his entire life. Yet when *The Moorish Maiden* met her unhappy fate, her creator was in Italy. And during these years from 1835 until 1842, a period in which he wrote his three novels and a series of stage-works, and undertook the long journey to southern Europe and the Orient, which he then depicted in detail in the great travel book *A Poet's Bazaar* (1842), he also published—quite quietly, one might almost say—a series of small volumes called *Fairy Tales Told for Children* (the seventh volume appeared in 1841), and also wrote another fanciful literary work in a related style, the *Picture Book without Pictures*, which appeared at New Year's, 1840. To begin with, these works aroused far less attention than the novels and the plays, and even Andersen himself did not attach much more importance to them than the soldier of the fairy tale did to the tinderbox.

As soon as something went against him, as soon as his works were exposed to criticism, Andersen became beside himself with worry and embitterment, and thought himself to be unappreciated, unjustly treated, persecuted. This attitude had its basis in his sensitivity, his instability, his burning ambitiousness; he did not wish to be content with anything less than the highest prize, but he was tormented at the same time by the horrible suspicion that his old rector, Meisling, could have been right—that he was not a genius but an idiot. He had a constant need of success as proof of his own value and of the existence of a loving God's paternal hand.

However, one cannot deny that he was exposed to many humiliations. If they were worse or more undeserved than those which customarily fall to the lot of men—and especially of artists—this is difficult to determine, but it is quite certain that only a few have suffered as terribly from them as H. C. Andersen did. One often has the impression that this alternation between successes and failures destroyed whatever state of healthy equilibrium his soul might attain, making his egoistic self-absorption ascend to dangerous heights.

There is good reason to take some sample tests from the chronicle of his misfortunes. In the closing days of 1830, Denmark was enchanted by an anonymous literary work, *A Ghost's Letters or Poetic Epistles from Paradise*. It was the departed Jens Baggesen who walked again, defending J. L. Heiberg's aesthetics with graceful wit against Oehlenschläger and his disciples, Ingemann and Hauch. Later on, the unknown author revealed himself to be Henrik Hertz, the rising star in the firmament of the Danish theater, friend, kindred spirit, and armor-bearer of the Heibergs. The elegant causerie in verse treated Hauch with great politeness, but Andersen, on the contrary, was disposed of with extreme contempt: he was presented as a chieftain of the rag, tag, and bobtail, of the wild and unwashed gypsies. It is said of him and his crude fellows that they have:

> *Not in the least discovered what significance*
> *A thorough discipline in poetry*
> *Has even for him who genius claims to be.*

Hertz had been one of Rector Meisling's best pupils, and one may suspect that he got his idea of H. C. Andersen from that source. Yet the view he expresses is also the one held concerning the eccentric natural genius by Heiberg's highly intelligent and highly cultured circles. It must have been painful for Andersen, the parvenu, to see himself ranked with the vagabond rabble; one glimpses something of *O.T.*'s symbolism here. And it was especially uncomfortable for him to know that the Collins, warm admirers of

Heiberg's whole school of thought, had read *A Ghost's Letters* with delight. Meeting Hertz in Italy, Andersen was compelled to follow the advice of his revered Jonas Collin—he had to be conciliatory and polite toward his adversary; and the relationship between the two authors did in fact become a rather friendly one.

In the spring of 1833, when visiting Paris for the first time, Andersen had not received any letters from home for a month; naturally enough, he began to feel both anxious and homesick. Finally the post office gave him a bulky envelope on which the postage unfortunately had not been prepaid; inside there was only a copy of the *Copenhagen Post,* which contained a lampoon, "Farewell to Andersen," composed with some talent and surprising wit. It asks how a man whose greatest delight is reading his own songs aloud, and who is ignorant of foreign languages, can get along in Paris? Who will listen to him? He will be sent home accompanied by a protest:

> *Your German is nothing, your Danish is naught,*
> *Your English is even weaker,*
> *And if you try French, the Parisians ought*
> *To say you're a Bengalese-speaker.*

This, Andersen wrote to Edvard Collin, "was the first greeting from the homeland!" He was profoundly distressed at this proof of men's wickedness, and the fact that he had to pay the postage did not make him any happier, poor and thrifty as he was. It should be added that the lampoon was a parody of a complimentary poem to Andersen, which had earlier been published in the same paper under the same title—a circumstance which is carefully ignored in *The Fairy Tale of My Life.* For the rest, Councillor Collin himself composed an announcement which was included in one of the paper's June numbers; in it he pilloried the anonymous lampooner with elegantly restrained phrases—one of the many touching indications of Jonas Collin's solicitude for his protégé.

An episode of this kind, of course, had no very serious import, however much it could embitter and poison Hans Christian's spirit; it was merely part of that witty backbiting which has always flourished so luxuriantly in Denmark, a country where people live close to one another. It was a more serious matter, however, when in 1838 the young genius Søren Kierkegaard, drawing up his whole philosophical battery in *From the Papers of a Man Still Living, Published Against His Will,* directed the guns at poor H. C. Andersen: *Concerning Andersen as a Novelist, with Constant Reference to His Latest Work, "Only a Fiddler."* The reasons for Kierkegaard's terrible salvo are swathed in mystery. It has been conjectured that, in his own capacity of a genius, Kierkegaard felt himself insulted by the genial type presented in *Only a Fiddler* and by the banal tragedy of that genius' fate: Søren Kierkegaard was indisputably familiar with more subtle tragic situations than the worry about where the next meal was to come from. Whatever the cause of the attack may have been, Kierkegaard demonstrated in a long and unusually learned and clever treatise that Andersen had written a bad and overly sentimental novel. "Like Lafontaine [the second-rate German author] he sits weeping about his unhappy heroes, who have to be destroyed, and why? Because Andersen is the way he is. The same joyless battle which Andersen fights in his own life is now being repeated in his poetic works." Christian, the fiddler, is not a genius at all, but rather "a weakling, concerning whom it is declared that he is a genius"; for the genius is not a tallow dip, extinguished by a breath of wind, but rather a conflagration, which grows in the storm. The whole of Kierkegaard's

In 1830, Hans Christian Andersen traveled to the island of Fyn.
There he met Riborg Voigt and before their romance was over
penned these lines to her:

> You have become my thinking's single thought,
> My heart's first love: it had no love before.
> I love you as no love on earth is wrought,
> I love you now and love you evermore.

From a daguerreotype, ca.1845

Andersen's last great love was Jenny Lind. In September, 1843, he
jotted in his diary, "I love her." But her emotions were only friendship and sisterly devotion, and she declined any thought of marriage.

From a lithograph after a painting by Ed. Magnus, 1846

own feeling of power is found in this image; he speaks of pride which, strengthened by opposition, refuses to bow its head. Of Christian, who is openly identified with H. C. Andersen, it is expressly said that everything about him is vanity, he wishes only to have attention centered on his person, to be admired; yes, he is even happy with a compliment in which scorn is concealed—provided that he can just wallow in the pleasure for a moment. A great many pertinent and subtle remarks are to be found mixed among the speculative odds and ends of Søren Kierkegaard's treatise; but one cannot term these remarks either friendly or considerate. Kierkegaard belonged to the camp of the aristocrats of the spirit, just as did the Heibergs, for whom Kierkegaard had a natural sympathy; and it was easy to look down with sublime contempt on the childlike and intellectually underdeveloped Andersen.

The blows dealt with the clubs of philosophical and psychological definitions could be hard enough, but it is a question whether the ironic whip of persiflage did not have a louder crack and a crueler bite. The smiling, refined, and restrained J. L. Heiberg made the lash cut the most elegant figures when he wrote his brilliant apocalyptic comedy, *A Soul after Death,* which was printed in *New Poems* in 1841. A friendly relationship had existed between Heiberg and Andersen for a long time: the poet had sought the great critic's favor, and had also received encouragement and support from him. But Heiberg, naturally enough, had not been able to shut his eyes to Andersen's weaknesses—neither his personal nor his literary ones; he had criticized Andersen's bad plays severely, taken them apart and put them back together again with his crystalline logic, and in the process had preserved the suavity which always distinguished him. Thus when Fru Heiberg, who had disliked her role in *The Mulatto* said that her fragile health did not allow her to play *The Moorish Maiden,* Andersen was quite beside himself. He behaved, so Johanne Luise Heiberg says in her autobiography, like "a child, an impulsive and naughty child. . . . 'That's mean of you, it's very mean,' " he cried out, declaring that it was Heiberg's envy of the poet H. C. Andersen which lay behind his wife's refusal.

One must keep this background in mind if one is to plumb the depths of the superbly funny joke in *A Soul after Death;* it should also be remembered that by this time H. C. Andersen had been acclaimed both in Germany and in Sweden—in the latter country by, among others, the students of the University of Lund in Skåne. J. L. Heiberg and the Danish intelligentsia regarded Andersen's trips abroad as efforts to get publicity. In the spring of 1841, H. C. Andersen visited Constantinople, and was thus in a milieu where mulattoes and Moorish maidens flourished. In Heiberg's comedy the Soul journeys to Hell, a realm in which Philistinism stands in full bloom; on the very evening of his arrival *The Mulatto* and *The Moorish Maiden* are to be given at the local theater. The Soul expresses his joy at Andersen's having achieved recognition in these reaches, a remark to which Mephistopheles answers:

> *Why not do here what's done in other places?*
> *Already the moon of his reputation*
> *Shines over the whole of the mighty Scanian nation;*
> *In Germany he lovingly embraces*
> *A glory beginning, I'd think, on the Hunsrück's reaches*
> *And ending north of the Swinemünde beaches.*
> *In Constantinople he means to print instanter*
> *A masterwork amidst the Seraglio's banter.*
> *He stands there in a literary park*
> *Quite like an Oriental question mark,*
> *And reads* The Mulatto *for the sultan's ladies,*
> *The while subalterns grovel and his pate is laden*

The Cup of Humiliation

With wreaths by the captain-eunuch—but in Hades
To you, as torment, he'll read The Moorish Maiden.

This is a parody on the coronation of Aladdin, which was Andersen's secret dream. Here one finds his megalomania, his self-advertising journeys to the north and the south, his eagerness to read his works aloud (something he gladly did in distinguished circles, and in time at a number of Europe's royal courts!), and the painful effect upon his listeners; the whole passage is composed in a festive manner, mordacious but without bitterness, and precisely on this account perhaps doubly humiliating. Andersen speaks somewhere about the devilishness of Heiberg's apparently innocent jokes: it was the sovereign calm, the absence of any hatefulness or unsophisticated passion, which created that infernal impression. It suited Mephistopheles. As a parting shot the Soul says:

> *They know him here, so I see: whatever*
> *Judgment they on that curious man confer,*
> *It tickles him just the same to be known.*

Andersen had to bear all these witticisms of Heiberg's with Christian patience, for Heiberg and his wife and his friends were much too influential for the ambitious Andersen to dare to challenge them. Besides, all the Collins were among Heiberg's warmest admirers, and old Jonas Collin entertained chivalrous feelings of admiration and friendship for the great actress, who, quite justifiedly, looked up to her fatherly protector with much the same feelings as Andersen had—she too was a child of the proletariat who had been saved from the abyss, and she too had received aid and support from the good and wise man. The relationship between Andersen and the Heibergs thus through natural necessity assumed an external air of friendliness, although the connection never became a hearty one. Whenever the Heibergs were invited to the Collins', Hans Christian had to be present, too, but he left early, without saying a word. One can only guess what pangs of jealousy and what humiliation he had suffered.

But he was not always silent. The most magnificent and wildest of his outbursts—it is like a storm on the North Sea, difficult to imagine as a part of the traditional Danish idyll—occurs in a letter of April 29, 1843, written to his hunchbacked friend, Henriette Wulff, the admiral's daughter. In Paris at the time, Andersen was being received with the greatest friendliness by that city's celebrities, by Victor Hugo and Alfred de Vigny, by Alexander Dumas the elder and Heinrich Heine, by the great actress Rachel, and by many others as well; he was already in the process of acquiring a European reputation, and he naturally overestimated the importance of the polite phrases he heard. And it was in this frame of mind that he happened to read a Danish newspaper, where was discussed the fiasco which *Agnete and the Merman* had made upon the Danish stage: the play had even been hissed. Ten years before, this luckless piece had almost brought about a rupture of the friendship between the poet and Edvard Collin, for Collin had flatly refused to admire the work; on that occasion, brave Jonas Collin had interceded, burning up the letter in which Andersen had given vent to his rage. Now the play had finally reached the boards, and the public's refusal to admire it was as energetic as the younger Collin's had been. Andersen was furious:

May I never again behold that homeland which only has eyes for my faults, but no heart for the greatness which God has deposited within me! I hate that which hates me; I curse that which curses me! As always, the icy blasts come from Denmark, and turn me to stone

168

in this foreign land. They spit upon me, they tramp me into the mud!
I know that I possess a poetic genius of a sort which God has not
often vouchsafed the Danes, and which I in my hour of death will
beg Him never again to give this nation!—Oh, what poison courses
in my blood during these hours!—When I was young, I could weep;
but now I cannot; I can only feel pride—hatred—contempt—I can
only give my soul to evil powers, in order to find a moment's relief!
—In this great and foreign city, Europe's most famous and noblest
spirits surround me with their friendly wishes, treat me as a kins-
man, and at home the street boys spit upon my heart's best creation!
—Yes, even if I shall be judged after my death as I am here on earth,
I shall say: "The Danes can be malicious, cold, satanic! They suit
those damp, mold-green islands which Tycho Brahe was forced to
leave, where Eleonora Ulfeld was imprisoned and Ambrosius Stub
was the butt of the nobility's jokes, and where many more will be
given the same bad treatment, until the nation's name will become
a byword!" Of course, I'm using the typical expressions of a poet
whose works have been hissed; if this letter of mine should be printed, Copenhagen would have a happy hour reading it!—May I never
lay eyes on the place again! May the ever-living God never again let
a nature such as mine be born there! I hate, I detest my homeland,
even as it hates and mocks at me! Pray to God for me! Pray that I
soon shall die, never again to see a place where I am a foreigner,
more foreign there than in any foreign land!

This, then, is the Hans Christian Andersen who was noted for
his good nature. The wonderful vision of the "mold-green islands"
and the obstinate repetitions show what a surprising power his
will to live possessed.

In order to do him justice, however, one must pass on to another
scene, in which he reacts in quite a different way to the humiliations visited upon him. Two years later, in 1845, the Romantic poet
Carsten Hauch published a long novel on contemporary condi-

tions which bore the title *The Castle on the Rhine; or, The Different Points of View*. There is no lack of strange and obscure matters in Carsten Hauch's career, and one of these is his sketching, in the novel, of an easily recognizable caricature of H. C. Andersen. It was all the more embarrassing since Hauch and Andersen, who had earlier had various misunderstandings, were presumably reconciled with one another—as a matter of fact, they were the best of friends. An intensive investigation of Hauch's novel, which is no masterpiece, is unnecessary; but one of the main figures is the author Eginhard, a self-centered and foolish fellow, who recites his poems in and out of season, tells about all the famous and distinguished people he has known, and travels around the world, urged on by vanity and disquietude, in order to establish the fact of his popularity, to enjoy it, and to advertise it. His soul is gnawed by doubts of his greatness and consumed by self-pity; because of his unswerving egoism he stands quite alone in life, with ambition as his only driving-spring. It has been prophesied to him that he will be feted by kings and emperors, and that the people of a great city will unhitch his horses and themselves draw his coach in triumph: "My songs shall be read beneath the plane-tree and in the tents of the nomads, the camel shall bear them through the desert, the Negro shall sing them in the shade of his palm, and my name shall be remembered thousands of years from now, when the last descendant of my persecutors has vanished from the earth." Finally Eginhard crosses the boundaries of madness; the prophecy—and it is the prophecy about the illumination of Odense which makes its ghostly appearance here—comes true, however, for as Eginhard is being driven to the madhouse, a laurel on his brow and medals on his breast, he arouses the glad interest of the mob, and his coach is indeed drawn by the masses. At the madhouse he continues to exist in his megalomaniac dreams, and a visitor sums up his situation thus: "He really isn't much crazier than he was in the days when he was regarded as having all his wits."

Hauch's description of Eginhard teems with features borrowed from Andersen's personality; of course, Eginhard also represents the boundless egoism of the artist.

Hearing of Hauch's novel in advance, Hans Christian wrote, in December, 1844, to Ingemann, Hauch's friend and fellow resident of Sorø: "I look forward with the greatest pleasure to Hauch's novel! He is a great and authentic poetic soul! Give him and his wife my hearty greetings." By August, 1845, the book had appeared; Andersen had heard stupid people whispering about the model of the poet who dies of sheer vanity in the madhouse, but he wrote to Ingemann that he did not believe these rumors; he sent his greetings to Hauch, assuring him that he is not in the least hurt —how could the noble Hauch have had an evil thought? But then Andersen finally got hold of the novel and read it, and on September 16 he wrote to Ingemann once again. It must have been a dreadful blow, and it was surely a scandal beyond compare; Hauch, after all, was one of the country's most famous authors, and his works were read everywhere.

Andersen wrote to Ingemann that he could no longer be angry at the rumor-mongers who had called attention to the model's identity:

> Yes, one is correct in saying: "That's Andersen!" All my weaknesses are collected here. I hope and believe that I have passed beyond this period, but I could have said and done everything this poet says and does; I felt unpleasantly moved by this harsh picture, which displays me in my misery. I think, of course, that a supplement is necessary if an accurate picture of me is to be given; I try to console myself with the thought that I also have a number of better qualities,

by which, in actual life, I become more bearable or—I might almost say—less contemptible.

Hauch himself may not have realized how great the resemblance between Andersen and his poet had become: "That which shook me and which burns in my memory is the unhappy poet's fate." Ørsted had once described the depression which could arise from the thought of the inheritability of mental disease; then Andersen had remained silent. "My father's father was insane, and my father went mad shortly before his death. Thus you can understand the effect the dissolution of the unhappy wretch in Hauch's work had upon me—his dissolution is a picture of me .... It is unpleasant to get sympathy from people who, even as they speak, are keenly aware of the striking truth in Hauch's depiction of my weaknesses. Nothing can be done here, nothing can be said; I can only let this sea wash over me." And then Andersen concludes with the request that his heartiest greetings be passed on to Hauch; "I have not written anything at all recently; I feel like wet wood which will not catch fire."

It can be safely said that the letter is a remarkable and an imposing one, bearing witness to a freedom from bias, a love of truth, and a goodness and wisdom which should scarcely have been imputed to H. C. Andersen, with his reputation for vanity and egoism. He bore great humiliations more easily than small ones, just as, on his journeys, he demonstrated more courage in the presence of real dangers than before those he imagined. He thus saw himself quite as clearly as a modern psychiatrist would; concerning his psychopathic nature and the legacy he had received from his father and his grandfather, he is in complete agreement with Hjalmar Helweg, the author of a shrewd medical study of him.

Despite everything, his legacy did not get the better of him; he bore both humiliations and triumphs, the envenomed and the exalted hours of his spirit, without collapsing beneath their burden. In the final analysis, he was perhaps saved from Eginhard's fate by two qualities which his intimate friend and stern critic, Edvard Collin, ascribed to him as he looked back over their friendship: his goodness and his sense of justice. "He struggled hard to keep free of personal antipathies and to form a just opinion," Edvard Collin attested.

Carsten Hauch gave him a splendid opportunity to make use of his goodness and his sense of justice, and Andersen did not do his work halfway. They were reconciled, and the friendship continued unclouded. In 1867, Hauch's heavy-footed friend, Peter Hjort, published a collection of letters addressed to him; among them was an epistle of Hauch's from 1829, in which, after the young author, Andersen, had been ridiculed for *A Journey on Foot,* the following cause for his popularity was given: "He throws himself in the dust and lets himself be trampled by anyone who has a notion to do so. He insinuates himself into every family, licks everyone's spittle, and is as vacillating and ungoverned in his person as he is in his poems." Upon reading these lines, Hans Christian made the following notation in his diary: "Thank God I didn't write it—how painful it must be for Hauch." And then he sent a hearty letter to Hauch in order to console him for Hjort's silly indiscretion; as a matter of fact, he paid a personal visit to his sick and aged friend, and fell into his arms.

Thus he dulled the point of humiliation, thus he conjured the ghost of his youth back into the ground—as it were to deny, finally and in the noblest manner, the picture Hauch had given of Eginhard's incontrollable egoism and distorted moral sense.

CHAPTER XII

The Goblet of Triumph

ANDERSEN WAS NO MORE THAN thirty-three years old when a great German poet, Adalbert von Chamisso, wrote to him, two weeks before his own death: "You justly belong to Germany's favorite authors." The opinion was rendered in August, 1838; the occasion was the German edition of *Only a Fiddler*, in which Chamisso had been enraptured by the poetry of childhood, portrayed, in his opinion, with incomparable skill.

Time after time H. C. Andersen emphasized that abroad—and first and foremost in Germany—he found the appreciation and the warmth so long denied him in his fatherland. There were periods when he persuaded himself that, at home in Denmark, he had to empty the cup of humiliation every day, while he merely needed to travel to German soil for the goblet of triumph to be raised in greeting.

One must grant that there were reasons for this assertion, even though Andersen generalized and exaggerated. He had attained world fame before he was universally recognized in Denmark as an author of classic greatness, and it was certainly the help from abroad which inspired, or at any rate hastened, his break-through at home. To a certain extent, this early success abroad was no doubt due to the fact that foreign readers had not had their opinions distorted by the personal weaknesses which aroused criticism and ridicule among Andersen's countrymen; more spacious conditions can also cause a good deal of pettiness to disappear, and envy, of course, always wreaks its cruelest havoc in confined and intimate circles.

That Germany took the lead is not surprising, for interest and enthusiasm are not customarily lacking in that country; furthermore, Andersen's work was extremely accessible to the German mind. In cultural and literary respects the whole of the north—and not least, Denmark—was closely allied to Germany, and during the Romantic age the connection was perhaps more intimate than at any other time. Most of the basic elements, both age-old and extremely modern, of Andersen's writings were common property of Germany and Denmark: fairy tales and popular beliefs, the Romantic concept of the world which Ørsted had transmitted to the north, the literary techniques created by the generations of Ludwig Tieck and E. T. A. Hoffmann. Quite the same conditions prevailed as in Esaias Tegnér's case; he too acquired genuine popularity in Germany at about the same time, he too was a Nordic master with roots in the ancient world of legend and in modern German culture.

Sweden, it should be noted, also gave Andersen a very warm and early reception; in 1837 he traveled to Stockholm and made friends on the Göta Canal with Frederika Bremer; and time and time again he was an honored guest at Skåne's castles and estates, as he was in those in Denmark—something of the old Danish climate survived amidst the Scanian aristocracy.[1] While visiting the Scanian estate of Hyby in 1840, he was invited by the students of Lund to come to the near-by university town, in order that they might honor him with songs, speeches, and food in the traditional Swedish fashion. In the evening, having decided to serenade their visitor, the students marched up arm in arm to the private residence where H. C. Andersen was staying, and doffed their blue caps as soon as the poet appeared. The lanky Dane was quite overwhelmed —never before had he been the object of such a public display of esteem—and afterward, hiding in a corner, he wept out his joy and his excitement. Following the students' cheers and Andersen's little speech of thanks, the spokesman of the students, Bernhard Cronholm, publicist and proponent of Scandinavian cultural and political union, stepped forward to utter some prophetically inspired words: "Someday soon, when Europe speaks of the great bard Hans Christian Andersen, do not forget that Lund's students were the first to bring you the homage you deserve."

This was the Swedish and the Lundensian overture to a European opera in countless acts. Andersen did not forget it. Once after he had been given an ovation at a Scandinavian banquet in Rome in 1846, he wrote to Fru Louise Lind, née Collin, his former flame: "If I'm to be honest, then I must say I like the Swedes best. In their manner toward me they're—the way I'm accustomed to find the Germans."

Amongst the Germans, Andersen had a wonderful time. In 1840 he wrote a long letter on the subject to Edvard Collin; he is, in-

[1] Skåne, Sweden's southernmost province, was "the brightest pearl in Denmark's crown" until the Peace of Roskilde (1658).—G. C. S.

cidentally, quite giddy with delight at his first railroad journey, from Magdeburg to Leipzig—"now I know what it's like to fly, now I sense the flight of birds in passage"—and in Augsburg, burning with interest, he had seen his first daguerreotypes. "Yes, contrary to what one thinks at home, I do have a reputation, and with God's help I'll strive to deserve it," he cries, declaring that he is "humble of heart." This is the theme on which countless variations, played crescendo, are constructed throughout the years. In Weimar during the summer of 1844, he had honors heaped upon him; Chancellor von Müller, Goethe's intimate friend, was his guide for eight days and in person led him to the Princes' Vault, where Goethe and Schiller rest. "And yet Müller is the most important man in Weimar, he is regarded here [these are Andersen's touching words to Edvard Collin] as your father is regarded by the best people in Copenhagen." Andersen was quite a success at court, and Grand Duke Carl Alexander of Weimar actually became one of his warmest personal friends, full of admiration for the poet and liking for the man. Their long and intimate correspondence does honor to them both, and the gifted prince gallantly held his shield before his Danish friend whenever it was necessary. H. C. Andersen became nothing more nor less than the heir of the great Weimar tradition from Goethe's and Schiller's time; at the Grand Duke's country residence he told *The Emperor's New Clothes* and *The Ugly Duckling* and many other fairy tales; he told them in German, and his narration was received with rapture. Reporting to Edvard Collin, he is forced to add: "You're smiling. Of course, people are always smiling in Denmark." Here they say that he speaks excellent German, at home he is regarded as having no talent for languages whatsoever. Here they beg him to continue, at home they stuff their fingers in their ears. It is a mystery —and with naïve frankness he writes: "After all, there must really be something in my personality which attracts people." His conclusion is inescapable, and yet he has begun the letter with: "My beloved Edvard! You whom I must address formally—an artificial relationship, to be sure, and one which goes completely against my nature—but enough of that!" And it is the same story when he arrives in Dresden. "I am really a famous man." He pinches his ear in order to make sure he is not dreaming.

The next year, in December, 1845, he is received at the court in Berlin: he is begged to read a single fairy tale quite as Jenny Lind is begged to sing a single romance. He comes upon his fairy tales wherever he goes in the city, the sculptor Hauch embraces him and calls his tales "immortal," the great Alexander von Humboldt declares that the name of Andersen is now being spread throughout the world, and the evening before his departure the King of Prussia bestows the *Roter Adlerorden* upon him. "This was my first decoration," he wrote in *The Fairy Tale of My Life,* "and I received it on the birthday of my benefactor Collin" (January 6, 1846); the award also had the happy result that the King of Denmark made him a Knight of the Dannebrog immediately thereafter. He went once again to Weimar, where court and town and newspapers were filled with his praise, and on February 21, 1846, he wrote to Edvard Collin: "Either I suffer terrible injustice in every respect at home, or else mighty Germany is a mere nothing in comparison with Denmark's intellectual world." (Unfortunately he wrote "entillectual," and Edvard Collin most assuredly gave a little smile.) In the same letter he utters the wish that the Collin family could accompany him on his sunlit way; he rejoices at the honor he does old Jonas Collin, but adds the melancholy note: "Even to my best friends at home I am merely—Andersen, the good-natured fellow, who has talent but entertains awfully important ideas about himself, while Denmark has great men of another rank." After trying to drop the subject, he returns to it, as if attracted by a magnet; here he is a prince, at home he is a beggar, and his beloved Father Collin, for all his goodness, pays no attention to the triumphs and honors of his protégé. He is dreadfull hurt, for "my Denmark lies in the house of the Collins."

It is quite true that the Collin family refused to succumb for a very long time. On July 5, 1844, Edvard Collin wrote about the bad summer weather, and then continued, with that disrespectful humor which is so typically Danish:

> But you scarcely pay any attention to the weather God gives us in those circles now being graced by your presence. They're really making an awful lot of fuss over you, but it makes me terribly pleased both because it satisfies you, quite justifiably so, and because it must annoy others—and that too with justice. See to it that you bring home a decoration, that would be heaps of fun.

Andersen soon came home with his decoration, but for him it meant something much more than Edvard's heaps of fun. On the same day many members of the family wrote to Andersen, and among them was Jonas Collin himself:

> *Dear Andersen*: It is no doubt superfluous for me to tell you that I—and all of us—read your Weimar letter of June 24–26 with the greatest interest and pleasure, and it is very understandable that you wish to make such trips, and need and enjoy them. Let us only hope that your home does not thereby become less dear and pleasant, for home is after all the place which ought to be dearest to one's heart.

The letter closes: "Farewell, farewell—your paternally devoted Collin," and H. C. Andersen could certainly be proud and pleased at it; but something was missing both in Edvard's cheerful jests and

Jonas' moral earnestness. The princess, feeling the pea of their secret reservations through all the cushions and pillows, twisted and turned on her luxurious couch. "I wish to be praised," Andersen had written in December, 1843, "not for my own pleasure, but so that your father will be pleased. I shall only be happy in the world's eyes, as a poet, when your father can say: 'I am proud of him.'"

But this goal was particularly difficult of attainment. J. L. Heiberg and Henrik Hertz, cultured, tasteful, elegant poets, were the family's favorites; they possessed the formal perfection which foreigners could not appreciate. Celebrating their family festivals, the Collins improvised witty songs, as Danes are wont to do, and it is significant that, without exception, Edvard Collin's products made a greater hit than H. C. Andersen's—and they are, in fact, more cheerful, more inventive, more playful. Likewise, the subtle, temperate, critical tone of the Collin ménage simply could not be brought into agreement with the enthusiastic and emotional compliments H. C. Andersen received abroad, and the transition was often painful for the returning traveler. With wise dignity, Edvard Collin has accounted for his stewardship in a letter to his niece, Baroness Jonna Stampe: "He demanded recognition for having made the house of Collin famous through his fame, but the Collins set no value on his deed." The Collins did not lack a sense of their own worth, but they were quite free of vanity or snobbery. They continued to feel affection for H. C. Andersen, the author, just as they had once felt affection for the poor, unknown youth; but their emotions were not changed by his fame, they did not flatter him, their words of praise had Attic moderation and their jests, Attic salt. It is surely worthwhile to ask if this treatment were not the best one for H. C. Andersen in the long run.

In any case, he got his fill of compliments from other quarters.

There was no mistaking Charles Dickens' warm admiration for Hans Christian Andersen. He called the Dane "a great writer." Strangely, during his lifetime Andersen's talent was more esteemed in other countries of the world than it was in his native Denmark.

Hans Christian Andersen posed for this photograph at the age of sixty. In an early poem, *The Evening*, Andersen wrote a humorous self-portrait:

> *. . . a gawky creature:*
> *He has a nose that's grown to cannon-size,*
> *And tiny eyes, like green peas, grace his features.*

Photograph by C. Weller

He was passed from grand duke to king to emperor, thanks to the letters exchanged between these lofty personages. Arriving in Vienna from Dresden in 1846, he met Count Szechenyi, the brilliant Hungarian philanthropist (and prince of the House of Vasa), and read *The Sweethearts* at Schönbrunn before an audience composed of archduchesses and empresses. Of course, all fairy tales—Andersen's not excepted—deal with kings and queens, princes and princesses; but one can safely say that few tellers of fairy tales have made as extensive a study of the actual phenomena as Andersen did. From Vienna he proceeded to Rome, where he celebrated the Easter of 1846; among the thousands of visitors in the Holy City, the world's great newspapers mentioned only three by name: "one of the three was your humble friend, whom you, on that former occasion, were too refined to address with *'du,'*" he wrote to Edvard Collin.

One readily gains the impression that Hans Christian had a special predilection for trying to win the friendship of crowned heads, and for sunning himself in the favor of princes; and, born as he was in the morass, he quite naturally had an incontrollable desire to climb to the highest tussocks, if only for safety's sake. Yet his constant concern with royalty also reflects his knowledge of the world's hard ways; in the society of his day, the court was a symbolic market place of popularity, a strategic point. If Andersen were alive today, he would devote a corresponding amount of attention to the international press—he by no means neglected newspapers, as it was. "From the emperor's palace to the peasant's cottage," he wrote of his reception in Austria; from the former locale he could most easily determine his rank in the latter. His reputation flew across boundaries of every sort. As early as 1837, after having described his German conquests in a letter to Henriette Hanck, he wrote the following Napoleonic words: "But how shall I capture France and England? I shall know no peace until I've won these two great powers." He speaks of his portraits, presently being distributed on the continent; he has even been praised in a Russian journal. "My name shines ever brighter, and that is the only thing I live for! I thirst after honor like a miser after the sound of gold; both objects of desire are vain, but one must be enthusiastic about something in this world, otherwise one will collapse and rot away." These words have a demonic air—they make one think of some character in Balzac. Hauch was on the right track in *The Castle by the Rhine,* as, of course, Andersen had confessed with moving honesty.

He outdid his poor father's hero, Napoleon, for he conquered not only France but England. Xavier Marmier and many other littérateurs sang his praises in Paris, and he succeeded in penetrating the famous Chinese Wall of Parisian society, a barrier which stopped most men. At the races in Vincennes one day, H. C. Andersen was allowed to sit on the royal tribune, at the side of Frederick, the Danish crown prince, the object of all eyes; and as always his thoughts went back to a little house beside a street in Odense. Arriving in Holland, he found himself the focal point of literary interest; landing in England, he took the country by storm like another Julius Caesar. "You need no letters of recommendation here," Count Reventlow, the Danish ambassador, said in 1847, "You are known in England through your writings"; and known he was, for on the same evening he met his ducal friends from Weimar at the home of Lord and Lady Palmerston. "This evening," Count Reventlow explained, "you have leapt into lofty circles which others take years to reach." For three weeks, night and day, his life was a continuous party, with gold, satin, roses, and blue-blooded extras among the exquisite decorations. Charles Dickens opened his home and his arms to him. On his way back to Denmark he stood in the railroad station at Ghent, waiting for the train to Cologne; and other travelers came up to pay their respects to him—they recognized him from portraits, or had seen him at social events in England without daring to lay claim to his attention. Then, in Hamburg, he met his first Danish compatriots: "Good Heavens, Andersen, are you here? You should have seen what a lot of fun *The Corsair* had with your sojourn in England; in a cartoon they sketched you with laurel wreaths and money bags! It was very funny." Standing by his window after his return to Copenhagen, he saw two well-dressed gentlemen passing by; they looked up, stopped, laughed, and one of them, pointing at him, said in an intentionally audible voice: "Just look there—it's our world-famous orangutang!" The story is told in *The Fairy Tale of My Life,* and it does not sound improbable.

Yet Andersen's public triumphs, superficial as all such triumphs are, should not lure us into ignoring the realities behind them. In Hamburg, one evening in 1845, Andersen was on his way to the theater with a German friend; their path led them past a prosperous and well-lighted house. The friend, the painter Speckter, persuaded Andersen to go in with him for a few minutes, although it was high time to get to the theater—the children of the house, he explained, had their little heads full of Andersen's fairy tales. The whole flock of children clustered around the visitor as soon as they found out his name; all of a sudden the wizard, the good sorcerer, stood in their midst, and with shining eyes they listened to the story he told them—then, a moment later, he had disappeared. The anecdote is an utterly enchanting one. Nurseries all over the world have been bewitched by Hans Christian Andersen, although their little owners have not experienced the same unforgettable good luck as the children in Hamburg.

Sight-seeing in Edinburgh with the silver-haired old banker,

Hambro, Andersen visited "George Heriot's Hospital," the castle-like building familiar to readers of Scott's *The Fortunes of Nigel*. The old doorkeeper, taking Hambro for the famous author, Hans Christian Andersen, did his reverences to the former gentleman. When the mistake was corrected, the doorkeeper looked with astonishment at the forty-year-old Dane: "So young! I've read him and the boys are reading him now! It's strange to see such a man—otherwise they're always old or dead if you hear people talking about them!" After the poor Scottish children had turned out to be acquainted with *The Ugly Duckling* and *The Red Shoes,* Andersen, true to his wont, wept a few tears. One can agree with the English author who wrote: "This is indeed popularity."

He heard his praises sung by the mouths of children and babes, and more than three kings swung censers before him. It would surely be excusable if all this went to his head a little. And he was not only the well-advertised darling of the public and of newspapers and of courts—serious literary minds, great men, authors of intellectual distinction paid him homage. There is no mistaking Charles Dickens' warm admiration, to which Dickens gave expression in a correspondence filled with hearty invitations and in demonstrations of hospitality. His daughters had admired the Danish poet from afar, and Dickens himself called Andersen a great writer. With naïve self-satisfaction, Andersen included in *The Fairy Tale of My Life* a rich selection of the gushing panegyrics which were dedicated to him by the poets, some famous, some not, of all the lands of earth. Many of these works stem from deep emotion and are filled with genuine poetry; to their number belongs the lyric which an Austrian poet, Hermann Rollett, improvised in Weimar on January 29, 1846, as he saw Chancellor von Müller standing together with Andersen and Jenny Lind in the

Princes' Vault, before the coffins of Goethe and Schiller. The poem deserves to be remembered:

> *Fable's rose, who have so often*
> *Charmed me with your perfume's wave,*
> *I saw you growing on the coffins*
> *In the poet-princes' grave!*
>
> *And with you beside each coffin*
> *In the hall as still as death,*
> *I a nightingale saw captive:*
> *Mournful dreams robbed her of breath.*
>
> *And in secret I was gladdened,*
> *Thrilled in my most hidden breast,*
> *That the poets' darkened coffins*
> *Were with such late magic blessed.*
>
> *And your rose's sweet aroma*
> *Wafted through the hall of death*
> *With the nightingale, whose mourning*
> *Had made mute her lovely breath.*

How could this poetic apotheosis of the nightingale and the rose have failed to move Andersen, whose last great love was Jenny Lind and who for a moment even dreamed of winning her?

At Uppsala, in 1865, Ernst Björck presented him with another handsome poem; in it, the feelings of Sweden's children toward the king of fairy-tale tellers were expressed, and one of its stanzas runs:

> *Behold, he comes, the king approaches,*
> *Prince of our dreams, our childhood's pride!*

And poetry, sprung from his heart's deep reaches,
Forever young, goes at his side.
She is his bride, he has no other
Save her he got from heaven itself.

Coming to these lines, Andersen once again repressed a tear; the old bachelor thought of Riborg Voigt and Jenny Lind.

He had even become a poetic figure; he was no longer ugly and grotesque as he had been in his youth. His long, thin form had something unique and fascinating about it, and his face was spiritual, sometimes downright handsome. He could travel around the world in pomp and honor, he could be celebrated as the great Danish poet.

Nothing could prevent him from gradually becoming a great man in Denmark, too. After he had been feted and spoiled and decorated by foreign courts, the royal house of Denmark likewise found itself compelled to make a great fuss over him. As early as 1844, Christian VIII and his queen, Caroline Amalie, had invited him to be their guest at the bathing resort of Föhr amongst the Frisian Islands on the west coast of Slesvig; it was no doubt the cabinet minister, Count Rantzau-Breitenburg, who had instigated the invitation, for he had been a friend and admirer of Andersen's ever since he had read *The Improvisator*. The visit to Föhr is described in detail in *The Fairy Tale of My Life,* but a more vivid description of the experience is to be found in a letter of September 5, 1844, to Edvard Collin.

Do you know what day it is for me today? On September 5 I arrived in Copenhagen for the first time, back in 1819; and today it's exactly twenty-five years later—what a strange act of providence! My heart grows strangely soft at the thought; twenty-five years ago

I came to Copenhagen with my little bundle in my hand, penniless and unknown, and today I took my chocolate with the Queen, at table I sat opposite her and the King, and Rantzau brought forth a toast to me and to the day itself. Isn't it strange to think back, my dear, dear friend? It was also on September 5 when I crossed the border of Italy, there to write my *Improvisator*. Have your father read this letter of mine; he will understand the emotion which fills me. At table today I quietly drank a toast to him.

Andersen gradually came to stand on a most intimate footing with Danish royalty: meeting the poet, Christian VIII could ask Andersen where he was eating dinner, and upon receiving the answer, "at a restaurant," would say: "Then come and dine with me and my wife instead, we'll eat at four o'clock." He had equally close connections with Frederick VII and Christian IX; in effect, he belonged to the highest ranks of the court.

And in "the King's Copenhagen," in the capital's society, he could not, of course, hold a lower rank than the one the monarch had accorded him. He was a member not only of the family of His Excellency, Jonas Collin, but of the Royal Theater, the focal point of Danish culture. He had his permanent seat there in the so-called court's parquet, and there he had taken his place quite early in his career, at the beginning of the 1840's, beside Thorvaldsen and Oehlenschläger, chatting in a friendly fashion with his neighbors. "As I sat with these great men, a feeling of pious humility went through my soul, the various periods of my life rose up before me, memories from the time when I sat on the last bench of the figurants' loge in the third gallery, memories from the time when, moved by childlike superstition, I fell to my knees on the darkened stage and recited The Lord's Prayer." This is the account Andersen gives in *The Fairy Tale of My Life;* one thinks of *The Ugly*

Duckling's conclusion, where the swans, bowing their royal heads, bid the outcast welcome in their brilliant circle.

And gradually, as the years passed by, Andersen perceived that Denmark too received him with warm admiration. In a letter of February, 1846, Edvard Collin had already protested to Andersen, then in Weimar, concerning the latter's jeremiads. "You are not hugged and kissed the way you are in Weimar," Edvard Collin admits, "but we aren't hostile." He compares the extravagant scenes in Weimar with "the coffee hours in the house on Amaliengade, when Ingeborg teases you and Theodor tickles you and calls you *pauvre pomme de terre.*" Then he continues:

> With your exquisite powers of imagination you immediately make up a story to the effect that you are scorned in Denmark and that you scorn Denmark, and both parts of the story are lies; for at bottom you and Denmark get along famously, and the two of you would come to a still better understanding if there weren't a theater in Denmark—*hinc illae lacrimae!* Your thoughts keep coming back to this damned theater, and that's what makes me angry: is this theater the whole of Denmark, and are you nothing but a writer for for the theater? Is it in this capacity that you are feted in Germany? Aren't you the author of the fairy tales for the Germans, too? And don't people love your fairy tales in Denmark? Perhaps more sincerely than they do in Germany?

In this letter, common sense itself speaks through the mouth of Edvard Collin. By 1855, Andersen had to give up his resistance; with the publication of *The Fairy Tale of My Life* in Danish, he settled once and for all the question of his triumph in the land of his fathers. He had conquered. He had achieved his life's goal. He was a great and world-famous man, such as he had dreamed of being since his earliest childhood. The ghost had been laid. His life was a fairy tale, and all fairy tales end happily.

The psychologically interesting fact is that the fairy tales, with their undertone of optimism, of a religious faith in the goodness of God, and their humorously playful view of life's adversities and men's shortcomings, could not have been written by Andersen before that moment in which he achieved his decisive success as a poet, before he had received confirmation of his calling. Having triumphed with *The Improvisator,* he entered that period of euphoria in which he recounted *The Tinderbox,* the tale of fortune's golden boy, of Aladdin, of Lucky Peer, of Little Claus. It is the oldest of the fairy tales, and it contains the basic theme in their great symphony, taken from Andersen's own concept of life. In *The Fairy Tale of My Life* this mood, out of which the fairy tales were created, has received its inalterable and dogmatic form. On this foundation he continues to write fairy tales until the end of his life: success is the tales' *sine qua non;* nor, at the same time, could that success exist without them—"nothing succeeds like success."

For there can be no doubt about the matter: nothing should survive of the whole reputation of Andersen, a reputation which he enjoyed so immensely during his lifetime, if he had not written the fairy tales. His fame should have withered away just like that of so many of his celebrated contemporaries; he should be consigned to the same oblivion as Ida Hahn-Hahn, Lady Blessington, and Lord Bulwer-Lytton; he should scarcely have aroused as much interest as Henrik Hertz or Ingemann, whose names are practically unknown outside Denmark; he should have attracted decidedly less attention than Johan Ludvig Heiberg. One can set up the following formula: he achieved a borrowed success to begin with, obtained fame on credit in Germany, and only thereby was enabled to make his life's great profits. That is the paradox of Andersen, his great miracle.

One cannot speak in lesser terms than these. For in and with the fairy tales he not only won that place among Denmark's leading poets, between Holberg and Oehlenschläger, to which he had unabashedly laid claim when, once upon a time he had written to Madam Iversen in Odense: he won much more. He put his fellow poets in the shade. His fairy tales are Denmark's greatest contribution to world literature, and no country possesses an author who has acquired a fresher and truer immortality than Hans Christian Andersen's. His place is beside Homer, Dante, Shakespeare, Cervantes, and Goethe. In 1845, Hauch had his madman, Eginhard, utter these ravings: "My songs shall be read beneath the plane-tree and in the tents of the nomads, the camel shall bear them through the desert, the Negro shall sing them in the shade of his palm, and my name shall be remembered thousands of years from now, when the last descendant of my persecutors has vanished from the earth." A hundred years later Eginhard's words seem to be the simple truth.

In her autobiography Johanne Luise Heiberg tells a story about H. C. Andersen which, although perhaps not completely authentic in its details, possesses an absolute truth nonetheless.

Visiting her in 1858, Andersen told her of his stay in England the previous year, when he had been the guest of Charles Dickens. One day, as he sat happy and content beside the dinner table at Gadshill Place, Dickens' country estate, he received a letter from Copenhagen; his correspondent informed him that his latest novel had been censured in *The Fatherland* by an anonymous critic. Andersen fell into such despair that he went out into a grove adjoining Dickens' garden and threw himself weeping into the grass.

There he was discovered by Mrs. Dickens, who had missed him at
the table; at first she believed that the letter had told him of the
death of someone dear to his heart. Then Charles Dickens himself
appeared; when Dickens expressed curiosity over whether the review had really been so bad after all, Andersen was forced to confess, amidst his tears, that he had not read it. This caused Dickens
to give his Danish friend a little lecture about the pride an artist
ought to possess: "I am not acquainted with your book, but if
you've written a bad book, that doesn't mean the end of everything.
It happens to us all, to great poets, too, and you know full well that
you are a poet. Do you think that your works would have been
translated into all the world's languages if there weren't genius in
them? Pull yourself together, and be a man!" But H. C. Andersen
could not regain his good humor, for, as he told Fru Heiberg, "I
cannot endure criticism."

Fru Heiberg's ironic story is, as has been said, an excellent one;
yet, in order to be completely fair, one must not forget that H. C.
Andersen had been forced to take deep draughts from the cup of
humiliation before he had a chance to taste the goblet of triumph,
and that for a long time he had had to drink from first the one,
then the other. Slowly but surely, Danish criticism also fell silent,
and the poet of the fairy tales finally achieved an exceptional and
privileged position: his weaknesses were taken into account, his
peculiarities were ignored, he was wrapped in cotton-wool and
made happy with homage, attention, admiration, and love. To
attain this status in a country like Denmark, where wit, irony, and
even malice are accustomed to run riot, was perhaps the greatest
and most unique triumph of Andersen's career. Official confirmation of his role as the nation's declared favorite came when,
on December 6, 1867, Odense named him an honorary citizen,
holding a torch-light parade and illuminating the city to celebrate

the event, just as the old woman had predicted long ago. "My life's fairest festival," he called it, touchingly loyal to his childhood memories, for he had walked through a good many arches of triumph in the course of his life.

This chapter about Andersen's triumphs has been a long one; but he himself would have found it terse, mutilated, incomplete—and rightly so. The subject is treated more exhaustively in the more than seven hundred pages of *The Fairy Tale of My Life*.

CHAPTER XIII

The Fairy Tales

ᚹᚻᚹᚻᚹᚻᚹᚻᚹᚻᚹᚻᚹᚻᚹᚻᚹᚻᚹᚻᚹᚻᚹᚻᚹᚻᚹᚻᚹᚻᚹᚻᚹᚻᚹ

Edvard collin has given a fine picture of Andersen as a teller of fairy tales before he wrote any of them down:

> In many of the circles to which he paid daily visits were little children with whom he concerned himself; he told them stories which he had partly made up for the occasion, and partly taken from familiar fairy tales; but whether the tales he told were of his own invention or borrowed, his manner of telling them was so exclusively his own and so vivid, that the children were enchanted. He himself enjoyed having a chance to give his humor free play; his speech came in an unobstructed stream, richly provided with expressions familiar to the children and with gestures to fit. He put life into even the driest sentence; he did not say: "The children climbed up into the wagon and then they rode away," but: "Then they climbed up into the wagon, good-by, father, good-by, mother, the whip

cracked, snap, snap, and away they went, hey, will you really pull there!" Those who have heard him read his fairy tales later on can only form a weak notion of the strange vitality his delivery had in the midst of a circle of children.

Here Edvard Collin emphasizes two aspects of the style of the fairy tales: their bold use of the spoken language and their plasticity. Nothing is unclear, nothing is vague; it is all precise, exact, just as in the imagination of a child. It has the oral directness of the theater, where everything must be expressed in dialogue or action. H. C. Andersen acted before the children. The dream of the theater, which had filled him ever since he was a little fellow in Odense and which had driven him to Copenhagen, had been realized here. The new genre was created by transferring the method from private life to literary creation.

In May, 1835, he published the first volume of *Fairy Tales, Told for Children,* which contained *The Tinderbox, Little Claus and Big Claus, The Princess on the Pea,* and *Little Ida's Flowers.* The second volume appeared in December, 1835, and the third, with *The Little Mermaid* and *The Emperor's New Clothes,* in April, 1837. In 1838 the first volume of the *New Collection,* containing *The Steadfast Tin Soldier,* was issued; in 1839 came the second volume with *The Storks;* and in 1841, the third volume. In 1843 the series called *New Adventures* was begun; the title no longer addressed itself exclusively to children. One volume followed another; from 1852 on a series of *Stories* appeared; and finally, as matters turned out, a little volume of *New Fairy Tales and Short Stories* was published just before Christmas every year until Andersen's death in 1875. There is no longer any doubt that Andersen was born so that he could write these fairy tales and stories: they are his contribution to world history.

Andersen complained bitterly about the lack of encouragement and approval which his first fairy tales met. One literary magazine advised him not to waste his time on fairy tales for children, and another praised the fairy tales of his old adversary, Christian Molbech, at his expense—Molbech's calm and simple manner was more tasteful. Had not Molbech himself once inquired in a review: "When will Andersen ever learn to write Danish?" He never learned; instead, he taught the Danes to write their language in a different way.

It may be true enough that the initial applause was weak, but it should not be forgotten that not even Andersen himself knew what he had wrought; a considerable time passed before it became clear to him. Writing to a friend in Sorø on May 15, 1835, he called the first volume of fairy tales a "bagatelle." To Chamisso he said merely that he had "expressed something of childhood in a special way." On March 16, 1835, he repeated the judgment of Ørsted to Henriette Wulff: "While," according to the physicist, "*The Improvisator* will make me famous, the fairy tales will make me immortal; they are the most perfect thing I have ever written—*but I don't think so.*" The words italicized here contain a clear protest from Andersen himself; one discovers, with a certain astonishment, that Denmark's brilliant physicist was also Denmark's only brilliant critic. He needed but the first volume to determine the fairy tales' value. Upon the second one's appearance, in December, 1835, Andersen wrote to Ingemann: "Many rank these fairy tales, strangely enough, above *The Improvisator;* in contrast, others, like you, wish that I had never written them at all. What am I supposed to think now?" The same uncertainty is evident in the introduction to the third volume, from March, 1837. "None of my works," it says there, "has been the object of such varying evaluations. While some individual persons, whose judgment I highly esteem, have ascribed to the fairy tales the most value of anything I have written, others, holding the opinion that they were quite unimportant, advised me not to write any more. These mixed judgments and the apparent silence with which professional criticism passed the tales by, weakened my desire to make further attempts in genre." He was silent for a whole year, but then the inspiration of *The Little Mermaid* came to him, and he could not resist putting the fairy tale on paper. The public must decide whether more volumes should follow, Andersen says in conclusion, but adds the prophetic lines: "In a little land the poet will always remain a poor man; *renown* is thus the golden bird he must hunt with special zeal. We shall find out whether or not I can catch it by telling fairy tales."

If one, after the passage of a hundred years, shall try to tell why H. C. Ørsted was right, one stands hesitatingly before the countless and eloquent reasons given by both Danish and foreign judges, and before the changing points of view from which various generations have observed the fairy tales. The truth of the matter—that they are incomparable—has been proved in practice, and no splitting of aesthetic hairs can help much one way or the other.

One can, of course, point to the style, the manner of narration, as Edvard Collin did, one can say that their imaginative plasticity combines the nursery's fresh naïveté with the theater's artful precision in a way which was only possible in innocent Denmark's cunning capital during the aesthetic Age of Gold, a period characterized by its high priestess, Johanne Luise Heiberg, in her description of Carl Christian Hall, the Danish politician and statesman; "Like all other cultured people in this period, he was extremely interested in the theatrical arts. Politics, this omnivorous hyena, still did not have the power to push the Muses and the Graces aside." This was the air Andersen breathed, while being, at the same time, no jaded product of the metropolis, but rather what the Danes like to call "God's word from the country-side." The result was bewildering and enchanting.

One can emphasize the fact that he saw human existence in all its manifold and vital richness simply because he had come up from below, out of the dark depths of poverty and want—more can be seen from the ground, as it were, than from the sky. And one can continue the thought: he possessed a great advantage over other poets who, although gifted with emotion and imagination, had never experienced elementary excitement—they had never gone cold and hungry, they had never trembled with mortal fear. H. C. Andersen had known these experiences, and so he had something to tell; from this reality stems his rushing *élan,* which is authentic—the dizzying tempo which takes the listener's breath away. His knowledge of reality was present at the very outset, in *The Tinderbox,* and it is the source of inspiration for all the fairy tales—*Thumbelina, The Ugly Duckling, The Little Mermaid.* Each of them is concerned with a question of life or death.

One can amuse oneself by applying a purely literary-historical yardstick to the tales, as Valdemar Vedel did in a learned lecture at the University of Berlin, held in connection with the H. C. Andersen Exposition of 1925. In this case, one will discover that Andersen, with extraordinary sensitivity and receptivity, absorbed the early nineteenth century's whole current of international Romanticism. One will discover parallels to and connections with his fairy tales everywhere, not only in folk literature but also in conscious literary work, and above all in the German Romanticists, those worshippers of life's magical elements. Andersen was a lightning-fast and omnivorous reader; he knew Tieck and Novalis, Hoffmann and Heine, Chamisso and Fouqué; he even stumbled upon Arnim's *Isabella von Aegypten,* to which his contemporaries paid all too little heed, but in which there were the flaming colors and grotesquely expressive contures he needed. Like Tegnér, he ruthlessly appropriated the material he required wherever he found it, and from Swedish soil, too: from Atterbom's *Isle of Bliss* he took the shoots for his *Garden of Paradise*, and they flourished better in Denmark than they had in Sweden; *The Water Sprite* of Stagnelius gave him that chord of yearning, for death or immortality, which he made ring so masterfully through the symphony of the waves in *The Little Mermaid*. But in making such comparisons, one should not forget the core of the matter, which Edvard Lehmann put his finger on in the brilliant essay, *The Primitive H. C. Andersen*: all these Romanticists and fairy-tale poets enthused about the mystical motifs of popular belief and superstition, they wanted to squeeze poetry out of them, but not a single member of their band could for a moment transport himself back to the world of primitive superstition—none save H. C. Andersen, who was born in its midst and preserved traces of it his whole life through. For this reason all the other fairy tales are paper work, literary decorations, while his are authentic products of experience—both those he repeats and those he invents. He is the earth's last teller of fairy tales; from the dark womb of Fyn's primitive peasant culture he came directly before the footlights of Copenhagen's Romantic theater. Since he was the last, he was also the first and the greatest. He preserved the old, primitive qualities, and added new and subtle ones to them.

He added, for example, nature poetry, depictions of landscape, which had no place in the old folk tales. The delicacy, the intensity, the splendor, and the beauty of his pictures of nature compose an essential part of the fairy tales' enchantment, but we no longer realize exactly to what extent Andersen was a revolutionary creator of new things, a rebel against literary stereotypes. In his poverty-stricken childhood he had sat for days on end, staring at a single leaf on the gooseberry bush, and he kept this ability to see wonderful worlds of beauty in what was commonplace, in what others scorned. Even in his last years he put together bouquets of grass and frostbitten meadow flowers far into the winter, he made the discovery that blooming apple-branches were still lovelier than carefully tended flowers in their beds; and in his fairy tales he reproduced real nature, the nature he had experienced as a little boy in the town and in the countryside, with elder trees and scraggy willows, with dock and thistles along the wayside ditches, dandelions and violets, field mice in the stubble and rats in the gutters. As Edvard Lehmann has so wisely observed: he saw everything which people had not wanted to see before; but his glance was unconstrained—it also saw all that was fresh, sweet-smelling, idyllic, dreaming, and bounteously happy in the landscape. His perception of nature had that naïve and ruthless love of truth which one finds in the unspoiled mind of a child.

The epicist was also a lyricist, and the lyricist was a psychologist besides. An extraordinary wealth of experiences, observations, and reflections is concealed within the fairy tales; one obtains the most forceful impression of this by studying Hans Brix's exceptional treatise on *H. C. Andersen and His Fairy Tales,* a work unique in its concrete astuteness. A drop of the heart's blood lies in each of the fairy tales, Brix says, and that is why they remain fresh and vital; one can follow in detail the process by which all the occurrences and the moods of Andersen's existence impregnated his imagination and, in accordance with their own secret laws, were crystallized into the fairy tales' symbolic script. It is realistic literature, saturated with life and actuality; one knows this from the unflagging interest the fairy tales arouse, even though one is not always able to interpret their symbols. The reader cannot remain indifferent. The true fairy tale, like the true dream, always has the force of a dark message.

It would scarcely be incorrect to say that the world, a hundred years ago, was conquered primarily by the poetic, emotional, Romantic, and mystic light surrounding the fairy tales, while today we are entranced by their wit, their quick play of humor. Making this re-evaluation, one must call up the most perspicacious of Andersen's friends as witnesses. H. C. Ørsted, the first commentator to grant the fairy tales their rightful place in world history, has also made the categorical statement: "Andersen is greatest in his humorous vein"; this was Ørsted's indefeasible opinion, although no one had repeated the physicist's Romantic philosophy—of the spirit which dwells in nature—more faithfully than Andersen had. And Edvard Collin, who never allows himself to become guilty of exaggeration (if it is a question of emphasizing his friend's virtues), bears enthusiastic witness on this one occasion: when he characterizes Andersen's humor. The songs Andersen made up for convivial evenings were not especially brilliant, Edvard Collin assures us, but then he adds:

In conversations where there was a touch of irony and his humor could be brought into play, he could be incomparably amusing. I have never known anyone who in quite the same way could seize upon a simple and essentially unimportant detail and then, not troubling himself much about the correctness of the matter, could make it bear fruit with his humor. Almost every day he had a comical story to tell about something or other that had befallen him; and it is not surprising that, after one such story, Commodore Wulff threw up his hands and cried: "It's a lie, the devil take me if it isn't, things like that don't happen to anybody else"—a scene of which Andersen himself then gave hilarious re-enactments.

The testimony weighs all the more heavily because it is given by a humorist who, in turn, lived surrounded by wits in a capital where an unusually animated spirit prevailed. One cannot refrain from regarding the fairy tales of Hans Christian Andersen as one of those fine products which Denmark manufactured for export on the world-market. And whether Edvard Collin liked it or not, the Collin household must be ascribed partial credit for the high standard maintained. In *The Fairy Tale of My Life* the express statement is made:

> Humor and the joy of living had their source in the Collins' home, which in this respect exerted a salutary influence upon me, preventing the sickly elements in my soul from getting the upper hand: the Collins' eldest daughter, Fru Ingeborg Drewsen, had a particularly strong effect through her bold jests, her wit, and her humor; when one's mind is as soft and elastic as the surface of the sea, such as mine is, then it reflects its surroundings.

Unfortunately, Ingeborg Drewsen burned her whole correspondence with Andersen before her death in 1877. Only a few isolated notes are preserved—bubbling with a fresh, uninhibited humor. She was the only person capable of saying to the great oracle, Heiberg: "But, heavens, Heiberg, now you're really being stupid!" To Hans Christian she dared to say exactly what she pleased; in a letter of 1838, a remark of hers about the improvement in his health is reported: "No, taking the waters hasn't perked Andersen up—it's the incomparable success he's had this winter with *Fata Morgana, Prince and Page,* and finally *The Flight.* It's added years to his life!" These were three plays, but not Andersen's; they belonged respectively to Heiberg, Paludan-Müller, and Hertz, and all three had been fiascoes. Andersen's fairy tales are full of this sort of ironic wisdom. "My sister Ingeborg was really the only one who, in everyday life, could safely joke with him," Edvard Collin says; "I can't say why, since he knew all the rest of us just as well." They had, of course, a spiritual affinity to one another: for both of them jest was a natural way of life, and hence nothing intentional and negative. He was not "in love" with her in the normal meaning of the phrase. Ingeborg Drewsen's sympathy for Andersen was passed on to her children and grandchildren, and it still blooms in her granddaughter Rigmor Stampe's wise and excellent book.

In private life, Andersen himself possessed this supple wit, and he was surrounded by it; it is a social virtue, and cannot be developed in isolation. The Danes sharpened their wit and their quickness of tongue on one another as slaughterers sharpen their knives on a whetstone. Edvard Collin adduces many examples of Hans Christian's lightning-fast presence of mind. One of his finest and most original replies, no doubt, was the one made to Heiberg, when the latter, in a fit of sarcasm about Andersen's Swedish triumphs, remarked: "You'll have to come along when I go to Sweden, so that I can get a little homage, too." The reply came: "Go with your wife, then you'll get it much more easily!" The thrust ("Advertisement!") and riposte ("No, true talent!") of opinion is elegantly paraphrased. When in his old age Andersen was visiting the Mendub of Tangier in the company of the British minister, he was required to drink two cups of tea, a beverage he detested, and then, to his horror, he saw the Mendub filling a third. But Andersen knew a way out: he declared that it went against his religion to drink three cups of tea, and the Mendub immediately yielded before this dark hint at the dogma of the Holy Trinity. One does not know which to admire most: Andersen's imagination, his insight into the Oriental mind, or his rascally smile. But the fairy tales bend beneath the weight of such roguish and graceful inventions as a hazel bush bends beneath its nuts—they, like all true wit, are improvisations; one can gratefully say that methodical whims do not exist.

Wit, of course, is closely related to maliciousness; at times the two words are used almost synonymously. One cannot deny that wit in this secondary meaning had also reached a splendid flower in Hans Christian Andersen's Denmark. Intimate backbiting flourished on the green islands. In Sweden, and perhaps in Norway too, things were and are a little different: either people are good friends, and then everything is politeness, irreproachable benevolence, and propriety, or else hostility is in the air, and then the stage is immediately reached in which all bridges are burned. In Denmark, on the other hand, people are masters of the ironic manner, with polite persiflage and disguised polemics. There exist exquisitely friendly letters between Heiberg and Andersen, and non-Danish readers must ask a Hans Brix to explain the jibes in them—otherwise, one would not discover the drops of venom placed inside the roses. H. C. Andersen had attained the highest rank in this freemasonry of witty malice. When it came to disarming innocence, no one could outdo him. The good citizens of Denmark were served a good portion of this medicine, but always in such a form that they could only laugh and try to make the best of it. How could one feel hurt by the story of a feather, a story that takes place in a chicken yard? And how could the Collin family be offended by *The Ugly Duckling?* And would not Edvard Collin have deemed himself both boorish and stupid if he had taken *The Shadow* as a personal insult and demanded an exact interpretation of the story? Nothing more clearly reveals the infinite subtlety, the ambiguity, the hesitation between pain and resentment and gaiety in these emotional relationships than the fact that Andersen in his fairy tales confessed his most intimate experiences and touched upon his connections with those people to whom he was closest and whom he loved best. A subtler, a more discreet, a more ingenious jest has perhaps never been made. It has something of the grace one admires in a dancer, making his way over a stage covered with eggs, or a juggler, smiling as he tosses his sharp knives into the air.

What a light-footed and sure-handed master of the game Andersen was! Telling the immortal story of *The Emperor's New Clothes,* he thought the whole time of his brothers in Apollo, and in particular of the distinguished and elegant Paludan-Müller; but just on this account it was vital that he did not reveal what he had in mind by a single syllable, a single mien—the faintest sign to the public would have been an unheard-of vulgarity, a piece of tastelessness beyond compare. As Hans Brix so pertinently remarks: H. C. Andersen has worked with gloves in order not to leave fingerprints; he has swept away the traces of his deed. And this is why he celebrates the triumph of having his readers for the next hundred years apply his fable to the fashionable greats of art and critical opinion—and his readers do it with happy enthusiasm, believing in their innocent conceit that the idea is their own. Andersen has outwitted them: this was the goal he sought.

Now and then there is an element of a naughty boy's rashness in Andersen's satire. In *The Flying Trunk* the merchant's son tells a story about sulphur matches which from start to finish is an ironic depiction of the Heiberg circle. Yet it becomes apparent from a letter to Henriette Hanck that Andersen originally wrote the fairy tale so that Fru Heiberg could read it aloud at a soiree. The soiree was cancelled, however, and Andersen was thus deprived of that unique pleasure to which he was evidently looking forward with keen anticipation. It is not likely that Fru Heiberg would have grasped the fairy tale's content straightway, and at any event the public would not; a scandal would not have resulted.

But one wonders if Andersen did not entertain a quiet hope that the clever Johan Ludvig Heiberg himself would have been able to read the cipher? If such was the case, then Andersen was paid back in *A Soul after Death;* there Hans Christian Andersen reads aloud to the sultan's family, just as the merchant's son does in *The Flying Trunk*—it looks suspicious. This hidden exchange of barbs has not escaped Hans Brix.

Happiness and joy emanate from the fairy tales, they are written in a spirit of triumph; that is why the first one deals with the soldier who owns the tinderbox, and the second has Little Claus as its hero—both are fortune's darlings. What created the productive mood in which Andersen wrote the fairy tales?

It seems as though it were sheer luck, at least in the soldier's case, pure magic; but in Little Claus the truth leaks out—it is a piece of nature's magic instead; behind Little Claus's naïve and clumsy innocence there are concealed inventiveness, guile, waggishness, just as in Andersen himself. Writing the fairy tales, he had the victorious sense of advancing through all the world's difficulties and trials by means of his wit and his humor.

The genre could have turned out to be a vulgar one, a crude and forceful joke in the clownish manner of Till Eulenspiegel, and *Little Claus and Big Claus* has something of Eulenspiegel's mood. But heaven had not cut Andersen after this pattern; his laughter was not boisterous and empty, his humor was not crude and without nuances. No one has had a finer, subtler, more highly strung, more sensitive spirit than he—it is for this reason that the third tale is called *The Princess on the Pea.* Nor was this enough: in his soul there lay depths of bitterness, fear, unrest, and melancholy; his seed-leaf had sprouted amidst suffering and want, deprivation and humiliation; and there was an ineradicable trembling in his whole being as in the leaves of an aspen. All these elements lay behind his smile, and therefore his smile became so brilliant and so enchanting.

The merriment in the fairy tales and their grace—these things expressed Andersen's own triumph over the shadows. Edvard Collin has borne witness to the fact that the basic mood in his friend's life was melancholy, and under this rubric he includes his vanity, his impatience, his suspicion, his unhealthy outbursts of emotion. He could get up from the festive board in the Collins' house with tears in his eyes, hurt, unhappy, filled with hatred, ready to cause scenes and scandals. After one such paroxysm he sent a messenger to fetch Edvard Collin's wife; when she came, he met her with a cry of despair: "Oh, what shall I do, I'm so full of evil and hateful thoughts!" In his youth he had lamented: "I'm an insane wretch, remember that there's something wrong with my mind!"

In poetic creation, in the fairy tales, there was a remedy and there was health, and liberation, triumph, and victory. There he has pressed the healing balm of humor from life's bitter herbs, there he attains a smiling equilibrium, there he tells of the ugly duckling and the shadow, of all his life's tribulations, with fairness, joy, and playful temerity.

It is for this reason that the fairy tales offer such a deep and exquisite pleasure to their readers: pain has been not forgotten but overcome.

But intelligence, *esprit,* is not the only factor in the fairy tales which delights the reader; he also rejoices at watching the imagination at work, he knows the satisfaction which arises when, like fireworks, colorful and surprising visions follow one upon the other. The child's imagination is highly developed, and that is why Andersen originally addressed himself only to little children; but he very shortly discovered that adults were equally enchanted, and then he abandoned the fiction that the fairy tales were told exclusively or principally for the young. What infinite enjoyment it must have given him to keep a whole public of large and small breathless with excitement—and, at the end, a public which embraced the entire globe! The pleasure a magician takes in swinging his wand is part of the enchantment which streams out of the fairy tales—a demonic pleasure, in Andersen's case as in E. T. A. Hoffmann's, but also an innocent one, white magic, not black. The demonic desire to perform, to draw attention, to be the center of interest, had made Andersen a scandal and a hissing from childhood on, it had branded him as being half-crazy, a monster of vanity. It was his creative and supreme imaginary life which shook the conventions of everyday existence as a lion shakes the bars of its cage. When this life had its chance to flame up unfettered in the fairy tales, then the final great symbolic figures were born, to become the common possession of all humanity; the youngest sisters and brothers of those primal figures, Tom Thumb, Little Red Ridinghood, and the Master Thief, emerged—Thumbelina, the little mermaid, the ugly duckling.

CHAPTER XIV

The Philosophy of the Fairy Tales

N̲o one denies that Hans Christian Andersen was a brilliant artist; but if we wish to take him and his fairy tales seriously, we must ask what sort of wisdom it is he preaches.

At first glance it seems to be anything but deep. Life is a beautiful fairy tale, and there is a loving God Who arranges everything for the best. Andersen takes the practical proof of this teaching from his own life story; the hopeful dream was realized as if through a miracle.

This is the basic type of all his fairy tales: that they treat of fortune's chosen darling. It can scarcely have escaped the author that not all the children of men maintain a magical alliance with the Almighty: on the contrary, some of them lead an unhappy life, in want and poverty, frustrated and betrayed in their fondest desires. Andersen does not close his eyes to any of these unfortunates, and he has a consolation for them, for the little match girl frozen to death, for the withered cripple in the cellar beside a metropolitan street: the joys of Heaven, bliss in the arms of God. Even the little mermaid, apparently excluded, will reach this goal by a detour. Thus the books always balance; we all become favorites like the ugly duckling, although some of us do not attain happiness save through that second sandman, the one who is called "Death." "Fantasos" could be a common name for both the sandman-figures, and when, still in the class room, Andersen wrote his first finished poem, it dealt with the two sandmen, and with the child who falls into happy sleep beneath Fantasos' magic wand.

Religion, a firm belief in an eternal bliss, is thus the foundation of the fairy tales and their optimism. However, Andersen was by no means an orthodox Christian. He resembled the picture he had given of his poor father, a seeker, a brooder, a doubter. Now and then he glorified the faith, the mystery of Christ, and the authority of the Bible, but it was more an expression of his longing than of his conviction. Even in his old age he quarreled with the pious ladies among his circle of friends, just as he had argued in his youth with his Grundtvigian tutor, Müller. In 1870, when, according to his diary, he declared the "connections of birth and family," which Christianity busies itself with, to be meaningless, he was excommunicated by the three noble ladies of Basnæs estate: "If I didn't agree to believing in the Father, the Son, and the Holy Ghost, then I wasn't a Christian." The storm was so violent that he was happy when—despite what had happened—Fru Scavenius of Basnæs pressed his hand as he left; before going to sleep that night he begged God to enlighten him if he were wrong. So much is sure: a year later, in October, 1871, he gave such pointed expression to his opinions that another lady, a follower of Grundtvig, declared that at best he could only be counted among the Jews. Something similar happened to Viktor Rydberg, of course, upon the writing of his great *Jubilee Cantata,* and, as a matter of fact, the two poets may well have entertained quite similar attitudes toward religion, although the Swede could give far more learned reasons for his stand: Andersen had also lost the faith of his childhood, and he was also an idealist, a believer in the spirit. He never abandoned his belief in a personal God. He fought eagerly against the doctrine of hell and eternal punishment; and he had every conceivable difficulty in holding fast to his belief in the immortality of the soul—in other words, he had to fight hard to maintain the very basis of both his own existence and that of the fairy tales. At the passing of his old friend and fellow poet, Carsten Hauch, in March 1872, he noted in his diary: "Is he now dust and ashes, dead, extinguished, burned out like the light which exists no more! Oh Lord, My God! Canst Thou let us entirely disappear? One feels dread at the thought, and I have become too wise—and unhappy." In Gothenburg in the summer of 1871, he met Viktor Rydberg and was struck by his "attractive and calm exterior . . . . We talked of life beyond the grave, and it was all so human and reasonable," the diary says. It was obviously not Viktor Rydberg's physical being alone which had a calming effect upon Andersen.

In essence, a belief in immortality was a moral postulate for both Andersen and Rydberg. Andersen once had a conversation with Oehlenschläger, in the course of which the latter, no doubt half in jest, said that Andersen was not content with all he could get on earth—to top it all off, he wanted to be immortal too. Andersen replied that he would become furious with God if He did not grant eternity to all those people who had never known a single joy in all their wretched days on earth. In the novel *To Be or Not To Be* from 1857, Esther, the heroine, develops a similar line of thought. "We perceive disharmonies," she says, "we see an unjust distribution of life's goods, we witness gifts cast away, and the triumph of evil, stupidity, vice, power—the triumph of Caligula. It is unthinkable, it cannot be true! Our sums here on earth will never come out even, unless we add to them the number: *an eternal life.*"

Noting such expressions of opinion, one could assume, it seems, that Andersen surely no more distorted the metaphysical urge for eternity, religious idealism, into an argument for the preservation of earthly injustice than Viktor Rydberg did. Marx has said that religion is the opium of people; but Charles Kingsley, a Christian idealist and also a contemporary of Andersen's, has given the matter an equally caustic formulation: "The Bible has become a mere police handbook, a dose of opium to make the beasts of burden patient beneath their loads." Did Andersen write his fine fairy tales so that they might be used in the same spirit? Did he have the sandman's magic lantern enchant sick children so that they would forget their pain—or forget to seek a cure for it? In principle, the two matters are very different; in practice the boundary between them often becomes blurred. Morphine is a boon for suffering humanity—a fact which, one guesses, neither Marx nor Lenin would dare dispute—but it is not a panacea; it has no use in the science of hygiene, nor can it prevent sickness; the man who tries to make it the basis of therapeutics is a charlatan, a spirit akin to those men who make an idyllic falsification of religion. Was Andersen one of their number? They were legion in that age, and one must ask oneself whether Andersen's moral and intellectual independence was sufficient to enable him to see through their sophisms. This is no vain question, for in the final analysis it concerns the content of truth in Andersen's fairy tales.

The request for a vote of confidence was made in all due order by the critical representative of the new generation, the realistic age—by Georg Brandes, who in 1869, to the very great pleasure of the old poet, wrote an excellent treatise on Andersen's fairy tales. Georg Brandes' admiration is provided with a number of question marks and reservations; he criticizes, among other things, H. C. Andersen's preference for tame and submissive domestic animals— even the nightingale, which is supposed to symbolize poetry, is a docile bird with monarchistic tendencies, and the ugly duckling ends in a castle park, where it swims around as a prisoner and is fed with cakes and crumbs from the table of the rich. "How can your enthusiasm, your pride allow you to let the swan end in this way?" Brandes cries pathetically. Let it die, tragically and magnificently, let it fly away unfettered through the air, rejoicing at its beauty and its strength, let it sink into the depths of a lonely forest lake—but spare it the approval of old swans and ducks, spare it the cakes and the crumbs!

This is indeed a very elegantly formulated criticism of Andersen's social attitudes, and no one can deny that Brandes put his finger on a sore spot. But at the same time one has a strong feeling that we no longer could formulate the accusation as Brandes did. It cannot be considered a failing on the ugly duckling's part, on the part of poetic genius, if it is too humble, if it shows too little arrogance at its strength and its beauty, if it remains among men and joins their community instead of mirroring its fascinating and tragic ego in a wilderness lake. In Brandes one detects the ghost of Romantic individualism from the nineteenth century's beginning, or else it is a sign of the superman who would appear at the century's close; it does not harm Andersen in our eyes if he fails to be demonic or autocratic. On the contrary: Brandes' enthusiasm for the wild, freedom-loving wolf seems to us to be a rather empty pose.

No, we should like to express our criticism in a different way. Has the ugly duckling, once he has succeeded in entering the paradise of the swans, forgotten his brothers in misery, all the other starved, mistreated, and hapless creatures? Did he lament only at his own misfortune, his own sufferings, did life's injustice merely consist in all the hardships he had to undergo himself, was he merely another of the world's many sentimental complainers? In this case Kierkegaard would have been right in his contemptuous criticism of *Only a Fiddler,* even though the philosopher himself was all too entangled in the prejudices of his time to find the correct perspective. Was Andersen, in other words, actually the incurable egoist, the literary hustler blinded by vanity, whom Carsten Hauch happened—quite by accident— to portray? Does the fairy tales' optimism, their free play of humor, simply mean that, after the poet himself is in the clear, his heart no longer bleeds so readily? And, that the sandman with his magic wand (or Fantasos with his morphine-filled needle) may take charge of the other victims?

If this had really been true in Andersen's case, then we still should not have the right to condemn him too severely, for this was the typical moral attitude of the nineteenth century's *bour-geoisie,* and one cannot require miracles of perspicacity or tolerance from Andersen. He was a child of the age of aesthetic ideal-ism, his intellectual energy was concentrated on the theater, art, lit-erature, poetry; and the refinement, the mastery, he and his kin-dred spirits achieved was dearly purchased at the cost of one-sided-ness, passivity, blindness. The world's center was the stage and the parquet of the Royal Theater at Copenhagen. Quaking, Fru Hei-berg spoke of the hyena of politics, and Andersen himself said on one occasion: "At the time when politics played no role whatsoever among us, our public life was the theater, the day's and the eve-ning's most important subject of conversation." The prerequisite condition for this attitude was that patriarchal despotism, the noblest virtues of which were incorporated in old Jonas Collin—

can one be surprised that Andersen remained unpolitical, and that he received his bread from the King's hand, as the swans did from the master of the castle? Failing that hand, he would have perished.

Of this remarkable systematic one-sidedness, which, seen from a sociological standpoint, is indissolubly connected with an exaggeratedly rich flowering of religious, asethetic, and moral ideologies, many traces are quite naturally to be found in Andersen. Georg Brandes has correctly observed that the distressing impression *The Fairy Tale of My Life* makes is not caused by the author's self-absorption—strictly speaking, an autobiography is the right place for it—but rather by the fact that Andersen's ego in this book shows itself to be so little interested in any objective idea, in what is going on among men, in the events of world history. To what extent he thoughtlessly accepted officially approved values can best be seen in his depictions of England. He noticed nothing of political problems and political strife, although his visit occurred during an election year, 1847—the Chartist riots were forerunners of 1848, the year of revolution. He portrays the political agitation in London, the speaker's stands, the election meetings, the excesses, the shabbily dressed people who, singing and shouting, came up in splendid coaches; he observes everything which passes before his eyes with a childlike curiosity, but he does not waste a thought on what these strange scenes could mean. He is deeply impressed by England's lofty moral *niveau*: "Here one visits a nation which is perhaps the only truly religious one of our age; here is respect for morals, here is morality; there is no need to dwell on the individual excrescences and aberrations which are always to be found in a great city." He speaks of home devotional services with Bible-reading for the children and the servants, a phenomenon he found in all the families he visited; it made "a beautiful and a good impression" upon him. That drunken ragamuffins were driven up to the election urns by elegant coachmen and footmen did not arouse any reflections within him, just as little as did other scenes of London life, scenes which he nonetheless could not entirely ignore. In an omnibus he saw a pale, emaciated girl, dressed in rags, hiding herself in a corner; on the streets he saw beggars, men and women alike, who bore on their breast a cardboard sign with the words: "I am dying of hunger! Have pity!"

> They dare not speak, for begging is forbidden by law, and so they glide past like shadows. They stand before one, staring with an expression of hunger and care in their pale, thin faces; they station themselves outside coffeehouses and teashops, choosing some person among the guests on whom they fix a glance such as only misery can possess; a woman points to her sick child and at the card fixed to her breast, on which one reads: "I have not eaten for two days."

But there are no beggars in the sections of the city where the rich live, Andersen adds. He no doubt suffered very much under the glances he received: the beggars of London had probably discovered his vulnerability. His own mother had been sent out to beg when she was a child, and he himself had walked the streets hungry.

He was glad to be back in Denmark in the stormy year of 1848. "Here alone peace had its home! Here one could still breathe freely, and think of seeking out art, the theater, and all that is beautiful," he wrote in *The Fairy Tale of My Life*.

But there were a number of points at which Andersen succeeded in freeing himself from prevalent catchwords. He distinguished himself from the vast majority of his Romantic fellow poets by never believing in the "good old days"—the great teller of fairy tales had no patience for that fairy tale. To a certain extent, this attitude of his perhaps was inspired by his intimate friendship with H. C. Ørsted, the liberal scientist; Ørsted's influence can easily be discerned in *The Galoshes of Fortune,* in which Andersen settles his accounts with Romanticism's enthusiasm for the middle ages. However, in the final analysis Andersen needed neither ingenious philsophical arguments nor learned historical comparisons in order to become conscious of these reactionary sophistries. Like all other genuinely poor people, he had made the necessary studies in his own self and his relatives; he knew the truth about the good old days at first hand, just as he knew the poetry of the stagecoach. Conservative panegyrics about the happiness and harmony of the past, about the healthy satisfaction of the spirit which more than outweighs its concomitant, an apparent poverty of the flesh, have stemmed, of course—directly or indirectly, consciously or unconsciously—from those privileged circles standing to profit by the idyl. If one allows members of the proletariat (or anyone else who has come to grips with the good old days) to bear witness, then the story has a different flavor. However well things went for H. C. Andersen, he was never ashamed of his origins; he never went back on his childhood memories or his family's experiences.

Thus there is no doubt at all where Andersen's deepest sympathies lie: with the unpropertied, the oppressed, and the cowed, with the people—the withered cripple in a back street, the beggar girl, the drunken laundress and her boy in his broken-billed cap. To be sure, he did not demand reforms or pose problems or incite to revolution; but although he stayed quite clear of politics, his fairy tales perhaps exerted a psychological influence nonetheless, an influence which then extended itself into the sphere of action: they had a chastening, a softening, a disturbing effect upon their readers. Edvard Lehmann attested to this fact when he wrote:

> Remember that the *Fairy Tales* were the first book we read as children, and that their gentleness toward the unfortunate became part of our initial concept of life. We heard about starving and freezing, about being mocked and crushed, and we heard the story from someone who knew whereof he spoke, from a poet who could make human existence itself speak through his words. And reality itself: for every detail is taken from reality, from the cap's broken bill to the grieving heart.

This is the influence Andersen had in Denmark, and not in Denmark alone; this is the influence he had on one generation, and on many. One thinks of the nightingale's promise to the sick emperor: that he would bring him news of happy men and of those who suffer, of the poor fisherman and the cottager's roof—that he would report whatever is otherwise kept hidden from the court and the throne. It is a program, of course, which Andersen did not realize; but the nightingale's words cannot be dismissed as exaggerations, either: attempts in this direction are to be found more than once in Andersen's works.

Andersen's social attitudes become most readily apparent in the strange tale he published in 1853 under the title *Everything in Its Right Place*. It must have been written just previous to its publication, and it shows that Andersen by no means let the revolutionary year of 1848 slip past him without a thought, a conclusion to which one might very well come after reading *The Fairy Tale of My Life*. The tale deals with the life of several generations on one of those Danish estates where Andersen, visiting as a respected and honored guest, got along so splendidly. His reception there did not keep him from making certain observations, and the more one studies them, the more respect one gets for the sense of reality the teller of fairy tales possessed. There were many contemporary historians and social philosophers who had ever so much more obscure ideas on the subject.

He tells about the old days—he begins more than a hundred years before the time of writing down the story—when the estate's masters, loving the hunt, fill the castle with their horses and their dogs and their merriment. One of the young gentlemen, overwhelmed by high spirits, pushes a poor goosegirl down into the mud of the moat, from which she is saved by a traveling peddler, who has likewise had a taste of the nobility's jests. "Everything in its right place!" was the cry as the girl was shoved into the mud, and "Everything in its right place!" the peddler repeats as he pulls her out, and plants in the earth a willow branch which the girl, reaching out, had broken off in her mortal terror. Years pass, the willow shoot grows up into a tree, the mighty squire, become a beggar, has to leave house and lands, and his successor in the castle is the peddler, grown wealthy through trade and wedded to the erstwhile goosegirl. Card games disappear and Bibles take their places; piety, industry, and thrift flourish, just like the willow beside the moat—a new dynasty has been founded. But the years continue their course, and when one has come to Andersen's own days, a blue-blooded family once again dwells in the castle: the descendants of the peddler and the goosegirl—the young barons practice with their bows and arrows, using the old family portraits of their ancestors, which have landed in the rubbish heap, as their targets. The young barons' tutor is a pastor's son, a youth filled with the thoughts of his times; taking a branch from the old willow tree, the ancestral tree, he has carved himself a flute. A great festival at the castle includes a concert, and the fine gentlemen tease the tutor, trying to force him to play a solo on his rustic instrument. At last he accedes; but it turns out that he has carved a magic flute—its wood has come from the mysterious ancestral tree whose motto is: "Everything in its right place!" The first tone from the flute resembles a locomotive's whistle, and it passes over all the land like a storm wind: the old baron flies down to the groom's cottage beside the stables, and the pastor's son finds himself sitting at the high table beside the young baroness, the daughter of the house. An ancient count from the country's oldest family is allowed to keep his place for "the flute was fair, and that's the way people are supposed to be"; but the witty gentleman lands on his head in the chicken house; the family of a rich wholesaler, out riding behind their four fine steeds, are blown out of their coach and can not even stand on the footman's dickey; two rich peasants, grown too big for their own fields, are blown down into the muddy ditch. It was a dangerous flute, H. C. Andersen concludes, but happily it went back into the owner's pocket—that is where one gets the expression "to change one's tune," he adds with a quizzical glint in his eye.

The revolution of 1848 had been broken off after the overture; the flute had been put back into the owner's pocket. Andersen had gone through approximately the same experiences as the goblin did in the grocer's house—that tale is also from 1853. During the night of tempest and fire the goblin's heart beat in warm sympathy with the student, and he wrapped his dearest treasure, the Holy Scripture, in his red goblin's cap; but when the holocaust was past, he continued his friendship with the grocer—"And that was quite human! We others also go to the grocer—for our porridge's sake." The self-ironization is subtle and witty, but *Everything in Its Right Place* offers a deeper perspective. The transition from a feudal order of society to the bourgeois-capitalistic era is brilliantly symbolized in the story of the old Danish estate, and in it Andersen has taken as critical and as just a view of the middle class as of the nobility. He had not sworn an oath of allegiance to either side.

In the Romantic little verse-drama about Christian II, *The King Is Dreaming* (1844), he has Dyveke, the king's mistress, utter the democratic thought: true nobility, that nobility which the Lord has created, has nothing to do with shields and scutcheons. But his feeling appears with quite a different clarity in the novel *The Two Baronesses,* which was published both in Danish and English in the very year of revolution, 1848, late in the fall. The theme of the novel has an obvious connection with *Everything in Its Right Place*; the chief character, the old baroness, is a sister of the goose-girl in the fairy tale, but her personality has taken a more original development. In her childhood she saw her father, Tall Rasmus, forced to ride a sawhorse as punishment for not being able to pay tenant's rent on his wretched husbandman's cottage, and when, creeping up, she tried to ameliorate her father's torments by shoving a stone under his foot, she got a taste of the master's riding crop—a truly fearful scene from "the good old days," Andersen remarks. The child from the proletariat becomes a baroness, the lady of the castle, but she never forgets the event, and even in her old age she still broods over the memory with bitterness and hatred in her heart. In her castle there is a secret chamber where she keeps her wooden shoes and the rotted boards of the sawhorse and a portrait of the master. Again and again she returns to the chamber, as if she were bewitched: "I knew those times, I remember the evil days when honorable men went to the dogs, when an honest peasant rode a sawhorse and an innocent child was beaten by the master's whip." Her frenzied hatred abates only in one of novel's final chapters; as a Christian, she decides to forgive and forget, she gives away the portrait and the sawhorse to be used for kindling:

Illustration from *The Nightingale*.

"At least they'll bring some warmth beneath the poor man's soup-kettle!"

One cannot mistake the fact: the injustice and brutality of the previous age pursued Andersen like a nightmare. Moreover, it must be remembered that neither the self-centered egoist nor the querulous sentimentalist is giving voice to his resentments here, for it is highly unlikely that Andersen ever endured severe corporal punishment, even as a small boy in school. Instead, he has become a spokesman for the experiences, sufferings, and thoughts of society's lower strata, the strata to which he belonged.

There is nothing which would indicate that H. C. Andersen ever forgot his origins, however high he climbed on the social ladder. On the contrary: one gets the impression that these feelings of human solidarity were best able to assert themselves in Andersen's old age, after his passionate ambition, surfeited with prey, had finally begun to doze a little. In 1867, on the way home from Paris, he stopped at Odense; a festival, bringing all classes of the town's society together, was being held to welcome a battalion which had just been transferred to the capital of Fyn; and the soldiers were greeted with songs and flying colors. Attending the celebration, Andersen told a friend about another visit he had once paid to the Odense riding school, where the ceremonies were concluded: as a little boy he had been there to see a soldier run the gauntlet. "How bright and beautiful our time is in comparison with those old days I knew," he burst out. His own father had been a soldier; as a schoolboy he had been present at that popular amusement, the public execution—it is not surprising that he could give such a vivid description of the moments leading up to the soldier's near execution in *The Tinderbox*.

In the spring of 1872 he came once more to Nuremberg, and he described the Romantic aspects of the medieval city with enthusiastic admiration. One can tell that he belonged to the generation whose feeling for the poetry of history had been awakened by Walter Scott. "You are in the city of the middle class, where artisanship became art," he writes, wandering amidst memorials of the past. But he closes by hesitating before the Spanish Coat, the Fiddle, the Spanish Boot, and the Iron Maiden. "And this was the Golden Age, brilliant and free, of the middle class," he remarks, "in those olden times whose praise we sing to the skies." Such is "the mighty and venerable city of the *bourgeoisie,* the Meistersingers' city"; in its atmosphere we perceive a cold shudder, a cry of pain. Quite humbly, Andersen agrees with an old woman of Nuremberg: "Those days are past, the Lord be praised!"

If one assembles all these testimonies, one is inclined to declare Andersen innocent of the charge that he got along much too well with Copenhagen's patriciate and Denmark's nobility, at courts and in castles. It may be that the swan bowed his neck in greeting; he also lifted his head in pride. It may be that he took his bread from his masters' hands; he had earned it honestly, and no one need begrudge him the crumbs. All the gratitude and friendship he felt for his benefactors—and primarily for the noble, the incomparable Jonas Collin—is accurately mirrored in the fairy tales. He had not forgotten the shadows of the past, and he kept his glance toward the future.

"Only a Fiddler" was the title he once gave to his hero and to himself. But the instrument he played on was, to be sure, not a doomsday trump, designed to make walls come tumbling down, nor a warlike bugle, for firing soldiers' hearts; his instrument always retained, perhaps, something of the rustic willow-flute's idyllic and pastoral tone—but "the flute was fair, and that's the way people are supposed to be." It played a melody which tried to put everything in its right place.

CHAPTER XV

Lucky Peer

ALTHOUGH THE FAIRY TALES became the main thing, for Denmark and all the world as for Andersen himself, their supremacy does not at all mean that he put his authorship's other aspects on the shelf—on the contrary: considered quantitatively, the fairy tales comprise only a rather small part of his life's work. In particular, he never stopped seeking to win the theater's favor; one could not expect that a Dane and a resident of Copenhagen would do so. He experienced a couple of inglorious failures, which threw him into utter despair, and several decided successes, which delighted him; to the latter category belong the Romantic Singspiel, *Little Kirsten* (1846), with music by Johan Peter Hartmann, and the comedy, *The New Lying-in Room* (1845). He often had his pieces played under the shield of anonymity, a common practice in this age of bitter competition and conspicuous envy; every now and again he succeeded in getting that stern critic, Heiberg, to grant him a measure of approval for his poetic touch and his inventiveness. But it is significant that he achieved his greatest theatrical triumphs only when he put his fairy-tale motifs on the boards, writing such "fairy-tale comedies" as *More than Pearls and Gold* (1849), *The Sandman* (1850), and *Elder-Bush Mother* (1851). Nor were these plays produced at the Royal Theater; they were given instead at the Casino, the new popular stage. There no one could prevent Andersen from taking the public by storm— actually, the success of these comedies was but a reflection, behind the footlights, of the fairy tales' unique popularity. In reality, his first great love—his love for the theater—remained unanswered; his plays have been given outside Denmark only on the rarest of occasions.

Fortune proved equally faithless to him when, in 1847, he attempted to follow in the footsteps of Goethe's *Faust* and similar weighty creations by writing a major drama about the Wandering Jew. The drama's name is *Ahasverus,* and its protagonist is the fallen angel of doubt and disbelief, who passes through world history as representative of pessimism. The drama contains Andersen's liberal faith in progress; and in its colorful variety of scenes, employing the world's many epochs and their celebrated men, his imagination can run riot; but no dramatic unity is achieved. A Swedish reader will note, however, that the play's basic thought and many of its details seem to have exerted an influence on Viktor Rydberg.

The novels and the travel books, on the other hand, were warmly received by Andersen's own contemporaries, both at home in Denmark and in the great world beyond; and they offer much which is also worthy of the attention of later generations. All in all, *The Two Baronesses* from 1848 is probably his best novel, and his social pathos shines through the figure of the old baroness. It is characteristic that, while the three earlier novels were more or less patent self-glorifications, *The Two Baronesses,* a realistic story of everyday life, provides an ironic and critical self-portrait; the "Kammerjunker's" arrogance and egoism is made the target of censure—although the censure, to be sure, is mild. In the novel *To Be or Not To Be,* written in 1857, Andersen treats a religious problem instead of a social one, and the autobiographical element disappears altogether. He speaks affirmatively, in H. C. Ørsted's spirit, of the natural sciences, of the world of technology, and of reason's power, while indulging in polemics against a narrow and intolerant "religion of the heart" and attacking superstition—here his need of the miraculous is not satisfied by a reactionary enthusiasm for the symbols of the past, but rather by a courageous glance into humanity's future. It is the artisan-philosophy of his unhappy father; Hans Christian has stuck to the shoemaker's last, although he makes his spokeswoman, Esther, quote Goethe's *Faust* as her bible, and his hero, Niels Bryde, cites Ørsted as his witness. The poet, the novel says, must be modern, he must employ the spirits of knowledge to build his Aladdin's castle, he must throw whatever is antiquated into the attic of poetry. Amusingly enough, Niels Bryde predicts the radio with the accuracy of an Andersen prophesying airplane traffic: some day people in Copenhagen will hear Liszt playing in Weimar.

On the boundary line between novel and fairy tale, even to its size, stands *Lucky Peer,* which appeared in 1870. In this witty story, sparkling with many humorous details, Andersen has returned to that inexhaustible theme, his own life story, yet he speaks more quietly than before; the hero is a true darling of fortune, he wins everything, fame, fortune, and love, but consequently he must pay a price—he dies in his hour of triumph. Otherwise, how could it be a story?

The book *In Sweden,* about Andersen's trip to that country in 1849, was published only in 1851. He describes the Swedish struggle, led by Gustav Vasa, for independence from Denmark with striking objectivity; it is not the only occasion upon which the "childlike" H. C. Andersen, the creature of fantasy and emotion, showed a wisdom and a fairness his highly rational contemporaries often lacked. He was substantially less a chauvinist than the respected and likable realist, Edvard Collin, or than the exquisitely polished jewel, Johanne Luise Heiberg. On Midsummer's Eve, 1849, Andersen was in Leksand, cutting out some new cookie-shapes for his good hosts—he was a master with the scissors, although he never became a tailor as his mother wished him to do— and at last he uttered the pious wish that a part of him might live forever in Dalecarlia, "in new cookie-shapes": he searched for immortality with scissors, too. With his picturesque descriptions of Lake Siljan he gave a direct inspiration to Vilhelm Marstrand and so to Scandinavian painting. Thus he had an enormous influence: in literature itself he is the incomparable teacher who, to take only a few examples, had Viktor Rydberg, August Strindberg, Selma Lagerlöf, and Oscar Wilde as his disciples. What a mixed bag of pupils—and what a cunning person the gawky village schoolmaster was!

In the north, then, he crossed the Dalälv, and in the south he got all the way to Africa, an experience described in the book *In Spain* (1863). This travel book surely does not betray its author's increasing years; on the contrary, it has an astonishingly bold impressionism in its style, and the poems inserted into the text are more direct, freer in attitude, hotter and sunnier than the majority of his previous lyrics. All the monuments of Spain's vanished greatness did not put him in an elegiac mood; he praised the modern age; and, taking his departure, sang:

Presently you have grown youthful,
For your monks you've chased away;
I predict: Spain will its flowering
In the future's book display.

Andersen had always suffered a great deal because of Denmark's damp, cool weather; now he is as if intoxicated by Spain's sunny warmth. He praises the fiery Spanish colors of red and gold, colors united in the cactus flower. He stands enchanted on a street in Malaga:

By the wall of the house stood a hedge of geranium's splendor;
There she sat on the marble stone of the stair:
So young, so lovely: she was a chestnut vendor,
And sat with bare legs and a flower in her hair.
With two lively eyes she sat and watched one there:
If one weren't an ice-man, they would him a Spaniard render.

In contrast to the woman of the north, whom he compares to a dreaming lotus on a quiet lake, he celebrates the Spanish beauty:

You possess magic, fiery Spanish bloom:
Child turns to maiden in a moment's room.
Here life is a kiss, sweet disappearing.
Burn me then to ashes, let me die.

In another little poem he says that the fairy tales of the north bud in the warmth of a tile stove, but here they grow wild everywhere in nature:

If you're young yourself, real flame and real fire,
Then you'll be consumed on a fairy-tale pyre.

228

In his imagination he has even embarked upon the adventure, and with drastic humor he depicts his awakening out of his ecstasy:

> *Where's my passport! Where's my inspiration*
> *Defend me*
> *Against the Medusa of the Spanish nation!*
> *The Inquisition's got me.*

There is an amazing verve in these lines: the fifty-eight-year-old poet has a buoyant vitality. It is as though youth and the erotic dream stirred his blood for the last time on this trip to Spain.

The author of *In Spain,* one should think, ought not to have been suspected of lacking a normal masculine nature. He had been in love several times. His youthful affection for Riborg Voigt was followed by the infatuation with Louise Collin, and, at the end of the 1830's, he had felt a strong attraction to the seventeen-year-old Sophie Ørsted, the daughter of his great and good friend, the famous physicist; but she became engaged to another and, simultaneously, Andersen believed that he himself lacked the necessary economic qualifications for marriage. His life's last great passion was directed to Jenny Lind. In 1840 she had not made any very strong impression upon him, but in 1843, during her appearances in Copenhagen, he caught fire. One can follow the story in his diaries from September of that year; as early as the tenth he jots down the word "enamored," and by the eighteenth the intensity has increased to: "I love her." Upon her departure, on the twentieth, he came down to the dockside customs shed, and at the last minute handed her a letter which, according to the diary, "she must understand." There is no doubt that she did understand the letter's author: she felt a strong sympathy for the great literary artist, who for her was both a congenial spirit and a comrade—like Andersen, Jenny Lind had ascended from society's depths by means of her genius. But evidently she never felt the slightest erotic affection for the writer, and, in some letters preserved from 1843 and 1846, she expressly declined any thought of marriage. Her emotions were only friendship and sisterly devotion; in 1845, upon their meeting once again in Copenhagen, the poet had dinner with her at the Hotel Royale just before her departure, and subsequently knew the bittersweet satisfaction of making the following entry in his diary: "She toasted me as her brother." The next day, October 22, there are the laconic words: "Said good-by to Jenny!"

Yet they soon were reunited, at Berlin in December of the same year. Andersen was so very sure that he would spend Christmas Eve with the singer that he turned down every other invitation for the evening. But Christmas Eve came, and he sat alone in his hotel room, on the verge of tears—opening his window, he looked out at the starry sky. (At least, that is the story he told; however the description, as Helge Topsøe-Jensen has pointed out, seems "a little artificial.")

The next morning, feeling insulted, he complained about his hard lot to Jenny Lind herself. "I thought you were visiting your princes and princesses," she retorted, according to *The Fairy Tale of My Life,* and then he confessed to her that he had said "no" to everyone for her sake, that he had been looking forward to the evening for a long time, that it was just for this reason he had come to Berlin. "You child," she said smiling, stroked his forehead, and arranged for him to have a Christmas tree on New Year's Eve. Then they sat together beneath the fir tree, Andersen got all the presents which hung from the branches, and Jenny Lind sang a great aria and some Swedish songs for him. But they were not alone, her chaperone was present; and the whole story got into the

newspapers, a sentimental picture abounding in atmosphere: the
two brilliant children of nature from the north, against a background of green fir branches and Christmas stars. Later they met
in Weimar and in London, but nothing more ever came of it than
just such poetic scenes. Then, in 1852, Andersen, who had been
jealous of the Swedish singer, Julius Günther, had to endure the
awful news that Jenny had married Otto Goldschmidt, a German
pianist, conductor, and composer. But Andersen bore his fate
resignedly, as he had before. When, in his old age, he sent her his
Lucky Peer, her reply was friendly but a little over-pious; she had
gradually developed into a religious bigot. It had been twenty
years since she had last written to him.

But during the 1840's she had played a great role for the author,
and the best of his fairy tales bear witness in a great variety of
ways to the inspiration she gave him. She is the nightingale, her
song is health and life, balm and consolation. Andersen
plainly regarded her vocal art as a complement to his literary
production, and, as far as enraptured natural poetry is concerned
there is certainly a resemblance. Yet the Swedish nightingale had
nothing of Andersen's humor; instead she possessed that lyric
pathos, directed to a single goal, which one so often finds in Swedish art. It was only in Europe's eyes that they belonged under the
same Scandinavian rubric.

The passion for Jenny Lind is the final one to be discovered in
Andersen's life. Beginning with his school days in Slagelse,
the unrest of the blood had caused him many torments, and in his
diary it is touching to read of how he longed for the physical presence of a woman. He was especially prone to such sensual excitement on his journeys to the south. But this urge on Andersen's
part never found a natural outlet; religious and moral considerations prevented him from establishing any sort of purely physical

relationship, although the struggle against temptation was now and again a hard one. Instead his sexual life found a kind of satisfaction in the pitiable surrogate which otherwise is a customary phenomenon of puberty; mystical signs in his diary betray his secret, and one can also detect torments of conscience and fears about the consequences the practice may have for his health. At times he evidently imagined that his neurasthenic exhaustion, a condition which in his case can be called the normal one, had been caused by his sinning along this line.

This is the background of Andersen's erotic innocence, which he no doubt preserved uncorrupted his whole life through, and which he confessed in *The Rose Bud*:

> *Rosebud: round and firm displayed,*
> *Lovely as a mouth of maid:*
> *I shall kiss you as my bride,*
> *Fairer still your bloom will bide.*
> *One kiss more my lips require,*
> *Now feel my fire!*
>
> *I'll confess, as well I should:*
> *Till now my lips had maidenhood!*
> *And no maid awaits me true—*
> *I must kiss, rose, none but you!*
> *Oh, you know not my desire—*
> *Now feel my fire!*

Atterbom once spoke of the "vestal purity" of his friend Törneros. An inevitable prerequisite of such vestal purity seems to be either a condition like Andersen's or some other more profound abnormality. Some researchers have chosen to burden Andersen with the latter alternative, but they are quite plainly wrong.

Neither his warm cult of friendship for Edvard Collin, the Grand
Duke of Weimar, and others, nor his love of children, contains any
element of perversion. He was a normal person and a normal man,
although a man whose sexual life had been stunted by an unkind
fate.

One would obtain a warped and incomplete—and thus an ambiguous—image of Andersen's nature by neglecting, for reasons
of propriety, to mention these aspects of his personality. They
have been so clearly illuminated in Hjalmar Helweg's psychiatric study that future misapprehensions would seem to be pre-
cluded.

In *Lucky Peer,* Andersen depicted his alter ego, and had him
showered with all of fortune's gifts, not merely with artistic
triumphs but also with a woman's love and with gold. In his own
life he had been forced to do without love; as far as gold is concerned, he had not been quite so hapless. The musical genius, Lucky
Peer, was able to set up a serene and cheerful home for his poor
parents—it is characteristic of Andersen that his imagination
found an outlet of this sort. It was never vouchsafed him to carry
out a similar deed in reality; he was still without means at the time
of his mother's death. But he gradually achieved a certain solid
prosperity; he could easily satisfy his personal wishes—to be well
or even elegantly dressed, and to make the long journeys he loved.

However, he did not become rich. This resulted in part from the
insufficient protection his age afforded in matters of intellectual
proprietorship; for, under any reasonably equitable system of literary copyright, Andersen would eventually have enjoyed a gigan-
tic income. And it must not be forgotten that he failed to take advantage of the economic possibilities which did exist. There
is an amusing anecdote about a conversation between Charles

Dickens and H. C. Andersen. Dickens, who lived from his pen and lived like a prince, asked his Danish friend and colleague what royalties he had received for the novel *The Improvisator*. "Nineteen pounds," came Andersen's reply. "Per sheet?" Dickens inquired. "No, for the whole book," the unhappy Dane insisted. Since the one party to the conversation was not very strong in English and the other was weak in Danish, Dickens was convinced that a misunderstanding had crept into their talk, and kept returning with energetic curiosity to the theme. Nothing could be done about the matter from a linguistic standpoint, however, and Dickens finally stood convinced and amazed. Financial and juridical improvements were in order.

It is worth noting that Andersen mentions the economic side of his authorship only on the rarest of occasions, and always in a lighthearted tone. Thus a striking contrast is formed to the ravenous hunger with which he watched over his fame and over the praise lavished upon him. As he planned his trip to England in 1847, King Christian VIII offered to grant him a subsidy so that he could make an appearance in keeping with his station—after all, he already had a great reputation in England. Andersen refused the offer with a becoming insouciance: he preferred not to correspond about money matters, he would rather write to his monarch unhampered by any ulterior or practical motives.

The Swedish nightingale seems to have understood the rewards of song better than the Danish poet; at least that was Andersen's impression. In England he introduced the old banker, Hambro, to Jenny Lind; the two got on famously together, he reports, discussing financial affairs and laughing at the childlike Andersen, who had not the foggiest idea what they were talking about.

In this case as in others, Andersen demonstrates an indisputable ability at putting his own childlike innocence in a good

234

light; but what he says is true, at least to a certain extent. In his old age, however, he was glad that he had become the master of a little fortune. Edvard Collin, the friend of his youth, had taken charge of his affairs; and he attended to them as sensibly and carefully, as devotedly and unselfishly, as he performed every other task he undertook on Andersen's account. Every New Year's Day, and frequently in between, Edvard Collin gave his restless friend a lucid and exhaustive report on his financial situation, for Andersen easily forgot figures, and time and time again he was seized by worries: perhaps he did not have enough money for his frequent and protracted journeys, perhaps he would find himself in straitened and perilous financial circumstances during his last years on earth. Edvard Collin could always pacify him: the small fortune was constantly growing, and at the end of 1867 he reported a sum of more than 14,000 rix-dollars, "apart from my friendship now and in the future," he adds cheerfully and charmingly. At the end of 1869, upon Andersen's firm declaration that he, God willing, wished always to have an untouched capital of 12,000 rix-dollars, Edvard Collin was able to assure him that he had over 15,000, and then, too, he would probably win the lottery on January 13! The experienced savings-bank director amused himself and his friend by taking out mortgages on castles in Spain in this frivolous way. "Money wants company"—a saying which is valid in every case, even in that of Andersen, the child of the proletariat: in July 1874, he confesses to Edvard Collin that, for safety's sake, he would like to attain a fortune of 24,000 rix-dollars. And Edvard Collin replies by return mail: at the moment his account consists of 23,842 rix-dollars and 15 shillings. There was really not much missing in Andersen's earthly happiness—but then, the hourglass had almost run out.[1]

[1] According to Svend Larsen's investigation, published in *Anderseniana*, 1953,

With the thousand rix-dollars of his poet's stipend from the Danish state, the thousand in annuities, and the author's royalties, which, despite the absence of proper laws, came trickling in from Germany, England, America, and Sweden, the old poet had nothing to worry about; even in the last summer of Andersen's life, in June, 1875, Edvard Collin had to break off his vacation hobby (moving manure in a wheelbarrow on his summer place at Hellebæk), in order to write letters repeating his assurances that his friend could get to be as old as Methuselah—he would still, if a human being can judge, never have to suffer any want. This financial disquietude was, as a matter of fact, only an expression of Andersen's general anxiety, which seized upon the most unimportant bagatelles. At the utmost, one can say that the man who had had such a hard time in his youth never got rid of his terror.

And still more significant is the fact that, his whole life long, he cherished a burning hope that he would win in the national lottery —Edvard Collin could not keep from joking about his ineradicable optimism. In the final analysis it was not for the money's sake, since he had more than he could use; in his imagination he drew up plans about which persons he would render happy when his number, 41,214, came up—a number which Edvard Collin faithfully renewed year after year at his friend's behest. In November, 1873, the number bore winnings of five hundred rix-dollars, which Edvard Collin immediately put into the savings account; but this was, of course, almost a disappointment: Andersen had always dreamed of getting the grand prize. In the diaries from his last

---

the estate of the deceased showed a residue of more than 53,000 crowns (about $7,571), somewhat more than 24,000 rix-dollars; this corresponds to a vastly greater sum in present currency. In contrast to his debt-ridden fellow poets, Adam Oehlenschläger and Christian Winther, Andersen had become a wealthy man.

years one can see with what febrile excitement he followed the drawings: like a child, he waxes fidgety, hopeful, and desperate in turn; he appeals to heaven and to fate with something of the same soft, ingratiating, penetrating glow which he, in his youth, put into his prayers to God about examinations, moves, and salvation from hunger. One finds the dulcet formulation: "I believe that something good still awaits me." One is reminded of beggar children in the Orient, who, pleading for baksheesh, employ such gestures and such a tone of voice that pockets are turned inside out all by themselves, and purses spring open with a snap. On November 10, 1870, he noted that Reitzel had sent him the first copies of *Lucky Peer,* bound in red and with gilded edges—and on the very day of the book's distribution there is a drawing in the Lottery: "I wonder if I myself am Lucky Peer?" The query is repeated year after year; in September, 1872, he writes: "It's really too annoying, I didn't win this time either, damn the lottery! ! ! But this evening I see that the 60,000 [the grand prize] have not been drawn for as yet, and I feel a strange flare of hope—may I win them tomorrow: what a lot of fun that would be, and may I use them well, in their entirety!" It sounds as though he already had them. Then, the next day: "I didn't win the least thing in the lottery. In a bitter mood. Fortune is no longer with *me.*"

The cat is out of the bag. It is not the money which lures him, he has no need of it. Instead, it is the feeling of being Lucky Peer, of being in alliance with God, with the mysterious inner principle of existence. This is the premise for his existence and the fairy tales' existence, and he cannot let go of it, as long as there is life and breath in his frail body. Until the very moment of death the poet of the fairy tales thirsts for new proofs of the truth which has carried him to victory: life is a fairy tale, and I am Lucky Peer.

Yet Lucky Peer, like all other children, did not get everything he wanted. He did not win the grand prize, either in love or in gold; but he got what he coveted most hotly, in the full measure that befits a darling of the gods. A few months before his death, he noted that London's *Evening News* had called him "the most-read poet of the age," and had ranked the fairy tales with the works of Homer and Shakespeare.

And this strongest urge in his nature: was it not ultimately a dark and confused form of something higher and more holy? Did Lucky Peer, in the last analysis, search for something other than fortune? On November 14, 1870, he spoke of Thorvaldsen and himself, the most famous of all Danes, both of them poor men's children—he believed, by the way, that Thorvaldsen's fame would outlast his own. Then he added: "Is this vanity? I wonder if I shall know someday? Lord, Lord! Is immortality a dream of vanity and are we merely toys of Thy omnipotence? Lord, Creator, *Father,* take not Thy hand from us!"

CHAPTER XVI

The End of the Fairy Tale

OLD AGE CAME RELATIVELY EARLY for Hans Christian Andersen, perhaps because the hard conditions of his youth had exhausted him, after all. He had many aches and pains, some real and more imaginary, but he kept his vivacity: he did not like to go to bed; trips, social life, attendance at the theater amused him, even though he felt poorly. His toothaches were frequent and violent, and in the last fairy tale he completed, *Aunt Toothache* from 1872, he succeeded in producing something humorous and graceful from even this earthly infirmity, a deed which can well be reckoned among the fairy-tale-poet's greatest triumphs.

Gradually he had become one of Denmark's great men. He had already been given the title of professor in 1851; in 1858 he was made a man of the Dannebrog; in 1867, Councillor of State; and on December 6, 1867, Odense celebrated his selection as the town's honorary citizen with a national festival, to which King Christian sent telegraphic congratulations in his own name and in that of the royal family. Andersen, who was the guest of the Bishop of Odense during his visit, saw the torches shining and the banners waving before the town hall, and as he stepped forward to the open window, his thoughts, no doubt for the hundredth time, went to Aladdin upon the castle balcony: "A poor boy, I too walked along those streets." But as the songs and the applause rose up around him, he stood there physically exhausted and psychically overwhelmed, the ice-cold air made his teeth throb unbearably, and he counted the number of strophes in the printed version of the song, wondering if he could hold himself erect until the end; he did so, somehow, his toothache disappeared as soon as the torches were extinguished, the eyes of the throng, filled with a friendly light, were turned toward him, and, despite everything, he felt happy and grateful. Among those who sought him out after the ceremony was an ancient widow, whom his parents had given a meal now and then; she remembered him as a child, and now she wept at the torches—"it's just the way it was when the King and Queen came to town." He liked to hear such things; they reminded him of an event which had occurred in May, 1866: sighting the Bordeaux steamer, all the Danish vessels in Lisbon harbor had run up their colors in belief that Andersen was on board. He got moral and aesthetic satisfaction out of events like these— he was still the poor boy. He continued to think of himself as such when, in 1869, he became a Commander of the Dannebrog, and when, on his birthday in 1874, he was named Conferential Councillor—a title, as he explained in a letter to his old friend, Grand Duke Carl Alexander of Weimar, with which Oehlenschläger and Thorvaldsen had been favored before him. These are no unessential details—they meant a great deal to him. He was delighted when he became a Commander of the Dannebrog's First Class in 1875, when foreign monarchs decorated him, when the King and the Crown Prince came repeatedly to visit him in his furnished rooms in Nyhavn, or when he was familiarly treated at Amalienborg Palace: all the members of the royal family received him on the ground floor, so that he could avoid going up the stairs—after one such visit he came home bearing the King's own traveling bag as a present, and it now stands in the museum at Odense.

One can attain a much better understanding of Andersen's sensitivity in these matters by reading of a dream which he had in October, 1867, at Basnæs, the Scavenius estate; he describes it in a letter to Henriette Collin:

> I thought I was in Meisling's house; it was just the same, down to the last detail, save that Meisling, amidst all his bitter mockery, called me "Councillor of State." Yet a change had taken place within me: I got up from the school bench, threw my books at him, and left the room; but now something else characteristic occurred, which revealed how dispirited I was in those days: I was afraid to show myself in the presence of your father-in-law, and so I turned to Edvard first, but he began a stern lecture, in the course of which I fortunately awakened.

If a frightened schoolboy is concealed within one's breast, then a decoration on the outside can be a comfort.

Old Jonas Collin, he too a Conferential Councillor (but on other grounds), Andersen's savior as well as fatherly protector, and one of those rare people truly deserving to be called noble, had begun to fade away during the early 1850's. Never left in peace during his days of power, he now sat alone a great deal, and, approaching his eighties, he passed the time by writing an autobiography, which is exclusively a "memorial of his toils." But he lived on in his quiet family circle until 1861, dying on August 28 of that year after a protracted and wasting illness, eighty-five years old. Andersen did not stand at his deathbed; he had invited young Jonas Collin, the grandson, to accompany him on a long trip to Italy, Switzerland, and Germany, and Edvard and Henriette Collin often wrote letters to the travelers from the old gentleman's desk in the house on Amaliengade. They sat and watched, listened to the patient's breathing, and waited for death finally to conquer the vigorous body, which, although it had taken almost no nourishment for weeks, still had some vital resources of strength left. Andersen, who, after his return home, had taken up abode at Basnæs, arrived only for the funeral. "It's a sad home-coming," he wrote upon receiving the news of Jonas Collin's death, "but we who held together before must now hold together still more firmly."

Among Jonas Collin's merits was, of course, his salvation of the friendship between Hans Christian and Edvard Collin. They remained faithful friends, even though they never used the familiar mode of address. Edvard was inexhaustible in his solicitude; the dryness and the abruptness of his nature became milder with the years, and he even learned to show his feelings. When this happened, Andersen was deeply touched. On May 22, 1873, writing from the Swiss Alps, he expressed his thanks for a letter, full of friendship and brotherly affection, which he had received from Edvard:

I have many friends, yes, some who take as lively an interest in me as they would if I were a member of their immediate family— the Melchiors, for example, but you, dear friend, are the oldest of my friends, from the time you helped me with my Latin compo-

sitions and were a little too much of a mentor toward me, until the
most recent years, when our relationship became completely unclouded.
You have also become so incomparably youthful and soft, in a
good sense of the word, since that serious and dangerous operation
of yours. All of your many admirable qualities shine through on
every occasion, and I am not the only person who sees you thus, you
are infinitely dear to me and I shall pray Our Lord to let you survive
me, for I cannot do without you. The words I write here come from
my heart, you will understand me. It is wonderful to have friends
in this world, friends such as I have.

Reading these lines, even Edvard Collin melted; on May 27 he
wrote in reply: "I am profoundly touched by your affectionate
statements concerning me in your last letter; I shall put it among
the other documents which concern my own person." In the voluminous
book which Edvard Collin published in 1882, seven years
after his friend's death, under the title *H. C. Andersen and the
Collin Family,* one finds nothing which borders on the panegyric
and a great deal that is critical; but it does contain some simple
sentences of great import: "I have looked into the depths of his
soul .... I know *that he was good."* The italics are Edvard Collin's
own.

Andersen never gave up his position as a member of the
Collin family; he was an intimate friend of several generations.
Edvard's brother Theodor Collin was his physician, Edvard's son
Jonas accompanied him on trips abroad, in the course of which the
young natural scientist had a chance to satisfy his passion for collecting
snails. On one of the trips, the younger Jonas Collin reports,
Andersen proposed that his companion should call him *"du"*;
the young man naturally put up some shy objections, but was
voted down: "You simply cannot say no, once upon a time your

father refused the same request, and it saddened me." Jonas Collin adds: "At this time I knew nothing about what had happened, and so we began calling one another *'du.'* " Edvard's sister Ingeborg, the Collin with the best understanding of the poet, had a daughter Jonna, who married Baron Stampe; from this marriage was born a daughter, Rigmor Stampe, who became Andersen's godchild and favorite. In 1918 she published her book, *H. C. Andersen and His Intimates,* filled with subtle understanding and wise admiration. The book represents, as it were, a final living testimony from the Collins' circle and a compensation for whatever the circle may have lacked in appreciation of the artist.

For Andersen did receive more appreciation in other quarters, and this was one of the reasons for the assiduity with which he visited other families during the last years of his life. The old man, feeling the chill gather in his bones, needed sunshine, he wanted to be spoiled, to be paid a little more attention than was customary among the Collins. Two wealthy Jewish families, the Henriques and the Melchiors, related to one another by marriage, were especially devoted to the world-famous poet, showering him with admiration, solicitude, and real devotion; they added luster to their name by having him as a guest of their circle for long periods, both in Copenhagen and out in the country: Melchior's handsome country house, "Rolighed" ("Repose"), beside the Øresund became in particular a second home for Andersen. One may not ignore the fact that Andersen's presence did give a certain brilliance to his surroundings, and that both the Henriques and the Melchiors were more sensitive to this side of the matter than the straightforward Collins had been; it gave them the strength for greater sacrifices and still more patience. And finally it must be remembered that the rich merchants had better material resources than did the Collins, a family of bourgeois officials. But not the least

244

shadow falls upon the relationship of the Henriques and the Melchiors to Andersen; the letters they exchanged bear good witness
to a sincere and considerate friendship on both sides, and the
element of unselfish devotion in Fru Melchior's attitude became
admirably apparent as she was transformed more and more into
a consoling spirit, a helper, a nurse.

But vying with Copenhagen's *bourgeoisie* one now found the
aristocracy, the country squires, with whom the poet Andersen
maintained close connections—he loved the historical castles, the
parks and the gardens, the avenues with their shadows, the moats
with their swans, the forest glades stretching down toward the
Sound or the sea: all those things of which he had given such
superb descriptions. Helge Topsøe-Jensen, the most outstanding
of our Andersen experts, has concluded that the poet visited about
thirty estates: he was at Glorup, the estate of Count Moltke, twenty-
four times (1839–69), at Basnæs with the Scavenius family thirty-
seven times (1855–72), and fifteen times at Holsteinborg, where
Countess Mimi Holstein, nee Zahrtmann, was the most charming
and sympathetic of hostesses. And Andersen got along splendidly
in these princely surroundings. Henriette Collin found herself in
a position to tease him a little: he no longer paid as frequent visits
to her and her husband's summer home, Ellekilde, a modest and
cozy place near Hellebæk. Writing to him on July 2, 1871, she
chided him by saying that a visit from him would seem "like royal
personages amusing themselves by seeing how their poor subjects
lived." Andersen himself put the blame on the strong gales and
chilly weather he would be exposed to beside the open sound; he
sought shelter in castle parks. But it is plain, for the rest, that certain aspects of his personality showed themselves to excellent advantage in distinguished milieus: he was really something of a
courtier and a diplomat, he had a certain fastidiousness in his blood,

245

like the princess on the pea—and had he not been hatched from a swan's egg? It was naturally a relief for him to move in circles where he had never been a comical, unpolished suppliant. In his old age he became a grand seigneur among grand seigneurs. Coming as a boy to visit his relatives at Holsteinborg, Kristian Zahrtmann, the great painter-to-be, met Andersen there; he looked at the poet of the fairy tales and described his impression thus: he was unbelievably large and rawboned, he made both an important and a fine appearance—but people were in the habit of calling him ugly. This was in 1861. As an old man, after he had given up the false teeth which were much too large for him, "he got a quite unusually handsome head," Zahrtmann attests, although almost everyone was blind to this beauty. It was not banal; it was expressive of his spirit.

One receives the same attractive impression of his spiritual nature from the letters and sketches of the charming Countess Mimi Holstein. Topsøe-Jensen has made the pertinent observation that she belongs to the second generation, to those who in their childhood had learned to love and admire Andersen through his fairy tales, and who now were becoming acquainted with the man himself. And for Mimi Holstein, who had first seen Andersen in her parents' home when she was a ten-year-old girl, he remained forever in a transfigured light; she seems not to have noticed anything of his weaknesses, of his personal peculiarities, and in her confidential letters to her husband she speaks of nothing save the happiness, the contentment, the poetic aura her elderly friend disseminated throughout the whole castle and the whole family. There is only one explanation for this: that he must have been irresistibly lovable toward masters and servants, toward children and adults —witty and amusing, both when he of an evening read aloud his fairy tales, recent stories or the old, familiar ones, and when he cut out paper dolls for the children, and when, late in the fall or even winter, times at which no one else could find any beauty left in nature, he came home from his promenades with unusual bouquets of flowers. If he had not really possessed such personal qualities and such social talents, his whole remarkable career would have been inexplicable and the fairy tales would have remained unwritten. But his all too intimate friends could not perceive this charming aspect of Andersen in quite the same unsullied purity as did the gentle, intelligent, and highly cultured Countess Mimi Holstein, filled as she was with unquestioning admiration. Coming to Holsteinborg once in December, he was met by a closed coach containing a heater and a basket of flowers. Then he wrote in his diary: "The sun was shining brightly. At the stroke of two I arrived at the castle and was warmly received by the count, the countess, and all the children; I got my customary two rooms, and a table filled with flowers was brought in; it was all warm and cozy. Elizabeth was given a volume of fairy tales:

> *Whenever in this book you read*
> *Its first leaf will be able*
> *To call you rosebud of the breed*
> *Born in the realm of fable."*

This was the old storyteller's everyday life at its most festive.

Every now and then there came times when he found life hard to bear. His frame of mind became all the more labile as the years passed, subject to attacks of anxiety and nervousness; his morbid fancies became ever more frequent and ever more severe. His intimates have told many tragicomic anecdotes about these notions of his, and one wonders if they have not left us with a one-sided picture of his last years. Mindful of the danger of trichinosis, Andersen was deathly afraid of pork; he fell ill if he ate fruit soup, and it was just on this account that he never failed to get it at the tables of his friends; he could become intensely excited, simply because he had happened to swallow the pit of a plum; minor accidents, bruises, and symptoms of illness could absorb his whole attention. He suffered from agoraphobia, and when his young traveling companion, Jonas Collin, who did not take his fear quite seriously, succeeded in getting him by the arm and leading him out onto an open square, Andersen—to the youth's astonishment—began to tremble throughout his entire body. For long periods of time he kept a piece of paper lying on his night table; it bore the words: "I am in a trance!"

His friends, among them Edvard Collin, were of the opinion that there was really nothing very seriously wrong with Andersen's health, since he was almost never forced to keep to his bed. A modern medical specialist like Hjalmar Helweg takes the symptoms much more seriously; Helweg confirms that Andersen had always suffered from a certain nervous weakness, and that in his old age he had to struggle harder and harder in order to keep going —in all the various meanings of that phrase. The most striking of his symptoms was the exaggerated reaction of his imagination to every happening. From the Spanish trip, Jonas Collin has noted such details as the following: when their vessel decreased its speed in the Bay of Trafalgar in order to take soundings, Andersen was convinced that they had gone aground. He himself was certainly not unconscious of his weakness. Plagued by a fear of scarlet fever, he wrote to Henriette Collin on June 5, 1869: "I have imagination, yes, I live by it for the most part, of course, but it causes embarrassment now and then, especially when one thinks it's not working, and it's just then that its reactions are strongest."

He was able to transform his imagination's instability into humor; Edvard Collin tells how Andersen, hoping perhaps to clear up some misunderstanding, sought out Edvard's wife, Henriette, but could not find her; on her writing desk he left the following note: "Fru Collin. I am sorry that you flee from me; I'm going now, day after tomorrow I'll start out on a trip, and soon I'll die. Most respectfully yours, H. C. Andersen." After having given vent in his diary (for November 10, 1870) to his gloom about the hardness of men's hearts, and having wished that he were in the grave, he concludes: "I am tired of living—this evening."

His painfully acquired harmony did however threaten to go to pieces now and then; he could lie awake at night, filled with resentment at some unjust or contemptuous treatment he had received long, long before. During his last years Jonas Collin sometimes found him distraught, weeping and complaining like a child; his animosity could even be directed at old Jonas Collin, the grandfather, his life's benefactor. But in such cases Andersen himself knew that he was ill, he sent for help, called himself evil, thankless, and hateful, and soon became calm again.

It was time that he had peace.

As late as 1872 he traveled all the way to Venice with his young friend, William Bloch, and in April, 1873, he journeyed to Switzerland with another young man, Nicolai Bøgh, whom he had invited on the excursion. When he joined the Melchiors at their summer place, "Rolighed," in July, it was plain to them that the trip had not refreshed their guest, but rather had drawn heavily upon the few resources of strength he had left. Cancer was devouring him. During 1874 he was unable to write a single fairy tale, and in the summer he traveled no farther than to Holsteinborg and Bregentved. From the latter place he wrote to Fru Melchior on July 12:

I don't have ideas for any more fairy tales. It is as though I had filled the whole circle with fairy-tale radii drawn one close beside the other. If I go out into the garden among the roses—yes, what a lot they've told me, and even the snails, too! If I look at the broad leaf of the water lily, then I see that Thumbelina has already finished her trip on it. If I listen to the wind—it's already told its story about Valdemar Daae, and knows no better one. In the forest beneath the old oaks I have to remind myself that the old oak told me her last dream long ago. Thus, sadly enough, I no longer get any new, fresh impressions.

The winter of 1874 he spent mostly in his rooms, nursing his cough, and he could not even eat dinner every Thursday with the Melchiors; but he succeeded in dragging himself to the newly dedicated theater, which he found bright, elegant, and comfortable, although he was unable to stay there for more than an hour at a time. The theater had not altogether lost the magic it exerted in the days when it turned the head of a boy in Odense, drawing him unto itself. On February 4, 1875, one of the guests at a banquet the Melchiors were holding spoke constantly of "the old Conferential Councillor"; and so, according to the diary, "I read my latest poem, *Copenhagen,* to the company, in order to prove that I hadn't aged so much after all." In the same month he completed his poem on Odense, and one can say that in general he still wrote handsome lyric poetry during this, the last year of his life. Toward springtime, it was suggested that a statue of him be put up in Copenhagen, while he was still alive; but upon seeing the sketch made by the sculptor, Saabye, he became enraged, saying quite bluntly that it would not do at all. The artist had represented the storyteller surrounded by children, who clambered about on his knees and his back; Andersen pointed out the lack of historical accuracy: whenever he read aloud, he refused to have anyone behind his back

or too near him. But the main reason for his objection was naturally another: He most certainly did not wish to be stamped as a writer exclusively for children. "My aim is to be a poet for all ages," he
wrote to Jonas Collin. "The naïve element is only a part of the
fairy tales, humor is the salt in them." To Saabye he said: "My
fairy tales are written as much for adults as for children; children
understand only the trimmings, and not until they are mature will
they see and comprehend the whole." With self-esteem and dignity
he thus sought to guard his work against superficial misinterpreta-
tions, and he was right in doing so.

When summer came, he was able to travel no farther than to the
Melchiors at "Rolighed." He fell ill with dropsy there; and his last
letter to Henriette Collin, of July 13, was dictated to Fru Melchior,
but the signature is by his own hand. On July 25 he received a
letter from the younger Jonas Collin, whom he wished to have as
his traveling companion on a final journey through Europe: he immediately dictated an answer: he was ill, to be sure, but he had by
no means given up the idea of the trip—nothing must be allowed
to prevent it. "I beg you to come, I'll tell you the very moment I'm
able to travel. We'll meet again. God's Will be done!" His wanderlust burned within him until his final hour. Fru Melchior added a
postscript, in which she said that he grew weaker every day. She
quotes some of his last remarks: "If I except my cough, my exhaustion, and my swollen feet, I really feel very spry." And: "I'm
quite moved by two things: H. C. Andersen's patience and Fru
Melchior's."

On August 4, 1875, he set out on his final journey.

He had coveted immortality more than anything else.

He had achieved immortality, in that sense in which we most
often use the word. He has become perhaps the most famous of all
Danes. His reputation and his name are indissolubly united to

those of his fatherland: in his work there lives Danish nature and the Danish spirit—perspicacity, intelligence, mellowness, and the friendly smile are fused with a bitingly sharp wit to become humor, to become what the Danes call *"Lune."* He is a Danish type, indeed, a Danish myth, and one would be justified in calling him the "Prince of Denmark."

But he also coveted immortality in another meaning of the word. He thirsted for something eternal, something imperishable. This is the longing for goodness and justice which penetrates all the fairy tales. He himself was no hero of the faith but rather a doubter and a seeker; he shrank and trembled in the presence of annihilation and night, like that other Prince of Denmark, whose words he used as a title for his last great novel, *To Be or Not To Be.* If, despite all his doubts, he could not give up the thought of eternity, this was most profoundly because he could not have endured the cruelty and the injustice of existence without it. He yearned for justice, and that is why his glance passed beyond earthly horizons. In this fragile and rebellious feeling he was surely not unlike that other mythical Dane, the first Prince of Denmark, Hamlet. Both had listened to the invisible bell which rings throughout the whole realm of existence, although many are deaf to its sound. His fairy tale of *The Bell,* about the king's son and the poor boy with wooden shoes and sleeves which are too short—both leave their pleasant, humdrum existences and, on separate paths, seek their way from the depths of the Danish forest so that they may stand on the shore of the sea, the eternal and infinite sea, listening quietly—is a tale whose symbolism admits many interpretations; it could also be applied to the two Danes who are most immortal.

Index

A. General Index

Index

Rasmussen, Jørgen: 12
Rauch, Christian Daniel: 178
Reitzel, Karl Andreas: 119, 153, 237
Rembrandt van Rijn: 24
Reventlow-Criminil, Count Alfred: 182
"Rolighed": 244, 249, 251
Rollett, Hermann: 184–85
Rome, Italy: 102, 128, 131, 146, 151, 176, 181; Palazzo Borghese, 151; Pantheon, 146; Tivoli, 131
Rosenvind (or Rosenvinge) (father of Karen Marie "Andersdatter"): 10–11
Roskilde, Peace of: 176 n.
Rydberg, Viktor: 210–11, 225, 227

Saabye, August Vilhelm: 250–51
Sabine Mountains, Italy: 131
Sala, Sweden: 145
Saxon Switzerland: 127, 142
Scania: see Skåne
Scavenius, Fru: 209, 241
Scavenius family: 245
Schall, Anne Margrete: 48, 51–54
Schiller, Friedrich: 70, 104, 177, 185
Schley, Ludolf Gottfried: 108
Scott, Sir Walter: 72, 78, 104, 121, 149, 152, 184, 223
Shakespeare, William: 40–41, 67, 70–71, 78, 84, 91, 104, 190, 238
Siboni, Kapellmeister Giuseppe: 55–57, 61–62
Siljan Lake, Sweden: 227
Skåne, Sweden: 142, 166, 176 n.
Slagelse, Denmark: 11, 18–19, 76, 80, 83, 85–86, 91–93, 100, 108, 231; Latin School, 11, 76, 80–81, 84, 86, 103, 116, 147–48
Slesvig, Denmark: 186
Småland, Sweden: 75 n.
Sørensdatter, Anna: 12, 17
Sørensen, Christiane: 17, 68
Sorø, Denmark: 91, 96, 106, 132, 171, 195

Sorrows of Young Werther, The: 112, 116
Soul after Death, A: 165–66, 205
Spain: 28, 143, 227–229, 248
Speckter, Otto: 183
Spiess, Christian Heinrich: 116
Staël, Madam de: 152
Stagnelius, Erik Johan: 158
Stampe, Baron: 244
Stampe, Baroness Jonna: 180, 244
Stampe, Rigmor: 202, 244
Stegmann (tailor in Odense): 42
Sjernsvärd, Karl Georg: 158
Stockholm, Sweden: 140, 175
Strindberg, August: 227
Suhm, Peter Frederik: 70
Sweden: 23, 28, 75 n., 109, 119, 142–43, 159, 166, 175, 176 n., 185, 198, 202–203, 236
Swinemünde, Germany: 166
Switzerland: 109, 128, 242, 249
Szechenyi, Count István: 181

Tegnér, Esaias: 108, 175, 198
Thorgesen, Madam: 57, 59, 60
Thorvaldsen, Bertel: 108, 146, 187, 238, 240
Tieck, Ludwig: 118, 145, 175, 197
Tønder-Lund, Frøken: 67, 70
Törneros, Adolf: 232
Topsøe-Jensen, Helge: 230, 245–46
Turkey: 143, 147–48

Uppsala, Sweden: 185

Van der Maase, Fru: 67
Varnhagen von Ense, Rahel: 145
Vasa, House of: 181
Vedel, Valdemar: 197
Vejlby, Denmark: 130
Venice, Italy: 249
Vienna, Austria: 143, 181
Vigny, Alfred de: 168
Vincennes, France: 182

B. INDEX OF HANS CHRISTIAN ANDERSEN'S WORKS MENTIONED IN TEXT